VENGEANCE: CHILDREN OF FAUST

Chris Ulm

Thanks to those few who believed in me.

To everyone who read and reviewed the book at every stage dating back to its infancy, who supported me with kind words of encouragement and provided harsh criticism at times; thank you. It has been a long and winding road with many speedbumps along the way. But to accomplish anything worth accomplishing, that is the only road to take, and it's worth it. Without my friends and loved ones, I would never have made it this far, and the book would not be what it is today.

Disclaimer:
This version of the book has not been professionally edited. As such, there may be small grammar and spelling errors that I missed. With that considered, I sincerely hope you enjoy.

Vengeance: Children of Faust

Chapter 1 - Change Is Coming

A gentle murmur of mixed voices and whispers reverberated in the background of my fermented daydreams. Swimming in the whirlwind of distant realities that clouded my mind; afraid to fight my inner thoughts, as I may soon forget them entirely. Tapping my pencil against the desk grounded my body to this world while my subconscious roamed free. The vacancy in my eyes was plain to see, though nobody would offer their gaze.

My body rested in the same place as every time before; propped upright in a familiar desk, bombarded by the perpetual white noise of a rowdy classroom. My vacant eyes went unaffected by their incessant chatter. However, intuition build by repetition slowly revived me from my mental wandering. The pencil froze and my dry eyes slammed shut. In a matter of seconds, the noise floor raised, and I was back in the world I knew; the world I hated.

I sighed; brushing aside the hair that had fallen in front of my eyes. A searing headache erupted as I grew increasingly frustrated with the noise around me. My glare shifted to the teacher who had her feet propped on an extra chair and was reading a book. Fed up, I twisted my torso and checked the clock on the wall behind me.

"One minute, thirty-two seconds," I stated quietly to myself.

Facing forward, I reached down to the floor and brought my bag up onto my desk and unzipped the largest pocket. One by one, I returned the textbook, notebook, and pencil to the bag and zipped it back up. Now it rested on my lap and I dug my chin on the top, breathing lightly through my nose. I noticed a drop in the chattering volume directly to my right, but only for a moment. As soon as I heard it, it struck me. Something round and lightweight bounced off the side of my head and gently clattered to the floor. Raising my chin off the bag, I directed my eyes to the wad of paper on the dirty floor as it came to a rolling halt.

My face was blank, for the most part as I looked away from the ball and up at them. A group of boys huddled around a single desk all looked away from my saddened gaze; holding back their amused snickers and trying to hush each other. I had no real reaction, with no words to share. Just one single thought in my head.

It's only Tuesday.

The monotone bell rang, and suddenly the noise became animated. Every classroom and the vacant hall was simultaneously alerted to the advancement of time. Applying unnecessary pressure to cram ourselves through the narrow doorways, fight every other kid for a path in the hall, just to lock ourselves in a small room and do it once more.

The chair I sat in for the past forty-five minutes was hit with recoil as I jumped up and flung my bag over my shoulder in one smooth motion. In a matter of seconds, the hallway flooded with other students and brought with them the task of swift maneuverability. The familiar stench of floor wax and hand sanitizer floated freely throughout the building, creating an accustomed coziness within me. I disregarded that feeling and instead focused on getting through the crowd.

The best way to cut through was to act as a thin projectile in the halls; tense up, bring your arms in close, and wade through the bodies. Easy enough; I've done it more than a hundred times and yet, there always a chance for something to go wrong. As I made my way toward my next lesson, I approached a blind corner without considering my speed. I took the corner fast, keeping close to the inner wall and ended up crashing my forehead into the chest of another student.

Rebounding off him, I regretted my decision to look up and see who it was. My heart sank the moment his large fingers clamped down on my shoulder. Making his attitude known, he stepped forward and pushed me into a set of lockers with restrained aggression. This guy was tall, almost enough to cast a shadow if I only lowered myself another inch or two. A light brown, military-style crew-cut and patchy facial hair designated him as a jock type. That judgment was reinforced by the stocky torso and testosterone defined facial features.

A sharp breath escaped my nose and a tense stillness radiated in our little dome. His music was blaring through his headphones, repeating the same heavy bass over and over, eerily enough it almost matched my heartbeat. Any comment or apology, I would muster as an attempt to get by quicker, would go unheard. So, I waited, keeping my eyes to the floor and body against the cold locker.

He then grunted and pulled himself away from me. Offering a final word before continuing his way, “Bitch.”

Removing my back from the locker, I waited quietly until the coast was clear. I started to laugh a little at my version of him. The whole time he stared me down, I imagined a big, dumb bull waiting to charge. Two things made this fantasy even funnier; the fact that he grunted, and I was wearing a red T-Shirt. Now and forever, Brent will be a bull to me.

I cleared my throat and wiped the smile from my face, knowing my time in the hall had just been cut down. I took the corner more slowly this time, then started my stride again.

The halls were full of nameless faces and clashing lives, all moving in unison every day. Rinse and repeat. Too many people I grew up around but hardly knew, made an uncomfortable aura around me, though I doubt any of them felt the same way. Personally, I didn't have the luxury of meeting with the few people that cared to hear my opinions. No one to talk to or get excited overseeing. Save for one or two friendly faces.

I started a light jog, cutting corners tightly and weaving through the other students; just keeping my head down. One minute of dodging bodies and I could see the open door at the far end of the clearing hall. Between where I stood and that door, was a water fountain that caught my eye.

As I made my way towards it, a few other kids formed a small line of three. Thankfully they moved quickly and in no time, it was my turn to drink.

The buttons on the side of the cold metal box were subject to jamming up, so I gave it two light presses than a hard shove. The water flowed proudly with a decent arc, waiting patiently to sate my thirst. I leaned forward a considerable amount and made sure to hold the button down tight. The water was smooth on my tongue and chilling to my teeth, but overall satisfying.

Through all the repetitive thumping of footsteps in the hallway and the loud sound of rushing water from this machine, I hadn't noticed a presence behind me. It wasn't until I heard chuckles that I became aware. The few gulps I had drunk were swiftly interrupted by two clamping fingers on my shoulder.

"Got her, get the door!" One of the voices shouted.

"Hey! What are you-" I was ripped away from the fountain and dragged on my heels by two assailants.

The third of the group had opened the door directly behind us which led to a single person bathroom. All of a sudden, I was tossed onto my back into the room. The impact caused my head to bang off the concrete floor and hinder me with harsh dizziness. Lifting my head up, I saw three blurry figures waver in the doorway. A large figure stood in the back and held the door open while the other two entered and placed their slender fingers around my arms.

They hoisted me up, and I gave little resistance while my mind and body recovered from the impact. They turned me around and propped me up on my knees before one grabbed a bundle of my short hair and reared my head back with a powerful grip. My eyes opened wide with the pain and I could clearly see where they had me.

One girl leaned in close to my ear and said in a low, menacing voice.

"Drink up, Kim."

I took a sharp breath before my head plummeted into the dirty toilet water. My legs attempted to kick, and my arms reached around but found themselves pressed against the edge of the bowl for stability; desperately trying to push up and get free, but it was two against one.

They pulled me up for a moment to allow me to breathe, but just as quickly forced me back down again. Then the flushing started. I held my breath the best I could, but water forced its way up my nose and into my mouth. Finally, I was able to kick in the right spot and catch one of them in the stomach which knocked them off me just for a second.

Having that much less strength holding me down gave me the chance to pull myself up from the bowl. I coughed hard, trying my best to get the water out of my nose and throat; escape was still improbable. This girl asserted her position by pulling hard on my hair until I screamed, but my scream was quickly subdued as her friend rejoined and shoved me down again. This time my head went all the way to the bottom and my nose was bashed against the porcelain.

The impact formed a pressure between my eyes and my stability wavered. They pulled me up again and turned me around, then released their grip. My swaying body couldn't hold itself and I fell to the side, nearly slamming my head into the wall but I managed to catch myself in the last second.

"Damn, she's a fighter. You good?" One voice chuckled to the other.

The voice was that of a girl with a cocky tone and a snicker behind every word. Authoritative and adult with a pinch of adolescence.

"I almost peed when she kicked me!" The other girl complained loudly. Her voice was much less dominant; clearly, she held no position of authority in any social circle.

I sat on the floor, hand wrapped around my own throat, coughing and gagging repeatedly; thinking about what I had ingested. The dirty water in my gut and up my nose made me feel nauseous. I looked toward them and saw the door open wide in the background. Standing tall like a bodyguard was that guy Brent. Then I refocused on the girls before me and it all started to make sense. The girl on my right, the one with a conceited stick up her ass was the only person in this whole school who would go out of their way to make my life miserable for any fickle reason. Stacy Kingston.

"God! What was that for, Stacy?" I yelled between rough coughs.

There stood a slightly taller, slender girl. She wore large silver hoop earrings that perfectly complemented her thick blonde ponytail and delicately trimmed bangs. A low-cut pink top revealed the slightest amount of cleavage that made it easy to distract any boy she wanted.

Her shoulder was only slightly burdened by the dense leather purse, which, no doubt carried enough makeup to stock a vanity table and constantly refresh the mask she wore.

She was gorgeous, but beauty is only skin deep with her; inside she was rotten and cruel.

She angled her head, gesturing to Brent in the doorway.

"Thanks for getting her bro, she's been dodging me all day."

"She had this coming, no biggie." He said in a gruff, angry voice.

I looked at her with an embarrassed, crude face as awkward streams of cold liquid ran down my face and curved around my nose. The majority of the water dripped off the tips of my short hair and soaked into my shoulders. All she did was grin in a superior way. I was angry, but there was nothing I could do about it; nothing I could get away with. She adjusted her feet and leaned in a slight amount.

"Well, let's hear it." She demanded.

Confused, I cocked an eyebrow. "Hear what?"

"Tell Brent that you're sorry for bumping into him, then maybe we will let you go."

"That's what this is about?" I asked dumbfounded. "You nearly drowned me because we bumped into each other in the hallway? I can't believe you!" I clenched my fist.

"I can't believe I didn't hear an apology. Don't you want to get to class little Kim? This will all be over if you just say it." She sang the words in a gleeful melody only I could hear.

"Maybe she enjoyed the bath? Another one couldn't hurt, she kinda stinks." The other girl stated her opinion; voice echoing between these walls. Brent then leaned against the door frame, exposing a gap into the hallway. If only I could break free and make a run for class, I'd be safe there.

"Excellent point Lynn; she does stink like a dog, but I still want an apology." She sneered.

I grit my teeth and looked past her. Locking eyes directly with the big guy behind her. But then, I looked to the floor. She grabbed hold of my shoulders but was surprised to find my body completely limp.

"What, you're just gonna let it happen?" She seemed genuinely surprised.

I spoke in a monotone. "I have nothing to apologize for, I did nothing wrong. If you think this is the right thing to do, then just get it over with."

She sighed. "You've always been stubborn." Holding true to her intention, she grabbed a tuft of hair right behind my left ear and dragged my head over the bowl once more. I hovered above, staring down at my own reflection as water droplets fell from my hair and disturbed the mirror. I prepared myself for the coming lack of air. Suddenly, a loud demanding voice shouted from the hallway.

"Take your hands off her!"

A pause, then she released my hair. My limp body regained its integrity before I fell forward. Peering towards the open door and past Brent, was a boy I knew. My savior for the day.

He called out, "This is ridiculous, guys. What's your problem?"

She giggled. "Oh, Joey, here to save your darling, Kim? How sweet." She said the last line with detest.

Brent pulled himself off the door frame and puffed up his chest.

"Got a problem, little dude?"

Joey exhaled through his lips and adjusted his eyes to meet the four-inch height difference.

"Only if you don't move along," Joey replied with fire in his voice.

"Y'think that leather jacket makes you tough? How about handing that over to a real man, looks a little big on you." He growled.

"Oh, That's funny. Because when my dad passed it down the family tree, he skipped my older brother and gave it to me. You wanna know what he said to me? *Perfect fit."*

The two stared each other down and unlike all other students who met Brent's gaze, Joey did not falter. He was stoic, confident.

Stacy finally put up her hands, admitting defeat.

"Alright, boys, no need to cause a bigger scene. I think we're done here."

She made her way to the door and slid between them, making an intentional move to brush her body against Joey's as she exited the bathroom. He didn't flinch.

Brent's fingers twitched as he stormed off down the hallway; leaving just the four of us. Stacy's face was direct, vile, and enjoying every ounce of tension. She got in close to Joey, making sure he could smell her minty-fresh breath.

She whispered, "You can't protect her forever. Don't forget who she left behind."

His brows were lowered with impatience.

"Just get lost before I get a teacher." He threatened, stuffing his hands in his pockets and tightening his shoulders. She smirked.

"Whatever you say, tough guy."

Joey stepped to the side and let her walk past him. Though his shoulders were slumped, his back was straight and his arms tight as a knot. When they were all gone, and down the hall, Joey took her place in the bathroom with me, making sure to prop the door open.

Acknowledging the safety, I pulled myself up to the sink, bracing my body against the cold porcelain. Still dizzy from everything, I waited to regain my composure.

"Are you all right?" He asked kindly. All the strain in his body was released, and his gentle touch helped me keep my balance.

I spit toilet water and mucus into the sink, then sighed.

"I'm fine. Thanks."

Water still ran down my eyes, and I rubbed them furiously. Noticing this he took a small step to the paper towel dispenser and removed a few.

"Here." He offered.

I looked at the paper, then at him, and smiled.

"You're always here when I need you, Joey."

Taking them happily, I folded each pair neatly on the creases. Using them to blow my nose and clean myself off the best I could.

"I do what I can. There's just, not much I can really do."

"You do plenty. I only wish you didn't have to." I spoke sadly.

"Someone has to watch out for you, not like you have a big brother to keep the bullies off you, and seeing how I've known you forever, I think I qualify for that role." He grinned.

"There's no one I'd rather have by my side. . ." My words trailed off, and I went quiet, staring at the cold floor. Reliving the events that had just transpired. I stopped drying myself for a moment and watched it continue to drip. Joey noticed I got quiet and moved a little closer.

"Hey kiddo, what's wrong?" he asked sincerely.

I found it hard to look him directly in the eye. It had been nearly a week since I talked to him last or even seen much of him for that matter. Yet, like always, whenever Stacy takes it too far, or if I am feeling more down than usual, he is always there to remedy the situation. Any situation.

"Kim?" He spoke again.

"Stacy's right. It's like I always need you to protect me as if I can't take care of myself."

"Stacy's a jerk. She seriously needs to quit this shit." He growled.

"I like to think she secretly likes me and has a difficult time expressing herself." I joked with decreasing emotion.

He caught the joke and let a thin smile form. He knew I was coping and played along.

"No, I don't think that's it." He placed a finger on this chin.

Feeling less pressure in my chest, I grabbed another paper towel and continued drying off. I lifted my head and just kind of staring at him. Today he dressed in tan, baggy cargo shorts and a long-sleeve shirt with dark green stripes on the sleeves.

His clothes were so baggy; he could fit at least two and a half more of his skinny clones in there with him. The look of disinterest was complete with his two signature articles of clothing. His typical dark beanie which covered his medium-length dirty-blonde hair and a worn, black with red lining leather jacket. That signature hat and hair complimented the shape of his smooth, angled jawline and soft cheekbones. No feature, not even his cute button nose could distract from his warming bright blue eyes, which were practically glowing in this dim bathroom light.

I admired his uncanny sense to dress and look at how he felt comfortable no matter what others may think of him. This school wasn't preppy, but there was a certain style people dressed in. Most guys wore Khaki pants, nice jackets to cover some bland dress shirt or plain tee. The girls wore a lot of accessories, loose blue jeans or skirts, and bright thin tops with nice zip-up sweatshirts. It was as if everyone's parents shopped in the same two stores at the same time.

Nothing close to how Joey and I dressed every day. My standard attire mostly consisted of red or blue T-shirts and stonewashed jeans. Apparently, that stands out as too simple around here and draws attention, as if I should care that much about what I wear.

As I stared at Joey, he could see I was spacing out. He gave me a friendly poke in the arm, and I snapped out of it.

"By the way, you wanna borrow my hat for the rest of the day? Not to sound mean, but your hair . . . Yikes." He popped his eyes.

"You and that dumb hat. I'm half tempted to wear it, so I can see your hair again. You know you look better without it." I poked fun at him.

His face went from a playful smile to simulated worry.

"Uh, never mind, I think I'll keep it." He got embarrassed, but the smile came back. He kept handing me fresh paper towels as I dried myself.

He started again, "Well anyway, I'm glad I came along when I did. I was looking for you because I wanted to ask a favor. But it doesn't really matter now." He shrugged.

"Sure, it does. What's the favor?"

He rubbed the nape of his neck. "It's a bit annoying, but when I was trying to get down the notes in English class, Mrs. Hern was going too fast, and I didn't get them all. Do you think I can borrow yours and I'll give them back to you tomorrow? Or, maybe even later today if I can secretly copy them during Science." He talked with his hands, gesturing for a handout. I looked at him with a day-dreamy stare, rolling up the last bit of paper towel.

"Notes, huh? This is what, the third time this month you've had to ask me?" I chuckled. He did the same.

"I've been busy with my Woodwork class. We have had a shit-load of projects one after the other." He was now loosening up his previous sharp attitude. Every word was spoken with a smile. A goofy smile he only wore with me.

"Well, if there's one thing your good at, it's putting all your attention on one thing," I said. I held the ball of wet towel in my hand and tossed it in the trash.

"I guess it's the least I can do for your help. My bag is still in the hallway." I pointed to it, still lying by the fountain.

"And don't worry about giving them back today. I don't want you getting in trouble during class, so just bring them back tomorrow."

He opened the door fully and held it for me. "After you." He acted like a doorman.

"You're such a loser." I laughed. Kneeling by my bag, I felt a slight rush of blood go to my head, but it quickly subsided. The zipper coming undone echoed through the vacant hallway and made me feel conscious about being here. He stood behind me while I dug for the notebook. He sighed loudly, but not out of impatience. He then leaned his back against the wall, placing his foot heavily against it.

"Man, Stacy really needs to stop this crap. I'm getting seriously pissed off at her." He was back on her.

"It was sort of my fault this time, I technically did bump into her brother. So, if we are gonna blame anyone, blame Brent."

"The fact is, that this whole thing was unnecessary." He sounded flustered.

"Not much we can really do. I've told the school board, but they can't do much else outside of warning her. They'd never suspend her because of her dad."

"Why? What's so special about her dad?"

"He's just close friends with the principal."

"Then why not stand up to her? Knock her down and stomp her throat."

I looked at him with concerned eyes. "That's a bit intense, Joey."

"Well, I don't actually mean that. But, like, maybe just show her you won't be pushed around anymore."

"I plan on just waiting for her to grow up. I mean, she's bound to get over it some time."

"What's there to get over?" He got a little louder, clearly, he thinks about this about as much as I do. "She has no reason to pick on you. She just does, and that's messed up."

"Well, then maybe you should ask her for me." I tried to keep my attitude on the *I couldn't care less what she does*, side of things.

Joey could see right through me, and he stopped arguing. He knew this was a circle he had no way of changing. It is how it is.

After enough sifting through papers, I found the correct notebook and handed it to him. He took it with grace, but also seemed worn down from everything. Still, he immediately tried to perk himself up.

"Thanks a lot. You're a life saver." He spoke with somewhat false enthusiasm.

"Consider us even." I smiled.

"How can we be even? You've given me your notes loads of times. I'll have to step in at least six more times to make it fair."

"Or you could just take down your own notes, so you can stop asking me." I chuckled and folded my arms.

"But then I wouldn't have any excuse to talk to you more."

A red-hot blush washed over his face, as did mine. My chest tightened; the very fiber of my being screamed to back down, retreat. But my words flowed anyway.

"I may not start conversations, but you're always free to talk to me, Joey. I still see you as my friend, despite everything that happened."

"I know. We all need time to grow." His words took a sharp turn towards panic as he glanced at his wristwatch. "Shit, I gotta go and so do you. Thanks again, Kim." He held the notebook tight and sprinted down the hall.

Gone just like that, so suddenly left alone, just staring off into an empty corridor. I'm glad he came to my rescue. I don't ever see him often besides in the hallways. He was like me, quiet and keeps to himself. However, he is a bit more scatterbrained than I am. He may be sixteen but has the maturity of an adult, only ever acting childish when he was with me.

I guess, even though we are only a year apart, he will always see me as a younger sibling. Someone who he doesn't have to maintain his posture around, and I am okay with that. I admire him.

I blankly stared into the hallway where he had run off, lost in my thoughts, thinking about everything all at once; the depressing thoughts of wanting to be a little kid again, being at my mom's daycare, and playing with other children. Getting to see my dad laugh and smile like he used to, so many faded memories that continued to haunt me in the simplest of times.

Anxiety set in for a moment, digging up calcified memories I have tried to bury over the years. Yet, time and time again, they return to me. I can't let them go; they are a part of me. *He* is a part of me. So much of my life was built by the things he taught me, the days he spent looking after me, and the words that brought me back to life. He is precious, but painful. With every good memory, he brings a horrid reminder of the past and how much things have changed.

In this state of remembrance, I had forgotten where I was. As if the world knew I was lost and needed to find my way again, the school's loud, punctual bell reminded me of my location and informed me that I was now late for my next class. I zipped up my bag, slung it over my left shoulder and started a mad dash to get to my next class as soon as I could. It just hit me; I didn't have History this block.

My previous destination, the door directly down the hall from me, was *not* where I am supposed to be. Feeling stupid, I tightened my calves and turned around, running in the opposite direction.

"Damn," I exclaimed to myself.

From the starting point that was the water fountain, I moved swiftly along the right wall and had two short left turns before I arrived at the already-closed door. Without hesitation, I burst into the classroom, panting heavily.

Everyone went quiet and just stared; their judgmental eyes burning a hole in my head. I looked to the floor, sighed, and gracelessly made my way toward an empty seat. It was clear to anyone that my hair was not supposed to look like this. Flat, damp, and dark from the water.

Compared to my usual puff and the signature waves near the ends that always curled into my eyes and ears, this mess was undeniably appalling. I brushed my fringe to the side and because of its dampness, it partially stuck to my forehead.

"Nice of you to join us, Kimberly." My teacher, Mr. Lane said sarcastically.

"Sorry about that. I had a little accident." I responded softly.

"Clearly." He nodded. "Is everything all right?" He asked in a bored, impartial way. This is probably the least interesting thing he has seen all day.

I looked around the room; despising the attention; above everyone's stares, I noticed Stacy *had* made it to class after all. She sat at her desk, ogling at me with a devious smile.

"Ms. Avery?" he called me again, persistently trying to start class.

In the far corner of the room, I heard a boy speak softly, but intentionally loud enough for us to hear.

"Ms. Avery?" He repeated with a deeper voice, followed by a few immature chuckles from the other students.

I, as well as the rest of the class, ignored the jesters.

Mr. Lane directed his eyes to my seat and impatiently placed his hands behind his back. With silent steps, I slid between desks and plopped my butt down, letting my bag rest beside me on the floor.

"As I was saying, everyone . . ." He continued with his intro to today's lesson.

In normal circumstances, I would try my best to participate, despite any bad situation. But today, I just wasn't feeling it. My nose still throbbed, and my lungs struggled to recover. Focusing on Math was not something I was able to do right now. Instead, vulgar thoughts of self-loathing infected my brain.

Thinking and thinking and thinking in circles. My knuckles grew white with the surmounting pressure. Anger crept around my veins, burning my insides with white-hot rage that was only just contained behind a wall of sadness. There was nothing more I wanted right now than to scream at the top of my lungs.

Yet my body remained idle, secretly fuming behind my mask of silence. One day, I will speak. Tell the world my story, my struggle. Perhaps, they will cast me aside once more; ever dismissive of my little ball of misery I call life. Or, maybe they will hold my heart in their hands, and cry. Shed tears of regret, begging for amnesty.

Circles, thinking in circles; I found myself back to rage again. Then back to sadness, and even a sliver of happiness, thinking about Joey. This continued for the entirety of math until I found a distraction in my hair. Thirty minutes into class and my hair started to curl as it dried. A slight amount of body returned but not enough to make me look presentable. Still, I rustled it, pulled at it, and attempted to manage the mess.

By this time, my nose had stopped throbbing. Things seemed to reset themselves in a way like it never even happened. However, not all scars are physical or heal the same. Suddenly the bell rang in my ears, shaking me free from this train of thought.

At last, it was time to head home. Leaving the classroom with little urgency, I contemplated my destination. Usually, I would make a straight dash for the bus, but today was different. I didn't want to get home so fast.

I wanted more time to myself, so I kept a slow pace, falling behind the rest of the herd. Eventually, I made my way to the front entrance and pushed through the layers of doors that led to the outside world.

It was a bright and warm day at the tail end of August; the perfect time to live here in the snug eastern corner of the country. Especially since I lived in a more rural part of the state, I don't have to deal with the salty ocean air or the heavy winds, just trees, and dirt back roads.

Just a cool breeze and slightly chilled air, while also having a fair balance of warm sunny days. I enjoyed the bleak weather just as much as I do the sun. Although it's safe to say most kids around here prefer the blazing heat.

I exited through the front doors of the school. The sun and its bright, ever-loving warmth greeted me kindly. A dusty scent of pollen carried itself with the light breeze and brushed past my nose. I stood just outside the open doors and held my hand above my brow line to shade my eyes.

As the sun's rays were absorbed into my skin, I felt the sharp bitterness of a harsh wind blowing desperately through the students as they left the building. Because my shirt and hair were still a bit damp from Stacy, the wind was going to feel twice as brisk on my way home. Oh, how I wish I brought a sweatshirt today.

I walked away from the school and followed the thin sidewalk toward the main road. Taking my time, I kicked random pebbles and bottle caps. At the same time, I watched the approaching stop sign that displayed itself as the way home. I closed in on the red sign, and I was met simultaneously with a large yellow bus, carting students. The bus was stopped for no more than fifteen seconds, long enough for me to walk a few long feet beside it. I heard one of the bus windows scrape open.

Without warning, something shot from the bus and hit me on the head. Something solid, then wet, but didn't hurt all that much. I staggered to the side and stopped walking. Slightly shocked, I looked down to see the open water bottle lying on the pavement in front of me. As my eyes focused on the bus window, I saw Stacy looking down at me with her friends, all laughing as they threw the bottle cap at me as well.

"See you tomorrow, dog-face!" She mocked.

I reached down and picked up the bottle and cap. I held on to it tightly, then glared back at them as they closed the window. I watched them intently, the angry thoughts spiraling. So many things I'd like to do to them; or Stacy in particular.

Apart from the sorority squad, something else caught my attention a couple of windows down toward the back of the bus. A girl was staring at me. I couldn't see her all too well, but I know I didn't recognize her.

That wouldn't be saying much if this wasn't such a small school. Everybody knew everybody's face here, bare minimum, even if they weren't personally acquainted. But this girl was misplaced. I didn't know her, and that struck me as odd. She focused on me through the thick glass. The moment she noticed me looking at her, she abruptly turned away, just in time for the bus to begin pulling away.

Maybe I was wrong. Perhaps she was just someone I somehow completely avoided seeing all my time in this town and school. Anything's possible. Trying to ignore Stacy's actions, I began taking in the fresh air and the shine of a new day.

I headed home; luckily, I did not live too far from school, about four miles. At least today, I had the comfort of bright and friendly sun to guide me and warm my shoulders, despite the chilly air.

I was walking slowly so that I may enjoy the outdoors as long as I could. People passed me on bikes or while jogging, but the farther I got from school, the fewer people I saw until I was walking completely alone. A car would pass here and there; some even passed with loud pounding music blaring through the streets.

Going about my business, I continued down the sidewalk that stretched along the main road, kicking bits of broken cement as I swayed. Not much scenery to speak of, nothing new anyway. Only tall, thick trees hiding a few small houses and driveways with the occasional river trench beside the road. I've seen them all a thousand times. About two and a half miles of walking along the main road brought me to a turn where the sidewalk ended, and the pavement quality was degraded. It was a long barren road that was surrounded by trees and stretched on farther than you could see. This long back road was bare and socially naked, with no occupied houses around.

After some time passed, the entrance to my road became visible in the distance; it was small and made of nothing but dirt and rocks. It branched off from this straightaway and pushed deep into the trees; hidden by the dark, dense forest. Silence and secrecy were the law around here, and all must obey.

Standing at the beginning of what was technically passed off as my driveway, I observed the house and let out a heavy sigh. To my left, I gazed at a tree that held a very small green sign with a name and number on it.

87 – Avery

I dragged along the fifty-foot dirt path that was labeled as my driveway. Half a minute and I arrived at the decrepit front door. My house was small, run-down and dirty. A mossy and dank screened-in porch was the first thing you saw, giving off a terrible first impression. The porch was so horrid and full of junk that it made us look like terrible, dirty people.

Up the few short steps and through the screen door; which doesn't close all the way and screams like a banshee were tools, paint cans, and an old torn-up couch, which decorated my humble abode. Just lying there, getting older and dirtier.

I obliviously knocked on the door and waited. When there was no answer, I noticed a small note stuck into the house by a thumbtack next to the door handle.

"Kim, out shopping. Be back later. —Dad" I read the note out loud, then scowled.

I took a step back from the front door and turned to face the driveway, with a sharp inhale. My mind was so full of random nonsense that I didn't even notice the car wasn't here. It only had one place to be, dead center of the driveway and I somehow missed it.

I determined my dad had been gone for a short while since his car has a distinct smell to it. Fifteen new air fresheners and overuse of wiper fluid. That specific smell was nowhere to be found.

"Great, after a terrible day at school now I have to sit here all alone in my own home," I said to myself, trying to feel less lonely by creating a conversation between me and myself. I took the note off the door and crumpled it, then stuffed the paper in my back pocket.

He left the door unlocked for me, which is surprising considering his paranoid attitude. The old bronze knob, however, forbade me from entering easily. The old mechanism jammed itself and forced me to be aggressive with the handle until it clicked and opened with a loud creaking noise. One of these days I'm going to snap that thing in half, maybe then we can finally get a new one.

The first thing I do when I get home is take my shoes off; my tired feet begged to breathe. I sat on the floor directly in front of the door and rubbed them gently, cracking each toe. I then stood back up and stretched my body, reaching my arms up to the ceiling and letting out a long yawn. My limbs felt stiff, so I jumped up and down a little to loosen up, then kicked my shoes out of the way and closed the door.

The first sight you would see when you walk in was the living room on your left and the kitchen on your right, no dividing wall. The kitchen contained a semicircle of cabinets lining the wall with a few appliances between them.

The living room contained a couch in the center, facing a TV against the back wall and complete with a couple of cheap end tables by either arm of the couch. Between the kitchen and living room, straight ahead from the door was a small archway that acted as a transition to the living quarters. A door to my dad's room was in the center and on the right around the corner was the master bathroom.

To the left of the archway and down a very short and narrow hall was an ascending staircase that climbed up over his doorway. Above his door was a rib-height railing that overlooked the entrance and living room. Just past the rails upstairs are three more doors. My bedroom in the middle, a tiny bathroom down another short hall to the left, and a small half door that led to an attic storage space to the right. That's it.

The first thing you noticed when you walked in the door was the smell. My house had a mixture of rotten wood and stale everything; a musky, sour smell that really stabbed your nostrils if you weren't used to it, which I was.

The smell was an accumulation of an overflowing garbage bin, dirty dishes, food left out, and a mass amount of half-drunk beer cans and bottles strewn about the living room and kitchen counter.

The ceiling fan above was spinning slowly. It made a gentle vibrant noise as the gears spun the blades. I walked in front of the couch, directly below the fan and pulled one of the strings that hung down. A soft whirring started up, and the blades began to spin faster.

"Ah, crap, wrong one." I groaned aloud.

I pulled the wrong string; I've always done that, and I don't know why. I had to pull the same string again and try for the other one.

It spun faster with each click until the whirring stopped and the blades began to slow back to their original speed. I stuck my hand in; getting stung by the initial smack of the thin blade, but then with each passing lap, the blades went slower and slower until they ground to a halt. I then pulled the correct string to turn on the light.

The house was dead silent now. I could hear that empty ringing in my ears. I didn't like absolute silence, so I cleared my throat and began humming a random tune. My shirt had dried a little but was still damp enough to bother me. I felt the damp spots with my fingers to judge how wet it was. Since no one was home and we didn't live near any other houses, I took my shirt off in the living room and bundled it up into a ball. Being a girl, I wasn't completely exposed.

I needed to take a shower for obvious reasons, but my dad gets pissed if I use his shower; I have my own upstairs after all. The thing is since my bathroom is so tiny, it's impossible to have a comfortable time in there no matter what I am doing. So, if he isn't home, this is my chance.

Without hesitation, I ran into the main bathroom, set my stuff on top of the washer to my left, and stripped down to nothing. I quickly cranked the shower on and let the water heat up. The water pressure in this whole house is terrible, but his shower is much better than mine. Wasting no time, I jumped in and cleaned myself up, using only a fraction of the shampoo I would normally use, so he wouldn't notice a difference in his bottle.

When I was finished, I grabbed a nearby towel from a rickety stand next to the toilet and first used it to dry off the inside of the shower and wipe the mirror. Leaving behind no trace of water, hair, or soap. He'll never know. Then I threw on my underwear again and gathered my stuff.

Now standing beneath the arch in the hallway leading upstairs to my right, I stopped and listened to the silence once more. I felt saddened. As much as I enjoyed this luxury and alone time, I would have much preferred it if my dad was here to greet me today. It's been a long one.

Then again, knowing him, maybe the silence is better. I felt the urge to speak.

"I guess I'll just do some homework, I'll be upstairs if you need me!" I said out loud.

Shouting at the empty living room as if my dad were here and would respond. Frowning, I lowered my head. The emptiness began to set in, and like a virus, it spread through my veins. For me, this was normal.

Nothing about being alone was strange to me.

The hardwood stairs creaked with every weak, ascending step that I took. As I reached the top, I could see the front door over the railing and my bedroom door to my left. I turned left and rounded the short corner down the short passageway into my bathroom. I inched passed the standalone sink and toilet on my right and stepped into the tub and shower combo.

I had to stand here to close the door most days unless I felt like scraping the hollow wood against my hip trying to close it. With the door shut tight, I placed myself in front of the mirror and looked at the room through its reflection. It was so tiny and lame, but I took care of it. All except for the hundred-year-old shower curtain that had yellow stains randomly splotched on the plastic.

My hair flew in all directions with the whipping of my head side to side. Taking the brush from the edge of the sink, I proceeded to brush away all the knots and loose strands; collecting them in a clump on the brush and disposing of them in the small trash bin. Once my hair was absolutely neutered, I ruffled it a bit and tossed my clothes into the corner behind the door. I forced my way back into the hall and noticed a pile of clean clothes next to my bedroom door.

It seems my dad did a small load and left it here. I was happy that he did that but immediately started thinking about how dirty this carpet probably is.

Nevertheless, I took a baggy long sleeve shirt and some slacks, threw them on really quick, and then slid the pile into my bedroom. At least I know how clean *my* floor is, so I felt better with them being there for now. The next stop was the kitchen for a snack. The stairs rumbled with my steps once again and I found myself wondering just how long before one of them would give out on me.

Entering the open kitchen, I paused to observe the surface mess. The fridge was standing before me with the sink directly to the right of it and the oven to the left. Everything else was cabinets; every surface was covered in some form of trash, stain, or tools. The sink was obviously a mess and the stovetop was slathered in grease, which would surely spit fire the next time it got used. In the fridge, I rummaged past some open cans of tomato soup, leftover hot-dogs from about three days ago, and miscellaneous unidentifiable gunk that my dad considered good enough to eat; someday.

Luck had finally found me when I stumbled across a ripe apple in the bottom left drawer. A brief wash and it was ready to eat. The first bite had a satisfying crunch to it and made me smile big, almost distracting me from my ever-growing loneliness. Almost.

I turned my body and leaned against the fridge, making sure not to bump into any of my dad's magnets which held many non-stack-able coupons. I observed the dirty white carpet in the living room and some sticky spots on the kitchen floor. I'd love to have access to a beast of a vacuum and mop bucket to give this place a new shine, but that won't happen.

With the apple devoured at an appropriate pace, I retreated upstairs to my room. The door opened slowly, and I took in the all too familiar sight once again. The pile of clothes I shoved in here was against the wall immediately to the right of the door, but it won't be there for long. The full-size mattress had its cheap headboard crudely pressed up against the left wall with the feet pushing into the center of the room.

A dark blue comforter, body pillow, and standard pillow lay in a jumbled mess on top. To the right of the bed against the wall was a single, short nightstand that housed two little drawers and a two-inch gap between it and the floor. On top was a picture frame and small lamp complete with a shade that didn't quite fit.

Beneath the bed was a small square carpet that acted as a sort of bridge from the bed to the dresser, which sat directly across against the opposite wall. To the right of the dresser was a tiny closet that only served the purpose of housing a few small boxes and some warmer clothes for winter. Its best feature was the standing mirror my dad attached to the outside of the door.

Lastly, my one small window was dead ahead as you are walking in the room. Its foggy glass allowed me to peer at a little man-made trail that cut through the dense forest. I've explored these woods many times, and there is nothing of interest out there. Even the trail ends abruptly giving it no real reason to exist at all.

Back on task; the clothes I shoved in here had to get taken care of. The dresser only had three drawers, granted, they were decently sized. Still, that gave me limited sorting options. Basically, the top drawer was underwear, socks, tank-tops, and bras. The second drawer was shirts, and the third was pants and pajamas. With the clean pile sorted rather quickly, I moved on to my next task.

I tossed my backpack onto the bed and walked over to it. Standing by its side, I reached into the top drawer of my nightstand and removed my CD player; then popped it open to find there was no disk inside. So, I tossed it beside my bag, crawled underneath the bed, and pulled out a shoebox that contained multiple CDs and old cassette tapes.

I sifted through the box and pulled out a disc containing a mix of classic rock and some punk. I smiled at its beauty and snapped the disc into the player. With headphones on, I pounced on my bed and was ready to do my homework.

For the next two and a half hours I flew through Geography, Math, and English; barely breaking a sweat. Once homework was done, I cracked my knuckles loudly then twisted my neck in a circle. The clock caught my attention.

"Eight pm." I crossed my legs and stiffened my back as I stretched then let out a long-strained yawn. In the middle of my stretch, a sudden loud thump came from downstairs.

I rolled off my bed and ripped my door open. Two steps out my door and I could easily see the front door wide open through the guard railing.

"Ah, shit." A low, raspy voice slithered through the silent house.

Taking the remaining steps up to the rail, I leaned my arm against it and watched the door handle bounce off the wall again as he kicked it out of frustration.

With little to no emotion, I called out to him. "Hey, Dad,"

"Hello, Kimberly." He said with a groan. "This fucking doorknob is gonna bust a hole in the wall one of these days." He griped.

"I know, the handle gave me some problems when I got home. I think we need a new one." I called out.

"No, we don't need a new doorknob. My dad used to always tell me, 'If it's old, it's good.' Therefore, we keep it." He grumbled.

I shook my head.

He set his keys on the nearest counter and started unpacking the three bags he was carrying. Milk, bread, chips, cereal, yogurt, and of course, beer.

"How was school?" He asked with an obligatory tone while putting things where they belong.

"Fine," I replied. "I just finished my homework." My words were dry; tasteless.

"Good. Anything new with you?"

"No, not really."

"You sound mad or something. Is that girl at school giving you problems uh, what's her name?"

"Stacy," I answered. "And yeah, she's still pushing me around, but I'm dealing with it."

He stopped for a minute and faced me completely. There stood an obvious shell of a man that I called my father. Broad shoulders, toned arms, and an uncomplimentary beer gut were his most prominent features.

The skinny nature of his face gave him a tired and generally older look, and the messy ear-tip length hair made him look the part of a hard-ass even more. His patchy dark stubble and stained 80's hair metal shirt gave me the indication that he had gotten up early for work. Probably filling potholes or something along those lines.

"In what way are you dealing with it?" He addressed me directly, before taking a moment to lean into the fridge.

"I'm just kind of avoiding her as much as I can, even though I'd rather just teach her a lesson." I chuckled lightly.

"We don't need you fighting anybody. Trust me, that can only end badly for everyone. Especially you."

"Oh no, kicking her ass is the *last thing* I wanna do," I said in an obviously sarcastic tone.

"Watch your mouth, young lady." He asserted. Then mumbled under his breath, "You definitely got your mother's sarcasm."

I sighed loudly. "Yes dad, I've spoken with teachers, but they won't do anything about it."

He put the last of the groceries away and went through his daily motions. Open beer, grab the remote, turn on the TV, sit on the couch, and do absolutely nothing. I have never seen anybody get so comfy, so fast.

"Well, if things get worse, just try to talk to the principal again or something. They have to do something about it." He said, now utterly disinterested because his brain was being pumped full of reality TV.

"Sure," I replied, not actually taking his suggestion to heart.

The short conversation died just like that. I stood by the railing and just watched him for a moment, then my eyes wandered around the house, then back to him. I waited for him to say something else.

Maybe something like, *'It's nice to see you. Why don't you come sit with me? Let's go for ice cream tomorrow, maybe a movie night?'*

Anything that would make it seem like he cared, but he was done for the day. Disappointed, I walked back into my room and eased the door shut.

Sitting on the side of my bed, I tapped my feet along the floorboards. The room had a soft yellow glow from the lamp next to me, giving the room an ominous vibe. My head pivoted as I observed all the dark corners, eventually resting on a spider web that stuck in the corner of the slanted ceiling.

Out of boredom, I flicked the lamp on and off. Dark, light, dark, light, dark. Surrounded by the void, I listened closely. The laughter from the TV, the creaking of an old house, the wind pushing through the trees.

Feeling trapped in the bedroom, I eventually gave in. Before long, I re-lit the bulb and moved over to the dresser to get changed. Almost immediately, the pajamas flooded my skin with warm comfort. Prepared for the night, I jumped onto the bed and lay on my back. Both hands stuffed behind my head and my legs straight out and crossed, the slanted ceiling had my attention.

I examined the tan paint-drip-pattern, making shapes and figures out of the various shadows. I had a friend up there, a little shadow that formed when only the lamp was on. A certain collection of longer than average drips cast a shadow that looked like a little man. He had spiky hair and a bird's beak of all things. Glancing up from time to time, I silently greeted him; making sure he knew I hadn't forgotten.

I thought back to when I first discovered him when I was a girl. The timeframe is foggy, but I've been told he replaced my other imaginary friends; whatever that means. I don't remember having imaginary friends, or any friends at all until my mom introduced me to Joey in her daycare. Ever since then, my beaked friend has remained here. I don't think he minds, as long as the lamp is never moved.

Chapter 2 – Dread

Unknown to me, a handful of hours had passed, and I found myself stirring on top of my blanket in a foggy state. The nap I fell victim to had released me, and I sat up in confusion. I knew I had been out for a bit, although I wasn't sure exactly how long a bit was. I hung my feet over the edge of the bed, readying myself to stand. The first two steps upright caused me to sway, but I quickly found my balance.

Standing by the door, letting my eyes adjust slightly before risking the stairs, I spun around and looked at my window. A blurry beam of fresh moonlight poured over the sill and dripped onto the floor. It seemed calm outside. I sleepily made my way to the window and opened it a little to let some air into this stuffy box. The room became many times more breathable the instant cool air whispered in.

I let the chill rush over my skin while staring into the void that was the forest behind my house. The only outside lights we had was a single porch light that only illuminated about fifteen feet into the driveway. Basically, anything outside of that was an ocean of secrecy. Nightmare fuel.

My throat was itchy still. With the heat in my body purged and my eyes focused, I made my way back to the door. Right now, the kitchen was calling my name, a murky glass of tap water was the unfortunate remedy to this dry throat. Upon exiting my bedroom, I felt the hot air once more and swallowed hard.

"Jeez, what did he set the thermostat to? Eighty?" I whispered to myself.

The first step descending the stairs was a loud one, although I wasn't worried. My dad is a heavy sleeper when he's sober, and I know he didn't stop at one beer after he got home. I rounded the corner on the stairs and casually walked to the kitchen. All the lights were off, making this trip a test to see how well I knew this place. All things considered, I made it to the kitchen without a hitch.

Suddenly a loud grumbling noise echoed behind me. I jumped but quickly reassured myself that it was only my dad and his obnoxious snoring from his room. Feeling just a little more edge, I hurried along with my task. A clean glass from the right side of the sink, a couple of ice cubes, and some not-so-great water from the tap. A couple of hard gulps of the semi-cool liquid and my throat was starting to feel better. I reached for the handle to refill the glass, then stopped. Setting the glass down next to the sink I opened the fridge once more.

The warm light poured out onto the floor, casting deep shadows everywhere. I looked around, squinting to shield my eyes. To my delight, I came across a brand-new jug of apple juice on the door beside the milk.

A sly grin crept up on my face. "Jackpot." I contained my excitement.

The fridge made a soft thump as it closed, darkening the room once more. Even with obscured vision, I could still see my hands enough to unscrew the cap of juice. Everything around me remained quiet and lifeless except for the sound of pouring liquid. I set the jug down on the counter. Taking the edge of the cup to my lips I began to drink, pacing myself as this juice was much colder than the water I just had. My throat adjusted, and the drink began to flow easier. Nearing the bottom, I tilted my head back to finish it up when suddenly I was shaken by the sound of an abrupt rustling noise from behind me. I spun quickly, nearly choking on my drink, I felt my back crack with the swift motion.

Heart racing, I peered into the darkness. Straight ahead, floor, ceiling, left, right. In the upward peripheral vision, while looking right, I caught a glimpse of something. My neck titled as I gazed up at the railing above. Only six or so feet above me, I swear I could see something there.

Just behind the rails, was just darkness. Yet, it was unique; this was like a black sheet that was darker than everything else around it. True, living darkness. My eyes rapidly scanned the area as confusion and fear rose within until I blinked. At that moment, a mere fraction of a second; it was gone. The atmosphere changed all at once, I felt fine.

Still, I couldn't shake this idea that I should be careful. I know I heard something move, although it could have been anything. A mouse, maybe a bat? Either way, there is nothing here that is a threat. Rationality forced me to believe that it was nothing and so I set my empty cup in the sink and put the jug away. Just before I could close the door to the fridge, the light inside flickered and went off. The cold air hit my front as I stared into the icebox.

"Um." I raised an eyebrow. I reached my hand down and pushed the little switch inside multiple times. Nothing. Not even the soft humming of the fridge itself. Confused, I closed the door gently and turned around. That feeling of unease slowly returned. Tiptoeing through the dark, I walked towards the front door where the panel of switches was located.

The furthest left was for the kitchen, but as I flipped it, nothing happened.

"What happened to the lights?" I asked myself, then proceeding to flip all the others. Resulting in the same concern.

My eyes had adjusted well enough to make my way back to the kitchen and find the miscellaneous junk drawer. All the while I kept my head low, making sure not to let my eyes wander to the railing again; for fear of seeing something.

I sifted as quietly as I could through this drawer. Rummaging my way through screwdrivers, nails, thumbtacks, a single spool of thread, masking tape, a small sewing kit with a variety of needles, and lastly a pocket Bible. All the way in the back, I found what I was looking for; a handheld flashlight. I wrapped my fingers tightly around it and rotated until my thumb landed on the button.

The beam shined bright at my command. A shimmering circle was cast on the floor, giving me a sense of control over the situation. Having retrieved a light I tried to close the drawer that I just now remembered has a broken slide wheel. Meaning I had to quietly, slam it shut.

Now, flashlight in hand, I dragged my feet over to my dad's room. Thankfully, his door is nice and quiet when it opens so I feel less like I am intruding. Walking into his room was like walking into a motel room on the first day; bare, almost no personality inside.

A full-sized bed directly in front of you with the headboard against the wall beneath a wide window. A dresser and a large mirror to the left and a closet and chair on the right. I calmly made my way over to the right side of his bed with the flashlight aimed downward.

"Dad, Dad, wake up," I whispered.

His response was nothing more than a loud snort.

"Dad!" I whisper shouted; still no response.

I sighed loudly, then had an idea. Lifting the flashlight up to my chest, I shined the ray into his eyes.

Immediately he jerked around, and his eyes burst wide open. He forcefully sat up while bearing a clenched fist; I jumped back for safety.

"Who-who the fuck's in my house!?" He shouted.

"Whoa, relax Dad! It's just me." I said shining the light under my chin.

Lowering his fist and panting slightly, he tiredly looked in my direction.

"Y-you're not him?" He mumbled, rubbing his eyes hard.

"Him? Uhh, Him who?" I offered a confused stare.

"What'r you doing?" He dizzily questioned.

"I. . . came down to get a drink and I think the power went off. Can you get up and see what happened?" I asked.

I watched him pause and take the time to allow lucidity into his numb mind.

"Why don't you? You already have the flashlight, what's the point in waking me up?" He snarled.

"The breaker is in the basement. I don't wanna go down there alone." I chuckled nervously, hoping he would sympathize.

He scratched his head and yawned loudly.

"Plus, I don't even know how to fix it." Childish fear circulated my gut.

He looked at me and grumbled, then lazily reached over to the floor lamp next to his bed and pulled the cord. The light blipped on; bright as can be.

There was an awkward silence where he just looked at me. The light clearly bothering his eyes, fluttering faintly as they begged for it and me to go away.

"But the kitchen—" I started.

"Probably blew a fuse." He said in his gravelly voice. "It's fine. All you need to do is find the switch that is facing the opposite direction and flip it around. A five-year-old could do it." He said condescendingly.

"Well, if it's so simple, why don't you go and do it?" I urged him.

His frustration grew. "For fuck-sake can you just shut up and do it, so I can go back to bed? God, all you do is bitch about everything inconvenient for you." He snarled, pulling the lamp string again.

The hard thump of his head hitting the pillow made me jump a little. For a second, I thought that sound was him moving to smack me. Almost the instant his head hit the pillow; the snoring erupted.

I gripped the flashlight in my hand and backed out of the room. I mumbled under my breath while walking through the house to the front door. I threw on my shoes and switched the porch light on. I swung open the front door and saw that there was no light.

"Are you kidding me?" I whined. "Of course, of course, the porch is on the same switch as the kitchen. Why wouldn't it be?" I mumbled to myself as I took the first treacherous steps out the door. The flashlight aimed directly at the ground in front of me cast such a short-range beam that I couldn't even see the tree line that was a cars-length from the side of the house.

Instantly, I was greeted by the same cool breeze that is keeping my room at an optimal temperature right now. I was indefinitely aware of how loud my steps were as the porch boards screamed under my weight. Each scrape of the sole, every rustle of my pajama pants, every breath I took hit the walls of the woods and were sucked into the endless abyss. I felt like I was in a glass dome underwater. Feeling safe in my bubble, until I see or hear something mysterious make a pass.

I turned left at the bottom of the stairs, moving away from the porch and keeping close to the side of my house. Using it as a defensive wall, knowing that the only mystery was to my right. As soon as that thought came into my head, I remembered seeing the black mass stand above me inside.

That thought instantly made my stomach twist, because now the roof was a threat. What could possibly be perched above? Waiting for me to advance just a little further before making a move.

My shoes scraped against the dirt and sand as I reached the back of the house and rounded the corner tightly. Just a few feet ahead of me, attached to the house beneath me and my dad's window was a deep red bulkhead. My flashlight illuminated this death trap, and my eyes wandered once more.

Shivering, I rotated my head slowly, peering into the trees that stand coated in thick, murky ink. No moon or stars were present tonight, giving the entire world a feeling of abandonment. My stare returned to the task at hand. Rusty hinges and chipping paint represented the door's outward appearance, giving off a foreboding aura.

I can't believe this. I thought to myself.

A steady wind picked up and whispered through the leaves, beckoning all the fears within me to animate and take over my subconscious. The shifting leaves skipped across the ground, creating the illusion of a hundred tiny footsteps running in circles around me. I spun around and shined the light in the woods. The small light barely reached the trees but could not penetrate past the line.

The instant I lit up the woods, I heard a small *squeak* behind me. A whining crack, the sound of an old tree being bent just a little too far by the wind, but there was no wind; I turned again.

Before opening the door, I got curious and shined the light upward and looked at my bedroom window. Expecting nothing but a reflection of light, my heart skipped a beat when I saw what looked like a faint shadow standing at my window; looking down at me.

As my body quaked, the flashlight was moving around in a way that altered the shadow. It became clear to me that this figure had been caused by the light hitting the lip beneath my window and casting an odd shadow against the glass

Even though it was debunked, it added to my suspicion. I could not help but feel an odd presence in this brisk night air, a presence other than my own. Something about it drew my attention toward the basement. I got a chill up my spine as I gathered my confidence and lifted the bulkhead door.

The loud rusted squeak of the hinges wavered through the trees, attracting more attention to this very spot. Crouching slightly, I shined the light into the hole. My heart raced; mouth dry again. Every nerve in my body told me to turn and run, but for some reason, I couldn't back away. I aimed the light down the stairs. The beam wobbled and shook along with my unsteady hand.

The steps screeched under my weight, forcing me to stop and wait for any sign of undesired accompaniment. It was so quiet. Ankle deep in unforgiving darkness. I could almost see the far back wall of the basement.

The fuse box was no more than twenty-five feet away, but my vision was limited at this angle. I hardly ever go down here; I didn't know what to expect. I swallowed hard and took another step, much too aware of my own heavy breaths. I tried to silence them as much as I could, but the stifling only caused my breathing to become sharper.

There's nothing to be afraid of, I assured myself.

With one final step, I dipped my head under the house and fully submerged myself in the crushing black. My golden ray of security was the only thing keeping me from running like a child. At the bottom of the steps was a little-beaded string hanging from above, the light switch. Relieved that I may finally have some more light.

I pulled the string and of course, nothing happened. Getting really irritated at these circumstances, I used my beam to check it. There I saw the base of a soft white light bulb inserted in the socket, but the actual dome was nothing but shark teeth. Following the clue, I examined the dirt floor and saw the shards below.

"Perfect," I muttered.

The darkness surrounded me at every angle, seeming more dangerous than before. Then, like a flashback, I thought back to every event tonight. How strange they all were. Am I dreaming all of this? Out of nowhere, powerful nausea punched me in the gut, which forced a dry wheeze to escape my lips.

Doubled over in sickness, I exclaimed, "Oh, man. What is this feeling?"

My body shook, the flashlight trembled between my fingers and the grip was loosened. The sickness brought a paranoia.

With my head hunched forward, I directed my eyes upwards, searching. Within a few seconds the feeling leveled out to a general upset stomach, and I let out a hot breath. Regaining my posture, I jolted forward for the box.

Three feet was all I covered when a loud buzzing erupted in my ears. I slowed; my knees began knocking together. I stopped and turned around, looking towards the only exit. Something was very wrong.

The longer I stared at the small gap, the more my eyes began to blur. I felt dizzy like I was going to pass out. The buzzing would not stop, but for some reason, it felt familiar to me. Like the vibrations were always there, my whole life and I only now was questioning its existence, but that's not true. I knew that, so why am I okay with it? Then my eyes caught movement. Not a shadow wavering from my light or the hair in my face. The movement came from the bulk door. It was closing. I watched in horror as the door moved on its own, completely and impossibly silent.

It was lifted straight up, the flat of the door facing the sky, then suddenly slammed shut. With that slam came absolute, unfiltered fear. I wanted to scream, I wanted to raise my fist and pound on the floor, hoping my dad would hear me. I couldn't. I felt like if I made any noise whatsoever, I would die. Turning again, I shined the light in every direction, trying to keep the darkness at bay. As calm as anyone could be in a situation like this, I lifted my feet and took baby steps toward the bulkhead door.

It was my only option besides sitting here all night. I managed to get within a few feet of it and turned once more to face the dead end. Cold sweat dripped down my forehead, and I stopped and held my breath.

One step backward, then another.

The third step would bring me to the base of the stairs but instead, my back was met with something solid. Something tall. I froze in place and let out the faintest of whimpers. My lips loosened, and teeth gritted shut. Eyes as wide as ever.

A sharp breath brushed its way down my spine.

"No!" I shouted, jerking forward and spinning around.

My beam drowned the stairs in the fickle yellow light. Nothing. At this point I knew I was stuck in some nightmare; I wanted that to be a reality, but I could not believe that this was in my head. Another low breath hit the back of my ear. This time I didn't shout or move away. Instead, I shut my eyes. Not by my own will but through some unnatural force, my eyes were closed, and my body began to vibrate.

I could hear something growing steadily all around me. It sounded like talking. . . No. These voices were in pain. The noise grew louder, drowning out the static that previously inhabited my mind. It sounded like a hundred dying children, beckoning me, insidiously calling my name. Everything was spinning, and for a brief second, I felt as though I was no longer in this world. Lost. Dead. The voices grew louder and louder, but no other intelligible words came through. All nonsense except for the last two.

Trust her. A tired, docile voice whispered in my ear.

My mind exploded. That internal combustion erupted into my reality. Screaming bloody murder, my hand released the flashlight and my legs propelled me forward. up the stairs. I rammed my head and shoulders into the steal bulk, pounding on it with clenched fists.

"Let me out!" I wailed at the top of my lungs. "Please!"

When I rammed it again, the door opened a little. I pushed against it with all my strength; it was way heavier than before. Like someone covered it in bags of sand.

As soon as the door flew open, I ran out of the basement; at first tripping over my own feet, I hit the ground hard but got up as fast as I could. As I rounded each corner, my feet slid on the loose sand. I ripped open the porch door and burst through the front. Locking the many various deadbolts and key locks slowed me down, but once those were in place; I felt safer.

Taking just a second to breathe I looked toward my dad's room, the door was open, and I could see him sleeping. But just behind his headboard, I could also see out the window into the backyard.

Directly over the bulkhead door. I didn't see anything from here. Then my eyes shot up to the railing; again, the coast seemed clear. This puts my mind somewhat at ease, and I was able to make my way through the house with less haste. I moved slowly, aware of every corner and shadow; still unsure if this was real or a dream. I made my way up the stairs, which were quieter than usual, and then entered my bedroom.

Thank god, the ceiling light turned on. I then noticed the room was ice cold, in fact, the whole house seemed to drop by thirty degrees. Then I remembered leaving the window open for this whole time. I closed the door behind me and moved to my window to shut it. I couldn't help myself. Stupidly, I looked down to the ground, and even with how dark it was, from here, I could see the door directly below me, was closed.

"I-it's. . ." I whispered.

My head jerked back; too afraid to look again. Then I shut the window quietly, locked it, and pulled the shades down.

I spun around and darted for my safe, warm bed.

Sitting straight up, I watched my door for a minute or two; then my eyes focused on my window, just watching. Paranoid doesn't even begin to describe how I was feeling right now. I told myself over and over it was just my imagination, or this was a dream. But I knew this was a lie, the fact is I had no real explanation.

The weight of my own body became more and more apparent as I waited up. With each passing hour, my body became lower and lower until I was lying down again. Sleep reclaimed me.

I always dream, everyone does whether they remember it or not. Not this time. Instead, my slumber was bombarded with voices from an unknown source.

The same voices I heard down below. I could not distinguish anything they were saying, but I felt their pain. I understood that they were suffering. Amidst all the cries and pleading, there was a constant in the background. Something that I only noticed after the cycle of moans begins to repeat. An echo of bubbling liquid.

Chapter 3 – Overburdened

I awoke the next morning with a stiff pain in my neck and both arms stuffed inside my shirt. Rolling from my side onto my back, I popped both arms through my sleeves like a turtle and stretched them as far as I could. Both elbows popped loudly, and a stiff pain jolted up and down my bones.

Still a bit foggy from sleep, I remained flat on my back for the time being; waiting patiently for my brain and body to arrive at an acceptable lucidity. Once I had finally rubbed the sticky dust from my eyes, I sat up and yawned loudly.

In the middle of the yawn that seemed to last for about an eternity, I was startled by a high-pitched beeping noise. Nearly choking on the ball of exhaustion in my throat, I stared at my alarm clock on the nightstand. I didn't have to reach far to turn it off. With the blaring silenced, I attempted to think about the coming day, but now I was distracted.

The alarm twisted my anxiety in a knot; making me much more aware of the little noises around me. I felt paralyzed. I pressed my back into the springs once again and stretched as far as I could. The very first thing that came to mind upon waking up was how badly I wished to smell bacon and eggs.

I want to head downstairs to see my dad wearing an apron and chef hat, cooking me a delicious banquet with a big smile on his face. Albeit looking like a doofus while doing it, but that's what would make it amazing. Together we could laugh, and joke. He could teach me the best way to scramble an egg and I would nod along, pretending I didn't already know how.

I smiled at the thought and let that dream linger in my head for a few minutes before cruel reality began to sink in once more. The more lucid I became; the more recent events began to crop up. Many small details, little inconsistencies came rushing back the more I tried to suppress it. But now it was too late, those dreadful thoughts were stuck in my head for the rest of the day.

Determined to start the day, I rose out of bed like a zombie and pressed my feet to the floor. Still, in my pajamas, I made my way over to my window, nearly tripping over a corner of the rug that had folded over. Opening the shades, I squinted at the new daylight. For just a second, I believed this day could go well for me.

When I looked down, I could see the bulkhead door was closed; appearing perfectly normal out there. And yet, I got a disturbing feeling staring down the door.

I imagined black smoke billowing out and making a dash for my window, or some kind of monster would open it up and reveal its long bony arm. These fears seemed ridiculous now, but last night. . . I don't know.

I stepped back and took my time getting ready for school. A white tank top under another plain old T-shirt, both zipped under a hoodie. Standard baby-blue stonewashed jeans and my only pair of sneakers. I wasn't going to be setting any new fashion trends today, and that's how I liked it.

As soon as I was ready, I threw my door open and made my way down the stairs. I noticed a distinct lack of eggs but didn't let that discourage me. Taking the corner with medium haste, I was met by the sight of my dad melted into the couch with an empty stare on his face and the news playing over the TV. I reduced my speed to see if he would notice me, but he didn't waver.

"Morning, Dad," I said plainly.

No response. So, I stopped just past the couch and stared at him, hoping he would acknowledge me at some point. I waited a minute, he hardly even moved. My rejected gaze fell to the floor, followed by a heavy sigh. With a lax jaw, I speed-walked out the door and hopped down the short steps; embracing the morning chill. Arriving at the end of the driveway, I glanced down the road to my left and could see the bus approaching from about half a mile away. A thin layer of fog rolled over the pavement, refracting the headlights and making the road glow as it got closer.

The bus arrived with a dainty squeal of its brakes and a low huff from the exhaust. I stepped up to the bus doors and waited for the driver to open them, but she seemed preoccupied with the radio. My eyes wandered to the fogged-up windows where I caught a glimpse of heads against the glass.

Some were sleeping, others just enjoying the feeling of cool glass against their face. Some were moving around and talking, but I guarantee nobody wanted to be at school today. It's Wednesday; halfway done. Finally, the doors opened, and I stepped up and took my seat.

I quickly found a place to rest on the left side of the bus. Like most other times before; I placed my bag between the wall of the bus and myself and used it as a makeshift pillow. The bus released its brakes and started the drive. Thankfully, my bus ride was short, so all I had to do was stuff my hands in my pockets, get warm, get comfortable, and wait. Today it would appear I lucked out, for the seat I chose was directly behind the one that had a heat blower underneath. Which means my ankles and legs would be toasty the whole way to school.

Though I would only get to enjoy the warm breath for a brief time. My road was second to last on the list of pickups because just beyond my house was a dead-end community that was a perfect spin-around point. In the direction, we headed now, was the center of town which of course led to every other road and destination.

We continued towards town for about a mile when we reached a fork in the road. Then continued straight, just past the wheat field which served as a marker to most people. Once you hit the field, you only have about a fifth of a mile until you hit the town. Cutting through the main road, we reached an intersection and this time turned right.

The small supermarket, located just as we turned down this road, was more busy than usual today. This area abruptly changed from supermarket to dense tree population; which continued on for a brief time until we came across the final pickup road on the right. It was at this point that my eyes eased shut and I allowed a half-sleep, half-awake state to wash over me.

Memories of exiting the bus that morning were lost to me; as was my first class of the day. Something had a tight grip on my skull all morning; an emptiness with a physical form at the foundation of my brain. Crackling and twisting, like it was being slow-cooked by a hairdryer.

It was during the second period when I finally noticed it. Barely audible, hardly dominant; a tired whirring chipped away at my ability to think clearly. I sat in drawing class, staring down as a blank sheet of paper with my pencil in hand. A half-assed doodle came to life on the page, in an attempt to distract myself. Even *that* proved only to annoy me.

Releasing the pencil onto the desk, I looked around the room for anything to focus on. I only saw minor pulses through my eyes as my heartbeat carried on. The substitute teacher dictated this period to be a study hall, and thus the room fell into complete and utter silence.

As for me, I wanted to work. I wanted to engage in classroom activities and feel productive, to hopefully scrape this funk out of my system. That didn't happen. Next thing I know. I'm being shaken awake by the Sub.

My eyes darted open as his loud, irate voice shook me awake. Loads of information blasted my brain when I came to the realization that I had slept through the class. My body shot upright and I looked right at him, a small string of drool hung from my lip.

"Miss Avery, I understand it's early, but school is not for sleeping. That's why you have a bed at home." He spoke sternly; clearly unhappy.

I wiped my mouth and cleared my throat, trying to find some excuse but was distracted by his big nose and grey beard.

My words didn't find a smooth exit; instead, happening to stumble out.

"S-sorry, I didn't mean-mean to." My lungs were deflated.

He hummed, "I only feel bad that you missed out on an opportunity to get more work done. So, here's what we're going to do." He laced his fingers and gave me a devious grin. Clearly letting his Substitute Teacher status go to his head.

"I am going to let you make up for lost time and spend lunch with me today. How does that sound?"

A light chuckle came from the front of the room and I had no response aside from looking away and gritting my teeth.

He spoke again, "Great, see you then." He spun around and walked back to his temporary throne.

The more I thought about it, the less I cared. What does it matter if I miss lunch? Not like I have anyone to sit around and chat with. Even Joey skips lunch to work on other projects. Sure, I was a little hungry, but it's not like that's new for me. The food here isn't anything to write home about. . . so it doesn't matter in the end.

When the bell rang, I maneuvered my way to the next one, then the next one. After the issue during Drawing, everything else seemed rushed. Like the world was moving at twice the speed today. Every class seemed to go by in a flash, and nobody else bothered me.

Not the teachers, not some jock looking for answers to a question, not even Stacy; which was the most unsettling. Messing with me was like, her favorite sport. I'm not really complaining, but I haven't seen her at all, and that worries me.

On the bright side, it only took half the day for the buzzing in my head to go away. You could almost say I was feeling back to normal; my normal being a tightly bound ball of angst and misery.

Lunch came, and I made my way to the art room again. The Sub was there, waiting patiently at the desk for me to arrive. I sat up in the front row of the classroom and quickly buried myself in my English literature textbook. Whether I was taking in the information or not, didn't matter. What mattered is that he kept to himself and so did I.

Though, of course, it was time for lunch which meant he came prepared. Ten minutes into our time together, he opened a loud bag of chips and unwrapped a sandwich. Now I definitely wasn't taking in the words I read. My stomach rumbled at the thought of food, but at the same time, I screamed at him from within; telling him to stop eating so loud.

As soon as the bell rang, I was out the door without a word. I entered the mostly vacant hallways and was pleased to find it that way. My locker was a fair distance away, so I had to be quick before the crowd swallowed me up. Turning right from the art room I made my way past a few doors, teachers' lounge, and the main hall that leads to the main office and other parts of the building.

I wasted no time and made it to my locker in less than a minute. That's when I discovered something conspicuous. Our lockers were tall, vertical, and thin; a little smaller than average shoulder width. They all had a number stamped at the top, and a combination lock about mid-way down to gain access. My lock was already undone.

A bad feeling spiraled in my gut as I observed my surroundings. This hall had filled significantly in the time it took for me to arrive, but no one looked entirely hostile, at least not towards me.

Still suspicious, I opened the door and revealed something resting on a stack of books. It was a yellow sticky note with messy, small handwriting. I leaned forward enough to read it.

Behind you.

"Oh sh-" Before I could finish, a hand reached past me, snatched the paper away and instantly plowed my face into a cold mound of mashed potatoes and meatloaf.

I reeled back and inhaled deeply, staggering a few blind steps backward. One eye remained sealed shut from potatoes, ketchup, and random gunk. The other angrily searched for the person that did this.

No surprise, Stacy and her friend were standing behind me with a very pleased look on their faces. I met her directly; random bits of food stuck to the ends of my hair and fell in front of my face.

"Are you freaking kidding me?!" I yelled. The rest of the hall went silent, now looking in this direction.

"What, you're not gonna say thank you? I noticed you skipped lunch today, so I thought I'd be nice and bring you today's special. I just didn't expect you to eat like such an animal." Stacy explained.

"I didn't skip it, jerk!" The crowd slowly returned to normal, ignoring the situation.

"Oh yeah? Then, where were you?" One of her friends said very snippily.

I looked at the girl. "I see you got promoted to lackey with lines. Congrats." I said angrily.

It was at this point that every other student in the hall either moved along or ignored the scene entirely. Stacy gave me a swift kick in the shin.

"Why weren't you at lunch?" Stacy reiterated.

With clenched teeth, I spoke. "I had to catch up on my work."

"She doesn't seem too grateful that we went out of our way to make sure she got food." The same girl chimed in with a cynical tone.

"No, Lynn she doesn't. There's always next time." She smiled, together they chuckled.

Tears were welling up in my fiery eyes. My rage boiled, but my body became weak. Timid. My legs began to tremble, and I felt the spot on my shin begin to throb.

"Y-you're such a—"

My words fell short; engulfed by the overbearing malice in her face. I'm a coward, a worthless child that can't fight her own battles. With a clenched fist, I sprinted down the hall as fast as I could. Unintentionally ramming into two other kids who were just having a casual conversation.

My head was low, everything was a shadowy blur, but I continued on. Running to a destination I had not planned for. This new hall I entered was twice as populated as the one before, which inevitably slowed my pace.

A few students, busy prepping for their next class, stood right in the middle of my way, leaving only a tight fit between them and the lockers. I tried hard to pretend I was invisible, that I could easily slide by them unnoticed and uninhibited. My main concern was the food that blatantly coated my face and hair. The embarrassment I would have to face if anyone were to confront me about it.

The tight gap grew close and I started to move faster until a locker opened and blocked my only way through. I stopped and lowered my head again, waiting for a new opening.

As quickly as it opened it closed again, revealing some guy on the other side who now stood where the door had been. I didn't look to him, but I could feel his eyes on me. We stood idle for almost twenty seconds before I took a deep breath and raised my head to ask him to move. But to my surprise, he had a strange curiosity in his eyes; almost awestruck.

Prepared for him to laugh, I stared him down with saddened lips.

"It's you." He said softly, his voice matching the interest in his eyes.

I continued to stare, albeit now less rigid than before. The blood rushed to my face as shame took hold. I didn't say anything; I didn't move or look away. It was odd, to say the least, but I don't think I recognized him. Which seemed unlikely given the size of this school and how long I've been going here. And yet, here stood a cryptic face.

He was slightly taller than me, skinny, and had a very lax posture. He had angular features, thin lips and shaggy medium length light brown hair, sort of like mine just a little shorter and less random. This guy had some pretty standout features, such as the two black earrings in his left ear and two more black ball piercings above his left brow. On top of that, he also had a small scar on the right side of his face along the lower portion of his jaw and extending up to his cheek.

As for clothes, he wore a simple grey T-shirt, no logo or insignia, and black skinny jeans. Above it all, there was one thing that stole my attention to the point that I felt almost hypnotized. The way he looked at me, with his narrow green marble eyes was magical. For a second, and not a second more, I could have told you his eyes were glowing there under the pale fluorescent lights.

Then to my surprise, he leaned in. Close enough to conceal his mouth with his hand; like passing on a secret message.

"The bathroom just down this hall is open. You're safe." He whispered in my ear, then slyly sidestepped, making space for me to pass. I was stunned but still aware of my situation. I gave him a short nod of appreciation, then ran past him.

The bathroom door slammed shut, and I wasted no time removing the nasty food from my head and face, letting both scenes play over again in my head. The gunk came off pretty easy, but the smell lingered in my hair and on my clothes.

On the outside, I was clean. But underneath the surface, I couldn't be farther from it. Staring into my own reflection, I cried. This pain I felt, there was no escaping it.

The tears didn't last. And soon, I was wiping them away; discarding my emotions into the trash with everything else. My body pulsed; cool goosebumps ran over my skin as a new thought formed. Who was that guy? It was a rare thing for a bystander to get involved in any way. Everyone besides Joey just goes about their day, minding their own business. Even I have seen this kid I know get bullied and just ignored it. It's the smart thing to do if you just want to get by, and we all understand that.

But this stranger was not from around here, I'm sure of it. There's no way the school board would allow him to have those piercings in. . . Come to think of it, there was a girl on the bus yesterday. I didn't recognize her either. This was all so strange.

I shook my head, trying to unclog my brain and re-immerse myself in my current reality. The day would go on, with or without me so I had to get it together. With a final glare into the mirror, I exhaled and opened the door.

The hall where my locker rested was almost completely empty. I still needed to swap out some books, but I needed to be fast. There's always a chance she's lurking for round two.

Thankfully, the coast seemed clear, and I was able to get what I needed and go along my way. Math came next, and I couldn't be any more neutral about it. Even though Math was one of my favorite subjects, I just had no drive for it lately. There's too much mold in my brain, too much chaos in my life; it didn't seem very important.

Arriving a minute late, I entered the room to receive numerous eyes locked on me. Not surprised by this, I just kept my head down and moved to my seat.

"Two days in a row, that is exceedingly strange." Mr. Lane observed, standing at the front of the room doing his daily intro.

I sat in my chair and kept my eyes on his legs. "I'm sorry," I muttered.

He could tell by the tone in my voice that there was more to this than simple time mismanagement. So, he ended it there.

He started up again, beginning class by handing out a worksheet that would help us prepare for an upcoming quiz. I received mine and stamped my name and the date on the top of the page. Admittedly, I had no interest in the worksheet, but after I examined the fifteen questions, I realized it wouldn't be hard.

About halfway down the page, I stopped to look around the room. It was mostly quiet today, save for two boys who always joked around with each other at the far end of the room. I didn't care about them; I was looking for Stacy. She was nowhere to be seen, which definitely relieved some pressure in my chest.

I finished the sheet but waited to hand mine in until somebody else went up first. Following behind them, I placed it on his desk. As I arrived, Mr. Lane looked up from his notepad and smiled at me.

"That was fast."

I shrugged, the energy to engage in playful banter was missing.

His smile flattened briefly, then returned bigger than before.

"Kimberly, if you ever need someone to talk to. . ." He started.

"I know. . .Thanks." I stated plainly, then started back towards my seat.

He called past me, "Oh, and once you have all finished, you can start reading chapter six."

Returning to my seat, I lagged for a few seconds before removing the textbook and opening it to chapter six as he said. Most students would be annoyed to have to read, but it was fine with me. I just wanted this day to be over faster. Granting my wish, the bell came faster than expected, and I was on my way out the front doors of the school.

Greeted once again by the hovering sun, I felt a lingering sense of déjà vu. Every day was the same as the one before, with only minor differences to break the illusion that I am being trapped within some eternal cycle of pain. Though some days, it really did feel like that.

Those were my thoughts as I sat down on the bus. Will this Hell ever end? Will it at least get batter in some small way, or will I spiral down into a deeper pit?

I guess I'll find out one day. I thought to myself as we pulled away from the school.

The ride home was a literal repeat of all the others. The same path, the same speeds, the same trees, and buildings. All scrolling by as nothing more than blobs of color and nothing more.

But then it occurred to me, that the things outside these windows weren't just blobs of color. To other people, this road may be their favorite to walk in the morning.

That home I so quickly dismiss is perhaps the most cherished thing in someone's life. These trees are the inspiration to some artist or writer out there. Everything has some meaning to somebody, even if to me they are just background noise.

I began tapping my toes into the underside of the unoccupied seat in front of me and humming tunes to pass the time. When the bus finally pulled up to my house, I stumbled down the lane and nearly tripped going down the steps. The bus took off, and my mind relaxed.

I opened the door to my home and ignored the loud creaking hinges. Inside, I was torn between happy and scared to see my dad bent into the fridge. As I closed the door behind me and removed my shoes, I noticed he had the trash can pulled up next to the open door.

"Hi, Dad," I said with a strained voice. He didn't respond, just like this morning.

He took something heavy from the fridge and slammed it into the empty trash can. I see how this was going to end, so I tried to play it smart and sneak past him to my room.

As I reached the archway, his voice commanded, "Stop."

I finished my step and halted, my mind lagging. Wearily, I looked at him, and he did the same.

"What?" I yawned.

He slammed the cold door shut, jars and glasses jingled inside. He walked with an authoritative strut toward me and harshly grabbed me by the ear.

"Ow, ow, ow. That hurts!" I shouted. He pulled me toward the fridge and leaned me over the trash can.

"Do you see this?" He sternly pointed inside the bin.

He let go of my ear. I looked down to see a few bowls of leftover food, two milk cartons, eggs, mayonnaise, yogurt, and bread all resting in a messy pile at the bottom.

"What happened?" I asked quietly, still nursing my ear.

"This is what happens when you let the refrigerator stay turned off all night and half the day. Spoiled food!" he growled.

"But. . . That doesn't make any sense. How did it all go bad so quickly?" I questioned.

"What does it matter? The food is rotten, and now I have to replace the stuff I just bought." He stated.

"I'm sorry, Dad, I went to turn on the switch thing as you said, but when I got down there, the door closed behind me, and I got scared . . . I-I didn't think—"

"No, you didn't. You never do! Oh, and that reminds me, you left the flashlight in the basement. I'm guessing you dropped it."

He reached behind him and tossed the flashlight into the trash. The glass pane was in pieces; It must've shattered when I dropped it. He placed his hand on my shoulder, and I went stiff.

I knew what this meant. What followed his shoulder grab? A hard smack to the back of the head, just like when I was a kid. But to my surprise, he squeezed tight for a moment then let go, giving a heavy, tired sigh. He angrily rubbed the top of his head. I watched dandruff sprinkle onto the floor.

"Just. . . Go to your room and don't come down until morning." His throat made a grinding exhale, choking on the words he held back. I wanted to move, but my legs wouldn't work. I was still waiting for the smack.

"Now!" he shouted.

My legs quaked, and I ran up the stairs as fast as I could, making sure not to slam my door behind me. Today, I counted myself lucky. This could have gone one way, but it didn't.

Usually, he would've tossed me around and then grounded me; no TV, music, or reading for two weeks. Oddly enough, he took mercy or whatever you might call it.

That being said, I was still in a bad mood, albeit relieved that I wouldn't be trying to sleep tonight with a lump on my head. Then it occurred to me that I'm not sleeping easy tonight anyway. Being in this room, this house again I could feel the unease rise once more. The negative energy flowed as a vibrant hot mist, suffocating all goodwill and positive thoughts. I am definitely home.

Tossing my bag on the bed, I pulled out a few papers, trying to occupy my mind but to no avail. I had nothing new to work on and there were no assigned chapters to read. I needed something engaging, something to soothe this angst in my head. My attempt at a solution was pulling out one of my favorite books from under the bed. I had all the best moments bookmarked with slips of paper, so I skipped ahead to a later section.

I read those ten or so pages but had a hard time immersing myself. The suspense, drama, and revelations didn't seem to affect me at all. For some reason, I just didn't care. The book was returned to its rightful place, and I spent the next short burst of time cleaning my bag. All pencil sharpeners were dumped, and paper splinters followed. Every notebook and textbook were meticulously organized by order of the day. My bag was immaculate.

Sliding it off my bed and onto the floor, I flopped down on my back and returned my everlasting stare at the ceiling. It occurred to me that I didn't do the best job cleaning up at school, but honestly, I just wasn't in the mood to shower again. I hate showering every day; it's such a pain. Even though this is kind of necessary, I will hold off until the morning.

I rubbed my dry eyes gently, trying to stay awake. I don't know why I felt so drained; it's barely six o'clock. I figure I got enough sleep during school to make up for last night, but that wasn't the case. All the dozing off probably added up to an hour, roughly.

My back cracked as I sat up and rolled off my bed. I dragged my feet and stood in front of the small window, staring into the trees. Thinking, for a long time, all manner of thoughts rolled around freely in my head. There was enough light to still watch the clouds slide past the tree line.

I never take the time to watch the clouds as I should. Today, they moved so very slowly; carried by a gentle breeze to an unknown destination. It just felt odd, placed in the woods like this. No surrounding lights and when it got dark, even the moon had a hard time reaching the ground. It was so desolate. So, forgotten.

I felt a strong emotion inside me begin to swell, a gloomy wave of displacement and disappointment in everything that I am.

"I wish. . ."

A tight fist curled up in one hand, then slowly released as the tension escaped. "I just wish I was somebody."

I pressed my chin between my hands as I leaned on my elbows in my windowsill. The sun was fading; lending its last fiery orange glow to the world before wishing us goodnight. I watched the sun fade away, and the darkness came. Protected by the nearby lamp, I stepped away from the window.

Right now, I felt alone, so I did something out of character. I moved past my bed and opened the bedroom door, letting the flooding noise of the television creep in. All lights were off downstairs, leaving the just flickering of pointless programs. I stood there briefly, just listening to what he was watching.

It sounded cheap like all the actors were inexperienced, and to compensate for their inexcusable lack of talent the director drowned out almost every interaction with an obnoxious laugh track. Still listening to the TV spouting nonsense, I crawled back onto my bed and shut off my lamp.

My head hit the pillow, and the blanket soon rested on top of me. The light from below rapidly flashed into my room, creating new shapes of shadows on the ceiling above. Eliminating any familiar shape, I rolled onto my side and faced the door, watching. Feeling just a little closer to him. I closed my eyes and imagined the two of us sitting on the couch, enjoying a crime drama or black and white movie.

"I wish . . ." Within a few minutes, I was asleep.

With the darkness came the fast-forwarding properties of sleep. I don't remember when it happened. You never do. In an instant, I could feel again. The bed sank as I shifted around, waking from my shallow slumber. Each stiff movement compressed or released the springs beneath me. I wearily opened my eyes in the dead of night. I could almost feel my pupils widen, absorbing any fraction of dull light trapped in the emptiness. I eased them shut again and imagined I was floating in the ocean without a care in the world; drifting on and on having no sense of urgency or reality.

Something shook my senses. Startled, I instantly sat up. My eyes roamed intently; scanning the flooded darkness for anything unusual. The only light was the same flicker from outside my open door, bluish-gray and constantly shifting the shadows cast by the railing. I let my eyes focus on that light. However, something was there, a dark mass just inside of the door that blocked some flashes. I never noticed it, until I did. I blinked once and the image I saw vanished.

I rubbed my eyes quickly and blinked a few more times, staring out into the short hallway. The darkness just outside the source of light seemed to flicker in every second. Shadows weaved and dipped, almost seeming alive. I bit my lip and hesitantly switched on the lamp.

The new light helped ease my mind by displaying a normal-looking bedroom and returning some sense of security. Unfortunately, the pit in my gut remained.

"Strange." My throat was dry enough to bring forth a cough.

I crawled out from under the sheets and sauntered toward the door. The way that these old floorboards creaked made you think you were one heavy step away from going through.

The crackling static helped me maintain a sense of awareness, a constant that assured my lucidity. The only way he would have left the TV on is if he fell asleep on the couch. Not surprising. I think he views the living room as a bedroom more than anything. I stood just before the frame and glared over the railing; fear grabbed hold once again. I wanted to close this door, but unfortunately, mine is the only door in the house that opens outward. Meaning to reach the handle, I would have to dip my arm into the living ink. On the frequent occasion that paranoia haunted my thoughts, I would have to turn on both lights to make it less scary. This time, however, I decided to just go for it. Despite the fear that something may latch onto my wrist was still a disturbing image.

Without thinking about it any longer, I flung my hand around the corner, took hold of the small handle, and used my body weight to assist in pulling it tight. With the door closed, my hand remained loosely wrapped around the cold bronze handle. I spaced out briefly.

The urge to yawn hit me like a brick, forcing my hand away from the handle and over my now-agape mouth. My body pleaded to go back to sleep. I waited there, unfocused eyes caught on the door handle, just contemplating. I have been sick of just getting home and going right to bed. I wanted my own TV, or a gaming system or something. Something to kill time with when I am alone. I sighed.

My body swung around one hundred and eighty degrees and took a single step, then instantly became rigid as my trembling gaze got stuck on something that stood apart from everything else. My heart became energized as my brain interpreted what it was seeing.

Standing at the end of my bed, just feet away from me, was that same deep dark mass, exceptionally tall with distinguished sloping shoulders.

"What the fuck?!" I yelped.

Out of instinct, I attempted to back up but tripped over my own feet. I fell over, hitting my head on the doorknob. Dizzy and frightened for my life. I stared back at the dark figure. I wanted to look away but was drawn to its head. The figure moved closer and the room spun around me.

Lost in a hazy warble, I could hear very distant thumping all around me. My heart? Or something else. The noise only drew closer, as did this silhouette. Then I felt something touch my shoulder. The physical sensation started to pull me out of my trance, but the feeling lingered still.

"No, no! Get off me!" I yelled. I thrashed around but found my body restrained by two large hands.

"Hey! Kim, it's me. What's wrong?" My dad's voice called out to me, still sounding distant in my ears. With each passing second, the natural feeling was slowly restored. The color balance in my vision became over-saturated, then simmered to a neutral level.

"Why are you screaming? What happened?" My dad was kneeling beside me, standing in the now-open doorway.

I could hear him plain as day, and the world seemed to fall back into place, but the man was still there. I couldn't look away.

My voice cracked, "Dad, look there. Don't you see it?" I pointed straight ahead with my finger.

The figure remained still, not threatened at all. Now it had something new about it. Eyes were staring back at me. A dull yellow glow that pierced through my skull and stabbed my brain at its core. The longer I stared, the louder the voices became. The same voices as the night before. Why were they here, what were they saying?

"I don't see anything. What are you talking about?"

"Are you blind? It-It's right there!" I shouted.

The water in my eyes suddenly erupted into a burning sensation, forcing them to close. This searing pain took me over so quickly as though the entire room was suddenly filled with a cloud of dense black smoke. The pain subsides as quickly as it came, and when I reopened them, the shadow man was gone. My hand dropped down and the look on my face was something close to confused mixed with terrified.

"I don't know what you're talking about, there's nothing there." He got a little angry; not at me but at whoever might be in the house.

He jumped up and walked around my room; checking everything from the closet, to under my bed. Anywhere someone could be hiding but found nothing; nothing at all. Not even a fold or impression in the rug where it was standing. The back of my head radiated with pain. I could hear him pacing around my room, being cautious, and checking everywhere.

My headache resurfaced, and he returned to me with haste.

"Are you sure you saw somebody? Are you sure it wasn't a dream?" He sounded genuinely concerned.

A new exhausted sleep tried to take me again, slurring my words.

"Yellow. . . eyes." I murmured.

The tone in his voice changed from worried, to deathly concerned.

"Yellow? Kim, talk to me. Hey!"

He shook me some more, trying to keep me awake. It was no use; my mind went blank.

□

Chapter 4 - Selfless Effect

There was a feeling. Something unrelatable that crept around under my covers as my mind lit like a fragile wick. Oxygen flowed through my system, igniting the fire in my soul that grew and grew until my lids peeled open. That feeling was gone, the mysterious sensation of sudden gripping loneliness. As though my room had just been filled by a crowd of unknown faces; and in an instant, they had vanished. Disintegrated, their dust filled the cracks of my wooden floorboards.

Feeling rustic and unable to focus, I lingered prone in my bed. Unsure of what day it was, I searched recent pieces of memory for something that matched with the feeling in my gut. A small amount of sunlight shined into my window through the treetops, warming my sheets and beckoned for me to sleep just a moment longer. For once I resisted the urge.

Lethargic and uneasy, I sat up and placed my warm forehead in the palm of my hand. Nausea corrupted my belly, but the thought of food still found its way into my brain, which only served to churn my empty gut with a hot whisk. It took a little more coaxing, but I finally dragged myself out of bed; a bit unbalanced but lucid.

Standing now, facing the open door, my thoughts settled back into the events of last night. I recalled the shadowy figure and how the world exploded into a fiery static. I remember my dad coming to my rescue, which seemed the most fictitious of the entire event. Still, those details alone weren't even the craziest thing to happen. After all, I have had vivid hallucinations before; a cocktail blend of insomnia and copious amounts of sugar spawned some strange visions in the past, but this was not that.

The yellow, glowing eyes burned straight through my soul. Remembering what I saw birthed a violent headache in the back of my head. Red hot and pulsating, my teeth grit tight. That sensation faded as my body suddenly sank into itself, as though my spirit had been tugged upward; lifted free from my mortal coil, and then dropped back down. My brain reset, and I blinked hard.

Having not moved an inch from the door I was suddenly hit with a keen self-awareness. Looking down at myself, I saw my ruffled clothes, stringy hair hanging every-which-way and the potent stench of my heated pits was enough to become red with embarrassment. Thankfully, I had time for a shower.

Moving as fast as my sluggish body would allow, I gathered an outfit for the day and fast-walked to the bathroom. I opened the door and watched as the edge barely avoided crashing into the sink. It happened every time, and yet I still anticipated the day they would actually collide.

I tossed the loose pile of clothes on top of the toilet then wedged myself in with them. Trapped in this tiny box, I stripped down to nothing and twisted the hot and cold nozzle to my preferred setting; somewhere around seventy-six percent hot and the rest cold. Taking two steps away from the shower, I was now met by my reflection in the mirror. On the edge of the sink below was a brush that I used to rip out any and all knots in my hair.

It was at that moment that any doubt of what actually happened last night was dismantled indefinitely. I dragged the brush down the back of my head and winced in pain. Apprehensive, I ripped the brush away and gently reached my hand back. Rubbing the sensitive area, I confirmed there to be a large bump. That missing chunk of memory suddenly became crystal clear. The doorknob.

Every segmented and elusive piece fell neatly into place, and the scene played over in my head from start to finish. The shadow was real, the eyes were real and my dad actually coming to my aid was real. And yet, I wasn't shaken by this. In fact, I was calm; almost dismissive. There was some part of me that completely accepted what happened and was content with moving forward. But there was another part that wanted to freak, that wanted to tell Joey or anyone about it. The motivation to act, however, was entirely nonexistent; at least right now.

With only a slight tremble in my hand, I set the brush down and leaned back enough to open the medicine cabinet behind the mirror. Inside I snatched up a white bottle with a red cap. An everyday painkiller that I normally would avoid taking, but today was an exception.

I twisted the broken cap and shook free loose two gel capsules, then returned the bottle to the shelf inside without a lid. As the cabinet door fully closed, I was met with my own reflection. Seeing it now, I could really pick apart all the depressing details of my tired face.

The purple bags drooping under my eyes quickly had attention taken by the dry skin on the bridge of my nose. For a girl, I didn't have movie star lashes or nice plush lips. If my hair was any shorter, and my boobs a little smaller, I could easily put on a baggy shirt and be a guy for a while without anyone noticing. Even if I owned makeup, I don't think I would use it; there was something about putting on a mask every day that rubbed me wrong. Maybe some eyeliner would be acceptable, but I had no way of getting it.

"I guess, it really doesn't matter. Nothing was going to fix this dog-face." I sighed.

I hastily stepped over the tub edge and placed myself directly into the waters spray. Out of the ten or so minutes of hot water, I was granted, I managed to lather and rinse successfully; but only just so. As the last suds slipped from my hair and skin, the water ran cold and shocked my system, forcing me to evacuate.

I don't know if it was the shower or the painkiller, but once I stepped out onto the old, dirty bathmat, I felt like my head was in a much better place. Now, with gusto I used a towel to dry the majority of my head and then threw on my underwear, followed by a tank-top, purple long sleeve swoop neck, and deep blue jeans that fit me nice and snug.

Now, looking back in the mirror I no longer saw a sad, sleepless, putrid dog. I saw a person, with average looks and bright blue eyes ready to take on the day. Fully dressed and wearing a fragile smile, I exited the confinements of the bathroom and stood in the thin hall with a ringing in my ears. Having been in the steamy bathroom for the past collection of minutes, I came out with a keen sense of smell and sensitive skin. The air that cycled through the house was thick and oily and smelt like rust and dusty fabric.

I took in a deep, disgusted breath and then released it slowly. Taking a few steps forward I reached into my room and retrieved my already packed bag, then thumped my way down the stairs. As I reached the front door to catch the bus, I stopped and slowly turned myself around. The moment I did, all sense of glee was forfeited. Exchanged for a surreal misery as recollected fragments of the house's history replayed. So many emotions, locked within these hollow walls and yet the silence was deafening.

An enormous sense of infuriating paranoia loomed over me. Every corner felt unsafe; every unknown aspect of my surroundings was a potential threat. The quiet was so thick, I thought at one point I could hear whispering. Bubbling.

I don't like silence; I never want my surroundings to be so empty.

I shook it off, cementing myself in my skin again. I wouldn't let my brain screw with me today, I needed to put myself back together and focus on what's important. School was my destination, and I was going to have a good day if it kills me.

Ripping my sweatshirt from the coat rack beside the door, I was off. The anticipation of a new day gave me even more of a jolt as I hopped down the steps and began my short walk to the end of the driveway.

The first thing that I noticed making my way past the surrounded wood was the air. Usually, it was a musky wet smell, consistently damp and smelled like mossy, rusted metal, and pine. However, today was pleasantly different. The air that entered my nose was nippy and clean. I zipped up my sweatshirt, pulled the layer of sleeves underneath down to my wrists, and took in all that clean air.

I arrived at the road and checked for the bus but didn't see or hear anything. Two minutes past me by and my excitement began to deflate again as my eyes wandered around the trees. While I liked living in exclusivity, a part of me wished we had at least one neighbor. On both sides of the house and for a square mile across the road was nothing but trees and trees.

It's isolating, makes me feel like nothing else exists outside of my dad and me. Until I'm reminded day after day that there is a world outside of this. For this reason, I stopped exploring the woods and seldom play outside anymore.

There's just nothing; I've seen it all. Not even many cars passed by because of the dead end. Then, as if on cue I looked to my left down the road and saw a shape emerge from around the furthest corner. It wasn't the bus, unfortunately, but still, I watched it grow and take on a shape. It was a large car, an SUV of some sort. As it drew nearer, I shuffled my feet and pretended not to stare, but I kept it close to the corner of my eye.

It passed by with a trail of exhaust smell that dissipated after a few seconds. I blinked and watched it go down the road until it disappeared. I sighed and looked up at the sky, taking in the blue for a moment before closing my eyes. It was so quiet out here, but this quiet was different than the one inside my house. Out here, it was organic and peaceful. Birds called on occasion, a steady wind rustled leaves and pines all around me and random twigs would snap as playful chipmunks bounced around the forest floor. I really enjoyed this feeling, almost a little too much.

Five more minutes went by without me taking notice, and I heard the bus ease up next to me. Caught off guard I rapidly blinked, acquiring the giant yellow mass that seemed to materialize from thin air. The double doors folded onto each other and opened, and the bus driver leaned a little my way to speak.

"Sorry, I'm late. Some jackass parked right in the middle of my turnaround." She explained in her raspy but peppy voice.

The bus driver was a middle-aged woman who used to smoke three packs a day and gained fifty pounds in the last month. She's a nice lady but definitely has a few loose screws. She hit somebodies' cat one time with the bus, which definitely horrified the younger kids that day; she tried making jokes to no avail.

I chuckled. "It's fine." Then stepped up and continued down the lane to find my seat. I rested my head on its hard surface and closed my eyes.

A few extra minutes of sleep wouldn't hurt. Thankfully the ride was longer today, but I never actually drifted off. Instead, my mind was occupied by a girl sitting two rows ahead of me singing out loud, listening to her CD player. Having that as my first distraction, I went off on a tangent and started to imagine the outside of the bus.

In my head, I watched a guy on a skateboard riding alongside us. His wheels and balance were immune to the bumps and sticks as he kept up and managed to ollie over every obstacle in his way. Whenever we would hit a large bump, he does some flip tricks or an impossible grab. He was a cool guy, fearless and skilled; someone I wished I could be. The bus slowed to a stop, and so did my skater boy. I figured we hit a stop sign or red light, but we hadn't started moving again.

Then, I felt something shake around me. My eyes opened in response and I looked up toward the aisle. A guy was standing there, a Junior with a large duffel bag. He slid past me and I took that as my queue to get off the bus. We had arrived.

I moved up the short pathway, still feeling chipper but a little slow now. Once I got inside, I took a seat in the cafeteria where all the students gather in the morning to wait for the rest of the buses to show up and school to begin. I sat at a mostly empty table, the only other kids there were a few of the nerds and some guy with his hood pulled up and his head down on the table.

I minded my own business and watched the clock. In about fifteen minutes the bell rang, and the herd began to move. Though I was awake now and somewhat exuberant, the first part of the day was mostly a blur.

Art went well seeing how our teacher had returned to school and I got to practice shading techniques. Gym followed, and today we had a free choice day, so a lot of kids got basketballs and shot hoops while I walked laps around the Gym and finished class by throwing a tennis ball at the wall. History and Spanish didn't hold any place in my brain, and then I got to eat lunch.

It was Thursday, which means we got the pleasure of indulging in some sweet potatoes and meatloaf. Apparently, it was the head chef lady's home recipe. It was during Lunch that my energy began to wane. I got my food and found a table to sit at where I wouldn't be bothered by anyone. Alone and mindlessly eating, I found myself slouching again, feeling disinterested; stuck in my head. Outside of engaging with my teachers, I hadn't spoken to anyone today. It has just been class after class with nothing in between to bookmark today in the future.

The daydreams began out of a need to entertain myself. At first, I thought about the skateboard kid again. But he was replaced by the room around me in a different context. In my head, I watched myself jumping from table to table, doing handstands, and the occasional backflip off a seat. Mimicking acrobatics and fighting stances from a few anime and martial arts movies I had seen. I had always loved watching people fight with such mastery; it was almost like they weren't fighting, but dancing.

In reality, my food had been consumed without me realizing it and I was just sitting there waiting; staring off into an empty space in the room. The space where my eyes rested and my mind ignored, then became filled with the body of someone walking my direction. I saw them but didn't see them at the same time. Nevertheless, they drew closer. A hand then waved in my face causing me to snap out of it.

"Yo Kim, you in there?"

I straightened out my back and looked past him, then to his face. It was Joey.

"Oh, what's up?"

"Spacing out, huh? What's on your mind." He asked casually as he sat down next to me.

I adjusted my seat a little and faced him more.

"Nothing, just random stuff, y'know?" I stated plainly.

"I do actually. So, listen, I got something for you."

I looked at his bag as he set it on the table. "Oh no, this can't be good."

"Relax, it's just your notes." He snickered, then removed my notebook from his bag and set it on the table.

"I'm not gonna lie, I forgot all about that." I chuckled. I looked to the floor to find my bag, locating it under the table between my feet. I left it there and unzipped the top, slid the notebook in, and closed it tight.

"It was super helpful, thanks again." He said cheerfully.

I nodded in response.

There was a brief pause. I didn't know what to say, my mind was too full of everything else right now.

He started awkwardly. "So, uh, how's your day been?"

I shrugged. "Okay, I guess, nothing much has happened. What about you?"

"Nothing, it's been quiet."

Another pause. Uncomfortable shuffling occurred in both of us.

"You workin' on anything cool in Woodwork?"

"Nothing you'd find cool. We had to cut a model car from a single block."

"Yeah? What kind of car did you do?"

He licked his lips, "I cut a really nice-looking Porsche, but got too confident and tried by making tiny little mirrors, but they snapped off." He explained.

"That sounds tedious."

"Somewhat, but it's not a big deal; I can just glue them back on."

"You gotta show me when it's done. I'd love to see it." I smiled.

"Psh, you don't care about cars. I bet you don't even know what a Porsche looks like." He joked.

I scoffed, slightly offended. “So? Doesn’t mean I don’t want to appreciate your work.”

He put his hands up defensively, “That’s fair. I’ll bring it over after school sometime.” He grinned deviously.

“Just show me here.”

“Why can’t I come over after school and show you? I know your dad would love it and I haven’t seen him in a long-ass time.”

“You *know* why.” I reminded him with a dry voice.

He clicked his tongue, leaning back in his seat slightly until he quickly jolted forward.

“I didn’t do anything wrong. He can’t treat me like I was never a part of the family. It’s not fair.”

“No, it isn’t but that’s the person he became after everything happened. You’re a boy, I’m a girl and he’s a hard-ass.” I stated.

He got this really sad, distant look on his face. I could tell he was remembering the past, cycling through so many things he’d like to say.

“I wish. . . it didn’t have to be this way. Your dad was always nice to me, they both loved the friendship we had. I just wish we could go back to that.” His voice was soft, clearly deep with sadness.

“A lot has changed. You know it isn’t so simple.”

The bell took this chance to strip away the building tension.

Before we could start moving, he looked me dead in the eye. A laser of intense examination formed between us, both searching.

“Maybe. . . it is.” He said plainly. Then looked away and stood up. I followed his motion and recovered my bag, slower now than before.

We walked together, a small gap between us, but still together. Joining the herd, we moved alongside them until we reached a junction in the hall where we had to split ways. It was admittedly a little hard to look in his eyes again, so I settled for his mouth. I could see he was looking at me whole-heartedly, but that didn’t sway my decision to put up a barrier.

“I’ll catch you later, Kim.” He spoke with a tired voice.

“Bye,” I responded and turned away.

Back to back, we went our own ways. Those old scabbing wounds that never seemed to heal had been peeled away again; the bitter blood soaking into my lungs. It was odd for Joey to get serious like that with me. It was especially odd to bring up the past and left me with a bad feeling in my gut. I’m just glad it was over for now.

Despite that little encounter, I wanted to stay true to my intention and make today a good day; so, I counted my blessings. No sign of Stacy so far and I hadn’t fallen asleep in class. Two good things weren’t much, but it was better than two bad things.

I casually continued down the halls, taking my time and trying to distract myself with everything I saw. As I walked through the hall, I noticed my old Health teacher, Mrs. Charleston engaged in something. From here, I could see her confined to her wheelchair trying to reach up to a notice board in the hall with a tack and paper. There weren’t many people around, but no one was stopping to help. So, I approached her from her right side and stopped.

“Mrs. Charleston,” I announced myself. She turned her head to me, still reaching.

“Kimberly, how are you dear?” She said strained.

“I'm good, how about yourself?” I asked, keeping tight to myself.

“I’d be much better if I could pin this without falling over.” She giggled.

I smiled. That's one thing about her that I loved, despite her situation she always kept a good spirit.

“Here, let me help you.” I offered.

“That would be wonderful, thank you very much.” She smiled, handing me the paper and tack then took a big recovering breath.

I took the items from her and stuck it to the board. The paper advertised an after-school club, the message was way too enthusiastic; trying its best to draw students in.

“Darn janitor Baily must've raised this board, seems like it gets higher every day.” She exclaimed.

“Why not have someone help you with stuff like this, I'm sure your students wouldn't mind at all.”

“Are you volunteering?” She grinned. “Because I could use your help with something else.”

Walked right into that one, I thought. “Sure, what do you need?”

“Just follow me.” She spun around and retreated to her room two doors down. Once inside she ushered me to the back of the room.

“I have a free period right now so if you could spare a couple of minutes helping me fix something, I would greatly appreciate it.” She asked,

“No problem.”

Mrs. Charleston was a sweet lady with a short brown perm, glasses, and a smile that stretched across her wrinkly face. Married for thirty years with two kids and a yellow Labrador named Holly, I’ve never seen somebody take her circumstance so carefree and joyous.

I followed her to the back corner near her desk, and there stood a tall, yellow-painted steel cabinet. She opened it up, and I could plainly see the problem. The bottom shelf had collapsed, and the books had fallen everywhere.

“That shelf fell yesterday, and I can't bend down far enough to pick it up.” She gestured kindly.

“I see.” I smiled. “I don't think it'll be an issue,” I stated confidently.

“Such a sweet girl.” She spoke to me as a grandmother would.

It's crazy to me, how a school of such negativity and bias, can still house people like her. You think they'd all be corrupt in some way.

“I'll leave it to you then, and don't worry about your next class. I will write you a late pass.” She turned and wheeled slowly to her desk.

I bent down on one knee and pulled all the heavy textbooks onto the floor. Creating a neat stack beside me, I lifted the shelf and examined it closely. Nothing wrong with the shelf, however the little pegs that held it up along the walls appeared to be the problem. One of those pegs along the right wall had popped out, a simple fix. I placed the shelf on the floor beside me and searched the bottom of the cabinet. I found the little guy stuffed in the back corner and used my fingernail to dig it out, then stuff it back into its designated slot. I placed the shelf on top of the pegs but noticed it was a bit off-balanced. Removing it again, I checked them all and saw the peg I had just replaced was a little bent.

Luckily, these things were cheap metal, so I just reached in and gave a little effort to bend it back with my fingers. The shelf was now almost completely balanced again, so I gathered the books and began stacking them neatly and evenly inside. After I had finished that I stood up and closed the doors; wasting little time approaching her desk. She saw me coming and looked up from the book she was reading.

"How did it go?" She asked, removing her reading glasses.

"It's fixed, just make sure to tell your students not to stack so many books on one side. I think that's what bent the peg and caused it to collapse.

"Is that all? Sounds easy enough to me." She sounded joyful.

"If I could suggest something. Maybe when you confront Baily about the corkboard, you could play nice and try to get some new metal pegs out of it. I'm sure he has some lying around somewhere." I crossed my arms slyly.

She chuckled. "Well, that won't be easy; he's a stubborn old fool but I'll try my best."

Then she reached to her right and handed me a slip of paper with her signature on it and the date. "Here's your late pass and thank you again."

"Absolutely." I took it graciously. "Have a good day Mrs. Charleston," I said as I walked away and left the room.

A little detour, but one I was happy to take. Now, I had a smile creeping out of the corner of my mouth as I walked down the long hall. Stuffing it into my back pocket, I took advantage of my pass and slowed my pace; enjoying the serene lane.

My thoughts wandered but I kept my eyes open for anything unusual or interesting. Most of what I encountered were locker doors left wide open, which I of course closed. However, I knew that if I was alone, there was a decent chance Stacy could show up, so I needed to keep my attention loose and watch out for anything suspicious.

Halfway to my next class, I ended up turning a corner to another empty hall; or at least it was supposed to be empty. Instead, I came across something peculiar. I stopped.

Standing completely alone in the dead center of the hallway was a girl I had never seen before. She was facing the direction I was, so her back was to me but I could see her head turning left and right, then her feet would shuffle slightly in either direction; frantic. It was plain to see that she was lost, which struck me as weird. Turning to her left a little, I could see her hands connected in front of her chest, holding a piece of paper. She stopped moving and stared down at it, then let both hands fall to her sides in defeat.

My heartbeat picked up steadily as my legs unstuck from the floor. Drawing nearer, I debated on just walking right on by. If it were me, surely no one would consider helping, so why should I supply the courtesy?

And yet, there was something about the way she held herself that itched my soul. I somehow approached her so quietly, that she didn't even notice until I was right up on her.

"Hey, are you lost?" I asked, stopping a few feet from her.

She turned sharply in my direction and stared at me, like a deer caught in headlights. She instantly broke any eye contact that was briefly established and redirected her vision to my shoes. She bit her lip gently, then replied hesitantly.

"Who? Me?" She asked, looking as nervous as someone could be. Her voice was docile, a whisper.

"Well, you're the only other person in the hallway," I stated sarcastically.

It was clear by the way she shuffled her feet that she wanted to flee.

"Do you need help?" I asked again.

She looked up again then turned her head to each side, like she was checking her flanks, then back to me, then the ground.

"M-maybe."

Okay? I thought.

There was a brief moment where the air around us just sort of stopped flowing. I stared at her with tired, semi-invested eyes while hers were low and dark. I wasn't able to get a good look at her face, but I did examine some of her other features.

Most girls in this school had long blonde or brunette hair. Hers was a little longer than mine; no more than an inch past her shoulders. The color was a shimmering black that that appeared to reflect fractions of the lights directly above. The top of her head was pretty tame, but once you got down to the ends around her face, bangs, and neck, the edges got sharp and jagged; almost choppy.

Most of her bangs hung down with the tips reaching just past her brows except for a small section on her left that was pulled to the side, pinned with a lime green hair clip. Her sides were the longest, proportionately. Just in front of her ears was a section of hair that resembled thin black daggers on both sides that shaped her face and reached all the way down past her jawline.

From here I could assess her height pretty well in comparison to myself, which seemed to be just a little shorter; though it was a little hard to tell due to her posture. She was rigid but leaning forward just enough to fold her arms in front of her chest like she was shielding herself. Similarly, her knees were basically joined together they were so close.

She was wearing a grey long sleeve shirt, that had sleeves long enough to reach her fingertips. She also wore a pair of dark blue jeans that looked like they had an elastic texture to them.

After I looked her up and down, and got a feeling of who she was, I exhaled and tried to re-engage.

"How about we start with a name. Mine's Kim. . . What's yours?" I felt way more awkward now but tried to sound confident.

"My name—" She paused.

Strangely, she then handed me the piece of paper she kept referring to. It was a slightly crumpled sticky note with a few classroom numbers and her name written on it.

Every other number except one was crossed out: E132. After a moment of examining the paper and all its contents, I recognized the number. E132 was the Math room. Looks like she's headed in the same direction as I am. I then focused on the name in the left corner.

"T . . ." I stammered "Tan–"

Now I was growing pale with awkwardness. Before I could try again, she suddenly spoke sharp, clear, and concise, but still quiet.

"It's pronounced Tansuke Hikono."

I blinked hard and looked to her slightly irritated face.

"Huh?" I questioned ignorantly.

"Ta–just never mind." She whispered. Then her face got beet red. She snatched the paper from my fingers, stuffed it in her pocket, and began walking away.

"Hey, wait!" I took half a step forward.

She stopped, still holding herself. It took a second, but she finally turned around; ever so slowly. Her arms still protected her chest and her eyes lingered around my waist.

I got to see her face a little better when she snapped at me. This girl was Asian but had a lighter skin tone than what I'd expect. Her thin face was complimented by the wide round eyes, that caught my attention the most. Her tiny nose and three small freckles beneath her right eye accentuated how big her eyes appeared.

While my eyes wandered, I noticed something else that really caught my attention. Both of her hands were bound in this tight, strange fist. Each hand was identical; the index and middle finger gripped over her thumbs with the tip of the thumb poked out from under the middle finger and over the ring finger. It didn't seem aggressive.

"Tansuke, huh? Sorry, I think I can remember that." I said, walking toward her.

She lifted her hand up and made sure the hair clip, pinning her fringe was still in place.

"Tansuke is my birth name, but I go by Tansu mostly."

Her voice was soft like velvet and she didn't appear to have any type of accent, except for a very slight stutter; which I think is just because she's nervous.

"Tansu is pretty cool. So, I take it you're new here? When did you move to town?" I smiled.

She still mumbled, "Almost three weeks. But today is my first full day."

"Really? Welcome, I guess." I chuckled.

"Thanks." A pause. She looked up at me for a second, then away again. "I think I recognize you." She said.

My left eye partially squinted in confusion. "What do you mean?"

"A girl threw a water bottle at someone from the bus. She kind of looked like you."

Now I was the one feeling put on the spot.

"Oh yeah, that was me," I said shamefully.

I rubbed my arm and bit the inside of my cheek.

"For the record, that girl is Stacy Kingston; dodge her if you can. Though, I don't think she'd go out of the way to bother you. She's too busy messing with me to find a new chew-toy." I faked a smile.

"Oh." She responded mildly.

Then something popped into my head.

"Wait, so if today is your first day, then why were you riding the bus before?"

"My mom brought me in yesterday to see the principle. She wanted to make sure I got my schedule and met some of the staff. They decided I should ride the bus home to *see how I felt* or something. Even though my mom will end up driving me to and from school most days." She explained softly.

"That makes sense."

I saw her shuffle again; obviously wanting to move along.

"Well, sorry for bothering you like this. I just saw that you looked a little lost and wanted to see if I could help in any way."

She nodded, without saying a word. I looked back down at the note to confirm where she was going.

"Okay, so it says here that you're heading to E132, which is the Math room."

"Yes." She replied.

"Looks like you're in luck. That's where I'm going as well." I stated while handing to slip back to her.

As the paper returned to her pocket, I initiated an unusual motion. It happened without my will and before I knew it, I was extending my reach to her; gesturing a handshake.

"Well, Tansu, it's nice to meet you," I said in a somewhat happy monotone.

After saying that, I felt instantly weird. I mean, handshakes are so incredibly lame, nobody does them anymore besides adults in business meetings, and yet here I was. I couldn't retract it now.

I watched her hands with a patient obligation. She squeezed her mangled fingers tighter and her thumbs let out a loud wet crack. To my surprise, she ogled down at my hand and let a faint smile creep on her face before wrapping her fingers around my hand and giving a fragile squeeze.

Butterflies erupted in my stomach and my eyes widened just the slightest bit. Her hand was indescribably soft and fleshy. It may seem silly, but I fully expected her to swat my hand away, make a joke, or even insult my gesture. But. . . she didn't.

I chuckled a little under my breath, then smiled the most genuine smile I have had in a long time. Our hands released.

"A-alright," I stammered, "let's get you to class. Oh, and don't worry about being late." I whipped out my pass with authority. "I've got us covered."

She timidly smiled but didn't say anything. I started down the hall and she followed close enough on my left side; the two of us moving at a snail's pace. I stared straight ahead but tried to shift my eyes over to her; get a reading on how she moved. At first, I thought she was afraid of the walls, but upon closer examination, I could see that wasn't the case. It was hard to tell exactly what was going on with her, but she wasn't *afraid*. It was more cautious, defensive even. I made a note of that and filed it away for later consideration.

This girl, Tansu, had my interest, I wanted to loosen her strings; get to know her a little. Five steps forward and I started again.

"Moved here three weeks ago, huh? If you ride a Blue bus, then you must live close to me, 'cuz that's *my* bus too. Which means you live on either, Moulton Road or Chase Lane or Red Hill road. . ." I listed.

She interrupted. "Actually, I live on Jassent Avenue."

Jassent? That sounded familiar. I tried to place it in my head, then remembered the other road past my house. The one where the bus always does its turnaround in the mornings.

"Oh, I know Jassent. Yeah, that's actually a little past my house. I don't think I've ever been there except for when the bus spins around."

"It's past your house? But it's a dead-end and there are no other houses between ours and the main road. My mom had us introduced to all of the neighbors and I don't remember seeing you." She stated.

"Well, no we aren't a part of that community. I actually live on Old Route forty-three. . . That barren strip of road that connects Jassent to the main? It's just before that old wheat field near the fork before town."

She looked at me like I was joking or playing a trick on her. "I don't remember seeing any other houses?"

I tried to clarify. "You don't really see it from the road. The driveway is pretty small and hard to see if you aren't looking for it."

She pondered for a minute.

"Well, that's nice that we ride the same bus. But I won't be on it very much, if ever."

"Yeah, you said your mom drives you. Still, that's pretty cool. I wish my dad would take me once in a while." I sighed.

The pitter-patter of our feet continued to echo in the empty halls. In this moment of absent words, I observed her feet from the corner of my eye. The way she walked couldn't be more different than me; fast and smooth whereas I was stumbling and swaying. She wore expensive-looking, black dress shoes. Which made me aware of my old and tattered sneakers.

Our pace was slow enough to keep a conversation alive, while not feeling forced; I kept it nice and steady and she made sure to stay with me. Searching for something new to say, I was a bit hesitant when I found it.

I cleared my throat, "So, uh, do you. . . wanna stay after school or something?" I asked nervously; my hands clammy.

Her feet came to a dead stop and her eyes fell to the floor. I quickly tried to find a legitimate reason for asking. Anything that made me seem less desperate.

"Erm, ya know, that way I can help you learn how the school flows and help you catch you up on some work." I quickly spit out.

Beating myself up in my head, I watched her stand there in silence.

Her feet didn't tap the floor, both hands remained limp; she was frozen in place. I stared and stared, equally pondering what my own intentions were, and how *she* may have perceived it. Then, I noticed something about her hair. A small collection of follicles that dangled over her face, was trembling ever so slightly. I could immediately tell the atmosphere around us had shifted, but I couldn't determine exactly in what way.

I knew that she was thinking really hard on something. Something I may never know about, that held her tongue second to second. Finally, she took a stuttering breath and spoke, keeping her head down.

"S-sure. I think that would be okay."

As she reset her position and started moving forward without me, so I caught right back up and got alongside her. I made an obvious glance over to her face and could see she had turned pale, her lips tight and head perfectly aimed forward.

Eyes wide, as though the fear of God himself, was struck into her soul. This girl was an odd one, but there is something endearing about her. Something that drew me in every time she spoke up.

I quickly added, "You just have to make sure to let your mom or dad know, or you can take the late bus with me if you want. It leaves around four."

"Four. Okay." She repeated.

At this time, we had finally arrived at the Math room door.

"Alright, here we are," I said.

She looked at the door; I could see she was examining every detail, trying to memorize its existence and location. Then she turned to me.

"Thank you very much. I really appreciate it." She replied, barely audible.

"Hey, no problem." I smiled.

I took hold of the door handle and pushed it open. Mr. Lane gave me a fed-up glare, but let it simmer when he noticed Tansu beside me.

"Kimberly. This is the last time you will be arriving late to my class unexcused. Next time will be detention."

We stood in the doorway, and I looked around the room. Everyone was staring but not at me this time. That's when I felt a tuft of air lift behind me. Looking slightly more to my left, I saw that Tansu had dipped half of her body in my shadow and was actively avoiding all of their scrutinizing eyes.

Feeling the heat from their collective spotlight eyes, I addressed him.

"Sorry. I was helping Mrs. Charleston with something but she did give me a late pass." I removed it from my pocket and showed it to him from across the room.

He rolled his eyes, then looked past me. "And who is this?"

I tried stepping to the side, but she moved with me. Everyone in the room began whispering amongst themselves and I couldn't help but snicker at her timidity. "This is Tansu, a new student. I found her on my way here and we got acquainted. That's why we're so late."

His eyes opened wide and his entire demeanor perked. "Ah! Yes, I was informed of you recently. In that case, thank you Kimberly for escorting her." He said gratefully.

I nodded and took a step in the door, allowing it to close behind us. I craned my neck to find two available seats close to each other but the only ones available were on opposite ends of the arrangement. On my way over to my seat in the back right, Mr. Lane approached Tansu and ushered her up front.

I sat down and faced forward only to see Tansu standing at the front, facing all of us. She was completely flushed red, her eyes directed at the floor and her fists balled up by her sides. She looked absolutely petrified.

"Class, I want to take a moment to formally introduce Tansu Hikono."

The room was dead silent. I made sure to look as invested as possible, to show her my support but she couldn't see me. I then directed my own eyes around the room, observing all of the disinterested kids who just wanted to leave the room as soon as possible. But most importantly, I found Stacy sitting three seats ahead and two rows to my left. Thankfully, she was looking down at her phone; not paying any attention to this event.

Lane noticed the silence and just sort of shrugged it off. He then patted her on the back and whispered for her to take her seat. She moved slowly to a desk near the door and sat down with as little confidence as I'd ever seen. It was clearly visible, even from here; the trembling.

That was the most stirring thing to happen in class. For the rest of the period, we went over decimal placements and how to convert large fractions into smaller fractions. I personally hated fractions but could get by. Throughout the short time slot, I made sure to glance over to Tansu and Stacy. Making sure Tansu was okay and checking to see if Stacy was interested.

Everything seemed to be stable right now. Relieved, I released my focus from her and engaged in the lessons. I shot my hand up as often as I could, maybe showing off just a little.

Class was coming to a close, which meant the last five minutes was pack-away time, as Lane called it. He sat at his desk and began working on some other paperwork while the students all gathered their things and prepared for the day to be over and done with. The bell rang and everyone squeezed through the narrow doorway, leaving just Tansu and I.

The two of us remained seated and just sort of looked at each other for direction. I smirked at her and stood up from my seat, and she did the same. She waited for me to navigate the desks and we met up at the door and we both exited the room.

The moment we stepped into the hall we were both startled by a woman standing just outside the door with a big smile on her face.

"Hello, Tansu." The woman spoke through her pearly grin.

She was still behind me but wasn't hiding this time. Instead, she maintained a defensive wall but approached this woman as if she knew who she was. I looked deeper and realized I *had* seen her before but only every so often. This was the guidance counselor.

"Are you ready?" She asked.

Tansu nodded and joined her side. I looked at them both a little confused.

"What's up?" I asked.

"Principal Whellard has some questions about her first full day, that's all."

"Oh, okay." I complied.

Tansu and I exchanged a look; one of a little half-smirk and head nod. Then, this lady started to walk down the hall and Tansu followed. I watched them move past the lockers, catching their shadows scrape across the grey metal doors until they had gone.

It took me a moment to get my feet moving. Once I had started, I decided not to linger and just head for the bus. The day ended with me stepping outside beneath the scrolling clouds, happy I wasn't walking home today.

Taking my seat in my usual spot, I was annoyed to discover the bus was full today. By the time it got moving, the other kids had stimulated a new headache. The only thing I was thankful for, is that they didn't bother me directly. I was allowed to stare out the window and replay the fresh memories of the day.

In ten minutes' time, the noise level had simmered and fewer students remained. Finally, I was able to let down my guard and just sink into the seat. A thought occupied my mind; this girl Tansu. She was something else, someone I couldn't quite place in any category.

Unique. The way she stood, how she always seemed defensive, and the strange little fist she was making. All of these things contributed to my curiosity and made me anxious to return to school.

I was interrupted by the familiar sight of trees as we turned down route forty-three. I watched my house go by and then started to pay more attention when we turned right down the road and entered a new strip.

A quarter-mile down this way and we turned left, only to immediately turn right to enter the private community. I sat up fully and looked out my window to see a house on the left, flat roof by design but still fairly large. Directly across was another two-story house with a nicely trimmed hedge out front and white picket fence protecting their grass.

The bus pulled past these two houses and then turned slightly right into the large parking lot for the community playground. They had a tennis court, basketball hoops, soccer nets, and plenty of stuff for kids to play on. All packed tightly in the corner of this place, surrounded by a dense forest.

There were more houses here, but I didn't pay much attention. The bus turned around and we headed back the way we came. Soon after, we stopped in front of my driveway and I stepped out onto the dirt. It was hard to explain, but as I jogged towards my house after such a long and genuinely satisfying day, I had this sinking feeling in my gut that it would somehow be ruined. I could feel the negativity steaming out of the front door, palpable and toxic.

Managing my expectations, I got to the door and jiggled the handle; locked. I sighed, then proceeded to knock loudly a few times. Almost five minutes later, I heard the locks click and slide. Then the door swung open, revealing my dad in all of his five o'clock shadow, tank-top wearing, beer gut glory.

"Hey, Dad." I greeted him with a fake smile; already I could tell he wasn't in a normal state.

He looked at me oddly and greeted me the same way he always did.

"Hello, Kimberly, where have you been all day?" he said with a slur.

"Uh, school, Dad."

He half scratched his chin. "Oh yeah."

His voice was slow, dragging at the tail end of every word.

"What're you standin' there for? Get inside."

With a tense grip around my bicep, he dragged me inside. His grasp and the stench as I entered the house confirmed my suspicion. He released my arm and went back to the door to lock it up. I stood there, awkwardly placed in front of the kitchen trying to choke on the liquor and skunk smell.

It took him nearly a minute to engage the locks, but once he had finished, he turned around and blankly stared at me. My shoulders were raised, eyes glued to his. Carefully, I removed my shoes and set them by the door, taking care not to get too close to him. Before I could step away, he started in with the questions.

"What did you do today?" He stood as an imposing figure with a slanted jaw and watery eyes.

"School as usual."

"Are you doin' all your work-k?" He stuttered.

I scoffed; it was transparently obvious he didn't actually care about my day. Not by the look in his eye; there were no lights on, no sense of who he was.

"Don't worry, dad, you won't have to deal with any heat from the teachers. I'm still averaging A's and B's." I explained with a tired droll.

"Meh, good." He slurred.

Without warning, he stepped away from me and staggered all the way to the fridge. The content jingled on the door and then he slammed it tight, returning to the living room with two fresh beers in hand. A loud sigh and mumbling groan filled the space as he sat down on the couch. I remained by the door, arms dangling by my side and eyes tracking his every movement.

I felt nothing for him; no sorrow, no pity, just emptiness. Then again, given his introduction a moment ago, if he got disinterested this quickly, I'm going to count myself lucky.

"I'm going to go study for a little bit," I whispered, hoping he wouldn't interject. He stared blankly at the television; my head stayed latched onto him as I slowly crept across the floor.

The chilled can in his hand dripped condensation onto his leg while the other waited patiently on the coffee table. I watched him slowly dig a fingernail under the tab, and then stop. His bloodshot eyes absorbed the mind-numbing properties of the flashing static. Putting him in a trance that lasted for almost an entire minute. Then, to my surprise, he sighed and set the unopened can on the end table next to him. His chin rested in his hand, kept up by his elbow that dug into the arm of the couch.

With heavy soles, I tiptoed up the stairs and entered my bedroom. Ready to make it my prison for the night, as well as the upcoming weekend. I didn't actually *want* to study tonight; if I left it for Sunday, then I could still have the work fresh in my mind. So, putting it off for a bit was an acceptable approach. Instead, I stood awkwardly in my room, examining everything within my initial sight.

My room was so bland, so empty and lacking any personality. It really struck me just how boring I am. I wish I had money so that I could buy some decorations. I could see it now; string lights, posters, a deep blue rug, and new wallpaper. Maybe a lava lamp or glow-in-the-dark stars to stick to my ceiling. Childish? Maybe; but I don't care.

A desire for nostalgia tickled my gut, and with gentle prance, I made my way over to my closet. Inside I was met with a small stack of boxes on the floor.

Near the very bottom was the one I needed, so with carefully applied strength and dexterity, I lifted the others in one single pillar and used my feet to slide the desired shoebox out from underneath. The stack rested again on the cold floor, and the prize was mine.

The lid came off easily and was gently placed to my side. I sat on the floor, criss-cross position, and started to dig through it. A few drawings I did as a kid was the first thing I saw, but once I set them aside, I found much better mementos. Just beneath the art, I pulled out a birthday card. The image on the front was that of a firetruck, the phrase, with letters formed from water shooting out of the hose, said;

I hope your 6th birthday is on FIRE!

I never understood this card. Why would a firetruck want my party to be on fire? Its only purpose is to put out fires. Which means whoever came up with this card didn't get paid enough to be creative.

On the inside of the card was a little note written in crayon. It was mostly indecipherable besides the person's name that signed it.

Joey N.

This was the first card he ever got me. While I am not one to hold onto birthday or holiday cards, this one holds a special place for me. I gently set the card down and continued my search. I pushed past trinkets and a stuffed sea otter that belonged to my grandma.

All these things were very important to me and gave me a warm spot in my chest, but none came close to the feeling the last item gave me.

At the bottom of the box, I discovered a little ball of cloth. I delicately lifted it out and placed in on my lap. Using as little force as I could, I unwrapped the cloth and newspaper that acted as protective layers. Inside, was a palm-sized glass unicorn. The body was thick, but the legs and horn were incredibly thin and fragile. The memory of this gift was fragmented but powerful.

Christmas morning around eight years ago. I was sitting on the floor in my pajamas at the foot of the tree, sobbing. My dad was in his usual spot on the couch sulking, feeling powerless, and lost. The entire day had been filled with sorrow and regret, and there was no changing that. Not even the most wonderful time of the year. Laid out before me was a select few presents beneath the tree, waiting to be opened. Unaware of the recent tragedy that befell our family. I could see them there, all the bright flashing lights and complimenting colors, but I didn't have the strength to move.

Finally, my dad stood up from the couch and without a word, began opening my presents and placing them next to me. Plastic dolls, CD player, some pretty blue ribbons and clothes. All wonderful gifts for my young self to receive but nothing got through. Nothing made me smile.

Not until the last one.

He stood up with a heavy sigh and reached to the angel on top of the tree. He took hold of its one remaining wing and set it on the floor. My eyes were drawn to the ruined tree topper. I could relate to it; missing such a vital piece of its identity, its symbol.

My dad stood in the way of my sight and crouched down. I looked up to him, and he presented me with a small red box, secured by a tight ribbon.

Tears still running down my cheeks, he said to me,

Sweetie. Out of all your gifts, you have to open this one yourself.

I did. Inside the little box was this very unicorn, I didn't think much of it then or even care until I read the folded piece of paper inside.

In very neat, slightly faded writing it read;

-Kiki

This little guy belonged to my mother and was given to me when I was a young girl. I promised her that I would hand this down to my own child and that I would also pass along the same message. . .

'A unicorn will only reveal itself to those with a pure heart and an open mind. When you do find it, follow it and it will led you to happiness.'

I ask that you carry this treasure and spread love and kindness to others, so they too can find their own unicorn.

-Love, mom.

That was my first Christmas without her. That was her last gift to me. I let this memory play on repeat for a few minutes, watching the light from my ceiling pass through and refract in the glass. I felt almost nothing at this moment; those feelings were buried years ago, but something inside me still writhed. A flicker of the flame within. I just couldn't let go.

Seeing the trinket again gave me goosebumps, I could not look at it for too long, and as quickly as it was found, it was re-wrapped and hidden away. The box was shoved back into the darkness just like the memories of her.

I looked around my room again, the air had a new feeling of renewal, in a sense. Now, I thought mostly about Tansu. She wasn't like everyone else I knew from school. I wanted to know about her, so I can understand her. I was feeling. . . Hopeful.

I wanted to talk to her. I know it hasn't been long since I've seen her, but I couldn't shake the urge. Without thinking, I bolted downstairs and stopped at the supporting wall across from my dad's room. Standing there I peeked around the corner to see my dad watching the TV, I don't think he even noticed me.

I removed the phone from the hook, and the dial tone buzzed. Then, I realized that I didn't even have her phone number. I shook my head, feeling foolish. I was just about to hang up the phone, then took it back, dialed a few digits, and let it ring.

The phone rang and rang.

"C'mon. . ." I whispered.

Nobody answered. Instead, the answering machine clicked and played the custom message.

You've reached the Nelson residence. I am sorry we missed your call, please leave a message, and we will get back to you as soon as we can.

Followed by a beep

"Hey. . . uh, Joey, it's Kim. I was just going through some old stuff and found that birthday card you got me forever ago." I chuckled. "Man, I really hope it was your mom that picked out that fire truck, 'cuz looking back on it now, you seriously just lost some cool points and the fact that you were a kid is no excuse." I acted cheerful, making it clear that I was joking around.

There was a long pause, a moment where I lost the point of this call and everything I was doing. I shook my head and snapped out of it.

"A-anyway, I'm gonna go, don't worry about calling back, you know how my dad is," I whispered that last part. "I'll talk to you soon, okay? Later jerk"

I hung up the phone and my false smile quickly faded. I sighed loudly as the feeling of loneliness and abandonment became quite apparent. I casually made my way back to my room and prepared myself for a quiet weekend. This wasn't anything new, unfortunately. Still, time went by slowly. For now, I attempted to kill boredom by drawing. Many papers, pencils, and erasers were spread out on my bed, there wasn't much room, but I made it work.

First, I tried to draw a cat, but the fur gave me way too much trouble and I had to scrap it. A waste of thirty minutes. Next, I drew a self-portrait, but that also came out wrong. I couldn't get my eyes to look symmetrical and the jaw was too pointy.

The worst of it was the inconsistent mess of hair that made no sense when you compared it to how hair actually looks, so that was junk as well. Now I just started to sketch random images on one page. Just to kill time while I brainstormed what to draw next.

Busy sketching away I finally moved on to a new piece, and as I drew, I began talking out loud to fill the dead air.

"Okay, so if I shade this and then I darken this line. . . No, dammit."

I violently erased a large section that I had just spent ten or so minutes working on. The eraser bits were all over my bed at this point. Becoming more and more frustrated I straightened out my back and cracked it, grunting out loud. The harder I seemed the try, the worse it turned out.

It was a simple sketch of the sky and moon looking over a grassy landscape all done with a number two pencil. But the shading was a mess. I couldn't figure out how to make the light from the moon look realistic in the dark sky and how it would cast shadows below.

A couple minutes later and I made a line way too dark, making it impossible to remove with just the eraser. Leaving the page forever scarred by the dark streak. I groaned loudly and rubbed my forehead. I looked over at the clock: it was past midnight. Apparently, time flew right by me. I jumped out of bed, letting the springs shoot eraser bits all over the place and headed downstairs. I left my room with the intention of being quiet, but I saw that the TV was still on, so I didn't try that hard to be stealthy.

My dad was dead asleep on the couch. I tapped my foot loudly on the floor to see if it would stir him, but it was ineffective. I crept up behind him and stood staring at the TV, viewing the world from his perspective.

The bright flashes of color lit my entire front and washed out my body, turning me into a ghost in the night, I felt empty and the longer I stared at the screen, the more irritated my eyes became.

I looked down at him, his head resting heavily on his left shoulder, snoring with his mouth hanging wide open. I watched him with laser focus, a spark of buried anger rose in me. Dark thoughts entered my head, and my brain swelled with malicious intent. I examined every detail of his pathetic existence, an incapable father that lived his whole life as a selfish jackass.

Now working part-time jobs and his primary concern was when he would get his next twelve-pack of booze. Leaving me, the only family he has left out to dry. How dare he. Clueless, self-loathing piece of shit that can't even bother to spend one waking moment with his daughter.

I clenched my fist and gritted my teeth. I thought about what my life would be like without him if he had died instead of my mom. My neck stiffened with angst, forcing me to rotate my head and snap the tension away. I couldn't help it. My nasty habit of falling prey to a single bad thought was hard to defy, especially in this atmosphere.

Shrouded by heavy, foreboding darkness that beckoned every negative emotion within to come out and play. I felt the need to satisfy my hate. Without the instruction of my will, my hand raised itself above his head. Each finger tightened forcing the veins to the surface. I imagined some psychic ability, one that would allow me to crush his skull from here with ease. My whole hand began to shake as I compressed this handful of air within my empty palm.

Suddenly, a loud slam came from behind me. I nearly jumped out of my skin and let out a harsh shriek that scratched my throat on its way out.

This succession of noises woke my father.

"The fuck!?" He woke from his slumber with a noticeable lisp.

He flew off the couch and smashed his shins against the coffee table, flipping it over and making him stumble to the side. Barely able to stand, he leaned up on the arm of the couch, then made eye contact with me.

"Kim?" I was surprised he could recognize me in his state in the dark.

"H-hi." I said nervously, "I was just stretching my legs and. . . Stopped to see what was on the TV, then I heard that slam." I explained with a noticeable shake in my voice.

"Well, what was it?" He scratched his neck fuzz, not even really awake. Just a miserable zombie. I came up with some random explanation. Whether it was for him or me, I'm not sure.

"I'm not sure what that was. The wind might've knocked something over outside?" I guessed.

"Humph, the wind?" he said, but without another word, he relaxed his body and lay back on the couch.

I stood dumbfounded. Mouth agape and completely appalled at the fact that this man, my dad, just got woken up by a loud mysterious slam which is potentially a threat to himself and his daughter. . . And he just lays back down and goes to sleep.

I scoffed. "Wow." I shook my head and looked around the bottom floor, trying to ignore his idiocy and focus on that noise.

I saw nothing in the dark. This reminded me a lot of the other night, those mysterious noises, and whatever the hell happened in the basement. Something is going on here.

I felt uncomfortable standing here. Vulnerable. I gave my dad one last look walked around the couch, heading to my room. I slowly moved up the steps; my brain felt heavy and somewhat foggy. Those same evil images of hurting him flashed again.

“Get out of my head,” I said as I softly slapped myself on the side of my skull, wishing the bad thoughts would go away. I stopped in front of my door and pondered. It may be late, but a shower sounded good right now. I was tense, and the thought of warm water all around me was already relaxing my muscles.

I walked down the short hall, using the walls as guides in the dark and squeezed myself into my tiny bathroom. I closed the door once the light was on and pushed the shower curtain to the side, the tub was yellowed, and the showerhead had a rust ring around its spout. Not the most appealing thing ever, but it couldn't be helped. I looked at it with stressed eyes, then got undressed.

The water took forever to actually heat up, all the while I shivered and held myself outside of the stream. I felt a hint of warmth and took this opportunity to slide myself in. When the water hit me, my body tightened then relaxed. A light steam started to rise from the water as the heat finally reached its peak.

The shower lasted about twenty minutes. The first ten was used to wash myself, then the last half was all about just soaking in the water until it suddenly turned cold and I was forced to jump out of the shower; nearly tripping over the curtain on my way out. I made the unfortunate discovery that I forgot to bring any clothes with me.

Luckily, there was a towel nearby, so I snagged that and wrapped myself up. Peering out of the bathroom door, I determined it was safe and swiftly slid into my bedroom. The dirty floor in the hallway stuck dirt and dust to my still wet feet.

Once inside my room, I closed the door tight and began drying my hair. Since I didn't have the luxury of a blow dryer, I spent nearly ten minutes making sure my hair was dry enough to sleep on. Getting ready for bed, I threw on a black tank top, pajama pants, and of course my socks. I never let my socks stay off for too long, even when I slept. Apparently, that was weird to most people. As Joey once told me, everyone he knows and has ever known always sleeps with socks off.

Not me.

I moved to my bed to clear it off for the night. All the papers and pencils were collected and neatly placed aside. Lastly, the sketchbook that held my most recent work lay in the center. I picked it up with tired muscles and observed the moon and sky closely.

The smudged moon in the sky didn’t look as bad as I thought earlier, but the clouds still needed work. I found it best to always take time away from a drawing, then come back to it. That way you can avoid artistic tunnel vision and see it with fresh eyes. I was making notes on what to fix and would come back to it another time.

With an airy slap, the book hit the floor. I took hold of my blanket, pinching two corners between my fingers, and began shaking it off onto the floor to get the eraser bits off and then reset the blanket. Feeling ready to crash, I climbed under the warm layers and clicked off the lamp. That wash really helped to release my nerves, making it so much easier to get comfortable.

Thankfully, after moving around on the bed for a few minutes, the warm and heavy blanket was too much to resist, and sleep took me quickly.

Chapter 5 - Breeding Hate

Today was Friday. The weekend was closing in, and I was not prepared to spend two days completely isolated. I had so many things on my mind that the entire first part of the day was missing from my memory and willfully ignored, my body moving on autopilot. The moment where environmental awareness finally crashed into my brain was Art. Now, I was fully awake and having a good enough time in class. The subject of study today aligned with my personal needs, light source shading techniques.

A quick sketch of a round vase was crudely doodled on everyone's page, and it was our job to draw a large circle anywhere outside of the vase. That circle acted as our light source, and we have to shade the vase appropriately. Personally, I was enjoying this. It was something that I found to be very useful and would apply to my art in the future. As things tend to go, whenever you are having fun with something, time moves faster. I found myself exiting the classroom with my next destination being the gymnasium. However, Gym was an easy class to skip out on. Seeing how I had perfect attendance in that one class, I wasn't afraid to miss it just once. I had another idea.

I moved with a light jog directly to the front office where my plan would unfold. As I ascended the main ramp, my feet were met with the red-tiled floor that formed the lobby. Cold cinder-block walls had a harsh glare reflecting off from the many large windows on the opposite wall of the office, looking out to the parking lot. On my right was the wall which housed a water fountain, door, and double sliding windows looking into the main office.

I stopped before them and was quickly greeted by a friendly smile.

"Ah Kimberly, how may I help you?" Mrs. Joans asked in her chipper politeness.

Immediately taking her fingers away from her keyboard, lacing them together and leaning forward.

"Hey there Melissa. I just had a favor to ask." I responded kindly.

"Oh, I'd do anything for ya, girlie, you know that." She spoke boldly. Her loud New York accent vibrated the glass windows.

I always got along with her, although a lot of students have a habit of making fun of her behind her back. Some even went as far as to makes jokes right to her face. She was a tall and skinny woman, with an older sense of style. Some targets of humor against her were her large, puffy haircut straight out of the eighties; which matched well enough with her gaudy earrings and long fake fingernails. When people really wanted to be cruel, they would laugh and poke fun at the large mole on her upper lip.

Despite all that, as far as I could tell, none of this had any effect on her. She is always smiling and constantly going out of her way to help students.

"Knew I could count on ya." I snapped my fingers and pointed at her, she did it right back at me.

This is how we acted towards each other, super lame and cheesy. If I got to see her smile shine on, that's all that mattered. Just behind her, I saw another office staff member walk over to the desk, snag a few sheets of paper then walk away.

"Well, now, what can I help you with?" She asked.

"There's a girl that recently transferred here. Tansu? I was wondering if I could show her around."

She gave a quick look of confusion, then started looking through a nearby folder.

"Was she not assigned a guide?" She flipped through a few pages. While at the same time, chewing loudly on some gum.

"Tansu Hikono. . ." She spoke softly to herself. "Ah, yes she was supposed to have Nicholas Trenton show her the ropes, but it seems he has the flu." She said with finger quotations, "I always knew that boy was shy, but this is just too much." She shook her head. I snickered.

"So, I guess that means the spot is mine?" I slyly grinned at her.

"I guess so little Missy."

She reached into a drawer beside her and took out a laminated hall pass.

"When you find the time, you can get this from me. This will allow you to bring her to any classroom and even outside to the sports field. Now, I would tell you not to abuse this kind of power, but I know you wouldn't do anything like that." She grinned

"That's great! Actually, is she free now? Because I'm good to show her around, I decided not to go to Gym today" I rubbed the back of my neck.

She gave me sly eyes, "Mhm. Well, let me check."

Her slender fingers rapidly tapped the keyboard.

"It just so happens she's in a study hall right now. If you hurry, the two of you will have around thirty minutes of freedom."

"That's perfect," I exclaimed

"Ya know what? I think it would be alright if you two had a little extra time. How about you take advantage of the two class periods?" She wrote something down on some loose paper.

"That's being super lenient. You sure that's okay?" I asked.

"Absolutely, the sooner that girl learns her way around, the sooner she can get her groove." She chomped on her gum and set the paper aside. "And I know I can trust ya." She winked.

I collected the pass from her.

"Awesome, thanks a bunch."

"Now, once you're done today, just bring the pass back to me, I only have the one, and I will be timing you. Also, you can get this from me around this same time for the next two days, but after today I can only give you this period to roam. So, don't dilly-dally, you hear me?"

"Of course. Thanks again."

"You're welcome. Now, Tansu is being held captive in the middle school Science room for Study Hall."

I nodded and quickly made my way there from the office. Down the ramp, turn right down a narrow hall, a left into a short hall, then right into another long straight pass. All the way at the end, the second door on the right was her class.

I approached the door with the 'Skeleton Key of Hall-passes' and entered quietly. Tansu looked up from the textbook she was reading and stared at me. Looking shy as always. I have never seen someone take up such a small amount of space on their desk.

Usually, people unload their bags and spread out, but she only had one textbook out, and it seemed as though its primary function was just a wall to hide behind. Mr. Kel looked up to me from across the room and smiled.

I quietly shut the door, trying not to interrupt anyone's chance to study and made my way over to his desk. So as not to interrupt the other students, I quietly shut the door and headed for his desk. Here sat a fairly fit, middle-aged balding man with thin-framed glasses and a tie so loud and full of obnoxious colors he teaches the class with a megaphone to be heard. He's a goofball and one of the nicest teachers here.

"Hello, Kimberly, what can I help you with?" He asked politely, wearing as big a smile as ever.

"Hey Kel, I was just wondering if I could borrow Tansu." I showed him the hall pass, "I gotta give her a little tour of the school and whatnot."

He adjusted his glasses and took the hall pass from me. He then held it above his head and examined it like it was a forged hundred-dollar bill.

"If that is a fake it's a pretty darn good one." He snickered at his little joke. "Guess I can't say no can I, but can you do me a small favor?"

"What's that?" I asked.

"Can you try to, maybe, convince her that I'm not going to bite her head off. My introductory jokes and approachable smile didn't work. All she did was go dead silent and look like she was planning on running away. I don't want her thinking I am some weirdo." He explained with his hands.

I chuckled. "But you are a weirdo."

He grinned and gave me back the pass. "Some help you are. Alright, you'd better get a move on."

"Will do." I then approached her and helped collect her stuff. She only had that one book out, so her bag was quickly assembled, and we were on our way. Once outside the closed door, she looked to me for answers.

"W-where are we going?" She asked quietly.

I positioned myself in front of her and gave her a big, confident grin then whipped out the pass, pretending it was a police badge.

"I'm going to take you on tour around the school. Show you the classrooms and introduce you to some teachers you may have."

She was a little slow to respond. In fact, for a second, I thought she wouldn't respond at all. She just kind of stared at me, then the pass and back to me.

"R-Really?" She muttered. "You'd do that for me?"

I lowered the pass back into my pocket.

"Uh, yea? Of course. Why wouldn't I? You're new, and I'd hate to see you wander around lost or have to face the embarrassment of bursting into the wrong classroom." I snickered.

She spoke very, very softly. "I wouldn't burst into a room."

"Not literally burst. . . But. . . Like, you know what I mean. It would just be awkward for you, and I want you to avoid all that."

She didn't smile. Instead, her head lowered slightly.

“Thank you very much.” She whispered.

I found it kind of charming how enclosed she was.

“Hey, no problem. Now come on” I gestured. She shuffled her feet a little, then nodded.

We moved slowly together. From the starting point that was this door, I moved us to the end of the hall on our right. I figured we would start at the emergency exit at the end of the middle school wing, then work our way out to the main hall and then to the lunchroom, branching off from there.

We reached the big red, glowing EXIT sign above a set of double doors and stopped.

“This is the door you hopefully, won't ever use.”

“Mhm.” She hummed.

“This is just a starting point, now we're gonna go back the way we came, and I'll stop at each door to explain what room it is, its number and who the teacher is. Okay?”

“Sure thing.” She finally let a teeny smile loose.

I noticed she wasn't slouching as much anymore. It seems like she is a bit more comfortable now.

This hall had some of the main classrooms, AP English, Foreign Language, and Reading and for some reason, they used one room for High School Biology. Each class was occupied right now, so I couldn't show her inside the rooms.

We reached the opposite end of the hall and were met with the first corner to round and as we got near it a couple of stray students came around the corner, a guy and a girl. Tansu was very quick to reposition behind me, placing both her hands on my shoulders and hiding as my shadow. I cocked an eyebrow, and half turned my head to look at her. I was about to ask what she was doing, but it became very apparent.

The guy was explaining himself to the girl as they went by us.

“Look, I told him I was gonna meet them at the diamond after school. Sorry babe, next time.”

She scoffed. “You always say that. If you don't wanna hang out, then just say so.”

“Lynn, C'mon, gimme a break.”

I recognized the girl that was one of Stacy's friends. She was there when I got a free lunch. As soon as they were gone and out of sight, she let go of me. I wanted to ask why she dodged them; they weren't even trying to talk to her. So, I found it a bit dramatic to hide. Then again, I still don't know her all that well. I guess it's just one of her quirks.

One thing was certain, it felt good to have her hide behind me. To have me almost protect her. I felt, powerful? Or something.

That brush in with the couple was the biggest excitement for a little while. The two of us were able to wander around the school, uninterrupted, to most of the classrooms and the auditorium. The whole time she remained mostly silent, only giving me a repeated set of responses. Little nods and whispers that affirmed her attention.

It wasn't until we exited through the auditorium outdoor entrance that she got more vocal. Or rather, her voice grew a little louder if anything. We walked along a paved path that led from the auditorium to the sports field out back, and I noticed her movements relaxed. Her shoulders weren't as tight anymore, and her head was almost raised to a normal level.

Our outdoor tour brought us to the baseball diamond, soccer field, and the shed which housed miscellaneous equipment. We were a good distance away from the school, and honestly, I didn't really talk much myself.

Seeing her relax combined with the fresh air and warm sun gave me a nihilistic feeling. Together, we just enjoyed the world around us. Away from the cement walls and oppressed minds.

Although, this wouldn't last. We were a good one hundred yards away from the auditorium entrance when I heard the bell blaring. Our first free period was over, and it would be smart to get back indoors. I cut this part of the tour short and directed us back inside. We didn't re-enter through the auditorium doors, I forgot that these doors wouldn't open from the outside unless there was an event being held.

Luckily, I knew of another door near the Wood Working room that was always unlocked. It took us a few minutes to walk around the building, but we were able to get back inside without any further problems. Once inside I took in the stuffy smell. It was plain and dusty compared to the real world. Her expression also retracted a bit, making it obvious to me that we both preferred the outdoors. We both waited a moment just inside the doors, and I gave a quick thought to how much time we had left. Neither of us had said a word since we saw we were locked out and before that was about a ten-minute gap of silence. I started to feel a bit awkward. Needed to fill the air with something.

"Hey, Tansu?" I asked.

"Yeah?" she responded.

I looked at her for a moment. She wasn't holding herself.

"What do you think about the school so far?" I asked.

There was something odd about her. The way she stood now, how her eyes examined many changing details around us, and most of all, her hands were loose.

"You know what? I kind of like it." She sounded happy, but still a bit undecided.

"Good start. How about the teachers? Any ones you like?"

"Hmm." She hummed. "That's a little different. With the school, I can appreciate the structure, the beauty, and the general atmosphere. As for the people, I would rather not get to know them too well, if I can help it." She said very straightforwardly.

Her tone had completely shifted before she was timid, barely audible, and simply afraid. Now, being here alone and having time to separate herself, her voice was more pronounced, stronger, and intellectual. She spoke very fast, fluent.

"Why is that? You can enjoy them the same way you enjoy the school. I mean, you can at least talk to them and become friendly."

"It's. . . Too difficult."

"I hear you, but hey, look at us. You seem to be doing okay." I said reassuringly. This made her blush a little and let out that fragile smile again.

"Well, you're different." She said, now reverted to a shy volume.

I was a bit surprised. "How so?"

"I don't know." She looked at me. "You just are. I don't feel so nervous when I talk to you."

"Nervous?"

"Just- I get really anxious around people. So, I just don't really try, but you have more color than anyone else. Something about the way you move and present yourself. You stand out. . . To me anyway."

My mouth was hanging a bit. I didn't really know what to say, so I chuckled.

"Well, you should always try. You never know what will come if it. Just look at me. If I didn't go out of my way to help you, you wouldn't have a friend helping you out."

Her eyes shot open and her cheeks turned beet red. The tiny freckles beneath her right eye were almost completely hidden beneath the rosy red color. "Friend?" She whispered.

I smiled, then nodded. "Ye, friend. Now, it's my duty as your friend to continue this tour and bring you to the library next." I said with a sarcastic excitement like I just announced a prize on a game show.

She hid her blush for a moment and once her face had returned to normal, she spoke loud and clear once more.

"But I've already been to the library for class." Then, as if feeding off my sarcastic, playful energy, she let out a childish groan.

"Well, I'm so sorry to say you're just gonna have to put up with it because I need to look something up using the computers." I gave her a mockingly aggressive tone, obviously joking.

Luckily, she understood my sarcasm. Most people don't.

"If I have to. I guess I can endure this." She groaned again. Then smiled.

We started walking along, keeping in stride with each other, and almost aligning our steps. As we walked, I slyly looked to her, watching her movements. I then noticed her hand. Apart from before, where her hands seemed relaxed, she now had that same weird fist again. It piqued my curiosity but wasn't that important to bug her about. My rationale behind it was, it's a nervous tick of some sort. Seeing how we returned to the halls, which grants the possibility of confrontation, only then did her first two fingers grip the top of her thumb.

As we turned down the hallway, the library doors could be seen up ahead.

"Since you'll be with me, can you help me look something up on the internet?" I asked her.

I swiftly turned my head toward her. We locked eyes for a moment. I felt a surge of fear with the unintentional glare and awkwardly looked down at her lips. I don't like making eye contact with people. Therefore, I figured out a small trick: if you stare at a person's lips or nose, you give the illusion that you are looking them in the eye as long as you maintain a fair distance.

"Um, sure. But do we have a lot of time to spare?" she asked back.

"Don't worry, we've got time. Melissa. . . I mean, Mrs. Joans at the front desk said we have two periods of freedom." I confirmed

"Okay then, I don't see why not. What is it that we are looking up?" she asked.

"Well, you're going to think it's weird, but I want to look up something paranormal, like a ghost."

She looked puzzled and suspicious. "A. . . ghost?"

"Yup." I looked away.

Great, she probably thinks I'm some sort of freak now.

To my surprise, she giggled. It was so petite, like a little machine gun of high-pitched child wonderment. Personally, I found it completely adorable.

"Sure, I love ghost stuff." She said with genuine cheer in her voice.

"Really?" Completely surprised, I looked back to her with my shock plain as day.

"Yeah!" she said with a gleaming smile. "What specifically are we looking up?" She seemed to get excited, albeit, still contained to a degree.

"Well, this is actually pretty serious. . . Or maybe not. I'm really not sure, it's something I think I saw at my house. It was super creepy. But like, it could have just been a weird, half-asleep, half-awake, hallucination thing?" I said in an unsure, babbling way, not really knowing what to describe.

Well, that sounded convincing, I thought to myself.

"Interesting." She pondered. "Maybe if we figure out what it is, we can exorcise it from your domain!" she said with a haunted-sounding voice. This made me snicker a bit. I definitely did not expect that reaction.

She just kept surprising me with how different she was compared to the first day. Almost the complete opposite now. She still seems a bit insecure, but she's much better.

The two of us walked through the door, Tansu naturally stayed close behind me, but I, unfortunately, got stuck holding the door open for a few other students who were leaving. Funny enough, one of the last kids to pass us was Joey. He noticed I held the door and stopped, allowing me to let it close.

"Hey, Kim. What's up?" He asked, seeming happy to see me.

"Nothing really, just gotta do some research," I explained.

"Oh, nice." He responded, then looked past me to see Tansu there. He raised an eyebrow and shuffled his feet a little.

"I don't know if you've noticed, but you got a tail rider." He chuckled.

I did as well, then stepped to the side, exposing her. "Be nice, this is Tansu."

She went completely red in the face and got behind me again.

"Oh. What's up?" He said with a smile, trying to see her past me.

She shyly nodded, acknowledging his words.

I gave him an amused look. "She says hi." I chuckled.

"Well, alright then. I, uh, won't keep you from your research. I'll talk to you later." He grinned and opened the door again.

"Later, Joseph."

He stopped and turned to me, halfway out the door. "Hey! You know better than that." He complained, sarcastically.

"Do I?" I sneered with a cunning grin. He shook his head, entertained by my attitude, and left.

As soon as he was gone, and the door was closed again, I looked to Tansu. She loosened up again and gave me a relieved face.

"Joey?" She asked.

"Yup, my oldest, and previously only friend. He's harmless, no matter how he might act."

She didn't say much about it, and neither did I. We had a mission, so after that minor delay, I approached the desk and got assigned a computer. We quickly took our seats, and I logged into my account. I slid the mouse and keyboard her way, and she positioned them comfortably.

In the meantime, I took out a notebook from my back, just in case I needed to take some notes. She seemed ready to search.

"Alright." She undid her fists. "What are we looking for?" Tansu asked as she clicked into a web browser. I waited, thinking.

I closed my eyes and tried to recall the events, digging deep to uncover any small detail that would help our search.

"From what I can remember, it was this black mass. It was really freaking tall and thin, but it didn't look like a monster, more like a person. Except their entire body was darker than the darkness around it. It disappeared quickly, but there were other times where I heard like, voices or movement at night. I don't know, a lot of weird stuff has happened, but I never found any solid evidence besides this shadow guy. Even still, I can't prove it was even there. My dad was in the room when I saw it, but he couldn't." I explained with fear and confusion in my voice

"That's really spooky. Where did you see this?" she asked.

My heart was pounding a little as I recollected the event, all the faint details creeping back to the front of my mind. The images I saw flashed wildly over my eyes.

"I heard noises everywhere. In the kitchen, the basement. . . But the only times I saw this shadow, was in or near my bedroom." I swallowed hard. Remembering it standing behind the railing at home,

She gave me a quick stare.

"From what you said, I can already say that maybe it was just a shadow man; there's a ton of lore about them, and they are generally harmless. Echoes of the past kind of thing. Or maybe you're right, and it was just a sleep-deprived vision?" she speculated

"How do you know so much?" I asked back.

"I watched a lot of scary movies with my dad." She chuckled.

I paused and seriously doubted that it was just an apparition. If I only just saw it, then maybe it could be explained that way. But the feeling in my chest, that vibration in my head along with those voices, that wasn't normal. I don't think those symptoms fall under the category of a typical ghost or shadow person.

"Besides that, what else could it be?" I asked.

She paused. Then leaned closer to the computer screen. I watched her flip through multiple pages, scanning, and scrolling. She must've been searching for ten minutes in silence. Until finally she leaned back and sighed through her nose.

“I think, you’ll need to be more specific. I can’t find anything different than what I already said.”

I thought harder and harder. I know there was something else, I had an itch in my brain that screamed at me to remember. What else? I put my hand on my chin and thought hard. Then it hit me. How could I forget?

“Yellow.” I broke the silence.

“Yellow?” She repeated

I glared at her. “In the dark when I stood tall in my room. . . I saw evil, solid yellow, glowing eyes, staring me down.”

“Glowing yellow eyes? That’s definitely important.” She turned her head back to the screen.

At that moment, the bell sprang to life and interrupted our search. Honestly, I was a bit relieved that we had to log off. A part of me really didn't want to know the truth, I just wished it would go away.

“Bummer.” She sighed.

“That's okay, its Lunchtime anyway, let's just try again tomorrow,” I said as we both stood up.

Both of us headed toward the door; I got close to the exit and realized I forgot my notebook on the table.

“Hold on, Tansu. I forgot something.” I turned around and ran back to the desk we were at.

I snatched it up but did so in a way that caused me to fumble the book and it fell to the ground. I averted my eyes quickly and looked at Tansu by the door. She stood off to the side, by the printers that were on a table by the door, out of the way of the stream of other kids going in and out.

When the notebook fell to the floor, it opened and landed line paper down. I picked it up and looked at the pages and I felt a chill run down my spine. That fear that was pushing at the back of my mind had taken over; the page that the notebook had opened to, has something inside. Something I had no explanation for.

In the center of the page was a rugged circle, almost like a solid coffee cup stain that bled into the pages. The stain didn't look like an ink spill or marker. No. This was familiar to me. This black puddle of mysterious darkness seemed to expand outward, slowly absorbing the page.

I was hyper-focused on this stain, and the more I stared, the more I began to distinguish depth; it didn't seem flat to me. Instead, I had the feeling that I could reach into this void, place myself within it. A steady whispering grew in my ears. Voices seemed to amplify from this book, from this stain.

I could feel my heart race, and I couldn't look away. It was as if everything around me vanished and I was all alone. I struggled to force a movement like I had woken up in the middle of the night with sleep paralysis, it seemed impossible to reanimate, until finally the blood flowed through my veins and I regained control. I slammed the book closed with unnecessary force, hands trembling. I nervously turned around, then back again, checking my surroundings. I started toward the lady at the sign-in desk, she looked back and smiled. I looked away and opened the book again and flipped through the pages, but something was wrong; the page that grabbed hold of my mind, was gone.

"What the hell. . ." I whispered to myself.

I tried to gather my mind, but I was completely distraught. I began to panic; my fingers became clammy and the notebook slipped from my grasp. As it hit the floor, I felt a hand touch my shoulder.

I jerked in place and whipped my head around to find Tansu there, looking at me with worry in her eyes.

"Kim, what's wrong?" She asked

"Huh? Yeah, I'm fine." I said with a visible shake.

"I didn't ask if you were okay. I asked what was wrong." She said.

I shook my head and replied, "Um, oh, sorry, yeah, everything is okay. It's okay." I tried to assure myself.

She had a concerned look on her face, then bent down to pick up the notebook.

"I just. . . Can you look through the book and tell me if you see anything weird?" I requested.

"Sure?" She seemed off-put by my request.

I watched her sift through pages and when she reached the end, she closed it and handed it back to me.

"There's nothing in there besides some doodles and English notes."

"So, nothing weird?" I asked again.

"Well, not weird but it looks like someone left you a note on the last page." She opened it up and showed me.

Thanks again for the notes, Kim! - J

Then there was a little drawing of, who I assume to be Stacy getting struck by lightning and her hair all frizzy. Seeing that brought me back to reality, and even gave me a good feeling in my gut.

"I thought I saw something else in there, but I guess it was nothing," I explained. This feeling I had made me want to vomit, but I didn't want to tell her exactly what I saw. I don't know why.

Then I had an idea. Call it paranoia, or whatever you want, but I wanted to avoid my house for a little longer than school hours.

"Tansu, you think it would be cool with your mom if you stayed after school with me for a little bit?"

"Hmm? Why would you want to do that?"

"I'm in no rush to get home, maybe we could hang around the cafeteria or better yet, I can help you with your work," I suggested, really hoping she would agree.

Her spirit was delighted, "That sounds fantastic. I'll call my mom from the office. I'm almost certain she will say yes." She giggled again.

"Awesome. I guess I'll meet you there after school. Let me know if anything changes, alright?"

"You got it, Kimmy." She gave a very small bounce in her step as we parted ways but almost instantly receded as she approached a crowd shrinking herself and almost becoming invisible to everyone else.

I was left there smiling to myself. Just playing and replaying the short time we have spent together. I really like her.

That happy notion could not hold my head above water for long. Soon after Lunch, which was uneventful, I returned to class only to be met with the inability to focus on anything else.

As I sat in various desks between different classrooms, I felt off-balance; like the room was titled and vibrating, but this sensation wasn't physical.

My brain was shrouded by a paranoia, an unease I could not shake, and the image of that ghastly figure and inkblot resurfaced over and over. I've done my best to ignore it, but this is too insane to rationalize. It's new to me but strangely feels like I'm being reacquainted with something.

Before I knew it, I was in Math. Placed in my usual seat, I rotated my head enough to see Tansu in the back. She didn't see me looking at her. Instead, her head was staring down at her lap, I assume trying to ignore Eddie beside her. Eddie was a troublesome kid, sixteen with facial piercings and usually an unruly stench. He wasn't bothering her, but it was plain to see she did not like being next to him.

My eyes were drawn to a paper that the teacher just slid on my desk. It was a pop quiz, and when everyone saw the paper, they groaned out loud. All went quiet except for the ticking of the clock. The first few questions were simple, easily solved, and able to distract me for a moment. But as I progressed down the page, my mind began slipping. Things I would normally know escaped me.

Nothing I read made sense to my brain and left gaps in my head. These gaps were quickly colored in with black ink, and the horrors set it once more. By the end, half of the questions were left unsolved, and I felt shame in myself. About ten minutes until the bell, everyone had finished with the quiz and were all waiting in silence for the bell to ring. It was around this time that an announcement came over the speaker system, calling for Tansu to come up to the office.

The teacher allowed her to leave and I didn't see her return. With Math ending, so did my day. Exiting the room and entering the hysterical halls, I felt a small weight lifted off my shoulders. I had regained some balance, and my surroundings became a bit clearer to me. At this moment, I was supposed to go with Tansu in the lunchroom to stay after school.

I was originally going to walk with her but seeing how she never returned, I guess I will just meet her there. I moved at a steady pace and as I entered the office lobby and peered into the wide-open lunchroom, I could see her sitting alone at a table. Waiting like a statue. I approached her boldly and sat beside her.

"Hey Tansu, what's up?" I greeted her, setting my bag on the floor beside me.

"Just waiting here for you." She responded softly.

"What was that call you got?"

"My mom didn't answer when I first tried calling her, and she just recently got back to me. She said it was okay to stay after and she will be here to pick me up a little later." She explained.

"Sweet. Well then, I guess we shouldn't waste any time, huh?"

We immediately dug into her Social Studies worksheet from earlier. Not my best subject, but I could manage. We flipped through her notes and started working on the answers of her take-home workbook.

It became clear pretty fast that she didn't really need my help, in fact, as I tried to explain something to her, she called out a mistake of mine. I was a bit embarrassed but mostly impressed. After Social Studies we moved on to Science.

For the most part, I was able to keep my brain on track, having Tansu here and directly interacting with her made it easier to stay on subject, and not let my thoughts roam.

There wasn't a lot of casual conversation happening, mostly just schoolwork which made the time fly by. Not to mention there was about fifteen minutes where she had to read through an entire chapter in a textbook; a task that didn't require my help, so I rested my head on the table and used my folded arms as a makeshift pillow.

We were both sitting at the table nearest the entrance, and as soon as I thought she was done reading, she went ahead and started the next chapter which means I would be waiting for another fifteen minutes. Going on about twenty minutes of resting my eyes, I began to drift off to sleep. Then I heard her rustling around, to me it sounded like she was putting stuff in her bag.

"Hey, Kim." She whispered.

I opened one eye, looked to her, and then opened the other.

"What's wrong?"

She had packed her bag and slung it over her shoulder.

"I have to go; my mom is coming." She pointed out the window that overlooked the front of the school.

"Oh, alright." I half yawned.

She looked a little uncomfortable. I noticed this and sat up completely, asking her, "Is something the matter?"

"Um, kind of but not really. It's just if my mom ends up walking over here, can you do me a small favor and try not to cuss around her?"

I scratched my head. "I don't swear that much, Tansu." I awkwardly grinned.

"I know. It's just, she isn't a big fan in general."

"Alright, I can bite my tongue." I laughed.

Her mom walked through the front doors and stopped at the office, eventually making her way into the lunchroom. I got my first good look at her as she made her way towards us. She was a little taller than Tansu and I, maybe late thirties, small crow's feet around her eyes, but nothing much to distract you from her pretty face that was almost an exact copy of Tansu's face. Or I guess that would be the other way around. She appeared astute, confident, and as gentle as Tansu.

She wore a blue swoop neck cardigan that was buttoned all the way up and long enough to extend past her waistline and partially cover her gray tapered pants. Her hair was the same shade as Tansu's but was less jagged, overall straighter, and kept. Long enough to go a little past her shoulders and her bangs were soft and mostly pushed to one side.

I stared at her while she walked toward us. For a moment, I felt a pit form in my stomach, because I thought of my own mom. Even though she died around eight years ago, I couldn't help but get a burst of emotion. That void remained. Her mom got to the table and presented herself first with a thin-lipped smile.

"Tansuke, are you ready to go?" she asked, at the same time partially eyeing me.

"Just about mom. But first, I want to introduce you to Kim. She's. . . my friend." The way she said friend was almost as if that one word was in a different language, and she didn't quite know how to pronounce it.

I gave a frail smile. "Hello." My shyness took over.

Her mouth opened a little in surprise. She fully looked at me and examined my features. I promptly became highly aware of my appearance. My hair, my slightly chapped lips, my apparel. I was ready to be judged, cast aside as undesirable but instead, she nodded and greeted me with a smile.

"Hello Kim, it is very nice to meet you. I'm very pleased to see my daughter has already made a friend."

She was extremely polite and precise with her words. I felt bad for not coming off as more welcoming.

"She's great, mom. She has been helping me catch up with school and is even showing me around during free periods." Tansu seemed really happy.

"Well." She clapped her hands together, "I would love to get more acquainted with your new friend, but that will have to wait until another time. I need to stop in at the town hall before we go home."

"Alright." Tansu paused. Then continued "Do you think. . . Maybe, she can come over soon? That way you can get better acquainted." She looked hopeful.

Her mom looked at me with this strange look. Somewhere between happy and seriously confused, then her gracious smile appeared once again.

"Of course, sometime soon."

"Thank you, ma'am," I said.

Tansu grabbed her stuff and stood by her mom.

"Bye," Tansu said to me, sticking really close.

"See ya later," I said back, as they walked away toward the front door and left. I had a warm feeling floating in my chest. Reflecting on all the fun we had today, all the interesting moments too.

Once they were fully gone, I stood up and burdened my bag. I walked myself over to the line that divided the office lobby and lunchroom and turned to face the lunchroom. I let my eyes wander around freely, unsure of exactly what I should be doing right now. My attention was getting stuck at any point of interest while the recent memories swelled.

At that moment, loud footsteps crashed through the hallway, coming up the ramp and caught my eyes. I saw Joey in a full sprint coming towards the lobby.

I called out to him, "Hey, Joey!"

He didn't slow down; in fact, once he reached the office lobby, he stopped, panting. He looked to me, his eyes caught mine for just a second, but they did not stay. Seemingly in a hurry, he bolted out the front doors.

I gawked at what I saw, watching the doors close slowly with a thump. That was a little odd. The look on his face showed distress–or fear? It's strange, I was worried about him, but had no urge to run after him. I wanted everything to be alright, but at the same time didn't feel any desire to help. What was wrong with me?

Then it occurred to me, back against the wall, staring off into the empty hall and lobby. I was all alone, again. I had to get home and seeing how there are no late buses today, so I had to start walking. My dad will already be furious with me for staying after school without asking him. If he even believes my story.

I wasted no more time and headed out. I walked the same path I have been walking for almost two years. Every crack in the pavement, every sign and tree was stagnant, the only difference between now and the last time was what trash might be on the ground. I moved fast, stressing my ankles to reach an acceptable speed, trying to cut down the four-mile walk into as little time as possible. I had to beat the night.

About fifteen minutes into a speedy pace, I slowed down a bit. I realized then, that I didn't really care if he got mad at me. He can yell at me all he wants, in the end, nothing he can say matters to me. Let him get mad, so I can get mad right back. Give him a taste of defiance.

I watched the clouds crawl along the sky, drifting past tall trees and revealing the dim blue sky above. The sun had left the sky, granting me an hour or two of light before nighttime would envelop the land. By the time dusk had begun to fade, I was within shouting distance of my road.

My shoulders felt weighted, and my mind burdened. I had no desire, no motivation to go home. I envied everyone who got to go home to a loving family and a stable environment. Come to think of it, I wanted to run away. Like so many times before the thought occurred to me and every time it did, it only made more sense. The last time I seriously considered it, I brought it up to Joey, who quickly shot down the idea.

He doesn't fully know what goes on at home, but he still made good points about preserving myself and being patient and strong. This time was different, I wanted to run away because of a small, nagging curiosity.

Would he even bother looking for me?

Yet, just like each and every time before, here I am walking down my driveway, a coward; ready to endure it all again. The instant I opened the screen door and took a step in, the front door flew open and I was met with an intense stare from my father.

"Where the hell have you been?" He spat in my face.

My hands began to shake, I couldn't even look him in the face.

"At school." I mumbled, "I stayed after to do some more work with a friend, but there were no late buses today, so I had to walk." I said cautiously. So much for being brave and defiant.

"What friend? Is it that boy?" he asked, clearly pissed off.

"No, it's nothing like that, Dad. Calm down." I pleaded with him. I quickly added, "I-I'm sorry, Dad. I should have told you, but you never answer the phone, so I didn't bother calling and-" he cut me off before I could finish.

"That's enough! Don't you lie to me! Never lie to me!"

I quickly became frustrated but sighed. Trying to keep the situation under control. "Dad, listen, you don't understand. Just let me explain."

He had no intention of letting me speak. He grabbed me by my short hair and dragged me inside.

"Dad let go! That hurts!" I yelped. The door slammed shut behind us.

Even though my hair was short, only reaching my shoulders, he decided to grab me as close to my scalp as his thick fingers would allow. Ensuring the maximum amount of grip, and pain, he dragged me across the living room and threw me down on the couch. I took my bag off and set it beside the couch, keeping my eyes on him.

I waited; arms loosely folded around my stomach. He paced around for a moment, looking toward me occasionally. My body was trembling, and my heart skipped. He was acting strangely. Drunk, yes, but compared to his usual stupor, he was seemingly lost in his own actions. There was something else about him like he was clashing with another identity.

I licked my lips and spoke with as much of a normal, non-shaking tone as I could.

"Did you start your medication again? Alcohol and these pills don't mix, you know that." I made a foolish guess.

He stopped pacing and glared at me, one eye half-closed, the other wide and full of fury.

"Dad, this is ridiculous. Just let me explain what happened." I argued with him. He faced me, shoulders straight and tight.

"No, because I will not tolerate your lies. For all I know, you could have been out doing drugs or fucking that boy." He shouted.

My chest was on fire with rage, I let my voice grow louder with each defensive word. "If you would stop accusing me for two seconds, maybe I could tell you exactly what I was doing."

"I won't listen to your bullshit Kim. Don't even try it!" He raised a clenched fist. I too clenched my fist, but let it go. This arguing was pointless. It's no use trying to talk to him like this. The best thing to do is remain calm, escape, and talk to him tomorrow.

"Okay, fine. Why don't you just lie down, and we can talk about this later? You look tired." I tried my best to talk him down.

He grunted angrily still and turned around then walked into the kitchen. It went quiet. Looking around the room, I debated on running out the door; there is no way he could catch me in this state; I doubt he'd even be able to start his car. Before I could solidify the idea, he reentered the room and advanced right towards me. I didn't even get to fully turn my head and see him before the back of his hand was whipped across my face.

Stunned, I placed my hand on my cheek and looked up to him. Tears formed in my eyes.

". . .Dad?" I whimpered

Then he swung again, this time I reacted enough to bring my arm into his path, absorbing his fist in my right forearm.

"Ach!" I cried in pain. Being knocked to my side on the couch, I positioned myself up with one hand.

"What are you doing?" I yelled in fear.

It's happening again.

“Shut the fuck up!” He threatened, aiming a deadly pointer finger at me. Sensing the danger, I slid myself to the opposite end of the couch, being halted by the arm. I didn't know what to do, I couldn't think. He had hit and hurt me before, but this was different. This time he wasn’t just drunk and being an asshole; he was full of blind rage. He never went this far, this fast.

He approached fiercely and took me by the shoulders and held me still.

“You think it’s funny to lie, huh? I deserve some goddamn respect.” He instructed with a deep, aggressive voice.

I swallowed a wad of spit and mucus and blinked a few times. Trying to maintain some strength.

“Listen to me, Dad. I just want you to understand that everything is all right. I’m doing well in school. I’m not on drugs, and I made a new friend. Everything is going well, and you have nothing to be angry about. I'm sorry for staying late at school, it won't happen ag-”

He cut me off again, this time with an open palm slap to the side of my head. From a full-grown man, a slap might as well be a full punch. He knocked me free from his grip, and I stammered off the couch and fell to my knees on the floor. My head was spinning. With no time to lose, I attempted to stand up and run away.

My tired legs carried me in a wobbly sprint towards the front door, but I tripped over his boots left beside the couch. I fell face-first into the end table and smashed my chin against the corner. I rolled off it and fell to the ground; everything around my lower jaw felt fuzzy and warm. Vulnerable and dazed, I rolled onto my back and tried to get ready to defend myself. He reached for my shirt, but I sloppily kicked him in the chest; knocking him backward.

“Get the hell off me! You’re crazy!” I shouted.

I was given another chance at escape and forced myself to my feet. He tried to stand but his body would not respond due to his intoxication. I barely got out the door, pushed through the fragile screen frame, and turned left at the bottom of the stairs. It was dark now, but I continued my sprint around the back of the house and ran blindly down the cut path into the woods. He stopped at the front door.

“Kimberly, get back here!” His voice swelled with raw anger, then almost like a switch of personality, receded to a potent sadness and regret, “I’m sorry. I didn’t. . . I didn’t mean it!”

I could hear his voice bounce off the thick tree's around me as I ran deeper into the woods. Led tears and blood ran down my face and dripped from my chin, leaving a trail of fleeting life and emotion. I cupped my hand over my chin to catch it before it got onto my clothes.

My feet carried me in a desperate, off-balanced sprint to a safe place; away from him. But I could only go so far in this state until my legs finally gave out and my breath was stripped away. I came to a dead stop and fell to my knees; panting furiously. The wet leaves were pushed into the dirt under my weight and the damp ground soaked into the fabric of my jeans. The chilled feeling gave me something to focus on, something to ground myself in reality.

I was alone. The sun would soon cease to exist, and I would be entirely vulnerable. A quick glance to where I came from revealed a portion of my house to be visible through the trees.

From here, I could see a large chunk of my bedroom window poking through the trees; ominous.

I took this moment to catch my breath and try not to think too hard. After a minute or two, I wearily brought myself to my feet and stared at the blood now drying on my palm. My chin throbbed and became irritated by the brisk air. The longer I stared at my own blood, the more furious I became. Hot tears of malice and fear flowed from my eyes without restriction or shame. I was broken, hating him, loathing myself. Regretting this life.

I clamped my fist tight and the remaining liquid dripped onto the ground, followed by a few more drops from my still bleeding chin.

"That. . . fucking ass-hole." I cursed.

I took a deep, stabilizing breath into my nose and released it from my mouth. This attempt to calm myself failed. My fingers were twitching, my bones ached with a desire to beat the hell out of him.

It was then that I heard a distant sputtering. The familiar sound of his ancient car attempting to start. The engine roared as this beast came to life and the tires matched the roar with a scream of its own; as he hastily drove away. You would think that right now, given the circumstance I would hope he crashed and burned. But that isn't the case. I hope he makes it back; I hope he has the guts to face me again because this is the last straw.

The sun had reached the moment of last light, and I finally headed back to my house. It had been nearly an hour of standing among the trees, contemplating my life up to this point.

I settled on the conclusion that life sucks and I must be strong to survive, however reaching my front door, I wasn't fully convinced of this philosophy. There had to be more to life than suffering; than being under someone else's authority.

Once entering the living room, I had a flashback of what just happened. Many blood drops leading from the end table to the door, now forever stained in the carpet, a constant reminder of his sin. My chest ran cold, but I pushed on, ascending the staircase and turning left to the bathroom. Once inside I saw my reflection in the mirror, face stained red and eyes bloodshot. The look on my face was a mix of exhaustion and hatred.

Firstly, I turned on the faucet and used a nearby washcloth to wipe the blood from my face, making sure to also dab the wound to clean it as much as possible. Once that was done, I opened the medicine cabinet and removed a box of band-aids. I attempted to cover the wound, but the adhesive would not stay. Instead, I opted for a few smaller butterfly bandages that could simply hold the wound closed and then taped some gauze over the wound in a very unprofessional manner.

At this point, it had stopped bleeding, but I feared the possibility of having to get stitches. I'm no stranger to pain, but there is something about someone pushing a needle and string through my skin that makes me shudder. For now, I will just keep it clean and covered.

Returning to my room, I dragged myself over to my bed and sat on the edge. The reality was silent, almost non-existent. Like I was a part of some unfinished, cobbled together daydream. Soon, I would wake up.

I thought I was fine, but after being alone in my room for a few minutes, dark thoughts had returned. Burrowing into my ear and cementing itself in my heart. My knees were pulled to my chest and my arms tightly wrapped around them. I had to act as my own safety blanket. I lost it.

The tears came, and so did the loud, child-like sobs. I tried to fight it, using my inner anger to snuff out the sadness, but it didn't work. In the end, I'm just a coward, and now, I hoped he didn't come home; so, I didn't have to face him again. I am powerless. I would do anything to escape this, escape him. My emotion poured freely into the air and spawned a thick feeling around me. The walls seemed to close in on me, and all color had drained away. Suddenly, a strange, visceral feeling surged in my gut. Not an upset stomach but actual searing pain. I let my feet touch to floor off the side of the bed, and I placed my hand on my stomach. My mouth hung open as I tried to take in air, but it proved difficult with this new pain. I don't know what caused this sensation, but it forced a new alarm to go off in my head. I was not alone anymore.

I looked up and around the room, completely silencing my breathing and forcing all my mental energy on looking and listening. Trying to confirm this paranoia. The more I focused; the louder some distant, artificial noise grew. I didn't understand what this sound was, but it was reaching me, not through my ears but my senses.

Like my body was wading through a pool of bubbling static noise that only I could hear. I focused and focused, and the headache grew until finally, I heard a voice. It was faint, like a pained whisper from across the room, from all directions at once.

"He. . . He's coming. Don't listen to him . . ."

My hands fell to my side and clutched the sheets. My breathing slowly returned, but only escaped as partial huffs.

"Who. . . are you?" I questioned the walls.

The voice responded, this time it was booming; screaming in absolute agony. *"A friend!"*

Fear found its place in my heart and I found myself backing up to the headboard.

"Friend?" I questioned.

Very suddenly, I went from sitting on my bed to standing outside my house in the middle of the driveway. My brain struggled to make sense of the world around me, but nothing had a solid edge. Nothing stayed the same for too long but never changed at all. The trees remained absolutely still one second but changed to decayed husks in my peripheral. The only constant was my barren, unlit house. For some reason, I didn't question this. I accepted it, at the moment as my life all the way up to now. Like it was and always had been this.

A girl was standing before me but never existed until I noticed her. She was masked in shadows, but key features were printed on my brain. Thin, tight skin and long, faded red hair. A deeper red was visible to me, one that stained the left side of her face and head, blood. I could not see her entire face, only bits and pieces flashed in and out of this reality. Nothing ever stuck with me.

I spoke. "How are you speaking to me. Is this real?"

She replied at a normal speaking volume but tired and sunken.

"To you, no. But I can see you, just out of reach. A voice led me here to the leak, told me to warn you. There is a piece of you here with me, with us. It's very warm."

"The leak?" I questioned.

She continued. *"I can try, to give you what's left of me. . . It may not be enough to stop her."*

"Her? Who are you talking about?"

"The red demon. . . Listen!" The girl screamed at me, but her face froze in a state of lifeless despair. "He will try to steal you, use you. You cannot let him."

A pause. My head pounded.

"If fate would have it. . . She is false, do not fear her power." She whispered.

My breathing grew harsher, more erratic, I felt a drop of sweat roll down my forehead.

"What are you talking about?! Tell me who you are!" I shouted. My voice bounced all around me.

"Lucy."

As she said her name, I felt a burning sensation begin to grow behind my eyes. Unexpectedly, her previously frozen body collapsed to the ground. Animated like a movie missing random frame intervals. Her arms pulled her legs close to her chest, just as I was in my bed. Her body froze again, and she began to sob.

"He's coming, he's coming. . ." She cried.

Her body slowly began to fade away, splintering, and turning to black dust before my eyes. Without warning, there was a loud ringing. The vision fading, I lingered in her last words. Unconsciously, I took in a deep breath and awoke, sitting up with great force; at the same time, I let out a fearful yelp.

My hair was disheveled, and my bangs were scattered, sticking to my forehead in odd clumps. I looked around; the room seemed darker than usual, eerily so. How long has it been. . .? When did I fall asleep?

Panting heavily, I wiped the sweat from my brow. Looking down, I realized the shirt I slept in was soaked through with sweat and my body was blazing hot.

Her name, Lucy, radiated in my ears. I tried to piece everything together, but nothing made sense, and thinking only serves to irritate my brain. I sat in my bed and looked down at the bruises on my arms. My nose crinkled with a grim expression. I directed my sight to the digital clock on my nightstand.

"3:32 A.M." I read out loud.

My eyes seemed a bit out of focus as they wandered in the dark. Everything was so still, so peaceful. I was fooled into thinking it would stay that way. Having been barely lucid for a little under a minute that pain in my stomach returned. As soon as it did my heart began to race and worry clouded my mind.

Not again. I thought.

Through my eyes, every shadow and dark corner began to pulse and sway as if the darkness itself was coming alive. I reached for my lamp to pull the string, but no light came. When my eyes returned to the middle of my room, I noticed something was missing. The pale moonlight that usually leaked in from my window, was nowhere to be seen.

It became instantly clear that it wasn't gone, but something was blocking its rays. In the corner of my eye, without looking directly at it, I could see that same shadow figure. Standing in front of my window. A lump formed in my throat and my body began to tremble as I came to the realization, that my dad might not be home to save me this time.

Then, I remembered the voice in my dream. Hide. But if I move, what will happen? If I don't do anything at all. . . What will happen?

Instincts overpowered rational thought and my body came to the decision to move. If the voice said hide, then I will hide, but where?

Without looking at the figure and bathing in a pool of sweat and fear, I quietly rolled off my bed and rested on my hands and knees out of view of the window.

I got really low and slid my body underneath my bed, pressing tight against random boxes. Laying on my stomach facing the foot end of my bed, I couldn't see anything in the room. It was silent, which made me terrified of breathing at all.

I rolled my eyes to the right, only turning my head the smallest amount and could see a sliver of orange light from the living room beneath my door. My dad, he must be home. Before I could think about my next move, the room exploded with deafening white noise. My fragile brain was being assaulted by this intense static and felt like it would soon shatter like cheap glass. I covered my ears in a desperate attempt to quiet the barrage, but it had no effect. The noise wasn't in the room, or even in my head. It resonated from within me, as though my soul itself was being shaken by some godly force.

I started to panic, no longer caring about my own noise level, I kicked my feet and groaned loudly with the pain this static caused. I desperately wanted to run but was stuck here underneath the bed. The temperature in my body skyrocketed and I began to squirm in discomfort. My teeth were bound so tightly together it felt as though they would soon fuse.

"Eh, eack!" I let out a small shriek of pain and soon my lungs refused to fill. Each breath exhaled shortened the next intake. I was suffocating.

Somehow, I found the strength to force a move. With one, came the next, and the next until finally I rolled out from underneath the bed and tried to stand. But my legs were numb, and I fell back down on the hardwood.

I opened my eyes to try to figure out where I was exactly, but my vision was solid white. To escape this situation, I tried to let out a scream, but nothing came out. I could feel my vocal cords straining to let out my voice, but I heard nothing over the white noise. With that failure, I began crawling on my hands and knees to the door.

What's going on? I asked in my head. What is all this?

Then, out of absolutely nowhere. Everything stopped. I was flat on my stomach and everything was back to normal. I paused, struck by confusion. My lungs filled with air again, but I held it in, waiting for something else to happen. My legs. . . No, my entire body didn't feel so heavy anymore. My breathing reset to a normal pace, and I carefully stood up. Turning around to face the window, I saw nothing but the soothing moonlight on the floor.

My hands continued to shake violently. I wasn't safe here, I still had to escape. I quickly turned myself back around to the door, but locked eyes with a physical person. Before my brain could even process what was in front of me, it spoke.

"Do not fear me, Kimberly. I have no desire to harm you." Its voice was cynical and confident. Almost cheery but incredibly devious.

The man was tall, so much so that he was leaning forward and slumping his neck to meet my eyes, but once he resumed natural, albeit still hunched posture, he towered above me. I was only average height for a middle school girl. To see his face now, I had to crane my neck and lean back slightly.

I choked on my own breath, fighting to speak with all my might until the words were forced out of me.

"Wh-What do you want?" I shook.

It was clear to me that this is the shadow person I have seen recently. Now fully exposed as an older man nearly as pale as a ghost and thin as a bone. His hair was gray and receding and all the skin on his face was weighted, causing more wrinkles than anyone could count.

A large nose and thin lips only added to his disproportionate appearance. He wore a very long dark-brown trench coat that was unbuttoned to reveal a black suit and red tie. His hands remained in his pockets and he just had this intent, somewhat crooked smile on his face the whole time.

Apart from everything else, there was one detail that stood out to me the most.

"Y-you have. . . narrow eyes." I stated with a dry mouth. The yellow glow of his irises almost beckoned me to come closer. Giving off a feeling of safety and closure, but at the same time instilling fear and distrust.

"What do you want with me?" I asked, hesitant to get an answer.

The figure continued, "I am here to grant you the peace and vengeance you so greatly desire. The bloodstained aggression that fills your heart can be satisfied."

Fear overrode all other systems, but my mouth still spat a hollow threat.

"I don't know what you're talking about. Y-you need to leave."

He laughed in a dry, bemused way. "And what would you do if I refuse to leave?"

"I'll scream, and my dad will come running up here."

He didn't say anything. He just stood there, not moving and smiling.

"What are you waiting for?" he started, "Scream."

I gulped.

"Only, consider this. If you were to scream, are you certain he would come to your rescue? Let's say he did and discovers nothing at all. Would he then beat you for wasting his time?" His eyebrows lowered.

"How do you. . ."

"I know what you have been facing, the conflict in your heart. That, my dear, is exactly why I am here. Now allow me to repeat myself."

He removed one hand from his pocket, I took half a step back. He then adjusted the tie underneath his coat and returned his hand to the pocket.

"I am here to offer you a deal."

"What kind of deal?" I asked timidly.

He licked his lips quickly; routinely. The room got hot and my legs started to feel heavy again. Without warning my knees buckled and I lost my balance. I fell to one knee and my breath had once again eluded me.

"What is this feeling?" I asked between gasps of breath.

"Your human body is weak. You cannot even bear to be in my presence unless I restrain myself. But that can change, you can be strong; like me."

I struggled. My head felt like I had a thousand dull pencils were being jabbed into my skull; a maddening sensation. Then a flash of that girl's decrepit face appeared beneath my eyelids. Her voice distant and echoing, barely a memory. I kept her warning in mind, as I asked this next question.

"What would you need from me, for this deal?" I asked with chattering teeth.

"To be blunt, your soul." He said casually with a cynical smirk.

"My soul? Like, my actual, real-life soul?"

He then took his right hand out of his pocket again. It hung loosely in the air. He extended his arm and offered it to me. I looked at his hand, examining the skin.

His palm was flat. There were no folds in the skin that any human would have and no fingerprints. His fingers were long and thin, the knuckles clearly defined. The tips of his fingers came to an acute angle; where his nails were yellowed and grown out just past the ends of his fingers. Moldy crud was smudged across his skin and nails, completing the outlook of filth and decrepitude.

Staring at his hand, I fell into a stationary void of memories. The actions of my dad today, a month ago, a year ago. Everything he ever did to me was compressed into a single sphere of hatred and despondency. Another collection of thoughts flashed in my brain. Thoughts of Stacy and all the times she bullied me, made me feel inadequate and less than human. Every single one of those memories coagulated into its own sphere and took its place beside my dad's.

Then every random student, teacher, and stranger who wronged me came together as their own collection. Burdening me with self-loathing and destructive rage. It was overwhelming, so much so that I intently focused on this hate and saw these marbles roll around in his palm.

I blinked a few times, and my mind became a bit clearer. His hand hovered before me, waiting. "All you need to do to obtain power is take my hand. Simple." He chimed.

His hand was almost magnetized, I could hardly resist it. In my mind, I could see myself taking his hand in mine. Over and over, a hundred times; a thousand times. Forever.

However, some semblance of good will hammered at the back of my brain. Joey, Tansu, All my teachers, the memory of my mom. . . The colliding energies spiraled in my mind, causing a violent storm of conflicting emotions. I had so many questions, concerns, but no way to express them. No solution to every question.

He spoke again.

"It is a tough decision I know. But ask yourself this. . . The next time that girl pushes you to the ground, the next time your father throws you into a wall, will you regret not taking my hand?"

I heard his powerful words but distracted by a feeling in my body, or rather, a lack thereof. I didn't notice until now, but the pain he caused me, the shortness of breath and disarray; had been lifted. Well, almost. It was still there, I could feel it in the air, but it didn't seem as powerful as before.

With tired ankles and a stiff back, I straightened my back and stood tall once more. An assurance was established and the fear I felt had nearly dissipated. He raised an eyebrow, looking slightly impressed.

"You can stand. I must say I am surprised. Your willpower is strong, as I thought. I see greatness in you, young Kimberly." He praised while uncertainty covered my face.

His expression then changed from impressed, to slightly annoyed. "What can I do to make you understand I am here to help?"

I didn't want to talk because even though he looked like an old, weak man, he wasn't. It was clear he is some supernatural being with insane power. I was terrified inside; I didn't truly understand what he was or what he was offering. I could only guess his true intentions.

"All right, how about some honesty from me?" He smiled. "That feeling you had moments ago that forced you to cower under your bed? That was me, trying to take your soul."

This petrified me. "You. . . What?"

That feeling before was him ripping at my soul? No wonder my entire body reacted. I thought

"Yes well, it seems prior circumstances led an old accord to run dry, as I feared. Which is why I am making you this offer instead."

"I don't know what you're talking about."

He paused. "You needn't worry. All you need to know is I desire your soul and in exchange, I will grant you power so great, you cannot be touched by anyone who means you harm."

"Even you?"

My words had no effect on him. The lack of response showed a disinterest in whatever I had to say. He was here for one thing and did not want to listen to much else. I thought it over one more time, but in the end, rationality and fear had won out.

"I. . . I don't think I can make the deal. I need time to think. This is just too much." I backed out, out of fear. My hand fell to my side. I could hear cracking coming from his bones in every motion he made as he slowly drew his hand back and relaxed it by his side, just the same.

"Very well, Kimberly, I must say I am a bit let down."

I sighed. It seems I'm always letting people down. Even in a situation like this, I managed to disappoint him.

"So that's it? What now?" I asked

“Well, I can honestly say I didn't expect to be denied. Steady yourself, child, for I will not give up. If you change your mind, all you need to do. . . is call me.”

He snapped his fingers.

Chapter 6 – Hollow Bond

Three light taps, a stirring in my bed. Two knocks, this time with reserved intent. My crusted eyelids were glued together like tree sap, the world was fuzzy and swaying as I rolled to my side; facing the noise. The door handle jiggled, and the hinges cried softly as the door parted open. My vision slowly adjusted to the daylight reflecting off my walls.

"Kim?" A voice spoke softly.

My sight became clear and I saw my dad standing with slumped shoulders in my doorway. In an instant, I was fully awake and sitting up in my bed on high alert.

He witnessed my harsh rise and froze. His gaze fell to the floor and his body seemed drained.

"I'm sorry to wake you." His words barely made it out of his mouth.

"I thought you should know it's almost eleven. You should get out of bed soon" My initial fiery stare had simmered once I saw how he held himself. He didn't look angry, or rigid; instead, he just seemed. . . Lost?

I spoke in a normal, but still groggy voice. "Okay."

He released the door handle and stood a little straighter now.

"You're actually talking to me." He seemed surprised, relieved, and confused all at once. He now looked at my face and saw the gauze sloppily taped on. His face sank some more; creating new wrinkles and divots.

Once he saw the gauze, the air filled with awkward tension. I had a few choice words for him but kept it to myself for now. Looking at him, I can see the defeat, so what's the point in kicking him while he's down.

He started again,

"I. . . Uh, remember what happened yesterday." He looked away toward the window. Shame replaced the awkward.

"Do you?" I whispered.

He spoke very slowly, tiptoeing his words.

"It doesn't count for much, but I wanted you to know. . . I am sorry."

My irritation spiked. "Sorry, means nothing." I huffed.

It was quiet again. He stood in the door frame but did not obstruct it. He usually boasted control and authority in his very presence, his mannerisms. Right now, he appeared almost childlike.

A child who knew they had disappointed their parents, except now the roles were reversed. I pushed the blankets that I somehow ended up under, off me, and hung my feet over the edge of the bed, still in yesterday's clothes.

Sitting on the edge and trying to avoid his eyes, I stared down at my lap. The dried mud was embedded into my knees and random drops of brownish-red were sprinkled all over my pants.

Truth be told, I was trying so hard not to start screaming at him or jump up and punch him in the face. I don't know why, but it just didn't feel right anymore. The contemporary rage spiraled around, but the energy and willpower had dissipated.

He sighed loudly, and I looked up to him as he took two steps in. The room was so quiet, I could hear a plane high above the house as it passed.

I was positioned right in the middle, and he came up to my left side near the foot of the bed.

"Can I sit?" He asked politely but still sounding gruff.

Without looking at him again, I scooted over to my right to make room.

"Thanks." He sat down, and the bed sank under his weight.

Another pause. Neither of us spoke, moved, or even breathed too loud. The interval between us did not last forever though and within five minutes he spoke up.

"Kim. I wanted to explain to you what happened, even though it won't change what I did. . . will you hear me out?" He asked permission.

I shrugged. "I guess."

"Well." He wasted no time, anxious to speak, "I want to start off by swearing to you, that I only had two cans, that's it. And you know me well enough to understand that two beers might as well be just water; I hardly get a buzz from that. But. . . When you got home, I don't know what happened. Suddenly I just felt this, uncontrollable anger towards you."

He gestured a swelling motion around his chest. "It was like, all I wanted to do, was. . ." His voice began to stutter, and he had to stop himself.

I could sense his emotion. This sturdy man with his feelings under lock and key was actually breaking, right in front of me. I looked at him, and my own anger subsided.

"I was fighting myself for control, and then you got hurt. The moment I saw you run out that door, it was like I lost a hundred pounds, and everything was clear again." He explained, almost not believing himself.

My voice still maintained a low, distrusting tone. "If everything was clear to you, then why did you leave right after?"

He sighed. "I wanted to go after you, but what would you have done if you saw me chasing after you?"

He looked to me, desperate for an answer.

"I would have grabbed a big rock and thrown it at your head," I answered with shame. He didn't seem bothered by this.

"Good." He replied.

I gave him an uncertain look.

"That's exactly what I would have wanted you to do because I was not in the right state of mind. I could have hurt you even worse. That's why I left, I had to clear my thoughts."

Even though we were merely inches apart, it felt like we were separated by a chasm of issues and angst. I moved another inch away, so I could turn my body towards him a little more. No longer did I want to speak to the wall. I wanted to address him personally. I want to see his face, his regret.

"Where did you go, dad?" I asked, starting to get mad. Though he was right, I could not ignore the feeling of abandonment.

He turned slightly as well. "Honestly, once I was in the car, I blanked everything out. I came-to later, driving down the highway without any headlights ongoing about eighty. I slowed the car down and pulled off to the nearest gas station and just sat in the parking lot for a while."

I stared at his face as it sank and sank. He was clearly depressed and confused, but that didn't change what he did, that didn't change my own anger. I stared him down, replaying, and rethinking everything. The more I stared at him, the more my brows lowered until I snapped.

"Do you have any idea what you put me through?" I shouted. His attention was spiked. "I thought you were gonna kill me, I ran for my life into the woods where I sat, all alone in the darkness!" My tears rose, cracking my voice and causing a full-body tremble to overcome me. My tears boiled over, and I was sobbing. . . Screaming.

"Kim. . . I-" He started, but I cut him off.

"No! You don't get to talk anymore. After all, you did and have done, you decided to drive away like a fucking maniac. . . What if you had died in a car crash like mom!? Then what? What would happen to me?" I shouted violently, tears flowing like a river.

Now I was confused at myself. I was truly angry at him, but also upset that he himself could have died. Why do I care? By all rights he should have died, he deserved it, I wished it. Then why am I concerned about that?

He went still, and the room was filled with the sound of my frustrated, restricted crying. I tried to hold my head up, but it fell forward, and my arms went limp by my side. Then something strange happened. As the tears dripped from my face and onto my legs, I felt both of his arms close around me. He had leaned in and was holding onto me so gently, trembling.

"Kim, I. . . I'm so sorry, I am. I messed up and can't ever take it back. But I swear it will never happen again." He wasn't crying, but his voice was unquestionably weak.

I didn't know what to do. My eyes were open wide, and my tear ducts stopped producing the rain. So many emotions exploded in my head. Anger and sadness clashed with empathy and regret; also throwing in happiness and relief.

In the end, my eyes closed, and my hand rose up, tenderly holding the forearm, which reached across my collarbone and loosely held my right shoulder. He was holding me.

A gentle side-hug was the first hug I've gotten from my dad in years. Come to think of it, I don't remember the last time anyone gave me a hug. This was, rare for me. . . For us.

He held me for a minute or two, completely still. I could hear his heart steadily beating through his emotional show. The ten-year-old in me cherished this moment as the long-desired father-daughter moment I so desperately lacked. But the adult inside understood everything about this situation and was torn in pieces.

Conflicted by a compelling moral obligation to tear myself away and continue my verbal assault, displaying raw impudence in the face of a man that diminishes me and long since relinquished his rights as my father in exchange for numbing potions of false vigor. Or remain idle and allow this moment, heightened by a sense of duty and appearance, to go on and forever give the impression of accepted repentance in his mind.

Caught in between, I lingered. Until I decided it was time to be let go. I took a breath, then attempted to stand. He released me without any struggle or defiance. On my feet, I let out all the air in my lungs, took some back in, and turned to face him. His face was less strict now, although his cheeks were slightly red. In my eyes, he genuinely looks sorry and that counts for something. That being said, I refuse to look past this and just let it go.

"You know, dad. It hurts to say this, but. . . I really, don't forgive you." I spoke with heavy words of guilt.

He scoffed in an amused way, biting the inside of his cheek. I decided, right then that for now, I would play nice. After all, I've never gotten an apology this sincere.

"Although." I grinned a little, "You did apologize, and I know you meant it. I won't forget that." My angst was receding. I won't fight back, this time.

I'm guessing he was still a little stunned with everything because he just kind of sat there and shifted eyes. Looking at me, then his feet, and back to me.

"Thanks, sweetie."

I shook my head, entertained by this side of him.

"Now can you get out, so I can get changed?" I said with a somewhat false grin. He placed both hands on his thighs and used them as supports to force himself up. Loud thumps echoed in the still air as he made his way out the door. He took two steps out and stopped, turning his head toward me.

"I'll just be downstairs if you need me."

"Sure," I spoke in a muted tone and closed the door behind him.

His steps continued down the stairs, and I took a moment to collect myself. Clearing my throat from the brief yelling and crying. On top of my dresser was a box of tissues I hardly ever used, until now. I took a few and used them to blow my nose and get all the sand out of my eyes.

Slowly but surely, I was repairing my disarray. Despite what had just occurred, I was still feeling bewildered by everything. Memories from a long time ago resurfaced and occupied my brain while I ripped my clothes off. I remember time and time again where he would get mad and smack me on the arm or grab me too tight, bruising my skin. All these things happened just long enough apart never to arouse suspicion at school or with friends. Except for Joey. He always had some eye for detail and patterns, and when he would voice concern, I made him drop the subject. Now, how could I possibly hide the bruises and most of all this cut?

At my dresser, I removed one of each article of clothing. When everything was replaced, a purple shirt, black pants, and a fresh pair of white socks. Lastly, I grabbed a dark gray zip-up sweatshirt from my closet and threw that on as well. Nothing felt better than a complete change of clothes. It was enough to lift my spirits, but not enough to keep my mind from roaming too much. But it simply couldn't be helped.

On top of what he did yesterday, I now have to worry about this man who appeared to me and not to mention that strange girl. My dad is one nightmare that I can somewhat handle, or at least live with for now. I can understand him in the way that we are both clearly human and I will be better at dealing with his shit. But those bright, piercing yellow eyes burned an invasive print of evil in my heart that at this moment carries a sickness. He is something unnatural, I have to be careful.

The whole thing gave me the creeps, yet oddly enough, was intriguing. The clothes I previously wore had been lobbed into a small pile to the left of my dresser to be taken care of later. I moved over to the window and examined the day just beyond the glass. The blue sky and proud sun illuminated every shade of green in the trees and gave me a serene, hospitable feeling.

There was a lot to consider and a lot to deal with, but I just have to continue being strong. No matter how much it hurts, I can't give up on life. I like to think there is a reason for me, for all of us being here and even though I'm unaware of that reason, I know someday it will find me. I will look back on this and appreciate the pain for making me who I am. Even if right now I am suffering, that is necessary for our growth as human beings. I gazed for a few minutes before pulling myself from the sill.

I felt an anxious pinch in my chest as I walked out the door. Breathing in the crusted air of the hallway and house, I sauntered over to the railing and peered over; ogling down to the floor below. I partially leaned against the railing, aware of my own weight and its fragility. I never did trust it. From here, I could see my dad standing in the kitchen, fully dressed in tan cargo pants and a white long sleeve shirt bearing some construction company's logo on the chest. He appeared to be spacing out, looking into the living room with empty eyes and sipping on a glass of water.

I called out to him.

"Are you drinking water?"

He blinked, sinking back into reality and looked up at me.

"Yup. Figured it would be a smart choice." He took a gulp and cringed at the taste. "God, I hate water."

"Why? It doesn't really have a taste."

"Yeah, it does. It washes over your teeth and gums and tastes like whatever was in your mouth before."

"If you say so." I half chuckled.

My ears rang with how quiet the house was. It was never this empty sounding unless he wasn't home. There was always some noise, whether it was the television, radio, or background noise from him working outside.

Right now, it was peaceful.

"So." He cleared his throat, "It's Saturday, got any plans?"

I shrugged, "Not sure. I have a lot on my mind, so, it would be in my best interest to distract myself."

He took another gulp and finished the glass, then set it in the surprisingly empty sink. He walked to the center of the room and gave all his attention to me.

"I'm thinking about running to the store, you can come too if you wanna."

I cocked an eyebrow, "The store?"

"Yeah, y'know, I got another job tomorrow that is gonna last until Monday morning. I'm going to someplace in Chester County to put up drywall in a big office complex. And I was planning on chipping in with some snacks for the rest of the guys."

I pondered for a minute. I'm kind of glad he won't be here tomorrow, and more so, that I can expect him to be gone instead of just waking up and finding him absent. Still, I feared being alone, now, and tomorrow. But that's a worry for a later time.

"Sure," I said with little emotion.

He let a tiny smile form at the corner of his mouth. "Great and it looks like you're ready, let's get going."

I didn't say anything, just turned and walked down the stairs. I met him by the front door and slipped my feet into my shoes while he stomped into his work boots. We got outside, and I embraced the refreshing air while he locked the door behind us. Among the random scents of mixed nature was a familiar one that plucked at my senses. Carried by the wind was the scent of his car and all of its fresheners, so blatant and clearly defined among all other smells that it was distracting.

Walking to the car, I felt positive and distant at the same time. I could tell he was happy that I am going with him, but it was clear he was uncomfortable as well. This was new for both of us.

His car was parked dead center of the driveway. A shiny, dark blue Sedan carried him from place to place. My dad, if he had the choice, would never own a car like this. He is all about muscle cars and the classics.

He has told me time and time again that his dream car is a '78 Firebird, specifically a bright flashy orange so it would be impossible not to notice his ride. However, even if he could afford a new car, there are two reasons he won't. One, he has a lot invested in this one. Many hours have been spent polishing and repairing this car to absolute perfection. After the accident, he told me that the insurance company covered all the repairs, but he still checks every component often to make sure it's all pristine. Sometimes spending precious food money on little parts that aren't the most crucial.

Second and most importantly, it was my mom's first car. So, he will never get rid of it, even if it's rendered immobile. He once told me that if the insurance hadn't covered the cost to repair, he would have gone broke fixing it for her. I paid close attention to the front passenger side where he said the collision happened. As I passed by the windshield and got a glance at the front seat, a pit formed in my stomach knowing, that is where she died.

Sentimentality is one thing, but I don't know how any sane person can go on driving in a car with such a personal history. I opened the back seat and climbed in, choosing to sit behind the passenger seat. He climbed in the front, and as soon as he started the engine, I put on my seat belt.

Nothing was said as he backed out of the driveway and on to the road. The engine purred, and we were off. The car ride started off bumpy but the closer we got to town, the smoother the roads became. I didn't ride in the car often. Most days if I left the house it was either by walking or the school bus; so being in here right now felt weird. Mostly being so low to the ground in a moving vehicle was somewhat nauseating.

I took the time to look at the interior and made a note of how clean it was. The house may be a pigsty, but this car was immaculate. No trash, no dirt, and nothing cluttering the floor or seats. He made sure to keep all of the tools he needed for a job in the trunk.

We reached the wheat field and stopped at the stop sign for a moment, still silent. He continued straight and after another two hundred feet, turned right onto the highway which passed through the center of town. It wasn't any more than five minutes before we took another right into the parking lot of a small grocery store.

The parking lot was empty so finding a spot was mindless. Once parked, the vibrating car was reduced to a simmering hush and then stopped. He turned his head and looked at me.

"Alright, I have to get some stuff for them like I said but do you want to go and get some stuff for the house?"

"Like what? You went shopping, recently didn't you?" I asked as I unbuckled my seatbelt.

"I was thinking, since I always buy the same stuff, maybe you can choose. . . Let's say, two boxes of cereal. Whatever you want as long as it stays under ten dollars. Just none of that organic crap." He instructed

My eyes lit up. "Really? I mean, I like that Oat & Flakes you buy but I would love to get something really sweet. Ever since I kicked the soda habit, I get sugar cravings, especially in the morning." I grinned widely.

"Maybe just one box will be enough." He lifted one finger and smiled, clearly joking. "Let's get a move-on."

He pushed open his door and got out, I did the same. We walked to the entrance a fair distance apart from each other, but still as a pair. The sensor doors slid open for us and we were met by the radiant glow of a clean store.

He grabbed two hand baskets by the door and handed me one.

"Go ahead and grab your cereal and while you're over there, get the milk too. I might wanna have some."

I took the basket by the handles and raised an eyebrow. "Dream on, this cereal is mine." I joked.

He shook his head, amused and we went our separate ways. Before I got too far, I stopped and watched him. Examining the way, he moved down the long strip. He stood with his shoulders raised, broad and defensive like a wall. His head low and making sure every step was a thump.

The facade of strength he displayed was completely unnecessary in my eyes, but I guess it worked for him. He then made a turn at the other end of the store out of view and I moved to the right, a couple rows down toward the cereal aisle. It wasn't a big store by any means but to me, it seemed huge. I must have walked up and down this one aisle, searching for exactly what I wanted almost ten times. I think the main problem was, that I was distracted.

I saw all the different colors of boxes and mascots, but nothing stayed in my head for more than a few seconds because I was stuck on a thought. My dad. His current behavior confused me. I haven't seen him scowl even once since we left the house. He always lived a one-man pity party that was permanently painted on his face.

But today I saw him smile and even chuckled once or twice. That alone is extremely unusual and now he brings me to the store and lets me choose my own cereal. This change of attitude was clearly a mask; a thin one at that. Then again, maybe it's not. Maybe he really is trying to improve, and these actions are genuine. It's hard to tell even if my instincts usher me one way.

I stopped pacing. Right in front of me was what I was searching for. Vanilla almond and granola cereal. Practically glowing on the shelf and begging me to take it, I snatched it up and set it in my basket. All previous thoughts had escaped me, completely overwritten by the sight of such a magnificent item.

Three more boxes down was another cereal that I grabbed but could not compare to the first. This was a colorful, fruity cereal I know my dad would like. Feeling satisfied, I made my way to the milk with a slight bounce in my step. I acquired everything and went to the registers to meet with him. The store was pretty empty, and I stood almost completely alone beside one or two clearly bored cashiers.

I waited there for about twenty minutes; never once did I see him move between aisles or anything. The weight of the milk in my basket became too cumbersome and I had to set it down on the floor. We have been here for nearly thirty-five minutes now.

Finally, I saw him turn a corner and spot me. Meeting with his eyes, I lifted my basket again and waited some more until he approached me.

"Got everything?" I asked.

He didn't say anything, just gave me a grunt which indicated a yes. I glanced at his basket, inside was a large pack of jerky, some crackers, pudding cups, and chocolate covered raisins. Not much considering how long he had been missing.

I saw the raisins and got excited. "Oh, could I get a bar of chocolate?" I asked happily, now thinking about chocolate.

He then mumbled to himself, but I didn't hear him.

"What was that?" I asked

He gave me an eye and spoke up, a little too loud. "I said, you can never be satisfied, can you?" He spoke sharply.

I was taken aback, and even the lady at the register was giving us funny looks.

"Uh, okay. Never mind." I said defensively.

He set the basket down and rubbed his face in his hands.

"No, no, it's fine." He sighed, seeming frustrated but trying to keep a level head. "You can get a chocolate bar."

He picked his basket back up and started placing his stuff on the belt.

I did the same but kept my eye on him. "You feel okay?" I asked him.

"Nothing, just a headache. That's all."

One after the other, our items were scanned, and the total kept rising. I didn't realize just how expensive jerky was until now. After everything was scanned and bagged my dad stepped up to pay. Thirty-three dollars and thirty-two cents. He pulled two twenty-dollar bills from his wallet and handed it to the lady.

"Hold on." He stopped and looked at me. "Did you get the chocolate?" He asked.

"Don't worry about it."

"Kim, I told you to get it." He said, irritated.

"Yea, but it's no big deal, really," I stated.

She looked at us, and I looked at her, then back to him.

He groaned, "Whatever."

He finished paying, and the lady handed him his change. After that, he took all the bags in both hands, and we left the store. It was almost noon now, and the sun proudly displayed that fact. There were almost no clouds in the sky, meaning it was a bit warmer than most other days.

Not that it was hot by any means, but just so comfortable in this sweatshirt. As we loaded into the car and set the bags on the seats to my left, I thought about the rest of my day. Honestly, I didn't want to do much today or tomorrow for that matter. It's the weekend and I want to sleep it away, especially after everything that happened. So much has happened in the past few weeks that I can barely keep track of it all.

All buckled and semi-comfortable, he turned the key and the car sprang to life. He rolled the car over to the exit and waited as a couple of cars passed by. After turning left, we were on the road again. I felt compelled to talk to him. He seemed on edge again.

"So, dad." I started, "this job tomorrow, is it going to pay well?"

He glanced at me through the mirror, then focused on the road.

"Eh, not really. I mean, it'll pay but we won't be leaving town any time soon." He spoke in monotone, although not seeming disinterested in me. "But money's, money, right?"

"Yea," I affirmed.

He looked at me again through the mirror, this time lingering longer than he should.

"Why do you say that?" He asked me, now looking to the road again.

"Say what?" I asked in confusion.

"Why do you say yeah like yip without the p?"

"Uhh, I'm not really sure, I just always have," I answered, staring at the passing trees through the window.

There was a minute of quiet, then he started chuckling to himself. I caught this and gave him a look, "What's so funny?"

He cleared his throat. "I just realized; Rachel used to talk to you in a baby voice almost constantly. It drove me nuts at times."

"Okay? What does that have to do with anything?"

"Your mom was mostly responsible for teaching you to speak when you were younger, but she always used that stupid baby voice until I got on her ass about it. I told her if you hear the words spoken like that, then that's how you'll learn 'em. You must've picked up on the way she said yeah to you."

I pondered that thought.

"You know, that kind of makes sense," I said a little surprised.

"Man, she was a character, that's for sure." He smiled to himself.

There was stillness between us, and I found myself drifting more towards the center of the car, looking at him.

". . . Dad?" I said softly

"Hmm?"

"Can, you tell me some stuff about mom?" I said very quietly, like a child.

"What stuff?" His voice was reserved too, now.

"Just . . . What she was like, and what she looked like."

"What she looked like? You're telling me you don't remember?" He almost sounded insulted.

"No. . . I really don't. There are no pictures in the house anymore, and she died eight years ago, so I don't remember all that well." I said sadly.

He took a moment to think, while also focusing on the road. I noticed he had slowed down significantly. The car merely coasted through town.

"Your mom was, an amazing woman, though I don't think that comes as a surprise. You look a lot like her, Kim. You have her eyes, her nose, and definitely her hair. Except, hers was long, reaching all the way down her back. . . I woke up every morning tangled in the stuff." He snickered penitently.

I smiled faintly, picturing what she would look like. Trying to piece together memories.

"What was she like?"

He adjusted himself in his seat and rubbed the steering wheel, clearly uncomfortable.

"Lively, for one. She had enough energy for the both of us. When we first met, she was really nice to me, treated me to lunch a couple of times."

"You guys met while you were at work, right?" I asked

"That's right. She was in college and I was there on a job. At the time it seemed silly to meet that way, but now it almost seems like fate." The look on his face was distant, and I started watching the road for him. To make sure he didn't go over the lines.

"She had. . . Aspirations. Our friendship was strong, we had a true connection right away. I got to learn so much about who she was, and why I was drawn to her. She was ambitious, and endlessly kind woman with enough patience to last but a temper that could ruin lives. She was perfect, in every conceivable way. She dealt with me, nurtured me when I was struggling inside. I stopped drinking for her, I would have stopped breathing if she asked me to."

I was dumbfounded. I had never heard my dad talk like this. For him, this was poetry. The expression he never allowed to be free around anyone, not even himself. I could see just how much he loved my mom, and how much he misses her.

"She loved kids. It was her dream to work with kids; teach them, help them grow, and become amazing people in the future. All she wanted was to change how you viewed the world, give you a different perspective than what may seem obvious. Her presence was magic."

I heard his blinker tick as he turned down our abandoned strip. We were almost home now. A warm feeling of collective remembrance and empathy swelled in the deepest pit of my stomach.

A nearly snuffed ember glowed once again as the spark was fanned by common compassion, for my mother. I adjusted myself in the seat, my eyes fell to my lap.

“Thank you, for telling me that.” I showed an uncomfortable appreciation.

He didn't respond.

The car then jerked left as we pulled into the driveway, hitting a couple of small bumps until we stopped, and the car shut off.

Everything went quiet when the car shut down. That constant vibration in the air and body became a fixture of normality in my mind. Temporarily tricking me into thinking that sensation would always exist. When it disappeared, I was left in a nihilistic state, a state that left me sinking into my seat and experiencing a level of relaxation that far surpassed my own bed. My eyes were lost in the trees as they swayed in the gentle breeze. I could so easily fall asleep here, right now.

Caught up in the sensation that was peace, I was not able to refrain my words. It was as if my brain didn't command the words, rather my soul did.

“Dad. . . Could you please, not drink today?” I asked softly, barely able to squeak the words past my cottonmouth.

His hand had grabbed the door handle, ready to exit the vehicle but he stopped and looked at me once again through the mirror. He sighed,

“I don't drink because I want to. I do it, because. . . I'm weak. People like me, we need things like alcohol to survive, to cope with life. Some people need a cup of coffee to function, some need a hobby, but me-”

I cut him off,

“You need mom.”

He turned away from the mirror, directing his eyes to me, but mine was occupied by the trees. I could feel his stare, almost hostile but mostly concerned I knew what he was looking at, the bandage. Personally, I almost forgot it was there, the sticky feeling already cemented in my mind as normal. But for him, it was a reminder of his sins.

“You're right. But I don't have that.”

“You have me.” Now I looked at him, and he looked away.

Ignoring my stare, he grabbed the handle again and opened it. As soon as the door flew open, I was released from my trance. In no rush to move again, I too unbuckled my seat belt. I slid out of the car and took the bags with me. My dad was right there to meet me outside the car.

He extended his arm for something to carry, so I handed him the snack bag. He took it and let his arm fall to the side. Before he turned around, he said,

“I won't drink, today. I can't promise you tomorrow or the next day.” He seemed on edge again. It didn't feel like it was directed at me specifically.

I nodded in affirmation.

Side by side, we approached the front door, ready to embrace the rest of the day. He took his time unlocking the front door, especially making sure that it didn't fly against the wall when he got it open. We stepped inside and took in that familiar, dank stench. He didn't seem fazed whatsoever. He set this bag by the edge of the counter closest to the front door, ensuring he wouldn't forget it tomorrow and I opened the fridge door to store the jug of milk. Standing inside the open door, I saw him walk over to the couch.

I called out to him, "Hey, can I have some cereal right now?"

"Sure, whatever." He waved, disinterested.

I smiled and quickly set the boxes on the counter and grabbed a bowl, then a spoon. All the ingredients came together, and I was ready for the burst of flavor. I took the bowl, after putting everything away and sat on the far-left end of the couch.

My dad always sat on the far right, towards the center of the room. He already had the TV on, set to a crime drama that I personally didn't like. It focused more on the drama between characters than actual police work.

I ate my cereal, surprised to find that it tasted as good as it looked. I ate it a bit too fast and was left feeling awkward as I held the empty bowl in my hands. The feeling was that compared to finishing a test too early and not wanting to be the first one to turn it in, in fear of the spiteful looks you'd get from the other students. In this case, I felt as though my dad would judge me for eating it so quickly, plus I had to walk in front of him to put it in the sink. So instead, I ended up holding the bowl for about fifteen minutes until I finally got up and deposited it in the sink.

At the sink, I debated on what I should do. Though he wasn't really saying anything outside of a random comment about the show, more talking at the characters than me; he was at least being civil. This is the first day we've really spent together in a long time, so why cut it short by retreating to my room?

I returned to the couch, not expecting much else to come of it but trying to enjoy the quality time, nonetheless. It was mid-afternoon now and we sat in near-perfect silence. After about an hour, he got up and returned with sparkling water to drink. I was proud of him, even though I know it will not last. He is still holding true to his word by not drinking today. At this point, I'll take what I can get.

As the hours passed and the sun had set, I began to feel drowsy. The program had shifted to a talk show that couldn't keep my interest for more than a minute and I was hardly able to keep my eyes open. I resisted sleep but was unable to resist its call. I slipped into unconsciousness for nearly an hour when I was startled by his sudden movement on the other end of the couch. I awoke with force and glared at him. He was only standing up.

"Did I scare you?" He asked with a light chuckle.

"Yea, a bit." I exhaled.

"I'm going to bed now; remember I have to get up early." He explained.

I rubbed one eye, "What time is it?"

He angled his head and peered at the stove's digital clock. "About eight."

I yawned. "Eight? Okay, I think I'll stay down here for a bit."

"Alright. . . I'll see you in the morning, Kim."

I laid myself out flat, pushing my feet to the other end of the couch where he had previously sat. I tried to get comfortable using the arm of the couch as a pillow.

"G'night, dad." I shut my eyes and listened to him walk away, closing the door softly behind him. The TV chattered in the background; incoherent words pricked my ears as I slowly drifted off into a deeper sleep.

The day seems to race by after this morning. For once, it wasn't leaning good or bad; just a day. But I'm glad neutrality was possible, and that I could cherish these little moments between us. These pleasantries eased me back into a dream and gave me a lasting comfort as the night grew darker.

I was awoken the next morning by the sound of rain hitting the windows. Laying on my back, my eyes peeled open and were met by the spinning fan blades above. The circulatory motion stole my numb mind and occupied it as my body became more aware of its own existence. With a creak in my back, I sat up. It was then that I noticed something on me. One eye half-open the other closed, I glanced at my lap. There was a small brown throw blanket placed on my body.

My dreary mind was fixated on it until I became lucid enough to process thought. Both eyes opened, and I was met with confusion, to say the least; as I don't remember falling asleep with a blanket. Then it occurred to me. This crazy idea that my dad, feeling a stroke of pity or compassion for his daughter, actually gave me a blanket either in the middle of the night or on his way out this morning.

I couldn't help but smile at the thought. I took hold of the blanket in both hands and pulled it up to my face, taking in the clean scent trapped in the fabric. I got up from the couch, folded the blanket, and lay it over the top of the headrest. Standing with a slump, I stretched my spine and cracked every available bone. It's Sunday and my dad will be gone all day long. Leaving me here to my own devices.

I wandered over to the kitchen and poured myself another bowl of cereal. I leaned up against the counter by the fridge and ate it right there, just letting my eyes wander around the living room. I debated on cleaning the house but felt no real motivation to do so.

Chewing on the clusters of granola, I glanced at the clock on the stove beside me, it displayed 10:37 am

"Holy crap," I mumbled, trying not to spit out food. "No wonder I'm stiff," I spoke out loud.

Realizing I slept for nearly twelve hours on top of sleeping in yesterday I had an epitome of time wasted. I quickly shoveled the rest of the cereal down and went to place the bowl in the sink when I saw the pile.

It was obvious that these wouldn't get done for another few days unless I did them now, so I pulled the dish-soap close, removed the dishes from the sink, and set them on the counter. We didn't have a plug for the sink, so I ran to the bathroom and snatched a small, old washcloth and a towel. I compacted the small one into a ball as much as I could and used it as a plug to keep water from draining and laid the towel on the right side of the counter.

When the left sink was full of soapy hot water, I submerged a few bowls and plates, giving them about five or so minutes to soak before I pulled them out one at a time and washed them; using the right sink as a rinse station and the towel for them to dry.

I'm no stranger to a pile of dishes, and I could handle them fairly easily. Able to fly through them in a matter of thirty minutes. The only thing that always proved difficult and I saved for last was the silverware. I hated silverware.

That alone took me an extra thirty minutes, as I found it difficult to hold back on precision and perfection between each and every fork tong. But finally, the dishes were drying, the sink was drained, and my fingers were pruned. Now that I am awake, it was time to start the day. The next task that popped into my head was schoolwork.

I wasted no time getting my bag and spreading out my papers on the coffee table. It was really nice being able to use a solid surface at home to write on and keep my stuff organized. I found it much easier to concentrate, now that my back didn't hurt from the awkward crisscross position on my bed.

My assignments were as follows; read a total of five chapters in various textbooks, complete two separate worksheets, and write a short essay for English Literature. With this setup, I was able to get my work done in just a couple of hours.

The last sentence was written, and the essay was done, leaving me with no more work for the day. Satisfied, I packed up all of my stuff and carried my weighted bag to the front door. Leaving it by my shoes for the morning, I walked back to the center of the room and checked the clock, it was almost two o'clock now. To think, by this time yesterday I had experienced so many emotions. I had already lived a full day, and now here I am, idle and starving for an activity.

As my mind often does, it began to wander, and with it, my body followed. Random thoughts sporadically appeared in my mind and just as quickly changed the subject as I paced around the house. My feet carried me to each picture on the wall, every piece of furniture, and every random item discarded on the floor. While I walked, I picked up bits of trash and threw them away, keeping up the healthy habit of cleanliness. I eventually found myself moving towards my dad's room, standing in the short hall outside of his door. The door was cracked, and I couldn't help but feel curious.

Coy, I poked the door near the handle, and it opened a small amount. All of the random thoughts I had, converged into a ball of wonder. With a full hand on the wood, the door opened the rest of the way, and I entered slowly. Everything looked the same as the last time I was here.

The bed beneath the window straight ahead, with the dresser and large mirror on the left, closet on the right. His room was barren, devoid of all personality. I moved toward the dresser and began to snoop. Not searching for anything in particular, just trying to kill the boredom and get an idea of how my dad really lives.

The mirror hardly reflected my image due to the grime and dust smeared all over it; it looks like it hasn't been cleaned in over a year. Part of me wanted to open his drawers, but that's a little too much privacy to invade, plus I don't want to see my dad's underwear.

On top of the surface was a rolled pair of socks, incense burner, crumpled pack of cigarettes,, and some loose change. Nothing of interest. I moved on over to his closet in the right corner and opened the door. There was a pull string hanging down which lit up the small box with a dim yellow glow. I saw a few shirts hung up and his laundry basket stuffed in the corner, completely full and smelling like sweat and food. There were a couple of boxes on the floor; inside the first small box was a bunch of papers, tax information mostly. Beneath that one was a box full of a few cables, remote, a bible, and a pocket watch.

The last box on the very bottom was by far the most interesting. At first, it seemed to be just a box full of clothes, but as I dug through them, I came to the realization that these were my mom's. I got a stomachache as I pulled out a few shirts and looked at them. My hands began to tremble as I pulled a red V-neck out and brought it into my face; taking in the scent. To my dismay, the clothes had no unique smell. Just an old box in the corner of his closet. Tainted by years passed by, forgotten.

The tension in my body was subdued and I returned the clothes to where they belong for now. Maybe, I will ask my dad soon about her clothes. He might let me have some. After that, I returned everything to where it belongs and closed the door. All I was doing now was killing time, but what else could I do?

I lumbered over to his bed but didn't see much in the immediate area to hold my interest. I checked underneath it but only found a large dead spider, more clothes, and the front page of a calendar from the year 1985.

It seemed to have no clear significance, just old trash. Standing up again, I sighed loudly as there was nothing in his room or this whole house to keep me occupied. Or so I thought.

Next to the bed was his nightstand. Spread out on top was more change, a coffee mug, screwdriver, and the lamp of course. The nightstand housed one small drawer and stood on long, wobbly legs. I grabbed the tiny knob and slid the drawer open, revealing its contents. As soon as I laid my eyes on what was in the drawer, my brain to swell with cynical ideology.

Innocently laying on its side, was my dad's handgun. An S&W .38 Caliber pistol. Fixated on the weapon, I swallowed hard and removed it from the drawer. Many drunken exposits burned the name of the gun into my brain. Though, I've never seen it.

It's heavy.

The weight of the gun was dense, concentrated in the center where it housed the loaded bullets. I've never held a gun before, so I fidgeted with it until the chamber popped open and a couple of bullets fell to the floor.

"Oh, shit," I swore and quickly bent down to retrieve them.

My palms perspired as I reloaded the weapon and closed the cylinder. I was completely encompassed by its craftsmanship and purpose. Just staring at the faded sheen and wondered just how many times this gun had been fired and why.

The longer I stared, the more it became clear to me just what I was holding in my hand. This small, seemingly insignificant contraption of metal could steal a person's life instantly. All you have to do is aim it and pull the trigger. I held the gun with two hands; one properly with my finger through the guard and the other wrapped tightly around the first hand, supporting the weight. I raised them both and held it straight out locking my elbows. Looking down the top of the gun, I aligned the backsight with the front post and held it there.

My finger on the trigger, I stopped and really imagined what it would be like to have someone on the other end of this gun. The power I would have over them, the ability to determine their fate. Live, or die. I held my breath and concentrated on the opposing wall. Then, seemingly without my own will but encouraged by a deep-seated desire, I inched myself over in front of the mirror and saw my own murky reflection. I raised the gun once more and locked onto my own image. I stared down the barrel and my hands began to shake with its weight. However, my image did not stay for long. Through the dust and grime of the mirror, my own reflection began to morph; taking a completely different shape. The shape of my dad.

Imagination or a vision, it did not matter to me at that moment. I was hard focused on the new target, ignoring the changing elements of the room around me. The air around me became heavy and hot, bringing sweat to my brow and stealing my breath. A loud, constant clicking vibration could be heard in the walls, echoing. My intent did not sway, my posture remained.

Then, I felt a surge of energy in my chest. One that shot outward and followed along both arms into my fingers; itching to tighten up. Boiling energy pulsated in my veins as the pressure around me completely changed again. Losing all color and becoming electrically charged. I felt nothing but angst and fire. Holding this gun in my hand, holding this much power, caused a sickness; a desire to wrought vengeance.

Without my own command, I began to speak out loud. My voice harsh and sharp. Like an inner demon using my body as a conduit for expression.

"Who cares that he had one good day, who cares if he held me once? He is evil, a man with no regard for anyone, not even himself. He deserves to die; they deserve to die!" A frantic breath seized my lungs. The hot moisture erupted from my mouth with every intake and exhale.

Suddenly a controlling headache took hold of me and my eyes slammed shut. My body swayed for a moment and my hold on the gun weakened. When I opened my eyes and stared along the barrel, I could see someone else standing there. It wasn't my dad, it was. . . Him.

The old man was there in the glass, overcast by shadows. My chest exploded in panic and my hands reacted with raw instinct. The finger which tightly wrapped around the trigger forcefully tightened. Then, it seemed that everything around me began to play in slow motion through my eyes. As I watched the hammer release and slam against the gun.

The cylinder cycled once, and I was left shaking in absolute silence. My eyes had forced themselves shut, bracing for the noise; but it never came. When they opened again, the mirror was reflecting only my image.

There never was anyone else. I redirected to the gun and pulled my arms back. Holding it delicately in my hand, terrified of it. Ensuring sensitivity, I turned it slightly and popped the chamber open again. All the rounds were there, except for one empty slot. My lips trembled, and a bead of sweat rolled down my face, soaking into the bandage.

I set the gun on the bed, making sure to treat it with respect and got down on the floor. Just beneath the bed hidden under its shadow was the stray bullet that I thankfully missed. I snatched it up and held it in my palm. Examining it closely, I discovered an oddity with the shell. A wrinkle in the metal where the bullet itself was planted in the shell was an imperfect distinction between it and the others. Unique.

Carefully, I returned it to the gun and then placed the gun to the drawer. Letting out a sigh of relief, I sat on the edge of his bed, nursing my headache.

"What's happening to me?" I asked myself, rubbing my temples.

As I rubbed, I noticed an aching pain in my muscles. My shoulders and back were completely stiff as though I just got done doing a day-long handstand. I straightened out my back, trying to crack it when I noticed something odd in my peripheral vision. The window to my left, above his bed, was black. The sun had completely set.

"The hell?" I jumped up in confusion.

It only now became apparent that the room I stood in was completely dark, outside of a small guiding light plugged into an outlet near the door. My brain spun as I tried to make sense of this.

It was, like, two or three when I came in here? How is it dark already? I thought to myself.

Then, a sinking fear interrupted my thought process. I turned around and looked right out of his door into the living room. The entire house was shrouded in darkness. I swallowed hard.

"Fuck," I whispered to myself.

Luckily, I stood by the nightstand, which had a small lamp, just like in my room. I quickly turned it on and was relieved to be absorbed by its glow. I tiptoed away from the bed and stood at the door, checked my corners, and stepped out. I wanted to get to my room as fast as possible, so I fast-walked my way down the short hall and took my first step on the stairs and stopped.

Looking up the stairs, I saw nothing at all. The only thought in my head was the railing and what could possibly be standing there. One step, then two, a loud creak then three. I slowly made my way up, and as I reached the top; my eyes had adjusted enough to see that I was entirely alone. I bolted into my room, flicked on the light switch, and shut the door. Once inside and protected by the light, I took in a deep breath and released it slowly. Sanctuary.

My body was so weak. I can't imagine how or why this happened. I sauntered over to my window and checked outside. The sky was painted black and blue with bright stars contrasting the vast emptiness.

I struggled to find an answer, only more questions. I know I have a vivid imagination, but when I was holding that gun, I would have sworn to anyone that my dad and that man were right in front of me. On top of that, the amount of hatred I felt was only matched by the fear in my chest. In my mind, he was really there, and I wanted to shoot him. I tried to.

Contrary to a sane mind, I felt an odd pride within. The fact that I pulled the trigger, despite the misfire, shows that I am strong enough to fight back. I am willing to stand up to him. . . Well, given the right leverage. The power trip I experienced felt amazing. Holding that gun made me feel incredible, so strong like I could do anything.

Is that why I saw the old man? He was showing me what he meant by the power to fight back? All I know, is I am torn up inside. I want this feeling to go away, but it feels almost natural.

The rest of the night was spent sitting there, on my bed. My mind circulating around one thing in particular.

That single bullet that escaped my grasp.

Chapter 7 - One Reason to Smile

The next morning, Monday, was tedious, to say the least. I woke up with weighted, dreary eyes. Having no idea when I fell asleep or where I was. Dragging myself out of bed, I felt lost and distant. When my feet hit the floor, a chill ran up my spine in anticipation of the day. My mind was not in the right place, but I had to go to school. Changing clothes was a slow, arduous process that I blanked from memory. Only noticing what I wore when I stepped into the bathroom. A basic red shirt with a sweater on top and blue jeans, nothing new.

Today, I skipped basic hygiene, only taking time to change the gauze and bandages. The tender flesh pulsated as the morning air made contact. The red and brown clumps of skin and blood stuck to the inside of the fabric made me wonder if it was infected. I hastily splashed some water over it and reapplied the bandages and a new gauze strip. I quickly brushed my hair and shook my head to give it some life.

Exiting the bathroom, I stumbled my way down the stairs and reached the kitchen, catching a glimpse of the clock above the stove, 8:46 a.m. School started an hour ago, and my dad was nowhere to be seen. My backpack felt ten times heavier than usual as I made my way down the front steps. His car wasn't here, which means I would have to walk to school. With a frustrated sigh, I began my trek.

I let my mind slide into obscurity as I walked along the roadside. Trying to recall the events of last night, but having a hard time getting a clear picture. The paranoia that suffocated my room haunted me all night, and the feeling lingered even now. The trees felt suspicious, every car was a ghost, and the chirping birds cried in agony. The world was different today.

Maybe it's me.

I didn’t know what to expect for this new week. What I did know is I have had enough drama to last me a lifetime. It's true, I really can't escape some version of hell, whether it's in my own home or at school. Although, I think I prefer school. Stacy was a threat, but I had Tansu to lift my spirits. Joey too.

I missed them so much, it feels like forever.

My legs began to throb in the final mile. One last stretch of flat road and I would be able to sit down. My body hurts so badly. From too much sleep to no sleep and then all the weirdness that occurred; I've had just about enough. I want some normalcy for once.

Something to balance the stress.

When I finally arrived at school, I refused to record anything of the first few classes. Having shown up over two hours late with no call, I had to listen to a lot of complaining from the office. Nothing I cared to hear or respond to at the moment.

Basically, I ignored reality. Not thinking about anything, just existing. Lunch had come, and I used the ambient noise of chattering kids to ground myself again. I couldn't eat, I could only focus on the constant barrage of voices around me.

For some reason, if I tried hard enough, I could zero in on a particular conversation. A table, twenty feet from me were talking among themselves, and I could hear them plain as day, just them. Then a different table behind me stole my attention when I heard my name, spoken in a hushed tone.

I whipped around and glared at them with wide, concerned eyes. One person saw me and gave me a funny look then whispered to someone else who also looked to me. They both turned away, and I returned my eyes to the plate of food I hadn't yet touched. My head was pounding.

I felt a little sick, so I grabbed my plate and threw it into the trash. The plate itself was not disposable, but that didn't stop me from chucking the whole thing. Lunch had only just begun, but I found myself walking past the occupied tables and making my way to the next class.

I stood outside the door and waited for the bell. As I leaned against the wall, hands stuffed in my pockets, my eyes became fuzzy. The lights in the ceiling seemed to expand their reach. Violently radiating in my eyes and causing my brain to swell. I couldn't break eye contact, a scene of raining glass played in my head, and I wondered how that shower would feel.

The bell exploded in my ears, and I hastily entered the room and took my seat. In those brief moments waiting for the rest of the class to arrive, I rested my head on the desk and closed my eyes. Nursing an upset stomach.

Next thing I know, I was being shaken awake.

"Kimmy? Hey, wake up." A faint voice rustled in my brain.

Startled, my eyes ripped open to see Tansu leaning over my desk, shaking me. She looked concerned.

Sinking into reality, I was immediately eased into a sense of security by her face. The pit in my stomach subsided, and normal thoughts began flowing into me. Groggy, I leaned back in my seat, using the hard plastic to crack my back and yawned. Looking around, I could see class was over, and most of the students had left. I looked back at her.

"Are you okay?" She asked.

With a playful tone, I answered, "Uh-huh. Why wouldn't I be?" I said then rubbed my whole face, trying to wipe the sleep off. I then scratched my head; my coarse fingertips scraped my dry scalp.

"Don't you love Math? How could you fall asleep?"

I shrugged, "Sorry, Tansu, I had a long weekend. I didn't get too much sleep." I chuckled.

She started again, "I mean, I'm not upset with you, but everyone was laughing at you, the teacher had to shush them." She looked embarrassed for me.

"And another thing. What happened to your face? Did you trip or something?" She questioned with concern on her face.

My words still fumbled, "Oh, yup, you guessed it. I tripped walking to my house. It's no big deal, really." I said nonchalantly. She didn't look convinced, if anything she looked even more worried than before.

Seeing her face quelled the storm in my brain. All of the aches and pains became trivial looking into her eyes, so much so that I found my gaze unintentionally locked. She looked away and blushed. I smiled at her coy behavior.

She spoke again, "A-anyways, schools over and I was wondering if you wanted to come over today. If you feel up to it?"

My eyes went from admiration, to ecstatic. "What, really?"

"Yeah, why not?" The grip she had on her bag strap tightened.

"I just didn't expect it. That's all."

I stopped to think. If I return home, who knows what mood my dad will be in? I might have to deal with his attitude and after everything that happened this weekend, I wanted nothing more than to spend time with her. The thing is, my dad won't like it too much if I don't come right home. As much as I want to just leave him hanging, the smart thing to do would be to call him first.

"Tansu, I'd love to come over today. I just need to give my dad a call and ask him."

"That's fine. We'll both go to the office, and after you ask your dad and get an answer, I will call my mom."

"Alright," I confirmed.

I climbed out of my seat and threw my bag over my shoulder. The two of us left the room and started to walk towards the office until I stopped. An upset feeling in my gut had returned, for a moment I thought I was going to puke.

"Hey, hold on," I said with minor urgency.

She stopped and faced me. "What's wrong?"

"You go on ahead and wait at the office, I need to run to the bathroom."

A small curl formed on her lip, displaying impatience. "Can't it wait?"

I slumped, "Not really. I don't think I've used the bathroom at all today. I'll be really quick." I promised, then without waiting for her to respond, I dashed in the opposite direction.

As soon as I turned a corner and was out of her sight, I slowed my pace. I played off a normal posture, even though the inside of my stomach ached horribly. Like a distant heartbeat, it thumped. Bringing nausea to my body. Then another yawn snuck up on me.

I dried the forced-out tears and observed my surroundings. I was alone. I continued my way to the nearest bathroom and the closer I got, the less sick I felt. While I walked, I placed my fingers along the lockers and dragged them across; bumping into the padlocks and listening to the clinging of the metal.

I reached the end of the hall, and the bathroom door stood wide open, but I didn't need it anymore. I don't know where that came from, though I suppose it wasn't a surprise. . . The whole day has been funky.

I turned around and started to head back, moving at a normal pace again. Approaching a turn, I leaned in a little, taking the corner tightly. Unfortunately, tragedy waited to greet me. Both of us unaware of the other, turned the corner, and bumped hard into each other. I rebounded off them and stopped moving, looking up to identify who it was.

Unfazed at first, I saw who it was.

"Sorry, Stacy," I said, my eyes quickly lowered to the ground. As they did, my attention was drawn to a pink liquid that had been spilled to the floor. I cocked an eyebrow and looked back up at her. Her eyes angled, and teeth flared. A faint, inaudible grumble leaked out from between her teeth as she held back harsh words. Her entire front and some of my own pants were soaked through with the slushy she was holding.

"Do you know how much this cost me!?" She snarled.

My mouth dropped. A pang of legitimate guilt weighed heavily on my heart.

"No. Oh no, shit. Stacy, I'm sorry. I didn't mean to." I pleaded with her.

"This cost me four dollars! Not to mention this outfit is now completely ruined. How am I going to survive detention without this?!" She threw the cup to the floor. The rest of the beverage spread out across the base of the lockers.

Detention? I thought.

"Well, I can't do anything about the outfit, but I'll pay you back the four dollars, okay?"

She placed her hands on her hips and glared at me. Then, to my surprise, she relaxed, letting her hands fall to her side.

"You know what, Kim, forget it. No harm done." She said plainly.

My mouth continued to drop, now hitting the floor.

"Are you serious?" I nervously chuckled, keeping my eyes on her.

There was no way she would just let this go. She's the same girl who stuffed broken pens in my bag, letting the ink leak out all over the inside all because I told the teacher she was texting in class.

"Yeah, it was clearly an accident. Just go get a janitor to clean it up." She shrugged her shoulders. Her face was still red with anger.

I'm not buying it, but if I have a chance to escape, I'm taking it.

"Okay. . . Sure. Again, I'm sorry." I apologized.

Cautiously, I approached her, both of us eyeing each other the whole way. Just as I got what I thought to be a safe distance away, a loud thumping rushed up behind me. My balance was ripped away as my body was propelled to the floor.

With a hard slam, I bashed my chin against the cold floor. My brain took a second to catch up with what just happened while also managing the new daze. I hoisted myself up on one arm and stared down at the floor, only seeing red. My one free hand cupped my chin, holding back the flow of new blood from the freshly reopened wound. My chin was numb but held a vibration in the center.

Lightheaded and maintaining a dizzy posture, I pulled myself upright and turned to her, still holding the bottom half of my face.

"Holy shit didn't mean for that to happen." She laughed out loud.

"What the fuck is your problem? You have issues you know that?" I shouted.

"I don't know what you're talking about." She giggled and confidently strutted away. I watched her turn that same corner and she was gone. I panted heavily, angry. Deceived, no longer feeling guilty about the mess or her clothes.

"Damn it all." I pulled my hand away and looked at the blood. "Crap."

Now, my feet carried me in a full, unsurpassed dash, leaving a trail of blood and smoothie droplets. My destination was now the nurse's office. After a minute, I made it to the front office and saw Tansu standing in the corner, waiting for me. As I approached, she noticed me coming and was about to greet me, until she saw the blood.

"Hey, what happened to you?" she called out.

I called out as I ran past her.

"I'll explain in a minute. Just wait there!"

"Uh . . . sure." She said.

Dashing past the office and Tansu, I bolted through the lunchroom, through some double doors into the gymnasium lobby, and continued down another short hallway into the nurse's office. The door flew open, and I stepped inside, panting as the door closed behind me.

"Hello." She greeted from her desk, fully focused on some work.

"Hey, can you help me out here?" I said, taking my hand away from my chin. She looked up from her computer and noticed the blood.

"Oh my! What happened?" She jumped up from her desk.

"Just opened up again." The blood still came out, but not as frequently as it had been. "By the way, someone should inform a janitor, I left a lot of blood in the Middle School Hall. . . Also, a slushy."

She rushed over to her cabinets and instructed me, "Go over to the sink, get a paper towel then sit over there." She pointed to a bed in the corner. One is primarily used for students that need to rest because they are sick or injured.

I did as she said, getting three sheets, folding them together, holding it in place, and then sitting on the bed. I waited for her to gather whatever she needed, just staring at the half-circle curtain above that could be used to give whoever sat here some privacy.

In less than a minute, she came over with a bottle, bandages, and more paper towels. She immediately cleaned my chin off and mopped up the blood that dripped down my neck and hands.

"How did this happen?" she asked, wiping down the cut.

I explained very, matter-of-fact "I fell at home recently and just now bumped it. Which made it open again."

After cleaning the blood, she took a brown bottle and poured some of its chemical contents onto a paper towel.

"I have to warn you; this may sting a bit." As it got close, I took a whiff of the medicated towel.

The stench was strong, curling my nostrils. She pressed the wet towel on the cut, and I felt the hot sizzle of hydrogen peroxide. I bit my lip hard while the pain escalated, then faded away. Leaving a radiating discomfort. When it was done, I gave a long sigh of relief.

She took a moment to observe it closely.

"Hmm, well, I don't think you'll need stitches. It's pretty deep, but it should just scar up a little. If you take care of it properly by changing the bandages and cleaning it often, then you should be fine." She said as she applied a new, identical wrapping.

"Thanks a lot. I'll be careful with it."

She looked concerned with me, even though I gave no indication that this was anything except an accident. I know she has kids of her own, so mother's intuition, I guess.

"Are you sure you're okay?" she asked.

"Yea, there's nothing to worry about" I smiled.

She still didn't seem convinced. "Alright. Come back if you need the bandages changed. Got that?"

I chuckled, "I will."

With that, I stood myself up and followed her to her desk where I signed a paper that stated that I was here on this date and that was treated. After that, I left the room and slowly made my way back to Tansu. Admittedly, my chin felt a lot better after she cleaned it up.

I arrived at the office to find Tansu looking anxious. She spotted me quickly and greeted me in a panic.

"There you are!"

I chuckled and rubbed the side of my neck.

"Sorry about that. I just had an accident."

"Was that. . . Blood on you?" she asked.

I nodded, "My chin reopened. It bled pretty well, but I'm fine."

"Jeez. Looked pretty bad from what I saw."

"It could have been worse. Sorry, I didn't mean to just run past you earlier."

"No-no it's fine." She smiled. "I'm glad you're okay." That gave me a warm feeling, and I smiled back.

"I'm gonna call my dad, Tansu," I said, walking past her and up to the front desk window.

"Alright. You should know, my mom usually shows up around this time, so I'll just ask her when she gets here."

"Okay," I affirmed.

On the other side of the glass was a different desk lady that I didn't know that well. I asked her for the phone, and she handed it to me, begrudgingly. I dialed my home number and waited for him to pick up. About ten rings in, the answering machine beeped, and I hung up the phone.

I know if he didn't answer during the first call, then he wasn't home. I don't know why, but he had an affinity for rushing to answer the phone. Even if he was mid-shit, he would dive out of the bathroom to pick it up.

I turned back to face Tansu and shook my head, "No answer."

"Oh." She looked disappointed.

"Forget it." I walked up to her, "I can still go over. He won't care."

"Are you sure?" She asked.

In my head, I knew he would be pissed. But right now, I really couldn't care less.

"Absolutely." I grinned, which caused her to give a reassuring smile as well.

We waited in the main lobby for about five or so more minutes when she called out the person walking to the front doors.

"Here she comes." Tansu's voice held a nervous and excited tone.

I too got nervous when she came in the doors and approached us. What will she say about the bandage? How will she judge my clothes and hair?

These worries were swept aside when she greeted us normally, not calling attention to anything I thought she would.

"Hello, Kim." She greeted me with a smile. She stood with her hands folded over one another and placed delicately in front of her beltline. A very proper, yet protective stance. I smiled as nicely but couldn't talk. My tongue was tied, and I left her lingering with my silence. She looked at Tansu.

"Are you all set, sweetheart?"

"Yes, mom. Um, would it be okay if Kim came over today? Just for a little bit?" She begged.

Her mom looked back at me, and this time I spoke.

"If it isn't too much trouble."

"No trouble at all." Her eyes closed as a big smile took over her face.

"Thanks, mom!" Tansu cheered

"Yes, thank you," I said in appreciation.

The three of us walked out the door, they stood side by side while I kept my pace slow enough to stay right behind them. We walked the short distance to her car in the parking lot, and we all climbed in. I got in the middle, and Tansu sat next to me behind the passenger seat. We were quickly on our way, and the car ride was quiet until we got on the main road, then her mom spoke.

"So, how was school today?" she asked the two of us.

Tansu answered, "Not a lot happened today. It was actually pretty boring."

"And you, Kim? Did anything eventful happen today?"

I nervously cleared my throat, "Just everyday school." I was so nervous my heart jumped out of my chest. I haven't been in a situation like this in a long time.

"Do you enjoy school? Tansu tells me you're very smart." Her mom said, glancing at me sitting in the backseat through the rear-view mirror.

"Heh, yeah, I like school. It can be fun." I blushed.

Tansu butted in, "She's great in school. We don't have a lot of classes together, and you should see her hand shoot up in Math! It's nuts. Oh, she can draw too!" She sounded way too excited for me.

I groaned, "Tansu." I bumped my elbow against her, she looked to me, puzzled.

"What?"

"Don't . . . hype me up like that." I said bashfully. "I'm not all that great," I reassured her mom.

"No, I think it's wonderful that you hold such passion for learning. The world needs more enthusiastic minds." She said with a cheer in her voice.

"I'm just trying my best, Ms. Hikono."

"Oh, so formal. Please call me Kari." She chuckled then followed up with a common question.

"What do your parents do for work?"

My blushing face sank a little, and my eyes redirected themselves out the window. "My dad does construction and odd jobs like that; kind of a jack-of-all-trades guy."

"That must be very convenient at home."

"Yea, he's great with clogged toilets." I crudely joked with a slum face. Surprisingly enough she snickered, even though it was a bad joke and dirty at that.

"And how about your mother?"

I paused. There was a thick silence that only I could hear. Only the humming of the car and an occasional bump in the road filled the gaps. I didn't want to state the facts right away, so I kept it vague.

"When my parents moved here a long time ago, she owned her own daycare center out of a separate studio apartment. I know she absolutely loved it there."

"That's very nice. Was she able to continue the profession here?"

Guess there is no avoiding it. I could continue to dodge the truth, but what would be the point in that?

"No. . . Actually, she passed away when I was young." I expressed sadness in my voice.

She looked at me through the rear-view mirror, then back at the road, then to me again. Sharing the sadness in her eyes.

"I'm, very sorry."

I reassured her with a little smile. "It's okay. It was a long time ago." I pushed some hair out of my face and cleared my throat.

"I hardly remember her anyways."

Tansu felt the awkwardness from her mom even though I tried to refrain the vibe. Then another question to follow up, to sort of change the subject.

"What do you see yourself doing when you get older?"

"Honestly, I'm not too sure. I sometimes imagine what it would be like working with animals or a teller at a bank. But I don't really have anything I'm working towards. More like, inspiration from whatever is around me."

"At least you have ideas. That's more than most people of your age. That being said, I wouldn't worry about it too much right now. You have plenty of time before you are faced with a decision. Ninth grade is a long way from adulthood." She chuckled.

"Yes, but I've heard it sneaks up on you," I added.

"Hopefully not," Tansu spoke.

The car continued to carry us down my own road and as we passed my driveway it was pretty clear that most people wouldn't see it if they weren't looking for it. I guess Tansu was right to be confused at seeing me standing there that morning.

We approached a turn and the car suddenly veered right, which caused us all to lean slightly. We followed this road for a quarter-mile, then made another left and followed the bend. Which led into the private community, one that I have heard about in passing but never seen. Important townspeople or people richer than everyone else lived here. That's all I really knew about it.

As soon as you took the curve, you could see four houses: one to the right, another straight ahead, and another next to that one and the closest, on the left. All of them big, and intimidating. The first one you would pass, immediately to the left, was the one we pulled into. Admittedly the smallest of the bunch and least kept, but far nicer than my own. As the tires came to a halt on the pavement, a small pit formed in my stomach along with a serene, affiliated sensation.

To the left was a nice brick walkway that connected to the pavement and leads to the front door and to the right was a large tree and boulder close to the road, decorating the front yard. Besides that, the yard was barren and green.

From what I could see they had plenty of yard space on the left and right before it was cut off by tree-lines.

The ringing in my ears was ever-present as I observed this new place. I've never been down this road before, seeing as the bus usually comes here first in the mornings before turning around to get me, and for some reason always dropped me off after school before turning down this road.

We all climbed out of the vehicle, each at our own pace; mine being the slowest. Moving around to the left of the car, we all walked along the walkway. I found myself feeling ashamed; seeing their house. I don't want Tansu to see mine at all now.

I haven't even seen the inside, yet, I already knew that it would be much nicer than anything I could offer. I followed up behind them and observed the outside of the house.

It had a shell-white siding and a dark asphalt roof. Every window was boldly outlined by a thick off-white frame, and the front door stood proud as lovingly treated mahogany.

Little flower buds guided our way on either side of the walk, and we reached the front door. Her mom unlocked it and stepped in first, but before we could take two steps in, her mom stopped me.

"Kimberly, if you don't mind, could you leave your shoes in the nook by the door? I want to keep this place clean as long as possible." She asked as she and Tansu removed their own shoes.

"Of course." I replied, quickly lifting one leg to remove a shoe, "Um, can I ask one thing?"

She perked up. "Yes, what is it?"

"Sorry, but can you just call me Kim? I'm not a big fan of people using my full name. Never have been."

"If that is what you prefer." She smiled tenderly.

We all left our shoes neatly by the front door. The first thing you saw in the house was this short hallway, with a nook on the right that had a coat rack and shoe mat.

To the left in the hallway was a little shelf on the wall. A few scenic photos were neatly placed on top, all symmetrically laid out on this beautiful hardwood floor. Once all the shoes were left on the mat, we stepped into the main room. The house had an open floor plan, basically just one big room with a few small divider walls. Directly to your right were the kitchen and dining area.

What stood out the most, was a short island in the center of the horseshoe counter layout. So many cabinets, top, and bottom, you could never fill them all and tucked into the right corner closest to the entrance was a small, but cozy-looking dining room with a medium-sized table and enough chairs for a whole family. Nicely accommodated by a few paintings and two tall windows looking out to the front yard.

On the furthermost right of the house was a small aforementioned dividing wall, which held a few countertops on this side, but on the other was a short hallway. Then on my left, I only saw a diagonal wall starting from the door and stretched out to about halfway into the house.

Then it squared off and formed the living room, sectioned off by a dark-green carpet and bright floor lamp in the nearest corner. The living room was simply decorated by a couch that sat a coffee table and a large TV surrounded by a hundred or more VHS tapes and DVDs.

Straight ahead were three doors aligned against a flat wall, but I didn't know what was behind them. That was everything I could see from the front door and with that, I was left with only amazement. From what I could see, I could tell that they had a good chunk of money but were humble and reserved. Very comfortable.

"Wow," I whispered. Tansu stood beside me, watching me look at her house up and down.

"Your house—" I started.

She looked at me. "What? What's wrong with it?"

"It's awesome." I grinned.

This made her chuckle. "I'm sure your house is just as awesome."

"If only," I said. "Hey, where do those doors go?" I pointed to the wall dead ahead.

She gestured with her left hand. "The one farthest left is the reading room; my mom loves to read. When she isn't reading for her classes, she's reading for fun." She snickered. "The one straight ahead is my room and I'll show you that in a minute. Next, to the right is the bathroom. Lastly, the door around the corner past the kitchen is my mom's room. And that's pretty much it besides the basement to the left around this corner."

I stepped forward, just detailing everything in this house, comparing it all to my house. Hers had live plants, clean end tables, a decent couch, and awesome-looking kitchen appliances and just about everything that my house didn't.

"You guys lucked out with this place. I really like it." I complimented.

Her mom jumped in the conversation. "The Realtor said the house has been on the market for quite some time. We had others that were up for consideration, but once we stepped foot in here, we were sold. It may be a little out of the way, but the inconvenience is worth the feeling of being at home."

"What makes this one more special than the others?" I asked. This time, Tansu answered,

"I had the same question before actually stepping inside. But once I did, I understood how my mom felt. This place is just so down to earth. It isn't needlessly complicated. Plain, I guess, and we can both connect with that simplicity." She chuckled.

Her mom spoke again, "We love it. It just felt like home."

It got quiet for a second, all the while my eyes still invaded every inch of this place from where we stood. I couldn't help it; I felt like a kid in a candy shop. Tansu cracked her fingers again, looking into the living room, seemingly spaced out. Nervous maybe. The house smelled un-lived. A little, too clean. Maybe she was self-conscious about it.

Her mom then separated from us, moving towards the dining area and taking a seat at the table in front of some papers. I looked to Tansu; she returned my gaze then gestured for us to move along. I nodded and followed her across the open floor towards her bedroom door.

We stepped inside and she made sure to close the door behind us. Once inside, I made mental notes of her layout. It was oddly plain, though I chalked that up to her still getting used to the move and not fully unloading in here. Still, it was cozy; she had a carpeted floor with a pink circle rug in the center, her wallpaper was white with very thin black vertical streaks scattered randomly. To the right from the door was her bed and a nightstand. To the left was a weird waist-high lip and indent in the wall with a few pillows and books; a reading alcove. Dead ahead was a small desk below the window, which had a laptop and some random office supplies scattered on it. To the left of that was the closet in the corner.

She took off her socks and tossed them into a laundry basket beside her bed then sat at the computer desk. She was the first to comment.

"I'm going to be honest. . . I have no idea what to do. I can't tell you the last time I had someone over." Her shoulders tightened to her neck as she plopped herself onto the rolling chair in front of the desk. I awkwardly placed my hands behind my back and watched her make shifty eyes all around the room.

I peeled my feet from the floor and tiptoed over to her bed, allowing myself to sit on the edge and cross one leg over the other.

"I'm right there with you." I chuckled, feeling a little distant.

From where we sat concerning each other, there was maybe a foot between us. She was turned in the chair facing me; I leaned forward, resting my tender chin in my palm. Her eyes eventually crossed mine, then instantly disconnected. "So, what do we do now?' I asked

"Umm, I'm not sure." She replied softly.

"Okay well how about we play a game of favorites?" I suggested

"That sounds fun, we can get to know each other a bit more." She smiled.

"Exactly! Alright, I guess I'll start." I paused and started searching for a question. "What is . . . your favorite food?"

"Oh! That's easy, Oatmeal and blueberries" She said with a big smile.

"That's, really modest; I expected something more exotic than that."

"Nope, you thought wrong. My turn, what is your favorite. . . kind of milk? Plain, chocolate, or strawberry?" She asked.

"Really. . . that's your first question? The way you want to get to know me is by first asking me what milk I like?" I gave her a confused, yet entertained look.

She shrugged in response, "I don't know what I'm doing." She said cutely.

"Well, the answer to such vital information is strawberry, no doubt," I answered with determination.

"Good choice." She said with a little nod.

"Wait, now I have a question for you that isn't favorites related. . .Do you put ice in your milk?"

She almost looked offended, "No! That's weird."

"Oh thank god," I exclaimed sarcastically.

"What kind of person does that?" She played along with the overreaction.

"Freaking Joey!" I half-shouted by mistake. "I actually got a shirt a while back that has, like, ice cubes and milk and a big red crossed out circle on it. I wore it to school to show it to him and he lost his mind; going on a rant about how the ice *does not dilute the milk.*"

She snorted, holding back a giggle. The whole time I was using my arms for emphasis, eyes wide and expressions overplayed.

"You know, I could see you wearing a shirt like that." She said with a thrill in her voice.

"Once upon a time I would." I scoffed, trying to put a leash on my energy.

"But not now?" She questioned.

"Well, no. That same day I got made fun of for the shirt. The school is so bland and lifeless that any form of self-expression is swiftly crushed. . . I should say, for people like me."

I could tell by her face that she didn't like my answer, particularly the self-exclusion. "And who are you when compared to *them*?"

"Nobody. If you aren't in some clique or group, you get targeted."

"That doesn't make sense." She said quietly. "You should always express yourself despite what others may or may not think. If you want to wear goofy shirts or color your hair or even shave your head, then you have the right to choose that for yourself. Don't let the expectation of others limit who you are."

"I agree, but. . . I don't know, it just doesn't seem worth it. Why give them ammunition? I go there to learn and see a few faces, not to stand out and get sucked into the social stigma. There are more important things than that."

"Don't you want more friends, or at the very least don't you want to make a positive impact in their lives by showing them who you are? If not, then why did you even bother with me?" She looked a little sad at the end.

"I definitely don't want to make friends with anyone else at that school, I know pretty much everyone and they all suck. I stopped and helped you because you were new. Yes, at first, I felt obligated to help, and to be honest I expected you to be just like them, but you surprised me." I smiled.

There was a brief silence.

Now, she wasn't avoiding my gaze. There was no head-turning or staring at the floor between us. In this bubble of contemplation, I focused intently on her face, or, her eyes in particular.

The window was bleeding in sunlight from her left side, washing the color from her face but refracting light through her left eye; that's when I saw it. My first impression at school, under those overhead dull incandescent rays, was that her iris' were black. . . I was wrong. I could see clearly now that her eyes were green. A mixed blend of chartreuse and shamrock, depending on the angle of the light. I tried not to stare too hard, but this revelation intrigued me.

"Your favorite animal?" She asked quietly.

Caught off guard, I refocused with a few light blinks and then grinned, "Nuh-uh you just went, and it's my turn. What your favorite season? And if you must know Cape buffalo."

"Cape. . . Buffalo?" She asked. "That is very specific."

"I watch a lot of nature documentaries and stuff like that. I love them because people often depict them as prey, food for the hunters, when in fact they are extremely deadly. So cool. But, weird, I know."

"No, I like that. That's very unique, I would have accepted cat, so I am pleasantly surprised. To answer your question, I actually don't have a favorite season. That's because I like them all equally." She giggled.

"What a cheap answer." I chuckled with her.

She tilted her head. "It's still an answer."

I sighed, leaning off my arms and stretching my back.

"Okay, I think I'm done with favorites; let's talk about something else."

"Like what?" She initiated again.

I scoffed, "I don't know, what do girls talk about?" I joked.

"Boys?" She answered, perplexed.

"Oh jeez, boys. I have nothing to contribute on that subject."

"What about Joey. What's your relationship with him?"

My heart ached for a sliver of a second.

"That's. . . complicated. He's an old friend, but we sort of had a falling out."

"What happened?" She asked.

"Meh, it's all so stupid." I stalled but she was becoming more invested.

"Were you two, like, together?"

My brow raised, "What? No!" I half exclaimed, "It's not like that. . . I mean, not like I have a problem with that, but it isn't. . . that's not. . ." I fumbled, all the while she let a devious smile creep across her face.

"I see." She said softly.

"No, Tansu you don't get it." I pinched the bridge of my nose, and sighed, "We weren't together or anything, it's just. . . I don't wanna talk about it." I simmered, taking a breath and releasing it slowly. She backed up and gave me a sly look.

"You can tell me."

I shook my head, then scratched the back of my head. "I let him go," I admitted.

Her grin disappeared, then she leaned in closer, but I kept my tilt back. My eyes had fallen to my lap.

"You heard in the car. . . that I lost my mom some time ago. Well, because of that I just closed up. He tried. . ." I shook my head, gritting my teeth, "He tried hard to stay close, but I wouldn't let him. I can't."

That made things quiet again.

"Sorry." She whispered.

I paused.

"But it wasn't entirely me. He has a sister, Natalia. . . I don't know all the details; he doesn't like to talk about it, but I know she's sick. Like, *really* sick to the point where she can't even get out of bed; he struggles to stay on top of his classes because of this. I help him out when I can, and I've been getting better at engaging him, but it's like, I put up this wall and I can't remember how to tear it down; be vulnerable again. I think he feels the same sometimes."

There was a long pause. She fiddled with her fingertips and I rested my hands on my lap. "Hey, can I ask you something?" I said softly.

Her eyelids fluttered. "Sure."

"What's it like having your mom around? I mean, my dad's my dad, but he isn't. . . soft."

She looked uncomfortable. Her lips were loose, a small gap formed below the peak and her eyes were heavy with thought. I could tell that she didn't want to boast about the one thing she has that I don't.

"She's. . . great; the best mom in the world, but you can only spend so much time with your mom before you want to tear your hair out. Even family can make you feel pretty alone sometimes." She laughed delicately.

"But things are changing. Now that I have you and you have me, we won't have to feel that loneliness anymore." She assured.

Suddenly there was a knock at the door that made the both of us jump.

"Girls, may I come in?" A fragile voice spoke through the closed door.

"Yes, you may," Tansu answered.

The door slowly squeaked open and her mom stood there and smiled.

"I hope you two are having fun." She said kindly.

Tansu nodded and I spoke, making sure to add gratuity to my voice.

"Yes, we are, thank you, ma'am," I answered.

She gave me a big smile, then directed a somewhat concerned gaze to Tansu. "I just wanted to check in, see if you two wanted a snack or something to drink?" She offered.

We each looked to each other and then back to her.

"I'm okay for now," I answered.

"Me too," Tansu replied.

Kari offered another tight smile and took hold of the door handle.

"Alright, I'm going to resign myself to the reading room. Let me know when you are ready to go." She ended by addressing me.

"Thanks, Mom," Tansu called as the door clicked shut.

Chapter 8 – Simpatico

After her mom had left us, things felt a little off. I personally had this feeling of misplacement; having reopened some old wounds and having the recent interaction with her mom made me feel somewhat homesick. I wanted to start another conversation but felt tongue-tied. I just. . . wanted to lie down.

I had no idea how she was feeling. There has to be some level of consideration for my emotions and how talking about Joey and my mom has affected me. Even though I was pretty good at keeping that instability under lock and key, there was no denying the potent sadness that flushed my face.

The springs of her bed creaked as I shifted my weight from one side to the other. It only now occurred to me that we should really switch places, simply because this is her room and her bed; so, it's kind of unfair that I got to sit here, and she is forced to sit in her chair.

Before I could bring that up as the stepping stone to a new conversation, she licked her lips and caught me by surprise.

"Kim, how old is your home?"

"How old? Why?" I responded with a partial yawn.

"I was thinking about the ghost stuff you mentioned before. Maybe someone died there and is reaching out to you."

I rubbed one eye, "Honestly I've been trying to forget about all of that. It's stressing me out."

"If it's just a ghost, it can't really do you any harm." She tried to be reassuring.

"That's the thing, I'm not sure it's a ghost," I stated plainly, knowing full-well that whatever this thing is, is more than just an apparition.

I was reminded of the deal. His yellow eyes flashed behind my lids with every blink. The moment I thought of him, his idea infected me like a virus, and nausea erupted in my gut. A burning, sour sting of corruption burdened my organs. I lost my breath, only to find it again as a stifled gasp.

"I need to know more about it." I stated somewhat dramatically.

"If-f you want. . ." She stuttered, sensing my energy, "You can use my laptop." She offered.

Her tender, docile voice aided in snapping me out of the growing trance. I swallowed hard, feeling more like myself with each second.

"Okay, yeah that sounds great actually." I nodded.

Rotating in her chair, she flipped open her laptop and typed in the password. I jumped off the bed and approached her left side, giving her the opening to switch places.

"Here ya go." She smiled.

She slid out from the desk and I took her place in the warm seat.

"Thanks. I hope I'm not being invasive or anything."

"Oh, I don't mind at all. I'll just be reading until you're done." She timidly smiled, her face looking a little red.

"All right, I won't be too long."

She adjusted her shirt and waistband then walked behind me, moving to the reading alcove. Once there, she grabbed a small stack of thin magazines and brought them over to her bed where she proceeded to lie down on her stomach, her head at the foot of the bed. She opened the fragile pages and began scanning the words and images.

As for me, I wasted no time in my searches. First, I started simply with keywords like *demon*, *ghost*, *yellow eyes*, *sickness*, and so on.

Ten or so minutes passed, and I did manage to find some new info about demons in general but nothing pertaining to my situation. Tansu occasionally asked my opinion of a pair of jeans or a dress she found in a magazine she was reading, other than that the room was ambient with focus.

More searches yielded similar results; nothing. I was getting frustrated and started tapping the keyboard more aggressively. I searched for *deal*, and demons which led to me to something I found interesting. Faust, a German legend of a man who made a deal with the devil. Although this tale was similar, it wasn't what I needed.

That was the single useful thing I found; after that the well was dry. Nearly thirty minutes wasted on the computer and I was ready to tear my own hair out. Though Tansu would have no idea the stress I was enduring right now, given my composure.

One final effort. Anticipation burning a hole in my brain, I strung together demon, deal, Faust, and evil. Page one, nothing. Page two, three four and five were similarly vacant. But there was this buzzing in my head, some stubborn gnat that coaxed me into clicking the next page over and over. Each number passed left me less and less satisfied and doubly frustrated. But my finger continued to click of its own will until I happened upon page twelve.

By this point, my vision was foggy from lack of blinking. A hard rub and aggravated sigh reset my patience and allowed my vision to uncloud. The cobwebs of my mind cleared as I read the list of links before me.

Third from the top, a page called, *a place for us all.*

The webpage loaded incredibly slowly, one line of text at a time. Once it was fully loaded, I skimmed over what appeared to be a personal blog written in nineteen-ninety-six.

Every entry started off with a date and ended with a signature L.C. Starting from the earliest pages, this girl spoke mostly of drama with her mother. A lot of fear for her well-being and the mystery behind her father's place in the family tree. Nothing too crazy, but relevant enough to grasp how this girl lived. It seems like a lot of this information was written in a few sittings, backlogging events from her past until she finally caught up to the present. That's where things got interesting.

In the latest scripts, she detailed newest hobbies. Feeling lost within herself, struggling with her emotions and identities, this girl turned to a group of misfit kids. A group that got together to drink and smoke their problems away. Inadvisable, for sure but from what I'm reading here, apparently these other kids helped her grow into herself. So, in the end, it was a good experience for her.

But then, she started talking about an old man.

This mysterious elder came into her life and appeared to have some unexplainable presence about him. Explaining how she can remember looking down at their conversation from outside of her own body; unable to deny his curiosities. After that first encounter, she started seeing him everywhere she went. Hidden among crowds, in the corner of her eye and persistently in her nightmares.

There were many times where she explicitly expressed concern for her safety but felt twice as afraid to ask for anyone's help. Though she had people to lean on, the assurance in confiding in them was slim to none; so, she remained quiet. All of this, leading up to a final journal entry.

I read it in my head.

I made a mistake. . . So much has happened in these past two days so I don't know where to even begin. All I can say, is I'm afraid. He found me again but this time I gave in to his temptation. I made a mistake. Now there's a voice in my head; she's watching as a type this and she won't stop. . . I don't know what will happen to me in these coming days, but I sincerely wanted to thank all of my readers. I owe you my life. - L.C

"L.C." I whispered to myself. Searching for a meaning behind the identifier.

I clicked out of the browser and closed the screen. This girl waited to ask for help, but it was too late. She tried to ignore the problem, but it didn't go away. Maybe it isn't too late for me? She was all alone and maybe if I'm not, things could be different.

My lower lip quivered. I have to talk to Tansu. I don't know what else to do. She needs to know. At least, it doesn't sound too crazy. Maybe she will understand? Or maybe she'll think I'm completely psychotic. I turned to her and just stared at her with gloomy eyes, indecisiveness plainly displayed on my face. She noticed my stare and put the magazine down gently.

"Are you okay?" She asked

I clenched my fists tight.

"Tansu, where do you stand on the supernatural?" I asked.

She cocked an eyebrow, then giggled. "I already told you. I used to watch a lot of those shows."

"I'm not talking about TV shows. I mean actual ghosts and demons. What do you think? Are they real?"

She didn't hesitate, "I suppose. I mean, anything is possible, right? It would be pretty cool if they were. . ." She paused. "Actually, no, that would be kind of scary. To be honest, I'd rather not know for sure if they were real or not. The suspense of the unknown seems more fun than a definitive answer."

"Close enough." I whimpered.

Not the answer I was really expecting. In any case, going off what she just said, I think it may be safe to assume she won't think I'm bat-shit crazy if I tell her about this man.

The problem is, how do I present this? Maybe I'll explain how it started, give it some background. It may help my case and god knows I need help here.

"Kimmy?" She was worried.

“I’m sorry. It’s just . . . There’s something I want to tell you. I just don’t know how. It’s nothing against you. I’m just unsure whether I can, trust you or not.” I looked to her, then turned away, my mind spinning.

She hopped off the bed and took my hand, guiding me. I followed her as she took me over to the bed and sat me down next to her.

“I’m here, whatever you need. You can talk to me.”

I sighed deeply. The pressure in my chest building. I want her to be my friend, I enjoy having her around. But I'm scared. I feel as though I'm lying to her.

“I don’t really. . . Know how to say this. We haven’t known each other long enough, but I feel like, I just need someone to talk to; without judging me. I need help.”

“Well, if you want help, then talk to me. If you want advice, then talk to me. I’m here. I don’t scare easy.” She assured.

In my head, it didn't make sense to come right out and say demon. Then I'd have to backtrack, explain everything after the fact. So, best I start from the beginning.

“I guess, it starts with my dad. But he surprisingly enough isn't the main issue here, but it does start with him.”

“Alright.” She was listening.

“He, uh, he sort of hurt me,” I spoke very slowly, choosing each word cautiously.

“He hurt you?” she said with minor disbelief.

“Like. . . physically. Verbally.”

She looked uncomfortable, but she slid herself a little bit closer to me.

“What made this come up?” She asked with care.

“For one, I don’t like to lie to people, especially my friends. And I did lie to you. . .”

She was following along with a look of worried determination. I pointed to the bandage on my face.

“It’s true. I did

trip. That’s how I got this cut on my face. But it wasn’t that simple. I tripped trying to get away from him. . . When he was drinking.”

“What’d he do to you?” She looked scared.

For a second, I backpedaled, changing my mind on how much I wanted to say. Anxiety hit me, and cowardice came over me like a heavy blanket. This is too much for me, for her. I can't do it.

I separated myself from her, sliding toward the outer edge of the bed.

“No. . . I want you to be my friend, Tansu. I don’t want you to leave now. Just forget what I said.”

“Don’t be silly, Kim. We are friends, at least I happen to think so. If something is going on, I want you to tell me about it. Friendships are built and maintained through shared secrets and trust in one another.” She smiled.

I got scared. My eyes changed to an empty stare.

She leaned closer, “Talk to me, please.”

I stammered, "I-I just. . . Talking about this stuff is hard, Tansu. It only brings back the terror, the neglected feeling inside. Just like with Joey; when my mom died."

I swallowed hard, she listened intently, "I wanted him to know what I was going through, I wanted him to help me, to hold me. But I was suffering, and, in my head, it was best to do it in silence. No one could remedy the situation, no one could quell the screaming. So why bring it up? When it would only bring depression to everyone around me."

I stopped and thought to myself.

That's why I left him there, just when I began to understand my feelings for him.

I finished, "I want to feel safe, to feel loved, and to love. But it hurts, to tell the truth about my life. That's where I am right now."

I turned my eyes to the wall and bit my lip, grabbing the fabric of my sleeve tightly. She noticed this and took my hand. I tensed up.

She moved my hand off my arm carefully and down to my side, trying to unwrap my stress. Then, she grabbed the sleeve of my sweatshirt and slowly slid it up my arm. A big purple bruise had developed on the top of my forearm where my dad had grabbed me.

She let out a small whimper and looked at me. I kept my eyes averted. The pressure of tears building behind my eyes was becoming too much to hold back. Next, she moved her hand to my face and touched the bandage's surface, then took hold of my jaw and gently turned my head toward her, I saw her eyes; the sadness and grief.

Shaking, on the verge of tears, I tried to calm down, but it was no use. I just couldn't. It's like I was absorbing all this information for the first time myself, reliving every second of fear. As the first stream of tears rolled down my face, she threw her arms around me and squeezed me tight.

This is not what I expected from her. At school, she is so quiet and keeps to herself, baseline afraid of interaction. But here, she was friendly. Tender and close. Like a sister. I hardly know her and yet. . . My body trembled, and breaths quaked. The whole time, she comforted me.

"My dad—he wasn't always a bad person." I cried. "But lately he's been so cruel to me, and I don't know why. I got this cut on my face when he started hitting me. I tried to get away, but I fell and—"

I paused to compose myself a bit. "There's something else . . . something I'm not sure how you will take."

"I can take anything, Kim. Tell me." Her own voice was shaking.

"There was this man in my room. I've seen him a couple of times and he always seems to appear from the shadows. Recently he offered me some sort of deal, some way out of this."

This caught her attention. She pushed me back but not in a rejecting way. Instead, the look on her face showed terror. She wanted to look me in the eye but struggled to maintain a full connection.

"A man, offered you a deal? What does that even mean?"

"I'm not sure. He said that he knew about my suffering and he could help or something."

She looked scared for me.

"I don't know what to do, Tansu." I shuddered.

It went quiet as I wiped the remaining tears and took a deep, revitalizing breath. "I'm sorry. I just. . . I needed to get it out and I have no one else to go to. I know I haven't known you long. So, I understand if you just want to take me home and move on. I don't want to make your life stressful." I said woefully. "I didn't mean to–"

"What? Are you kidding me?" She sounded almost jittery. "Look, I don't know how I can help, but I won't abandon you. Yeah, it's kind of a lot to find out about a person. But you don't have to face this alone. I promise I'm not going anywhere." She said with a sincere smile that boosted confidence.

"Really?" I was shocked.

"You bet."

She took it better than I thought. One thing she had going for her, was determination. You wouldn't guess that she held such powerful traits; seeing how she was at school.

She is really inspiring to me. Something about the way she approached a huge ordeal like this, with her chin held high and ready to take on the challenge, made me feel so much better about the whole thing.

"So. . . This deal–what was it he offered to give you?"

I pulled on my sleeve and scratched my arm underneath the fabric.

"It's weird. He said that he would give me power?" I said with my own disbelief. "I guess to get back at people who hurt me."

"Power? What kind of power?"

"I have no idea, really. I know nothing about this sort of thing."

She pondered for a second. "Well, in any case, you definitely shouldn't take it. I mean I've seen shows and movies on this kind of thing and it never ends well. Just . . . I don't want anything to happen to you." She said sincerely. I looked into her face and let out a long, tired sigh.

I was confused at her intent. She sounded sincere, but I had my own disbelief that she was just humoring me. No way would she just accept this so casually.

"To be fair, this isn't a show or movie. It's real and it's happening to me. But I won't take it. The whole thing creeps me out. He seems very. . . clingy."

"Why do you say that?"

"Besides this feeling in my gut, I also found something on the computer. Some sort of blog post, written by some girl who was posting about something similar. . . I'm honestly amazed I found it. . . But when she said no, he didn't leave. Then she disappeared."

"How do you know she disappeared?"

"She stopped posting one day after writing out some heavy stuff."

"Isn't it possible she just stopped blogging and moved on to other things?"

"Well, of course, it's possible, but you didn't read it. It was ominous. It's still on your laptop if you wanna look at it"

"Actually, yes I would." She stated.

I reached around her and set the laptop on my legs, then reopened the page. She stared at the screen for a few minutes, concentrating. She occasionally let out a heavy sigh or adjusted herself.

When she was finished, she moved it to the side and closed the lid again. She didn't respond at first, just sort of stared at me. Then to her own legs.

"It seems that you have very limited information on this whole thing. There isn't anything really concrete with this situation, I'm not sure what we can do right now."

"I know. I didn't expect you to have any answers, I just needed someone to know. I'm hoping it's nothing serious, and that it will go away. If not, then I'd rather not face this alone."

"I hear you." She said quietly.

I then realized just how selfish this whole thing was. I am too afraid to handle my own problems, so I drag her down with me; what if he's dangerous? What if he doesn't want anyone else to know and he hurts her?

My heart silently thumped, now feeling guilty that I just spilled my guts in front of her and potentially endangered her. A long silence lingered. Both of us just stared at the floor or walls, thinking. Neither one of us knew what to say or do.

A soft knock came from her closed door.

"Tansuke, dear, would you and your friend like a snack? I was going to make grilled cheese." Her mom called from behind the door

Tansu perked up and suddenly sat very straight and symmetrical.

"Yes, Mom, that sounds great." She replied.

"All right, ten minutes."

"Okay."

I spoke, "That's sweet of your mom to make us food."

"She loves to spoil, and I hate to refuse her. Are you hungry?"

"I could eat," I said politely.

"Then let's go take our seat at the table." She stood up and walked to the door. I followed close behind her.

"Tansu." She stopped, mid-reaching for the door handle.

"Yes?"

"Thanks for listening and caring." I smiled. She smiled back, but somehow, it felt less sincere. A sinking feeling invaded my gut.

Eighteen minutes later, we were sat at the table with her mom apologizing for it taking so long. But I wasn't one to be less appreciative for it taking a little longer than expected. The grilled cheese was mouthwatering compared to the food at school or home. The happiness I felt sitting at the dining room table and eating with these two was something I had always wanted. It was a great feeling; all the tension from the conversation in her room was gone, and we were able to hold a nice long conversation about school.

However, I was fully prepared for this to be my first, and last meal here. When we finished our food, her mom unpacked a few board games for us to play with, games I had no idea how to play. Like, Yahtzee and Mouse Trap. It was fun, despite my ignorance.

Time went by, and I became wary of the time. The sky was glowing a dim orange, and I had to get home soon. Tansu began washing the dishes from earlier while her mom put the games away. I stood awkwardly, not knowing what to do until her mom called me over into the living room.

"Kim, you'll have to tell me where you live so I can bring you home now."

I replied, "No, it's fine. I'll walk home, Ms. Hikono."

She was astonished by my response.

"Walk? Dear, it's almost dark. I can't let you walk home this late." She laughed a little.

Hearing this made me happy. That was something I didn't get too often; concern for my well-being. The only time my dad showed any concern was if I did something or was planning on doing something that may affect him in some way, like his image and things like that. He doesn't like to deal with my problems, so he stays out of them.

"I guess you have a point. Okay, but only if it won't be too much trouble."

She giggled "It's not. Now, go get your shoes on."

"Okay." I grinned, then fast-walked over to the front door. I threw on my shoes and called to Tansu.

"I guess I'm going home, are you coming too?"

She turned away from the dishes and smiled softly, "No, I have to take a shower before bed. But I will definitely see you at school."

Her mom walked up beside me and slid her dainty feet into her slip-on's,

"Alright, cool I'll see you then." I waved goodbye as I opened the door.

"Bye, Kim." She waved as well.

We headed outside, and I hurried over to the car. I was a little too excited for a simple car ride and immediately slowed my pace to a casual walk, but still moved with purpose. Nearly bumping my hip as I rounded the front of the car. Standing by the passenger door, I looked through the glass and her mom climbed it. I opened the front door a little.

"Um, Ms. Hikono, can I sit in the front seat?"

She gave me a puzzled look. "If you want to, it's okay with me, just as long as your seat-belt is on."

I grinned widely, then jumped in the front seat and strapped myself in.

"Thanks, I've never ridden in the front seat before."

"Never? Well, I can say that it's not very exciting." She said, amused.

"It has to be better than looking at the back of the seat," I replied

We were on our way. Just her mom and me.

This was sort of a good thing because it gave me and her mom a chance to get better acquainted. Partway down the road, she initiated a conversation,

"Did the two of you have a good time? I hope Tansuke wasn't too quiet for you."

I fiddled with the belt strap over my chest. "Not at all. She was talking as much as I was and yeah, it was fun. I haven't actually spent time with someone my age outside of school for a long time. And, can I say something?"

"Kim, you don't need my permission to speak. Please, relax and speak freely." She giggled. "You have excellent manners, but I think you need to work on your confidence if you don't mind me saying."

“I have confidence. It’s just. . .” I thought about how I always tiptoe with my words around my dad and around the people he would invite to the house. I always had to keep quiet out of fear of being scolded.

“Well, I just wanted to say that you have a gorgeous house and I was curious to know what you and your husband do for work. Tansu mentioned something about classes?” I asked politely.

“I spend a lot of time teaching young minds. In my spare time, I give private lessons, but my main occupation is teaching college students.”

“Oh really? What fields?”

“Hmm, my lectures mainly consist of English Literature, Poetry Workshop, and, funny enough, Marine Biology.” She said softly.

“Wow, that’s a lot of stuff to teach. How do you know all that well enough to teach it?”

“I took a lot of classes through my own college years, and I just love knowledge. Everyone deserves a chance to learn.”

We took a turn, and it hit a light bump, making the car rock. Staring ahead, I watched the pavement scroll under the car. She was taking the drive slowly. It was a little unsettling, seeing the road coming toward me right in my face. But I was enjoying it the whole way.

“Do you plan on going to college, maybe need a tutor someday?” She winked at me.

“Heh, it’s possible. I just don’t know yet. I try not to think about it too much. It stresses me out, but I’m keeping my mind open.”

“Good. As long as you are considering furthering your education, then that makes me happy. I just hope Tansuke does well in this school.”

“She’ll be fine. I’ll watch after her. You can count on me.” I said with confidence.

“Thank you, Kim. She needs a friend like you.”

A long pause.

The car approached my driveway. “It’s the next right coming up, just slow down because it's hard to see.” I pointed forward.

Realizing I was about to be home, I thought about my dad. He would probably yell at me for coming home in a strange car this late after school. He has the right.

I just hope he’d understand I wasn’t doing anything wrong. Still, I prepared my ears for a good long yelling.

“You can drop me off here,” I said the moment we turned into my driveway. The brakes cried softly, and we came to a stop. The headlights flooded the front of my house. She clicked the switch down to the low beams then turned to me.

“Here we are. I hope to see you two together again.”

“Me too.” I stepped out of the car and held onto the door.

“Have a good night, Ms. Hikono.”

“See you soon.”

Chapter 9 - Stitched Wounds

The scrape of my feet against the coarse sand and dirt of my driveway echoed in the empty woods that swallowed me. The day had been long, but my mind was active enough to pick out noises that pinged my brain as noteworthy. A rustle of high above branches or an acorn crashing to the forest floor. But nothing auditory held precedence over the visual stimulation I discovered among the shadows.

My peripheral was wide; warping with my swaying feet. I stopped; my feet locked in place just beside his parked car. My neck twisted in both directions; stiff and creaking. This is the very spot I stood in that dream, with Lucy. That makes two pieces of this odd puzzle without a place to fit. The Leak; I remember her naming it with auspicious implication. Yet, here I am without a clue.

My first step out of this spiraling circle of thought and potent energy was a stumbling one. Approaching the door, I felt a keen sense of caution wash over me. My body became tense, preparing to respond in some frightful manner. But as I opened the door and found the house entirely dark, that feeling simultaneously dissipated, yet densified.

The house was deathly quiet; so idle that my very heartbeat shook my ribcage with every thump. My hushed breaths stifled as I focused on hearing, but there was nothing. I closed the door behind me, engulfing myself in the container of living shadow. Cautiously, I flipped the light switch and to my surprise, it worked. The living room was filled with ambient yellow light and the ceiling fan above slowly began spinning in response. I sighed.

My shoes slipped from my feet with hesitant aggression, then I carried my weight across the carpet.

I couldn't shake this feeling that the walls had faces; that the very air I was breathing was toxic and consuming from within. I reached his bedroom door and noticed it was partially open. I lightly pushed it; the hinges creaked loudly and revealed my position.

"You in here?" I whispered into his room.

The light from the living room poured in and revealed ruffled sheets on his bed; vacant. My lower lip flexed inward and I sucked saliva to the back; swallowing it along with this fear I felt.

Then, something I can't quite put into words happened. Each hair on my body became rigid all at once, my skin became cold and my ears were suddenly stuffed with cotton. Muffled, feeling like I was floating, my heartbeat accelerated, and my limbs became heavy. I could hear it, plain as day; the blood coursing through my veins. I focused intently on this violent rush of thick liquid but became quickly distracted by another sound.

This sound was of equal volume but somehow *behind* my blood. In the background of the darkness, beneath my very feet was a frantic mumbling. There were no words I recognized, only lisps and chortles; barely considered verbalizing and more along the lines of incoherent babble.

At that moment, I made a solid fist and smacked myself in the side of the head. This action sent a minor wave of prickly skin tickles through my body and the cotton feeling lessened; the mumble faded into obscurity. Another smack and my normal state returned, the only difference is now I have a throbbing headache.

I tried to think about what this experience was, but I couldn't form a thought longer than a few seconds before some itch on my skin pulled me away. My feet walked me out of his room without my will and I found myself ascending the staircase unfocused.

The headache persisted, except now I was burdened by macabre images of dead children, fire, and rotting flesh. These scenes flashed before my eyes with every blink and left my gut wrenched and balance staggered. In the back of my mind, I could hear whispers, names, and stories I could not decipher. All of this chaos slowly burning a hole in the back of my skull until finally I reached the top of the stairs and fell to my knees gasping for air.

As I lay hunched, I traced the sensation of icy wet fingers gliding down my spine and throughout my hair. Evil snickering bellowed from the forest beyond these hollow walls and left me feeling trapped in my prison of flesh and bone. I wanted to give in; I wanted to lie on the floor and wait to sink into the depths.

"What's. . . happening in here?" My limp mouth spit out. "Dad, come home please."

It was then that my eyes shut, and I fully embraced the darkness. The fingers which glided along my back became coarse; rigid. I could feel nails scraping and plucking; my shirt started to get warm; saturated in some unknown fluid and some indescribable pain took hold of me.

Then, against expectation, a new image started to become clear behind my eyes. Dusty, torn, and flaking; it was an image of my mother. Her face, her wonderful gleaming smile just as I remember pierced through these negative thoughts and with it a word.

Stand.

I released a shaky breath, cherishing the burning desire growing in my gut, and pressed my palm into the carpet beneath me. With great effort, I lifted myself off the ground, and with that strength, the fingers began to release me. The air around me was thick yet chilly; I could see past the veil and clearly observed the outline of the railing to my right. My eyes tracked down and I took a tiresome breath. But from my lips, fell a thin wisp of fog; like a wintery exhale but this fog was black; heavy. A rough cough erupted from my throat as I got up onto my feet, ready to surpass this nightmare.

In the thick of silence, a metallic clang made itself known. My ears perked and my eyes widened as I listened for another noise. I followed the sound into my bedroom, past the bed, and over to the window. Looking out into the forest proved useless. It wasn't until my eyes lowered to the ground below that I saw it; the bulkhead door was wide open.

I waited there, watching the bulk for a minute or more; just reliving that horrible night over and over again. So much has happened and yet, so little has changed. Here I was in the exact same spot, waiting to see that long arm reach up and rip me through this window. Instead, I heard another noise. This sound was much quieter than the last, intentionally so. I only barely managed to hear it behind the intensifying breaths I took, but I knew exactly what it was; the front door opening, then a muffled click.

I waited, listening for a few seconds but found it strange that though I heard it open, I never heard the door close. I turned myself around only to see that the hallway was pitch black.

The living room light had been switched off and now the house was forfeited to shadows once more. Then a light wooden tap snaked between the walls. A creak, then another. Then a loud creak and a pause. I stood with my back to the forest, watching the gap between the door and frame, my shaking eyes focused on the stairwell edge. I froze as I heard another wooden tap.

My eyes shifted around the room, danger blaring in my ears while I scanned every inch for a weapon or escape. I had nothing, nothing at all and the taps continued to grow closer. Finally, I saw something move at the top of the stairs. My vision was blurry, less optimized for the dark due to the overwhelming stress I was feeling. From what I could tell, someone was standing at the second step from the top; part of their face, torso, and hand was outlined, jutting out from the bathroom hallway wall.

My entire body screamed, begged for me to throw myself through this window to escape, but my heart mellowed the slightest amount. Because even though I was cornered and surrounded by mystery, I recognized this aura. How could I not, I've only been around it my whole life.

"Dad?" I churned out.

The figure took the final ascending step and it became clear to me by the outline that it *was* my dad. But. . . he moved *differently*; there was no sway or stupor. It was as if he had complete euphoric control over his body, but still, he was slow. One step after the other took seconds to plan, second-guess then follow through.

"Dad, what's going on? Were you in the basement just now?" I asked fearfully.

He was quiet, as expected. It took him far too long, but he finally made his way to the foot of my bed and stopped. His posture was slumped, head lowered and shoulders drooping. Paranoia vibrated throughout the room and the whispers I had heard on occasion began to slowly rise from the floorboards; an obsessed babble as quiet as a pine needle falling to the earth below, but somehow audible to me in the most unique way.

"Kimberly-Anne. . ." He started.

My brows lowered; face pensive.

"Where have you been?" His voice was monotone, yet accusative.

I took half a step forward, a gesture of peace.

"I was at my friend's house, dad."

He didn't respond.

"I-uh, I'm sorry, I should've called but I never planned on being out that long. Time got away from us."

He sighed heavily.

"Us. . . Who's us?" he asked with dread in his voice.

I awkwardly scratched the side of my head; the feeling in the room was a strange mix of pressurized fear and everyday scolding.

"My friend Tansu. A new girl at school I've been helping out." I tried to keep my answers short and to the point.

I looked past him to the door, then to my lamp and back to him.

"Hey, uh, can I turn on a light? I'm getting a little freaked out in the dark." I lightly scoffed.

His head then raised a little, "No. . . I don't think so. This will all be so much easier if I can't see your face." His words trailed off and his head lowered again with the last word.

What he said made my lower jaw tremble. "What does that mean?" I asked, trying to keep calm. But the whispers were growing, burrowing into the soles of my feet and worming their way through my nervous system. This whole room was alive but stagnant.

He took a heavy barefoot step towards me. My eyes looked to his midsection where both arms hovered with tension; both fists tightly bound by his waist. I retreated but found my back bumping against the window frame behind me; I had nowhere to go.

"You're scaring me," I gave a sweaty huff.

He took a large breath and released it with a low crazed chuckle.

"I'm scared too baby, but I have to do this. If you can't say yes, then he can't have you!"

Suddenly he lunged forward, his left hand reaching out and taking hold of my forearm. I shrieked as his fingers clasped around me and immediately, I started throwing my free fist at him.

"Get off me, you're crazy!" My voice rebounded off the surrounding walls.

He took my punches to the face and shoulder but wasn't fazed by my efforts. He then spun me around and strung my own arm across my neck and pinned me to his torso; securing me with his right leg coiling around mine.

He then screamed in my ear. But this wasn't a scream of authority like all the other times; this was a scream of terror. "Don't fight me! Please just stop fighting. . . and let me do this."

Still, I struggled. With every ounce of my being I fought and fought; using my free left hand to slap and punch at anything I could reach, all of it ineffective.

"Let me go, let me go! You son of a bitch, I swear to god I'm gonna kill you!" My voice wailed.

My eyes slammed shut and I focused on thrashing the best I could, but he wouldn't let me go. Then, without warning, I felt something cold and warm fall on the back of my neck. It dripped and rolled down my shirt one drop at a time. My muscles slowed themselves, but my eyes remained shut; I could hear his whimpering. . . he was crying.

Suddenly his grip tightened, and his voice became hoarse through the tears. "I was a fool to think it would be so simple; that he would just let us go. No, this is how it has to be." He spoke through grit teeth.

With his grip around my arm tightening, so did the pressure in which he held me. My own arm slung across my neck tighter than before; choking me slowly. I could steal a breath or two as I fought to get free, but it wasn't enough. I could feel the swelling of my head as oxygen became less frequent.

My eyes squeezed tight and I fought for every breath, but then something strange happened. Behind my lids, I could see a faint glowing light. It was like a fire in the distance, hidden behind a dense fog on a cold winter night. But this light wasn't red or orange; it was purple.

I opened my eyes and my room had that same faint shade layered over the black. Using my free arm, I reached up and dug my fingers into his wrist and slid my nails across his forearm; all the way down to the elbow. He screamed in agony as my nails sliced through layers of pulsing flesh; collecting wet bloody chunks of his skin underneath my nails.

He reared back, releasing me from his grip and grasping his arm. I fell forward, attempting to recover my breath. However, just as I turned myself around to make a run for the door, I was met by a dense fist to the side of my skull.

Rolling green hills and a barren blue sky decorated my vision. A wide-open range of short-trimmed grass accompanied by the smell of a summer's day had been laid out before me. Standing in the middle of a field, I felt misplaced. Not even the wind accompanied me. The isolation brought happiness and an emotional reprieve. I had no recollection of this place or how I got here, only bliss with the solitude.

Now, looking down at my hand, I saw my open palm. On impulse, I closed it tight, then opened it again. The folds of skin that were woven around my muscles and bones made it what it was and what I knew it to be. The psychological perception was real enough, but the physical sensation that I should experience was nonexistent. I knew then and smiled.

The grass flattened itself out as I began to walk forward, making my way toward a nameless destination. No thoughts in my head, no feeling to overbear me. Complete solace. But out of nowhere, appearing around a corner that wasn't there, I came across a small house. No driveway and no windows. As I was alone in the wasteland of a field, the grass around the house was tall and dead. A single tree stood falling over; many discarded leaves adorned the earth in a fiery autumn pattern.

I approached the house with confidence. I took up my arm and made a fist to begin knocking. I paused. Just before I made contact with the door, a knock came from the other side. Self-preservation fled my bones and I reached for the handle. When I opened the door, I found the room to be filled with some strange liquid; however, the liquid did not spill or become disturbed by the opening of the door in any way. Hesitant, I looked behind me once more, then inserted my index finger into the pool. I was then ripped from where I stood; sucked directly into slow-spinning water and spun in a half-circle.

Once inside the water, I found that breathing was not *impossible*, but it wasn't the same as taking a breath. This pool vitalized me in a way that I couldn't grasp or explain to another living being.

It was murky, brown, and full of thick bubbles all rushing to a surface that didn't exist. It was hard to see, with my regular eyes but that issue was quickly remedied when that hazy purple filter slid over my eyes.

This ocean I was in had no walls yet seemed contained to a relatively small space. The more I floated around the more I understand the limits of its space. Oddly enough, attached to nothing but somehow not moving were a few metal looking boxes above. One was open on the bottom and dripped whitish-blue algae looking substance. I felt drawn to the color but at the same time revolted by it.

A shattered glass feeling in my chest pulled my eyes away from the boxes and redirected towards the limitless floor below. It was complete utter darkness, but not at all vacant. I stared into the abyss, unable to move or think. Then I saw lights; two at first, then six and then twenty. All igniting up two at a time, each of them bearing a bright purple glow.

At that moment I started to drown.

Chapter 10 - Faust

At first, my breath didn't come to me so willingly. The muscles that worked in conjunction to contract my lungs and steal the air around me pushed back against my instruction. Any air that managed to get in was jagged and cold; unsatisfying.

I didn't know where I was; I didn't remember the last thing to happen. The only thing I had a complete understanding of, was pain. My eyes peeled open but observed nothing but black and blurriness. It was difficult to open them through the cotton beneath my skin, but once they were open, they stayed. It was only a matter of time before minute details of the ceiling and light fixture above drew themselves before me. I waited patiently, allowing myself to become further invested in my apparent reality.

My body attempted to move but wires seemed crossed somewhere inside. Whatever signal I sent to a particular limb was misinterpreted and discarded. A refrained panic started to build in my chest as I struggled to move any part of myself. Eventually, my fingers twitched, and paralysis released me slowly. My skull was pounding; each tendon in my neck repeatedly tensed and released without reason or provocation.

All of the air I took in came through my nose, but that cavity seemed too narrow. The more awake I became, the more oxygen I required. Naturally, I attempted to separate my lips but found that simple task impossible. More than that, the very act of flexing my lips drove an indescribable pain into my jaw and teeth; reverberating down my neck and reversing back, scattering over the flesh of my face.

A soft whimper pushed from my nose and my eyes were now fully open; an exasperated breath overcame me. Shaking, I wobbly rose my hand up to my face and touched the delicate skin of my cheekbone; it was numb yet sensitive. Moving down slightly my tips were interrupted by some thin strand poking up from my skin. My hand came away and I immediately attempted to rise but found my movement sluggish at best.

With a raised torso and feet protruding forward, the blood came rushing to my cold body and reignited my awareness. I could see now that I was still in my bedroom, sitting up on my floor in front of the bed, facing the window. Just then a searing headache crushed my temples and forced me to submit momentarily. The pain simmered and I took a second to breathe.

Then, with great effort and determination; I pressed my hands into the floor beneath me and attempted to stand. With shaky joints, I managed to get myself high enough to use the edge of the bed for support. Finally, I was on my unsteady, aching feet just swaying and listening.

Just like that, my perceived isolation was shattered by the sound of a quiet whimper behind me. I whipped my body around, in the process sacrificing balance. My body fell to the side and I caught myself on the bed again, now facing the direction of my door. Laying against the wall in front of the mirror was the shape of my dad. He appeared to be unconscious, haunted by some frightful dream by the way he continued to gasp and twitch.

This radiating agony in the front of my skull persisted as I dragged my feet across the room, over to the light switch. I reached it with relative ease and slapped my entire palm over the toggle. With the switch flipped, the light above flickered on. My eyes winced with the new light; momentarily blinded. My eyes were still focused on him as the light cast short shadows; and what I saw sent my mind spiraling.

His hands; from fingertip to wrist were soaked through with deep red blood. The blood was on his shirt, face, and even dripped onto the carpet. I followed the drip trail with my eyes; it connected us from where I awoke to where he is now. It then occurred to me and I looked down at my shirt. I noticed my shirt saturated in blood, along with my fingers and neck. My heart rapidly pounded, as I gathered the obscure pieces and glanced up to the closet mirror only to notice it was smashed into pieces.

Cold, I directed my body to the open door and my legs propelled forward in a slanted dash into the short hall. The house was dark just like before, and it was then that the memories of what happened started to come back to me.

Using the walls for balance, I moved down the hall and turned into the bathroom. The light came on just as before and all of a sudden, the world went deathly silent.

My feet could hardly support my weight. The edges of my vision started to blur and shake with the new information that raped all rational thought. Stricken by grief and overwhelmed by my life's greatest horror, I counted the threads in my head. Seven thick black stitches were sloppily carved in and out of my flesh. Interlacing over my lips and sealing my mouth shut with only a small gap for breathing.

Bringing both hands to my face, I touched my numb chin and gently glided my fingertips to my mouth. A wretched sickness bubbled in my gut while I attempted to wrap my head around exactly what was going on. The urge to vomit crawled its way up my throat but was forcibly held down and swallowed. Then my legs gave out and I found myself falling backward, crashing into the wall behind me and dragging down onto the floor.

I tried to scream, but only a growl came out through my gritted teeth. Every oral motion made the flesh of my lips burn and vibrate with unrelenting pain. Just having the knowledge of what it was, amplified my perception of everything it produced.

Nothing made sense. My dad was a miserable obsessed bastard, but he wasn't capable of this. Pulling myself up to the sink once more, I stared into my own eyes for a few seconds, then back to the blood that stained everything from the underside of my nose to the bottom of my chin. Attempting to vindicate the situation was futile, the fact remains that this is my current reality. Understanding that, with all the proof laid out before me, I started to cry.

Dizziness kept a tight grasp on my brain and body while the tears rolled down, leaving wet streaks through the dried blood. I turned my head left and right, searching for something to cut these wires. With shaking arms, I reached up into the dirty medicine cabinet before me and ripped it open. The force of my grasp tugged at the loose screws that held it against the wall and jostled its weakened supports. The entire thing tilted, and random pill bottles and bandages spilled out onto the counter and in the sink. The loud crash pinched my ears and reminded me of the pursuing headache.

My eyes caught a glimpse of shining metal fall in the sink. It was a pair of hair trimming scissors. I observed them closely; they didn't seem all that sharp, but they were scissors after all. Bracing myself for the pain, I clamped my eyes tight and stretched my mouth open to its absolute max; about a quarter of an inch. New blood trickled out as the thin wires sliced into my flesh even more. Hot tears poured from my eyes, and a gasping cry erupted from my throat. Droplets rained down to the tile below, quickly forming a small puddle of prior life energy.

My hearing was, at the moment, hypersensitive. Every drop of my tears and blood that hit the floor boomed in my head, causing me to feel even more nauseous. The curved blades slid on either side of an individual string and snakingly hovered there.

The first snip didn't cut. Instead, it pulled the top and bottom of the single string inward, tugging at my lips more. I snipped two or three more times on the same thread and looked back into the mirror. Nothing changed. I kept trying but no matter how many times I tried to cut them, they would not break. But I wouldn't give up; with every attempt I ripped more blood from my mouth and grew desperate with every failed snip.

My hands were violently quaking now and finally, my mouth gave way; slamming shut and at the same time I released a loud furious grunt and threw the scissors into the shower.

A sea of emotions came over me. I was drowning in fear, anger, and depression; unable to cope with this. Above all other emotions, rage took precedence; it built up inside me, sweltering like a burn in the summer's heat. Barely able to form a word, I grumbled, "N—o. . . J-esus fu."

I cupped my face in my hands, the hot festering tears and fresh dribbling blood created a melancholy mixture in my palms. My world had come crashing down around me. The stitches would not break, and yet even if they had, what would I do? An act such as this could not be ignored or hidden away. Punishment would find him, but these scars would remain for eternity and life as I know it will shatter. It's all over for me.

In an instant, I could feel my skin crawling and every hair on my arms and neck stretched toward the ceiling. My breathing became stifled; fearful, I choked down a gulp or two and held it. A sizzling, electric zap shot down my spine, causing my entire body to yield. As the jolt stung my senses, my eyes shot open. A few more breaths found their way into my lungs; and then, the agonizing sensation began to subside.

There was an odd sound murmuring through the air. I couldn't pinpoint it, but I knew it was real. I recognized it as a soft hissing; similar to air escaping from a tight seal. Then a loud pop which hit me like a smack to the head. This made forced a seize upon my bones and my gaze jerked to the ceiling. The light on the wall above the mirror intensely flickered, irritating my vision with its persistent assault.

A very noticeable change in atmosphere pressured me from behind and I whipped myself around with fear upfront. Mere inches from me, with his back against the wall, was the old man. He leaned carefully back; head tilted to gleam at me behind the casted shadow from his bowler hat.

His quiet yet booming voice filled the room. "It seems something terrible has happened to you."

I could hear a delightful sneer in his voice, almost a faint chuckle behind each word. Then I saw his expression switch from intrigued to surprised.

"What is this? You've been silenced?" A dirty grin then split his face. "Ah, I see. . . the fool." He snickered.

A light sigh slipped from his mouth and now his appearance was relaxed; joyous.

He continued, "I tried to warn you, Kimberly-Anne. You children are all the same; hesitant, defiant. . . However, as I promised, the offer still stands."

Seeing him again, under these conditions brought a churn to my gut and prick to my nerves. My own face was empty; devoid of everything that I was before. The muscles beneath my every inch of flesh were held in place by years of filtered hatred and paralyzing anger; all exploited by this *shadow man*.

Impatiently, he extended his hand; palm flat and fingertips aimed at the center of my chest. The very atoms that made up my skin rejected all that he was, but I didn't retreat.

"We both know why I'm here. Your heart has made a decision, but has your mind?" He coaxed.

Still, a desire for revenge plucked my brain stem like a guitar string. Trapped in this whirlwind of confusion, I decided upon one thing; I want this, and he knew it.

I can't go on like this, my life; everything I've worked for is gone. Stolen from me by a capricious, self-loathing pile of nothing. I have crumbled to pieces; stomped into unrecognizable dust one too many times. I *want* power; I want to fight back. I will take it upon myself to rip the apologies straight from their hearts. My response was a fragile nod.

"You understand the conditions?" He asked.

Again, I only nodded. Tears mixed with dried blood stained my entire lower face, stuck in a heated expression.

"Very well." He leaned back and let go of my chin.

His hand lowered and stopped just before my chest. Extended politely, he awaited my final decision; but I was hesitant.

"What's wrong?" He asked in complete seriousness, almost impatient.

There was something I had to know. My jaw trembled as I stretched my muscles, trying to talk.

"W-what" —I struggled to get my words out— "is your. . . name?"

He gave me a devious smile, dirty teeth fully exposed but he didn't respond. I watched him, living through the pain I just inflicted on myself by speaking. We stared intently at one another, then it became clear. With a final huff, I clasped my hand around his.

The edges of his smile twitched, "Call me. . . Sin."

There was a pause, then he swiftly pulled his hand back. I retracted mine but found there was something clasped tight between my fingers. I opened my fist to reveal a light glowing purple stone. A dim, skuzzy brown mist began to surround my hand; shrouding the stone and creating a dome of musky heat. A spiral of smoke, resembling a miniature tornado, linked this filthy sphere wrapped around my hand to the mirror. Spawning from the stone's reflection.

I saw a light flash as the gem sank and disappeared completely into my palm, but the glow persisted beneath my skin. I watched it move like a worm, shooting up my arm, past my collar bone, and finding a place to reside behind my eyes. I felt it there, pulsing. Alive.

My heart pounded as my lids pealed opened. A shockwave coursed through my spine, making me arch my back and crank my neck. It felt like battery acid was being soaked into my skin. A loud whirring erupted in my skull.

I felt something invisible. Familiar hands lashed out from behind me and desperately clawed at my clothes and skin while raw, hot energy forced itself into my pores.

These devilish fingers ripped at the back of my hair, pulling and ripping each individual strand. All the pain was real; every ounce of horror. Already, this unknown process was unbearable to me. I was not so determined anymore. All my adrenaline was gone, and my drive for revenge was depleted.

What the hell have I done?

He stood opposite of me, watching this change; this violation of my mortal human body. The room around me was completely shrouded in thick ink. My head was thrust back downward, thrashing the muscles in my neck as this supernatural hold was released.

Winded, I glided my fingers through my hair, trying to ground myself. This strange pressure invaded my space, like gravity itself was being amplified. I shot a glance at the mirror and witnessed the thick glass crack in various places. Simultaneously, the floor beneath my feet splintered and beveled; shattering the tiles I stood on.

The reflection I saw started to warp and so did my perception of all that surrounded me. The whispers came again, but this time I could understand them. A thousand voices, a thousand souls screamed my name; acknowledged and cursed me for taking his hand. Among the voices were a select few that loudly wept, just barely noticeable behind the droves of cackling insanity.

I focused on the voices but only now noticed that my hair started to darken and grow with every excruciating moment to pass. So many elements attempted to pry at my focus, driving me mad with the bombardment.

Every single hair on my arms began receding back into my skin, vanishing completely and leaving a burning pain in their wake. The same burning could be felt all over my body; everywhere outside of my head.

I groaned loudly, and I clenched my eyes shut, trying to fight the pain but it was far too intense. I wanted it to stop; I begged for it to stop. Horrified, I tried to scream for help, peeling my mouth open as much as I could.

"Geeeaaahhhhh!" The most bloodcurdling, panic-induced muffle of a scream erupted from my lungs. Every bulb in this tiny bathroom promptly exploded and rained shards of glass in every direction.

I gasped for air, whining, and panting. My hair had grown down to my lower back, becoming more jagged and rough; dirty and oily. The pain in my scalp began to subside but I was not allowed a moment of peace. Still watching myself in the broken mirror, I was drawn to my eyes. Both eyeballs felt frozen beneath the lids. My pupils were shrinking and expanding rapidly.

Suddenly, I felt a pop behind both eyes. Then a cool rush of blood began to drip out from my eyelids and nostrils. I cupped my face in my hands as it dripped down out from between my fingers. I had no control of the earthquake in my body. The agony that flowed into me was insurmountable.

Now, I begged for death. Quickly changing my mind and only wanting this to stop, but it wouldn't. The pain just kept coming with seemingly no end to look forward to. Every single part of my body reacted in some way. My skin felt like it was frozen, but my veins felt like they were pushing boiling oil, twisting and churning through every section.

All of the sudden, I felt nothing. Saw nothing. The whirring noise stopped, and my world was left waiting. Everything was dark; there was no noise, no taste. . . nothing.

Am I dead?

That question echoed in my head as my eyes slowly peeled open. I was lying on the floor. With little effort or resistance, I stood up, swaying, and nauseous. My vision focused down at my body, and I could see it. My skin was smooth yet coarse like bone; the tone a washed grey. Sliding my palm along my chest, I determined I was bare; like a mannequin.

I pinched my cheek—nothing. Not a single ounce of discomfort. I leaned against the ridge of the sink for additional balance. When I opened and closed my hand, it felt absent to me. As though I were a ghost inside myself. It was alarming but felt natural.

My hair was the next section of focus. Running my fingers through the absolute black strands, I noted dry coarse edges and an unnatural flow. It was much longer, thicker, and wilder than ever before.

I touched my lips and felt the strings; all seven were accounted for but strangely enough, they did not restrict my ability to move. I opened my mouth as wide as I could and felt my jaw release a satisfying pop. I took it all in, watching myself in the mirror. Trying to find something in my appearance that resembled the old me. I felt. . . wrong. Physically; like I was wearing someone else's skin, someone three sizes too small.

Finally, I stared intently into my new eyes. They were no longer a reflection of my mother's beautiful baby blue. Instead, the whites had gone black and the iris' morphed into a mixed purple. There was no pupil in the center, just the mesmerizing glow. I noticed in the spider-web reflection of glass that the darkness behind me was easily visible with these new eyes.

The last observation was my sustained injuries. All the tender flesh had healed. The bruises, aches, and tremble were no more. I was. . . reborn.

The anger was back, but it was not so lustful. Instead, I was calm. I didn't feel like myself. I was more confident; pleased with this turnout. I could tell this was a new beginning for me and a new chapter for everyone against me. My eyes closed. Everything was quiet except for the low ringing in my ears. All the screams of pain that had just filled the night air were gone.

The only remnants of chaos were the cracked floor and shattered mirror. Now only holding misplaced sections of glass in the frame. Smiling devilishly at myself, I slowly turned towards him.

He had an unexpected look on his face, still looking as serious as ever but slightly confused with my form.

"So, does this. . . come with instructions?" I asked sarcastically; pessimism and rage backing my voice.

He just stared at me, clearly not amused.

"Is that supposed to be a joke?"

"Hah, I guess not." I gave a wide, evil grin.

I rolled my shoulder, brows lowered and nostrils flaring. I heard saliva drain down his throat as he swallowed hard.

"This is peculiar." He seemed a little confused.

I continued to grin, blinking heavily once, then chuckled. I'm alive, unlike my entire life before now. Being someone, something else, was exactly what I needed.

This is what everything has been leading up to.

Chapter 11 - Coexistence

There I stood, breathing lightly through my nose, slight huffs. Brief and dense. The face I wore was a satisfied, minimally crazed expression. A strange sensation of ants burrowing into my skin covered my body. The old man stood in the doorway. Our eyes met. I saw him in a different perspective now, not a terrifying thing, hiding in the shadows, but as something else. Something I can't quite explain.

"How do you feel?" He asked me, though I had the feeling he already had the answer.

"I feel bound. My skin's elasticity seems to be gone and yet, I don't have any problems moving. If that makes sense?"

"There are many changes in this form, and you will come to understand them in time." He said plainly.

My legs were heavy, and the rest of my body strained. Constantly fidgeting and readjusting my feet and arms, all the while, feeling my body with my hands. Amused and intrigued by these odd sensations.

"So, with this power. . . I can do anything I want." I sneered.

Right now, I was calm, consciously planning every detail of my revenge. In this state, I felt like myself; but not the Kim that dragged her feet through her daily life. I was more than that; I was the person I imagined myself to be in my daydreams. Confident, untouchable, and superior. But there was this cockiness in my throat. A spiteful tongue that licked the back of my teeth. I was still me, just another version; one I had locked away and occasionally fed emotional scraps too. However, I couldn't shake this tickle in my brain. Like jostling windchimes swaying back and forth. A hum, harmonious, and aware. Then it occurred to me.

"W-wait. Will I ever be myself again?" I asked.

"It isn't a *complete* transformation. It's a demonic parasite that I attached to your soul. It merely *shares* your body until you lose yourself."

"A demon sharing my body?"

"Yes. . . and no. It isn't exactly a *demon*; in the way you know but genetically it can be classified as such. They are called *Teufel*, a creation of mine with many unique properties."

As if awaiting its introduction, this presence made itself known. Inside my head, I could hear something. Scratching. Digging. Something deep inside my brain reverberated like the wing beat of a fly, undulating in a dark room. Just barely noticeable, but once noticed, impossible to ignore. He walked up to me and rested his hand on my shoulder. The previous icy touch of his skin was mute to me now. He spoke gently,

"Kimberly, you are no longer alone." With that, Sin vanished completely.

At that moment, a stabbing pain erupted in my head. My hands shot up and took hold of the sides of my skull as it thrashed in place.

"Hmm, look at what we have here." The voice greeted me through a static filter.

"Are you the Teufel?" I asked hesitantly.

Then another shock to my brain and suddenly, I watched my body move on its own. Arms rotated themselves. Shoulders spun and cracked. I did not command these movements, but I did not feel that control was lost.

"This body of yours is frail." She said.

I then made a fist and looked at my knuckles. She was quiet. Her voice sounded like a thousand different tones mashed and ground together with an electric distortion layered over it. Every word pounded my head like a drum, causing a rippling headache that drowned my head in a deep wave of pain. Immediately, my boasted confidence shriveled under the scrutiny of a truly superior force.

"So, you are. . . A demon. My demon." I asked frightfully.

"Are we here to talk or are we here to drink blood?" She asked impatiently.

"Well, erm-" I mumbled.

She screeched. "Don't waste my time!"

I felt an electrical surge shoot through my spine. My body became numb and heavy in an instant. I fell to one knee, convulsing and panting. I felt it completely; her energy swirling in my bones; she was now taking full control of my body. The strain took hold for what felt like minutes when in fact, it was almost instantaneous. My shaky knees lifted me to a standing position, it was time to move.

I carried my weight to the doorframe without hesitation and I noticed something. The frame, as well as the sink and a hanging photo on the wall, seemed to be a little lower, but they were unchanged. In fact, I had grown taller; maybe three inches or so. I also noticed that my limbs and torso had become much thinner; lanky.

I let loose an evil grin, thrilled to be in this form, and walked out the door. Confidence overcame me as I indulged in the comforting darkness. I placed my fingertips on the wall and slid them along as I made my way to my room, humming softly.

Reaching the open door, I peered in and noticed nothing in here had changed. He was still there, leaning against the wall and unconscious. I took one step in and the vibe was instantly disturbed. The latent energy emitting from my body tipped off his subconscious and stirred him from his deep slumber. A sharp intake of air, he raised his head with a slanted face.

He groaned at first, slowly but surely sinking back into this world; unaware of what was truly happening around him.

Eyes fluttering, he reached up and placed his hot forehead in his palm, wincing. "Aw, god, my head."

He straightened his back with a hefty exhale and looked forward with glazed, numb eyes. I stood in his peripheral inside the doorway, just a blur to him but recognizable as the only other person in this house. He chuckled a little and shook the daze away. Mimicking lucidity as best he could, he gazed towards my shape.

"Kim. . . that you? I had the most fucked up dream." His words slurred, "It was so creepy; I-I can't really explain it."

He then rubbed his neck and realized the crusted substance on his hands. Reacting to the peeling dried blood, he examined his arms.

"What t-the hell!? Is this. . . Is this blood?!" He exclaimed.

Reality came crashing down right on top of him. He frantically scanned his environment, trying to get a feel of his surroundings. Then he looked up toward the previously blurred figure that stood before him, but his vision was no longer clouded.

"Kimberly?" He sounded normal now, afraid.

I stood tall in my new glory. Dense black hair waving in front of my face, partially obscuring the demonic purple glow of my eyes.

"You're. . . not Kim." He panicked.

"Hello, Alex." I snarled playfully.

"How do you know my name? Who are you?" He was terrified.

"Aw, that hurts my feelings. How could you not recognize me, Daddy?"

We snickered. He looked so confused and said nothing at first. After a brief moment of contemplation, he responded.

"No, no that can't be. You are not my daughter, you're. . ." His mouth shuttered, "You're one of them." He shouted.

One of them? I thought, then quickly disregarded his comment. My devilish grin switched to fury in a second. And I shouted back at him,

"No! You made me into this!" I took a step closer. "Everything. . . it's entirely your fault! Losing mom wasn't enough for you? You had to go and throw your only daughter into a sea of loneliness! What kind of man. . ." I huffed; my voice cracked from the screams.

My jaw clenched tight; teeth fully exposed like a rabid dog's. Something sparked in me; my emotions were unstable, constantly switching between the horror I felt, and the bloodthirsty joy this demon produced.

He started, "Sweetie, I—"

"No! You don't get to make excuses." I bellowed, clutching my head between both hands. "I hate you. . . I hate you!"

The sanity I held so dearly shattered into little pieces. My mind disengaged all reason and forgiveness and focused entirely on negativity and the unfiltered desire to relish in snapping every bone in his body.

I took a few steps closer, giggling under my breath until the madness ruptured and grew into boisterous laughter. He didn't move away, just watched as I moved casually.

I abruptly stopped and then lunged myself at him. Making a rock-solid fist and punched him square in the face. His neck snapped to the side but rebound back to its original position.

The first punch wasn't meant to be that hard, but I could instantly see the blood pool under the surface of his skin. Seeing red, more punches followed. He didn't even try to defend himself as a flurry of fists repeatedly collided into his jaw, cheek, and skull. My own strength was unknown to me, but it would seem simple punches were very, very effective.

I stopped, allowing his head to wobble and tilt. My dad was tough; all those stories he used to tell me about fights and beatings came off as horseshit back then. Now, I believed him. He withstood some hefty hits and still held his chin high with pride; spitting blood onto the floor and directing a swollen glare at me.

"C'mon demon, I know you've got more than that. I've been down this road before." He smirked.

My lips mirrored his and accepted his challenge. With one hand, I clasped my fingers around the top of his head and raised him up to eye level; with only his curled knees barely touching the carpet. The muscles in my arm and shoulder flexed but felt unburdened by his weight. He winced in pain, then stretched his legs out to support himself.

I threw him back into the pile of glass from the mirror. He caught himself but lodged wide shards of glass in his hands. He forced himself back to a sitting position and let out a pained sigh; then started panting rapidly.

That's when he did the only intelligent thing so far; he looked past me and made a dash for the bedroom door. I let him pass, smiling, and determined.

"There is nowhere to hide. You can't outrun your past." I whispered playfully and walked, following him.

He scampered down the stairs, tripping over his own feet, keeping himself from falling down by using the rails. At the bottom, he made a sharp left and stopped. Looking up, he saw me standing at the top of the steps, watching with glowing eyes. Without wasting any more time, he rammed through his own bedroom door and fumbled to the floor.

I was right behind him, taking my time and enjoying his fear. He crawled along the floor, leaving blood prints and scuffs behind him. About halfway to the bed, he attempted to stand but was unable to keep his balance. Tripping over his own feet, he fell beside his bed in front of the nightstand. Desperately he scrambled to the drawer and pried it open.

Hyperventilating, he whipped his head around and witnessed me glide my feet over his blood trail. I saw his eyes avert to my hands as they suddenly jerked. A sharp pain seized my fingertips, uncontrollable shaking and then fresh blood dripped from under my nails. All ten of my nails had become pitch black, then grew outward. As they grew longer, they each became jagged and sharp like thin bones.

I could feel them pushing out, forming from nothing, and yet extended two feet out from their origin. It was painful, even in this state but I didn't flinch. I let them grow until they reached their pinnacle. Once they stopped, I raised them up to meet my gaze.

Beautiful. I thought.

He stared at this display of inhuman modification; his confidence diminished. He then turned his whole body to face me, shoulder propped against the nightstand and legs limp outward. Proudly wielding my new weapons, I closed the small gap between us and watched him intently. The air between us was thick with so many emotions. Impossible to count or consider each one, but not easily mistaken by either party.

In one swift motion, I bent down slightly and jabbed my newly formed claws into his gut. A wet piercing spurt echoed in my ears as his organs ruptured and muscles tensed around the thin daggers. He gave a harsh, bloody gasp and quivered. I felt the warm, thick liquid pool over my knuckles; this sensation was euphoric to me.

I leaned in close and whispered, "Do you feel that? That's your blood. *Now,* do you see the pain you have caused me?"

His eyes fell to the floor, half-closed and lazy; draining. He responded with raspy exertion, "It was. . . only a matter of time."

I laughed at his pain; blinded by the madness within. To my surprise, he slowly lifted his hand up and reached into the open nightstand drawer. With a chortle enforcing his very last hope, he brought forward his only means of attack and defense.

The cold steel of his .38 caliber pressed loosely against my forehead, finger on the trigger, and tears drying on his face.

Amused, I licked the strings over my mouth. "Really? You would put a gun to your own daughter's head? What a *great* father you are." I taunted.

"You are *not* my daughter. Give her back to me!" He declared with a stutter.

For a second, my neck snapped to the side, then reverted back. Deliberately, I placed my skull against his gun just as it was. My voice was muted, but hers was present to the world. The ever-shifting control we juggled had been completely taken from me.

I found myself in a ghastly form separate from the current scene. There was nothing around me but shimmering darkness and occasional flickering mist; like little angry thunderclouds floating freely around me. Everything I could see was nothing at all and yet still something to me. A blue and purple hue saturated my vision as I glanced around this vast emptiness; listening to the words as they fell from the demons' mouth.

"You cannot demand that which you abandoned. She doesn't want you, not anymore." Her words echoed around me, cementing me in this place for the time being.

I was spectral, transparent, and unable to move but quite able to peak through nonexistent curtains to see what she saw. I felt some powerful urge to sleep, let the world slip away and curl into a ball of miserable peace. But something kept me lucid; attached to the real world.

A wretched barrage of regret violated all senses and, although I was unable to verbalize my anguish, I screamed inside my head which only proved to vibrate the fabric of this place. It was silent. My nonphysical body emitted a shockwave of rebellious texture.

"She chose *me*, she chose *hate*" The demon spoke again, "Although, it's funny, she isn't quite committed anymore; it seems her devotion has wavered. Right now, she is watching this; pounding on the very walls I built to hold her. But I can feel it in her heart, she wants you dead."

He snarled, "You're lying. She may be an angry kid, but she cares about me as I care about her."

"Oh, tell me how much you care, please. Right down to bringing her into this world just to hold up your end." She snickered.

His expression faltered. "Y-you don't know what you're talking about."

"Don't I? I have access to all of *her* thoughts and memories. . . every word she had ever heard and has since forgotten; even from when she was a baby. You desperately tried to justify your actions, confiding your sins to the child you sold. All for what? Love?"

"You shut your goddamn mouth!" He screamed, sweat profusely dripped from his brow and tears continued to pool and run down over his mouth. The screaming only caused more pain to surface.

Aggressively, I ripped my claws out from him, causing him to fall forward, groveling in agony. He kept the gun raised, focused intently at its target. Then he took his free hand and clenched his stomach tightly, attempting to hold in the blood.

I watched this play out through the mysterious veil. Upset that this demon was standing in my place. This is my revenge, not her personal playground. But I was locked apart from my body.

The demon's eyes then diverted to the wall. She was listening to my sadness, my loss.

"Tsch." She scoffed.

Out of nowhere, I found the spectral form entirely gone. A harsh blink washed away the burn in my eyes and I found myself in control once more. The muscles that held my arm upright relaxed and every knot in my shoulders and back untwisted. I blinked again and turned my head to crack my neck once more. I was given control.

"Dad. . ."

"Kim? Is that you?"

I nodded.

"I. . . I'm-" he said.

"Save it. I don't want an apology." I growled.

His bottom lip quivered, spirit broken, and left to rot in these final moments. The sight hurt me; much more than I ever thought it would. However, a big part of me was cherishing it, a part unrelated to the demon within. I redirected my eyes to the side a bit, avoiding eye contact.

"Then, I won't give any. Maybe now, it's time you learned." He spoke.

I blinked and crossed my arms, like a petulant child.

"Your mother—" he started.

My eyes went back to him, turning my head sharply.

"Your mother was so beautiful, an amazing woman no doubt. You remind me so much of her it breaks my heart." He seemed to be calm, lost in his thought.

"Rachel is dead because of me."

My heart pounded, causing a disturbance in my breaths. Things went deathly quiet. I felt the rage build up again in my chest. I took hold of his shirt collar and fiercely pressed my forehead against his. The horror in his eyes was genuine.

"What are you talking about? You told me she died in a car accident!" I practically spit the words in his face. My voice was booming, deafening to those close enough. My own palms felt damp, growing slick with anticipation.

"A car crash. . . I still can't believe you bought that for so long." He paused. "It was my fault. I should have known better, but I loved her so much. . . So very much."

He looked sad and broken, not just on the outside, but mentally.

"The story I told you, how we met, is true. But I didn't convince her to like me. . . not entirely on my own; I had help, from him." He spoke to me, so full of sorrow and regret.

"Him," I repeated, making the connection.

"It's a long and complicated story, but the important thing is. . . I fucked up and destroyed any chance I had at earning her love. Then he offered me a deal. I took it and right away she came back to me. She loved me. . . She loved me!" He coughed violently for a moment. Then with dry lips, he continued, "He told me that in exchange for this, for the love of the woman of my dreams, he wanted one thing-"

I watched him closely. "Your soul," I stated.

His eyes met mine very fast; hollow and remorseful.

"No. . . Yours."

My chest became constricted, eyes wide open.

"He told me to have a child. That was my end of the deal. Have a child for him to claim. So, I did."

"Y-you offered me up before I was even born, so mom would love you?" I growled.

He started to wheeze, his words trailing off.

"No, you don't understand! I tried to protect you. When you were born, I ran. I took us, the three of us, and moved here, trying to get away from him. But he followed, and he was angry."

I gritted my teeth, the anger still present, rising steadily with every word he spoke.

"Because we ran-" he started to whimper. "-*I* ran; he took her away from me! He murdered her." He started to cry like a full-grown baby.

"All of that is the reason, the truth leading up to years of abuse, neglect, and hate. You stitched my fucking mouth closed!" I shouted in disgust.

"I didn't know what to do. I was never meant for love; I was never taught to care for others. When she was taken, I just gave up. . . Nothing mattered anymore. I never even wanted to have kids." He cried.

Slowly he adjusted his torso position, trying to find a better way to lean.

"And now, I understand something. By killing her, he broke *our* contract. He had to come after you himself and propose a new deal for your soul!"

"You knew he was visiting me and did nothing. You coward." I snarled.

"What could I do? He isn't human, Kim. He's something else, but I did do one thing . . . The stitching *was me*, all me. He may have clouded my head with false accusations of lies, but in the end, it was my hand that forced the needle. You just have to understand! You couldn't say yes to him!"

His eyes glimmered with sadness. The emotional stress inside was real; I could see it through and through. He was sorry.

My shoulders rose, breathing intensified. Everything started to make sense. That being said, one thing remained clear to me; his ignorance, giving up. Unforgivable.

"I don't care what bullshit excuse you have. The truth is, you abandoned me; left me in the darkness when you could have helped. You could have been there for me!"

"Whenever I tried to be there, to be a father, he messed with my head. You have no idea what kind of monster he is; what they are! . . . but now-"

My mind was being torn in so many different directions. It was impossible to clarify or rationalize any particular thought. Instead, they just meshed together. An amalgamation of distrust, fear, and ambiguity.

"I'm sorry, Kim" he muttered, head fallen onto his shoulder. "I'm so sorry, Rachel." He cried hysterically.

I didn't respond. His eyes were fully focused on mine. Absorbing the purple glow, searching for a glimmer of his daughter. My eyes suddenly sharpened. Lips spread wide again and oozing evil intent; I hunched forward.

"Shhh. I think you two had long enough; I almost couldn't crawl under this flesh again." The demon giggled with fake sincerity, every word harbored hostility.

He relaxed his muscles and his eyes became soft. "This gun. . . if you hadn't talked to me, sweetheart, I would have used it on you. But now that I'm sure. . ." Shaking, he tightened his hold on the gun, every possible outcome circling in his mind. Lifting it with a visible struggle he clenched his bloody teeth together and frowned as the barrel pressed against his temple.

The demon spoke, "It's too late to save her from fate, she is condemned to a life of misery since the day she was conceived. But don't worry, I'll take good care of her. I will guide her down the proper path." She paused and became more serious, "But the only way that can happen is with you gone. If you can't do it, you can bet I will."

Looking into his eyes, she had a different tone now. Focused, almost trusting, a very contradictory manner of speaking. He stared into her black abyssal eyes; searching for any glimpse of me.

"Kim, be strong."

I felt my finger twitch very suddenly and as it did, a loud ear-shattering bang echoed through the house, nullifying my ears and devastating the silence around me. Red, warm liquid splashed the front of my face and a new horror burrowed itself into the back of my brain.

As I trembled, my gaze shifted between the copious amounts of blood splashed on the nightstand and the newly formed crater in my father's skull. My skin soaked through with his life, I shuddered.

Terror animated; my heart sadistically shook within its brittle cage. Turning in circles, the overwhelming feeling of being surrounded took over. An invisible cacophony of agonized emotion stabbed my senses from every possible direction, near and far. I glanced at the floor, then the ceiling. A dense cloud of energy surrounded me, and, in that instant, there was pressure behind my left eye as if a large bug were trapped in my skull and desperately tried pushing my eyeball out to escape.

The burning sensation forced me to swiftly cup my face and rub both eyes vigorously, grumbling in pain. Suddenly I was thrown backward onto the floor. I tried quickly to sit up and stand again, but some invisible force pressed me flat on the floor. Then came an explosion of pain throughout my body.

At that moment, I caught another glimpse of my father's face. A dark mist began to fall from his eye sockets, pouring out onto the floor like a fog machine.

The smoke rolled along and, with a mind of its own, flowed directly to me and shot into my eyes.

A horrendous scraping ravaged my eyes, a crackling fire, unlike anything I've ever experienced before. The force pinning me released and I was free to roll into a tight ball as my screams filled the room.

"What's happening to me?!" My body flipped itself over onto my stomach and started forcefully ramming my head against the floor. My forehead split open and blood dripped.

"Stop fighting it!" The demon inside me demanded.

My stomach churned what felt like boiling water, causing me to gasp and squirm. Then, I took a deep breath and released it in one hefty cough; with that exertion came wriggling black smoke.

The smoke encircled my body; floating a foot above for a moment, then instantly shot down like daggers into my eyes. My mouth opened, and I let out a terrifying scream. My body was thrashing around in pain without me telling it to. It seemed as if time were stretching on forever, but ever so slowly did I return to myself again. That nightmare subsided, leaving my spirit shattered and eyes vacant.

Both ears rang with silence. Eyes wide open, tears and blood trickled down my cheekbones, I tried to move, but my body was completely numb. For a while, I lay there, catching my breath, staring at the ceiling in complete disarray.

Every few minutes, I felt a pulse in my spine and my body would twitch. The only thing that I felt was total emptiness buried in my gut. I tried to move again and this time my hand responded. All ten fingers cracked with the gesture and soon enough my arms were released from lethargy. One by one my limbs awoke, and I was able to stand again; heavy, but upright.

It was hard to keep it up. After standing for a few seconds, I felt the blood rush to my brain. My vision got blurry, my body swayed, and a headache set in, but only for a moment; then I was fine. I stood there in silence, hardly breathing. His body was lying there like a rock, motionless. It was not supposed to go this far.

The mirror above his dresser reflected my image. Me, not the devil I harbored within. My pale, pasty skin soaked in blood. Mixed emotions overloaded my brain. I did not want him to die. All I wanted was for him to understand what was becoming of me, but what he told me about my mother—that pushed me, I felt sorry for him. All these years, he had to live with that pain alone for reasons I still don't understand.

My entire right arm started to shake uncontrollably as I came to an abrupt understanding and I lost it. My mind went blank as I fell into a pit of sorrow and loathing. I cried hysterically. I fell to the floor, pulling my legs to my chest, crying, bawling like a baby.

All these years of trying to stay tough finally broke and I was like a little girl again, a little girl without a mother or father to hold me while I cried. I had to hold myself. The only one to provide comfort was a bloodthirsty demon, whispering in my ears. Everything was quiet except for my sobbing. I stood up wobbly and awkwardly. Panting, arms hanging loosely in front of me. I took one hand and put it over half my face and closed my eyes. Reality seemed to melt away, the sadness and anger weighed on my soul. Yet, I felt oddly at peace.

In the end, he had paid for what he had done. I was satisfied no matter what he said or what I thought. However, I did not prepare myself for the loneliness.

A long, unknown amount of time was spent just waiting in one spot; thinking, rationalizing, I decided the best thing to do was take another step forward, then another. Continue my existence physically, with only the basis of my human instinct to guide me.

Each and every step was heavy and instantly forgotten. Momentarily regaining my ability to understand where I was, happened on rare occasion. In what felt like seconds, I had changed out of my clothes, throwing on clean ones and was now holding a black trash bag. Inside was the bloody remains of what I had been wearing.

Standing at the front door, I took a step into the night air, nearly dragging the bag behind me. I walked into the dark, unafraid, and spacing out. My instincts guided me again, and I blanked on the journey into the woods. Again, I became aware dumping the bag behind a thick tree in some random spot in the woods.

I felt the crushing loneliness surround me; blind and hypersensitive to every tiny noise. Surely there were animals nearby, listing to me as I rustled about. I did not fear them; how could I now? Turning in a slow circle, I saw a glimpse of my house through the brush. I was maybe, fifty yards down the trail, somewhere close by to where I ran previously.

Staring into nothingness, I contemplated while I could; before sorrow grabbed hold and left me a shell. I sat on the forest floor; pulling my knees to my chest and gently placing my chin on top. It was chilly out here.

The idea now, that I will never be held by family again crept into my soul. The only one left to hold and comfort me was me. I'm all that's left. Out here, though, I could feel no attachment to the events that took place. Only me, trees, and the sky, and yet, I couldn't let go of the thought of him. I started to speak out loud to myself.

"All I wanted, Dad, was for you to care and pay attention to me. Take an interest in my life and stop being so cruel." My eyes were getting glassy, I felt the tears again.

"Although, I'm also to blame. I could've tried harder and maybe talked to you about how I felt. I just assumed you wouldn't listen. Now, there won't be a second chance. You're gone, and it doesn't matter anymore. . . I *did* love you, but I can't ignore the things you said as you died. The lies you told me all my life, and now I know that he too is a liar. He gave me this power, he's using me." I sniffled.

I raised my chin and watched the tremble in my arms as they were wrapped around my legs. The blood still soaked into my skin haunted me.

"I don't regret it. I need this for now; there are other threats, and I am beginning to think, based on what you said, that he is the biggest threat I need to watch out for."

A heavy sigh fell. My face got hot with tears of rage. I bit my lip and glared at the ground. The intensity in my eyes could burn a mark into the soil where I was staring. My heart felt like cold stone. With all these thoughts in my head, I got nervous thinking about facing off against that man, that demon.

"I would have never even dreamed that something like this would happen to me, demons and death taking over my life and now. . ."

A static filter suddenly vibrated in my head. "You have me." the voice called again, reminding me of her presence.

"I have you," I whispered.

"It's quite amusing to hear you talk to yourself, so naive and innocent." She snickered insanely. As she spoke, I could feel my brain swell and quiver with each word.

"You want this body, huh?"

"I *need* it. For that to happen, you must kill again and again and again. Become a shell of who you were and take a swim in the depths. Let all your anger out through me, and soon enough it will become second nature."

"Why, why do you want to be strong? What does he want from you, from me?" I groaned.

"I am here to do as I please. You are merely my passing vessel." Another chuckle. Cynical and plain.

"No. . . You're in my head" I stabbed my pointer finger at my temple. "Not the other way around, which means you do what I say," I stated.

"You're saying you control the voices in your head? Impressive. Not many insane people can say that." She taunted, obviously being sarcastic.

She was pissing me off with her manner of speaking.

She finished, "We'll test your resolve sooner than later."

The headache started to calm altogether. Her influence subsided, and my brain reset itself.

"Sleeping." I slurred. "You must be sleeping now."

She is intimidating, but as much as it bothers me to think this, I'm not all that afraid of her. Since I plunged my hand into my father's gut and watched as his skull and brains exploded; the fears previously embedded in me shriveled and died. Sin and this new demonic companion of mine did not scare me as they should.

It all just melded together to a neutral state that bred a lack of clemency. The fear and pain coming and going like a strobe light. I am tired of feeling pain; tired of this Hell. There was no clear alternative to facing the situation I was in now.

It took me over an hour of sitting on the cold, damp leaves to plan the next step. The cops, school, and how I am going to live now that I am orphaned. Once I was sure of what I was going to do and say to the police, I wearily headed back to my house.

As I saw my house draw nearer with each step, a swirling sensation formed in my gut. It's funny, seeing it from here. There was no difference, no indication of the horrors that have been and just took place within those walls. . . Maybe it wasn't. Maybe I would walk in, and my dad would be on the couch watching TV as always.

Just maybe.

Chapter 12 – Rebirth

A blissful daydream fluttered around in my head.

Crystal clear memories of a time so very long ago, or so it seems to me now. The day was Friday, the final period before the day would end and the students would be free to leave. Anticipation was higher than any other day because this weekend introduced the start of winter vacation. However, not everyone was so thrilled to be returning home.

At first, it didn't quite stick with me, but I noticed the signs as the day progressed; something was wrong with Joey. This was a particularly rough time for me, and he did his best to avoid, and comfort me. Seeing him in this downtrodden state sparked a nurturing instinct and I gently pressured him, but he wouldn't budge.

I knew that as soon as we boarded our separate busses, I wouldn't see him for at least a week; so, I had to do something. Without any pretext, I asked him to meet me in the gymnasium after school. As expected, he gave no immediate answer. Even still, after the final bell rang and the school emptied of students, I stood alone in the vast bright room and waited.

If I remember right, it was nearly fifteen minutes before he showed up. The door opened with a whisper and he strolled in; head aimed down at his feet. When I greeted him, the response I got was an echo of my own voice around me. I waited, watching him stand with his hands by his side and his hat pulled over his eyes. I had no choice.

With a playful yell, I called his name, followed by *heads up.* He lifted his head and in the same motion pulled the hat from his vision; just in time to dodge the basketball, I lobbed in his direction. The ball bounced with an airy spring and dribbled until it hit a nearby wall; rolling back in my direction.

We stared at each other; the sorrow clearly visible in his bloodshot eyes. My face was, timid. Then, I shook off the weight on my shoulders and put on a joyous façade. Taking a few steps to retrieve the ball, I tossed it to him again and said, *let's play.*

He caught the ball and held it tight to his chest. Then, with a sensitive smirk, he dribbled once and tossed it back. The energy around us changed and we played for a short time. It wasn't competitive; just friendly attempts at making a basket and the occasional joke between us. It was therapeutic. I could see that with each passing handful of minutes, he was loosening up; whatever plagued him wasn't at the front of his thoughts, which is all I could hope for.

But then, something happened. I don't know how long we played for, but Joey tried to make a shot from the foul line and missed. The ball rebounded off the rim and was sent careening to the bleachers. I snickered and made some comment I can't recall, but then. . . he just stopped. Standing there with his arms limp by his side, he stared upward towards the ceiling; weeping.

It's bizarre to think that memories such as these can find me as I wander around in the dark; arms stained with blood, returning to my lifeless home. The door was still open, undisturbed by the light gusts that slithered through the trees. I shut it firmly walking in, a fragment of me was careful not to slam it, but the rest of me knew why that wasn't necessary anymore.

My vision was mostly clear, albeit shrouded by swollen tear ducts and a lack of focus. I was easily able to make my way over to the phone, mounted on the wall just outside of my dad's door. I stood there aching, breathing through my partially agape mouth when it occurred to me. Touching my lips, I confirmed the stitches were no longer a part of me; somehow.

Before taking the next step, calling the police, I casually moved over to the sink and began washing the blood from my arms and hands. It came off easier than I thought; just some soap and hot water did the trick. I'm not sure if it had anything to do with the demons' skin being present, but it's almost like the blood never fully soaked in like it normally would. I didn't understand, and I didn't care.

Clean and dry, I stepped away from the sink and dug my feet into the carpet by the phone; removing it from the hook. Immediately, I was harassed by the impatient dial tone buzzing into the still air. Again, I traced over my cobbled-together story and tried my best to keep it simple. Three clicks and a ring.

"9-1-1, please state your emergency." The woman on the other line asked calmly.

I exhaled with a staggering breath.

"Hello?" I responded low, emotionless.

She hesitated for a brief moment, "Hello. Is everything alright?" She asked.

"No." I visibly shook my head. "It's my dad. . . he," A real choke took hold of my throat, "I just found him dead in his room." I muttered; my voice weakened.

She didn't speak right away, but I could hear a faint tapping over the line. "He's dead? Can you tell me what happened? . . . are you safe?" She added.

"I'm safe. I-I don't know, I just got home from a friend's house and he was. . . just lying there, with his gun." My jaw trembled.

"Can you give me your name and address please?" Her voice seemed more invested, hurried.

"M-my name is Kimberly-Ann Avery, and my house is number Eighty-Seven, on Old Route Forty-three," I explained, exhaustion clear in my voice.

"Thank you, Kimberly, I'm dispatching paramedics and a couple of officers now. Is there anyone else at home with you?"

I sighed, acting a little to make my voice sound more fragile than it really was. "It's just me and my dad."

"Alright." She went quiet briefly, "They should be there in roughly six minutes. Can you stay on the line with me, so that I know you're okay?" She said sweetly.

My brow twitched. Rationally, I knew she was doing her job and trying to make me feel like everything will be okay, but it won't, and she knows that. It bothered me, but I understood why.

"No, I. . . I'm okay. Thank you." With that, I hung up the phone.

Silence welcomed me back and I patiently waited by the phone. Less than six minutes more was all I had to bear, and I would be free from this. Then again, this isn't over. The police will investigate, and what will they find? A self-inflicted bullet wound, true, but additionally five puncture wounds in his abdomen. Something I had no reasonable explanation for. However, I have an alibi in Tansu. There is no way they could link those stab marks to me. No way.

I couldn't sit still any longer. It had only been three minutes, but it felt like thirty. I moved to the living room, and approached every piece of furniture, reliving associated memories new and old. All the while listening to my slowly rising heartbeat and the deafening void. Strange; now that I have this demon in me, I didn't resonate with those voices. I hadn't realized just how present they were, what impact they had on me until they were gone; or at least, dormant.

I could hear them, the sirens growing closer in the distance. My pacing stopped and I watched the front door. Thirteen seconds passed and a rapidly flickering blue and red lightshow blasted through the small gaps between the door and its frame. The sirens had ceased but the lights continued to flash. They were here, but it wasn't until a loud knocking on the door that my mind was reanimated. I was ready.

I arrived at the door with moderate haste and took a deep breath.

"Police. Open the door!" A deep voice commanded from the other side.

I took hold of the crooked bronze handle and pulled it inward, instantly blinded by the bright lights. I raised my hands up to shield myself from the flashing, but it was too late; my vision was completely taken over by blue and red. The epileptic barrage infected me with severe disorientation.

"Miss, I'm going to need you to remain calm, okay?" A voice spoke intently through the lights. I could see his silhouette, accompanied by two other dark figures behind him. The man before me had raised shoulders with his gun in hand. He then lifted one hand and motioned for the two shadows behind him.

"Check the house." He commanded.

The guy at the door took me gently by the shoulder and pulled me onto the porch with him while the other two officers entered my home, unaware of exactly what they would find. The fickle strings of my nerves twisted in a ghastly knot with the truth so close yet hidden in plain sight. I almost let a pleased grin slip free but kept it together for the show.

This man stayed here with me, scoping out the place from the doorway, waiting for his men to return. The cops did their routine sweep and after a few moments, they came back to the entrance and reported in; they found his body. The cop that greeted me at the door holstered his gun and kept one hand on my shoulder, guiding me towards the driveway. I kept my eyes lowered, shoulders tight and breaths sharp. We moved together and passed the two paramedics hauling over a lightweight stretcher between them.

We stopped on the dirt at the bottom of the steps, the lights still slapping my skull. I turned away, back to my house. He stood in front of me, the lights splashing his face and revealing some details. He was a tall, African American man with a bald head and neatly trimmed short beard.

He gave a heavy sigh, "I-uh. . ." He awkwardly stammered, "I know you're going through a lot right now, but I need to take you down to the station and ask some questions." He stated solemnly.

He was uncomfortable, I could tell, not just by his voice or looks; I could *feel* it, in some weird way.

I wanted to act like I was devastated; display my sadness that genuinely existed but I couldn't. I was just so tired; so very lost. With a dry mouth, I replied, "Sure. I'll do my best."

He nodded and gestured me towards the lights.

A tickle in my brain stole my attention away, slowing my pace.

"Ooh, we get to ride in the police car." The demon commented in my head with sinister glee.

I cranked my neck, "Shut it." I whispered

". . .we should kill them too." She said completely serious.

I then lifted my hand up to my mouth and bit down on my index fingers knuckle; using the pain to distract myself.

I climbed in the back of the police car, flexing my hand to keep the blood flowing. I was surprised to see the seats were made of a dense, smooth plastic with notches dugout on the lower back section. I've never been in one before and found it extremely disconnecting with the mesh fencing between front and back. Though, that's probably a good thing for me.

Secured by a belt strap, I leaned forward and stared at the clean floor. Focusing on my breathing and keeping my mind blank. The front door opened and closed quickly, and the same officer called in on his radio; listing off situational codes. With that, he switched on the siren and backed out of the driveway.

We flew down the road at a much faster speed than I've ever gone on this road. I lifted my head and glanced out the window, watching the trees light up from the passing flashes. It was, mesmerizing; the way each flash appeared as a snapshot. Blue or red hues painted the freezeframe of reality and burned themselves into my retinas; I could watch this forever.

As we drove, taking speedy turns and ignoring stop signs, I listened to the nonsensical chatter that buzzed through his radio. It kept me grounded, focused on something other than the festering itch in my brain.

Ten minutes later, the sirens and lights were switched off and we pulled into the station. The two of us stepped out of the vehicle and were met halfway to the door by another much older officer who gave me a saddened look and led the way.

I followed like a lost puppy, too fragile and afraid to go anywhere on my own, or rather, that's how *they* viewed me. Once inside, I was directed down a maze of long white hallways decorated by some plastic plants and pinboards. Every door we passed was shut and the lights off, clearly discernable through the small glass windows in each one. This place was quiet, echoing every step and scrape.

Eventually, we came across a single room. It looked just the same as all the others except this one was awake; ready for me. I went inside and stood there, feeling scrutiny and shame. In my mind, judgment was present; my clean clothes could not hide the disheveled hair, eye bags, and pale skin. But looks were unimportant right now; all that mattered was my story.

The cop that guided me left without a word; closing me in the room and leaving me to my devices. A clock on the wall plucked at my brain with its incessant ticking. I huffed, quickly irritated. This box looked like an interrogation room from a movie; bleak, gray, and not at all inviting. All that it contained was a large, heavy-looking table with four chairs.

I sat on the one farthest from the door; facing it with dreary anticipation. Not very long after I sat down, a lady came in.

"Hello, Miss Avery." She said sharp and quiet.

"Hi," I replied in monotone.

This woman looked to be in her late thirties. Average height, dark-brown hair pulled back in a bun. Her eyes were rounded and blue. Tired, but still keeping the look of authority.

She had a rounded jawline and a semi-thin figure, looking as if she had lost weight, but maintained some minor loose skin. I didn't get any sort of hostile vibe from her but kept my defenses raised. She sat at the opposite end of the table, spreading out some folders, loose papers, and two pens.

"My name is Eleanor Curlin. Are you okay to speak with me?" she asked, politely yet firmly.

I nodded.

"Alright. Now, can you tell me what happened to the best of your ability?"

I started off bland; clearly drained.

"I was at my friend's house; I went over after school and when I got back home, I found my dad. . . like that."

"Did you see anything suspicious around the house?"

"Like what?" I wearily stared

"Any sign of a break-in or a struggle?"

"No, I don't think so."

She scribbled on her clipboard.

I shuffled my feet. "I mean, the house was more of a mess than usual," I added.

"As in, there could have been a fight?" She prodded.

"Maybe? But he isn't very cleanly, so there wasn't any stark difference. Why do you think there was a struggle? He shot himself." I said boldly.

"We're just working with all the information we have at this moment. My initial report shows multiple stab wounds to his abdominal area and *that* is the part we are having trouble understanding." She spoke very straightforward, clearly, she was taking this seriously; almost to the point of forgetting I was the victim.

"I see. Sorry, I don't know anything about that." I mumbled.

"Did your father have any enemies that you can think of?" She switched to a nicer tone.

"Tsch, he was a pretty big jerk with a long history of being a jackass in public. I'm sure some people didn't like him around here. But I don't think anyone would've done this."

She took a moment and read through some papers, familiarizing herself with documents based on my family and life. I twiddled my fingers, watching her slyly. Eventually, she stared back at me, now stern again.

"He does have quite the colorful history between here and Florida. . . Do you know if he had any other habits, apart from the drinking?"

"What, you mean like drugs or something?"

She shrugged, "If he was on some street drug, it's possible the stab wounds were self-inflicted, followed by the gunshot."

"He took anti-depressants, that, on the best of days didn't work very well. He wasn't very good at remembering when to take them and not mixing them with alcohol. . . But he wasn't on anything else." I stated, slightly annoyed.

She tapped a folder on the table with the butt of her pen, "I'm not trying to label him or insult you; I'm just going off of the files I was given, and it clearly states a reputable history of substance abuse."

I placed both hands on the table, palms flat, and leaned forward slightly, "So, then, you're thinking my dad was blitzed out on some drug, ended up stabbing himself multiple times and then shot himself in the head?"

"I've seen crazier. Either that or someone was invited into the house and stabbed him without leaving so much as a hair behind linking them to the scene."

The two of us got quiet for a long time. I folded my arms on the table in front of me, leaning on my elbows for support while she scanned over her files and looked at me. I don't know what she was looking for; it's a suicide, plain and simple. At least it is to them. Sure, the additional wounds are weird, but they can't find anything else through me. All I want is to sleep, just sleep for a day. . . a week.

"Kim, I know this is hard for you. . ." She started.

Something about her statement set me off. That bold-faced lie, the false alignment with my emotions.

"Do you?" I said, just under my breath.

Her eyebrow raised; face tight.

All at once, I felt my irritation. Bones tightened underneath the muscle and my fingernails dug into the table.

"How do you know what this feels like? My dad was an abusive drunk; he didn't care about me or anything apart from that damn TV and booze! Now he's *dead* and I don't even know if I'm happy or sad that he's gone! So how can you *possibly* sit here and tell me that *you know how I feel,* when *I* don't even know?" I screamed, almost hysterical.

Out of nowhere, I felt like a thousand eyes were on me, watching and urging me. I got anxious. Paranoid. In this cynical sadness, I started to laugh in between cries.

"When I walked in and saw him dead, I felt happy. Happy that he couldn't hurt me anymore! He was dead. I'm free, and I won't ever have to see that empty face again. But—" I cried out.

She didn't say anything. Just looked upset. I brought my hands up to cover my eyes and catch the few tears in my palms. Unable to continue.

She finished my sentence for me,

"But at the same time, he was your dad, your only family." She sorrowfully dragged her words. "I'm sorry. I didn't mean anything by that. I'm just trying to say that I am here to help you. I want to help—" She was looking nervous.

"Shut up! Just shut up." I wailed.

Tightly clamping my head between my firmly bound hands, the fumes turned to a bolstering flame and I was back in this mentality again. My eyes scanned the room frantically, examining the tight box I was in. Table, woman, notepad, a stack of papers, clock, ceiling light, and four chairs. I saw that Miss Curlin reached to her side; getting ready to subdue me. I jolted upright from my seat and grabbed the chair, lifted it over my head, and turned toward the officer. She unclipped the stun gun, and then everything froze in place. In the blink of an eye, I was no longer in the known timeframe of reality.

Everything was dark. I saw nothing, but the surrounding emptiness. The officer was there, accompanied closely by my pale-skinned, black-haired demon. Curlin was stuck in mid-sentence, mouth agape; the reflection of evil took her hand to the woman's neck and extended her jagged black claws.

"So much anger so quickly resurfaced. That is good; now let it go and take a nap. You need the rest." She mocked.

She stretched one hand to me, the same way Sin did when we made our pact. I swooned, eyes blackened and face limp. A serene plucking of some stringed instrument swirled around my head like a lullaby.

"You can do whatever you want. Nothing can stop you, not her, not any of those pigs beyond the concrete. You are invincible." She beckoned.

This illusion of madness was layering thick in my mind. Labored breathing and fierce eyes, I ravaged the raw, untapped power inside. In this hallucination, I set the chair down, the legs echoing with contact. I walked forward and stood face-to-face with the beast; seeing her in front of me, not a reflection in the mirror was disturbing; because I could see my features in her face. Twisted, re-forged as something not quite human but still resembled me. The stitches over her lips held my sight.

I couldn't resist. I wanted to feel that power again. I wanted to show them that they don't understand my pain. They can never understand. They lie about their feelings. I reached for her hand; the demon grinned.

Before I could make contact, a different hand met mine halfway, taking a gentle hold and stealing my sight. Shocked, I turned my head to find a vision of Tansu smiling at me from the surrounding mist.

A sudden twist in my stomach immobilized me, forcing me to rip my hand away and take a retreating step. Tansu and the demon stood side by side; a duality of my soul. Everything melted away and I was back in my mind, still holding the chair above my head with murderous intent. My brain reset and released that built-up tension slowly. I was shaking, balance faltered with the weight I carried. She noticed my expression changed, returning to docile and cautious as I carefully lowered the chair back onto the floor.

She lowered her stun gun and watched as I took my seat, eyes fallen to the table.

"I'm sorry, ma'am. I'm sorry for my outburst." I apologized.

A burning headache radiated. She too sat again and let out a long breath.

"That's okay. I can't imagine what you're going through; but I do want to help, really." She smiled.

I nodded tiredly. "Miss Curlin?"

"Yes?"

"Do you guys have any more information on how my mom died? My dad never talked about it. He only ever said it was a car accident, but I never knew what to believe with him."

"Your mother? Um, let me check these files; I'm new to this district so I'm still learning how they sort everything." She said nicely.

She sifted through some papers, stopping now and again to read before adding the page to a growing stack.

"Rachel Mcguille. . . Here we go." She chimed, "A lot of what we have is an eyewitness account from your fathers' statement. According to him, they went for a drive late one night, when she started having severe chest pains. He stopped the car in a parking lot to try and help, but. . . she didn't recover." She paused to take a breath and skim the page, "The official report says she died of a heart attack, at three thirty-two in the morning." She said with shifting eyes and a lick of her lips.

My eyes twitched as I watched her closely. In my head was a digging noise that stirred contempt and indicated something wasn't quite right.

"And. . . what does the *un-official* report say?" I demanded with an acidic edge on my tongue.

She looked to me with a crook in her jaw and an uncomfortable shift in her shoulders. "The uh, autopsy concluded that her cause of death was rapid heart decay. There wasn't any real explanation for this, so they kept it out of publication." She read off, sounding sad but also interested.

I had a knot in my stomach, feeling uneasy, my mouth was dry.

"Is there. . . anything else?" I asked.

She skimmed the pages again. "Um. . . Yes, your father indicated there was another person present; someone, who witnessed her collapse. But he failed to give a description or name."

Another person? I thought

"Thank you." My vision warped with a lasting headache.

"Of course. Now, there is one other thing we need to go over. As you can imagine, this process is extremely involved and you being this young, you cannot live on your own. Is there anyone you can stay with for now? Any relatives in town?" she asked.

"No, it was just us here. I barely know the rest of my family." I said shamefully.

"Are there any family friends? Guardians or anything like that? Because if you have nowhere to stay, then we will find a home for you."

"A home? What kind of home?"

"A foster home. One that will provide for you until further notice."

My nerves spiked. Immediately I thought about Joey and Tansu, how my relationships will fade into obscurity if I am taken away. Without them I have. . . Nothing at all.

"Yes, in your case, with both parents deceased and no immediate family in the area, you will have to move in with a relative. If they will not take you, then you will be moved to a group home. When you turn eighteen, you can go wherever you like. Until then, we have to make sure you are being properly cared for."

"*Properly* cared for?" I laughed inside, head spinning.

I had no family that would want me; hell, they probably don't know I even exist. Besides, I know from what my dad told me that anyone connected to us is on the other side of the country. It's pointless.

There was no way going to a foster home would be good for me. I know that almost everyone there would come from a broken home. They would all have issues and our issues would collide. I would end up killing them; plain and simple. Then again, maybe I could stay with someone here, even if it's just temporary until we figure something else out.

"Um, I can ask my friend Tansu or Joey if I can stay with one of them." I sniffled.

"Tansu. . . and Joey?" She scribbled a note on her clipboard.

"Yes. Tansu and her parents just moved here, and Joey has lived in this town since we were kids, but I know he isn't exactly in the best financial situation at home."

"So that leaves that Tansu girl then." She confirmed.

"Yeah, but I haven't known her long at all. I'm not sure how she would react."

Writhing guilt swept my system. The idea that the problems in my life can cause such a ripple in someone else's; changing the way they live or their perception of me. I don't have the right to invade their lives on such a personal level, but I don't know what other choices I have.

Miss Curlin bit her lip, thinking. "Alright, here's what we can do. For now, we can contact your friend and see if you can stay there for a short time; then we'll go from there. If they don't take you, we will arrange for you to stay with someone from the station."

She then stood abruptly, making sure to collect all the papers in her arms. I stood as well, feeling the weight of exhaustion pull me down.

"Oh, I almost forgot. Did your father have a will or any sort of documents detailing what would happen to him or his belongings after his passing?"

"I don't think he ever wrote a will, but I do know that he's mentioned being cremated and have the remains buried with my mom. He never wanted a wake or funeral or anything; and it's not like he had insurance or enough money to cover something like that." I said with a hollow voice.

"No funeral, and no wake." She repeated, making mental notes.

"Hey, Miss Curlin?" I asked

"Yes?"

"Could I possibly have something to drink?" I asked politely.

She had a look of longing on her face, then a slight grin. "Of course. We have soda in the break room. Would that be okay?"

"Actually, a water would be fine. I kicked the soda habit some time ago." I chuckled awkwardly.

"Water it is then." She smiled, then scribbled a final note on the clipboard and left the room.

I scraped the soles of my feet against this cold floor, listening to the light squeak the rubber made. I didn't want to be in silence; so, any noise would do. She came back rather quickly.

"All right, I passed on the information to someone who may be able to help you. At least for tonight." She said with a wide smile.

"That's great. Thank you." I responded wearily.

She then sat at the table and handed me a large glass, with ice and water. I started to drink it, but the glass was heavy. My muscles felt weak, and my head weighted. Between sips, I set the glass on the table, pretending it was an act of good manners to not chug the water. In reality, I had to put on the facade that drinking from this glass wasn't such a challenge. The nausea returned with the chilled liquid filling my empty stomach. The silence lingered while she read through her notes and together, we waited patiently for someone to come and get me.

The longer I sat there, the more my limbs started to relax. My neck became stiff and my eyelids began to close. I struggled to stay awake, but I felt mixed up inside. Something I can't exactly explain. The room went dark. At least, it did for me. Passed out right there in the seat for who knows how long.

A warm touch shook me awake, forcing my eyes to shoot open violently. With this sudden burst of energy, I let out a frightened gasp and lashed my arms out in defense; by doing so, I knocked the glass off the table and sent water in multiple directions.

"Hey, hey, it's okay. It's just me." Miss Curlin put her hands up flat, showing that she wasn't a threat.

Panic was blaring in my ears, but soon these sirens calmed down, and I remembered where I was.

"I'm sorry. Did I fall asleep?" I asked a little confused.

"You were out almost an hour and a half." She smiled invitingly, "I have good news. Everything checked out. I spoke with your friend's mom and explained the situation. She agreed to take you in tonight."

She tried to sound cheerful, but I could see in my bloodshot eyes that she was tired too.

"Another thing." She continued, "We had some officers pack some of your clothes, backpack, and toothbrush. They pretty much filled three duffel bags with your stuff before they left your home. It's all waiting for you at the front desk."

"Oh. Tell them thanks for me if you see them." I spoke slowly. The grogginess still hung on. I looked at the clock on the wall: quarter past one in the morning.

"So Tansu's mom said it was okay for me to stay there? Are we waiting till morning to go?"

"No, we're going there now if you're ready."

I looked around the room and saw the glass of water spilled on the floor. Luckily, the glass didn't break. That thing was damn heavy, so it must be pretty dense. She saw that I was fixated on it.

"Oh, don't worry about that; it's just water."

"Sorry." I frowned.

"It's no big deal." She smiled.

Her radio suddenly buzzed, and she paused to listen. She turned the small knob on the top to lower the volume down to a whisper.

"Well." She clapped her hands with false enthusiasm. "Ready when you are."

On the move, I followed her back down those long-crooked hallways. The blinding lights assaulted my eyes and cast a black shadow wherever I went. I could almost feel their heat warming my shoulders and head as we moved swiftly beneath them. My skin felt dirty in this light, corrupted, and split. I didn't want to be in this place any longer.

Departing the station an arm's length apart, we were met by the misty sheet of rain descending from the pale grey sky above. We rushed through the gentle trickle and climbed into the cruiser. Surprisingly, I was relieved to be back in here, this time without the sirens. Relieved, but somehow less comfortable.

The drive to their house felt longer than it should have. The pitter-patter of the raindrops hit the moving cruiser with refrained aggression. I attempted to stare out the side window, focus on something other than the pounding of my swollen brain; anticipating sleep. But I was far from the dreams; farther now than ever before. A departure from normality, I was afraid.

To stay awake for this haul, I kept a duffel bag of clothes on my lap. The weight bouncing on my body was enough to ping me in this world every so often; keeping my body grounded in reality while my mind attempted to cope. My attention was drawn to the little droplets of rain running down the backseat's window, and I wondered.

If rain were alive, how would it feel? Would it feel sad that its life started off falling from the sky? Falling at high speeds with no concept of what they were speeding towards. Its brothers and sisters simultaneously crashing down to an undeserving world. Every destination unknown, unfathomable to something so small and insignificant. Whether it be absorbed into the dirt, a larger pool of water, or anywhere else; it didn't have any choice.

It falls, destined to be mixed and mashed together in a sea of long-lost cousins and siblings; an endless cycle. Perhaps, we are one and the same. Living our lives day by day, thinking that we have meaning. Yet, one way or another, we all end up in the ground. Mixed and crushed and turned to dust; recycled. Just like every person before and after us. Everyone whose lives were affected by our existence will end up just the same.

I could feel it, as the street signs turned to trees; the sleep tried to drag me under. A thin line of consciousness warbled beneath my feet like a tightrope. Drawing nearer to my destination, I considered what Tansu's reaction may be. Will they accept me as I am; broken and orphaned? Will they cast me aside the moment opportunity arises, or will they take me in and glue my pieces back together? The idea pressed a knot against the walls of my stomach.

We turned into the driveway and my nerves were pulled tight once more. I don't know how much more of this anxiety I can bear for the night, but I have no choice. The driveway light was on; a lighthouse in the stormy night. As the cruiser eased to a halt and the taillights blasted the house on the other side of the street, the front door opened wide.

I moved the bag from my lap and set it on the seat beside me, turning my eyes away from their home; groggily moving about. I forced the door open and set one foot on the ground, however before I could even fully turn to step out, I was instantly greeted by rushed footsteps and a powerful hug.

My heavy body leaned on hers as her tight arms embraced me. She was crying softly, unable to speak right away. My arms too closed around her as I looked towards the house to see Kari stepping from the front door with an umbrella raised.

"Kimmy, oh my God, a-are you okay?" She whimpered

My voice was dry; churning from exhaustion, I stated. ". . . I'm okay."

I pulled myself back but kept both hands gently laced on her shoulders; she did as well. I could see her face in the light within the vehicle; small details washed away by the pale-yellow glow. Her eyes were wide, arrant sincerity beckoned my hollow gaze. Seeing her cry, seeing her face red and distraught by this; triggered some rusted emotion at my core.

"What happened?" She asked softly.

I struggled to find a word or phrase to convey my thoughts. My tongue became taught, refusing to give any indication as to what happened. It was too difficult for me, right now.

Miss Curlin had exited the vehicle to meet with Kari. They both took turns glancing in my direction, swapping whatever information was needed. Tansu and I waited here in perpetual silence; for once she was the one prodding me for a response and I was hesitant. But we didn't have to wait here long; in a short time, Miss Curlin and Kari returned to the car on our side.

"Okay girls, everything is all set; you can go on inside," Curlin stated.

I took a good look at her mom through the refracting lights and lifting rain. It was clear by the droop in her face that she was distressed; we all were. An overwhelming sadness, pity, and regret over something she had no control over.

Tansu helped me carry my bags up the driveway and inside. I gave a final wave to Curlin from the door as she backed out and eased away into the night. I gave a sigh of relief through my nose and closed the door.

With the door shut and thick silence lingering, I spent a considerable amount of time just facing the door. Unmoving, quiet. I could feel them behind me, watching as my shoulders rose and sank with every tired breath. For a moment, my eyes closed, and I felt like I was floating. Then, my eyes opened, and it felt like a dark veil had been lifted off my body.

I turned to face them, cheeks red and eyes dark; peering. They returned my stare with concern until I smiled. Butterflies invaded my delicate belly and I felt at peace. Wearily making my way to the living room, they each followed and joined me on the couch. I was ready to tell them what happened.

At first, they were quiet; just listening to me recall the event. I tried to keep my eyes low, so they wouldn't see the lack of emotion I had. But I had to connect with them, at least once or twice and when I did, it only made me feel that much worse. Kari especially had this dreadfully pale stare. She felt awful, knowing that just hours ago she had dropped me off; unaware as to what I would be walking in on. Though, that was *her* fiction to live.

Tansu was red in the face; tears resting at the edge of her lids and only seeping through at the end. For her, this seemed to resonate, she felt my pain in the way I conveyed it on a deeply personal level; whether it was empathy or something more. Either way, the two of them shed more tears than I did by the time we reached the end of this transitory circumstance.

It was two-thirty now; and neither my body nor mind could stay awake any longer. It was obvious to them that I needed rest, so Kari stepped away to retrieve spare blankets and a pillow. Tansu stayed beside me, watching my head dip forward as I fought for consciousness. When she returned, I took the pillow with gratitude and propped it up against the arm of the couch. Tansu slid off the couch and gave me room to lie down; choosing to sit on the floor while I got comfortable.

Kari said goodnight and assured me that things will be alright before heading into her bedroom; leaving just the two of us. My back throbbed as I flattened out and stared up at the ceiling. It was strange to see a different ceiling; a different peripheral. But in a way, I liked it; it was new.

"Hey," Tansu whispered

"Yeah?" I kept my eyes directed to the ceiling.

She then reached out and placed her hand on my left shoulder; I twitched.

"I'm here. You know that, right?"

"I know."

She paused, letting the stillness fester before she abruptly stood up.

"Hold on." She ushered quietly.

She then dashed through the dark into her room and came back out seconds later with her blanket and a pillow.

"What are you doing?" I asked.

She pushed the coffee table to the side with her feet and then plopped the stuff onto the carpet in front of the couch.

"You're not sleeping out here alone."

"Don't be foolish." I said in a low voice, "Sleep in your bed, I'll be fine."

"Nope, you didn't convince me." She smiled and sat down on the floor, spreading out the blanket.

I sighed, lacking the strength or willpower to argue at this point.

She nestled herself in close to the base of the couch and wrapped her body tight in the blanket; a little cocoon for the night. The room felt warm to me; a little stuffy under the blankets. My vision started to get swimmy and every joint or muscle between my diaphragm and my little toe thumped like a piston. Yet on the outside, I was inexplicably stable; calm.

"Hey." I pushed a whisper.

"Mm?" She grunted, barely audible.

"Thank you. . . really."

The response I got was soft snoring; she was out. I smirked; feeling a new warmth in my chest. Closing my eyes, I let the images of my imagination run wild. There were no voices, no scratching, and no fear.

Soon enough, I was asleep.

Chapter 13 – Misplaced

The next morning, I woke in a lagging, fugue state. A bright light shined through the living room window, illuminating everything around me and creating a dome of heat that bellowed through the thin panes of glass in the dining room. When my eyes finally absorbed my surroundings, they shot open, forcibly bringing me upright in a fright.

"Where the–" I started as the memories of the previous night had started flowing freely once more.

"Oh, that's right."

The memories of recent events soaked into my brain with each passing second. Still groggy from sleep, I foolishly let these thoughts be my first of the day, and with them came a sickening boil in my gut, stewing for a minute or two. However, my eyes wandered as my brain circled. I could see my new surroundings, and they were enough to break me from this trance. Tansu and her mom took me in, in those early morning hours. This is my new home. I looked down at the floor, Tansu wasn't there. The house was quiet; only the occasional sharp chirp from the smoke detector in the kitchen pinched my eardrums.

My legs begged for me to move them, so I dragged myself up and stretched my entire body. While extending my arms up as far as I could, something popped, and my chest started to pound harshly. Following my chest, my lower back began throbbing. It was extremely uncomfortable. It occurred to me that maybe my body was reacting to the transformation.

That whole foreign process must've put a huge strain on my body. Everything on the outside hurt and everything on the inside felt backward.

I retracted my stretching and paced in a circle, trying to walk off the stiffness. It seemed to be working. Then I noticed a piece of paper on the pushed aside coffee table:

Kim, I apologize for not being able to stay home with you today. I couldn't take the time off from work so suddenly. You should know I spoke with Miss Curlin and she had a word with the school. You are more than welcome to take time off. You don't have to return until you feel up to it and they will hold all your work for you. Also, regarding your personal items left back at your home, I was informed that you would have to wait until their investigation was over and then you could re-enter the house with a police officer to gather anything left behind. I will be home as soon as I can, and the bus will be dropping Tansu off around 3:20. You should rest for the day and try not to think too hard. If you need me, I am just a phone call away. -Kari

"Kari," I whispered softly. *Such a pretty name, it suits her.* I thought to myself.

I set the note back on the table with a frown. A small breath of sadness brushed me, a realization. They left me alone. Maybe I assumed too much of them, I rubbed my sore arms. Now becoming a bit depressed, I let my arm fall loose by my side and sniffled. The thoughts of them only doing this because they felt obligated or maybe to help poor old me, the girl who lost her mom and dad. The thought of that just made me feel like crap. A waste of space.

An odd feeling touched me. A small trickle slid down my upper lip, over the bump, and down my chin. My eyebrow rose in confusion, and I wiped at my mouth. To my surprise, I discovered a deep red smear of blood on my hand, and more of the substance immediately flowed from my nose.

Out of nowhere, a fierce headache seized tight. The dizziness tackled me and stole my balance. Trying to maintain my composure, I stumbled somewhat, but let myself sit on the floor to regain my breath. The thumping rose in my head, then sank just as quickly.

"Damn," I panted.

Looking down at my arms. My skin was pale and the veins in my wrists eagerly pushed to the surface; deep blue and pulsing hard. Another jolt hit me, causing my eyes to go dark and body limp. They reopened seconds later, and I found myself collapsed on the floor; numb.

"W-what is this?" I struggled to keep a steady breath and stay calm. Fear reared its ugly head into my thoughts.

My bones started shifting under my skin, twisting, stretching, and then relaxing. A grinding breath crawled up my throat, drawn from the pain of these strange involuntary sensations. Suddenly a snap in my lower back forced my eyes to clamp shut and a high-pitched squeal to erupt from my throat. In the darkness under my lids, I could see flashing faces, looks of haunted torment, all bombarding my mind as clear as day.

I saw many faces. All unique and wearing different emotions but carrying the same adolescent features. Appearing and disappearing like flashes of lightning. Illegible whispers crowded my ears from every direction. Then there was only one, one face just staring at me through my dark eyes and all went silent in my head.

I panted heavily, trying to control this coarse sting in my bones. It was persistent and unchanging. That last flash with a face I could not make out was staring, watching the core of my brain, looking into my soul.

Minutes passed. The face had vanished moments ago, but I remained there. It was so quiet for me. Frozen in time, listening to the echoes of crying souls that were no longer present. My halted mind was awoken by the sound of a light jingling.

A wind chime.

First, I tried to move my legs. They responded, then my arms, my head. I quickly, but shakily pulled myself to my feet.

Another jingle pinged through the house. Following its docile sound, my head turned to the dining room window. The small chime dangled outside one of the windows, overlooking the front yard. Its tiny noises brought to me by the wind. I swallowed spit and held my breath, listening, waiting for the second seizure to hit me. It never did.

"Are you okay?"

I nearly jumped out of my skin. Spinning in a quick circle, I saw there was no one except for me in the house. I remembered again about the demon inside me.

“You. What was that just now?” I asked worriedly. “That pain—it was surreal; like my *soul* was being torn.”

She chuckled “Oh my, you guessed it.”

“W-what do you mean?”

“That sensation is the result of you claiming your father. A bit delayed, being your first time using, but it shows that we have moved on to the first stage of my advancement. In other words, I have gotten stronger, and therefore you have gotten stronger.”

“I’m glad you finally give me a decent response. Before, you pretty much slapped me for trying to talk to you.” I said a bit snarky.

“Yes, well, your ignorance will only hinder me. I am not one for secrets. Ask the right questions and you may find answers.”

“So then clear up my ignorance. Tell me more about that soul rip feeling.”

She snickered. “It’s simple. Whenever you and I claim a life, a fraction of your soul is sliced off and sent to a special place for holding; waiting for the rest of you. I simultaneously grow to fill that lost space; feeding off the life essence of whomever we claimed.” I could hear the grin on her face.

“And what happens when all of my soul is gone?”

“As I told you before, your body is meant to be mine and this is how it is done. Your soul isn't taken after you die, your soul being taken is what will cause you to die; leaving just me.”

I tried to wrap my brain around this and not throw up at the same time.

“H-how do I avoid using you? Can you just take control whenever you want?”

“This is a question you should already know the answer to. Didn’t he explain this?”

“I, uh, no, I think he did. I just don’t remember. Sorry.” I apologized; feeling dumb.

She groaned in aggravation. “Like most, your personal trigger is anger but with trace amounts of fear. Those are the core elements allowing me to step through the door.”

“So, what, I can’t get mad without you making me kill everyone around me?”

“You can get mad all you like. The anger that allows me to loan you my power is different. Raw and unexploited fury. Swollen and putrid. It’s a kind of energy within you, fueled by years upon years of hate and suffering.” It sounded like she was getting excited talking about my hidden rage.

I knew all along I had issues, but I didn’t imagine they’d be this intense. As I rotated my hands to see my palms open and close frequently, the folded skin was numb. My fingers twitched randomly.

“So, where do the pieces of my soul go? And what will happen to it. . . me, when it's all there?”

“You are linked to the place of my birth by the contract you signed. When the set is complete, you will awaken in darkness. In this pit, you will experience your absolute worst nightmare, your greatest fears and regrets will be used to strip your soul of its humanity. Thus, creating fuel for new life.” She grinned.

I swallowed hard but almost didn’t believe her; figuring she was just trying to scare me or is blowing it out of proportion.

“This place. . . does it have a name?” I asked.

My ears then popped. She didn't respond like she got bored and left. Only, there was nowhere for her to go. So, she was ignoring me. I gave her a minute to answer before I determined she wouldn't.

"Great. Good talk." I sighed sarcastically.

This girl, this demon, was mysterious. She always had an angered edge to her voice but was also introverted and lax. I was curious to know more about her, more about all this. There are so many questions I have, and she is the only source of getting these answers. My face still had some partially dried blood on it. So, I took the bottom of my shirt and rubbed it all away. Still wobbly and swaying, I rotated my neck and forced it to crack. Within two minutes of uncomfortable dizziness, it lessened to a manageable inconvenience.

"Hey, are you still there?" I asked out loud. Nothing. "Listen, I just had one more question. I just realized I don't even know your name. Do you have one?" I asked nicely.

My skull buzzed once more.

"No, I never learned my name before I was placed with you."

"Then, what will I call you?"

"I don't care. It won't make a bit of difference to me anyway." She expressed aggravated impatience again.

"Why do you sound so pissed at me? What did I do to you?" I asked with the same bitterness.

She said nothing. I could almost feel the smug grin on her face as she chortled to herself. Fine then, if she didn't have a name and didn't care what I called her, then I'll come up with one. Something fierce and proud but brooding and mysterious. I thought hard, but every name I came up with seemed dumber than the last.

I began pacing back and forth, moving away from the living room, stopping at the dining room window, and staring off into the side yard. The chime was still now.

This little view provided no inspiration but did leave me with a sense of peace in my chest. The outside world ended up distracting me, so I moved around the house and stared at the floor, thinking of a name. On my fourteenth lap around the living room, I stopped. It hit me.

"Alice. I'd like to call you Alice." I spoke to the walls.

I heard a soft snicker. "Alice, huh? Took you long enough to decide that."

I shrugged. "Do you like it?"

"It doesn't matter to me. My purpose here does not change if I have a name or not. My only relief is that it is short."

"And what purpose is that?"

"I told you; wear your flesh."

"What else? What comes after that?" I urged.

"So full of questions." She snarled, "None of which interest me at the moment."

With that, I heard a soft whoosh sound, like a tiny gust of wind, shot my eardrum and I felt no more static in my head, no more buzzing. She had left or something along those lines.

"Mysterious. Definitely mysterious." I sighed with a loss for words. She was an odd one. I'm not yet sure what to think of her. Still, I got some answers. Next time, I'll ask her the other hundred questions. For now, I need to find my place again. This house was my new temporary home along with a new temporary family. At this time, I took the note from the table again and read it two more times. I understood better now.

To them, this was a sudden change in events. In order to afford a house like this, her mom works hard. She's obligated to go to work, and Tansu has school. She just moved here; she can't afford to miss a day right now. That makes sense.

I dragged my feet and sat back on the couch, still feeling groggy. The pillow I cuddled with for the past few hours had been dropped to the floor at some point. For now, I left it there and rested my head on the stiff arm. The new day's sunlight was shining through the window and hit sections of my cool body.

I lay there in silence and peace for half an hour. Not thinking, not speaking. Just lying there, eyes closed, hands placed comfortably behind my head. I almost fell asleep again, falling in and out of dreams, ultimately keeping lucid. Thinking about where I am. What had happened last night and those faces I saw.

But the thing on my mind I kept circling back to, was this demon inside me. When she was quiet, I couldn't feel her, yet there was an itch at my core. Some inclination that she was with me, but it wasn't incredibly obvious.

My thoughts were completely focused on her. Who is she? What is her real goal here and can she be trusted? I know nothing of her, and she is so strange, so dynamic. I need to know more about her, but how do I get her to answer my questions? She stopped talking when I pried, but she didn't act secretive. She is just toying with me.

My stomach growled. Apparently, my body was ready to start the day. I let loose a huge stretch, then rolled off the couch. Then I had second thoughts: is it wrong for me to go through and eat their food? No, of course not. It's not wrong. They took me in. Neither of them is here. It's no big deal for me to get a bowl of cereal or something. It may not be wrong, but it does feel weird.

Nevertheless, I made my way to the kitchen. Nestled cozily into a corner to the right of the door as you walk in, the kitchen was clean and organized. Nothing left out on the counters, a clean and mostly empty trash can, and a few pictures stuck to the fridge by small magnets.

I stepped up to the fridge and observed the pictures. One was a photo of her mom, wearing glasses, and sitting in a chair reading. Another was Tansu, blowing out candles at a very young age. She was getting help from a man, presumably her dad. They were both smiling. Just below that was a picture of Tansu. In the photo, she was sitting on a bench outside, holding an acoustic guitar in her lap.

She looked into the camera and had the biggest smile on her face. She looks so incredibly happy and lastly, I saw a picture of who I'm still guessing is her dad. A profile shot, a slightly heavier guy with round glasses and a crew cut.

He seemed to be wearing a uniform. A Red Cross patch was embroidered onto his shoulder. It occurred to me that I haven't seen or heard much from him. This got me anxious; thinking about where he could be. . . if he was even still around.

One thing is certain: Tansu sure looks happy in these photos and none of these were taken in this house. My stomach growled again, reminding me of its hunger.

"All right, all right, calm down I'll eat something," I spoke to my belly. The kitchen was pretty plain looking but had a lot of cabinet doors.

A horseshoe-style cabinet layout, top, and bottom, consisting of about fourteen cabinet doors. Not including four more doors located on the small island that was placed in the center of the kitchen. I began my hunt.

It didn't take as long as I thought it would and I found a box of cereal in the island doors. Fiber and oat cereal. Never had it before but the picture looks good. Clean bowl, milk, spoon, cereal, and a comfy seat at the dining room table. My stomach was pleased with me. I happily finished the last bite and drank all the milk along with it with a big sigh of relief.

I set the bowl down on the table and let the food settle. The house was so quiet it made me feel lonely. Without wasting any time, I brought my bowl to the sink then started walking toward the couch but stopped.

I moment of consideration, then I spun around and returned to the sink. Taking time to wash my bowl and spoon, then leave them to dry on a towel by the sink. Feeling proud of myself, I returned to the living room and sat down.

Tansu would be home from school soon and I needed to occupy myself somehow. TV is a decent distraction from negative thoughts, although it would probably help if there was something good on. Nothing but talk-shows and children's cartoons.

I settled on some random nonsense and lowered the volume to a quiet murmur. Instead choosing to focus on a magazine on the coffee table. It was centered around models and fashion; something I noticed Tansu had an interest in.

Flipping through the pages I found myself slightly more intrigued by the subject but in the end not interested enough to alter my standards. But I can see why some people like it; so many unique styles and choices that reflect your personality. Then, without warning a gurgling in my stomach brought back a sickening feeling all at once; stealing my attention away from the pages.

I set the magazine down and stared at the floor. This pulse in my head dimmed my vision in a loop. I started to focus intently, not just on what I saw but every feeling in the air around me. The wind chime outside pinged softly, not audible but present in my ears. Looking at the nearest window, my eyes were burdened by vivid colors and glaring light rays. With the pulse in my brain, those colors deepened and retracted rapidly; flickering.

Staring through the window, I noticed a tree on the other side of the road. I couldn't see the exact detail, but I could feel the energy of what I imagined to be a squirrel perching on a branch; he was gnawing on something. . . and I could hear it. Then I switched my attention to the bathroom behind me, turning my torso and head to stare at the partially open door. A drip in the sink flicked my eardrum every second or two. The walls in my eyes were warped the slightest amount; curved in a way to screw with the depth of my vision.

I rubbed my eyes hard, breathing casually through my nose. A chill ran up my spine and I focused on nothing at all. Just the tops of my hands as they draped over my knees; trembling.

The thought of my fists bludgeoning my father's skull abruptly beamed into my brain. The impact of my bones against his and how I felt nothing from the collision had my attention. Curious, I reached to the coffee table and grabbed a ceramic coaster. It was solid, but with little effort, I snapped it in half like a cracker.

I'm strong. . . even now. I thought.

My neck was stiff, I didn't feel right. Then my eyes wandered around the house until they landed on a pile of bags by the door; a moment of consideration, then a motion of interest.

Inside one bag I shuffled through a mound of clothing. Mostly shirts and tank tops in this one. Another bag contained a few pairs of pants, then socks and underwear. I blushed at the thought of some guy, even a cop going through my underwear and packing them. I'm sure he just grabbed them by the handful without a thought, but I still felt a little awkward.

The third and final bag was full of miscellaneous things like my toothbrush, hairbrush, a box of pads, some makeup I never used, and multivitamins. I thought that was everything, but underneath of all of this junk was one final item. My sketchbook. I smiled when I saw its spiral-bound spine and tan cover but decided to leave it alone for now but noted that it was there.

I returned to the first bag of clothes and unpacked a pair of pajama pants and an old shirt. Sanding right in the front hallway, I peeled off the jeans and shirt I slept in last night and changed into something more comfortable; considering I wouldn't go anywhere for the entire day. Amazing, how a change of clothes can alter your perception of yourself and how the day might flow. I set my dirty clothes aside for now, in the corner of the same bag and zipped it back up.

With a loud yawn, I scratched my right ear and rustled my hair; trying to fix it but moreover just pushing the mess to one side. It was almost time for Tansu to get home. With a sloppy grip, I twisted the handle and opened the door fully. The fresh, warm air poured into the house, heating my skin on contact. I inhaled this atmosphere deeply, taking in every ounce I could. Leaving the door open, I turned around and looked at a clock mounted on the wall in the hallway. Tansu would be dropped off in about fifteen minutes.

With one last knuckle crack and an eye rub, I stepped outside, shut the door behind me, and found a decent-sized rock planted in the front yard and sat on it to wait for her.

Waiting in the yard was peaceful, they had a beautiful green lawn, grass cut nice and even. Every few minutes, a new breeze would roll in, not too strong, but enough so that it would brush lightly against my skin and lift my hair. The perfect kind of breeze. Like nature was giving you a hug. The fifteen minutes went quickly, and the bus was late, but not by much.

As if it knew I was waiting here, the bus came barreling down the road then passed the driveway. Then, in a minute or two it turned around and came back this way.

The brakes cried out loudly and then a low hiss. The doors opened, and I glanced at the windows. All the kids inside were staring at me, giving me weird looks. I saw Tansu move down the aisle as her usual self; head down, bag pulled tightly in. She stepped down the few short steps and looked up to see me sitting on the large rock in the front yard. She smiled. I did the same.

With another low hiss, the bus closed its doors, retracted the mobile stop sign, and pulled away. She walked up to me with a gentle stride.

"Hey," I called out.

"Um, what are you doing?" she asked with a little smile.

"Waiting for you, I just woke up and wanted some air. But it was close to drop off, so I waited here."

"Oh. Thanks." She said.

"You okay?" I asked. She was now standing in front of me. I let my legs dangle and sway off the rock.

"I'm fine. Are you?"

"Good as I can be," I said with a hopeful tone.

"Good."

There was a somewhat long pause. A breeze rolled by and gave me a chill while at the same time lifting her hair in random ways. She looked weighted, almost sad.

"Hey, wait here a minute." She suggested.

"For what?"

Without an answer, she jogged into the house. I shrugged and kept myself planted on this rock until she came back. It didn't take long, maybe two or so minutes but when she finally exited the house and re-approached me, I saw she had a small black item in her hands.

"Give me a smile." She demanded cheerfully. I saw what she had as she held it in front of her face. A little digital camera.

"Whoa, hold on. What's the camera for?" I put my hands in front of my face, blocking her view.

"I need a picture of you since you are going to be part of this family one day." She smiled lightly.

"Do you really need to do that now? I'm filthy." I complained, keeping my hands in front of my face.

"No, I don't. But I might now think of it later."

"Then I'll remind you." I chuckled, keeping my hands raised.

"Too late, I'm already here. Now move your hands." She demanded.

"But–" I sighed. "Okay, fine. If you really feel the need."

"Yes, I do."

She lifted the camera again and I positioned myself on the rock, giving the desired angle for a profile shot.

"All right, I got a good one." She turned the camera off. "On the topic of pictures, do you have any that you'd like to place anywhere?"

"Pssh, nope. Honestly, the last time we took a family photo was a long-long time ago. I think I was maybe three years old?" I said uncertainly. "We weren't really the take-a-picture type of family."

"Oh, that's sad."

"*Thanks*," I whispered sarcastically.

"Oh no. I didn't mean it like that." She apologized.

"I know. I'm only joking."

She shuffled her feet. "At least now we have one of you."

"Looks like we do."

She walked to the house. I slid off the rock and followed her. She seemed tired, considering what time she fell asleep, then having to go to school. Just to cope with the day and stay attentive, I'm sure she was beat.

When we got inside, she quickly moved to her bedroom and tossed her bag on the bed. Then, she entered the bathroom and remained there for a few minutes before exiting and meeting me by the dining room table where we both took seats across from each other.

She then placed her elbows on the table and leaned forward cupping her face. "Tired?" I asked.

"Yeah. I'll probably take a nap later." She said.

"You look like you need it. Must've had a hard time sleeping on the floor." I joked.

"It wasn't bad." She smiled, "How are you holding up. . . really?" Her voice had genuine concern in it.

I sighed, "It's hard to describe, ya know? So much is going through my head that I think my emotions are kind of shut down."

"I understand. Do you think you'll be returning to school any time soon?" She asked.

I didn't say anything at first; my brain was lagging behind a little.

"Oh." She became a little nervous. "Not that you need to go back anytime soon! But just. . . You know. . . In case a teacher or someone asks me." She panicked.

"I'm not sure. I do wanna go back, but it's a bit more complicated than my own wants."

Thinking back on the events of that night, the brutality, I got the feeling that this was only a fraction of what she was capable of. That scared me. School is just a breeding ground for hatred and stress. I need to find out more about her and how this whole thing works before I can return to school. I don't want any accidents.

"It is complicated, isn't it?" She spoke softly, troubled.

I looked to her with quiet intent, examining her body language. Tight, head low, and hands in that weird balled fist again. She was a spitting image of the first day I met her.

"Well. . ." She started, "You can return whenever you like. I know it's difficult but I'm sure you'll know when the time's right." She smiled.

I licked my lips, taking time to pause and absorb her words.

"So, uh, how was school? Am I missing a lot?" I asked.

She pondered, "Um. . . We had an assembly this morning instead of first period. The principal stood up in front of the school and told us about your loss."

An angry butterfly ripped around my chest. "They had an assembly?"

She nodded. I was in complete shock; this idea that the school felt it important enough to gather everyone for an event in *my* life, was downright insanity.

"He said we should all respect your privacy and send you thoughts and prayers." She gave a tender smile.

My stuttering breath receded as I let that image simmer. I leaned back in my chair, tipping it on its two back legs and balancing it there.

"Anything else?" I asked, admittedly impatient.

She rubbed her eyes, "Mm, Joey found me in between class and asked me about you. His face was red, and he looked angry. . . or scared. After that, I didn't see him for the rest of the day."

Joey. I thought. A frown overcame my present face and I allowed the chair to drop forward, my body heavy.

"Also," She started, "That girl Stacy found me. She asked about you too." Her voice was softer now.

"*Great.*" I groaned sarcastically. "Let me guess, she's gonna hold lunch for me every day until I get back?" I shook my head.

"I'm not sure about lunch, but she told me to give you a message. . . the message being. . . her pushing me into the lockers and storming off."

My lungs tensed, "She did what?"

Tansu exhaled and shrugged, "It's okay. I think she's just a little confused with her emotions right now."

I made a fist on the table. Clearly, she could see my teeth were grit behind my lips and my shoulders were tight with building rage.

"Don't get upset, Kim. I don't want you to get into a fight over this." She said worriedly.

A crick in my neck forced me to rotate my head. A hot breath slid from my lips and my vision was clouded with thoughts of violence.

"Don't worry. It won't be a fight."

Chapter 14 - Unity Under Stipulation

It's jarring to think that two weeks can pass by so quickly. So much time wasted sitting around in my pajamas, just thinking. At least, that's how it was at first. The first few days were occupied in that regard; empty. It all hit me like a wrecking ball; stagnating every drop of potential I had to recover, leaving me to waste away without a word or care.

As the weekend came, the attempts Tansu had made to bring me to life, almost worked. I was able to find momentary joy and distractions in activities they undeniably forced me into. Movie nights, homecooked meals, riding along while her mom ran errands. These were things I had always dreamed of doing; simple fantasies just out of my reach until now. It could only be described as wonderfully fulfilling most genuinely but contained within. Outwardly, I had little energy to emote.

As fate would have it, Monday came, and the foul stench of isolation found me again. During the first few days into the week, I didn't sleep. Stricken with nightmares of my father's blown out face and the pit that awaited my arrival. I stayed awake all night either watching TV or sitting in silence as Tansu slept on the floor. Brooding, bleeding inside. Stagnation introduced decay; a virus that infected my will to try and take a single step.

I fell apart from them, and they watched my hollow form idle on the couch day by day; helpless. It was sudden; one bad night led to such a drastic change in my emotions. It was a rut I had not discovered until now, and their words could not reach me. In my own swollen skull, Alice stood watching as the world fell out of orbit in my mind. She held my hand, calming me with melodies of intrusive desires that were symmetrical to my own malicious dreams.

Mid-day when no one was around; my anger was aroused. Driven to madness by vivid hallucinations of my father, I nearly gave in to hunger. My skin became chalky white and my eyes had virtually turned black.

Then, the strangest thing pulled me down. That little wind-chime outside the living room window. It stabbed my brain with high-frequency pings and allowed those visions to dissipate. I was grasping at straws; every single ounce of anger was a risk to those around me.

In passing hours, I found myself spinning in so many directions; like a roulette of who I was to be for the next chunk of time. It was impossible to find a balance. So, I had to opt-out of feeling at all. Become numb, to save me and my new family from the manifested torment. If I began to slip too far into the depths, I had to shut off. With no immediate threat, I could avoid the anger by suppressing everything I was. Alice had means of getting me upset; she could play with my mind, but she couldn't always push me over the edge. Not without real provocation.

That being said, I hadn't hit my lowest point. At times, I was able to find that light; a sliver of myself. It could last five minutes, or it could last the day. This told me that I wasn't entirely gone, I was still alive. I had a chance. These nightmares, this imbalance, was nothing more than coming to terms with my fate. Understanding my situation and what it meant to be *me* every day in preparation for whatever future I may have. I was growing; learning.

I knew there was hope because Tansu and her mom could still make me laugh, they could still make me smile even on the days where I was lying in pieces. I cherished that, held onto it, and used it as fuel to keep my positivity intact.

Wednesday night.

I was wide awake in a state of swimmy consciousness; keeping my constantly cycling mind occupied by late-night television. The volume was off, and I had subtitles turned on as not to disturb Tansu as she slept on the floor. Every so often I glanced down at her, admiring her tenacity; she hasn't slept in her bed since that night.

It was a lonely night, just like all the others. As silly as it was to feel this way, I was insulted that Alice had been ignoring me. In the first week, she would speak, urge me to do something nasty, and insult me for *being too weak*. After that, she went silent, biding her time.

This bothered me more than it should because I had questions. Now that I was in a more focused mental state compared to the past two weeks, I had more than just a burning hole in my brain. All of this is the result of my father's mistakes; now, it's my life on the line. As much as I regret my own decision, I'm in this. And there lies the hurdle I cannot get around; I don't know what any of this is.

Rolling onto my right side, facing the inside of the couch; I closed my eyes tight. Searching deep in the depths of my mind, I listened for any faint signature, any bead of energy that she left behind while she skipped around the complex caverns of my being.

"Alice?" I whispered into the black.

The air was mute; cold. I focused on her face, beckoning her image to come forth.

"C'mon how long are you going to ignore me? We *need* to talk."

Still, I waited. Not a scratch nor a buzz. No indication she existed at all aside from the tiny pressure in my skull. Almost ten minutes passed and still, she ignored me.

"What do I have to do, to get you to respond?" I asked, getting flustered.

In the silence, an echoing tap, like a heavy door had unlatched and slowly creaked open. I winced in pain but kept my composure.

"You want to talk? I want to provoke some aggression in your pathetic life." She snarled.

"Jesus, finally you speak. Why do you continue to ignore me?" I complained.

"Why would I give courtesy to a sack of ignorant meat. I am not here to *be* your friend; I'm here to kill your friends." She said cynically.

"I gathered that. . . But I was thinking. . . Or, hoping we could talk, and you could fill me in on this stuff." I asked timidly.

"Talk, are you kidding?"

"No. You're in my body, so I think it's fair that I know a little about you and Sin. Plus, don't you think it might, uh, benefit you somehow if we got to know each other?"

"You sound like a stupid child. You want information, I want blood."

I swallowed hard; a thought just occurred to me.

"If you want blood so badly, why haven't you attacked Tansu or her mom yet?"

"Now *that* is a good question. Believe me, I want nothing more than to tear into their fragile bodies, but you haven't made it easy to break through. You have presented many opportunities but I'm finding it difficult to maintain a tight grasp."

"What does that mean? I *know* there were a few times where I was sure I'd lose control but aside from some light skin and my eyes changing to purple, you didn't come out."

"For one, you weren't angry enough. You did get upset, but I need that raw anger; the explosion of absolute chaos. . . Still, it's odd. All I can say is there's something about you, little Kiki." She mocked, flaring her nostrils in frustration.

Kiki? My throat went dry, "How did you. . . know that?" I asked sincerely.

"Your memories have left an impression; a scar to reopen. Real-time thoughts are different, though. As I said, I know who you are, inside and out. That's why I'm confident in waiting; my time will come." She explained with a sneer.

"Well then, now I *really* need to know about you. It's not ideal for you to know me entirely and for me to be left without a clue." I whispered.

"It's kind of funny, watching you pled for information. So much to learn."

"Then help me. You can start by telling me who you are."

"Alice. Fool, you named me." She replied.

"No, I mean, who were you as a human? Don't all demons start off as a human before they turn evil or something?"

"Hmm." Her vocal cords vibrated. "Okay, here's the deal—"

I interrupted her. "Can you not use that phrase?" I sighed.

"Sensitive, are we?" She snickered. "All right, I will answer your questions, but not here. Not in this house."

"Yes, here. I don't want to wait any longer." I stated.

She paused. "Do you want to risk a conversation like this so close to those ignorant to your plight?"

"Then where?"

"Where you met me for the first time is where you'll get to know me."

"You want me to go back to my house?" I questioned.

"That's right." I could hear the grin on her lips. "I'm sick of being here. If you want to talk, those are my conditions, maybe I *can* convince you to play this game and be of some use. Who truly knows what will happen?" She cackled.

I pondered it for a moment. This may actually work for me; I needed to return home and see what else I can get anyway. Plus, at this point, I'd comply with pretty much anything so as not to be left in mystery. She could be asking for a lot more of me.

"Fine. I'll go." I agreed.

Carefully I rolled off the couch and stepped around Tansu as she lay in her tight cocoon. I crept across the floor to the front hallway and opened one of my duffel bags. I changed out of my pajama pants and into a pair of jeans then dug through and found a tight-fitting long sleeve shirt; just some random grey one I didn't even know I owned.

In the hallway, I reached up to a shelf above the hanging coats and found a flashlight to light my way. The door opened quietly, and I was met by a grey-blue sky with minimal stars and a crescent moon. Not much overhead light to guide me, but enough to not feel engulfed by emptiness.

Moving stealthily out the front door, I shut it gently behind me. The first real challenge was the driveway light sensor, but I was able to move along the side of the house and cross over the lawn until I hit the pavement.

After getting out of sight, I began my trek with anticipation in every step. I kept the flashlight tucked in my back pocket, not willing to use it now otherwise someone may see me. I stuffed my hands in my pockets and lifted my shoulders up; it was a bit colder than usual. The walk was long and unsettling. The looming seclusion that oozed from the trees quickly pressured my imagination.

I continued slowly along the ocean of charcoal until I reached the first turn. There were no houses on this road, so I felt secure enough to test the flashlight.

Paranoia rampant, I aimed it forward and measured the distance in my head; about twenty feet of yellow light. I kept it on for the time being, but by doing so I became more aware of the encroaching dark. The atmosphere was muted; nearly devoid of all sound apart from my own footsteps.

At this time of night, I had to be wary of my surroundings. Wild animals such as bears, raccoons, and coy dogs wandered through here. Though it may be because of my developing narcissism or blind stupidity, I was not afraid of any wild animals. Still, I cautiously scanned the trees; left and right. Though the start of the forest was ten or so feet from the road, I could see every individual trunk and bush. Outlines plainly distinct from the shadow; almost glowing to me even without the flashlight.

My house was a three-minute drive; so, give or take twenty minutes to walk. Safety was forfeited, but I did not feel entirely threatened. Retracting off my vision, I focused on what could be heard. In this state of focus, I could hear a new sound in the distance grow. Rising up louder and louder with each step was the melodic tune of chirping pond frogs; caressing my ears from both sides.

Confirming life to exist should be uplifting, but the synchronized cacophony of assorted nature was unpleasant at the very least. I picked up the pace with suspense in my gut. By this time, I had taken the final turn which led to the long strip which held my home.

A tap on the pavement behind me pinched my eardrums. I whipped around, blasting the flashlight where I had already been. Almost perfect silence; I held my breath. Alice started to breathe; she was viewing attentively.

Turning back to the road ahead, I took another step. Unsure of what sense to rely on, I settled on what I could see. Another minute passed and I came upon my old driveway. I hardly recognized it as my own, although, identifying the overturned, rusty bathtub at the end of my driveway proved it to be my former home. This tub was left by my mom.

She turned a junk tub into a beautiful garden accessory, filling it with soil and planting flowers. At the time, it gleamed proudly in the daylight and was indicative of the carefree nature of this home long ago. That was then, now the dirt is dry and the plants degraded from years of neglect. It lay now as a relic of the past.

The forest that surrounded seemed to engulf the driveway. Tall and short trees alike hung lower than ever before; drooping with an invisible weight that made the driveway appear almost like a tunnel. I found it cryptically amusing to be so deeply fearful of the place I once called my home. Despite the unknown, I gathered my courage and made my way into the dark. The wind blew through the trees, rustling leaves and sending a chill across my body. As soon as I could see the front of my house, I stopped.

"There it is," I whispered.

Chapter 15 – Food Chain

A neutral gaze occupied my face. The porch door had been ripped from the hinges and tossed in the walkway. Staring down at it; the flashlight beam revealed a laminated piece of paper stapled to the wooden frame. *Foreclosed.*

My stomach flipped. My eyes reentered to the front door within the porch and it too was open; seemingly kicked in as it clung by only the bottom hinge. This feeling in my gut was potent; a saturated nostalgia bubbled within while at the same time fighting a vibrant disconnect. It's difficult to explain but the building had this *mass* to it. A dense aura that rolled from the confines, like sludge water. My back straightened; I felt at home, truly, but not in a familiar way. Not in the way as correlating this place with years of memories; but some unnatural interpretation.

I could hear the wind skip leaves along the road, but the trees around me did not move from their slum. Even more strange, I didn't have an awareness of animals or even bugs. No chirping crickets or frogs, no chipmunk, or even a mosquito. It was like, as soon as I stepped foot on this driveway, I entered another dimension. Still, despite my comfort with the silence, I felt a suspicious need to remain unnoticed.

I skulked up the front steps, wincing with every board squeak. The moment I stepped within the crooked doorframe; I was hit by an overwhelming atmosphere. The air I breathed in was almost like breathing in a cloud of dense concrete dust that refused to settle. At the same time, it smelled like a sponge soaked in used, festering toilet water and set on fire and slapped against every wall. All culminating to form a nauseating wave of decadence that pierced my chest and sent the rhythm of my heartbeat out of control.

"Do you feel that?" I asked with a low cough.

Alice didn't say anything back, but her buzz was ever-present. The living room was immediately struck by my beam as I whipped it around haphazardly. The house was a complete disaster, and that was saying something. I moved at a slow pace; sliding my feet instead of lifting them, observing as much as I could in this low light.

It looks like the police were content in just doing their initial duty and then leaving this place to rot. The fridge was tipped forward, the couch was entirely missing and the tables in the living room were warped; as though they were left in the rain. The carpet was stiff and crunchy; dust kicked up with every shuffle I made. Even the railing above, outside my bedroom door, had a few broken poles knocked out to the floor below.

"Looks like some looters came here and had a field day. Maybe even a party." I said as I kicked an empty bottle of alcohol. "Not that I can prove that by alcohol alone," I said while shining the light around.

I moved toward the staircase that led to my room, nervous to head into deeper darkness, but determined to explore and wait for Alice to talk. The second step I took up the stairs collapsed under my weight, bringing my foot down through the board. The wood scraped my ankle very slightly but not bad enough to cause any concern. I pulled it out and pressed on toward my room.

I noticed immediately that as I moved up the stairs, the paint on the walls was almost. . . melted. Patches of dark spots and chipped drywall lined the stairs and the steps themselves felt unstable.

"This is ridiculous. How could this place fall into such disrepair so quickly? Even if people came in here and ransacked the place, I couldn't imagine it'd get this bad." I said, honestly confused.

I kept the light bouncing back and forth from the steps to the wall on my left. I slowed my walk when I noticed a streak of blood descending down the staircase. The memory of my dad running for his life played back in my head. I did my best to avoid stepping on the copper stains.

"Mm, the air here is perfectly toxic. It reminds me of my womb." The demonic voice gurgled in the back of my head.

"Finally! Are you ready to talk?" I asked as I reached the top of the stairs. The door to my bedroom was closed.

"No, not right here. We must talk face-to-face, through the mirror."

"Ugh, why? Why can't we just talk now? I don't want to spend too much time here. It makes me sad.

"Because it is said that mirrors are a gateway into a person's very soul. I find the irony in that statement very fitting to your situation." She chuckled creepily.

"And why is that?"

"Because I enjoy seeing your worried face every time you see me standing behind you in every reflection."

"Not every time. Do you do that just to mess with me?"

"Only to remind you of your purpose. Besides, won't you feel better talking to me directly instead of speaking to the walls?" she said.

"I suppose."

The door handle to my room was missing, so I just pushed the door open. My room was surprisingly clean. Not clean, just not as messy as everything else. My heart thumped loudly as I entered my previous living space. I saw the old blood that stained my floor.

My window was broken, and my mattress was gone. I didn't want to go in, but there is one thing I wanted to check. With silent footsteps, I shuffled to the closet and slid out a large box. The cardboard had grown moldy, and a rotten stench flowed from the closet, a damp and sticky smell that gave an impression of death and decay. Everything in the box seemed to be intact, the birthday card, stuffed otter, an art award, a #1 Student ribbon, and a whole lot of meaningless rewards and memories; I cared for none of that. Only one thing in here had my interest. All the way at the bottom, still wrapped in cloth and the newspaper I removed my precious memento.

Before unwrapping it, I swallowed hard, trying to stay hopeful. I want this, I need this to come home with me. It's all I have left, it's all that keeps me connected to her. I let out a steady breath and removed the wrapping. To my dismay, the delicate unicorn inside was broken in two.

I felt tears well up inside, but I held them back. Only letting out a frustrated tongue click and harsh sigh, “Tsch. . . Of course.” I took the note that was folded tightly with the destroyed shelf piece and stuffed it in my pocket.

That’s it. I didn’t want to see any more. I left the room immediately after. There was nothing in there for me. Only horrible memories. Instead, I entered the bathroom. The shower curtain was torn down and lay inside the tub. I propped myself with a straight back and weak knees, facing the mirror. The cracked glass that I stood in front of not that long ago was whispering to me. My chest pounded, remembering Alice being fused with my body. The pain. I tried to ignore this haunted feeling.

“Okay, are you ready now?” I asked impatiently.

There she was. Multiple images of Alice reflected from the broken mirror. She is usually sporting a devious smile, but for some reason, she wasn’t. She looked kind of sad.

“Now, let’s make this fast. I don’t want to be here for too long. I have a lot of questions for you.”

“Well, you came all the way out here just as I asked. What is it you want to know?” she said with a straight face.

“I’m glad you are so quick to comply.”

“I am simply being fair. I think it’s time you know what’s really going on. There’s a lot more to all this than you may think. Things he neglected to mention and that is why we are here tonight.”

“I never imagined you to be one of fairness.”

“Well, I’m a bit different than what you might think.”

I was pleased that she would fill in the blanks, considering I know nothing about demons, the old man, or who she even is.

“Okay, I pretty much have a list of things to ask. I guess I’ll start with, who are you really? Like, were you ever human? And things like that.”

“I am what you see.” She folded her arms. “A demon created by Sin. No, I am not human.” She paused. “Though, in a way, I guess I used to be.”

“What do you mean by that?”

She began to explain, “Sin gathers human souls as often as he can. The natural law forbids him from merely snatching the soul from a living human. So instead, he bargains. Humans willingly exchange their souls using a deal.”

“Okay.” I was following along so far.

“We were all human once; before he collected us and crushed our existence into a fine paste. Mixing us in a cauldron of shit-water where we fight to grow.”

“Wait, we? What do you mean we?” I asked.

She grinned. “You can’t honestly believe there is only one of me. I have a family.” A lump formed at the bottom of my throat.

“A family? How many of you are there?” I asked. Admittedly, not really wanting to know the answer.

“A hundred, before a lot of us were eliminated mysteriously. Sin cannot replenish us that quickly, so a more accurate guess would be close to twenty right now. That leads me to why we are here tonight.”

“All right.” I ushered her to continue.

"I am the most recent Teufel to be plucked from a fresh batch. My brothers and sisters have all been in this world for much longer. Most, if not all of them, have dispensed the human they shared the body with and are free to hunt." She said in a concerned way.

"So, what's next for us, then?"

"I help you get the blood you sold your soul for and then you go crazy. Tormented by guilt or whatever heinous brand you give yourself. A smooth introduction to madness makes it easier for future transformations. Whenever a Teufel lends their power to a human, the soul is shaved and replaced by the Teufel's essence. Eventually, there is nothing left of the humans soul, just the Teufel. That is when we completely take over."

"Yeah, you mentioned that before, but you didn't answer where the human soul goes."

"A place where the human becomes a demon like me. My place of birth."

"In the end, you are all out for the body? But why? What is the purpose? What is the reason he makes you and gives you to us?"

She paused briefly and sort of adjusted her shoulders like she was uncomfortable.

"In the beginning, there was only one of us. The Firstborn. None of us know anything about her. Who she is, where she came from—all we know is she is favored by Sin. . .We, Teufel, are afraid of her, you could say she's our Boogeyman. Her name is Crism."

"Crism? That is an odd name." I stated.

"Every one of my brothers and sisters is given their name just before they are given to a human. In fact, you are the only person to actually name their Teufel."

"I guess that makes us special." I snickered quietly, trying to make the mood a bit lighter.

"It seems." She said softly, another pause. Then she continued, "He used Crism's indiscriminate thirst for death as a means to steal souls. As far as we are aware, he then used the ones she collected and made us out of them. We are then given to children like you, who then use us to kill which sends your traded souls, piece by piece, to where they will be used to make more of us. It's endless. All you are meant to be is my vessel until I am strong enough." The way she explained it was like she was lecturing me for some other reason than my own curiosity.

"Strong enough to do what exactly?"

She got a big smirk on her face. "To walk on my own, to hunt and become the strongest. We all strive for the status of Sin's right hand, a Deity."

I sort of expected her to say something like that. I moved on to another question, trying to shotgun as many questions as I could.

"You said before, you were born just recently. Then how is it you know all this if you have only been alive this long?"

She placed her finger to the side of her head, pointing to her brain.

"All of the Teufel share a sort of information bank. Things such as each other's names and faces; enough information about who our father is and what our purpose is. Being made from human souls grants us basic functionality and intelligence. We all vary in this field, based on whose souls made us."

"I still don't understand why, though. Why does he put you here? What is the reason for making you and giving you to kids? Just so we can kill and help him make more?" I questioned.

She began to laugh quietly to herself. I perked up. "What's so funny?"

"You. So damn curious. I love it. We need that curiosity. I will guide you, don't worry, but you still need to ask the right questions. You are learning, yes, but there is much more for us both to discover. I only know he wants us to become stronger than our competition."

I stopped for a moment and let my thoughts gather. I thought I was making progress. Not that I haven't made any at all, but she has more to tell me. Much more. She wants me to think, not just give away the answers.

"The right questions—okay then. These things we have gone over, it's all what he wants and that's fine, but what is it that you want?"

Her face shrank from laughter to pensive, very quickly. "Excuse me?" she growled.

"You can look into my past and hear my thoughts. I can't do that to you. I can tell that you are different than what I originally thought you to be; just a bloodthirsty demon out to kill everything. That isn't you. Not completely at least, I can feel it."

She paused. "And just what makes you say that?" she playfully sneered.

"I-I'm not sure. It's just a feeling in my gut. The way you talk about them. Your family. It sounds like you separate yourself from them in a way. Like your intentions are somehow different. I could be wrong, but that's what I hear in your voice." I explained.

She stared at me for a few seconds, examining my eyes.

"Let's just say I am not interested in his plans for me. I do what I want." She hissed.

"Well, what do you want?"

"It is part of a Teufel's core design to have one goal. Do whatever it takes to become more powerful. I align myself with that aspect of life, however, I do not want to become his partner, his ally. . . I want to do what I want, become so powerful I cannot be controlled by him, or anyone."

She licked the front of her teeth, slowly moving her jaw left and right with greedy desire. Her words shook me and brought out a deep fear up from the pit of my stomach.

"Oh, just great. You are a bloodthirsty demon who wants to be unchained. Awesome." I said sarcastically.

She growled, "You don't understand what it's like. You may have been beaten and bullied, but never starved or tortured at the very core of your existence. . . Not yet anyway."

"Starved? But. . . You were just born. . ." I was a bit confused about what she was getting at. Was it a metaphor?

"Tsk. Before this, you dumb fuck. In my place of birth where my essence was formed. Where we all waited for human souls to be dangled above us. Fighting, shredding our way to eat them. Those who ate enough, became more mature, growing stronger, and stronger. While I withered away."

She started to get heated, the air around me became stuffy and charged. I could feel her rage building.

"Every. Single. One of my siblings got a fair share of souls, while I was cast out! I don't blame them. It's nature, survival. However, therein lies my resolve. They will not stand above me anymore. No one will. I have no personal hatred for this world or its people, in fact, I love the potent negative energy that flows in the very air you breathe. So thick, so powerful. But I will eradicate this world's life to gain enough power to surpass the goals of my siblings. I will not settle for the position of a lowly demi-god; I will be the real thing. Even Sin will bow before me!"

Her eyes started to glow furiously. Her brows dense and angled. I swallowed hard. My mouth was dry as a brick and my stomach hurt. She closed her eyes and relaxed, opened them again, then smiled.

"Unfortunately, when it comes to the food chain, I am at the bottom. You may find me strong, but I am at my first stage of development. I need to feed, we need to kill, or we will remain at the bottom and become targets."

"And once they find us, we will have to fight? If we survive, then you will continue to kill and grow stronger. And eventually, you will rip your way out of me." I said in a depressing tone.

"Let me be clear. You are my meat suit, that is all. I have no choice but to work with you due to my somewhat premature birth and the general nature of Teufel. Unlike my brothers and sisters, I understand the value of partnership, but my end goal remains. I will do whatever is necessary to follow my path." She spoke down to me.

I sighed, not feeling all that confident. I spent a minute contemplating my place in this world and what I'm going to do about all this. This deal is much heavier than I thought. At first, I just figured I would have some superhuman powers and use them to make people stop messing with me.

Instead, I have a literal demon in me who has a family of apparent assholes. This isn't what I signed up for. Then my thoughts redirected to another topic.

"So, your siblings—how much of a threat are they really?"

"Considering all the facts. Many may not be interested right away, given how weak I am. Although, I can think of a few that may drop everything to come after me. If they are Whole, we have a serious problem." While she explained this, I watched her smile. It crept across her face, revealing a few shark-like teeth behind her stitched lips.

"Why? That seems a bit pointless. Don't they have better things to do than come after us?"

"That is the better thing to do. Even at my lower stage of development, my spirit is still more valuable than an abundance of ordinary human souls. That leads to my own question. Now that you claimed your father's life, what will you even be using my power for? That bully at school?" She chuckled.

"Nothing. I don't want to hurt anyone else. This whole thing was a mistake. I know it's too late, but if I can avoid hurting Stacy, I will. I don't know what I'm going to do."

"You will find that while I am with you, your desires and rationale won't be entirely up to you. Even if you changed your mind and you want to remain a Good Samaritan, you'll find that it's easier to give in to the hatred. That's just how it goes."

"But I don't want to be a homicidal maniac! I never wanted that."

"You can't lie to me, Kimberly. I know you liked the feeling of being in control of your father's life. You can't deny it." She growled in confidence.

"That may be. Even if I enjoyed it, just a little, that doesn't change the fact that it's not who I want to be."

Alice seemed to be getting impatient. Her gaze shifted slightly toward the door and the floor. Here and there, she would look around me.

"If you aren't going to use my power to kill and fuel us, then what the hell are you going to do with it?" she shouted.

I went quiet. If there is anything in this world I want to hold on to— then I thought about Tansu and her mom, Joey, and all the people who are kind to me. How much they care.

"I. . . Want to protect."

"Protect." She stifled laughter. "You want to protect people with the evil power you traded your soul for?" She was now laughing out loud, an insulting laugh that belittled my only real desire.

"Not people as a whole; I want to protect Tansu and those I care about!"

"You can't protect them unless you and I become stronger than this. To do so, we need to kill. It's the only way."

"I don't need to be all-powerful. Only strong enough."

"But what you think is enough strength to remain safe from ordinary people is simply not enough against the real danger that will inevitably come. You can't just decide you don't want to participate. They don't care. They will find you either way and kill you. If you are keen on sticking with these people, they will surely die once we are found. So, we have to kill, to get strong." She gritted her teeth.

"I will find another way, but as long as I am sane, I cannot follow your means of progression," I argued, not giving an inch.

She looked into my eyes. Eight different sets of her purple irises reflected through the broken mirror.

"Tsk, another way. What a fool." Alice scoffed in disbelief. Then her eyes widened for a second or two and her shoulders tensed up. I noticed this slight change.

"What's wrong?"

Alice flashed her teeth and looked into my eyes from the mirror. She was smiling so big, so dangerously. All of a sudden, my entire body started to vibrate. Not shake or hurt. Just vibrate, like my own personal earthquake.

"Wh—Alice, what's happening?" I asked her, flipping my hands around, staring at my palms I watched my body as it uncontrollably bounced in place. Then all together, it stopped. My brain was suddenly filled with a resonating headache that bent me forward a little.

"Protect other humans with power from the devil. That is interesting."

A loud voice came from the doorway. This voice bounced off the thin walls around me, hitting my ears from every angle. Utterly confused and feeling misplaced, I turned my head to the doorframe.

I was scared of this sudden presence behind me, calling from the darkness. I felt uneasy. I wanted to run, to scream. My childish instincts screamed at me to call for help. Something else clicked and I straightened my back. I was now angry that someone was here, intruding.

“Who are you and what the hell are you doing in my house?” I said angrily, trying to hold my confidence. I couldn’t see his face or features– just a pale mass.

He chuckled. “Your house? Funny, if this is your house, where have you been? I was looking all over for you.” He spoke softly but seemingly pushing his voice to reach me. There was a faint giggle to his words like he was trying to contain himself.

“It seems as though I have excellent timing. You two were talking about me, no?”

“Talking about you?” I questioned.

Alice stepped in. “He means we were talking about my family.”

He stepped closer, revealing who he was. A complete stranger in my eyes. A teenage boy around my height; wearing a blue sweatshirt, gray cargo pants, and a thick black cross necklace around his neck. He had almost shoulder-length choppy and greasy black hair. Eyes as wide as could be and mouth containing a large, beaming sneer. The boy’s face seemed calm, just grinning along, confidently standing with one hand slipped into his back pocket. Most importantly, his eyes were glowing a radiating light purple, just like Alice.

“Hello, brother.” She greeted.

"Your name is Alice? That doesn't sound right." The stranger grimaced.

When he spoke, I got this tight feeling in my head; not painful but pressurized.

Alice spoke in my head, "No, it doesn't. I wasn't given a name; she gave me one instead." Her words echoed in my skull, but he could somehow hear them.

"You're like a newborn baby. Dropped here without an identity, being forced to adopt the moniker a lowly human assigned you. It was a pain to track you, that's for sure." He said with a long sigh.

She didn't respond. Her energy was balanced; calm. She was disinterested in his words; keenly focused on every motion no matter how slight.

"So, how long exactly have you been in this world, sis? I read your signature and got here as fast as I could. The Ditch just couldn't wait to spit you out, huh?"

"If you are insinuating that I am weak, you're simply wrong." Alice purred.

"The Ditch? What's that?" I interrupted.

"The Ditch is our birthplace; where we grew and fed."

". . . Stupid name." I said plainly.

"Really? Is that all you have to say about it?" Alice questioned sternly.

"With everything I'm learning recently, a bowl of water for demon souls isn't all that crazy-sounding, okay?" I said.

He took the conversation back.

"Alice." The mystery boy snickered, "I gotta say the girl you're with, she's kinda cute." That caught me off guard.

"Cute?" My face got hot. Thick awkwardness filled my gut as his violating eyes slid across my skin. Repulsed, my shoulders tensed up.

"Delicious, in fact." He snickered.

"Umm. . ." I looked to him, then his feet, then back to him. I didn't know how to respond to that. He breathed in deeply through his nose, then let it out of his mouth.

"Oh, the things I am going to do with your corpse. Maybe I'll leave you alive, so you can experience my passion. Tell me, do you have any experience? Or is this going to be difficult for me?" He asked through a dirty grin. The words held a playful tune with them.

"Okay, that's enough!" My face was glowing. "Tell me your name and why you're here right now!"

"Oh, want to get acquainted first. How nice."

Alice answered for him, "His name is Destro. I don't think I have to explain much about his personality." He took a step closer in this small bathroom. We were practically face-to-face.

"Destro," I repeated, "what are you here for?"

He cocked an eyebrow at the same time his lips pressed tight, stifling laughter.

"Wow, you sure got paired with a stupid girl." He said mockingly to Alice.

“Excuse me!” I shouted. “You’re talking to me right now. Got that? Don’t piss me off.” I threatened.

“Piss you off? Oh, but that’s the idea.”

He squinted a little and watched me closely. His stare was definitely intimidating. Not only that, but I could also see the literal hunger in his eyes. The way he scanned me up and down and the way he licked his chapped lips, he wanted me in ways that I didn’t want to think about.

He gave off a strange aura. Being this close to him, I experienced a heatwave; like he was radioactive.

Suddenly he threw his arm forward, a tightly bound fist stopping just short of my nose. A slight wind tickled my face with his movement. My eyes went wide; mouth dropped a little and my entire body quaked in response.

“It’s true. I’m not here to play nice.” He continued.

With a sudden harsh grip, he took hold of the front of my shirt, pulling me toward him. With his other hand, he reached down and grabbed my left leg, digging his fingers into my mid-thigh. He took one big step back into the doorway and threw me behind him. I slammed into the outside wall back first and my head followed with the momentum. The back of my skull crashed into the sheetrock, cracking the wall and bringing a disorienting swirl to my eyes.

I fell to the floor, lying on my side trying to recover my stolen breath. He stood beneath the doorframe, crossed his arms, and looked down at me. Still clutching to my lost lung, I peered at him with one dizzy eye.

He then hunched down and grabbed hold of my hair.

“Ack! Bastard!” I slapped and grabbed at his arm, but he yanked on my hair, making me screech out loud. I punched hard at his arm and was able to knock myself loose from his grasp. Thinking fast, I stepped backward down the hallway towards my room and faced him. Breathing heavily, I raised one leg and kicked at him, but he reached out and grabbed my leg with both hands. Our eyes connected, mine full of worry and his vibrantly glowing with confidence. He used the grasp on my leg to swing me into the wall again. My shoulder hit hard, but he didn’t release me. Instead, he gripped tighter and swung my body with ease in the opposite direction.

He released me with the swing and sent me screaming into the overhead railing. My body smashed into the decaying wood and left me hanging in the air for what seemed like a minute until finally, my limp body crashed to the living room floor below.

My body bounced like a deflated basketball and a harsh gasp of air shot into my lungs. The dust sprang upward, then rained down on the floor like snow falling in slow motion. I coughed violently. Stunned, I lay still, lightheaded, unable to feel my back or legs.

What I could feel was scattered cuts and deep bruises forming along my spine. My muscles went numb, but my skin screamed in pain. A warm, wet sensation engulfed my backside.

“Argh.” I grunted “My back.” The hyperventilation started, and my vision began to pulse as fear overloaded my system. The pain I felt was sharp and thumping; cold.

“It’s not broken. You’re just in shock. Get up quick!” Alice demanded.

“I-I can’t move.” I cried.

“You goddamn child, move it!” she shouted angrily.

My voice broke, “Alice. . . Help me!” My lungs stretched.

“I don’t have an opening; you aren’t angry enough!” She roared.

Destro began his victorious strut down the stairs using those rails to guide his hands. The light echoing footsteps made their way down and over to me.

“Wow. . . sad.” He laughed creepily as he slowly moved and sat down next to me; his legs crossed.

“Tell me. Where were you all this time? I’m pretty good at tracking energy, and I came all this way just to find this dump abandoned.” He poked my cheek with his finger in a playful way. “Your energy is so dense; how are you projecting it like that?”

“Get bent, asshole,” I said with bared teeth, biding my time.

“Not nice.” He sang playfully, then he made a fist and crushed it into the center of my chest.

“Gah,” I hacked.

My ribs bent inward with his hit and a soft crack reverberated through my bones. His fist retracted and every breath I drew caused a stabbing ache in my torso.

He gave a satisfying groan, then got serious in a way. His face flattened, lips solemn and considerate. “Listen; if you could do me a small favor, I’ll make sure to kill you quickly when he’s done, okay?” He requested, staring down at me with conceited eyes.

“What. . . are you saying?” My wide eyes confided in his, searching for intent. His insidious gaze slowly melded the answer in my head; the pieces fell into place.

“I just gotta know one thing, before we begin.” he began, followed by a fierce punch to the side of my head.

The sharp impact forced a violent twitching to seize my fingers and wrists; then they relaxed. Gently, he placed one finger on my forehead, not pushing it, only enough for our skin to connect. He closed his eyes, and with that, mine rolled into the back of my head. He was pumping energy into my brain, invading my mind and scraping against Alice’s own soul.

I was suddenly withdrawn from my body; sunken into the floorboards and found my wispy body floating in a vibrant sea of trees. Gliding along the ground, I was forcibly drawn into the forest; gaining speed without any way to restrict my nonexistent body. The trunks and leaves melted into colorful streaks as my blinding haste drove me forward until I stopped.

Where I rested now was outside a window of a house; moss and pine needles decorated every inch of this forgotten relic, but I could sense energy inside.

“Lucas. . .” A hushed, child-like voice brushed through the trees.

The window grew closer; there were bars between the outside world and the black walls within. The world shut down in an instant, darkness overtook the sky and only a faint orange glow crept between the steel beams. Inside, a body rested on a bed; sprawled, lifeless arms dangling to the floor.

A new voice beckoned; fearful, shaking. “I’m sorry. . . It wasn’t my fault. It wasn’t my fault.” He cried.

The single bulb on the ceiling suddenly got brighter; revealing the body of a little girl; torn open and shredded inside. Her soulless gaze looked to me outside the window; grey.

A searing pain swelled in my gut as I drank in the emotions radiating behind these bars. A well of passionate sadness bleached my flesh and forced tears from my very soul. It was, unbearable; the feeling I experienced could not be described in words.

Then, this reality was pinched, and my eyes rolled back down to see Destro pulling his hand away.

“A girl; sweet and innocent. Her energy is so. . . polite.” He whispered; then grinned at me, “I wonder what was shared with you? Doesn’t matter, I’ll tell you what, how about I kill you now and then dash over to your friend’s house and skull-fuck her until her brain oozes out of her ears?”

Again, he raised a fist and punched the side of my head; further setting in the concussion. After that he wrapped his fingers around my throat and pressed down, bending my neck and restricting my breathing to only tiny huffs.

I lay on top of broken beams and shattered glass, eyes half open; my dark surroundings spinning out of control, head feeling fuzzy and vacant. I didn’t say anything. My brain was distant and silently building hatred. A cool touch then stirred up the fire within. He laid his hand on my hip then slowly moved it upward, sliding it gradually under my shirt. Slowly, so slowly; he began to rub my stomach. Ice-cold, rough hands, persistently caressing my lower belly.

“Hmm, maybe not. Maybe he can have you still; after all, I promised him a hosted Teufel.”

I couldn’t move; not on my own, no matter how much I tried. Just random misinterpreted twitches throughout my limbs. The darkness around me enveloped my eyes as they eased shut, consciousness fading.

“Kim,” Alice whispered, her electric voice booming in my ears, waking me, provoking my hunger. She spoke very calmly, almost comforting. My eyes shifted around ecstatically under my eyelids, searching for any light. Any blip of safety.

“You are too afraid.” She whispered.

Now his other hand came down to my waist. One finger pushed under the waistband of my pants. Then he started to tug downward on the beltline. His breathing was full of perverse motivation. Loud, raspy.

“Fear is not enough. . . You want my help?” she hissed.

A cool breeze brushed my skin, a breeze that did not exist to anyone else but me. My pupils, restlessly dilating.

“Get up. Get angry!” she commanded. “Just what are you willing to fight for? Not yourself, clearly. So then, what is worth getting up for?”

His guiding hand rose upward, fingers gliding toward my chest. He stopped, looked at me, and leaned in, his mouth less than an inch from my lips. The stench of his breath was suffocating. He then pushed out his tongue, trembling breaths proved his lust. Drool trickled onto my lips and rolled down my chin. My face blank and distant.

Alice whispered, "I know right now. You are considering giving up. If you do, no one will be around to protect her."

"Protect her. . ." my dimming brain was attempting to reanimate.

"She will die unless you kill."

"I, will kill," I whispered, losing myself.

Destro's hand had risen up my shirt, his overgrown nails tickled my rib cage as he grabbed hold of my chest with remorseless aggression.

The pain it caused forced my brain to jolt. With that stimulation, Alice spoke again, softly. "Get up."

Suddenly, there was a detonation in my head. In an instant, my skin flooded to a milky gray. The previous coating of pale human flesh peeled off and fell to the floor like a flaking sheet. My eyes reopened, with a dense glistening black, complete with purple irises. Before the rest of the change could take place, I jolted forward. With a piercing scream, I slashed my hand at his neck, claws shooting out lightning fast.

Lucky for him, he reacted quickly and jumped backward, rolled on the floor and stood himself up quickly, taking his arm to his mouth, wiping the drool away. No more smiling.

"You're too late with the change. I got a good feel, and now there is no stopping me. I will have you." Destro bolstered.

I could move freely once again. The power of Alice flowed through me, numbing the pain in my back and slowly repairing anything cracked within. My body reacted at full strength and carried itself with a smooth transition, lifting myself to a standing position.

My knees and spine cracked violently while I straightened out. The transformation was not complete. My hair was still short and brown. My skin was white, eyes black. The claws extended. I remained the same height and I did not become any skinnier. It was a strange state. Rushed, premature. I could still feel it building inside.

"Get out of my house." I snarled furiously through clenched teeth.

"I'll leave when I'm finished with you. Then I'm gonna take your girlfriend." He challenged.

"You rotten son of a bitch!"

"Rotten? To be rotten, I would have had to start out as something pure. Don't be absurd." He giggled.

I licked my lips as aggression settled in my heart. With full intent to kill, I hurdled toward him and swung my jagged claws, but he was quick.

He dodged to the side once, then I swung again, and he dodged a second time. The house was small, he could only avoid me so far until he would be cornered, but the same goes for me. A final fist from me darted straight for his face. This time when he stepped to the side, I grazed his cheek with my knuckle. With the contact of our skin, he brought his own hand up, backhanded my fist, and made a quick jab at my face. He whacked me in the nose and giggled as he stepped back. It didn't hurt much. It was just a playful tap. In the living room of a home that was no longer mine, we stared each other down. I scratched my nose where he tapped me and planned my next move.

At this time, the rest of the transformation smoothly sank in. The black hair poured out of my skull and my body took on her shape. She opened her eyes once the form had settled.

"Much better." She grinned confidently.

He straightened his back, then unbent his arm. In the glimmering darkness, a solid white bone sprouted from the underside of his arm starting halfway down the underside of his forearm and extending a foot past his right elbow. This strange bone weapon unsheathed from his skin like a sword. He brought his forearm in front of his face. The blade now curved around his side and the sharp end was facing me.

"Let's see if you can keep up." He snickered, then blitzed me. Immediately slashing at my neck, I pulled back, narrowly avoiding a vital hit. In response, I tried a sweeping kick at his legs, but he jumped up and planted his feet down onto my leg, bending it inward. This did not hurt me.

I threw my hand down quickly, grabbed his ankle and pulled upward, making him stagger backward. While his footing was lost, I rose fast, jumped forward, and swiping my claws at his face. He immediately planted one foot down and brought his arm in the way of my attack. My claws connected with his hand.

One single nail stabbed through the back of his hand, coming out the other side and stopping just short of his neck. A drop of sweat could be seen gliding down his cheek.

"Close one." He hummed melodically.

It was strange to move with Alice. Sometimes our actions were directly controlled by me, sometimes it was her and sometimes I couldn't tell who performed the action. We moved separately, but at the same time, we moved as one.

Blood dripped to the floor. A steady stream flowed from his hand. We both froze like that, eyes locked. His twisted smile was unbroken. My eyes filled with rage.

"I've only just woken up. You're lucky I didn't stretch first." Alice replied with cockiness.

"Y'know, this hole in my hand is going to be quite a pain. I'm gonna make you pay for it." Destro said confidently.

"If you happen to make it out alive, it'll be healed by morning!" Alice shouted with aggressive glee.

His face suddenly went lopsided. Struck with confusion, he asked,

"Healed by morning? What are you talking about?"

Alice gave him the same look of confusion, then laughed, assuming it was a joke. I ripped the jagged nail from his hand, and swiped with my other free hand, approaching from his left side, coming down at an angle toward his head.

He pulled his head back just enough to dodge. While my swing followed through, with a heavy momentum, he lifted his arm and brought the blade that protruded from his elbow down onto my lingering forearm, tearing through layers of flesh. The sound of my skin opening up, exposing the bare bone, echoed in the empty air. The pain flooded me and forced me to fall back.

"Damn it." Alice snarled.

His hand didn't even seem to bother him. I stepped backward and held my arm loosely in the other. Destro let out a slow breath from his mouth, planning his next move. I didn't hesitate and lept at him, this time I hurled a fist at his face, but he did something I didn't expect. He swiped his hand in between my fist and his face, and in the path, his hand followed, a trail of purple energy was left behind; creating an energy barrier exactly where his hand had wiped. My fist collided with the barrier with an airy slap.

I swung again, and again and again. Every punch I threw was interrupted by this manifested energy wall, wherever he swiped his hand and just as quickly disappeared as the next one formed.

I skipped a beat and held back a swing, but in that gap, he made the wall anyway in prediction to where I was going to attack. He saw my face gleam as I used my opposite hand to swing at his gut, leaving him no possible way to block. However, he returned my grin with one of equal pleasure. The barrier formed, but he allowed his hand to linger and then he pushed it forward; the slate of energy moved in front of his flat palm and smashed into my nose; sending me stumbling backward and wide open.

He took this opportunity to punch my chest and gut two or three times before finishing off his combo with a wide swing from his arm blade. In the second it took for him to switch from standard punches to his blade, I extended my claws in the path and blocked the gut slash. Bright purple sparks shot out from the bone and claw impact.

The heat between us was fierce. No more words were spoken, just an exchange of satisfied and pensive stares. Impatiently, I lept at him and sent my right arm forward, claws out like a sword jab. Calmly, Destro stepped to the side and I missed completely. My claws stuck in the wall behind him. They went deep into the wall, getting caught in notches and old studs, leaving me trapped and fully exposed.

We did not try to break free, instead, we just remained there, arm outstretched and hooked in the wall.

"Ha-ha-ha!" He mockingly laughed "Look at how pathetic you are!"

Destro gawked. I stood awkwardly, still in the same position as I was when I stopped.

"Alice," I said worriedly.

"Hold on." She whispered.

Destro walked up to us and leaned his back against the same wall right next to where I was stuck. He folded his arms.

"That was the worst attempt I have ever seen. You put up even less of a struggle than the *people* I have killed, and that's saying something."

We breathed evenly and calmly assessed the situation. I was worried, but Alice had a plan.

"Brother, I warned you not to underestimate me, didn't I?" she cackled. He raised an eyebrow, still leaning like a cool guy. Suddenly my nails burst out from the wall he was leaning on, piercing straight through his chest and belly in four different places. This time, it was *his* blood splashing outward, followed by a massive gasp from Destro.

"Geeeaaahhhhh!" he screamed, clutching two of the pencil-thick claws that protruded from his torso. Choking on blood, his eyes caught mine.

"You bitch, how did you do that?" When he shouted, even more blood expelled from his mouth, staining his teeth and lips.

"Do you not have an ability yet, brother? That's too bad because I have my claws *and* a trick or two." Alice gloated.

His body shook and was breathing sharply.

"I'm going to kill you!"

Alice's response was to rip her claws from the wall, thus pulling them out from his chest as they returned through the wall. He stumbled forward a few feet, creating distance between us.

I didn't understand how she did that. It was as though my nails bent inside the wall, but they weren't that long. They just went in one place and came out the other, as I understood it.

He stared us down, breathing and bleeding heavily. Not saying anything. Just watching. I stood still and waited.

"Get your eyes off me!" He shouted frantically. "You two are one and the same, looking at me with such disgusting lust. All of you are the same. . ." He covered his face with his hand, it sounded like he was crying.

"Just like this demon. Everyone just loves me for my body. . . Nobody ever cares and when you're done and satisfied, you'll move onto someone weaker than yourself. Shit. Piece of shit. She didn't deserve it!" He cried out.

He hunched forward, gripping his own head, blood dripped from his mouth.

"Aly, you can't be. . . you should be at rest!" He began to cry out.

"What's happening to him?" I asked, watching him thrash in a two-inch space. Alice said nothing.

Then he became calm; his face vacant. He let out a long breath, then lifted his head. With the tremor his body gave, he continued to stare at my face. I noticed that my face was steaming slightly. The small cuts and bruises sustained from going through the railing were slowly healing, giving off a light mist of dead skin and dried blood.

"What the hell are you doing?" Destro asked fearfully.

"What do you mean? These small wounds are nothing. I can heal them without effort. Just as you, with that hole in your hand." Alice admitted.

"Of course, we can all heal, but not like that! That's just. . . How?" Destro shouted, confused, and angry. Jealous, even.

Alice and I were both astonished by his words. I spoke to her in my head, "What's he talking about? I thought you guys all had this healing power?"

"We do. He must be hysterical." She explained.

Out of nowhere, Destro grunted and straightened out his back and looked to the ceiling. His torso shot hot red blood like a sprinkler. He began to groan loudly. The house echoed and shook with his deep yell. His body started to shake; his arms straightened out.

His body gave one final spastic motion. He then braced himself on one knee and looked upward at me. Everyday pale skin complimented his brown eyes. His hair receded a few inches and was a lighter brown now. He was human. Or appeared to be.

His face was frightened and angry. Large, tired eyes glared at me, it was easy enough to tell that he was just a kid, but this kid has an immense sadness. Something that screamed inside of him. I could tell just by looking at him.

With blood still spilling from his chest, the first move he made was to slick back his near shoulder-length hair, moving his bangs back and slightly to the side. Random clumps fell back in his face and stood tall in other places, but he just continued to stare. Now with a demented grin.

"I will be back someday, and I will finish what I started. I can't wait to rip your throat out an' tear into your corpse."

Even with the serious wounds, he was covered in, he turned and bolted out the front door. Like a wild animal that just escaped its cage.

Neither I nor Alice even thought of going after him. In his absence, the buzzing in my head picked up. My mind went blank for a second and both eyes rested.

I collapsed to my knees, keeping my back straight and looking to the ceiling. My teeth snapped together, and a soft groan came from my diaphragm. The moaning grew louder and louder as my white skin began to rise off my body, revealing the tan skin beneath. My hair quickly receded back to its normal length and regained the color, the rest of the reversion took place, and my groan was silenced.

Shaking, trying to regain my breath, I stood myself up again. My eyes fluttered open and I examined my ordinary body in all its glory. Relieved.

"H-holy crap." I stuttered.

"Well, it seems he hasn't disposed of his vessel yet." She spoke inside my head.

"He was just like me then? A human with someone like you inside."

"Pretty much, though I didn't expect it. I thought everyone else had taken over their host by now. It seems I was wrong."

"He's your brother? You have a damn scary family."

I thought I had control of myself, but as soon as I reverted back to my human state, my body got really hot. I couldn't stop shaking and my breaths were irregular. Placing my hand over my heart, I felt the beating, rapid rhythm of hysteric emotional overload.

Just like my entire life under the thumb of my father, this affected me deeply. I can handle a hit or two, and the verbal abuse isn't as bad, because of Stacy. But being thrown over the railing and then nearly—the things they did to me were nothing compared to this. I feared for my safety, my sanity.

"Get ahold of yourself." She said with detest.

I cupped my face and tried to breathe slowly. What do I do? What do I do? I silently contemplated for a couple minutes until I gathered the strength to stand tall and rub the emotion from my eyes. Alice noticed I was coming back to reality and waited patiently while I gathered myself.

"In any case, you did fairly well for a scared little girl." She said sarcastically.

"Screw you. How the hell do you expect me to react?" Her belittling sarcasm annoyed me.

"Well, I didn't expect you to be down and out that quickly."

"He threw me over the railing!" I yelled.

She paused. "How's your arm feeling?" she asked.

I took a look. The cut was a downward gash, placed just below my elbow, on the outer curve of my forearm. It was deep but not bone-deep. The wound was radiating beneath the skin and felt very strange. The pain was unreal, sharp, and burning. I should be passing out from this and yet, it was bearable. Hurting and not hurting at the same time, almost pulsing in and out between tolerable and agonizing.

It was bleeding a lot, but less now than when it first split open.

"Why does it all hurt so much now, but when you take over it doesn't hurt that bad?"

"As long as I'm with you, I can focus my raw energy into the inflicted areas and speed up what your body already does. When I take you over, my power is unbound at that time, which basically means my healing starts going bat-shit crazy with your wounds, making the whole thing practically instant, if the wound is small enough. Normally you wouldn't have sustained so much damage, given how much denser my skin is than yours, but the attack came from another Teufel, so it's different."

"How long will it take to heal? I noticed the smaller cuts have already mostly vanished."

"Something like this will take no more than eighteen hours to close up and recover. And you should know that wounds this bad will leave scars. Thin ones, but they will be there."

"And, what did you mean by the attack is different because it came from him?" I asked, twirling my arm to observe the slice. It was making me a little sick.

"There is dark energy behind each attack, confusing your body and disorientating your cells. However, it is, at the same time being healed by the same energy that damaged it. Your body simply doesn't understand. Don't worry about it too much. It'll be healed by tomorrow." She said.

"Sounds good to me." I sighed. "Any idea why he got so spooked when he saw us healing like that?"

"It's odd, for sure. We can *all* heal faster than normal humans. Things like, our strength, speed, skin density, and reaction time are enhanced to a certain degree from our host's own attributes. Additionally, we each have a unique melee ability, like my claws and the capability to use our Demonic Energy to use hidden abilities that are only limited by our creativity and energy capacity. However, it would seem my own healing factor is greater than the others, or at the very least his."

"How do you even do it? Does it just happen by itself or something?" I asked.

"For me, it's intuitive. Human souls give off all sorts of energies. The way I see your soul is a little blue ball that occupies space behind your eyes. Well, that blue ball is shrouded by a dusty aura. Those particles are raw life energy that I can harvest. I can use it to accelerate everything your body already does to heal wounds. Minor cuts and bruises are easy. More serious ones can take longer if I do it while idling. But if needed, I could focus more of my energy and really speed it up; at the cost of my own vitality."

"I would've just taken it's magic for an answer." I made light jazz hands to emphasize that I just don't get it.

"You asked, don't get sarcastic with me, runt." She huffed.

My knees were stiff, and my ankles made light snapping noises with each motion. I started to pace back and forth, keeping blood flow to my legs, forcing my body to move to ward off the dizziness.

"Do you see now; why we need to get stronger?"

I breathed quietly through my nose, thinking.

"How strong. . . How strong do we have to be to take on anyone?" I asked timidly.

She took a deep breath as well, "There is a stage we can achieve; one so powerful that it's an entirely separate transformation. But no human can endure the physical toll; it's a power only a Whole Teufel can manage. Even then, its rarely ever done."

"What is it?" I demanded an answer.

She sighed, "It's called Ascend."

"And that power will keep every threat at bay? Keep us safe?"

"That type of power requires a body trail. The exact thing you are so keen to avoid."

A pause stifled us; each thinking in circles. . . Wondering exactly how we could survive this with our goals being so unique among our peers. It was a mess, truly a godforsaken fate to stare down this path.

"You knew. . . Didn't you?" I started.

"Knew what?"

"That he would be here. That's why you made me come back because you wanted to fight him."

She snickered.

"If I hadn't, then he may not have found us for a while, with you laying low, it makes it harder for Teufel to pinpoint our exact location. We needed this fight."

My eyebrow twitched in anger. "You brought me here to fight him. . . He could've killed me!" I shouted.

"But he didn't." She stated the obvious, her words fiery and sharp.

I stopped talking and let my thoughts roam. I felt sentimental. Alice was not as evil as I thought. Manipulative, yes. Of course, she is a demon, but not by choice.

She knows we are in this together and we have to work together; she wants us to get strong. My eyes were drawn to my arm again. Her power was working fast in the sense that the bleeding had mostly stopped, just leaving the amplified pain.

My voice started with a squeak and carried on quietly,

"You know, before all this, I never *wanted* to kill anyone. I mean, sometimes I thought about it, but without you, I'd never have been able to actually do it. This isn't really what I wanted. Now that I'm here."

"You aren't the only one who wants something different, something more."

"I know. . ."

Her tone then changed drastically. Sad yet determined.

"They will fall to their knees at my mercy and I will become infinite, I will not suffer any longer."

"Do you even want to hurt this world? Be honest with me, do you actually like hurting people?"

"It's in my nature. I get pleasure, excitement from causing pain, and watching others suffer. Ultimately, it's the sloppy necessity. But humans don't matter much to me. The only blood I want is Sin's."

My chest shuddered with her effervescent desires.

She finished. "Unfortunately, Destro decided to run like a coward, so we missed that opportunity of growth."

"We kind of let him go, to be fair."

"I wanted to go after him, but for some reason, I couldn't move my legs," Alice said.

"Were you scared?"

"Absolutely not. I mean, literally could not move. I'm not used to fusing with you and we didn't exactly ease into this fight."

"Oh."

There was an itch on my shoulder. I scratched and adjusted my shirt. Shaking off the splinters and dust, I took in a deep breath and let it out slowly.

"You want to kill your father, huh?" I shifted my legs around. "How ironic. For him to give you to me, I used you to kill my father. Now you want to use me to help kill yours. That's a funny turn of events. . . I still don't get why. Why would he allow them to come after us freely? Why is he wanting to kill me if he helped me in the first place?"

"You stupid, ignorant girl. He never cared about your plight, he has his own agenda, his own reasons. He needs every piece on the board." She inhaled then abruptly shouted, "This is all just a game!" Her scream bounced around my head and vibrated my eardrums.

Her yelling triggered a sudden rage in my chest.

"Well, I won't play!" I snapped back.

My heart pounded silently, feeling anxious and scared. I clenched my fists tight out of protest to my fate.

"I don't want to do this—" I paused. "Although, I like your plan of killing him. If he is gone, then the deal is broken. My soul will remain mine, right?"

"Maybe, but the problem is getting to the point where we'll be able to kill him. You have no idea what it will take and at this level, it's foolish."

"Somehow, we will kill him and everyone else. Anyone who causes so much pain to innocent people deserves no mercy." I said angrily.

Alice smiled a huge evil grin. "You are a fool, and that's good because we won't be able to get this done any other way than a foolish one."

"I am not foolish. It's because of him that my life is so ruined. *He* caused all of this. . . So, that means that he has been the true source of my torment. I'm going to use the power he gave me. . . to destroy him. But not before I get answers, I want to know the truth behind my mom's death."

There was a silence, an extended period where we just examined each other's motives, our personalities. I got uncomfortable after a while. My average self-sank in.

"Things are going to be quite different now, aren't they?" I stated.

She scoffed. "Let's get going."

"Yea, we need to make sure he doesn't go after Tansu. I'm worried."

"I wouldn't concern yourself. We all drifted together and collected nothing but vague memories. I saw what you did, and I'm sure his vision was just as *unclear*. Even if he did get more information than that, he now knows that if he tries, we can beat him. . . Let's go home."

"Did you just call it. . . Home?" That gave me butterflies. She didn't respond, I continued, "Hey, I want to know that through all this, I want to trust you. Can I?"

"Maybe."

"I guess I'll take that over nothing."

I stood there in the living room, clutching my bleeding arm, nursing it the best I could. My back ached as well. I could feel cuts being scraped by the fabric of my shirt. I was sore all over, but she said I'll be okay by tomorrow, at least for the most part. I looked at the floor, all the broken rail pieces scattered around.

My dad would have been so pissed if he was here to see this. After a moment of lingering, I twisted my stiff neck causing the bubbles to pop and the rigid pressure released. I was so incredibly worried about a lot of things, and yet, for the first time, I'm not alone. I have people in my life, people I care about. I now realize how precious life is, how fragile.

They are worth protecting. I will protect them because *only I* can.

Chapter 17 - Left Behind

A dream. Various positive sentiments happily swelled in my dreary head while the pleasant visions played out. A scene I can't quite remember, but absorbed joy from, nonetheless. It was fleeting; ambiguous and opaque. There was no narrative or characters, just. . . her; smiling down at me.

For once, I awoke calmly. My eyes remained shut but in an instant, I was lifted back into reality; the dream nothing but a ghost behind my eyes. The springs beneath me squeaked as the weight of my body shifted to the center. Laying on my back, I pulled the blanket up to my chin and kicked one leg out and onto the floor.

Breathing through my stuffy nose, I allowed myself to ease into the new day. However, a sudden piercing ring from the telephone shook my eyes open and jumpstarted my heart.

All at once, I was forcibly submerged into my daily conscience. Groggy; I lifted my arm to rub my eye but felt a stabbing pain in my back. My spine arched upward a slight amount, then settled. Warm and fuzzy tingles fluttered around my skin, gently subsiding as I grew more conscious. I rolled over, now facing the inside of the couch; trying to muffle the piercing noise. But it was no use. Frustrated, I groaned and rolled back toward the television.

"Dammit, will you shut up!?" I barked with a dry mouth.

The ringing was persistent. Fed up, I pressed one hand against my forehead and set my bare feet onto the cold rug. My eyes slightly perked open, now staring at my naked toes. Searching the floor, I discovered my socks laying flat by the front-right foot of the couch.

Must've slipped off while I was sleeping. I thought as I picked them up and slid them back on.

I proceeded to roll my shoulder, making it crack three times. Every joint was tight from a restrictive night's sleep. I don't blame the couch; I blame my inability to relax.

Finally, the ringing stopped, and the answering machine began talking, but the caller hung up. Pointless. Consumed by a loud yawn, I rubbed my eyes. The skin beneath my eyes throbbed, and my eyeballs felt dry as sandpaper. I cupped both hands over my face and pressed against my skull, now rubbing intensely, getting as many morning itches out of the way as I could.

In the background I could hear a loud stream of water coming from the bathroom; it was still early. I confirmed that it was before school by glancing at the kitchen and reading the microwave's digital clock. It was clear that it was Tansu in the shower getting herself ready.

I stood up from the couch and dragged my aching feet into the kitchen and looked at the calendar on the wall next to the fridge. It was Thursday, a lukewarm morning. A moment of understanding struck me; everything about who I am settled in my brain and I was awake. Staring at the dates, I poked my index finger against today's square.

"I'm going to school today," I said to myself in monotone.

Semi-confident, I sauntered over to the closet by the front door and pulled out my backpack, along with a duffel bag. Lazily dragging them to the couch, I began unpacking a few things to wear. As I dug and shifted the clothes, I lamented in the fact that I no longer had a dresser, just these bags. Although her mom did tell me that they would arrange for me to have those things very soon, I couldn't wait for that. For now, this will do. I don't really mind this, but it would be nice to have some storage and my own bed again.

It didn't seem like it at first, but apparently, Tansu's room is big enough to squeeze in a second set of living, which is great. Until then, I had the couch and my bags. When picking out something to wear, I looked to my arm. All that was left of the deep wound was a long line of pinched skin, a very thin scar that covered almost the length of my forearm. I can explain this in any way I need to. For now, I wanted to avoid that as much as possible, so I grabbed a typical long-sleeve shirt and a pair of cropped jeans. I changed my clothes very quickly in the living room and set my dirty pajamas aside to be washed later.

Just as I got my shirt pulled over my head, I heard a door open. Tansu emerged from the steamy bathroom, with a towel wrapped around her. She stood in the hallway, holding the towel up over her chest with one hand and using her other hand to dry her hair with a washcloth. She didn't notice me at first. I was just admiring her; she was so pretty, much more attractive than I found myself. I was a little jealous and happy that I knew her to be a nice person. All the good-looking kids at school were jerks. She then turned to shut the door behind her and noticed I was awake and staring at her.

"Morning, Kim." She shuffled in my direction. "How are you feeling today?" I averted my eyes, awkwardly staring at my bag. I blushed. She's coming toward me in nothing but a towel.

"Don't know yet. I just woke up." I chuckled, pushing my messy, dirty fringe to the side and over my ear. "Tansu, don't you think you should get dressed?" I tried my best to look away but not make it seem like I was ignoring her.

She looked down at herself, then back to me and smiled, showing teeth.

"Oh, don't worry." She opened the towel to reveal that she was wearing underwear and a bra. Nothing overly exposing. "I'm decent." She stuck her tongue out then covered back up.

My expression went right to surprised and a little red.

"Well, that was surprising." I chuckled, feeling a little weird. I couldn't look directly at her.

"How do you mean?"

"Well, you're so damn shy around people at school. For you to open your towel like that is just uncharacteristic, I guess. Hell, I'm not really shy, but I still don't feel comfortable enough to do that."

"Well, I'm not doing anything. I mean, it's just underwear and it's just us here. I don't feel weird or anything, at least not with you." She said nicely.

"If you say so." I yawned again.

"Anyways, why are you dressed and up this early?" she asked, twirling some hair behind her head.

"I decided that I'm going to school today."

She looked at me with a slight tilt to her head.

"Are you sure? Do you think that's a good idea?" She sounded concerned.

"Not really. I just can't stand being cooped up all day. It sucks. Honestly, I'm nervous, but I need to go back some time, might as well be now."

"Yeah, I guess." She lowered her eyes to the floor like she was pondering some faraway thought. "Well, that's good, I'm proud of you. Lemme go get dressed. The bus will be here in about twenty minutes. I'll see you when it's time to go." Tansu said.

"Okay, I'm going to make sure I have everything in my bag."

She closed the bedroom door behind her, and I continued my backpack preparation. The first thing that caught my attention was a blue-covered notebook; the one I lent to Joey. I thought about him and relished the thought of seeing him soon. This is going to hit him hard as well. He is more concerned with the issues of others than the things that go on in his own life. He's going to be crushed when he hears. If he hasn't already. I zipped up the bag and threw it over my shoulder.

Tansu wasted no time getting dressed. When my backpack hit my back, she exited her room. I turned around to see her standing there, and my jaw dropped: a tight luminescent green t-shirt with a small cartoon tiger as a decal, accompanied by a thigh-high blue denim skirt and long black-and-white horizontal-striped leggings. The outfit was completed by a few bracelets, a green hairpin holding a bundle of fringe, and Converse sneakers. I was a bit awe-struck, to be honest. She approached me and took her bag from the floor, all the while I stared at her. She finally noticed.

"Kimmy, you okay? You sure you're up for school today? You look absolutely exhausted." She waved her hand in front of my face.

"I-I'm fine. It's just—" I smiled big. "You look great today. I can see you took a few tips from those fashion mags. I mean, seriously, where'd you find that skirt? It's really cool." I complimented her.

She turned beet red and rubbed her arm, rocking her body a little.

"You like it? My mom helped me pick out a few things for the new school year when we arrived. I've never really expressed my style until now. Is it too much?"

"No way. It's perfect. Seriously, I might have to fight off every boy in school. Maybe even a few girls." I winked. This got her even redder than I thought possible.

"I don't think that will happen, Kim." She said with puffed, embarrassed cheeks.

"No, really, you're gonna turn some heads, so be prepared for that."

She smiled kindly. I could tell she felt good about herself today. I'm glad she's opening up a little.

"The bus will be here soon. Let's go wait outside." She suggested.

"Good call." I then yawned.

As we waited by the road, I thought about how weird it would be going to school again. In reality, it hasn't been long, but it feels like school was another life I left behind. The thought of going back and being met by their judgmental eyes flipped my stomach; I can only imagine their reaction if they even knew the story. Undoubtedly, I will be confronted by someone. I'm not sure if I'm ready for that.

Tansu and I waited in silence; she was engrossed in the scrolling sky and my eyes were dropped to my feet. She noticed my slum and tapped her elbow against mine; stealing my attention and returning my wanting gaze with a tender smile. A smile that assured everything would work out okay.

When the bus pulled up and that nostalgic squeal of the tires hit my eardrums, my mind began branching off in random directions. Overwhelming thoughts of every class and teacher I would endure once again coiled around my throat and drowned me in itchy nerves. I took my seat with a heavy thud and tried my best to breathe.

Tansu sat across from me and pressed herself against the wall. It was quiet. I avoided staring out the window and instead traced over the folded leather patterns of the seat in front of me; allowing my vision to blur and those random ideas to fill my head. Until finally, I focused on a single one.

It was something I hadn't agreed with myself on; a difficult subject. It was Joey and how I would have to face him. I knew he would be upset for a variety of reasons; but which would he throw my way? Which manner of guilt will he bring up? It doesn't matter. . . I will admit to my faults. I will agree with his frustration and I will accept my punishment. Because I miss him.

My chest pounded along with the bumpy road. In a few minutes, we would arrive, and I would be in for the hardest fight so far; keeping my emotions in check. I can do this.

Turning my head to Tansu, I extended my voice.

"Tan."

She looked my way.

I spoke again, "If you see Joey before I do, tell him I'm in today."

She smirked, "Will do."

"Thanks."

The bus then took a slight turn onto the school driveway. The seven or so kids on the bus began moving around; slinging on their bags.

She kept her eyes on me, observing the tightness in my body. "Are you doing alright?" She asked.

I shrugged my shoulders, "I guess. Just nervous."

"I'll make sure to see you between every class. Keep your spirits up." She jeered.

I half-chuckled, "That'd be awesome."

In a minute, the bus eased to a halt and the doors opened. Everyone lifted themselves with dramatic displays of exhaustion and sauntered down the lane. We followed suit and stepped down onto the blacktop. A scattered hoard of deployed kids' bottle-necked the main doors. We found a place to fit with all the rest and it was there that I got my first taste of the day.

At least five different people took notice of me and couldn't help but stare. I made brief eye contact with one or two and only established a peripheral glance before directing my eyes to Tansu's back in front of me. I knew that there were more, but I didn't want to acknowledge them.

Waiting in the cafeteria before the first bell; Tansu followed me to a distant corner far away from the main collection of students. From what I could see, most here didn't notice, or didn't care.

But eventually more and more caught me in their scanning gaze, so I lowered my head and tried to hide behind my hair. I was still too tired to deal with anyone right now.

The first bell jingled, and everyone dispersed. Stricken by fear and reminiscence, I wandered the halls like all the hundreds of times before. A part of me was indeed glad to be back; I missed the smell of chemical floor cleaner, hand sanitizer, and grubby fingerprints on every locker. It was almost therapeutic to imagine myself walking down this hall as if these past two weeks never happened. Being here now, I could just about see that being true.

But I couldn't escape this foreboding aura that kept every person I slipped past an arm's length away. I was not hidden or unnoticed, as I wanted to be. It was just the opposite. However, no one approached me, perhaps that is thanks to Tansu being by my side at the moment. But she quickly said her goodbye as she split off into her own class.

I did my best to ghost through the halls and made it to my first class without being stopped. I sat in the back, back straight, and body tight. The class soon filled, and the teacher rose to the front of the room for the day's introduction. I was immediately noticed, but no attention was called to my sudden presence. I believed it to be intentional, a courtesy on my behalf.

My first class started out uneventful but notably pleasant in comparison to my expectations. Still, I found it hard to remain focused for long. It was very, very apparent that Alice was awake. Her presence fizzed in my brain like a carbonated whirlpool.

The teacher then rolled down the projector screen for a video about historical artists and the impact they had after their death. As the lights dimmed and the video started, a voice sprouted in my head and startled me.

"So, this is your school," Alice spoke loudly, trying hard to keep my attention on her.

I didn't respond, just shifted my eyes around; checking the people around me. Paranoia was apparent as her raspy voice churned.

"Now I see why you were so angry; this place is festering beneath the surface."

Can they hear her? I thought to myself, eyes widening with every rushed glance around the room. No one reacted in any way.

"Look at you; a prowling wolf among sleeping sheep. If only they knew what you were; what you have done." She snickered. "We can show them."

In my head, I whispered. "Get lost, Alice. Not today." I visibly scowled.

To my surprise, she listened. I felt her energy subside and the headache I didn't fully realize was there, simmered. I sighed, rubbing my eyes and keeping them locked on the projected lesson. The video continued for about twenty minutes at a low volume until it reached the end and the lights were switched back on. The teacher stood before us and started in on the questions.

It didn't take too long before the bell rang, and I slipped out of the room. One class was done; easy enough. The next class came quickly as I raced down the hall. I wanted to get there before anything could happen. I couldn't shake this feeling in my gut that the air was wrong somehow, but that didn't deter me from pushing forward.

The gym was my next destination. I was able to get there quickly; almost excited to spend the entire class running in circles around the basketball court. All of this energy piling up inside me needed to be released healthily, and this was a perfect opportunity.

Entering the double doors, I saw most of the class was gathered at the bleachers, waiting for the coach. I entered as another student left and then stopped in the doorway when I saw their eyes on me. They *all* stared intently; confused, frozen. I looked at them with tight lips and one hand on my shoulder strap.

"They're staring at me," Alice said; discomfort upfront.

In my head, I responded, "Definitely not." I licked my lips and continued; joining the group but keeping my distance. They released me from their scrutinizing eyes, and we all waited for class to begin. A few minutes after the bell rang, the coach exited his office to start the day.

"Alright everyone," He firmly clapped his hands together, addressing us. "We're going to have a free period today, I have to-oh, Kimberly, I didn't know you'd be joining us today." He stared at me.

I grit my teeth and shifted in my shoes. "Uh. . ." My dry throat itched, "I didn't tell anyone, Coach Miller."

It was clear in his face that he was trying to sort out an appropriate response; tilting his head up slightly with lowered brows and a contemplative eye. "Well," He cleared his throat, "It's good to have you back."

A heated discomfort filled the air, giving a chill up my spine.

"A-anyways, free period; like I said. Go nuts." He gave a wide fake smile and walked away from the group.

We all moved to the other end of the gymnasium and split apart to change in the locker rooms. Most of the girls stayed relatively close to each other; changing in the open while I, as well as another two girls, separated and changed in single stalls.

Exiting the locker room in a looser shirt and shorts, I immediately started my jog around the room. Instantly liberated, I relished in the light flicks of wind as I picked up speed. The gust pushed through my hair and scraped by my ears. I was fast; my legs carried the weight of my body with ease and the way I rounded corners was tight and smooth. I supplied little effort and my muscles surpassed my own expectations.

Ten laps; half a mile without slowing down. A couldn't help but smile with this accomplishment, but I knew the reasons why; it wasn't entirely my doing. I glanced at the others as they shot hoops, played catch and a few girls walked along the edges.

Another ten laps made a mile and I reduced my speed to a fast walk. It had begun affecting me by lap fourteen. My heartbeat picked up and my breathing was irregular; perfect. All this pent-up energy was being expelled, leaving me feeling more and more like myself.

Feeling the gentle heat rise off my skin, I fluffed my shirt and closed my eyes. In my mind, I imagined the borderline of the basketball court. I pictured my feet moving along the center of the thin red line and as I came up to a corner, I slowed and took the turn; balancing on the edge. It was vividly clear, even with my eyes shut; I could feel where I was, where they were. Opening my eyes, I confirmed my feet to be exactly where I thought. This gave me goosebumps and made me wonder how else I have changed; how much of the change was me and not her.

"You should lift the weights." Alice chimed in with a joke.

I scoffed lightly, finding her comment a little funny.

"Maybe I can finally dead-lift more than thirty pounds," I responded with sarcasm.

Just then, I felt a tickle across my skin. Following that sensation, I turned my head to the center of the room and swatted my left hand in the air. A tennis ball hurdling in my direction was slapped away and send flying towards the doorway. My feet firmly planted themselves as I stared in disbelief at my own action. A quiet girl, Bonnie, was the one who lost control of the ball and gave me a shocked look as well.

Eyes unstable, I saw two of the guys playing basketball witness my deflection and watch for a response.

"S-sorry, Kim." Bonnie apologized hastily.

She apprehensively stared from behind her round glasses and wispy bangs. I smirked at her.

"It's. . . it's no problem." I said softly, throat dry.

"Nice reflexes." She added, relief present in her voice.

She hurried over to retrieve the ball and I continued forward with my cool-down lap.

Admittedly, that scene didn't make me feel on the spot. It did, however, make me feel really cool for a brief moment. I only wish people I knew and cared about could've seen that. I pondered as I rounded the next corner before starting another jog. I wanted to test myself, run as fast as I could to see how well my body would keep up. I imagined the fight with Destro, and how quickly Alice and I dodged and attacked; I wondered how it could translate to something like this. But I knew where I was and what was acceptable behavior. If I ran full speed, it might draw attention.

Two more laps and the coach came back out to give us a ten-minute warning. It was time to get changed and clean ourselves off. Returning to the bathroom, I crammed into the same stall and changed back into my jeans and shirt. Normally, I would use the towels the school provided to wipe the sweat from my body, but that wasn't necessary today.

Within a few minutes, I returned to my backpack and slung it over my shoulder; ready to embrace the hallway once again. Right now, I wish I had my CD player to at the very least, set a barrier. I knew I could sense their discomfort that everyone around me, all day, had a portion of consideration reserved for me. The bell rang.

The noise level rose with the filling corridors and I quickly fell victim to the sting in my skull. My stride reduced and I felt my head swell; my senses were fluctuating. It was bizarre; there was this piece of me deep inside that I could feel reaching out and connecting with everyone around me. The heat they emitted, the vague summation of their emotions; little inklings of what they felt were imminent at a minor level.

I was like an antenna; receiving various signals from my peers. The more I listened in and embraced the flow, the dizzier I became. All at once, my body swayed and I braced myself against a set of lockers.

Let go. . . Ignore it. I thought to myself, but a high-pitched ringing erupted in my head; and with it, came the voices.

Disembodied murmurs at first. Random nonsense that didn't apply to anything at all. But then, I could hear people around me. My eyes shot open, bloodshot down to the other end of the hall where I saw two people sharing a conversation. They each looked in my direction, then whispered.

Look. I heard. *It's her.*

They must be fifty feet away, but I could hear their whispers.

Tension rose in my chest and a cold sweat formed on my brow. Instinct triggered and I jolted from the locker, moving swiftly down the hall towards my next class. As I slipped past numerous faces; I collected phrases.

Is that? . . . Did you hear about her dad? . . . Kim. . .

Every uttered word was expected and discarded. The school was quickly informed of my attendance, but no one would confront me. That's all I wanted.

"Oh good, the worms are wriggling in your ears. You sure you can keep it under lock and key?" Alice's voice overpowered the others; essentially muting the world excluding her.

I reached a turn that was lacking in students and slowed my pace, then responded as calmly as I could.

"I knew the risks coming here today and I know what will happen if I let you win. But that won't happen."

In this more secluded hallway, I moved by three different students all leaning in their lockers. The screaming voices expanded one final time before receding a bit; giving me a chance to breathe.

"Are those voices I hear. . . Are they coming from The Ditch?" I asked under my breath.

"They are. You're connected after all."

"I wish they'd shut up. Every time they get riled up, for whatever reason, it sets me on edge."

"Yes, but when you are in that mental state, your senses heighten. It's useful."

I shook my head, "Not here. I just want to be normal. . . at least for today." I groaned, already tired.

Up ahead, I caught movement and looked up to see someone wearing a hoodie turn the corner; coming my way. It was clearly a guy, keeping his head low and just going about his business. But as he drew closer, I found myself gradually moving away from his lane, closer to the wall.

The moment our paths crossed; my entire body was shaken. A creeping electric wave slid across my skin from head to toe and back, and I stopped.

Turning my head to his back, I watched him continue down the hall without a change in his posture.

Alice seemed to *hold her breath*. Before uttering a soft, curious "Hmm."

I felt it, something familiar but with a different taste. "You think. . ." I started.

"I don't know." She answered.

A deep breath filled my lungs and I marched on to my next class. Somehow, I was inexplicably calm. Which to me made no sense, but I can't deny the lack of trembling in my bones. Strange.

I made it a few more feet down the hall and tried to immerse myself in the quiet. When suddenly a voice shouted from behind me.

"Hey!"

Expecting no one, in particular, I turned myself around and finished my step before coming to a dead stop.

"Joey." My mouth became loose.

He ran towards me; the guy in the hoodie still went along his way in the background. Joey had this glowing face and an excited stumble; like a little kid at a playground. He reached me, stopping a short distance away and stood tall with glee.

A flutter in my gut brought excitement to my eyes as I took in his image. Every day, nothing new, he wore the same old hat and leather jacket and black skinny jeans.

I was almost awestruck, seeing him like this for the first time in weeks. I didn't know what to say, so I stared.

"You're here. I'm. . . so glad." He smiled big, cheeks turning red.

"H-hey, Joey. It's great to see you. How've you been?" I stammered nervously.

Almost immediately, his bright smile started to fade when he noticed my outward appearance. Depressed baggy eyes, red nose, and slightly dirty hair. I wasn't my best, I knew that.

"Kim. . . You look, different." He slouched.

His now frowning face caused mine to sink; feeling slight shame.

"I'm tired; but I'm here and that's what counts, right?"

"You're right. But shouldn't you have maybe slept or taken a shower first?" He gave a misplaced grin.

I frowned. He took note of my low demeanor and reeled back the jokes.

"Hey, relax. I'm only joking. You look fine." He smiled again.

I didn't say anything. I was stuck in a perpetual middle ground. On one hand, I was ecstatic to see him and wanted nothing more than to spend the rest of the day catching up. One the other, that wall I built years ago was still holding and now, there was another layer.

He noticed my silence. "You good, bud?"

I shrugged. "I suppose. How about you? How's. . . uh, how's shop class; did you finish the little car?" I asked neutrally.

He shook his head; amused. "Nope, don't ask me how but I managed to break it in half." He admitted, holding back a bemused grin.

I raised an eyebrow, "How did you man-" He cut me off.

"Ah, don't ask. Not my finest moment."

I snickered to myself. “Hey, did you see Tansu at all?”

“What, today? No, not yet.” He said.

“What about when I was gone; did you see her much?” I asked.

“Oh yeah, I spoke to her a few times; asked her how you were once I heard the news. She wouldn’t say much. . . but she did give me her number so I could call you.”

A pause.

“How did you hear, by the way?” I asked quietly, pressing my back against a locker.

His posture changed; becoming more slouched.

“They had an assembly. They didn’t say a lot, besides that, your dad passed away and. . . that you wouldn’t be coming back for a while.”

A lump formed in my throat. “What else did they say?”

“Not sure. As soon as I heard that, I left. I ran straight to your house, but you weren’t there. I couldn’t get any closer to the road, I just felt so sick.”

His voice was becoming raspy; less effort given with each word as he receded. A tremble in my lips introduced the feeling of tears as potent regret filled my chest.

“I’m sorry Joey.”

“Don’t be. It’s not your fault. . . I just wish I knew the truth. All I had was the lies and rumors being spread throughout the school.” Joey let his bag slide from his shoulder and rest on the floor and crossed his arms firmly.

“Why didn’t you call me, Kim? Why couldn’t you tell me what was going on?” He asked dejectedly.

My tongue tasted like cardboard and blood. I bit the inside of my cheek, frustration rising as I beat the hell out of myself within.

“To be honest. . .” I began, choking on my own words, “I never even considered calling you, or anyone. Not until it was too late to have meaning. Things have just been different lately; complicated.” I half-explained.

He sighed; a dry tension surrounded us.

“I can’t imagine. Can you help me understand? I don’t wanna be left behind; not with this.” He asked with trepidation.

I rubbed my neck, then scratched the icy flesh. “I know. . . My dad, he killed himself. I was at Tansu’s and when I came home, I found him.” I stated.

His eyes shifted between mine, though I was not connected with his gaze. I could feel his trembling begin, that soul shredding chaos erupting in his body. Confusion. “Jesus.” He muttered. “I-I don’t know what to say. Your dad was nice to me when we were younger, and I know it hit hard after your mom passed. . . but to-” He tried to come to grips with it.

“It’s, whatever. I’m sort of over it already.” The words dripped from my mouth as a light-headed wave washed over me.

“Over it; are you serious? I hope not, that’d make you a psychopath.” He joked while still refraining from sounding too playful.

I shrugged, “No. I’m completely sane.”

“How could you say that then? I know he had his problems, but he was still your dad.” He pleaded, concern in his voice.

I glared at him; slightly aggressive but still in my slum. "Joey, I don't want to be an ass-hole, but you really didn't know my dad. Not how he was after my mom died."

He bit his lip, frustrated. "How so?"

I scoffed, looking away from him down the hallway. "You want the truth?"

"Of course." He didn't hesitate.

"Fine then." I locked eyes with him, a fire in my stare. "He was an abusive drunk. Mostly verbal, but when he felt extra ballsy, he'd hit me, push me and grab me." I stated harshly.

As my words slapped him in the face, his expression became more and more horrified. That horror then turned to anger, and a balled fist was the outcome.

"He- I knew it. I fucking knew it." His teeth crashed together; holding back years of suspicion and building angst.

I watched him struggle inside. My heart was racing but my outward appearance was stone. "That's the truth. So ya, I'm over it."

He jostled his feet but remained before me. "Kim I-" He started.

"Don't. There's nothing you could've done." I assured him with a neutral voice.

He stood awkwardly for a moment; looking to me, then down the hall, and to his feet. "I don't know how I feel." He admitted.

"Welcome to my world." I tapped my foot, releasing the stress.

"I heard you and Tansu were living together now. That's good; I'm glad child services didn't take you away. I don't know what I'd ever do without you." He chuckled, trying to find a lighter tone.

When he said that, I was overcome by a hostile sadness. The idea that he still holds me as such a centerpiece in his life frustrated and confused me in so many ways.

"You'd probably be happier not having to worry about me." I sulked.

His face went straight. "Why would you say something like that?"

I bit my lip. "Because it's true. You shouldn't waste your energy worrying about me."

"I worry because I care." He stood upright and stepped closer. I pressed my back tightly against the locker, backing away as much as I could. My hands began to shake.

"Why are you still here, Joey?" My head lowered and my voice cracked. I wrapped my arms around my body, holding myself tight.

"Why am I- Because you're my best friend." He spoke from his heart and now held a new look of fear on his face.

"Your best friend? What kind of friend would. . ." I stopped and let out a huge, hot breath of angst.

"I abandoned you. I couldn't let you get too close; it would have destroyed me. . . destroyed *us*." I whimpered.

As he spoke, I heard the profound sorrow in his voice. "That kind of pain isn't something you should face alone. I can help; I know what it's like to be burdened by grief." He pleaded.

"Yes, but this is different. I couldn't before and I can't now. Not now. Not after everything that's happened." My eyes welled with tears.

He threw his arms up a little, "If anything, now is the time to let me in! Don't ask me to watch you wither away. I can't do that again, Kim." He shed the first tear. I looked up to his face and saw those rosy cheeks swelling and his eyes bloodshot.

I bit my tongue. My voice got quiet, so quiet he had to lean his head in slightly.

"I have known you for so long Joey. Your mom always treated me like a daughter, your whole family is some of the nicest people I've met. If I involved you at all, you and everyone you love would be in terrible danger. You don't understand."

"Danger? What are you talking about?"

My jaw trembled as the tears stacked.

"No," I whispered.

My mind started to break away from my current reality. My soul felt tugged, drifting away from where I stood and being lifted high above the school. I felt the air shift and the world turn; blissful winds swept my conscience away and brought me to a place where I felt safe. A box. My ears were muted; his voice could not reach me here. I could forget, let go of what ails me, and just float.

He reached out and grabbed my left bicep gently; this action snapped me back to reality. I twitched, then relaxed. My face was dampening from the hushed crying. I felt his eyes on me; waiting for a response. I sniffled and started breathing heavily.

He released my arm. "I do understand." He said with the heaviest, miserable tone I have ever heard from him and my heart hit the floor. He started to walk away. My chest got stiff and my breathing nearly stopped.

He's leaving.

My thoughts began to spiral out of control. A thousand invisible punches smashed into my chest and gut, wobbling my knees and forcing me to the floor. I moved my left hand to my throat and held it, trying to steal a wisp from my lungs; but only light gasps escaped and a small squeak of fear. I cried, my knees resting on the dirty floor.

This is the best option. It kills me, but at least he will be safe. That's what I told myself over and over as his footsteps got quieter. It was at that moment that I truly understood how he must have felt that day and every day since then.

He came to visit me after my mom died. He wanted to see me and be a shoulder for me to cry on. I heard him at the front door, tried to force his way past my dad, but only got knocked to the ground. I remember my dad yelling at him; cursing and threatening him.

Joey never gave up, he ran into the woods and snuck around back, grabbing a handful of dirt and throwing it at my window. A shard of glass from a broken bottle was in the dirt and ended up slicing his hand. I saw him waving to me from the ground below; his hand dripping blood, but still had a smile on his face.

I will never forgive myself for being so heartless and I will never forget the defeat in his face when I stared him down and closed the blinds. In my head, that was it. He was gone from my life. However, when I saw him next, he still greeted me happily. He didn't bring my mother up, he just tried to make me happy. He didn't learn anything about her death until a few months later when I broke down in front of him. I took my anger and sadness out on him. Ruthlessly.

Still, he continued to be my friend no matter how many days I avoided contact or got angry at life. He was always there when I needed him and especially when I didn't. He is the greatest person, the greatest friend, and I. . . I can't do this.

"Joey!!!"

My feet carried me as fast as they could until I was upon him and threw my arms around him. On my toes, I buried my face into the back of his neck and cried out loud.

"Please don't leave me. Please don't go." I burrowed my face deep into his leather jacket, taking in the old familiar smell.

It was quiet. He didn't respond at first, he didn't even take a breath. To my surprise, I felt both of his hands gently touch my arms. Then he spun around and took hold of my shoulders, eternally gazing into my eyes. A frail smile crept on his face and he closed the gap between us. My eyes were wide open, looking over his shoulder with my nose stuffed into the jacket.

"I'm not going anywhere." He tenderly spoke into my ear.

I let my eyes ease shut and my body relaxed a little. The tears started to dry up. We held each other in public, observed by who knows how many others. I felt total bliss. Because for once, there were no demons, no threat, no pain. Just us. To speak, I pulled my head back just enough to uncover my mouth.

"There is so much I want to tell you. It just isn't safe." I whispered timidly into his ear.

"Not safe?" He questioned.

"Just. . . listen to me. A lot is going on; things that you'd never believe even if I told you. I can tell you one thing; just one. Someday soon, I will sort all of this chaos out and things will go back to normal."

"Like they used to be?" he whispered somberly.

"Better." I let out a gleeful, smile, and laugh, "So much better. You just have to bear with me, okay?" I sniffled.

"I've been patient this long. I can wait." He leaned back and held my shoulders again. That sincere, love-filled smile of his just kept me entranced. Then he did something I never saw coming. He leaned in very slow and quietly kissed my forehead. Just a light touch, just enough to express what he could not easily say. That wasn't all, he proceeded to remove his jacket. The faded black leather, with a dark red lining, was now draped over me.

"I'll see you later, Kim." My arms fell limp to the side. I watched him as he stuffed his hands into his pockets and walked back down the hall, his bag swaying by his side.

When he was out of sight, my fingers moved on their own to my forehead and touched the space where his lips were placed. Then I dug my tired grip into the jacket that he placed on my shoulders and lifted the leather to my nose where I inhaled deeply. I had butterflies and an uncontrollable smile was slapped onto my face.

Maybe today wouldn't be so bad after all.

Chapter 18 – Chains

A metallic grind reverberated through the semi-vacant hallway through my locker door peeling open. The contents seemed detached from memory. Pens and pencils well-stocked; tucked neatly in a fabric sleeve that hung on the inside of the door. Lining the walls were a couple of drawings I had done throughout the year that weren't entirely garbage. Not as personalized as some students prefer, but enough to know this space is mine and mine alone.

Hanging on a small hook within was a long sleeve shirt I wore weeks prior; it smelled like old perfume and paper. I removed it from the nagging hook and stuffed it into my bag to be brought home and washed. The bell had already rung but I had no intention of going to class. I needed time to myself; so, my plan was to sit in the lunchroom and wait, seeing as lunch was coming up next anyway.

A long series of relaxing breaths helped me balance the thumping of my heart. Setting my bag on the ground I pulled both arms through the overly long sleeves and removed his jacket. Holding it in front of me, I admired the stitching in the leather; the red lining and popped collar. I smiled so wide that it made my cheeks hurt. Then I hung the jacket up on the hook and placed my fingers on the sleeve, gliding them down and closing the door.

In the hall where I stood, I saw two or three other kids either just getting to their locker or closing it and rushing along. I started my slow walk to the lunchroom, each step taken with minimal haste. Even though I was supposed to be in class, I figured any teacher who saw me would not get too upset if they saw me wandering, given my situation.

I walked by many doors; some open with a lecture boasted into the hall while most others were closed and only visible through the small windows every door had. I peeked through those gaps without slowing down and caught glances from other people; though I wasn't fully looking at them, just looking in general.

Every so often, I would catch Alice's face in a reflection; she was present but reserved. I knew she was watching me, observing my feelings, and soaking in the electric atmosphere. All this stress and negativity was like inhaling vitamin vapor. I'm surprised she was being so complacent; perhaps she was first assessing, and planning. Only *she* knows.

I reached the end of this hall and turned left down another long stretch with only lockers and two bathrooms. No one else was around and I instantly felt relief with the open space. However, it wouldn't last long. As I rounded the corner, I heard one of the classroom doors open and close behind me. It wasn't worth noting, so I continued along.

A new dilemma burrowed its way into my head; when the lunchroom fills with students, I will probably be confronted by at least a few other kids. Neutral people that exchange greetings and short conversations on occasion. I know I can't avoid it forever, but I don't entirely feel like dealing with that scrutiny.

Maybe Tansu and Joey will sit outside with me; get some fresh air and forget about it all.

That thought brought a hopeful gleam to my eyes. And yet, there was a pit in my stomach. A tinge in my chest that almost felt like a warning. Then it occurred to me; in the shadow of my own footsteps was another set trailing me. It wasn't obvious at first, but it became all too clear when I slowed my own steps to let them pass, and they didn't. The distance remained the same and the dynamic charge around me was consistent. I stopped.

As expected, the pitter-patter behind me came to a halt as well. I listened, gathering hints and feelings of who it was that would be following so close behind. It was sickeningly familiar; obvious to anyone with an inkling of our history. I would be stupid not to recognize that very particular presence.

I closed my eyes; my entire mood shifted.

"It's true. You're back." Stacy opened the conversation.

My eyes slowly peeled open and I turned around to see her standing ten feet away. Her arms were loose by her sides and there was no purse or handbag over her shoulder. In her hand was a large keyring with a laminated tag on it; a hall pass.

"I am." I said in monotone.

I could feel Alice looking through my eyes. "Hmm, what a *lovely* girl. Her blood is flowing so smoothly."

When Alice spoke, I got a jolt of cynicism. My lower lip trembled, holding back a wide grin. I kept myself steady and let the feeling subside.

Stacy began, speaking in an odd sincerity that I didn't think she was capable of.

"I. . . I saw you through the door, and wanted to talk to you." Her voice was docile; gestures minimal.

"Oh yeah? I'm sure you've got lots to say." My voice was rigid; irate.

Her face looked tired; she wasn't wearing her usual snide look and confident pose. She was different; humble. I've never seen her face so soft and unwound.

She could tell my defenses were raised; an invisible barrier of distrust and hate separated us, but her side was quiet.

"I just wanted to say. . . that I'm sorry about your dad." She spoke with zero hostility.

My jaw unhinged and my expression lessened. "You're sorry?" I repeated.

She nodded, clearly uncomfortable.

My heart began racing, confused, and scared of her true intentions. *Don't trust her. Never trust her.* Our colorful history taught me that and this is no different. My irritation spiked.

"Sorry. . ." I mouthed again.

Alice stepped up and started prodding my mind. "What a fickle word. Do you honestly think she feels any remorse? It's a ploy; she wants to weaken you like before."

With her words came a chill that twisted my spine and caused my breathing to shake. I couldn't look Stacy in the eye, instead choosing to look at the floor.

"Oh yeah, you must feel *so* bad for me. That's why you were picking on Tansu while I was gone, right?" I declared with a constricted throat.

She bit her tongue, "That was. . . a lapse in judgment. I don't know why I was doing that, but I stopped."

She then got a little annoyed, whether it was at me or herself I wasn't sure. "Look, I just wanted to give you my condolences like a normal person and get back to class. So, again I'm sorry and sorry for your friend too." Her words were less sincere and rushed.

I processed this; conflicted by her change in heart and my own. Underneath my skin, I was writhing. Unable to accept her words as truth and instead choosing to twist them into some malicious desire to harm me further. But was she capable of such cruelty?

"A word; sorry. Apparently, that's powerful enough to wipe away everything she's done. You must be joking." Alice mocked. "Where is that fire I tasted when the cop pressed your sensitive buttons? I want to see that explosion; I want to feel that hate. You've wanted this for so long!" She growled.

I didn't need Alice to pump me with demented confidence; I was already there. But a single thread of my conscience held me back. But, it's strange. All the while I was fighting to stay myself, I had forgotten the reason. Searching through the archives of who I am, revealed no motive; nothing to keep me from this. It was all a blur, and for a second or two, I had forgotten my name.

She rotated on an axis and started to walk back the way she came. My head twisted and compressed with confusion. A sudden shockwave of dissonant fury soaked into my pores.

"She's luring you in. . . so, take a step." Alice's words slithered.

I felt an uncontrollable pressure seize my muscles. The microwaving buzz in my brain urged my feet forward, slowly. My head hung low and my shoulders were slumped. Then, a burst of power from within hurdled me forward and I reached out for her shoulder. Spinning her around with violent force, I met her eyes with mine. I drank all the shock in her face and could sense her fear in the way she leaned back. I jabbed my finger at her nose, teeth flared like a rabid dog's.

"After everything you've done, you think you can just walk up and say you're sorry!?" I snarled.

She looked scared, "I just. . . I realized I was wrong in a lot of ways. I know saying sorry doesn't-"

"Doesn't what? Make up for your bullshit that never had a reason or explanation?" I threw depravity in her face. "It doesn't even come close." I planted my feet on the floor, my voice growing louder; more distorted.

"Hey, back off. If you don't want to accept my apology that's fine. But I was trying to be a better person and I figured you might appreciate that just a little." Her brows lowered.

"Maybe the old me would've like to hear it, but not anymore." My voice wasn't entirely my own. There was some filter breaking through; static and low. I didn't notice this change or anything else; I was blinded.

"Whatever!" She half-shouted. "I'm gonna get back to class now."

Then, I lost control of my body for just a moment; but a moment was all she needed. In a split second, my fist went from being balled by my side to vaulting at her face. Three knuckles contacted her lower jaw, lashing her head to the side with a snapping force. A splash of blood flew and landed on the floor as well as painted my knuckle.

She staggered a step backward and then fell down onto her ass. The impact was so fast; so sudden that her brain was lagging behind. She held her jaw, shaking as the deep purple bruise began to form.

"W-what the fuck, Kim!?"

Once her brain caught up with her body, she lifted herself up on one shaky arm and wiped the blood from her split lip. I didn't realize right away, but the whites of my eyes were now a shallow black, and my irises were glowing purple. But Stacy didn't see my eyes; her vision and mind were dazed from the long-overdue punch.

"I can't believe you just hit me! That was uncalled for!"

Before she could get another word, I was taking a full stride in her direction and throwing another fist her way. This punch collided with the side of her head; knocking her flat on the ground. My eyes were wide, demonic, and lacking any humanity or sympathy. I crammed my fist around her neck, lifting her up off the floor. She gasped for air, placing her hands on my wrist, trying to pry it apart.

"K-Kim, what are you d—let. . . Let me go!" she begged. I looked into her eyes again and she could see mine; the terror set in.

I gave a devilish grin and released a high-pitched cackle that echoed through the halls. The lights in the hall began to flicker rapidly until some of the bulbs burst with a deafening pop. The glass rained down upon us, lining the floor with hundreds of razor shards.

The newfound veil of black shrouded us in what felt like a new world. The power that flowed through me was seeping out into the hallway. Some locker doors began to slightly crunch inward, and posters taped to the concrete walls tore and fell down. My power created an invisible whirlwind of pure hatred that surrounded me unceasingly.

I tightened my fingers around her throat, crushing her windpipe. She clawed at my arms, trying to break free. Gasping for air, she opened her mouth wide, squealing. Out of nowhere, I felt a stabbing pain in my spine, which caused me to drop her. I cringed forward as my bones began to stretch.

Stacy watched in disbelief as my hair began to lengthen and turn black. Every single strand stretched and pulled away from my scalp, drawing small beads of blood to the surface and rolling down the side of my head. My fringe now covered my eyes, but the glow of my irises shined through the gaps. My skin was overcome by the deep light-gray tone and my mouth dripped blood to the floor as the stitches sealed my lips together.

"What. . . are you?" she cried.

Silence.

Alice closed her eyes and lifted her head, letting an easy exhale push to the ceiling. She opened her eyes and looked down at Stacy who was frozen in place. A grin split across my face, "To you, a nightmare."

My head lowered and the grin disappeared. Intent eyes locked on to her and my body idled. Stacy slid back a few inches, her body unresponsive. Amused, I stepped forward and reached out; taking hold of her by the collar bone. Her breathing hastened as I slid my thin fingertips behind the fragile bone and paused.

"Say you're sorry." I licked my lips.

"I-I'm. . ." She could barely talk. "I'm sorry."

With minimal effort, I pulled my hand back, snapping her collar bone outward. Horrendous screams erupted from her chest and her hands shot up to the protruding bone.

"Stop screaming!" I shouted with a gurgling moan and punched her in the chest; knocking the wind out of her. Before her screams could start again, I gripped her head tightly and planted her face to the floor. Small shards of glass dug into her skin as she attempted to pull away, as well as recover her breath.

She struggled; wriggling like a worm cut in half. Then, I proceeded to drag her face across the floor through the massive amount of glass. The razor dust stabbed and tore through her flesh layer by layer; leaving a trail of deep red blood.

Her cries were muffled by the lack of air and the floor beneath her mouth. At the end of the drag, I raised her head up a few inches and she took the moment to inhale deeply. But there would be no reprieve, not so soon. As she drew her breath, I smashed her face back down to the floor.

Her head bounced off the cheap tiles and a loud crack noise filled the hallway as she hit. Her nose was now pouring blood, along with her split lip and the many lacerations on her face. She was still.

I released her head and ogled at her bloody face as it lay on the side. I delicately lay my palm over her ear and jostled her head side to side; then stood myself upright. An evil grin decorated my face as I absorbed the scene. I felt calm; not entirely submerged in this reality. In my mind, I was living out a twisted fantasy dreamt up while I cried alone in my room as a child. But here, in the real world, Stacy was dying.

A twitch caught my attention. Stacy's eye started to open but it was clear she was in a traumatized daze. I watched her arms and legs come to life and her body slowly started to receive proper signals. A shaken flutter pulsed from her lips but that was all. She was petrified to do anything, but still, she made a brave attempt to get up. Alice raised an eyebrow; impressed.

"Wow. Look at you; guess that tough girl shit isn't entirely an act." Alice complimented.

Stacy somehow managed to get to a down-dog position. Barely able to hold her head up, her arms trembled uncontrollably. The sight of her face dripping blood to a growing pool beneath was exhilarating; empowering. I almost forgot this feeling; it was beyond description. I wanted more, I had to have more.

I lifted my leg the slightest amount and pushed her over with a light thud. "Oops." Alice giggled.

Stacy limply fell to the floor and rolled onto her back. Her mouth opened wide and she did her absolute best to breathe and contain herself.

"P-please stop." She cried like a scared child.

Alice sighed, disappointed with her resolve. "And just how many times have *you* been asked to stop?"

"I know!" Stacy abruptly yelled. Her chest rose and fell rapidly; her terror animated. "I'm a piece of shit! I did so many horrible things to you and I'm so sorry! Just please. . ." She hollered, blubbering with her face soaked in bloody tears. "I want my mom." She finished tenderly.

I leaned down to her level, placing my lips close to her ear, and this time it was *me* that whispered. "So do I."

Then, I felt a new presence. Lifting my head on high alert I directed my gaze down the hall where we had come from. Around the corner was still well-lit so I could see a shadow on the wall as this person approached the corner. I watched carefully as they turned and stopped the moment their eyes met the dusky black.

"What in the world?" The voice asked out loud; referring to the damaged lights.

Blurry and concealed, I stood myself up above Stacy's immobilized body and turned fully towards them. A deep shadow was cast over the left side of his body from the hallway light above; it was the History teacher Mr. Kel. I closed my eyes and *felt* the room around me.

"And so, it begins." Alice snickered happily.

Kel, oblivious to the horror beyond the veil, stepped into the darkness. His feet crunched on broken glass, but he persisted forward. As he drew nearer, I stepped to the side and aligned myself with the locker doors.

My right hand tensed. Slowly, silently, a single nail grew out from my pointer finger until the tip hovered above the floor. He was a few feet from us and stopped. His vision had adjusted enough to see somebody on the floor.

His heartbeat was audible to me, as was the shifting of his eyes in the dark. Holding my breath, I remained undetected to his left and watched as he leaned forward. "Is that-" He started.

Then, I ambushed. Erupting from the shadows I threw my single claw at his neck and slashed right through; leaving him staggering to the side gripping his throat. Hot red blood spat out with force and painted my face and teeth. All balance evaporated and his frightened body thrashed into the other lockers.

Gurgling loudly, the body fluid emptied from his veins and down his shirt. He looked around desperately when his eyes caught the glint of my own. Open wide with satisfaction, I watched his fall to the floor.

Alice spoke, her voice electric and sharp. "Your soul is dirty; I can feel the despair and regret. Shame, it isn't much, but I'll take it all." She stated and then fully extended her other claws.

Kel glared desperately at us as the life drained from his body, helpless to do anything about it. With claws fully unsheathed, we motioned to finish him off. Just as I threw my claws at his chest, I felt the tiniest gust of wind brush past my face. Within a blink, a new silhouette stood between the two of us. This new arrival had a tight grip around my wrist; stopping my attack an inch short.

My arm trembled as I continued to apply force. Then I felt a cooling wave of new energy rinse over my skin and instantly my offense turned to defense.

Attempting to pull my arm away, I caught a peculiar glimpse. In the dark, I could see the glow of another Teufel's eyes beneath a dense hood.

"Impossible! There's no way you could have snuck up on me." Alice stated worriedly.

This character didn't respond. Most details were lost beneath the hood, but I could see it was in fact a boy. His eyes were fixated on ours but strangely enough, there was no hostility, no blaring alarms in my ears.

He seemed docile. All except for his grip which was unlikely to escape without extreme force. Simultaneously, our ears perked up as a soft clamoring approached the same corner Kel had come from. Both of our heads whipped to the side, but the stranger took this chance to do something unexpected.

He lifted his free hand from concealment and directed a single fingertip to my forehead. A soft purple glow emitted from the tip and vanished into my skin as he jabbed me. In that motion, my body tripled in weight and crippling dizziness squeezed my head. Disoriented, I stumbled in place while he held me by the wrist.

"Shit." Alice groaned.

Out of nowhere, a blinding white light sprouted from nothing to my left. I glanced over and was absorbed by the enveloping glow that seemed to cast no shadow and had minimal effect on the darkness around us. The light morphed into a standing rectangle; a door, I quickly gasped. It opened inward and released a mist that rolled along the ground.

The stranger spoke very low. "This cannot happen." And then plunged us through the frame with inhuman strength.

We landed on what seemed to be the softest sand I had ever felt. The shock he induced had dissipated but was quickly replaced by a new agony. Lying on my side in this blinding area, I angled my head to look back through the doorway where I could see the stranger illuminated by the effervescent light. He looked at me with patient eyes and a tight-lipped frown. His purple eyes dimmed and revealed the gentle green beneath. It was him; the boy I didn't recognize.

Peering through the door, I glanced past him and saw a few more people happen upon the scene. He turned to face them and endure their terrified screams at the sight of Mr. Kel and Stacy. Then, the door shut without making a sound.

All at once, the gravity around me started to crush my body. A new furious thrashing of my very DNA raped my body with unparalleled force. This feeling in my skull and throughout my veins was similar to the night where Sin attempted to pry away my soul.

"Alice!?" I screamed in pain.

"Hold on!" Her voice echoed.

She then rolled onto her stomach and spotted another door fifteen or so feet away. She dug her elbows into the sand and began crawling frantically with every fiber of her being. Every second that passed, I could feel my existence being snuffed away. The blood which painted my skin flaked off and floated freely in the air before turning to dust; cleansing me. Looking through the layer of black over my eyes, I started to sink inside my own consciousness, fading and falling in an infinite loop. Everything, even parts of me that I never knew I could feel, was experiencing an agonizing gouging sensation that left me unable to speak, think or react in any way besides watch as the door drew closer.

With a final effort, Alice dug one foot into the ground and launched herself the closing distance and busted through the door. We rolled out, back into the real world, and hit the floor with my full body weight.

Chapter 19 - Pieces

A slow rushing wind slipped between my ears as I lie unconscious somewhere unknown. I could feel my body on top of soft carpet, but my mind was swimming in a dream that wasn't my own. A series of rapidly flashing images invaded my eyelids and assaulted my senses with screams, voices, and hysterical tears. Faces of children, dirty and unspeakably sad; locked in a room with minimal light and comfort. Then, aggression infected the air and chaos ensued. The children became hostile; eyes red and teeth gnawing. A piercing ring filled the air and the room became black.

A fearful burst stabbed my gut as the visions settled and I found myself living in this scenario. However, the children weren't vicious; they were mismanaged. A group gathered around me, or rather, the person whose eyes I stared through and cruelly taunted. Their disembodied voices were offered in a limerick I could not interpret but felt degradation from, regardless. My mind kept pace with the motion of this ghost and watched as the group pressed my body to the floor.

One single boy, a heavy-set kid without a face hovered above as my arms were restricted and revealed a broken shard of glass. Struggling was useless as the glass cut deep into my flesh; chest, arms, and legs. No skin was safe from the jagged blade. I felt no pain, aside from that of enduring this macabre scene. A final cut was inflicted, one set distinctly apart from the rest. Then I watched in disbelief as a purple filter flooded my vision and the blood quickly followed.

Every child in this open room, slaughtered. The scene lasted all of forty-three seconds, but to me, it felt like an hour. This estranged, disturbing vision ended with my gaze catching a vivid reflection in a mirror placed high above the mantle of a stone fireplace. The body my spirit inhabited was that of a little boy with shaggy brown hair and a fresh cut on his cheek.

A soft hum ignited in the background of complete darkness. Then, a fragile ping determined my location and gently plucked me from the veil. Another metallic tick echoed from a place I knew. Inhaling as if it were my last breath, I awoke crippled on the floor. Reality settled in around me and another ring slipped through the cracked living room window.

"The. . . windchime." I declared with a dry mouth. "I'm home?"

Leaning my head to the side, I confirmed myself to be prone on the living room floor of Tansu's house; just behind the couch.

"Can you move?" Alice spoke.

I winced, "Yeah." My voice strained.

Sitting upright, I allowed the blood to rush to my head before looking around. I was definitely back home; this isn't a dream or illusion. A nauseating bubble circled in my gut and incentivized me to remain seated until it calms down. Which was fine, I felt groggy and weak; the last thing I wanted to do was get up and walk around.

"How did we get here?" I asked out loud.

She pondered. "That Teufel. He opened a Rift and tossed us in." She explained briefly.

"What's a *Rift?*" I asked. At the same time, I touched my face and observed my hands; there was no blood anywhere on me.

"Its what you saw; a doorway. When a Teufel is powerful enough, they can open doors that led to a place they have been or know of in detail. An easy way for us to get around when we become Whole."

"If it's a way to travel, then why did it hurt so bad?" I asked, recalling the fire inside me.

"Human souls aren't supposed to be there. It's a crossroads of energy that directly conflicts with what's left of your purity. It's complicated."

"I'll say." I sighed.

Then it hit me. "Wait! That Teufel is still at the school!" I stated fearfully.

Alice seemed calm, yet perplexed. "The fuck is going on? Why would a Teufel not take the chance to kill us. . . and instead, send us away?"

I laid back down, spreading my arms wide across the floor; staring at the ceiling. "Shit. I don't know. It feels weird to say this, but I don't think he's going to hurt anyone."

"I felt it too," Alice confirmed. "I say again; the fuck is going on?"

"Hell if I know. What happened back there!? What you did to Stacy. . . and Kel." My fist bound tightly.

"What *I* did? Believe it or not, most of that was you!" She redirected the accusation.

"Me!?" I shouted.

"You went from mildly annoyed to blazing hatred in an instant. Don't get me wrong I was pretty fucking glad, but as I stepped into your skin there was a shadow overlapping me. You did something." She snarled.

"I don't even know what that means. What could I possibly have done? It was you who was in front and I couldn't stop you!"

A click from the doorway snagged my attention and I quickly angled my head to see it opening. A sharp release of the bus's brakes entered the house as Tansu stepped inside the short hallway. She immediately noticed me on the floor and dropped her bag by her feet.

"Kimmy!?" She exclaimed before half sprinting towards me.

I sat myself up again and she moved around to my front.

"Tansu, what are you doing here? School isn't out yet."

Her face and nose were red as can be and the look on her face was shock and horror.

"H-how did you get here? When?" She asked

Thinking on my feet, I stammered. "I-uh. . . oh, I got a ride from the nurse a little bit ago. I didn't feel good and lying on the cool floor was helping." I awkwardly brushed it off. "Why, what happened? You don't look so good."

"Stacy just got rushed to the hospital and Mr. Kel is. . ." She froze.

I swallowed hard, "He's. . . what?" I leaned forward, hoping to God she would say he was going to the hospital as well.

"He's dead!" She cried out.

I pulled my head back and directed my eyes to my lap. "J-Jesus. How did this happen?"

She was trying to keep her emotions in check and ended up joining me on the floor, crossing her legs. "I guess there was this boy who just entered the school and attacked them. No one knows where he went or even who he was." She said fearfully.

"That's all they saw, was this boy?"

She shook her head, "I think. . . I'm not sure. They announced the emergency over the P.A system and everyone gathered in the lunchroom. I only heard what the other kids were saying before we got on our buses."

I closed my eyes; tired. Thinking.

"Are you alright? You seem really shaken up." I asked kindly.

"Of course, I'm shaken!" She spiked, "How could something like this happen!?"

I sighed, "I don't know Tan. The world is a crazy place."

There was a short period of quiet where we both sat and contemplated the situation. I didn't have much to say about it and she didn't know how to process all of this. Alice was listening, enjoying her fear.

Out of nowhere, the house phone exploded with a piercing ring. We both jumped in place and looked over to the kitchen wall where it hung. Tansu was quick to stand and remove it from the hook.

"Hel- Yes. . . We're both here. H-hol. . . Hold on, I'm putting you on speaker." She took the phone away from her ear and pressed a button.

"Okay, we can both hear you." She moved in my direction with the phone in hand.

"Can someone please explain to me what happened!" It was Kari, and she sounded frantic.

Tansu gave me a worried look; which I returned with a tired gaze.

"Miss Kari?" I said.

"Kimberly? Are you alright?" She asked

"Yes; we both are, don't worry. Um. . . What happened was, a teacher of ours was just killed." I said simply, but apprehensive.

"Oh my goodness." She gasped.

Tansu stepped in, "And a girl in our class was also injured but they took her to the hospital. Everyone else got sent home and the police are there."

"I can't believe it. I'm heading home right now, so you girls just stay right there."

"We will," I said

Tansu added, "Please be careful driving home."

She gave a flustered exhale, and in the background of the call, we heard the car door shut and the engine turn over.

She continued, "Did anybody see who did it? What do we know?"

Tansu responded, "Some students and another teacher, Mr. Lane I think saw some of it. But they never identified him as a student."

She scoffed, irritated, "This is exactly why schools should take security more seriously." She griped; offering a completely different tone than I've ever heard from her.

“Shit happens, we can’t prevent every bad situation.”

As soon as I realized I swore, my mouth cinched tight and I looked to Tansu who returned my stare with an annoyed frown. “Um, pardon my language,” I added.

“In any case, there are measures that can be taken.” Kari sighed.

Tansu fidgeted with the clip in her hair, “I’m sure whatever precautions can be made, will be implemented now.”

Tansu held the phone close to her body and nodded as her mom spoke. The two of them exchanged comforting words but I, on the other hand, started to experience some severe discomfort. At first, it started as a chest pain which restricted my breathing. That then escalated to a pounding crack behind my ribs that crawled all throughout my joints and muscles. I started to rock back and forth, hiding the pain as best I could but my irregular breaths gave me away. She looked over, “Kim?”

I panted “I’m fine.”

“Mom, hold on a second.” She then set the phone, speaker, down on the floor and inched closer to me. “You don’t look so good.”

She placed her hand to my forehead and her brows raised with the heat emitting from my skin. “You’re on fire! Here, let me get you some water.”

“Tan, please it's alright I’m-” I feebly excused. My entire body was experiencing some astronomical shock.

“Mom, just get home when you can.” She spoke into the phone quickly while standing up.

“Lock the doors, sweetie. I love you.” Kari answered.

“I love you too.” Then she hung up the phone.

Quickly she jogged over to the counter and retrieved a clean glass and ran the sink until the water became cold. Meanwhile, I was struggling to keep this stifling pain inside. Hot knives pressed against my stomach and lungs and almost made me pass out. Those old acquainted haunting voices returned, and I knew exactly what this was.

Alice was absorbing Kel’s essence.

Chapter 20 - Dichotomy

"Are you sure?"

"Tansu. Relax."

"No. You just had an episode or something! Talk to me."

"I told you, it was anxiety or something. I just, I need to catch my breath."

I held the empty glass in my hand and had one knee raised, sitting up. She was hovering over me, overloaded by everything. I stared at the floor below and listened to the buzzing all around us with patient observation. An icy surge ravaged my bones every so often; becoming less frequent as time went on. I couldn't stop seeing his face light up in the dark. Occasionally, Kel's face would fade away and my dad would appear. I felt sick inside; wrong. This is the guilt I have to live with, and the wound just keeps getting deeper. I'm not sure how many it will take to break me, but I do know that it's easier than before, and that scares me.

Alice started snickering.

I spoke in my head, "What?"

"You still hold on to those fleeting moments as if they mean something."

"They do to me; I'm still human. These things hurt." I explained.

"That is an obligation to your soul. Think of it this way; we just became stronger. One step closer to Sin, right?"

My face became tight, "Yes but this isn't how I- . . . forget it. It doesn't matter." I forfeited the argument; we've been here before.

"One more finger surrendered to The Ditch. Feeling a little empty?"

"No. I'm exactly who I am; nothing less," I stated.

"Are you sure? Because I feel a little less cramped." She grinned evilly.

The glass slipped from my hand and hit the floor. Startled, my head rose. Tansu was still with me, quietly watching with a persistent cause. I gave her a smile, trying to make her understand she didn't need to worry.

"I'm good, just spaced out."

She returned my smile with a tiny one of her own. I could see the adrenaline had simmered and she was beginning to calm down. Looking at her now, I could see how it affected her. The redness under her nose and the darkness layered over the green of her eyes. I felt sorry for her; guilty on top of that. The secret that plagued my blood stared her down with animalistic tenacity, and yet she smiled; blissfully ignorant.

A low rumble quaked through the floorboards. Without my command, my left hand stretched to the floor beside me and felt the vibration. Tansu's lack of movement indicated this was not a force she could feel. However, she was keen on my reaction when I rotated towards the front door once again. She craned her neck to the side and joined me in my stare for a brief time until the front door opened.

Kari jiggled her keys free from the handle with worry painted on her face. Tansu was already rising by the time she entered halfway under the doorframe.

"Mom!" She jeered, moving swiftly to meet her.

I remained here but chose to stand as well, finding the sway inside manageable.

"Tansuke, dear. I'm so glad to see you." She dropped her handbag and wrapped her arms around Tansu. They shared a slow rocking hug and then separated with wide smiles. I couldn't help but smile as well witnessing their affection.

I faced them, awkwardly placed in the center of the living room with my hands idle by my side. Kari glanced over to me; fresh tears pooled at the edges of her eyes. She extended an arm in my direction and lovingly moved towards me. My expression was taken back by her motion and my body became taught.

"Kimberly, are you doing okay?" She asked kindly as she repeated the process and hugged me tightly. My arms trembled, hovering over her back as my chin loosely lay on her right shoulder. Hesitant, I let my arms form to her shape and return her gesture.

Something inside me suddenly sparked to life. A crusted, abandoned emotion I have long since buried was breathing for the first time. My cheeks got hot and my chest pounded. "I-I'm-" I stammered. Then embraced her fully.

A mothers' hug.

She released me with a deep inhale, then stepped back between us.

"Mom," Tansu started. "What's going to happen now?"

Kari reached behind her head and started to undo her high bun as she spoke.

"The school will be shut down for some time while it is still an active crime scene. You said a student was taken to the hospital?" She looked between the two of us. Tansu nodded. "Then they will question her as soon as she is stable. After that, we can only pray they find whoever is responsible." She released her hair and looped the hair ties over her wrist.

I asked, "And if they don't find them?"

"School will eventually resume, but things will change. Something like this will deeply affect the children and parents." She said nervously.

Kari's eyes lingered on me for an unusual amount of time. I gave her a confused look, "What?"

"Do you feel okay? You look pale." She said.

Tansu joined in, "That's what I was saying. She had this-"

I cut her off.

"I'm just tired." My hands went up defensively. "This was my first day back don't forget; a lot of stress before all of this happened." I tried not to sound too annoyed.

"Are you hungry? I can make you something."

It was weird to admit it to myself, but their concern for me was almost irritating. So long have I lived a life on disregard that I felt out of place being presented with such basic consideration for my well-being. I had to retract my initial responses and just go along with it.

"Y-yeah, food sounds really good right now." I blinked hard.

"Tansu? How about you?" she asked.

"I don't know how much I can stomach right now." She said wearily. "In fact, I think I'm going to wash my face with cold water."

She passed by the both of us and headed towards the bathroom.

Kari called to her, "I'll make a little extra, in case you change your mind."

She looked to me again and smiled, "What are you in the mood for?"

"Anything." I chuckled nervously.

"Something simple?" She winked.

I nodded along, admiring her trying to keep the tone light despite how obviously stressed she was. "I'll let you know when it's ready; I think I have an idea."

She then moved to the kitchen and I retrieved the phone from the floor where Tansu set it down. I carried it with me over to the living room where I sat down on the couch. The cushions sucked me in, and I instantly felt relief. My back cracked and my feet cramped; the transformation was becoming easier to handle but still left me feeling so drained.

The phone rested on my lap and I just stared at it, listening to the ambient noises in the background. A few pots being handled by Kari and the sound of rushing water in the bathroom. So lively. I was delighted to have movement around me that was not to be considered hostile; it was comforting.

I then had an idea. Taking the phone in my hand, I dialed a few digits and let it ring once or twice before bringing it to my ear. The ringing continued a few more times before it was picked up.

"Hello?"

"Hey, just the man I wanted to talk to." I greeted casually.

"Kim?" He responded.

"How're you doing Joey?" I greeted.

"Erm, fine I guess." He sounded the same as all of us.

My fabricated upbeat voice quickly switched to refrained seriousness. "I'm glad you made it home alright."

"Yeah, you too. . . Pretty insane, what happened." He said quietly

"I know. It's hard to believe that could happen in this little town."

"A lot has changed lately. Seems like there's a new demon around every corner with all the bad shit happening."

"I hear you." I sighed, "That's why I'm calling. . . to make sure you're okay and to let you know I'm thinking about you."

He happily chuckled, "Thanks bud. Glad you finally remembered how to work a phone." He joked.

"Oh, shove it." I laughed. "I'm getting better."

I kicked my feet up onto the coffee table as I talked, then immediately retracted that motion and instead crossed one foot over the other by the table leg. One arm folded over my stomach while the other held the phone loosely to my ear.

I continued, "Have you heard anything else?"

He cleared his throat, "Actually yeah. Jessie's at the hospital and he's been keeping us posted. As far as I know, she's stable but pumped full of painkillers, so she won't be talking for a bit."

The bathroom door opened and stole my attention away for a moment. Tansu emerged looking a little more awake and less shaken as she joined her mom in the kitchen.

My focus returned to the call. "Jessie? Why's your brother there?"

"He and Brent are like, best friends so when this all went down, he headed up there."

"Oh, gotcha. Well, I'm glad she's okay. Hold on a sec." I cupped the mouth of the phone and turned halfway around, "Hey, Joey said Stacy's gonna be okay!" I called over to them.

Kari responded first with a relieved sigh, "Oh, that's wonderful."

Tansu smiled at me as she helped by filling a steaming pot of water with noodles. I smiled back and then turned forward.

"Sorry, I wanted to give Tansu the good news."

Joey scoffed in disbelief, "Weird to hear you say that."

"C'mon Joey, just cause she's a bitch doesn't mean I want her to die," I remarked snidely.

"Could've fooled me." He joked.

"Believe it or not, I bumped into her before everything and she apologized to me."

"Bullshit." He practically spit.

"No, I'm serious. I mean, I still told her to get bent but it *was* nice to hear."

I could hear him raising a hand, "Alright-alright let's not get into that. It feels almost taboo."

"Yeah, I guess you're right."

A timer beeped in the background.

Tansu called over, "Kimmy, the noodles are done."

"Okay!" I called back, then spoke normally back into the phone.

"I gotta go. If anything changes with her, let me know, alright?"

"Will do. Talk to you soon." He said nicely.

"Alright, bye."

"Buh-bye." He clicked.

Setting the phone face down on the coffee table, I stood up with weak knees and made my way over to the kitchen. Kari was straining hot water into the sink and Tansu grabbed some bowl and forks. I watched them with a keen smile, enjoying the simplistic family moment that would stick with me for some time. It truly is about the little things in life.

Kari spoke to me, keeping her attention on the noodles.

"I hope buttered noodles will do. It's all I could get together without making a big meal."

"Are you kidding? It's perfect." I grinned.

Tansu spoke, "What she really means is she's a lousy cook." She snickered.

I nudged her with my elbow and gave her an amused look. Her shoulders tightened; bowls close to her chest as she scurried away to the dining room table.

"I can't argue with that." Kari admitted, "Nakito was the cook, not me."

A hard clang of rattling silverware caught me by surprise. I spun around and saw Tansu rigid, staring out the windows into the side yard. She held the stack of bowls on the table with harsh pressure. I looked to Kari, who returned my confusion with a saddened breath through her nose.

She carried the plastic bowl of fresh noodles past me and set it on the table, then paused to give Tansu a reassuring hand on her shoulder. I waited until Tansu began moving again before I took my seat at the table. I sat with Kari on the kitchen side; facing the windows and Tansu sat across from me with Kari on my left.

The food was passed around and the three of us started eating. Amidst the scrape and clang of our forks, Kari wiped her mouth and started another conversation.

"So, Kimberly you mentioned earlier that your friend from school is doing alright?" She confirmed.

Before I could say anything, Tansu spoke ahead of me.

"Stacy isn't her friend; she's a bully." She said with audible irritation.

"I see." Kari reacted in monotone.

I spun my noodles in the bowl, thinking of a response.

"She is a bully, but she wasn't always like this. Once upon a time, we were friends. . . Well, sort of; we had a lot in common in grade-school and we went to each other's birthdays. But then my mom died, and she changed; we both did."

Tansu looked interested, "I didn't know that."

I shrugged, "It wasn't worth telling. To this day I don't know why she started being so mean to me. Just, one day on the bus she told me she didn't want to be friends anymore because my family *is the worst*." I divulged.

Kari set her fork down on a napkin, "Did your parents know each other?"

I considered in silence for a moment, "Uh, not like they were friends. I know her mom has worked retail in town and probably saw my parents around. Her dad still manages a factory two towns over, I think. That's about it."

Tansu responded next, "Maybe they didn't like each other. I mean, adults are older, but it doesn't mean they're any more mature than us kids; maybe they had something going on and it trickled down to you."

My lower lip raised, "It's possible. But honestly, it doesn't matter to me. I have a feeling this whole thing will force a new perspective on her." I took another bite.

"I'm just happy she's alive. One death is far too many." Kari commended.

"Me too." I said softly.

"Anyways," Tansu said, "Mom, how was work?"

"Boring, actually. But that just means I have good students."

"Dedicated to learning?" I smirked.

She looked happy, "Absolutely. It makes it really easy to grade papers when they all try their best."

My food was dwindling, so I slowed down a little. "Must be rewarding being a teacher."

Tansu had finished her food and pushed the plate away. "Yeah but she quizzes me on really advanced stuff just to make me feel stupid."

I chuckled.

"I do *not*." She defended herself.

Tansu gave her a baffled look. "Do too!"

Kari rolled her eyes, "You're exaggerating."

I didn't say anything; just watched. Although, this talk about her career made me think about my own future. The future I probably won't live to see. This planted another seed in my belly to add to my garden of anxiety. I receded in my chair.

"Thank you. . . for the food." I said softly, a faint smile on my face as I stared at my own lap.

They each looked to me with a melancholy change in the atmosphere. I stood myself up, taking the bowl in my hand.

"Oh, Kim don't worry about that; I'll take care of it." Kari gestured.

I set the bowl back down, strength fading from my arms as several disputing emotions found their way into my core. I looked to them with tired eyes, but a smile on my face. "I'm gonna go to the park."

Tansu's expression heightened, "The park? But it isn't safe."

I nodded, "It'll be fine. I won't be gone long. I just want to clear my head."

Worry in their eyes, they didn't argue. "Just be back before dark," Kari asked. She too stood from her chair, and Tansu followed.

"Can I go with you?" Tansu asked.

"No, Tan. I wanna go alone."

With a gentle stride, I made my way to the front door and slipped my shoes on and made sure my laces were tight. Then I exited the house and embraced the wide-open space around me. A heavy burden was lifted from my chest the moment I took in the fresh air and a pleasant aura surrounded me. Instant relief entered my pores and my steps were carried with optimistic introversion.

Turning left at the end of the driveway, I walked along the side of the road past the other nearby houses. Directly across from Tansu's place was another house with a picket fence that two small children were playing behind. I glanced at them, listening to their jeering and absorbing their playful energy.

A small side yard of well-kept grass lay between the house and the parking lot of the playground. I stepped across the grey pavement and moved towards the collection of equipment for kids to play on. A slide, monkey bars, spinning corral and a seahorse spring-rider.

All of this seemed like fun if I was a little smaller; but I had my eyes on the swing-set to the left of the jungle gym. I stopped a few feet away and watched the middle swing steadily sway back and forth with the rolling breeze. The sky was blue, and the clouds were minimal. The temperature was fair if only slightly chilly in a short sleeve. An electric crackle rose in my skull which caused my equilibrium to shudder.

"You wanna talk?" I asked out loud.

Spinning around, I looked for any bystanders. Behind that house with the fence was a soccer field that a group of kids were playing in; too far to be concerned with. In the parking lot were two cars parked; one empty and one with a guy seemingly taking a nap behind the wheel.

"Don't you?" Alice responded wickedly.

I took my seat on the middle swing and kicked off the ground. Staring off at the distant trees while I started the conversation.

"Alice. What's gonna happen to Mr. Kel? . . . His soul, I mean."

I felt her kind of shift herself around inside, "We absorbed his essence. Your relationship with the deceased plays a big factor in how much strength we gain; so, it was a fair amount." She explained, sounding annoyed that she has to keep telling me these things.

"So, you mean, the closer I am to somebody, the bigger the boost?"

"Essentially. When your father took his own life, he was still inflicted by my Demonic Energy when we stabbed him; therefore, his essence was released to me. It was huge; the first usually *is,* given the context of our purpose. Kel was just your teacher, but a mentor nonetheless."

I kicked harder off the dirt below me, catching wind with my rising momentum.

"Are their souls trapped in me?"

She scoffed, "No. Their souls go to wherever it is they are destined. But their life force is mine."

"A part of them is still in there. I can feel it." My hand gripped the fabric over my shirt. "When I dream, it isn't a mimic of his voice I hear, it's him. And Kel. . . his face is going to stay with me forever."

"Don't be so hard on yourself. That guy wasn't so innocent." She paced around.

"What do you mean?"

I could hear her sticking her tongue out in disgust. "Believe me, a dirty soul is more than fulfilling. But he had a sour burn." She paused, "When we consume their energy, we get an idea of who they were. Imprinted memories and coagulation of their knowledge; its how we grow from being mindless killers to beings of drive and purpose."

"And what was so bad about his?" I asked apprehensively.

She was reluctant to answer.

"Tell me."

Her face was pensive. "Meh, he was a good dad but an unfaithful husband."

"An affair? That isn't so gut-wrenchingly horrible like you make it sound." I stated.

She snickered to herself. "All I'm gonna say is he really enjoyed his job."

I dug my heels into the ground to stop myself. Closing my eyes, I shuddered; picturing the image she presented.

"Oh." Was all I could muster.

My feet kicked off again. The wind lightly whipped past my ears and kept my focus there. Everything around me was muted as my thoughts roamed.

"Do you thi-"

"Shh!" Alice cut me off.

My feet raised off the ground and I kept swinging, now holding my breath with wide-open eyes. I could sense Alice scanning, expanding her energy all around us to detect something. Low monotone whispers crept into my ears as the atmosphere changed.

"Behind us!" Alice shouted.

As fast as I could, I lept off the swing; using the previously built momentum to send myself forward. Hitting the ground with an awkward stumble, I turned around to see another person standing a few feet behind me wearing a long flowing cloak. Their hand was extended, palm open and fingers partially clenched right where my head would have been on the backswing.

The cloak covered them completely except for the outstretched hand and arm; their skin was grey. One thing that stood out to me, was how short they appeared. I could rest my chin on their head without a problem.

"Is that the same Teufel from before?" I asked in a panic, realizing Tansu and her mom were only a few hundred feet away.

"N-no?" Alice stammered, "Their energy is much more powerful."

My teeth grit tight but worry tainted my expression. I kept my eyes on their head, trying to glance past the shadow cast by the hood but there was nothing to see. The hood was baggy and extensive; entirely obscuring their face behind the fabric. Their hand retracted; brought tightly over their chest with the fingers still firmly angled.

Then, this person extended the same hand to me. This time, their palm was aimed at my face and in the center of the skin was a glowing sigil. Odd parallels and intersecting lines hovered an inch off the skin and pulsed with hot energy. With tender aggression, this person crushed the sigil in their hand; shattering it like glass. The moment the pieces burned to the ground; the world became still.

In the corner of my eyes I could see the sky had grown dimmer; but not dark. The grass which surrounded this sand had ceased to move; there was no wind. Directing my eyes without moving my head, I looked around and saw the trees too were frozen in place.

"Not good." Alice griped.

"What do we do?" I responded

"Fight. There is no other choice."

I had to get angry enough to start the transformation. That wouldn't be too hard given normal circumstances, but I had already changed today. My body and mind are drained from earlier which would make the process invasive and dangerous. I had to try.

Before I could focus my thoughts on negativity, the new stranger lifted their other hand; now directing both to me. The sleeve glided down their thin arm and revealed what appeared to be darker folded skin. This arm seemed damaged somehow. They pointed two fingers at me with the odd arm and then flicked them inward. Following that motion came a small gust of wind from behind me. That gust quickly sharpened into the accuracy of a pencil and drilled into the back of my skull. It hit me like a piston and completely disabled my ability to guard as I lingered forward.

A flick of the wrist and a similar hand gesture created another spiraling bolt of wind from my side. This one entered my ears and caused my vision to go white for a moment, and a stinging ring to deafen me. I fell to the side, catching myself on one arm and trying to shake off the daze. Pissed and disoriented, I dug my fingers into the sand and pulled up a handful of the loose grains. In a swift motion, I threw the sand at their face and started a dash as a follow-up.

To my surprise, the sand stopped mid-air and then dropped to the ground. I was already in the middle of sprinting towards them with a fist ready when I saw this occur. Stricken by shock, I let my guard down and my sloppy fist continued on. They reached out and caught my fist in their left arm and drove their knee into my pelvis. Before I could react in any way, the hand which held the sigil before clutched to top of my skull and held me there.

"No-no-no-no!" I screamed

A white-hot wave began soaking into my head and with it came a brutal shakiness.

"Kim!" Alice called to me, her voice becoming lower and quieter. "Break free, you have to-" Her voice faded, and my vision quickly disappeared. My mortal body was no longer real; I was floating. . . no. . . falling. Farther and farther, I dropped; the wind rushing into my ears as I was dragged into limbo. I couldn't struggle; there was no body to fight with.

I didn't notice for a long time; that I had stopped falling. That I had a body again. A white dot centered through my eyelids and awoke me to immediate discomfort. The light expanded as it filled my sticky eyes. Feeling misplaced, I moved my legs and arms, feeling the slab beneath me. A small beam of light shined down from the ceiling, illuminating about a five-foot radius around me. The longer I stared, the more my eyes adjusted, and I could see that the light wasn't a bulb; it was a hole.

Hundreds and hundreds of feet above, the light poured in with me in the middle. Outside of this circle was nothing but total darkness and silence. The realization of my surroundings slowly began to take over.

Chapter 21 – What Makes Us

"What. . . where am I?" I asked; irritation growing. "I can't remember. . ."

The room I was in had a stone floor. Every noise I made created a soft echo that traveled a large distance before bouncing back to me. Faintly, I could hear distant water dripping randomly. Trying to wake myself from this grogginess, I walked with disrupted steps in the confines of this circle.

I noticed something. My legs moved swiftly and both arms dangled; influenced with the current of air. They seemed thinner than before; less dense, as did the rest of my body. Continuing another lap, I grabbed my wrist, then my shoulder and waist to confirm. I felt the bone and muscles; starved.

In the background, I noticed what sounded like a heavy door being slid open. I turned my head around and around, trying to find the source of the noise. The darkness did not lift. No direction had been revealed to me. Feeling uneasy, I closed my eyes and held my breath, cutting off those senses and using my instincts to guide me, but to no avail. I could not determine the direction of the sound.

"Alice?" I whispered aloud. But even a whisper carried into the black, returning to me with a sinister giggle. She did not respond. I slowly crept toward the edge of the circle and stood there; toes meeting the darkness. Afraid, I took a deep breath.

"Sitting here won't do me any good. You rest for now, just. . . not too long." I said as I stepped into the dark. Two steps in and I already felt like I was walking towards a cliff.

I tried speaking in my head but found it difficult to narrate. Speaking to myself felt fuzzy and backward. I could hear my footsteps echo around me, but the sound seemed to narrow the further I got. My awareness of everything became limited and more confined; I concluded by this that I had wandered into a thin hallway of sorts. This was confirmed as my feet stumbled side to side and my shoulder bumped a wall.

I placed my hands on each surface beside me and used that as my guide. It felt mossy; jagged and at odd slants. Taking my time, I glided forward, following the subtle curves in the walls.

After I walked for what seemed like an hour, my eyes had adjusted to the darkness, yet I was still unable to see more than a few inches in front of me.

"I'd probably be better off walking with my eyes closed. This is ridiculous." I complained.

I kept trying to remember what happened last; how I got here but all I could see was the swing set and a dark sky. It was hard to keep my balance for more than a few seconds. I found myself leaning to the side, then leaning forward, just wavering back and forth. Not being able to see the floor, walls, or ceiling made it extremely difficult to orientate myself.

This time I leaned a little too far forward and I bashed my nose into a wall. The inside of my nostrils went cold with pain. I pinched the bridge of my nose and rubbed it up and down and shook off the numbness. I pressed both hands against it and felt the barrier, dragging my hand across the stone surface. I followed it to the right, keeping one hand on the wall.

Then my hand fell back into the empty air. A new hallway continued to my right and felt no different than before. I pressed on down this mysterious corridor; relentlessly moving with confused purpose until my knees started to throb.

Completely randomly, I caught a glimpse of a faint glow dead ahead. I attempted to focus my vision, but it didn't help. Distrust layered over my optimism and anxiety set in. The darkness could be playing tricks on me, but I had no choice other than advancing forward. As I drew nearer to the light, it grew slightly brighter.

I finally reached what seemed to be a cracked open door or passageway. The orange glow appeared to be a faint light source pushing out from the small opening. I released a long, tired breath. Anticipating potential disaster.

I felt my way around and found the newly discovered door handle. A cold, steel ring was located in its standard placement. I wrapped three fingers through the loop and strained myself trying to pull the door open further. Every inch that it opened revealed more of the faint orange light into the hallway. It dragged along the stone floor, echoing endlessly behind me.

For a moment, I thought I heard a light snicker behind me. I didn't stop, and with great effort, I was able to pull the door open enough to slide in.

Before entering, I turned myself around, panting and eyed the hall I had come from. The dim light illuminated only a tiny fraction, revealing nothing to ease my worries. I slowly turned back to the door. Just as the darkness was to my back again, I heard a very low, barely audible giggle. Once more, I whipped around with a spike of fear in my chest.

I felt my mouth move, as if to say *hello*, but caught myself before any air could escape. It was silent, apart from the stressed ringing in my ears. I hurried into the room and tried to close the door behind me, but it wouldn't budge. I looked around the room I was now in; soaking in the claustrophobic nature. Two torches were slotting into separate wall sconces on the far and close end of the room. One to my right just beside the door and one in the back-left corner. The room itself was about ten feet long and maybe around eight feet wide. The walls were made of jagged stone and the floor smooth as concrete.

Above me, was a brown; misty void. There was no ceiling, nothing solid to limit my verticality but whatever ghastly substance swelled above my head, was not to be disturbed. Only after staring into the murky air above, did I notice thin brown strings dangling; like little hairs cautiously swaying with every one of my movements.

Within the room, itself was a dirty, overturned bathtub with wilted roses and a significant amount of dry dirt spilling onto the floor. Partially submerged into the ground in the back-right corner, was a bicycle with training wheels. Its front wheel was swallowed by the floor, and it jutted out of the ground like an abstract art piece. Lastly; there was another door. Immediately to my right as I entered, stood a tall rusted steel door decorated with deep scratches and a dozen or so bold, hefty rivets.

The door was cracked open nearly an inch; and inside spewed a threatening aura that quickly drove me closer to the opposite wall. I crept through the room, stumbling and falling over my tired feet until I reached the mounted torch at the far end. I removed it with a cumbersome grunt and lugged it over to the bathtub in the center and jabbed it into the soil to force it upright.

Naturally, my eyes lingered on the door. The other torch was mounted just beside it, but the crack allowed no light to pass the frame. I watched the flame flicker while simultaneously enjoying the heat from my personal torch. Now that I had light, I observed my body. Holding my arms out, I could plainly see that the meat and muscle had been sapped right off the bones. My fingers trembled as I lifted my shirt to see my stomach was inverted; ribs exposed. As for clothing; I wore elastic skinny jeans, tennis shoes and a red short-sleeve shirt; nothing out of the ordinary. Digging through my pockets, I found nothing at all.

"Alice? Are you here?" I spoke to the walls; voice dry and husky.

There was still no response; no buzz or electric impulse. My skull seemed vacant; as did the rest of my body.

"Great." I sighed.

Time passed me by, not knowing whether it was day or night or if those things I once knew even existed here. I was all alone and sat on the edge of the tub, taking minute-long shifts watching the open door and the other alike. The tiny room that confined me was maddening. The only options I had were to remain here or go back out. There's always a chance I won't find this place again; which wouldn't be too upsetting but that also leaves the chance that I won't find *any* other room again. And I will be wandering for eternity.

I had to bide my time; figure out a solution. This room seemingly had no other exit. That, and it possessed strange properties. The longer I sat in silence, the more I started to hear things. Things that certainly didn't exist. Voices of people I knew but distorted like an analog playback through the world's shittiest radio. These voices weren't just random words and phrases; I recognized them as memories.

My dad's voice, getting home from the store and smashing the door handle into the wall by mistake. That was one that I easily recognized and could identify. This replayed a memory I had nearly forgotten. Printing an image of him standing by the front door with his usual scowl. I smiled.

Something else caught my attention amidst my reminiscing. A wave of air pulsed into this room; completely silent. I caught a glimpse of the shockwave enter from the door; pass over me and bounce back like sonar. The wall of energy sizzled my skin for a brief moment. I perked up, darting my eyes with a stoic expression.

Candles. . . A voice muttered.

I looked to my right, then left; searching. My mind was becoming hazy.

The voices bombarded me by the hundreds; they were soft, hardly existent. I was only able to catch certain phrases or words.

Imagin. . .ary? What about the others?

"What others?" I whispered without commanding myself to.

Three separate voices responded.

I will help you- medication agai- it won't hurt.

"To make her. . ." A flash image of my mother stole my vision before burning away. ". . . Love me"

Find your parents. . .demons aren't real- Just a poke, and. . .

The voices changed. The same three remained consistent one after the other. Deep and conniving. Fearful and concerned. Snide; cocky.

Come. . . this has to stop! Sleep forever. . .

"Forever." I slurred, "Happy-"

Birth-. . .day!

"To-"

Good. . .night, Kiki

My eyes shot open and my head violently lashed to the ceiling. The strings above had grown like vines; twisted and corrupt, reaching for me. They stopped the moment I caught them and slowly, with a wet dragging sound; returned to the ceiling and vanished among the mist.

I was curled up; knees pulled to my chest and my arms wrapped around them tightly. Cold. Looking around, I saw the bathtub and bike were gone. The torch lay on the floor, still burning next to something new. A little silver box. The licking flame reflected off the spotless metal and I reached for it with haste. Inside the box, I was surprised to find a single strike match. Confused but pleased; I stuck the match in my pocket and made a mental note that it was real.

The song of horror had stopped, and I couldn't remember a thing they were saying. But with the quiet, came an innate sense of danger. The walls seemed to swell whenever they were in my peripheral; breathing. It came in again, though I had forgotten all about its first visit immediately after I sat down. A seemingly friendly static cloud twirled in the room; entering and exiting the door every so often. Taking a few seconds to tickle me then disappear. It's like, it was trying to lift me up and carry me back into the void. Then it was gone, and I forgot it had ever been.

My arms trembled thinking about the second door. Itchy; dirty. A small cough snuck up on me, then turned quickly to rough wheezing. I was freezing cold; my weakened body was not taking this environment well. Something was missing, something that left me feeling undeniably hollow.

The thought of Alice had redirected my thoughts to Sin. If it weren't for him, my life wouldn't have gone this way. No demons, no horrible nightmares, no voices. I could live a normal life, with normal problems. . . Then again, if it weren't for Sin fucking with me and my dad, Tansu and I may not have become friends. Joey and I would still be so distant. Truthfully, it's because of Sin that I was able to grow and come to terms with the world around me. He gave me a different perspective, but at what cost and for what purpose?

People died, because of me. People have been hurt and my own soul has become tattered and dry. He has a plan, a reason for the Teufel and us children. Whatever it is, I'll stop it. I'll kill him.

This unease drenched my skin and left me paranoid; but inexplicably exhausted. I couldn't seem to maintain a steady breathing pattern and comfort was impossible given my starved body. I begged to rest, just sleep for an hour or two but found myself dangling on the edge.

All of the sudden, a harsh sound broke through my senses. I yelped and stood as fast as I could; ready to take action but all at once feeling my own weight drag me down. The torch acted as a short-range flashlight but left the hallway and corners black. My heart pounded out of my chest, mouth salivated with fear and anticipation. I waited for another noise.

On edge, I scanned the room. My breathing slowed to a trickle of air while I waited. It seemed like the room had reset itself to lifeless; me being the exception. That static from before re-entered the room, nearly invisible but so very present. It slithered along the ground and caressed my ankles; then receded again.

I heard a jingle and remained still; placing the memory of the windchime in the front of my thoughts. Then I heard it again; it wasn't what I thought it to be. This metal was different; more dense and heavier. Then, a scrape.

My breath ceased as my eyes gravitated to the door in the corner. I stared with terror, and witnessed the door begin to creep open another inch. Unexpectedly, a low moan erupted within the room. My hands began to tremble as the horrifying cries of the anguished cracked the stone walls and vibrated everything.

A childlike dread came over me. "Please stop. Please stop." I desperately whispered to myself, covering my ears and pulling my legs to my chest.

The moaning increased, growing louder and louder until I felt like I was surrounded by the undead. My ears rang like a cheap alarm clock. My eyes focused on one singular point amidst the chaos. The torch nearest to the wall had been snuffed. All that was left was a small ember. That entire corner of the room was impervious to my own light; rendering it a mysterious impenetrable black that vibrated with the earthquake inside my skull. As I stared at the void, I could feel an unexplained pressure build around my eyes. It wasn't apparent at first; however, as soon as I fully noticed, I reached up to rub them.

"Lost!" A demonic voice shouted.

I covered my ears and shrieked, losing all sense of balance and falling onto the floor without catching myself. Landing on my side, I curled my knees and dragged myself to the farthest wall; clutching my body tight against it as tears started to roll down my face. All confidence was gone; I cowered.

To my surprise, the moans had begun fading out. Receding until they were null. I paused, back against the wall on the floor; waiting with a nauseated face for a new sound. Watching both doors, hoping some creature wouldn't come sprinting in at me.

I played false scenarios of demons, strange creatures and Sin repeatedly assaulting my small fortress individually or all at once. Every projection ended with me being torn to shreds. Unfortunately, a different reality emerged. Patiently contemplating; I slowly came to realize the only remaining torch was dimming fast. I quickly directed my eyes to it just in time to watch it spit smoke and die out. Now, both torches were nothing but soft glowing embers; little beads of red and orange. I shuddered.

My wrist twitched; silently debating on lighting the match but ultimately declining my desire. I have to get out of here; I was being hunted but had nowhere to go. Nowhere that was safe for sure. Every step outside this door was a gamble, but every second in here was potentially just as detrimental. I just had to believe there was a way out; a light at the end of one of these hallways. A doorway to my home.

The playground.

It hit me. I recalled the swing set and that shrouded figure. Whoever it was, attacked me; did something to me. Either they put me somewhere apart from my own world, or this is some type of trick. This reference to recent events sparked a new motivation.

"I have to escape." I bolstered myself.

I stood very wearily and recovered the burnt torch. Carrying it with me to the doorway and laying it with the glowing embers beneath the frame. Its light may be insignificant, but in these halls; it may be my only beacon if I need to return.

A chill ran up my spine and I turned my head to see the door in arms reach. The silence coming from that room was unnatural; so quiet it was practically screaming. I felt no life from within but could not shake the tragic energy. With regret in each step, I walked out of the room and lingered. The nothing welcomed me again and I casually peered behind me to watch the dim fire dust on the floor grow smaller.

Back at it again, wandering in the empty stone halls I had just recently escaped. I moved cautiously, but with a fierce determination. After ten or so feet into the dark, I noticed something.

My vision was not entirely obscured. I wouldn't say that what I saw was light, but there was a new depth to how far I could see. Almost like a prior smog that hovered in front of my eyes had lessened but the world didn't change. I think I did.

I could see the walls in my peripheral. The hall I walked down varied between four feet to eight feet wide and had an occasional slant to one of either wall. My steps had lost their echo; each scrape and tap were snuffed the moment the noise was birthed. It was so quiet now, so impossibly empty. Looking back over my shoulder, I saw nothing new, but the second I turned forward I saw something.

A few feet in front of me, was a single school locker attached to the right-side wall. I paused, staring at it hesitantly before advancing a few steps. I then noticed that above the locker was a light fixture like what the school had; except this one was dangling from the stone ceiling.

I got right underneath the light, with the locker a few inches from my arm and looked up the see the same strings from that room before. They were gripping the light, protruding from the ceiling through a pinhole of smoke and murky liquid that swirled in place. The light was broken; splinters of glass crunched underneath my weight.

A tap on the metal drew my eyes to the locker. It was rusted and full of random dents. Another tap, more persistent. I reached my hand up to grab the latch and open it but was interrupted by a slight jolt in my brain. My shoulders raised with the electric touch and my head whipped back down the hall. Something was telling me not to open this door. My hand lowered, and another tap reverberated from within. I stepped away, and continued down the hall, keeping my head turned until the locker was out of sight.

I swallowed hard; mind spinning with questions. Re-centering my focus, I found the hallway had changed; it tricked my sense of location as it now curved like a snake's body, taking me in new twisted directions. When I wasn't walking into a slanted wall, I tripped over the uneven ground. Wandering blind and unbalanced; my only company was the echo of my own footsteps.

"Echo. . ." I whispered in realization.

It had been very noticeable how my echo had not existed in this particular hall; now it's back but seemed delayed somehow. It wasn't true, in the sense that every step was consistently paced; almost like, my footsteps were trying to be matched by someone else.

I stopped dead in my tracks.

Instinct told me I was alone, but everything here was twisted; backward. I freed the restraints on my mind and let it roam free, trying to hear, or feel or smell anything-anything at all. Something that would either prove my isolation or led me to anything new.

There was. . . an anomaly. Barely registering in my senses, but it was there. Up ahead I felt a difference in the air. A lack of pressure coming from one section of the wall. I placed my left hand on the wall nearest to me, at first to steady myself, then I followed along some more. The echo was gone. I carefully used the wall as my guide and followed it for a minute or two until my hand slipped off. When this happened, I slowed to a stop and turned my head to the left.

In an instant, my shortness of breath had gone. I no longer felt claustrophobic in this never-ending abyss, because I could tell that I had found a new room—an open room with much more breathing space.

Mixed on whether I should feel happy to find a new room or not, I bit my lip and stared at nothing. The debate began; and I wanted nothing more that to have Alice's opinion. Where is she?

I lingered here, recalling the other room and the oddities within. This one was darker than the hall but felt entirely dead. Another jingle of that heavy metal plucked in the distance, further now. I didn't pay any attention to it. Instead, my legs carried me forward without a thought. Into the room I went, blind to anything within.

A horrid stench filled my lungs the moment I stepped under the frame. A prickling stab lashed up and down my body; submerging itself under my skin and remaining in a pocket of flesh beside my heart. It crackled and spurred before ejecting itself through my back and flying out the door.

My body lurched forward; falling on my knees and dry heaving at the floor. I loudly expressed my disgust, then, immediately, a creaking sprouted from the center of the room. Drool connected my lips to the floor as I panted heavily.

Hunched forward, gripping my throat; I wearily choked. "Who's there?"

Five feet in, and my brain now screamed to turn and run. But still, my legs brought me upright; wobbling and queasy. Another fearful step, then one more. It didn't get any easier to breathe in the ghastly air. I stopped breathing to try to listen, but the very moment I went quiet, I heard a shrill exhale from directly behind me. My heart dropped. I flipped around and saw nothing with my eyes, but I could feel it: an aura of intelligence. Another entity was here.

My skin crawled. Along with my own panicked breaths, I started to hear another. They too were moving around, perhaps lost in the dark just like me. Could it be? "Alice." I said.

A reflection. In the middle of the room, set delicately on the floor was a crystal-clear reflection. It completely stole my attention and got me to advance a step. The object was so small, I couldn't quite make out exactly what it was; but I knew in my heart. There was nothing here to cause it to reflect like that, yet there it was; clearly visible. My feet dragged forward; eyes fixated. A deep gurgle skittered past the doorway behind me, but I ignored it and kept on track.

I reached the object; now standing in the assumed center of the room. I bent down to retrieve a single bloody bullet and held it up close to my face. Overcome by emotion, my empty stare shed tears of remorse in silence. I clutched the relic tight in my palm and took in a shaky breath.

"Dad. . . I want to go back."

Back.

A voice prodded in the dark.

My brows lowered. "Sin. Wherever you are. . . coward, I will find you. I swear."

Fate. Another pained gasp slipped through the corridor.

My fist wrapped tightly around the bullet until the tip dug into my flesh. I twitched and opened my palm see the casing emit a faint blue glow; then begin to sink into my hand. The gentle blue light lingered beneath the surface, then shot up my arm and disappeared. A shuddering breath escaped me.

I smiled but was immediately taken by the sound of a low, continuous squeal at my back. Turning completely around, I looked in the direction of the door and witnessed something that wasn't there before. I could see the frame I entered; and just beyond that was a completely new door slowly opening a slight amount.

I walked towards it, a new feeling underneath my skin gave me confidence. Warmth. However, I couldn't help but feel like there were four or so other people in the room with me. People that didn't want me to leave but were helpless to stop me. I stepped back into the hall, and immediately a barred gate slid from the ceiling and connected with the floor. I spun around and stared at the metal bars.

The air became thick again. A low wind rushed behind the bars but could not escape the walls; instead it just spiraled; scraped the bars.

"Kimmy?" a tender voice called from the back of the room.

My heart spiked, the voice. . . it was- my hands snapped to the bars; taking hold of them with tightly bound fists. I pulled myself close to the metal and stared intently into the dark.

"Tansu!?" I cried.

Every ounce of my collected mind was thrown out the window and I was sent into full-on panic mode. I started pulling on the bars, causing them to creek and bang. There was something inside, I'm sure of it.

"Tansu! Are you in there!?"

There was no response, nothing at all. I continued to pull at the gate, but it was useless. My arms ached; my back was throbbing. Then, to my complete and utter dismay, she screamed. She screamed at the top of her lungs, until it was cut short by a bloody gurgle, and a hard collapse to the ground.

I stopped prying and stared in horror; waiting to see a movement or light. I desperately reached into my pocket and removed the match; but a moment of clarity gripped me and left my hand shaking. My teeth clamored, and I slowly released the gate; backing away.

"It's not real." I stated fearfully. "No. . . that's not you in there, Tan. I know what your soul feels like. It isn't you."

I blinked once, and in that fraction of a second; the gate had vanished. It was just a wall now, like it was always just a wall. I aggressively wiped my eyes and turned again, facing the door that had recently appeared.

"How many doors. . ." I started.

My feet firmly planted themselves at the edge of the second frame and I pushed the heavy metal inward. It scraped over the stone and buried a grinding stab of angst in my chest. A deep sadness overwhelmed me as a dense mist began to pour from the door. Brown, black and heavy, it crept along at waist level.

Light. . . A male voice entered my right ear.

"Dad?"

It was his voice, but it sounded raspy; tired. This room had magnetic properties. As I stood here, weakened by everything; I felt the center of the room tugging at me. The mist that rolled pushed out and waded back in like water; but I remained here.

I waited again for something to happen, Tansu's screams still echoing in my head. Nothing changed, nothing moved.

"Light." I repeated, then curiously looked to the match. "Okay."

Kneeling down slowly, I submit to the fog. I held my breath, clutched my nose and pinched my eyes tight. It was difficult to move my arms while submerged in the smoke, but with an extreme effort, I was able to strike the match on the floor and light the flame. Close to the fire, I felt clean air. My eyes opened to reveal that the fog was pushed back by the emitted dome of light. Releasing my nose, I took a steady breath and stood up; the fog rolled back to my ankles.

The light was nearly blinding to me after this time in the black. Still, even with this, I saw nothing in the room. That is, until the flame left me.

Like magic, the fire lifted off the wooden tip of the match and started to freely float to the center of the room. I watched it closely as it hovered over what appeared to be a table and chairs. It lingered at the center, and then shot straight down; it was dark again.

I took a step closer, and the light sprouted once again. I blinked, and something appeared in front of the dim light. Difficult to make out at first, but the longer I stared the clearer it became. A silhouetted figure sat in a chair, blocking the hovering glow, causing the light to seep around the edges of this person. They were sitting at the table, facing away from me.

I took another careful step through the mist, making almost no noise as I moved a few inches in and to the right. Trying to get a glance at their face or the light source. I could see it clearly resting on the center of the table; a candlestick. It was stuck in something, giving off immense heat in the chilled air.

The whispers rose again, and with them came the goosebumps across my skin. Charged all at once, the figure rotated its head in my direction; stopping at their shoulder.

It was me. . . My body, my hair; but without a face. Completely blank, she ogled in my direction. The whispers started to laugh as a melancholy tune rose from the cracks in the walls. The same strings draped from the ceiling and lashed out again at me, coiling around my hair and pulled at me. I slapped them away, gasping in fear and trying to retreat but the mist was so thick I could hardly move. Then suddenly, I heard metallic scraping come from directly behind me.

The door.

I whipped my head, wincing in pain as the strings became sharp and thrashed my forehead. The door was closing. My eyes shot open and I used every ounce of strength my frail body could muster to charge the doorway. The palpable sadness that suffocated me in this room dragged me backward, but I was able to get a hand on the frame and use it as leverage to pull myself out into the hallway.

I hit the floor; flipping onto my back. The door continued to slide while I recovered and sat up part-way. Looking back into the room, I saw my faceless double waver like a ghost. She was standing there, facing me.

I didn't see it before, but it was visible to me now. One leg and one arm on the same side. . . and a head. That's all she was. A broken husk missing over three-quarters of a full-body; hardly able to keep itself upright.

Shocked, I couldn't help but stare as the door slowly crossed over my vision. In the background, a fierce expansion and flicker of the delicate candle revealed three more shadows sitting around the table.

I'll be here, when you are ready. She sobbed without a motion.

The door closed.

Instinctually, I pulled myself to my feet and started a mad dash back down the lane I had come from. I moved swiftly, yet awkwardly with exhaustion at front. The foreboding mystery before me did not sway my desire to be free. My destination was the same room as before; with the remaining embers. I've had enough of the dark; enough of this place.

Desperate, I didn't hold back and ran as fast as my frail body would allow. I ran at full throttle, falling to the side and nearly tripping over every jagged bump. I could sense the open space in front of me, but at the pace that I moved, this prediction was inaccurate.

By the time I felt the wall, it was too late. My face and shoulder crashed into the wall at the bend first; carrying the rest of my body with the momentum until I rebound backward and landed on the ground in a daze.

Before long, my mind was forfeited.

Chapter 22 – Reconciliation

The penetrating light washed over my blanket and stabbed my crusted eyes. Rolling over to face the window, I relished in the heat that tickled every hair. Groggy, I pulled the blanket up to my neck and cuddled closer to my pillow. The heat beneath the blanket was soothing; for some reason I felt like I had been freezing for a long time. The ringing in my ears was ever-present; resting in my cloudy consciousness.

I yawned; the remaining sleep dribbled out of my body and left me feeling more awake by the minute. I rolled onto my back, rubbing one eye and peeling the other open. I was in my room, in my bed; at home. Taking a moment to stretch, I allowed the day to revive me and quickly rolled off the bed and placed my feet on the floor. As I did this; I felt something odd. Like that singular motion was shadowed by a hundred similar motions all just microseconds apart and all directly wired to me.

Shrugging it off, I stood up and peered to my clock. The time flashed twelve o'clock; the power must've flickered at some point. A blinding light from the window cast a long shadow over the door and warmed my back as it bounced off my carpet. I sighed happily and started toward the door. The moment I touched the bronze knob, a stabbing jolt crushed my mind and hunched me forward. A vivid flashback of my head colliding with the knob invaded me and then all at once released my body. I gasped, taking in air while still holding the knob.

"The hell was that?" I asked out loud. A sweltering lump formed on the back of my head; I reached up and gingerly touched it, feeling the sting.

Confused, I turned around with my hand still on the knob and stared at my room. The light from the window was nearly blinding. I couldn't see the trees or even the edges of the frame; just yellow and white burning light. With this intense ray, I saw the deep shadows cast by the bed. Stealing my attention for a moment; I saw something strange. A shimmering silhouette rested in the dark of its frame. I bent down slightly to see and what I saw twisted my stomach. It was me.

A transparent; flickering version of me cowering beneath the mattress with glowing blue eyes. But as I noticed her, she turned to a fragile smoke and sank into the floor. My jaw trembled as I came to the realization that things are not as they should be.

Turning back to the door, I prepared myself for more oddities. It opened with ease, and in the same motion, the light outside my window lowered; leaving the entire upstairs shrouded in darkness. But that same light seemed to have rotated around my house and poured in through the lower windows. I could see just past the railing, that the downstairs was lit up like it was the middle of the day.

I paused; feeling angst in my chest. Then I heard a light ceramic bump. Curious, I advanced a few steps and placed both hands on top of the railing. My heart nearly shriveled, and I choked on air. My dad was sitting on the couch, fully dressed and sipping coffee with a newspaper in hand.

I wasn't sure why; but all I wanted to do was run down there and give him a big hug. Like, I haven't seen him in a decade. However, another vibration slithered over my neck and forced me to turn. Looking down the dark bathroom hallway; I watched a pale figure with no discernable features stroll proudly out of the bathroom. Their shape phased in and out of existence every inch or two until it reached the bedroom door, then it was gone.

I swallowed the lump in my throat and slowly turned back to see him take a sip. A trembling smile crept on my face and I casually strut down the stairs. Rounding the corner, I was again blinded by the light. That's when he noticed me. Setting his cup on the table, with a careful thud, he gave me an unsure glare before smirking and setting the paper aside.

He looked at me, knees straight and elbows resting on top. He appeared just the same as ever, except he was cleaner. His scruffy facial hair was neatly kept, the mess on top of his head was combed and trimmed down. He wore a blue long sleeve shirt and jeans that distinctly lacked holes or stains. He was smiling but maintained hesitant eyes.

"You're here." He said in a low, content tone.

My jaw was trembling to the point where it was difficult to speak.

"D-dad?"

"Hi pumpkin."

I took a wary step forward and stopped. "What. . . is this?"

He directed his eyes around, then centered back on me. "A collection of fragments. . . it's hard to explain."

"Are you real?" I asked cautiously.

Ominous shadows hovered above the rail; swelling and reaching but were unable to slip past the burning light. I could sense this presence, but kept it set aside.

"Yes. . . but I'm incomplete." He sighed.

"Incomplete?" I questioned.

"I'm, what you took."

I looked at him in disbelief. Out of the corner of my eye I saw more partial images move about the room. These pieces expressed our shapes and moved around the house; mimicking our daily rituals. I saw myself, lag from the sink to the door and back to the couch without moving any space between. I saw his body blink around at random, idle for extended periods at ten times the speed and continue.

"Your. . . his essence," I confirmed.

He nodded. Then, he straightened his back, smiling at me. "Hey, can you come here? I wanna talk to you."

I didn't hesitate in the slightest. By his word, I looped around the coffee table and sat on the couch beside him. I was entirely transfixed on him, tracing over the flawless details of his skin, eyes and voice. But something else captured my attention. The TV was on, whispering at a low volume; it was *her* voice that got me to turn. Looking to the screen, I saw my mother holding me in her arms as a baby; rocking me back and forth and singing. My expression widened, but before I could invest myself further, the screen went black.

I looked to him, who returned my expanded pupils with a saddened grin. “Sorry kiddo, there aren’t many pieces of her here. You might not get the full picture with broken bits.”

Licking my lips, I nodded in disappointment. “Will I ever see her?”

He rubbed his hands together, biting his lower lip. “You might. She still thinks about you; I hear her sometimes.”

“How?” I breathed intently.

“I couldn’t tell you.” His hands wrapped around each other, closing as one balled fist between his legs. “but-uhh, how are things?” He asked.

I shrugged, “. . . I’m not sure how to answer that.”

“Can’t be that bad; after all, *I’m* not around anymore.” He smirked.

My eyes lowered, “Don’t say that.”

“Sorry.” He apologized, “What about school? Or Joey?”

“I only just went back to school, and it didn’t end well. It’s possible I could return at some point but. . . I don’t know.”

“You always were emotional” He chuckled.

“But now there’s a consequence. People got hurt, dad; I killed a teacher.” I admitted, sorrow dripping from my lips.

“It wasn’t you, Kim. It’s that demon, it’s what they were made to do.”

“You know about the Teufel. . . I remember.” I said.

“I know a little.” He sighed, “But that’s a different story. I want to focus on you. . . Are you and Joey alright?”

“He’s good. Well, better now that he got to see me. All this business with Sin has made it difficult to live normally. Seems like my life was thrown on a demented treadmill and gets kicked up to eleven every now and again.” I tried to force a laugh, but it fell short.

“I know the feeling.” He scoffed, “When I first met the old man. . . I’ll tell you what, my life was fluctuating. Good, bad, awesome and shit. Just back and forth.”

A moment of silence separated us. I kept my head down, listening to the random bumps and voices that moved around the house without a physical form. He looked at me, many emotions washing over his face.

He took a breath in his nose, feeling uncomfortable. “You look different.” He started.

“A lot’s changed.” I answered quietly.

“But you’re still you, right?”

“More or less. It’s getting harder to tell every day.” I tapped my foot.

“It’s stressful, but you’ll get through it. I know you will.” He lightly bumped his shoulder into mine.

“How can you be so sure?”

“Ah well, you’ve got your mother's tenacity and my *‘fuck it’* attitude.” He boasted, “With that combo, you can accomplish anything.”

I scoffed “I guess. But I don’t think it’ll be enough.” My body lowered; the weight of responsibility weakened my stature.

“You’re right. Not on their own; but you’ve got so much more than that. The power inside you is real and so much more than you can imagine.”

“What, Alice? I don’t even know where she is. Without her, I’m worthless. Just a depressed, lonely, miserable waste of space.” My words trickled to sadness at the end and my head lowered.

He placed one hand on my shoulder and assured me, “Don’t talk like that. Not my Kim, not my little girl.”

A skittering set of voices wisped past us in the living room. Words and breathing played at ten times the speed; there and gone in seconds.

“That little girl is dead. She was too weak to handle this life.” I said dreadfully.

“Then, you’ve already lost.” he stated.

I raised my head and looked to him with wet eyes. With that, a quake seized the walls, and everything began to shake around us. We both looked around, confusion painted my face and he wore melancholy acceptance. He reached out with both hands and touched both of my shoulders. The sincerity in his eyes shouted a thousand words he couldn’t properly convey, but I knew.

A change in the casted shadows behind him caught my eye. Looking past his head, I saw the light outside the windows rotate around the house. Then a click to my right. I reacted to the sound and watched the front door slowly ease open; the light entered just the same, but it was less intense.

My dad took hold of my chin and pulled me back to his eyes. “Don’t pay attention to that.”

With his touch on my flesh, I felt a burning singe in the middle of my chin and watched him retract his hand. There was blood on the top of his thumb; that same blood now rolled down my neck. His face tensed and he gave a frustrated sigh. “I’m sorry.”

“I-it’s okay.” I assured him. “Why. . . does my body react this way? The door handle in my room-”

“They’re triggers.” He interrupted, “It’s all a part of your image of me. This house. If you were to stay here, you would see much more than shadows.” He answered with caution in his voice.

“Are you suffering here?” I fearfully asked.

He smirked. “Are *you* still suffering, from the things I did to you?”

I shook my head, *no,* but averted my eyes to the TV. The blank screen reflected the two of us and I nodded.

He released my shoulders, “I see.”

When my gaze returned to him, I saw blood trickle from the corner of his lips. He was still smiling as his shirt very slowly soaked through with blood.

“Dad?”

“This-this happens sometimes. . . it all cascades until it ends as I did, then it loops.”

“What can I do?”

“Leave. You can’t be here when the loop starts. I thought we’d have more time, but. . .”

I shook my head again “I don’t want to go! I can’t leave you here.” My voice strained.

His lower lip quivered, suddenly stricken by powerful emotions. “You have to.” He reluctantly said.

“Dad, no. . . wait!” My body lurched forward, and both arms wrapped around him. The rumbling got louder, and the shaking intensified. The front door slapped against the wall over and over, cracking as the light outside of the house began to shrink in the distance until nothing but a frail glow leaked in through the windows.

Feeling the chill of dark, I held him tighter. “I-I love you.” I muttered.

Everything around me ceased with my words. A deafening ring came to life in my head with the complete silence that befell us so abruptly. The chill had stifled, and the house felt empty. Still shaking, I retracted my body and gawked at his wide-eyed expression. There was no blood to be seen.

His eyes started to get red and puffy; then, the tears fell.

“I love you. . . Kimberly. Thank you.”

Chapter 23 – A Place for Us All

I stared lifelessly at the ceiling; eyes agape and deadpan while my unconscious mind gradually settled back. As I grew cognizant, a sharp gasp drove out of my lungs and my eyes slammed shut. The blistering dry lids scraped my eyeballs and forced a vigorous rubbing to ensue. Scratchy and pounding; I allowed my vision to adjust. Sitting up on the lumpy floor, I scrutinized the wall where I had collided and followed it to my left to see the hallway continue. Down this stretch, I could barely make out that incredibly faint glowing ember.

Impossible. I thought.

Dizzy as I was, I maintained my doubtful stare until this inconceivable view cemented itself in my mind as truth. The halls had shifted, and I was back. Prying myself off the floor, I fell into the wall again but caught myself; using it to assist me. Once I was standing again, I gathered my breath and moved to the orange pinprick. All the while, I dug deep into my brain and remembered where I had been.

I smiled, feeling a led weight in my gut disappear.

Tired of feeling tired, I shot hot air through my nostrils and lifted myself off the wall. A new fire lit itself in my belly and I was more determined to escape than ever before. So, I carried my body with vigor to the ember, ready to face whatever was next for me. However, this was merely a delusion brought on by a need to survive.

Arriving within feet of the door, my powerful strut was brought to an abrupt halt when the glowing ember suddenly erupted to a flame. A loud, crackling rush of air bounced down the halls and the new light expanded in a wide-reaching dome.

One arm crossed over my chest, I paused with bated breath. Focused on the bright flame, I allowed its heat to draw me closer. Caution second to curiosity, I tip-toed closer to the door, never once looking away. That is, until I saw something move. Behind the fire was the once cracked door now drawn wide open. I stopped as I saw a shadow move within, just beside the reaches of the orange radiance.

The stick burned just the same, and I observed; growing more impatient.

"Were you in there this whole time?" I commanded a response.

A brief pause, then a gurgling slither sprouted from the black. I drew in a low, provoked breath and stepped forward. Another shifting beyond the veil; a whimper.

I stopped just before the torch and peered into both rooms. In the original, I took note of its vacancy. No relics to be found and no dangling strings on the ceiling. From here, I could only see a rectangular wavering light extended into the mysterious doorway. I felt it; pain. Colorful, brutal pain.

"Enough." I spoke to the nothing, "I'm done with this. Whoever you are, come out!"

A hushed wind rustled my lashes, coming from the doorway. A sharp clattering; like pebbles rolling down a concrete slide, rose and sank. My nose was wet with anxiety and the confidence I held in my chest wavered if only for a moment.

". . . F- . . . fear." A deep, monstrous bellow churned from within. Its voice was hoarse; fractured with a varied mix of vocal tones. Soft and petite like a child, wet and mucus-filled like an elderly woman. There was a certain quality or texture to the voice that made every muscle in my body constrict.

From the left side of the casted shadow, a hand reached into the light and took a gentle hold of the doorframe. The hand was wrinkled, brown and had a mix of long and short fingers. The nails were thin and broken, yellowed and at least three inches in length. The hand comfortably clasped the door in the upper third of its height, indicating something massive hidden just feet away.

Its voice boomed again; not hostile but *wrong* somehow.

"Mo-mmy? Where. . . is mommy?" It almost sounded like it was crying beneath the words but laughing in its voice.

My fist clenched, mouth becoming dry. "What the fuck?" I whispered.

The hand slid down the frame; lowering itself to my waist level. My eyes tracked it every inch until it stopped. The knuckles were wrapped in dirty bandages and the flesh itself was scarred and stretched; mutilated. I kept watch of the hand but failed to notice the creature's head lurching past the edge at the very top of the doorframe.

I only noticed when the glow of its purple eyes radiated with its increasing hunger. Keen now to the obvious, I tracked up the edge with an appalling gaze and retreated a step. Halfway exposed to the flickering light, was a dreadfully thin, long face with a crooked open mouth that doubled its natural length. Stretching out from the skull with serrated teeth and torn cheek ligaments. Gristly patches of long twisted hair protruded from the mostly bald skull. Swaying lifelessly in front of its wide, menacing iris' that rested in the abyssal sockets.

A considerable amount of drool slipped from its slack-jaw and dripped to the floor. The hand slid back up the door, all the way from the bottom to the top. The door itself was estimated to be six and a half feet tall, so this thing was undoubtedly massive.

Its jaw closed enough to scrape the teeth together before opening wide again. The creature's eyes shut, concealing the purple glow, then it slipped behind the frame again; withdrawing its hand. My heartbeat pounded against my rib cage as the situation was firmly established.

Hidden again in the second room; I hesitated. I heard a shuddering breaths tremble inside, then, it unleashed a blood-curdling scream. This scream physically pushed away the darkness that engulfed it. Exposing the creature hunched down; it's back rigid and arms clasping the sides of its head. The scream blasted a spiral of hot wind between the frames and directly at me.

My arm raised to block the gust, but it relentlessly blew my hair around and forced my eyes shut. Before I could react, I felt its hand reach out and wrap around my shriveled waist. It ripped me from the hall, crashing my torso into the doorframe before being pulled into the dark room with it.

The scream dissipated as I was raised up to the monster's face. I dug my fingers under its palm but was struck by the creature's horrifying stare. Razer needle teeth lingered by my neck as our eyes met inches apart. The glow of its iris' illuminated my face and left me mesmerized.

"Yes. . . I *am* lost." The creature sobbed.

I huffed fearfully. "Get away from me." I grit my teeth; attempting to appear strong, but ultimately revealing myself as powerless. Its stare was almost draining what little energy I had left. It was hard to breathe; to stay awake.

"So much. . . darkness." It whispered, sounding afraid. "Forest!" It cheered happily.

My head bobbed once or twice; I was losing consciousness fast. Then I felt that same old spark that graced me many times before. We both sensed it; the creature lowered me from its vision and looked behind me through the door. I turned my head as well to catch a glimpse of the electric cloud roll along the floor and stop at this door. A metallic jostle echoed through the halls, and then it retreated.

The creature released me; interested now in the cloud. I landed on my tailbone and fell the rest of the way onto my back. The monster almost seemed stuck in curiosity; momentarily frozen. Its body was visible to me now, as I sat up and the light returned to my eyes.

It was abnormally tall and lanky; easily over seven feet. Its entire body resembled what I saw on its hand; loosely wrapped in blood-soaked bandages with charred oily skin and horrible disfiguration. The legs were skin and bone and had backward knees like a deer. It was missing a foot entirely and the other had overgrown human-like nails. Its torso was wrapped in what appeared to be a shirt, long since decayed and shredded over time.

The arms, as previously established were nearly the length of its full body each and dragged on the ground by its side. The head was held tight by a thin, craned neck and strangely; what appeared to be a little red bow drowsily lopping on the top of its head.

Then, its body began to shake intensely. A loud, wet snapping drag spit into the air as the monster hunched forward. From the tall arch in its back, dirty white vertebrae shot out, becoming jagged and curved. The fin of bones curved forward; coiling over and past its head. Bodily fluids ran down the newly birthed bone structure, dripping onto the floor.

"Home. I want. . . go!" Its words brought an immense sadness into my chest. It didn't sound malicious, more scared.

More bones shot out from its elbows, knees and shoulders. Randomly erupted from the flesh, the creature was covered head to toe in various bone daggers.

It spoke quickly. "Suffering-suffering." Then screamed, "SUFFER!!!" The monster lunged for me.

"Get away!" I hollered back, crawling backward.

One of its extremely long arms reached down and grabbed my ankle then pulled me back under its mass. I stared, petrified at its tight skinned face and watched as its inward crushed nose began to drip a mixture of red and black liquids. The beast opened its mouth again and it snapped closed very quickly. Then it opened wider and wider.

Right then, I understood something. I was weak; without Alice, I am truly nothing. Always have been. I was a scared little girl who got much more than she bargained for and now, I stared down the inevitability of my death. This is how he must've felt. How they all felt.

Without warning, the beast's head slammed down onto my right shoulder. Its teeth plunged deep into muscle tissue; shredding through the meat and crushing my bones. My eyes widened, and my jaw dropped.

"GAAAHHHHHHH!!" I struggled and thrashed to get loose, throwing my fists into the side of its head; but my efforts were wasted. The more I moved, the more it tore into me. Flesh exposed and blood flowing, my arm felt like it was gone already.

"Oh god. . . f-fuck. No!" I struggled and yelped. "Let me go-o, please," I begged.

To my surprise, this creature did not laugh at my pain. I was accustomed to malicious figures bolstering laughter in my face. . . Instead, it cried. Absent of tears, but prominent in saddened whines and heavy breathing. All the while, just biting into my arm harder. The longer it went on, the more the beast and I cried out. Together.

Against all expectations, it loosened its powerful jaws and backed away. Blood ran from its mouth and sloshed to the floor. The same blood flooded out from my exposed veins; hanging, protruding sloppily at the edge of my skin. Regrettably, I focused my eyes on my arm. My skin was shredded to ribbons, and visible bone and veins felt the chilly kiss of the air.

The veins squirted deep red blood. The very thing that was essential to my survival left me so fleetingly. I didn't know how to react. My mind was not prepared for a situation like this.

It then placed one long finger on my chest and lightly dragged it between my breasts, down to my belly button and back up until its fingertip stopped at my neck.

It gave a sad voice again, "I ca-n't stop. Want. . . die."

Its finger lifted away and up to its mouth where it licked the wrinkled flesh. It then turned itself around and started to move towards the back of the room. For a moment, I stupidly thought I would be left alone. But then, I felt its hand wrap around my ankle and start to drag me along with it further into the room.

"Stop." I softly urged; my arms raised above my head as I was forcibly brought along. "Just stop!!!" I screamed out furiously.

As I did this, it released my ankle and quickly hunched over me like a wild animal, grunting and dripping spit.

A new voice called from deeper in the room. "Calm."

The beast raised its head and craned it over its shoulder.

"Oh man. . . what now?" I panted, groaning with irritancy.

"Good girl. Now, come here." The deep, feminine voice commanded.

The monster lifted itself off me and slowly lumbered to the back of the room; leaving me amidst the darkness with no sense of exactly where I was.

Propping my chin on my chest, looking down towards my feet, I saw a shimmering blur; like a heatwave in the summer.

Then, that blur split from the middle out into a wide window and a massive amount of light poured in; blinding me temporarily. Once my eyes refocused, I could see. . . trees. An overgrown saturated forest, and the monster standing just in front of the living image. It moved through the barrier; undulating reality as it crossed the threshold.

The other voice spoke, hushed but with a twisted joy in her lips. "Keep searching. You'll find your mother someday."

An exasperated sigh from the beast, then a low cry and the projected forest blipped away. The all-consuming dark returned, and I watched.

Within a blink, I could see a new shape take the place of both the monster and the haze. Details were obscured but hearing the voice and determining a few features partially outlined in the dark gave me a hint. It was a girl.

"Little lamb?" She called out in a hushed voice.

She hid in the shadows. Again, I saw two more bright purple iris' hovering beyond the veil. But these were different than the beasts; a lighter shade. My arm felt heavy and almost nonexistent. But this place had strange properties; the pain was horrendous but at the same time, manageable. It was difficult to move, but still, I summoned a large portion of my strength and pulled myself to a half-sitting position, my arm limp and dragging me down.

"Show yourself." I demanded.

By her command or by mine, two more torches mounted on the walls spit into flame. One on my left and the other on my right; both about fifteen or so feet away and each dome meeting my body in the middle. Without any words or time wasted, she took a step forward, just enough to be in the freshly spawned light.

This girl stood confident with a fascinated, raised chin smile that sent goosebumps up and down my skin. She had an unnatural sway to her; as if she couldn't keep her balance. Her hair was long and ruby red; wild and thick down to her lower back. She wore human clothes: unsurprisingly enough. A tight-fitting dark grey long sleeve shirt that was ripped and stretched from the neck seams over to the right shoulder. She had black loose-fitting sweatpants with the ankles rolled up halfway and no shoes.

Her human-like appearance was quickly diminished when I noticed the two serrated black horns protruding from the top of her head; gripping tightly to her skull like a demented bull. I shivered, trying to keep focused, but everything was wavy and distorted.

Out of the silence, a soft humming crept its way into the atmosphere. A familiar tune.

"Mary had a little . . . Lamb." She whispered very slowly—so raw and gentle, every word dragged itself out.

"Lit-tle lamb, lit-tle lamb." She snickered like a child. "Ma-ry had a little lamb. . . Whose, fleece. . . was white as coal. . ." She finished abruptly; a trail of prolonged breath followed. I panted uneasily.

The girl smiled still. "Hello, Mary, where is your lamb?" She asked kindly.

"Who are you?" I asked angrily; tiredly.

"I have more than one name. Everyone I kill that has had a chance to speak gives me a new moniker. I'd much rather you call me by my chosen nickname; ya know, whore to whore?" She sighed, pleased, "Just call me Lust." She said with a sharp hiss.

Her voice was deeper, more mature than she appeared. She had exceedingly thin features like Alice and wore that same grey skin except hers was a darker tone. Her face was rounded at the jawline but came to a soft point at the chin. Her brows were defined and low; scowling but showing a yellowed grin. Curiously, her face had strange black markings. Like tribal tattoos that started at the bridge of her nose and extended in a curve over and under her eyes. Just barely visible by her wrist beneath the sleeve were more black marks that assumingly extended up both arms.

"Lust?" I repeated. "Another Teufel. . . Seems like you guys have been hunting me down." I snarled, trying to ignore the fluctuating throbbing in my arm.

"That *is* the point of this little game. You should know that by now." She spoke to me in a very condescending way; like I was an ignorant child.

"I'm well aware."

She took a long pause, crossing her arms before speaking. "I must say, I'm disappointed. From the condition you left Destro in, I figured you'd be more."

"What are you talking about? You found him?"

She cocked her head, "Of course. He took a blind jump and landed a few towns over. I tracked his energy and he told me all about you. All except, of course where to find you. . . for that, I needed help."

I looked at her with confusion on my face, but it was all slowly falling into place. "The Teufel in the cloak?"

"Right." She said. Then she reached into her pocket and removed a small bronze coin broken in half. "They came to me when I struggled to find you and offered me this trinket."

"And what exactly is it?" I asked.

Lust pointed to me, "You were given one as well. Though you won't find it in these pockets. The coin allows me to enter your mind after you have been awoken as your very soul."

"S-so it's true. The pieces were there but it was too difficult to think clearly here. It all makes sense. . . we're inside my mind." I explained.

"Oh yes. Such a wonderful relic to allow me in my current location to murder you inside your own consciousness. . . but, it has its limitations."

She returned the coin to her pocket and started to look to each corner. "I am bound to this room alone. . . but I was able to summon Minerva here through my own overlapping bubble in the real world. . . still, she drew you in just as I'd hoped."

I glared at her, becoming angrier by the second. I thought about the thing she called Minerva and recalled its saddened cries for its mother. "That creature. . . it had Teufel's eyes, but it wasn't like us. Just what the hell was it?" I demanded an answer.

Lust frowned just the slightest amount before her confident scorn returned. "Minerva was. . . a failed experiment. Just like you, little Kim."

I took offense to that. "You think I'm a failure? I'll show you." I growled.

"Like you showed my brother? Please, he was weak, as *you* are. And I will eliminate you just the same."

I pulled myself up a little more; the pain flooding back but not burdening me entirely. With great effort, I stood myself in a hunched position and stared her down. "If- if I'm my soul, right now. Then where is Alice?"

Lust tapped her chin with her pointer finger with a false bemused look on her face. "Somewhere for sure. But she won't be bothering us. I had Minerva lock her down nice and tight."

My brows lowered. Another piece to the puzzle was set in place. Her face *did* seem familiar to me, and now I know why. "Coward. . . Lucy." It clicked.

Her face went straight. "How do you know that name?"

A satisfied face washed over me, "She warned me about you a long time ago. Told me you were a coward."

"What, you think she helped you? How does that information do you any good?" She grinned wider.

"Heh. Because I know you aren't as strong as you say you are. You only killed Destro because I softened him up for you. You couldn't track my energy because you don't have good enough senses. And you had to invade my mind and use your pet to weaken me further before killing me yourself. . . Pathetic." I taunted.

My words had no effect on her. She just smiled that creepy smile and swayed side to side, occasionally twitching. "Whatever it takes to win." She sang. "You *will* die, and your essence will contribute to my throne. Be proud of that." She paused to twist her shoulder in place. "Besides, Destro had the sharpest sense of us all; he was the only one that could pinpoint your location. But from what he said, even *he* was disrupted upon getting closer. Curious."

"Curious," I repeated with a scowl.

She took a step towards me and casually brushed the hair out of her face and continued that motion to the hair that surrounded each horn. She took a moment to pull some of it down and fix loose strands.

"Horns, that's new." I observed.

Almost looking happy that I pointed them out, she rubbed one hand up and down the side of her right horn. "Do you like them? I'm truly excited to take your essence. With you a withered husk in the dark; Alice will feel the drain on her own Anima and will be so easy to claim." She sighed despondently, "If only you'd been a good little sinner, you'd have been strong enough to prevent all of this. Lucky me I suppose."

"Seems more like a curse to me. . . Living a life of constant bloodshed and pain; murdering anyone in your way all for what? Power? A chair beside daddies' throne?"

"You didn't hear me before? *My* throne. I will kill Sin too and become all-powerful."

I grinned, holding back a chuckle. "And yet, until then you're just a scared cockroach, scurrying from shadow to shadow; searching for your next crumb."

She took another step forward "That's where you're wrong. Most Teufel fear death; losing out on their only chance in the game. . . but me? When I stole Lucy's skin, I made the most out of it."

The more she spoke, the more excited and demented she became, "On my second walk, I slaughtered an entire shopping center. Women, children, the elderly and every cop that was foolish enough to respond to the distress call."

She paused and pressed her right ring finger to her lips. "Oh, I'm sorry, I forgot. You wouldn't know what a thrill that is. . . just a taste" She trailed off.

"No, I don't because I'm human; I have a choice. Sure, I've made mistakes, lashed out and blamed everyone else but me. . . I've betrayed not only myself, but the ones I love for revenge; but I'm no monster. . . You are. You Teufel wear our skin, make us lose our minds and commit heinous acts against our own until there's nothing left. For that, I will kill Sin. End this cycle of suffering and atone for the wrongs I've done." My words became stronger, more defined by the end of my speech.

She watched me, smiling on and on with patient composure.

"Are you done? Because I think we've talked long enough, Kimmy."

My finger twitched.

"Don't you dare call me that. *Nobody*, but those I call family can use that name. I won't allow it!" I howled.

"And what will you do? Kimmy-Kimmy-Kimmy!" She giggled, taunting me. "If you haven't noticed, you're all alone."

She gestured around the room, lifting her hands in a shrug motion, emphasizing that there was no one else.

Suddenly, she cocked her head sideways, expression as wide as a deer in headlights.

As defeated as I already was, I stared her down. I don't know why. This blind confidence was stupid. Maybe I am a fool. All I know is I am not going to let them jerk me around. I am not weak. Making sure I stood as straight as I could, I planted my feet, took a step forward and never broke the line of sight.

"I won't give up. Even if Alice isn't here with me, I refuse to stand here and die without a fight."

She raised her head to the ceiling and gave a giggling exhale before returning her determined expression to me. "I don't think the word *fight* applies to you right now."

Quickly, she closed the gap between us and punched me in the side of the face. I fumbled backward but somehow kept myself upright. My right arm was nearly limp, but it had enough strength by now to raise up and use to block. My other hand reached up and touched the tender flesh of my cheek before reconnecting our stare.

"You hit like a little girl." I mocked, fire in my voice.

Her face widened with happiness "Ooh! You've got a spark. Where is this sureness coming from?" She hunched down low and extended both arms out to her sides; curling her fingers and preparing herself.

I repositioned myself and brought both arms up in a loose fighting stance. "Shut up. We're done talking."

My only option now was to bide time. Alice is here, somewhere in my mind. Maybe she will feel my soul breaking and rescue me before its too late. All I can do is hold out as long as I can.

"You know what I find so wonderful?" She asked.

"The sound of your own voice." I responded in annoyance.

"Funny. No, that your soul is unlike your human body. Which means it can take much more of a beating before burning out!" She finished her words with a shout and dash in my direction.

Again, her fist collided with my face but this time my body was lifted off the ground and sent backward, slamming into the wall by the open doorway. I crashed into the wall, flattening out and sliding down to my feet where I caught myself but tumbled forward. Before I could fall to the ground, she ran up and caught me by placing one hand on my shoulder and holding me steady.

Then she pressed me against the same wall with one hand and looked me dead in the eyes, inches away. "You could never hope to lay a finger on me, Teufel or not."

She aggressively pulled me off the wall and slammed me back into it, over and over. My head followed the momentum of my torso and slammed into the wall repeatedly until the room started to spin. She stopped and let me dangle loosely; held up only by her hand.

She leaned in close to my ear, "If you hadn't already transformed once today, your soul wouldn't have been so brittle. You might've made this a little less pathetic." Her sing-song voice plucked at my nerves.

My head draped, and my arms dangled. My shoulder blades and skull were screaming in pain, but I would not fall into unconsciousness.

"Fu-." I whispered.

"Hmm? You say something?" She replied.

Lifting my head up, I glared at her with blood in my teeth. "Fuck you."

Disregarding the limitations of my aethereal body, I raised my left fist and threw it at the side of her head with as much strength as I could muster. It connected with a hard thud, but something was immediately wrong. She was smiling still; seemingly unaffected by my attack. Then, I felt the surging sting shoot up my arm. My eyes tracked to my knuckle where I saw that her hair had turned rigid like needles. At least a hundred hyperfine wires pierced straight through my hand and protruded out the other side with a bloody glisten in the torchlight.

I gasped sharply in pain and a thunderous quake engulfed my arm. She then released my shoulder, causing all my weight to go forward and get knotted in her razer hairs; tearing and pulling violently at my flesh.

My foot instinctively went forward to catch me, but she swept my leg out which caused me to fall to the side. As I fell, my fist was ensnared further by the hair and I was left hitting the ground with my fist still curled and stuck.

I screamed out loud. "S-shit. . ." I attempted to get back up and pry my hand loose, but she was already releasing me. Her hair returned to normal and she immediately planted her bare foot into my chest and knocked me back down. I hit the ground with a limp roll and came to a stop on my back. My hand curled to my chest and spewed blood from the tiny pinholes.

"Dirty. . . move." My voice cracked. "I bet you're enjoying this, huh?"

My fragile body shook as fear overcame my fabricated assurance.

"I am. But not nearly enough; I'd like to hear some confessions." She opened and closed one hand.

Panting, distracted by my hand and shoulder; I glowered with one eye partially open. "What do you mean by that?"

"I want you to admit. . ." She paused before stomping her foot on my wounded shoulder. "That you were a mistake!"

"Ack!" Saliva shot from my lips and my only free hand grabbed the bloody mess as she reeled back.

"You're an insignificant mound of self-loathing garbage that deserves to burn along with this world." Her face was straight; impassioned by some deep hatred that shined bright in her eyes.

She stepped back and watched me struggle; rolling onto my stomach and lifting myself up to a kneeling position with one arm. Feeling the spotlight burn bright over my skin, I took many staggering breaths and hoisted myself upright. Swaying, dizzy from it all; I stood at a slant. Both arms dangled by my side, my head crooked and gawking at her with darkness forming in my eyes. This withered husk I inhabited was fading; there was nothing to be done.

She hummed, "I am. . . impressed; truly. You've surpassed my initial prediction. But, that's just more good news for me. A defiant soul like yours will be oh so satisfying to ingest."

Without warning, a hot shockwave blasted out from her body and pushed me back onto my heels. Recovering my balance, I leaned forward and braced myself for what was coming next.

Her entire right arm started to glow a light dusty purple; black particles spiraled out and around her arm as the sleeve was shredded away by, her raw output of energy. It seems I was right in the fact that the skin of her arm was tattooed just the same as her face. Black angled snake tails ran from her collar bone down to her wrist; then extended to her fingertips as the new energy polluted the air.

I watched with tired eyes; the sound of her power bounced around the walls like a shrill crackle, but all I could hear was a muffled metallic jingle. Desperately clanging now, the sharp noise rattled on and on in the foreground of my ears; stealing my attention away until her voice grounded me.

"It's time. . . to expire."

Lust dashed forward with unearthly speed, followed by a harsh gust of wind that flattened the fabric of my shirt and knocked my hair back. She was close to me, frozen in place with a proud look on her face. Then I felt something odd. My waist and upper legs got warm top to bottom; wet. An intolerable amount of pain abruptly consumed all of my being and forced my eyes to lower and witness the violence. Her fist, still emitting a soft glow had been punched right into my gut.

Hot blood spewed radically from the newly formed hole in my abdomen. At that moment, I vomited the same blood, spitting some onto her unflinching face. The nightmarish mixture fell to the ground, painting her arm and both of our feet. I couldn't scream; I wanted to let out the most horrible, guttural admittance of pain I could, but it would not come. Just the sound of my soft gurgles slipped by my agape mouth.

My legs swayed, vision blurred and with a harsh pull, she ripped her fist from my body, sending me crippled to the ground with a wet splat. Now I lay prone. The screams finally erupted.

"Arrgghh . . . Holy-" Heavy wheezing ravaged my lungs, "Jesus, what the fucking-" I cursed.

My entire body was on fire; insides spilling out onto the floor.

"And there we are." She proudly called, "Let your screams echo in the hallways of your mind! They make me go mad!" She said. Her body shivered intensely.

I continued to cry, let every emotion out until I could no longer gather any breath and my soul began to fail.

"Where is your gusto now, little girl? You were trying to act so tough and look where that got you!" she snickered. "On the ground where you belong."

She then placed her barefoot on my throat. I gagged, and she applied her weight onto my neck.

"S-top." I struggled; blood filling my mouth.

"Tsk, tsk, tsk." She clicked. "Oh, how sad you are, little Kimmy. So weak, a lowly child begging for death." She growled.

"You don't know. . . anything, about strength." I respired. In response to that, she gave me a hard stomp, forcing all airflow to be blocked.

She grinned widely before bending down to my level. I tried to stay awake, fighting it as best I could. Unable to move or defend myself, she reached her hand to my face, placed two fingers on my lips and opened my mouth fully.

"Do you remember when my father first came to you; that feeling of dread? You knew it would end this way, but you ignored your instinct. Lucy did too." She smiled, then gradually slid her two fingers deeper into my mouth. She lingered there just a moment.

"Humans; vile and abhorrent little things. Purity is a lie; none of you are saved from this cruel fate. It's better this way. . . The world I will create will have order. You humans will be slaves to the fiends and remaining Teufel, without a worry or care about your meaningless futures."

Her fingers sloshed around the pooled blood; I was drowning.

She continued, "And I have you to thank, Kimmy. I will recognize and accept your contribution, to make this a reality."

Her fingers became rigid as she jabbed them both down to the back of my throat and deeper. My eyes went as wide as they could, and a soft scream bubbled from my lungs. Unable to breathe, I reached up with one arm and tried to pull her hand out, but it was no use.

There was nothing I could do; I was completely at her mercy. A playful chuckle entered my ears and quickly, she jammed her entire fist into my throat, tearing muscles and breaking my jaw like a dry twig.

This feeling—I was accustomed to it. The helplessness, the fear. Just like my entire life before me, at school, with my dad. Being trapped by another, with no way to escape.

Then violently, she ripped her fist out of my mouth and punched me in the forehead on the rebound. Everything went black and swirly. Unable to cry, unable to scream, I lay there in a dreadful daze.

My vision was gone now. That punch to my head was more than enough to cripple the rest of my movements and restrict the signals my soul was trying to send. A loud buzzing erupted in my ears, blotting out her words. She mocked me, ridiculed me, but I couldn't hear.

Slowly, everything began slipping away.

There was. . . a cage.

In the blackness of my fleeting existence, I floated down a river of obscure dark liquid. My raft consisted of sinking paper and delicate stitching holding it all together as the thick liquid attempted to soak through. The current was docile, quiet.

A wide-open space with clouds and a personal sky of dark red and murky brown overshadowed the infinitely expanding verse I waded through; there was no destination and no beginning. I found it there, resting on the shoreline half-buried in the sand. Once noticed, the cage seemed to stand out above the abyss; a three-dimensional object on a two-dimensional plane. My dilapidated craft magnetized to the shore, and I was able to dock.

The cage itself consisted of thick, rusted bars with gaps big enough to slot in a finger or two but no more. A small rectangular sheet of metal with a single keyhole in the upper third appeared to be the only means of entry. A grimy russet aura swirled within the bars; confined by some magic barrier incomprehensible to me. I closed the gap and planted my feet in the sand; staring with mindless indulgence.

Observing the keyhole closely, I discovered a crack that slowly spewed an airy vapor of similar substance. I followed its floating pathway with my eyes back across the river to a door that rested on the opposite shore. This door was reminiscent of the Rift I saw before but wrong in a way. It was open wide; decayed and black within.

Turning my attention back to the cage, I allowed my eyes to linger on the crack. Without my command, I reached out and began scratching at the gap. The river of blood grew lonely with my absence. Bit by bit, I clawed at the metal, but was quickly taken hold by vibrating tendrils. The living whips of murky blood stretched from the river and tied around my ankles, chest and neck; attempting to drag me back into the perpetual flow. I struggled against it, continuing to scratch away with unparalleled desperation. There was no noise, not a whisper, grunt or splash of liquid.

Then, the mist within took on a shape; saturating with familiar colors and tones. It was her. . . him. . . them. My friends and family. It cycled between their appearances with rapid aggression; burning their faces into my retinas until the smoke began to shrink. Shrink down to the size of a small child. It birthed a new form, the shape of Alice. She seemed afraid; black tears drained down until she curled up into a fetal position before changing one last time.

It was me. . . I was just a kid. Sniveling and afraid; but my skin was white, and my eyes blackened by some unholy influence. Tainted to the very core. Terror coated my face and I reared back my fist; then punched the lock. The worn metal shattered to the sand and the small door unhinged itself; allowing the smoke within to freely escape and pour into my skull.

Chapter 24 - First to Fall

Lust reared proudly above me. Her hand covered in blood and other bodily fluids, dripping to the cold stone floor. My soul lay on the floor, eyes agape and mouth slacked. She raised her hand up and looked at the stain with a dirty grin.

"Fun." She stated happily.

The room was cold with silence and she looked around; searching not with her eyes but with her energy.

"Now that her soul is deceased, her body will be a husk; and your Anima will transfer to me without fail." She grinned.

My slanted head pointed to the open doorway; the flickering shadows of torchlight caused the pool of blood to glisten. She waited; staring at nothing with some bizarre sentiment in her eyes. Minutes passed, and still, she idled. Until finally she let loose a tender sigh and stepped forward. Her shadow cast over my face as she moved around me and started for the door.

Her fleshy steps echoed, and the torches began to dim. As she reached the frame; she stopped. A look of concern washed over as she felt disturbing energy. Eyes shooting to the floor, she witnessed the smooth slab of concrete crack abruptly. A single pebble floated upwards from the split; hovering right in front of her face and continuing on to the ceiling. More stones rose, each growing larger as more of the floor cracked and the room itself began to shake.

Her teeth slowly clasped together with a wide troubled expression. Turning sharply back into the room, she witnessed me rise from the floor with wilted limbs and a heavy body. A powerful flowing surge of misty brown and purple energy swirled around me; causing gusts of abnormal wind to lash in every direction. The sound of this rushing air was deafening and crippled her ability to think rationally.

"H-how?" Lust gasped angrily.

My head was straight; mouth closed tight and eyes beaming at her trembling posture. My eyes were. . . glowing; producing a vibrant, fierce blue light with an outer purple rim, which engulfed not only my iris' but the entirety of my eyeballs.

I could see the wind but could not feel its rage on my skin. I watched Lust stand under the door frame, waiting for my next move and trying to solve this puzzle before her. But aside from that, I could sense something else. The electric smoke that so desperately reached out to me, had a voice.

I could hear her; and the chains. . . chains, not chimes. Instinctively, my right arm raised, and I snapped my fingers. The snap calmed the storm around us in an instant and at the same time, sent a response.

Lust glared, becoming angrier by the second.

"That's impossible! Your soul was diminished; snuffed! What is this power!?" She stepped forward, "It's Teufel at the core, but infused with you. You're. . . an abomination."

My hand lowered and I looked to my shoulder; my wounds remained but I felt no lasting pain. The energy felt neglected; but at peace that we were united.

The cage held a missing piece; a piece that was stripped away from me so long ago and felt the sting of loneliness. Now, we are complete. I am whole.

I took a deep breath and grinned proudly. "Looks like, we both have questions." My voice was gravelly.

Then she got a demented smile on her face. "No! I don't care what you are; all this means is I will get more than I asked for." With that, she charged at me.

The hair on her head grew sharp and stretched down her right shoulder; engulfing her arm and turning it into a spiked gauntlet that she rapidly threw at my face. She closed the small gap quickly, but I remained still. My body reacted on pure instinct; which allowed her to get this close to me, before making my own move. Rendering a counterattack, impossible.

Her fist swung at my head and I ducked; the needle hair skimming my own and pulling loose a few strands. In the same motion, I rose up into her torso with a fist of my own; punching her in the chest and launching her upwards to the ceiling. Her head and neck crunched into the smooth ceiling and her body fumbled back down but she landed on her feet with a stumble; then rested in a crouched position.

This time; I was the one rushing in. Swiftly, efficiently, I slid up to her and kneed her in the chin, then I reached out and grabbed her by the face where I somehow shot a hot pulse of energy directly from my palm and sent her flying backward towards the door. She slammed to the floor and skid on her back until her head was in the next room.

"Dammit!" She snarled before her eyes opened. When they did, her anger was quickly switched to shock as she looked up to see another figure standing above her.

I reset myself to a basic stance and stared with curiosity too. With a thought, the flames on every nearby torch; to both my sides, the floor and the one just outside this door burned bright all at once.

My heated face reverted to a biased glee, "Alice!" I called.

Alice looked down at Lust who stared back with grit teeth. Then she turned her eyes to me and gave me an enforcing smile. "Finally."

My glowing eyes simmered to a dim radiance, and my guard was dropped. Lust quickly pulled herself to her feet and stood in between us, eyes darting back and forth. Then, she composed herself with a deep breath.

"This. . . this is quite the surprise; I'll admit."

I heard Lust speak but didn't focus on her words. I was looking past her at Alice, who stood tall with a confident posture. She wore nothing at all, and her hair was disheveled. On her wrists were tightly bound clasps with dangling broken chains that dragged on the ground; at least five feet long.

With her being so close to me, I noticed a slight burning on my skin and looked to see my wounds healing themselves. Relieved, my own energy began to subside, and my eyes slowly returned to normal.

"No matter." Lust stated. "I'm more powerful than five Teufel! I can take both of you at once."

I scoffed, "Wanna bet!"

Alice shushed me, "Easy." She was calm. "Lyumick. . ." She started. Lust turned sharply to her.

"You have no right to use my true name."

Alice sneered, "Ah, you would prefer one of your many aliases, then; *deceiver*. You may be able to fool humans with your tricks and illusions, but I see right through you."

"And just what do you see?" She confidently sneered.

"I can see your Ascended form but don't exactly *feel intimidated by it."*

"You should be; the weakest of us all should not haphazardly toss around conjecture." Lust said, offended.

"Why does everyone keep calling me weak?" Alice's voice was irritated and tired.

"Because the Ditch does not lie. You underdeveloped, shrill, starving little wretch! You should never have been granted life and yet you were plucked." Lust's hair was growing sharp again the angrier she got.

"The mysteries we live with. I will have my answers one day, but for now; why don't you drop the illusion and show Kim what *I* see."

She huffed, shoulders getting tense before she finally straightened out and sucked in a charge of breath. "All this talk is pointless." She looked to me, glaring with fierce eyes over her shoulder. "You haven't even seen my true power. When I'm done here, I am going to find where your corpse fell and kill every last human in a five-mile radius, little Kimmy." She threatened with acidic detest.

Alice folded her arms, the chains clanged together. Then, I felt that same heat start to rise from Alice's skin. Her face scrunched in and her brows became sharp. "I don't think Kim would appreciate you calling her by that name. You don't have the right."

"And just how do I earn such a right?" She played along, turning back with twisted glee.

"Neither of us can flaunt that name; *she* chooses. It's a human thing, respect it."

"Listen to yourself. Her body belongs to *you*!" Lust switched back to serious but kept a small curve to her lips.

Alice was still smirking arrogantly; looking to me, then back at her. This entire interaction was perplexing; I didn't want to say anything at all. Just watching this surreal moment unfold was entertaining and sickening.

Alice spoke, "I can see you are vexed. A loss of composure will led to mistakes." A misty, cracking static sweltered in the doorway around Alice. The walls blurred in my peripheral and the flames were slapped around.

Alice took a step forward, and Lust retreated the same step. Then, Lust snickered and began to step toward her. The atmosphere rose with each second as this rage infected the air.

I released the tension in my limbs and stepped off to the side; allowing them to have this battle. I placed myself beside a torch along the sidelines and watched with bated breath as Alice stepped into the room and they sized each other up. Lust made a dash.

She approached quickly, but Alice planted her feet. Lust used the momentum from her sprint and punched her square in the face. With a loud wet crack, her head was knocked to the side. But she quickly reset her neck and leered; no effect.

Alice pulled her head back slightly and threw her hand in a horizontal motion just short of Lust's face; missing on purpose. The chain followed and wrapped around her neck. Alice grabbed the end of the broken link after it circled her throat a few times and held her in place, lifting her up by pulling the two ends of the chain. Lust gagged first, then laughed. She brought her hands down on the chain, imbuing her flesh with demonic energy and cutting through the links.

The chains broke and unraveled from her neck as her knees bent. Immediately after the chains broke, she sprang upwards; hitting Alice under the chin with a solid uppercut. She staggered backward, and Lust reset her stance; keeping her defenses raised.

"Is that all you've got!?" Alice dug her heel into the ground and lunged forward; sending a hard punch her way. Lust spun herself around, using her thick mass of hair to absorb the impact. Alice's fist got lodged in the thorn-like follicles; many thin strands pierced straight through her hand and fingers.

"Don't talk down to me, filthy cur!" She spat viciously.

Lust then bent forward, pulling Alice in closer to her back then sent a reverse mule kick into her gut, bloodily ripping her hand free and sending her skidding away.

She came to a dragging halt on her feet, dust kicked up and sprinkled back down. She stood tall, sweating but her face unchanged; determined. Lust jumped at her with a yell, and while in mid-air, she gripped a section of her own hair and ripped it out. The clump of fiber merged into a solid red dagger and was swiftly lashed at Alice's face. She stepped back enough to dodge, but as Lust landed from her pounce, she immediately lunged and swung horizontally with frantic, animalistic movements.

She managed to land consecutive hits on Alice's gut and chest; sending bits of blood and flesh to the floor. I watched from the sidelines; my body twitching and almost reacting to every move they made.

The flurry of slashes ceased, and Lust stepped back, panting. Alice slightly bent forward, watching her own blood drain from her stomach and chest.

Then, Alice started to cackle insanely. "So, this is the extent of your power? I expected more from your *Ascension*." She mocked.

Lust spit to the floor and gripped the hair blade tightly. Then, her face sank as Alice reared her head proudly and was engulfed in a blinding white glow. The two of us shielded our eyes as the lasting flash spread across the room; accompanied by a low hissing sound.

In a moment or two, the light had faded away, revealing the true potential behind her healing ability. All the wounds Lust had just inflicted were gone.

"Wha—" Lust growled, her arms losing strength.

Alice recovered her breath, then let her glare flatten.

"Care to try again?"

Without thinking, she ran forward once more. The blade crumbled to loose fibers and instead of throwing a punch or a kick; Lust instead lept onto Alice and wrapped her limbs around her. Alice didn't struggle, only held her breath for a moment.

"All tricks, am I? I'll show you, bitch!"

"You've proven only that you hug like a man. Am I supposed to be impressed?"

"Not yet." She sneered then contracted her arms and legs, tightening until both of their bodies shook from the pressure, and with a loud grunt, Lust revealed a hidden technique.

The hair on her head retracted down to almost my length. Then, the hairs bunched up under her skin and collectively shot out from the flesh of her entire body; becoming solid and unbreakable needles. A hundred or so of these thorns pierced Alice and sent a burst of blood in every direction. Her eyes shot open and more blood fell from her lips. She gasped a raspy breath, and then it went quiet again.

She recalled the thousands of needles and hopped off Alice, backing off a few steps. Alice was still standing but angled back with her face directed above. Her arms hung loosely behind her and she was entirely riddled with small holes; dripping blood everywhere.

As expected, a steady white steam began to pour from Alice's wounds. The more steam that came, the more Alice straightened her back and returned to her normal posture.

Lust gave a high pitch growl and blitzed again.

"Not this time! Die!"

Alice opened her eyes and took a sloppy step forward; meeting Lust face-to-face. Without missing a beat, in a fraction of a second; Alice shot her hand straight up under Lust's chin, her fingers pointed upward, and claws fully extended.

The static sound of energy transferring from one person to another left a soft thump to bounce around us, then a long hush. Their eyes focused together; noses touched. A slow stream of blood flowed from under her eyeballs and a raspy breath escaped through her flared teeth.

Alice moved so fast, with such immense force, that she drove her claws straight through Lust's skull from under her jaw. Lust's face was stuck in shock, and her eyes slowly started to drift down and to the side. Then something unexpected happened.

Her outward appearance almost flickered before fading into a different form. She was mostly the same, all details exact except she had no black markings on her face or arm, and her horns disappeared. Her hair remained the same length but was tamed; more neatly kempt.

Alice lifted her foot up and placed it on Lust's chest to hold herself steady, then pulled her hand inward toward her own face and pushed Lust's body with her foot. With the push and pull, her claws violently shredded through the skull and flesh; cleaving out from behind her face. She fell backward, hitting the floor with a loud thump, her entire head now looking like it went through a woodchipper.

I watched with sickened amazement, inching forward as Alice gawked at her bloody hand; retracting her claws.

“You. . . holy shit.” I said, fixated on the corpse.

My body was exhausted, I felt the burn in my bones while stumbling forward to meet her in the center of the room. She looked at me with ghastly neutrality before offering a slight smirk.

I said, “Y’know, it’s really weird to see you standing with me and not in a mirror. Is this what people see me as when you take over?”

“Of course.” She grunted

There was an awkward pause. Alice started fidgeting with the clasps around her wrists.

I sighed, “I thought Lust was so strong. She gave off this energy that terrified me, but she wasn’t all that strong, huh?”

“You are in a weakened state here; it was easy for her to manipulate your perception. Don’t be so hard on yourself.”

Despite her words, my eyes dropped to the floor.

“Destro. . . And Lust. They both defeated me so effortlessly.” I said sorrowfully.

“Don’t whine. Did you not just hear me?”

I raised my head and we locked eyes.

She continued, “What you did, just before I got here. . . what was that?” She asked, an edge of worry in her voice.

“What do you mean? I thought that was your power going through me?” I responded.

“No. . . not in here. I *am* my power; *you* are your soul. . . we cannot overlap in that way here. That was Teufel power. . . and it came from *you*.” She pressed her lips together, confused and frustrated.

“I-I don’t understand. Teufel power in me? B-but. . .”

She scoffed. “None of this makes sense. Lust getting help to invade you, my early birth and now this?”

“It’s complicated, I guess.”

“It shouldn’t be!” She shouted angrily.

We gawked at each other for a moment, then she simmered with an annoyed exhale. I aggressively rubbed my forehead and then sat on the floor; allowing my body to rest. I looked to her, watching closely as she pried the chains away; discarding them to the side. The way she moved was the antithesis to who I understood her to be. Her shoulders were slumped, eyes low and emotionally flatlined. There was so much going on inside her head; things I don’t even want to challenge.

“Alice?” I said quietly.

She was now wiping the blood from her hand. “What?”

I smiled, “It’s. . . really good to see you.”

Her eyes shot to me and they lingered there. There was a connection between us; charged and resonant. Her brows retracted from her constant anger and her shoulders rose with a breath. “You did well.”

My head lowered and my smile grew. “Thanks.”

Her voice was quiet, but sincere. “I’ve been reaching out to you the moment you woke, why didn’t you respond?”

“I was confused and freaking out. Everything was foggy and I didn’t know what to trust.”

“You had me worried.” She admitted, turning away.

“You were worried? Alice. . .” A tight ball formed in my chest.

She was hesitant to respond, “If you died, I would have died.” She said irritated.

I snickered to myself. Out in the real world, I may not understand when she’s being genuine or bratty; but here, judging by how she held herself it was obvious to me. “Sorry, about that.”

Lust’s body then emitted a purple light from beneath her flesh; stealing both of our attention. The refracting glow painted the skin of my face and caused a burning sensation. I quickly stood up and moved away from the body while Alice approached it. The corpse then started to flake away; crumbling into tiny pieces and floating upwards, collecting in a dense pile about four feet off the ground. In mere moments, the body was gone and, in its place, floated a hand-sized purple stone that gently lowered to the floor.

Alice snatched it from the air before it touched and let it rest in her palm. I dragged my feet to her and stood on her left side; the two of us taking in its cold illumination.

“What’s that?” I asked.

“This is an Anima; our soul and relevantly, our eye’s color. Because I knew you were going to ask.” She said blandly.

The stone itself was clean-cut in some places and jagged in others. Like it was professionally sliced by one guy and smashed with a hammer by another. It was thin; about three inches wide and five inches long with a fat top and thin bottom.

“It’s cracked.” I stated, noticing a small split in the upper half.

“Damaged, maybe?” She guessed.

“*You* don’t know?” I doubted.

She shook her head, “Doesn’t matter. *This* is the true reward. *This* is why we fight. Lust’s own power along with the essence of every human she has killed. All mine.” She spoke blandly.

Half excited, mostly tired, I responded.

“Awesome. So, what do we do with it?”

She held the stone loosely and then closed her fist around it. A bright flash of light burst out between her fingers and with the flash, Alice jerked forward; gripping her wrist tight as it sank into her skin. The light faded away and the stone was entirely gone.

As she absorbed the stone, I felt a new pressure on my body. One that buckled my knees and almost caused me to lose my balance entirely. A loss of breath worried me, and I fearfully looked over my skin. The color had drained slightly, and my spine felt weakened. I’m. . . withering, with every kill.

Feeling almost ashamed, I separated myself from her; moving to the deeper part of the room. Along the way, I stepped over where Lust's body had rested and kicked something metallic. Reacting to the noise, I bent down and retrieved the half coin she possessed. Hardly able to stand, I forced myself up and moved towards the back again, dropping it in my left pocket.

There was a very, very long silence. Alice stared mindlessly, but intensely through the doorway while I paced; thinking. I shivered, feeling disturbed and utterly gross at the entire situation.

I started, "It seems like every day just brings new mystery, huh?" My voice echoed.

"I'm interested to find the answers. Only one can provide them, and now, we are that much closer."

"I know. . . but. . . The Teufel are giving us--me, so much trouble. How can we ever hope to beat him?"

"We have to try." Her voice was monotone; distracted.

I stopped pacing and dug my heel into the ground.

"If we face Sin and lose; we'll both die. If we face Sin and win- then what happens?"

She shrugged. "You? You'll probably die either way."

Hearing her confirm that for me, draped another led veil over my head. My lower lip quivered, and a sorrowful series of breaths escaped me.

"I need to get out of here." I whispered. "Do you know how?" I asked.

Alice crossed her arms, forfeiting her train of thought and keeping her attention on me. "No idea; but you're right, being here probably isn't good for you."

"So, do we just wander the halls? You know your way around, right?"

"Not entirely. This place and how we overlap is intricate and not two or three dimensional as you'd imagine. Everything I need to know is brought to me as if I had known all along. So, no, I don't typically travel the halls. . . besides, they are ever-changing as you grow."

"Well there has to be some sort of exit, right?"

"Hmm." She hummed, "Did she mention anything about how you or she got here?"

I paused, trying to skim over recent events. It took me a second, then I gasped lightly with realization. I reached into my pocket and removed the coin half. "She had this." I held it out, "Said it allowed her in."

She walked over to me with moderate haste, "Let me see it."

Watching her move, physically in front of me was still jarring; I couldn't help but stare. Taking it from my hand, she observed the bronze closely.

"This is a strange relic. I don't know much about fiendish artifacts but I'm certain it's a powerful spell of some sort."

"Do we have to recite, like, an incantation or something?"

She snickered, "No, not for something like this. I imagine it's temporary bonding magic. Given that it's half a coin, I'd say you were probably given the other half; and that's what established a bridge between you two."

I blinked a few times, repeating her words in my head. I was getting fuzzy now, tired. "But I don't have any other coin."

"You must." She dropped the coin back into my hand.

"I checked all my pockets when I got here." I said, whining.

"Check again." Alice demanded.

Rustling my hair in the back, I fixed some loose strands and then patted myself down. Everything was just as expected, until I got to my back-right pocket. I froze and shot her a surprised glance. Sure enough, another half of the coin was there. Removing it with haste, I held the two coins out in front of me and saw they were indeed a match.

"I don't understand, I'm sure it wasn't there before." I griped.

"Lust probably cast an illusion on you. You must've found it and she made you forget." She twisted her wrist, cracking it. "That's what I would have done."

"Well," I took a breath, "Here goes nothing." I slowly joined the two halves in the middle and watched intently as a spark connected the pieces and they merged into one with a soft clang. The moment they joined together, I felt my brain swell and shrink rapidly. This sensation crippled me to the floor and stole my vision.

I felt the space around me change in an instant. An expanse of open-air surrounded me, and an all-revealing ray poured down from above. Blinding white swallowed every inch of my body and I started to rise without a word or sound. Excruciating pain consumed me in a fiery white whirlwind of memories and voices. Spinning through a lit tunnel, I braced myself and witnessed the pinhole light above grow wider and wider.

I reached the top and took in a massive gulp of air as my body sat up. My overly sensitive ears were assaulted by the harsh slamming of rain all around me. My vision was still white, but slowly reset itself and I was able to look around to see where I was. The park; I'm back.

The rain-soaked through to my very core and I shivered intensely. The park was empty now and the daylight was fading. A few scattered streetlamps by the parking lot and soccer field lit patches of the land and messed with my eyesight as the streaks of water passed through and around the downward beams.

"You're awake. . ." A quiet, female voice whispered from behind me; just barely audible behind the crashing water. "I suppose, that means you found it."

My brain responded with hostile aggression, but my body was unable to follow such a drastic command. I felt my spine grind as I slowly rolled to the side and planted my hands in the dirt, crouched and facing the voice.

It was the Teufel in the cloak that attacked me. Their cloak was dark, heavy from the rain, but they stood in a laxed manner looking down at me.

"You." I growled.

The storm bombarded my ears and made it hard to think.

The comforting burn of Alice's static erupted in my head. "I'm here." She announced.

I nodded, then started to bring myself to my feet. "Just who the hell are you." My nose crinkled.

The stranger lingered a moment, arms loose by their side. Then, to my surprise; they turned and started to walk away from me.

One of my feet twitched and took a half step forward, "H-hey, wait! Don't you walk away from me."

A sudden rough cough stole my lungs and forced my eyes to close as I controlled the wheeze. In four or so seconds, the cough let up and I redirected my eyes to where she was. But to my surprise, she was now standing all the way at the far end of the grass, by the tree line; looking back at me.

"That's like. . . five hundred feet." I exclaimed softly.

“Don’t follow them, Kim.” Alice demanded, the usual tone in her voice.

“Are you kidding me? After everything that’s happened today, you think I’m gonna let them walk away without giving me some answers.”

“Don’t be an idiot. We’re lucky to be alive.”

I scoffed, already moving across the grass. “What’s it matter? According to you, I’ll just die anyway. So, fuck it.” I snapped at her.

That got her quiet, but she was still up front. I used a lot of my strength to jog at a steady pace across the lawn; trying not to slip on the soaked grass. Sure enough, the cloaked figure was waiting for me by the tree line. Panting, I arrived at their feet and followed them a few more steps inside the thick forest. Here, we were safe from the rainfall.

Much of the noise was dampened by the abundance of trees, making the pounding of my head much more bearable. I took a second and whipped my head around to throw as much water off as I could. Still freezing, I rubbed my arms and breathed heavily.

Alice still complained, “This is a bad idea.”

I ignored her and instead kept my eyes on the stranger. They stood like a statue; face obfuscated by shadows. I didn’t sense it before, when they first jumped me; but Alice was right. The power coming from this person was something else.

I gathered my courage and stood with confidence. “Enough games.”

The stranger gave a very slight nod and rigidly moved their arms. In a very articulate, leisurely motion; they grabbed the cloak at the center and pulled loose a dangling string. This string unbound and the entire cloth became loose until it slid off their body and onto the dirt. Their entire appearance was revealed to me; and I felt Alice’s soul run cold.

It was another girl; she was short with exceptionally petite features. Skinny and gray like Alice but composed, unlike any other Teufel I’ve seen. Her right eye was unnaturally wide; open to the fullest and had a very noticeable hazel iris with an outer rim of honey yellow. The other eye was closed; seemingly sealed shut judging by the coagulated skin and scars that surrounded it.

That entire half of her head, face and body was damaged. In the less than optimal lighting, I could see what appeared to be horrendous burns and creased flesh. That skin was darker, tight to her bones and leathery.

Under the cloak, she appeared to wear a ruffled, loose-fitting lavender shirt with three-quarter sleeves and a lot of abuse in the fabric. She also wore light grey slacks that looked just as old and beaten; with many tears and stitching’s throughout.

Nearly all of her hair on the burned side was gone; leaving only a few hanging strands around her ear. Notably, like Lust, she had a hair color that stood out among Teufel; a light cyan with very faint lighter streaks. The hair itself seemed lifeless in some places; shorter in the back but long at the bangs. Inconsistent lengths at best. Mostly, it resembled Alice’s in the way that it was sharp and risen off the skull. Like a short bouquet of knives.

The way she looked at me was zombified, yet scarily aware from her deadpan wide eye. Her posture was rigid; a straight back and limp arms and slightly downturned head.

Alice, now keen to the stranger's appearance, went on high alert.

"No! You should not be here." I've never felt this from her. She was truly afraid at her core. I sensed her stagger, shrivel down to a modest level.

This new girl was looking into my eyes, watching Alice. I couldn't look away from her penetrating gaze. She was unblinking and hardly breathing.

"It is nice to finally meet you two." She said normally, almost robotic. "I am impressed with your fighting prowess, Alicia."

"Don't call me that, you whore." Alice barked.

"So easily offended." She whispered, holding a tone of regret.

"Why. Are. You. Here!" Alice seemed skittish, overall defensive and reserved.

"Alice, who is this?" I asked in a hushed tone.

Her eye switched between mine, looking dreadful.

"*They* call me Crism." The girl answered.

My skin crawled at the revelation of her name. I recalled some distant conversation, where Alice told me about the Teufel's greatest fear. I scanned her up and down in disbelief; at this point, I began regretting my decision to follow.

"Crism. . . you attacked me. *You* helped Lust invade my mind." I accused with irate distrust.

She nodded very slightly. "Please, refrain your anger; there are reasons for my actions."

I grit my teeth. My body, mind and soul were exhausted beyond anything I've felt. "I. . . am so sick of this shit. I want answers, not riddles!" I shouted.

My outburst got Alice riled. "Kim you dumb-shit! Don't agitate her."

"No," Crism said, "She's right. The two of you deserve clarity, Alicia."

Alice's breath became more unsteady. Part of her wanting to stand alongside my frustration and lash out, the other far too timid at her legend status.

"That isn't my name." She held back her voice.

"Using the full version of your assigned name bothers you?" Crism asked quietly.

"Yeah, it does! Because it isn't the name I was given." Alice snarled.

"Fickle, I see. . . Amusing." She said then continued.

"It's true. I discovered Lyumick after she attempted a blind jump to find you. I kept my identity hidden and offered her a chance at your soul. However, this was to benefit you; not her."

"I was tortured; killed, even! I only managed to survive because. . ." I stopped.

She blinked once, "Because you found it; just as I'd hoped you would."

Alice stepped in, "That other energy. What was it?"

"It's Kimberly's. From the moment of her birth, her soul was linked to The Ditch. A preparative establishment meant to allow easy transfer of a Teufel as soon as she matured. However-"

I interrupted, "When Sin broke my father's deal, the connection remained." Crism nodded again. "How could Sin miss something like that?" I questioned.

"He is. . . distracted. The task of maintaining Teufel Anima, archiving his studies and. . . well, he is imperfect."

"But *you* knew." Alice said.

Crism responded, "I closely monitor any Teufel that catches my interest. You have never been alone, Kimberly."

My legs wobbled; breathing was difficult. Crism noticed my wariness.

"Are you well?"

My hands clasped my head, "It's just. . . All this time, I grew up hearing voices, feeling uneasy in the dark and having a disturbing sense of people. You're telling me that it's because I've had demonic power inside me my entire life?" I groaned, feeling sick.

"As an infant and child, the power was inconsequential. But it grew alongside you, adapting to your biology and broadening your senses." She explained.

"My dad used to tell me, that I always had new imaginary friends; then just as quickly forgot about them. Who were they really?"

Crism raised her chin, noticing the slight lift in the rainstorm. "My assumption; damned souls in The Ditch coming across your reservation plot and interacting with the piece of you."

With everything she was saying, I found myself rubbing my arms and shaking my head steadily. A light chuckle came from my throat, which turned into a peal of twisted laughter. Alice became worried, and Crism just stared on with her dead eye.

I settled; just staring at the ground. "Now, a lot of what Lucy said to me makes a lot of sense."

Alice chimed in, "So, explain something to me." She held detest on her tongue. "Why are *you* telling us any of this? What are you scheming?"

"As I said, I am interested in you. A Teufel who has set aside homicidal tendencies to work along-side their host. . . and a human who not only doesn't fear the Teufel bound to her soul but has a unique power of her own, hidden away. This combination will be significant, in time." She said.

Alice kept an intense stare laser-focused on Crism; taking note of any minute twitch or shuffle. "You expect us to trust you? You are the devil to us Teufel." She scowled.

"You treat me with such hostility." Crism replied.

"Yeah, it's been a fucking stressful day."

She blinked again, "Not one day. . . You have been unconscious for twenty-nine hours."

My jaw dropped. "Twenty-nine? What about Tansu, and her mom, didn't they notice my absence?"

Alice barked sarcastically, "Oh yeah, real smooth! Go ahead and tell the murderous *demi-god* who you're most concerned about. Idiot!"

"I am well aware of her bonds, Alice. As I said, we have been watching for a very long time. Your family has been gifted a mirage in your absence."

"Sorry, I. . . don't understand." I questioned.

Crism adjusted her bare feet in the dirt. "Yes. It's a simple spell. A version of you has been inside for this short time; constructed from memories of your interactions together. A physical form does not exist, but they convincingly perceive you."

"So. . . they were brainwashed to see *me,* based on memories of us together? That's, kind of fucked up."

"It was necessary and is quite dependable in most scenarios."

Crism then crooked her neck to the side, as if hearing her name; looking along the forest edge with small concern in her eye. "Time is short. Sin knows nothing about what has transpired here. Unfortunately, we need more time before any definitive action can be made. . . You must be hidden." She continued to speak, lacking urgency, compassion or sentiment.

My head weighed me down; but still, my hands were pressed into the cold soil and I dragged myself to my feet. My back throbbed, and the chill soaked into my clothes was very apparent. "I'm not going anywhere. My friends and family won't live alongside some mental copy of me for the rest of their lives. Besides, if something goes wrong, who will be there to protect them!?" I passionately argued.

"You will remain; I promise you that. . . I am referring to you, and Alice's essence. Now that my theory has been confirmed, and your true self has come to light; we cannot risk your unique vigor falling into another Teufel's hands."

Alice retracted her spiteful attitude, affirming that this situation was not the danger she had rightfully expected. Now, latent curiosity bubbled on her tongue. "What exactly are you planning?" She asked in a low voice.

Crism paused. In the background, the rain continued to lift slowly; leaving a haunting mist behind.

"At this moment, I need to hide you; before it's too late. I do not wish to make the decision for you, it is entirely your choice." She requested.

"No." Alice griped, "I don't like this, not one bit."

"Well, I don't know what to think." I admitted.

We each paused. Then Crism spoke. "I will respect your decision. . . But, please consider it. You do not understand the gravity of importance."

I gave her an annoyed, but thoughtful look. "What'll happen if I agree?"

She slowly lifted her right hand up and directed the palm at her face. A white spark of electricity zapped between each of her fingers, and that spark expanded into a small sphere of light that quickly condensed into an object. A ring.

"This will mask your life force entirely. Not even Sin can detect you."

"But why!?" I yelped. "Your vague information is making this so much harder. If everything happening behind the scenes is so important. . . if I'm so important, then why can't you just tell me!?"

"Because we need more time. You want to kill Sin; I know. You will have your chance, but not in haste."

Alice took over, "If we aren't strong enough now, with our combined ability; then how will *hiding* help us in any way?"

"You must have faith in us. Everything has been considered and everything is going in the right direction." There was no sincerity in her voice.

She extended her hand to me; the ring resting in her palm. "I implore you to wear it."

Eyes shifting, biting the inside of my cheek; my heart was racing. It was impossible to know which choice was the right one; but if she is telling the truth, at the very least this will give me time away from the threat of demons. The way I see it, my soul is already damned; so, I might as well take any chance at peace while I can.

I scooped the ring from her and held it just the same. It was warm to the touch; almost vibrating. It was silver, with a black band around the outer edge and a small diamond shape emblem embedded on the outside.

"This ring is made up of my energy; in time it will dissipate. The moment you put it on, it will be bound to you until its time runs out. The very instant it is bound, you will be masked, and Sin will assume you dead."

I chuckled nervously, "Don't see any downside to that."

Alice scoffed at my ignorance. "Fool. That means that as soon as it dissipates, you'll be back on the map."

"Right." I sighed heavily. "Meaning I'll be a target."

She nodded, "I suggest you practice transforming without aggressive triggers. With your newfound energy, the synchronicity between you two will be more manageable."

Alice cocked an eyebrow, "We can change without her getting pissed?"

"It's been done before." She answered plainly, then twisted her wrist. "Sin will waste no time finding you once the spell wears off. You mustn't divulge this interaction."

"What do I tell him, then?" I asked, rolling the ring in my hand.

A pause. She turned her head away from me, back to the woods except this time, her body followed in rotation. Her back to me, she gave one last warning. "It is likely, that he will *not* want to talk."

With that, raised one hand with a limp wrist and flattened her palm; aimed into the forest. That motion spawned a Rift a few feet in front of her. The piercing white door materialized from nothing and waited for her entry. As the door opened, it inhaled the thin air around us and almost knocked me off balance. She stepped through without hesitation, and the door shut tight behind her. Then it was gone; without a trace.

I stood at an angle; weariness getting the better of me with contemplative depression on my face. My eyes shut and I listened to the pitter-patter of the remaining rain. It was peaceful; despite the horrors I had been forced to endure. I felt almost calm. The ring was clenched in my fist at my side, patiently waiting for my decision; but I could not bring myself to make a choice.

The thick space between Alice and me was apparent. I knew she felt embarrassed and exposed. Being chained away by her sister; and now Crism makes an appearance with a mysterious plan. I don't know who is having a bigger crisis right now.

The cold air all around me iced over my deflated lungs. A sharp intake reset my heart rate and reminded me I was alive. It was difficult to focus on breathing, balance and awareness. Too many scenarios and memories bounced around my head. My eyes were bloodshot from the stress and my very core felt ajar.

It took a long time to move again. Dragging my feet across the open field towards the parking lot; I contemplated their reaction. I wondered how they would describe my behavior; seeing as a ghost held my spot in this time of absence. My body wobbled and dipped with every approaching step; but once the house came into full view, I smiled.

"I just wish I could have normalcy for a little bit." I clasped my hand tightly around the ring.

"I don't know Kim." Alice responded, sounding just as tired as me. "This whole thing with Crism rubs me the wrong way. She's a murderer of Teufel. When one of us starts to get strong, she challenges and defeats them. It makes no sense for her to help us."

"So what, should we just ignore this?" I groaned.

"We leave this place and go on the hunt. Find and kill my siblings so that I may become strong enough."

"You? What about me, us?" My pace slowed.

She went quiet for a second. Then, her tone changed. It was solemn, full of regret.

"We're a team. . . But you know what happens when we get stronger. Your soul won't live long enough to face Sin. I have to do it. . . I will face and kill him and reap your vengeance."

I shook my head. "That's not fair. What if she's right and we *can* defeat him with this power I have? I mean, we don't even know the extent of it. I say we do what she says and wait it out."

"It would be foolish to wait." She was irked again.

I stopped dead in my tracks, halfway crossing the barren parking lot. I detected her impatience dwindling, and then she was gone. Crawled back to wherever it is she goes when there's nothing more to say. Alone again, my feet carried the wilted mass of my body in perturbed silence. Hoarse breaths occasionally shuttered from my lips as I closed in on the house. The hurt in my heart spiked and left me isolated on this planet. It feels like forever.

The nearby streetlamp flickered softly; its vibrant ray spreading like a fire across the rolling fog. My head lowered to the ground; white knuckles and a tightness in my chest. "I. . ." My voice cracked, and the tears rolled down my cheeks. "I just want to be human again." I sobbed.

Trembling in the parking lot with looming grey clouds threatening another storm; I cracked.

Chapter 25 – Home

Reaching the front door, I idled quietly with the ring pinched between my index finger and thumb. Twirling it gently, my decadent gaze read the welcome mat letter by letter, over and over. The chirping of crickets and buzzing of faraway streetlamps accompanied me in this time of despair; tethering me to the ground and reminding me of reality.

My body felt normal, yet abstract. The proper weight, muscle and sway in my limbs aligned with my embedded perception; however, I still expected to find that room behind every blink. Another illusion; a false escape. It didn't seem all that irrational to believe I never escaped. That this was the reality my remaining consciousness conjured up following a ruthless death. At any moment I would find myself floating. . .

But that moment never came. I did indeed escape the pit but was thrown into a deeper hole. In truth, I wasn't debating on what Crism said; my mind was made up the moment this ring touched my flesh. I just wanted to make sure this was real. Whether Alice liked it or not; I choose peace. If only temporary.

The ring slid on my right index finger with ease. Once it reached the knuckle, it tightened very slightly then sent a jolt through my hand. I twitched with a soft grunt of discomfort, but it diminished almost immediately. What followed was the sensation of submerging my whole body in water. The world was muffled, and a thin veil of heated air blurred my vision as the spell went into effect. Seconds later, everything returned to normal and I was left feeling uneasy.

Alice remained quiet. I knew she would be upset, but only for selfish reasons. I know she'll get a sense of cabin fever; unable to release the energy into any meaningful target. But I plan on doing as Crism said; practicing.

A new sense of identity washed over me and I lifted my head with a smile. For once; the anxious pressure screaming paranoia was null and I felt almost free.

I hastily opened the front door with new vigor but had to remind myself of the time. Slowing my entrance; I shut the door behind me silently and absorbed the enclosed atmosphere within the hall. The house was dark except for a small nightlight on the wall directly ahead and the flickering light from the television.

I tip-toed my way across the floor, discarding my damp shoes in a shoe tray by the door. Unfortunately, the rain soaked through everything, so my socks left a small foot trail across the carpet. I made a straight path from the door to the bathroom; glancing to my left at the TV and seeing some cartoon playing and a lump of blankets on the floor.

Inside the bathroom; I shut the door and felt the whir of the ventilation fan above kick on. I stripped out of my clothes immediately and bundled them up; wrapping them in a dry towel and placing it in one of two baskets. In the other basket was a pair of my pajamas. They had been worn twice already but one more time couldn't hurt; besides, I'll be taking a shower in the morning anyway.

Before getting dressed; I used a small hand towel to dry my body and hair. Refreshed, I exited the bathroom and stopped outside the door; taking the time to stretch. Each toe cracked; along with my ankles and lower back.

Lightheadedness flushed over me and wobbled me as I advanced towards the couch.

Stopping behind the couch frame; I leaned on the spine and watched the TV flash colorful images. the silence all around me helped me immerse myself into the program for a moment or two; liberated from any fears of demons or the darkness behind me.

My eyes tracked down and saw Tansu lying on her back; blanket folded down by her waist. One hand rested under her shirt and lay flat on her stomach; while the other was crooked up by her head, laying flat by her ear. Her mouth was slightly open and a somber transfer of air in and out came from her lips. So tender and naïve; I couldn't help but smile with tearful eyes at her image. Up until now, I wasn't sure about this world; but now, I knew I was home.

Carefully, I moved around the couch and climbed over the arm to take a seat. My blankets were bunched up at the far side, so I rustled with them; trying to unravel the mess. But a clump of blanket flipped over the edge of the couch and plopped on her face; stirring her awake.

A feeble grunt and gentle adjustment before she pushed the blanket aside and her eyes peeled open. The child-like gaze fell on me and her chest fluctuated with new air.

"Kim?" She questioned groggily.

I placed my feet on the floor and leaned forward on my elbows, "Tan. Sorry, I didn't mean to wake you." I whispered apologetically.

She yawned and rubbed the sleepy tears from her eyes; leaving them puffy and red.

"What time is it?" She asked.

I leaned back and looked to the microwave,

"Almost eleven." I answered. Then looked back down at her.

She nodded, her muscles lagged, and eyes fluttered. Then she smiled, "Hey," She spoke slowly, "I think my headaches gone."

"Your headache?" I replied.

"Mhm."

I played along, "Oh," I said, "glad to hear it."

She opened her eyes a little more and looked at me; her smile growing. Mine grew too, and I gave a light chuckle.

"Hey, Tansu, will you do something for me?"

"What's that?" She slurred.

I took a deep breath and blissfully exhaled. "I want you to sleep in your own bed from now on."

She ogled with a spacy expression, but eased into lucidity, "But. . . I don't want you to-"

I cut her off, "I'm not alone. Not with you and your mom so close-by."

"What if you have another nightmare? I don't want you to go through that without me."

"It's okay; really. You've done so much for me; you both have. I can never repay your kindness and I will never forget your sacrifice. You can rest easy, in your own bed." I assured her.

She gave a look of unease.

I reached down and extended my pinkie finger. “I’m okay; I promise.”

A pause, then she released her apprehension and wrapped her finger around mine. “I believe you.”

“Good.” I snickered. “Now, get up and sleep comfy for once, will ya?”

She sighed in a pleasant tone, then threw both of her arms above her head and let out a long stretch and murmur before hoisting herself up and tossing her blanket over her shoulder. I grabbed her pillow and followed close behind into her room. Ignoring the light switch; Tansu tossed the blanket onto the bed with a feathery thud and I mimicked with the pillow.

She stood at the foot of her bed, facing it with reluctance in her bones. In my heart, I understood what she was feeling right now. In her mind; this was selfish of her; abandonment. Yet, she was rationalizing my perspective and was having trouble finding peace with this. So, I extended my hand and placed it on her shoulder. She relaxed and then turned around to face me. A pause; then she quickly stepped forward and gave me a tight hug. Butterflies swarmed my belly and I was encapsulated by this moment.

Tansu spoke kindly, “I’m so proud of you.”

Her words crumpled my chest, I couldn’t speak. So, I squeezed harder. In a moment or two we released, and she stepped around the side of her bed and crawled in. The springs settled with her weight and she expressed a shiver before releasing her weight.

I watched her for a minute; appreciating every little memory we have shared. I wondered exactly how this past day had played out for them; if they will remember it how they lived it, or just the same as every other interaction. I regret the fact that they were touched by my corruption; but was relieved that they were no longer in danger. At least; for now.

It didn’t take long before low snoring came from her bed. I looked to the shaded window; a light breeze lifted the curtain slightly then settled and I left the room.

A beep from the fire alarm caught my attention but was quickly disregarded. The TV illuminated the front of the couch but cast a deep black shadow behind it, across the open space. Transfixed by the flashing shadow, I paused and watched with numb legs. The flickering light gave me vivid reminders of the stone rooms and the nightmares within my own mind. Clear images of the torches, hallways and the cage bombarded my eyes and caused a ringing to erupt in my ears. Minerva’s cries of anguish, calling for its mother as she chewed my flesh disturbed me and for a moment, I saw her crawl from the inky black. A blink, and it was gone; never existed.

I shook my head violently and scratched my scalp. I wasn’t afraid of the memories, but I couldn’t forget them. They are a part of me; experienced on a deeper level than my average insight. Those moments are ingrained in my very soul; they will fuel me.

With gusto, I stepped across the deep shadow and rounded the couch again. I let my body collapse onto the couch and quickly wrapped myself in the blanket. Positioning on my back, I stared at the ceiling. Listening to the whispers of the TV, the peaceful breathing of Kari in her room and Tansu’s renewed snores under her blanket.

The ice maker in the fridge deposited a batch, and the outside light finally clicked off. A near twenty minutes passed with me not moving at all, waiting for a word from Alice. Waiting for a drip of water to fall from the ceiling and land on my head. Any rotten stench or mind-numbing buzz, a groan or even the smell of a freshly burnt-out match.

I *knew* that I was free, but I could not shake the illusion. Maybe, it was a side effect. Having Lust and Minerva within me; releasing Demonic Energy and damaging my actual soul infected me; my perception. It will surely fade, but for now, I couldn't shake the writhing under my skin.

My body was at ease while my thoughts grew restless. This overbearing sensation of eyes behind me grew too powerful. Ensuring secrecy and silence, I reached out to the coffee table and snatched the remote. A tingling warmth coated my flesh as anticipation rose.

The remote rested loosely in my grasp, finger on the little red button, dangling by the floor over the edge of the couch. Embrace the fear. Release my constraints; my crutches and prove not only to myself, but to Alice and Sin that I am not powerless.

I pressed the button.

The hushed commercial ceased; leaving a vacant ringing in my ears. The night swallowed everything in an instant. . . I am awake. This is real. *I am awake.*

Stagnant in a dreamlike stillness, I glared where the TV had been, my eyes swirled with many magical colors of the air. My back felt hot, and my breath escaped my lungs as the hairs on my body stood on end. I closed my eyes and saw their faces. Everyone I've ever loved in this word, standing by my side. Even Alice. For all the wrongs we have done, and every mistake that I have made; it made me who I am.

Everyone. . . I exhaled and left my lungs empty.

In time, I will face him. Whatever my future holds for me, whenever fate decides my time has come; I will not back down.

I will have vengeance.

Chapter 26 – Elapse

"Shouldn't you get moving?" Alice nudged impatiently.

I heard her voice but gave no indication I was listening. Dry, nostalgic judgment focused keenly down the forgotten driveway and on the crumbling outer image of my old home. Both hands stuffed in my pockets, I squinted as the sun rays shifted over the left side of my face; sneaking between the swaying leaves above. A swift breeze coated in a damp chill kissed my exposed skin and made me thankful for this leather jacket.

I popped the collar and zipped it halfway up my torso; unable to break my gaze. The saturated memories frozen in place behind those decaying walls still spoke to me. I remember everything, despite the allotment of passed time. But I also remember the house in a slightly different light; one where my dad drank coffee.

Alice pushed again, "Why would you even stop? You can barely keep your eyes off it on the bus."

My body tensed as another wind spiked up, then I turned away; continuing down the long-familiar strip towards town.

I kicked a stray rock, "It's hard to move on. I can hardly believe that that was my life at one point." I said with a straight face.

She perked up, "We can burn it down if you want."

I grinned, "Maybe someday. For now, I think we'll stick to the forest."

Alice scoffed, "Trees don't make interesting opponents; there's no danger, therefor no experience gained."

"What're you talking about? We've made a lot of progress, you and I." I said with abstained optimism.

"Our idea of *progress* is vastly unalike."

I shook my head, smirking at her cynicism.

Within the confines of my pocket, I rustled my hand around; caressing the ring with my thumb and reflecting on the days gone by. It was hard to distract myself from this view, however. The road before me was glistening with an explosion of greens and yellows. Every tree had an abundance of leaves that housed a playground for many chipmunks and birds. The docile banter of nature swelled from every direction and fixated me in the dead center of it all. I could hear everything; every stream of water, snapping twig and rustling blades of grass. It all depended on which I chose to focus on.

"Y'know, I missed this; walking to school, I mean." I observed the edge of the road, then up to the partially clouded sky.

"You have a lot of memories along this pavement." She responded in a flat tone.

"Most are repeats. Still, I never get tired of it." My words were laced with pleasant remembrance.

In my pocket, I felt a slight chill wrap around my finger. It twitched, and the pressure embedded by the ring almost loosened in a way. I closed my fist tight and pressed the tip of my thumb against it. A burn in my gut grabbed my attention.

"Alice, how long has it been?" I asked.

She sighed; her breath pulsing with static discharge. "Six months."

My feet slowed but trudged on. "Six. . . Tansu's birthday is coming up." I noted.

I sensed Alice shaking her head, "Don't detract; you and I both know."

". . . I should get her something nice." I spoke to myself; moving quicker now.

She grimaced; teeth bound, then she relaxed. "Oh, I know; give her the gift of clarity. Introduce us." She sang with sarcastic glee.

"Ew, don't do that; you sound like Lust."

She snickered, "A piece of her must have stuck. But really, it would be funny. *Happy birthday, I have a demon inside me. Alice, say hello.*" She mocked my voice.

"Yeah, a real riot. She'd flip her shit and I can't even imagine what you'd do. . . Oh wait, yes I can." I said in a playful tone.

"Bet her essence tastes good." She sneered.

"Alright, we're done with this." I stated firmly.

Adding a new bounce to my step, I tried to keep my spirits up. Another day back at school without worry or care of the supernatural. Just as it has been since Crism gave me this ring. My initial goal is to make it to class before the second bell; that way I can prove that Tansu is wrong. I've done it many times before.

I removed my hands from my pockets and unzipped the jacket; feeling warm from the walk. At this point, I had made it to the hayfield and intersection. I stopped by the road signs and waited for a car to pass; exiting my strip. After that, I crossed the pavement to the other side and started my shortcut down Bodge road.

Going against traffic, I braced myself from the overhead sun. On either side of me were houses now, with small front and side yards and expensive mailboxes lining the street. Almost no trees this close to the road, so I had no coverage. To my right, one driveway had a car jacked up, and an air pressure tank kicking on every few minutes. I could smell firewood and spotted a light plume of smoke coming from a chimney stack.

Passing by the car undergoing repairs, I slowed once I reached a house on my side with a tall chain-link fence surrounding the property. Almost immediately a hefty thumping ran at me on the other side and I reacted with a slight jolt in my chest before the dog was halted by the fence. It barked loudly at my presence; and I stopped to observe its hostility.

A light brown rottweiler with tight angled eyes and perky ears snapped at me. I observed it with wonder in my stare and curiosity in my posture. He had lifted himself upright with his front paws digging into the fence as he barked nonstop. But as my eyes intensified; the dogs barking became weaker. Finally, he let off the fence and paced back and forth, watching me closely. His tail abruptly lowered, and he let out a shrill whimper before turning back to the house.

Alice sneered, "Now *he* would make practice a bit more fun."

I looked back to the sidewalk and continued on, "I'm not fighting a dog." I said, annoyed; adjusting my bag straps.

"You already fought Destro; what makes this mutt any different?" She joked.

I ignored her comment and quickly forgot about the dog. Pushing on, I started a light jog; knowing I had wasted time and had to make up for it. This strip of road was short and held about five or so houses between each side. Once I was clear of them, I approached a small pond before a wide turn.

This pond on my left was sparsely decorated by lily pads, some floating sticks and low hovering bugs that made the water look filthier than it actually was. Normally I would stop and appreciate the collection of water but not today.

I rounded the turn and the sidewalk transitioned to dirt and more trees came into view. This road was a straightaway with more trees to my left and a few trees with the center of town poking through on my right. This road was no different than the others besides the fact that it mostly consisted of birch trees and some large rocks along the forest edge. It continued for nearly a quarter of a mile before meeting in a four-way intersection.

Decelerating at the bold stop sign, a few cars had met up here at each line and waited to make their turn. I glanced down my left to where the small-town road met up with the main highway and saw a lot of traffic coming and going. To my right, which led into town, was a few cars backed up and most of which were turning in the same direction as me.

One car on my left had an opportunity to go but saw me idling here and waved their hand behind their windshield. I noticed and accepted their gesture to cross. Hurriedly, I jogged ahead and moved on the appropriate side; going with traffic. This road I was on was deliberately pasted with No Smoking, No Guns, and a big blue sign with a Black Bear silhouette; the school mascot.

I was in the final stretch, so I picked up the pace one last time and ran alongside the road. Cars passed me by either way, and even though I didn't have a watch; I had a good feeling I was right on time.

Arriving within three hundred feet of the front doors, I heard a bell ring and for a moment feared Tansu would be proven right. However, to my liking, the hoard of students began moving by the front doors and windows from the cafeteria. I smirked, brushing my slightly messy hair to the side and moved to catch up with them.

I joined the crowd; easily inserting myself into the flowing river of bodies. I started craning my neck in all directions; keeping pace.

Alice spoke, "Looking for your friend?"

"Yeah, gotta shove it in her face that I made it." I answered out loud.

A guy in front of me turned his head, and gave me a funny look "What'd ya say?"

I gawked at him, "Huh? Oh, nothing." Avoiding his direct stare.

He squinted slightly, too tired to care and faced forward.

Alice snickered. "Idiot."

I gave a sour expression and lowered my head. The crowd reached the main diverting corridors and started to split off in all different directions. Classrooms, lockers, bathrooms; wherever they needed to go first. Then, I felt a sort of ping in the back of my head. Alerted to a familiar sensation, I planted my feet in the floor and looked to my left.

"Tan!" I called over.

Perking up, she followed my voice and saw me moving towards her.

"You made it." She exclaimed.

I rubbed the underside of my nose with a confident grin, "Told ya. No problem."

She noticed the jacket, "I see you're finally wearing it. I bet he'll be happy about that."

I shrugged, "I just hope he doesn't want it back. Does it look weird?" I asked.

"Hmm." She pondered, "It's a little big on you. Otherwise I think it reflects who you are." She smiled.

I leaned in slightly, expecting more detail, "In what way?"

She giggled, "Just a tad standoffish, from a distance, but soft to the touch."

Alice butted in, "Is she mocking you?"

I shook my head in response to Alice but spoke directly to Tansu. "I think that's pretty accurate. . . And hey I like what you've got goin' on there."

She blushed. Today, she wore her hair back in a low ponytail that left a lot of her bangs still drooping forward but held to one side with that same old lime-green hairpin. Her shirt was a simple white tee and on top of that was a dark blue button-down cardigan snapped all the way up. Light toned khaki pants and a thick black belt completed her outfit and gave off strong *Kari-inspired* vibes.

"Thanks." She said shyly. "We should probably get to class."

"Heh, yeah. I'll catch you later Tan."

"Bye, Kim."

With a wave, we split off to our own destinations.

The noisy clamor of people beginning their day surrounded me. I felt calm, more or less; though I faced grim reminders everywhere I looked. These walls no longer housed memories of lectures and soliciting; they were scarred over. I remembered the first day the school reopened; after the accident with Stacy.

Taking my first steps down these halls was overwhelming. At the time, two weeks had passed, and nothing was ever done. Their number one priority was her well-being and Kel's arrangements. The guy who they pinned the blame on vanished without a trace and I got away with it.

Still, I remember what it was like to be here after those two weeks; how sick I got. All of the raw, potent energy just wriggling through every ounce of air; all the angst, fear, loathing and scathing distrust. I absorbed it all; vulnerable in my new spiritual state. But now, I've grown accustomed to it; I enjoy the sensation it gives me. There is clarity with the people who walk among me.

I made it to my first class before the second bell, and the lessons began. Like every day before, time dragged the second the classroom door closed. I took my seat and let my bag hit the floor. The hard-plastic chair welcomed me with immediate discomfort, and I adjusted myself to a half-lying, half-upright position; crossing my arms and yawning. My eyes eased themselves shut, and I listened to the other students as they arrived, talking and laughing along.

Art was either the most interesting thing I will hear all day or equally the most boring, mind-numbing tasks. Today was a little different. We were given the task of sketching two things; something you love and something you fear. A speech outlining duality followed and were left with ten minutes to consider.

I wasted three pages with quick doodles; brainstorming. The jacket I wore was hung up on the back of my chair and gave excellent cushion when I leaned back; stressed.

I decided to start with my fear; thinking it would be easy. But it wasn't. There are many things I fear, but none I should express as part of a stupid drawing assignment. I don't know what I feared most anyway.

So, I drew a door. A single, steel door with a small barred window at the top half and bold metal rivets punched throughout. I could've spent all day drawing the things I am afraid of and yet, I struggled to find many things I loved. *Things*, not people. As far as memorable or special possessions go, I don't have many. No trinkets, photos or hand-me-downs to treasure.

Next to that, I drew the first object that really stuck with me as special, even though I have had almost no real interaction with it. A windchime; like the one we have in the yard. I felt close to satisfied with what I presented, but guilty that they were only acceptable quality.

I'm over-thinking it. This assignment probably won't even count for a major grade considering how close we are to the end of the year. But I handed it in nonetheless and waited. The rest of the class finished up and turned in their papers; they took their seats. With ten minutes 'til the bell, most everyone rested their heads or talked.

Once the bell came, every nearby door burst open and the same cluster formed. I exited into the hall, throwing on my jacket followed by my backpack and started like every other day before. But, not even ten feet down the hall, I was immediately stricken by a muscle spasm in my chest. This swayed my balance slightly and I braced myself on the lockers to my side.

Wincing, I glared down the hallway with half-open eyes and my vision started to pulse with the beating of my heart. The lights above me dimmed and one by one the students phased out of reality. My eyes slammed shut and when they reopened there was darkness. Broken light fixtures swinging above, bloody shredded corpses on the floor and deafening silence.

From the nothing sprouted a whisper that grew into a commanding yell. "Hey!" Alice shouted.

All at once I was back in my eyes and lifted myself off the lockers. A cold sweat formed on my upper lip and I went into a tight panic. Immediately I sprinted forward and located the nearest door that wasn't a classroom.

I burst in and slammed it behind me. Pressing my back against the cold metal, I caught my breath and stared at the hanging string in the center of the room. More flashes of the stone room bombarded me as I reached for the string. I pulled it and the light flicked on.

Whipping my head around, I realized I had run into the janitor's closet. A small, dank room with a plastic bucket sink and mirror to my left. Many brooms, mops and wet floor signs filled the tight space and a musky bleach smell burned my nostrils.

"Another one?" Alice warbled.

I spoke softly, "Yeah. Not so bad this time."

"A lot of stress in the air today; you shouldn't be so empathetic."

I pushed off the door and approached the sink, placing my hands on the edge and staring at myself in the mirror.

"I can't control it." I responded hoarsely, my breath tightening.

Behind my head, through the reflection, I saw Alice sort of fade into the light. She looked cynical as always but a little less upfront about it.

"Your mind and soul were never meant to carry this burden. I'm surprised you've held it together this long."

I smirked, "I'll take that as a compliment."

On the edge of the sink was a roll of brown paper towels. I peeled and ripped a couple of sheets and wiped my face. "Y'know, I always thought anxiety attacks were overdramatized in movies and TV. . ." I swallowed hard.

Alice gave me a look that could almost be considered worried. "I think you're closer to the PTSD side of things. Though, there's more influence than just your mind."

I nodded, "This is the third time this week."

"And each time has taken you longer to break free."

I raised an eyebrow, "How long was I stuck?"

She shrugged, "Forty or so seconds, I think. Some kid with glasses ran to get a teacher."

"Crap. Guess I'll wait here till after the bell rings."

"You'll be late." She said plainly.

"Just like old times." I joked.

Trying to settle back to normalcy, I exhaled until my lungs were drained completely of air. Then, I took in a big breath through my nose, tried to ignore the bleach scent, and let it out. I got my breathing under control, so now, I watched my reflection. Alice remained; no emotion.

The light flickered above me, adding to the overall feeling of claustrophobia and misplacement. Getting up close to my own reflection, I slid my pointer finger across my chin and examined the tiny horizontal scar. It was barely noticeable and had almost no bump to the touch; I nearly forgot it was there.

I ruffled through my hair and felt the lack of density. Ever since I cut it short when I was eight, my hair has always been the same length and texture. Just above my shoulders, fluffy with dense waves at the ends. . . I haven't cut it in these six months.

Three inches doesn't seem like much, but it wasn't just about the length. Overall, it's become less dense and the waves at the ends were less dramatic. On top of that, the weight was noticeable to me. Though, strangely enough; I liked it like this. Now with Alice being a part of me, I've taken a liking to the added length and the feeling of hair in front of my eyes.

Outside the door, I heard the bell ring. Now late; I lifted myself off the sink and opened the door a crack. I peered out into the hall, ensuring caution in every motion. On the other side of the hall, ten lockers down I saw three boys by a water fountain conversing with no regard for their level of volume.

At a glance, I recognized them by face and name but not association. They were Juniors, using their free period to just hang around apparently. Andrew; a tall, well-structured athletic type with short blonde hair and glasses. Danial: one of the few darker-skinned kids at this school who wasn't usually seen without his precious trumpet. And Alex; a husky, quiet guy that I didn't know much about.

Danial happened to turn his head and see me poking out. He gave a confused squint and then bumped elbows with Andrew.

"What'cha up to?" Danial asked loudly.

The other two snickered like kids. Exposed, I clicked my tongue and stepped out into the hall. "Just, uh, ya know. . ." I fumbled.

Andrew stuffed his hands in his pockets. "Nice jacket." He said while chewing gum.

No longer caught off guard, I raised my chin and glared at them with delighted egotism. "It is."

Danial leaned in a little, "Got your boyfriend in there, Sophomore?"

I couldn't help but smirk at their arrogance. In my eyes, it was laughable having them harass me.

"Whatever stirs a conversation. You're welcome to wait around for him to come out." I mocked.

Andrew laughed at my taunt, "We're just fuckin' with ya."

"You're Kim, right?" Alex asked quietly.

I shrugged, in a, *here I am*, kind of way. "Why?" I responded.

His bottom lip curled, "Nothing."

"Alright then. Well, I gotta go."

I casually walked past them with an amused stride. They didn't say anything else to me, and instead returned to their banter after I went on by. In the clear, I relaxed my back and walked normally; immediately disregarding the encounter like it never happened.

Off to the gymnasium. I wasn't really concerned about being late; but I kept going at an ordinary speed. Seeing as this was the last quarter, the hallways were decorated with projects and photos from the school year. Many unique works to marvel at and get distracted by all things I have become jaded to.

Arriving at the gymnasium, I gave the teacher a quick apology for being four minutes late and entered the bathroom to change as most others left. Today, we had a list of exercises to complete before moving on to whatever activity was planned. Ten laps around the court, stretches, twenty sit-ups, ten push-ups and more stretches. After that we split four teams and set up the badminton nets long ways across the Gym.

Personally, I wasn't all that interested in badminton today. I sat on the sidelines and spun my racket in my palm; pondering some faraway thoughts. When I did get tagged in, I couldn't motivate myself to get invested and mainly played defensively. Luckily the opposing team wasn't playing competitively, and we were all just killing time. Although, I think Alice enjoyed the game on a fundamental level.

By the end of class, a sleepy numbness entered my blood. A large yawn erupted and left my eyes watering. Like all the other students, I headed to the bathroom to change. In standard fashion, maneuvered myself away from the locker area and carried my clean clothes to a private toilet stall. The echo of the other girls' voices kept me entertained; gossip and immature comedy were prevalent in here.

I held the bundle of worn clothes against my hip and strolled out of the bathroom in a black T-Shirt with a white star on the chest and the pants I wore on my way in. One by one they all filtered back out and returned to their bags. I hoisted mine over my shoulder and waited for the bell.

After it rang, the day was feeling repetitive and my focus waned. I had to shut off my ears to get around the constant chatter in every direction. A headache grew while I weaved between faceless students. Alice was staying with me today, it seems. Normally she would have checked out by first period, but she's still here; almost like she was watching out for me.

I closed my eyes for a moment or two; continuing to move down this straight corridor. I took ten or so steps, relying on my special awareness to guide me. Suddenly, I felt an aura stopped in front of me and I peeled both eyes open in time to see Needy awkwardly in my path.

His shoulders raised up the sides of his neck and he offered a nervous grin. My tired eyes immediately recognized him. Short, intentionally messy looking hair and thick round glasses with a kangaroo pouch white sweater and blue jeans. His face had rounded cheekbones and thin lips, complimented by a button nose and brown almond eyes.

He noticed my dazed expression and tensed his body. "S-sorry. I didn't mean ta' spook you."

Allowing the atmosphere to invade me again, I took a breath and warmly smiled. "What's up, Needy?"

He gave an entertained look, "You're still using that nickname?"

I adjusted my feet, "I'm not the only one. Plus, it's a funny story. . . I'll stop if it bothers you."

A few people made wide arcs around us; disrupting the flow of traffic. He waved nonchalantly, "Nah, it's kind of refreshing."

"Did you *need* something?" I emphasized.

"And there it is." He giggled.

I rubbed the ring meticulously, "I couldn't resist."

"Of course not. But no, I didn't. I stopped to wipe my glasses and you were coming at me like a zombie. If you didn't snap out of it you would've plowed me over." He rubbed his shoulder.

I then yawned loudly; triggering a yawn in him as well. "Yeah. . . sorry, I lost the plot for a minute. Got really tired out of nowhere."

I stuffed my right hand in my pocket, feeling the chilly bite from the ring.

"Not getting enough sleep?" He asked.

"Actually, I've been sleeping a lot better lately. I used to have a lot of nightmares, but they seem to be happening less and less."

"Nightmares, huh?" His voice trailed off; bearing the weight of truth as he understood my past.

"Like I said. . . better lately." I emphasized.

"Right. Well, anyway, I don't wanna keep you. Keep your eyes forward, alright?" He smirked.

"I will, thanks man."

He nodded slightly and then curved around me in the opposite direction. Onward again, I kept my head raised. The next class came and went without burning any new information in my brain. All the teachers knew focus would be hard to gather at this point; so, they were doing their best to keep lessons simple and easily absorbed.

I tapped my pencil along; chin resting in my palm with a glazed over look and sleep prying at my eyelids. Alice had stepped away from my vision much later than usual. I no longer felt her buzz which made me feel even more empty; thus, enhancing the zombie state.

Just when I was over the day, the last bell before lunch rang and a new spark ignited in me. Food; that would inspire anyone. With haste and keen awareness, I jogged down the halls and got to the cafeteria as quickly as I could. A bustling hunger presented itself; whining like a dog with a treat dangling overhead.

Stepping into the new bubble of noise; I slowed and observed the droves of students either sitting at the circular tables or waiting in line. I joined the impatient line and let my eyes wander around; taking each crawling inch as it came.

It was pretty tame today. Usually laughter or some overzealous group was being obnoxious, but it seems like everyone was either tired or just not feeling it.

I didn't see anyone I was interested in at the various tables; but when I looked ahead through the line, I saw Tansu alone. She was about ten people ahead of me and clearly rigid like always. Seeing her gave me a jolt of happiness in my chest and I debated on calling out to her; but decided to just wait until after we both got our food.

But then, a guy and girl approached from her left and nonchalantly cut directly in front of her. She didn't react in any way, besides lowering her head a little. My gleeful face quickly switched to pensive annoyance while the guy wrapped his arm around the girl's shoulders and held her close. The line advanced another step, and I watched Tansu drag her feet forward.

Not fully attentive, the pair ahead only took half a step and Tansu ended up bumping her forehead right into the guys back. She bumped off of him and retreated herself; which only made her bump into the girl behind her.

"Watch it!" The girl scoffed.

Tansu then balled up between them; her shoulders tight to her neck and her arms under her armpits. The pair ahead turned their heads and chuckled before taking a step back and pushing Tansu again. Which, in turn, bumped her back into the other girl.

The girl, who I now saw to be the bratty rich girl Brianna, snapped at the guy. "Really, Brent?" Her voice was like biting a metal fork, "Push her the other way, not at me."

He looked at her with a dirty grin, "What?" He mockingly stretched his word, "She bumped me first."

By this point, I gave up my spot in line and started moving up the side with a huff in my breath. He removed his arm from his girlfriends' shoulder and started to jab a finger in Tansu's direction. I saw this action and sucked in a short breath, then reached out and wrapped my fist around his meaty digit. He paused, mouth ajar with confusion.

His head rotated to me and Tansu also looked up; both of her fists now wrapped tightly in their little odd ball.

"Let go of my finger." He said, still caught off guard.

I didn't say anything; just kept my fiery glare on him. The cockeyed stupor on his face shifted to an entertained smirk and then he tried pulling his finger out of my grip. It wouldn't budge; I had my hand so tightly bound around his finger that the air bubbles in his finger cracked with the third pull. Now, the rest of the line was privy to our little encounter and were all looking in this direction.

His bemused gawk changed to angry quickly. "Let my fucking finger go."

"First," I started, "Apologize to her."

His head shook, "What? Are you serious?"

My voice was stiff, deeper. "Haven't you embarrassed yourself enough already, Brent?"

His girlfriend inserted herself, "Get lost, bitch."

I didn't even give her the courtesy of a look; and, instead I tightened my grip, causing his knuckle to turn purple and his face tensed. I scrutinized every muscle in his face as he held back the pain.

Then, I felt a soft touch on my arm. My eyes shot to the sensation; it was Tansu's hand resting gently on my sleeve.

"Let him go." She requested quietly.

Without hesitation, my grip released, and he ripped his hand back; holding it gingerly.

"Psycho-fuck!" He shouted.

Brent and his girlfriend then faced the front of the line and pushed their way ahead. Snarling at other students and cutting straight ahead for the door. I wanted to go after him, but she suppressed that urge. I closed my eyes and tried to reset myself. Back to normal, I looked at her and smiled.

"Tan, you can't let people like *him* push you around."

She chuckled; her nervous fists unclasped. "Oh yeah? And what would you have had me do? Push him back?" She said sarcastically.

Amused, I threw my head back with a sigh, "I'm just saying, stand up to them. Let them know that you aren't just a mound of dirt to be kicked or stomped on."

She cocked her head a little. Her hair fell to the side. "Okay, I'll be sure to do that." More sarcasm.

The lane returned to its normal pace, and we were almost inside the buffet. More people had arrived in the cafeteria and so the noise level rose accordingly; making it slightly more difficult for me to focus on one conversation.

"Eventful day?" She asked.

Three other lines of dialogue skipped around in my head.

"Somewhat. I was getting tired, but I think I'm awake now." I gloated.

Brent and his girlfriend exited on the other side of the room with their food. They moved together with a superior strut until they reached a table with a couple other people and took their seats.

I watched him but spoke to Tansu. “How about you? Anything happen since this morning?”

“Not besides what just happened.”

I flicked my tongue in disgust, “Meh, Brent’s a dick.”

“It’s sort of my fault; I wasn’t paying attention.”

“Oh, I saw everything. He had no right to treat you that way.”

She went quiet for a second and I continued to watch him. Only now did I see that at the very same table; was a familiar face. Obscured by twice the makeup and longer bangs; was Stacy herself. Brent sat beside her and leaned in close; whispering something to make her smile the slightest amount. He rubbed her back and pushed the tray of food he brought over in front of her with a kind smile. She stared at it without any change in her expression; hands held tight between her legs.

Remorseful neutrality washed over me when I saw her; the way she kept her head low and face hidden. She hasn’t been the same since that day. The arrogant, self-assured, beautiful *miss everything;* was now too afraid to go anywhere without her big brother.

The visceral scars she hid behind the pasty muck and her hair were the product of a truth she never came forward with. In a way; I almost wished she didn’t wake up. Because the way she is existing in and out of her own mind; isn’t living at all.

I walked blindly forward; keeping with Tansu’s stride. Breaking my sight away from them, I looked forward and stepped again; now entering the buffet line. I took a tray and ogled at the assortment of food; picking out whatever caught my stomach’s attention.

We both got our lunch and moved towards our usual seats with minimal haste. The two of us found and sat at an empty table and unraveled the plastic spoon and fork from the rolled napkin. The collection of miscellaneous junk that passed as a wholesome meal around here was no less a letdown than every other day.

“Awesome, sweet potatoes! I love these.” Tansu expressed contained excitement.

“Come on, really? How can you enjoy this crap so much?”

“My mom wanted me to grow up not picky when it comes to food. If I didn’t eat all my cereal, she would make me sit there until I finished it all. No matter how soggy it got.” She chuckled.

“That’s gross. My dad got annoyed if I left food uneaten, but he just said *screw it.*” I lifted a spoonful of applesauce and ate it quickly.

“I think you should give the food a break. It’s not bad at all, I’ve had worse.” She defended it playfully.

“I mean, I used to like it. . . but I’ve been eating this cafeteria food for a while now. So, I’m tired of it.” I smiled.

“I can’t argue with that, I guess.”

We both shoveled a few bites and set aside the conversation for the time being. The clamor of other kids was less intense and I was able to relax my neck muscles and just space out for a moment.

Then, a new voice approached.

"Yo, what's goin' on?" Joey came forward with a tray of his own.

"Hey, Joey. Take a seat." I greeted kindly.

"Sure, sure." He beamed, setting his tray on the table across from us and sitting down.

Immediately, I noticed a big difference in his appearance.

"No hat today? That's a bit odd for you." I started.

His hand shot up to his hair and covered it partially. "Shut up, Kim. I had to wash it sometime." He grinned.

"When was the last time?" I leaned in with a sly look.

"I don't know, honestly." He snickered.

"Gross. How much mold was inside?" I ate another spoonful of applesauce.

"Who knows? I spent maybe an hour chipping away at it"

We both snickered at the dumb joke and I noticed Tansu had gotten quiet. I glanced from the corner of my eye and saw her smile was gone; now just quietly eating.

"You, all right?" I asked.

"Mm? . . . Mhm." She hummed with a little shy nod.

Squinting with concern, I jabbed my food a few times and collected a bit on my fork. Joey kept the conversation alive.

"I saw you and Brent going at it; what was up with that?" He said between chews.

"First off, chew your food, dude."

He cleared his throat, smiled with pinched lips and swallowed.

"Second, he was being himself; need I say more?"

He got a little serious, "You stood up to him?"

I set my fork down, "Yeah?"

"Funny. 'Cuz, I seem to remember saving you from Brent and Stacy not that long ago." Sarcastic insinuation lathered his voice.

I leaned on my elbows, "Actually, it was forever ago. I'm a big girl now."

His lower lip raised, "Alright." Impressed, he leaned back a little and continued eating. "I mean. . ." he chewed, stopped and swallowed before continuing, "I *was* gonna go over there when he started shouting but then he stormed off. So, I had your back."

Out of nowhere came a loud sneeze. The two of us both reacted sharply and saw Tansu with her spoon hovering in front of her mouth and face covered in squash.

Bright-orange wet mushy food spattered all over her face and left her red with embarrassment. My mouth halted wide open just as I was going to take another bite; the three of us frozen. Then, he and I exploded into laughter. I dropped my spoon and buried my face in my hands, laughing so hard my chest tightened. He leaned back and almost fell off of the table's bench.

Tansu just sat there, dumbfounded and motionless; food sliding down her cheeks. A crude expression started to form and the redness only grew.

"It's not funny, you guys." She trembled ashamed.

Hastily, she looked around for a napkin. Joey had taken large breaths to calm himself while I wiped the tears from my eyes. He snatched up his napkin and handed it over to her with a few giggles still seeping out.

"Sorry, Tan but that was funny." I chuckled a little. She pouted and wiped the remaining food from her face then pushed her tray away.

"I'm glad you're enjoying yourself." She responded stiffly.

I nudged her gently with my elbow. She looked back and gave me an assuring smile; now I knew she was okay. So, we continued on as though nothing happened. I finished up my food, Tansu was drinking her strawberry milk, and Joey stuffed the last bite in his mouth, then stood up with his tray.

"All right, I have to go." He said.

"Where ya off to?" I asked.

"Heading down to the library. I have a slideshow to work on. Have to cram it together for end period."

"Hey, at least you're making a solid effort."

"Don't I always?" He smiled.

"Nah." I joked.

"See you two later!"

He walked off and the silence continued. Of course, the room was as loud as could be.

I spoke up, "All right, Tan, what's the deal?"

"With what?" she replied.

"I think Joey may get the idea eventually that you don't like him. The way you go quiet when he's here."

"It's not just him." She whispered.

"I know, but I mean I'm not asking you to throw yourself at him, but maybe just acknowledge him a little. Who knows, you two could be friends. I mean you've talked before. It wasn't so bad, right?"

"It's just hard; you know me. . ." She said, almost sounding ashamed of herself.

"But you were able to open up for me; why not for Joey as well?"

Again, she folded her two fingers over her thumb and applied pressure.

"Maybe someday." She answered.

The bell blared over everyone; signaling the end of lunch period and urging us to move forward with the day.

"Time's up." I stated.

She nodded and we each stood up with our trays and disposed of them in a trash can on the way out. We walked side by side; a small space between us where our hands shifted with every step. A misstep on my part bumped our hands together and, in that moment, I experienced a slight sting in my finger.

"Oops." Tansu said; her eyes tracking to our hands.

I noticed she had stopped walking, so I planted my feet and turned my head to see her retracing back and bending down to the floor.

"Oh no." She exclaimed sadly.

She turned back to me with her upturned palm extending out to me. Time seemed to move in slow motion when my eyes fell on the object in her hand. A slithering pit of burning oil formed in my gut as I reached out and took the object in between my fingers.

"Kimmy. . . your ring broke?"

Chapter 27 – Incubi

At the end. . . will you rise?

A cracking, bubbly voice; indiscernible as man or woman pried at the foundations of my blackened mind. Blips of color and indescribable shapes phased in and out of my perceived reality. There was a low tone, deep and perverse; paralyzing.

Then; light. A vision of scrolling clouds rushed by my perception at immense speed from every direction. An explosion of fire and electricity sent a wave of invisible energy in a dome and created a pocket within the dense smoke and engulfed me as I descended rapidly without control. Spinning, fumbling like a ragdoll, hundreds of miles above the ground; an opaque smudge of colors spattered my eyes and blinded me with the passing speed.

A jolt harassed my enflamed body; surging from my index finger and shooting through to my heart. A drag pushed up against me and stabilized my motion; decreasing the overpowering descent and allowing me to face the earth below. The wind blasted my face still, but I could see something approaching below; a house. Impact was inevitable, as I had no control over my body; for I was a slave to memory.

Raging gusts lashed my face and body; picking up speed as I watched the ground approach with horror. Behind me in the empty sky, I could feel a presence scream a name I couldn't comprehend; reaching too short. Just before crashing into the room; my mind was overcome by a vision of bodies sprawled out on the floor as a living flame swallowed everything.

I existed behind my eyelids for a period I couldn't discern. A second or a year; impossible to tell. Spiritual and lacking perception; a conscious void where there was nothing and everything. All at once, I was awake in a room with my back against a wall; as though I had been forever. Pressed in fear, not knowing what form I took, I witnessed a shadow peel itself from a layer of nothing in the air. Sprouting lanky limbs and a slanted posture, it took on a human shape; distinguished indefinitely by the yellow glow of its eyes.

The disturbing shadow relaxed its weightless appendages and started to sway. Misty sections of the ghostly outline were washed away like blood in water; remaining on the surface like oil in rain.

Crying. I was crying.

I feel. . . you. Awake?

Random layered voices equally whispered and screamed in my ears. Its skin peeled off section by section, revealing bone and blood. A sickening white sphere at the center behind its rib cage pulsed in fragility; like a little sun it warmed everything around it. The skin then reformed in a macabre tornado; reshaping the entire body into a new one.

My mother. She was grey with darkened eyes and veins like tree roots spreading across her face. I felt the illusion tug at me, giving me an awareness of my own form. She smiled and then the skin burst outward again, froze in bloody chunks, then sucked back into the same shape; this time with a hole punched through her chest revealing a stopped heart.

She spoke to me, in a deep, pained voice.

Are you happy?

As if leaning in for approval, I anxiously nodded; "Yes."

Her voice changed to static, giggling.

Are you sure? That seems unlike you.

Her face suddenly flooded with blood originating from her hairline. She wasn't smiling. I watched her slowly drag her fingernails across her throat and peel the skin back. No blood fell from the lacerations; but once he reached the end of her neck, her head tilted backward and fell to the ground. The head hit the misty brown floor and many thin strings sprouted up to suck it into the void.

The neck stump did not bleed a single drop. Instead, a black bubble erupted up from the hole and burst. When it did, a bundle of dark tentacles made from solid shadow's burst out and extended up twice her height.

They whipped and thrashed in the air which caused her body to become unbalanced and fall over. The shadows slithered along the floor and attempted to snag my ankles. Another unique voice yelled to me from behind. Upon turning, the wall was gone, and I was met with the face of my father.

The wounds I caused in his belly remained, and the right side of his head was exploding outward from the self-inflicted gunshot. He laughed at me.

His mouth moved, but the words that he formed were nonsense. He cocked back his arm and threw a fist forward; but it wasn't his fist that connected with me. His hand had changed, morphed into a spool of thread with a thousand needles pointing outward. The needles shredded my face and sent me crumbled to the ground where the tentacles returned and spiraled around my body. Like snakes; they constricted my bones and left me screaming in agony.

I can set you free.

A familiar, but unrecognizable voice whispered.

Lashing around, I whined and begged. "Anything! Save me!"

A lumbering inky puddle rose up from the ground in front of me feet; stretching over ten feet above me thrashing about on the ground. The bubbling black tar took on a thin frame resembling a decayed tree and sprouted a face that I loved. A face with big eyes and three freckles.

Kill?

"Save her!"

The shape twisted again; spinning rapidly then settling on the form of Sin once more.

Save!?

The voices screamed.

I sobbed, "Kill. Save me."

Stop. Please.

In an instant. . . I became lucid. I remembered who I was; what I am. With the power of comprehension, my skin turned grey and my eyes exploded into a radiant purple. This change allowed me to rip free of the shadowy bindings and climb back on my feet. The ink body shriveled to my eye level and molded into his crooked shape. He greeted me with a silent, filthy sneer and tilted head.

Who are you? He cackled.

There was no hesitation. I took a confident strut forward and raised my hand back; claws extended and ready to strike. But something was wrong.

All at once the two of us were boxed in a tight room and there was a soft whimpering coming from the walls. My expression changed to worry, and my bones became weighted. Sin himself lost his snarl and his face went blank as he shriveled down against the wall; sobbing.

Perplexed, my hand lingered behind my head. The longer I stared at the shriveling body; the more I began to recognize details in my peripheral. A bed immediately to my left with pale grey light soaking into the blanket. Then another on my right, identical in every way aside from color. A three-drawer nightstand melded into the wall behind him as his appearance obfuscated into a pastel, darkened mass. A blink, and the walls had texture, the floor turned to carpet, and a tender scent of fabric softener entered my nostrils.

Screaming in my chest shook me and caused a retreat in my steps. My arm lowered while my feet stumbled until I could see the two beds side by side with a small walking gap between them; headboards against the wall and nightstand placed centered. In front of the stand was a huddled, cowering shape painted by shadows. A sliver of the face was revealed by a blue-tinted glow creeping from the left.

The nightmare was over, and I found myself in a whole new terrifying reality. Looking down at my arms and chest, I raised my hands before my face and witnessed the milky grey slowly sink back to my everyday paleness. The claws retracted themselves and the filter of vignette purple disappeared from my vision. A heavy panted overcame me as the power released me front its grasp.

Hard crashing into my world, my lungs stretched, and a sharp pulsating took hold of my brain. Glaring to the shadow, I slowly pieced together the scene.

"Tansu?" I whispered; saliva pooled in my mouth.

She sat on the floor; knees raised in front of her with her arms shielding her face. Her face soaked with tears and eyes screaming in fear; paralyzed. The memories from the day leading up to this reentered my brain like a storm cloud. Drowning me with images and sounds of whatever completed the mystery.

Fear. . . Palpable fear swallowed me; I remember. Leaving school, coming home and throwing up for an hour. Something almost unreal crashed into my brain and left me empty; waiting. I slept. . . I know I slept but that nightmare. . .

"No." I ushered.

A snap in my head broke me free from this circle of thinking. My arms fell limp to my side as an overwhelming sadness overcame me. I stared at her with a numb expression, waiting for her to react. All she could do was whimper; take in stifled breaths every few seconds.

A whirlwind of every emotion I was capable of, swirled around me. My eyes became bloodshot, dark bags prominent beneath and a hot breath flowed. I kept trying to tether myself on this floor; keep centered to reality and confront this. But I kept getting lost, searching for my words, any kind of nonhostile response.

A high pitched, bass-filled buzz crackled in my head. Alice provided concern in her voice.

"Why did you stop?"
In my head, I struggled to even respond. "Was it. . . me, or?"
She seemed frantic, "Are you confused?"
I jerked, visible to Tansu's watch.
"What's happening?" I replied to Alice.
She seemed baffled, "We were talking for nearly ten minutes? About the heat in the air, the pressure in your veins."
Stuck in this head-fog, I closed my eyes. "I was dreaming." I whispered out loud, ever so softly. "The sky. . . falling?"
"You weren't dreaming?" She seemed genuinely confused. "You stirred *me*, told me you were afraid of Sin and what would happen when he finds you. . . I suggested we kill your friend for a last surge of power." She admitted with a slum voice.
"You what!?" I choked in my head.
Her arrogance emerged, but she was restricted by some culpability; so, she kept her sharp tongue leashed. "I meant it as a joke. . . *You* said yes."
Red with fury, I crooked my head to the side away from Tansu; teeth grit.
"I would never say that."
Alice pulled back; her own head throbbing with the situation. "Kim I-"
"Fuck off, Alice. Don't even talk to me right now." I snarled.
Turning my eyes back to Tansu, my heart sank as I fully understood the situation. My right hand twitched and began to rise on its own; reaching out to her. Like a cornered animal, she thrashed in place; pressing her body into the nightstand and nearly toppling the lamp over. I retracted a bit and hushed her.
"Shh," A tremble in my jaw, I tried to speak. "It. . . It's me." I stated fearfully.
Tansu shook her head. "No." She huffed between words, "That-wasn't. . . Kimmy?" She questioned.
Her arms raised and blocked her face, but the trembling receded the slightest amount.
I let my body relax to the floor; brain swimming in fog. My panting slowed; a seriousness invaded me. "Tansu, I need you to breath."
She kept her eyes locked but pulled herself more upright against the stand. One leg slid out and her arms lowered just a bit. The terror pouring out of her had an acidic taste to it; bitter.
A deep sigh, "Now you know."
"No, I don't." She cried. "Who are you!?"
Dejected, I frowned. "Tansu, it's me, Kim."
Her head shook side to side fiercely. "N-no! No, that wasn't Kim. . . Please, get away." She recounted, trembling again.
"It *was* me, and also her." I said shamefully.
"Her?"
With a clenched fist and a loss of my determined self, I bit my lip hard. My eyes caught hers and they froze like that. A minute of us holding an invasive stare; she could see me, the real me. The truth was sinking into her brain slowly. Her muscles began to soothe and her posture drooped.

We disconnected, and I instantly felt a drain take hold of my body. Empathetic to her sensitivities, I held my breath and retained the emotion I drew from her. With a dry mouth, I looked to the floor, then back to her.

I took it upon myself to stand; she kept a close watch. Placing myself on the mattress, I let my legs dangle between our beds with her on my right.

"You want to run, don't you?" I asked neutrally, trying my best to keep my emotions under control.

A pause. She gave no answer in her eyes or body.

"I know you're afraid," My voice was trembling, "Will you listen to what I have to say?"

There was a release in the pressure around us. She started dropping her defenses and the tears were drying; recognizing that the threat had subsided. Keeping herself on the floor against the nightstand, she spoke. "Tell me." Her voice was frail.

I felt a smile in my soul, but no physical reaction came forth. Lifting my head, I saw the light from the moon pour onto the bed from the window and focused on that.

I exhaled through my nose, "Do you remember. . . back when we first met, we were looking up ghosts?"

"Yes." She responded quietly.

I nervously snickered, "There was something in my home. It uh. . . It wasn't a ghost." I looked to the floor. "It was a demon."

That got her attention. "What?"

I hesitated to answer, "I can't-it's hard. . . to say these things. I don't know how." My hands gestured.

She almost got annoyed, "Just tell me."

I bit my lip, "It's insane, it really is. But, okay, here we go. . . A while back, I met this old man in my house; the *ghost* we were researching. But he wasn't a ghost, his name is Sin and he's a demon." I messily explained.

Nausea in my gut made me twitch and twist my neck. Her face was stoic; reading me. Scrutinizing every expression and every minute detail that could be picked apart as lying or insanity.

"A lot of bad shit was happening between me and my dad and. . . he offered me a deal."

"A deal? What does that mean?" She asked.

"It. . ." My mouth went dry. I nervous cough spit from my throat, "It was a deal for power; revenge."

"And you took this deal?" She replied, disbelief in her throat.

"I did." I said shamefully.

Tansu then stood up very quickly, both hands balled in her odd fist and she said herself on her bed just opposite of me. I raised my eyes to her and gazed deeply into her mixed expression. Fear, sorrow, atrophy and confusion. It was clear she felt stuck, unable to force herself to leave this room, but incapable of accepting what she was being told.

"You accepted a demon deal?" She said plainly.

I nodded.

Her eyes shut tight and she rubbed them furiously before pressing both hands into the top of her thighs with a crude face. “What was that just now, Kim?” She asked angrily, “I was ripped out of my bed and thrown to the floor by what I thought to be a horrible nightmare. . . but then it changed into *you*.” She fought with the words coming out of her own mouth.

Hearing her recount that gave me goosebumps, followed by a deepened sadness. “Her name is Alice. . . and she is my gift, upon accepting the deal.” I swallowed hard, “She’s a demon, she resides within me and takes control when I lose it.” I explained with sorrow.

Her crude expression switched back to worry, “I don’t believe this.” She placed her palm on her forehead and leaned back slightly. “Demons. . . If you had told me this a few hours ago, I would have laughed at the idea.”

“You’re taking this well; considering.” I awkwardly stated.

She leaned forward and began rustling her hair, “I-I don’t know *how* I’m taking this. But talking to you, now, after that. . . I’m listening; so, keep talking.”

I was almost relieved to hear her say that, but equally stressed that this was the situation. “I gotta be honest, it’s a lot to take in.”

“But you will tell me the truth, right?” Her voice was still slightly panicked.

“You have no reason not to believe me now.” I assured.

She nodded, “Okay. . . Then, tell me everything.”

I heard her speak but couldn’t take my eyes off her. All I could see was a shadow overlapping her face; a ghastly image of what may have happened if I didn’t come to. My heart raced, and a dry burn engulfed my eyes.

I cleared my throat, “The demon I was given, Alice, is known as a Teufel. They’re like this energy with a mind of its own that Sin gives to children. The whole point is that the Teufel take control and kill the people who were cruel to their host. Whenever they kill, the human’s soul is shredded until there’s nothing left and the Teufel claims the body.”

“They kill people who were cruel to. . .” I could see she was piecing things together and didn’t like the picture it painted.

I interrupted her thought process, “But that’s not all. Like I said, Sin gives Teufel to children; meaning there’s more than just one. The Teufel are hunting each other, slaughtering their siblings for power.”

“And you’re a part of this. So, you are hunting them as well?” She questioned.

I shook my head, “No. I want nothing to do with the fight. . . But Teufel have found me before; I had to fight off and kill two of them.”

“You killed demons?” She scoffed; almost impressed but at the point of disbelief.

“I told you it’s insane, but that’s the truth. Tansu, these things are monsters and will stop at nothing for power. They overpowered, tortured me and fucked with my mind. I wanted to run away, get far from this place; but that would leave you vulnerable. I couldn’t. . .” A sudden dagger of emotion pierced me, and a quivering sniffle came forward. “In the beginning, I thought I was doing the right thing. Everyone that hurt me got what they deserved and more, but I would take it back. . . I would take it all back in a heartbeat. I was wrong and now, I’m out of time.”

I was talking to her, but moreover expressing all my faults to myself.

"Why would, uh, Alice, want to kill me?" She asked apprehensively.

I pinched my nose; the snot squished, and I snorted it back. "Because Teufel get stronger whenever they kill. She's afraid; desperate, we both are. But this shouldn't have happened; we had an understanding. I would *never* allow her to harm you or anyone I cared about." My lungs seized, and the anguish in my soul tormented me. "And yet. . . I almost couldn't stop her."

She leaned in slightly, compassion at front. "Kim."

This time, *my* body became taught. "No, Tan; nothing is safe. I can't be trusted and now they can find us again. . . It's all falling apart." I huffed; my back rose aggressively as I tried to suck in air.

She then reached out one hand and placed it calmly on my knee. I jerked but eased myself. We locked eyes; mine dripping tears and hers shimmering with my image.

"It isn't. Kim, I'm alive; you didn't lose."

There was a static charge between us. Hostile, but forgiving. Sharp, and rounded. Indiscernible at a glance, and impossible to understand when analyzed.

"I. . . I don't know what else to say. I'm sorry doesn't even touch it." I whispered shamefully. My body hunched forward and my hair fell freely. Guilt came over me like a tidal wave. "Tan, you know I'm not a bad person, right?"

She paused, then eased the next words out with a soothing, dulcet voice. "You aren't bad. Bad things happened to you, and you did the best you could."

"H-how can you say that like it's some sort of excuse? I've done terrible things. Stacy. . . My dad, K-" I stopped, the hurt building. "There's more evil inside me than anything redeemable. There always has been." I shakily admitted; thinking back to the cage.

"That isn't true. Kim, what I saw. . . it terrified me; I feel sick at the thought." She stammered, "But it *wasn't* you, not really. Not my Kimmy." She sympathetically smiled.

Hot tears swelled beneath my eyes; I didn't fight them. Her breathing was prominent, short and balanced through her little nostrils. My eyes fell to my index finger where a faint red mark etched into my skin where the ring had been.

"I'm tired." I cried softly. "Tired of feeling this way. I was almost free, I thought."

To my surprise, she sat up from her bed and moved to my right side. Sinking into the mattress beside me and resting really close.

She reached her hand up, and I turned to her. She slid a finger under my eyes and wiped the led tears away.

"I won't damn you for your mistakes. You were hurt in ways I can't even imagine. . . I mean, *demons*." She half-exclaimed with a light chuckle. "A lot of small details are starting to make sense now." She whispered; her sorrowful eyes tracked over to the window. My wet face looked up at her while my lower lip quivered.

"Y-you're too much." I giggled through despair.

"What would you expect?"

"I expect you to kick me out, call the cops or do something to throw me out of your life. What I did was unforgivable; how could you possibly take everything in stride like that?"

"Because. . . I know you were trying to protect us. You haven't given up on yourself, not completely; so how could I give up on you?"

My lips were dry, lungs stifled and hands clammy. The queasiness in my gut slowly dissipated by the effect her words had on my soul. I had nothing to say in response. Her head rested against the side of mine. She was warm.

She started again with a heartfelt whisper.

"I know you're scared. I can see it when you stare out the window when you can't sleep, when you don't eat. Now I know."

My hushed, hollow words followed, "Are you trying to convince *me* that you care, or yourself?"

She didn't say anything. Then pressed her weight into me, providing comfort in a time of distress for the both of us.

"I'm sorry. . . for everything." I apologized.

"You're only human." She sounded tired.

I exhaled through my nose. *Only human*, I repeated over and over in my head. Allowing my weight to be supported by her, I crooked my head and allowed myself to breathe; process. Tonight, I was perhaps seconds away from murdering my family again.

"The nightmares," I whispered, "so long have I been without anything so intense and vivid." I raised my hand this time to examine the mark left by the ring.

She took note of my motion, "You know, I always wondered where the ring came from. Was it important?"

I scoffed, "It's complicated." I answered vaguely.

"I'm sure you have a lot of stories to tell. Part of me wants to hear them; another part wants this to be a nightmare of my own."

I spaced out for a moment, feeling like my body was made of a fine mist, slowly being carried away by a persistent current of air. A chirp of the smoke detector inside the hallway reestablished my conscience.

"Hey Tansu?"

"Yes?" She sounded tired.

"I will do everything in my power to keep Alice under lock and key, but if you ask me to, I'll leave right now."

She lifted her head off of me and placed both of her hands in her lap. I awaited her response in deafening silence; anxious.

"You don't trust yourself?" She replied in monotone.

"No. I don't. The fact that this happened at all, means its unsafe." I fearfully sighed.

Then, she did something I never thought she would. She pulled her left leg onto the bed and sat on her foot; turning to face me completely. Then the placed both of her delicate hands on either side of my face and held me steady facing her. My eyes went wide and hers slightly peered. There she gazed deep into my iris' and I was fixated on hers as well. She held that position for thirty seconds without moving, without a word.

"I trust you." She smiled and released my face.

A warm sensation tickled my spine and my skin bubbled with goosebumps. My teeth clattered just behind my lips as they pressed tight and a grin returned.

She yawned, crooking her head back and finishing with a low yelp.

"You should get back to sleep." I said.

A nod, "I want to sleep in. Saturday is my favorite day to do nothing after all." She joked.

"I hear ya." I patted her leg and stood myself up; a numbness in my spine made it hard to find my balance. Tansu scooted herself to the top of my bed and started sliding her legs under the blanket.

Raising an eyebrow, I addressed her. "Uhm, what're you doing?"

She paused, both feet under and sitting upright. Keeping her eyes down at the blanket, she sighed. "I want to prove that I'm not lying; when I say I trust you."

"So, you're gonna sleep in my bed with me?" I questioned, face getting red.

She reached across the nightstand and retrieved her pillow, placed it behind her and plopped her head down. "Yup."

Another tingle in my chest. "Ya know; you really are something else."

A few steps in the dark carried me around the foot of the bed to the left side and I cracked my toes before climbing under the covers as well. It was weird, sharing a bed with someone; especially being how small the mattress is. But we positioned ourselves back to back and curled up with our pillows.

"Goodnight Tansu." I said hushed.

"Go-od night. . . Kimmy." She was slipping already.

The room got quiet; heat permeated beneath the blanket giving me a deeper comfort. Idling on my side, eyes wide open and staring at the wall; I listened to the sounds of the house settling. Just outside the glass, I could hear a light trickle of rain begin to form. I focused on that for the time being.

Her breathing was shallow, and her mind easily stirred; so I tried my best not to move around. As much as I wanted to just go to sleep, I couldn't; there was something else I needed to do. Sliding one arm under the pillow beneath my head and the other placed between my curled legs; I closed my eyes and searched for an image of Alice. I found her waiting with crossed arms; stoic.

My heart spiked and I spoke in my head.

"You. . . bitch, what were you thinking!?"

"Don't put the blame on me alone; you and I were conversing, remember?" She stated.

"I remember throwing up after school. I remember Kari making me tea and telling me about which teas help with what ailments. Then we played cards and watched movies before going to bed. That's all." I listed furiously.

"You weren't asleep that long. I saw you standing in here, right *here,* with me. You were freaking out about Sin and the ring and asked me how to survive. I told you to kill your friend." She was clearly irked by this confusion. "I thought, *hey, finally we're making progress*!"

"Well that wasn't me. You should have known better." I snarled.

She licked her teeth and began plucking at the stitches. "You know how fucked we are, right?"

My anger lessened and a disgruntled slum layered over me. "The ring is gone. . ."

"Which means they will find us. A Teufel, if not Sin himself."

"We're strong though." I boasted with minimal confidence.

"No, we aren't. Maybe we can manage a Teufel; but not Sin. You *know* I'm right. . . killing your friend will make us strong, perhaps strong enough to challenge him."

"Alice." I squirmed under the blanket; feeling the need to punch a wall. "You better shut up right now. If you hurt Tansu-"

"-then what? You'll pout and be angry with me? Please, I couldn't care less." She scoffed.

My gut twisted. A wriggling sharp jab made its way under my skin; triggering a cynical snicker from my lips. "I'll kill myself. . . I promise you. If she dies, I'll drag us both into the Ditch. Get that through your thick skull." I threatened.

She stared into nothingness with a tight look of frustrated disbelief.

"Then, it is all pointless."

Chapter 28 – A Pierced Heart Can Be Sewn

The soundtrack to the following morning was murky at first. Struggling to find warmth beneath the weighted sheets; I rolled onto my back only to have my arm limply fall on something solid. My awareness accelerated and I picked up on a light sigh from beside me and peeled my eyes open to see Tansu curled up under the blanket facing away from me.

Sitting up gradually, my head shifted side to side while I searched for my brain. Letting the memories of the night before rush back to me, a small pit formed in my gut and an itch dug into my neck. I scratched aggressively, which transitioned into a powerful stretch. My eyes were drawn to the window where I examined the colorless lawn and trees from the mattress. A loud crashing rain splashed the glass as a gentle wind pushed the curtain slightly through the inch gap.

I shivered, feeling the chill slither into the room. I hurriedly got out of bed and snapped the window shut. Turning back to the beds, I got a good look at Tansu's face. She was sleeping still but had a tight pinch to her face. I made my way over, off-balanced and still foggy; then placed my hand over her forehead. She was hot.

I exhaled and pulled my hand back; using it to adjust my shirt before hobbling over to the closet. In the background, through the closed door, I could hear the TV playing what sounded like a news broadcast. My stiff shoulders made it difficult to open the closet and rifle through the hanging shirts. But I was able to gather an outfit for a lazy day and got changed at the foot of the bed; keeping a watch on Tansu to ensure she was still asleep.

Dressed in a tight long sleeve grey shirt that featured a white lightning bolt decal on the chest and some basic black jeans; I exited the bedroom with little clamor. In the open now, I checked my surroundings to see the TV blaring, most of the lights on due to the gloom and Kari's bedroom door open.

I saw her pass by the door once, carrying some clothes in her arms. A pressure in my bladder made me rush to the bathroom and start the day off as most should. Then I washed my hands and face and brushed my hair; still getting distracted by its length.

Alice didn't show up in the mirror; which I took as a good thing. The last thing I needed now was to see her smug face and get all pissed off. Now, feeling a bit more alive; I strolled out of the bathroom and tried to stay positive. Kari was now in the kitchen. I could see the clock as I approached; it was ten in the morning.

"Morning." I greeted with a scratchy voice.

She perked up and turned to me with a smile; the crow's feet ever-present by her eyes.

"Good morning, Kimberly. How are you?" She asked.

"Meh, pretty groggy but I'll live." I chuckled.

"Did you sleep well?" She set a notepad down and focused on me with a smile.

“Not really. I had a nightmare, so Tansu climbed into bed with me to make me feel better.” I snickered, “But she made it kind of hard to stay comfortable.”

She raised her brows in wonderment, “She did that?” Then she smiled big, her cheeks growing red. “Well, can I make you something to eat?”

My stomach squirmed. I was hungry, but nauseous at the idea of food. “Oh, that’s okay.”

She gestured to the stove, “Are you sure? It won’t take long at all.” She smiled.

“Thank you, but my stomach’s a bit iffy, so I don’t wanna waste your time if I can’t keep anything down.”

She giggled, “Well alright then. If you need me, I’ll be gathering up all the laundry.” She folded her hands in front of her.

“Okay. And if you need my help, then just yell at me.”

“How about I kindly ask?” She teased.

“That’d be preferable.” I responded in the same manner.

A bright exchange, and then she walked away; entering the bathroom next to gather clothes. I loitered for a moment, just spacing out. A dizziness held onto me; cementing me in place for a little longer until I forced a step.

Entering the kitchen, I rummaged through the fridge and snagged a carton of orange juice; extra pulp. A clean glass was quickly filled and emptied, then rinsed off in the sink. It wasn’t food, but at least I had something in my belly.

I yawned again and listened to the news. Reports of heavy winds and minor flooding by the pond were repeated between the hosts. I think what I needed today was a nice walk, rain or no rain. Being wet didn’t bother me all that much, but the cold that came with it was another story. These days, I’ve been weak to cold and even a drop of five degrees was very noticeable to me.

Tansu’s mom then came out of the bathroom with a filled basket of laundry.

“Is she up yet?” she asked.

“Not when I came out. I don’t think she’s feeling well.”

She got a concerned, but accustomed face, “Why do you say that?”

“I felt her forehead, she was a little warm.”

A little nod, “In that case, can you try and wake her for me?”

“Shouldn’t we let her sleep it off?”

“Yes, but I’d like to prevent it if I can. She has a tendency to suddenly come down with a cold. Just like her dear old mom.” She smiled softly.

“You get sick easily?” I asked.

“Unfortunately. I always fell ill and made a world of stress for my parents.”

I crossed my arms. “That must’ve been awful.”

“At times; but I wouldn’t change it if I could.” She smirked, a twinkle in her eye.

“Why's that?” I raised an eyebrow.

A light blush, “Well, if it wasn't for my Asthma, I would never have met Tansu's father; Nakito.” She smiled, “But that is a story for another time.”

My hands transitioned to my pockets, “So, that's why your diet is so strict, and you keep this place so clean.”

“I suppose.” She giggled. “Although I think it's more of my habitual nature. I was born a clean-freak.”

"I wish I had that tendency; I enjoy cleaning some days, but mostly it's just a daunting task, at least, it was at my house." I snickered.

She glanced down at the laundry and hoisted it up a little to get a better grip. Noticing this, I realized I was holding her up.

"Okay, I'll try to get her up; but no promises," I smirked.

"Thank you."

She continued walking, taking the dirty laundry towards the basement door by the living room. I lumbered to our half-open bedroom door and pushed it open all the way. Peering into the desolate, still chilly domicile; I listened for her breathing. It was steady, with a frail mucus grind.

I stepped in, and as I made my way over to the bed, I picked up a few random articles of dirty clothing and tossed them in the basket beside the door. I reached her and knelt down beside the frame; seeing the muscles in her face had loosened. I whispered to her.

"Tan, wake up."

She didn't react. I leaned in a little. "Hey, Tansu, wake up. You're sleeping the day away." I nudged her shoulder a little.

Her eyes clenched, "Leave me alone." She replied in a dreadful tone.

I paused, then nudged her again. "But your mom wants to—"

"Go away!" Her eyes shot open, bloodshot and volatile. Shocked, I pulled back, and raised my hands defensively.

She glared at me with an intensity I had never seen on her. I stood up, and her eyes tracked me; she still clutched the blankets up to her neck and remained very still. A little peeved, I huffed and dropped both hands.

"Fine, waste your day." I tried not to sound so annoyed.

She then threw the blanket off and sat up; propping herself on one arm and shooting me a fiery stare.

"Get. Out." Her eyes were red like she was about to cry, but anger held a tight grip on her emotions. My face slacked; caught off guard by her direct, sharp words.

I struggled to find a response. Everything that presented itself reflected the tinge behind my ribs. Raw and angry; combative. I had to literally bite my tongue so as not to snap back at her. Then something odd happened. Tansu's baggy eyes shut tightly; she blinked a few times and her face sank down, innocent again. She put her hand on the top of her head and scratched. Her arm wobbled and she laid on her back.

My rage started to leak out. "What the hell was that about, huh? Where did that come from?" I growled.

"Where did. . . what, what are you talking about?" She said, holding her hand over her forehead now with searching eyes. "Wow, my head hurts." She groaned.

I retracted, "Wait, you don't remember?"

"I was sleeping. . . that's all."

The spinning of my brain ground to a halt and I closed my fist tight, then let it go. "Man, I don't think your mom needs a thermometer, you definitely have a fever."

"Yeah." She slurred, "I don't feel too good."

I noted the pressure around me; like the room was underwater, the walls pushing inward. A copper taste slid across my tongue as I calculated this feeling.

I offered cheer in my voice, "Hey, its Saturday; take as much time as you need. I'll have your mom come in and check on you."

She nodded; closing her eyes and breathing through a stuffy nose. I pulled the blanket over her and let the heat swell. Lingering briefly, I looked back to the window and watched the wind carry a varied rain across the yard.

I left the room with worry in my bones. The angst I felt was lifted upon entering the open space again. Feeling despondent, I emptied my mind of everything it stored and started to wander. The bleak nature of the day affected me the opposite to how I usually feel. Downtrodden, murky grey often acted as an inspirer to me; motivating me to work. But after what just happened, I almost feel hopeless.

Dragging my feet over to the kitchen, I lifted my chin and stared at the cabinet doors. Every notch in the wood, scrape and imperfect stain stuck out to me. To think; all of this wood was once alive. Now, repurposed; selfishly. I couldn't stop staring, mentally wandering in existential nihilism.

Last night hung heavily over my skull. Threatening to crush me if I allowed it to pervert my thoughts once again. Maybe it's possible that my own energy leaked out into that room and made her sick. After all, revisiting my own home I personally witnessed the ruin; decay.

"Kim, dear?" Kari stole my attention.

Slow to respond, "Hmm?" I hummed without turning.

"Are you feeling bored enough to help me with the dishes while this load washes?"

I stared for another few seconds then switched my eyes to the sink.

Two pots, a single pan and cutting board, plus a few plates and cups were all stacked in the stainless-steel bowl.

"Sure." I agreed, still not looking at her.

She approached from behind and placed an appreciative hand on my shoulder as she passed and stopped at the sink. I twitched at her touch, then slummed over to the hand towel; drying duty as usual. Typically, I found this menial task enjoyable at a fundamental level.

The news in the background kept her entertained while she started to wash the plates. It had no hold on me, however. My muscles were almost moving in slow motion; just dragging seconds behind any command I gave. I couldn't stay focused; I couldn't keep up. Tremendous guilt bled from my soul; an inescapable mindset that screamed *you don't belong here.*

I was fixated on that. The night prior and every horrible nightmare I endured behind the scenes reinforced this idea. Anything I said to convince me or anyone else otherwise, was a selfish lie.

Wet dish, dry dish. Place on the rack. Wet cup, dry cup. Place on the rack. Repeat, repeat, repeat. Without my will, the chore was being completed. I was watching myself from a thousand feet above my mortal body; cursing at the vessel that deceived everyone she loved.

My arms slowed almost to a complete halt. I repeatedly dried the same plate; wiping in circular motions with a grip that loosened with every lap. Kari finally took note of my silence and caught me doing this.

"Kimberly?"

At the sound of her voice, I was ripped from this process and dragged back into my body. With the spark of consciousness, my hands jolted and knocked the plate from my grasp. It fell and abruptly shattered on the floor; exploding ceramic shards across a short-range.

"Shit!" I cursed; immediately kneeling to recover the pieces.

"Wait, I don't want you to cut yourself. Here, let me get the broom." She hurried to the dining room and snatched the broom from the corner. Returning quickly and dropping the dustpan to the floor. I grabbed the dustpan and held it for her with wide eyes and frustrated shame across my face.

"I'm really sorry about that." I apologized while she slid the largest pieces into the pan.

She giggled. "Don't be. I'm sorry I startled you."

I scoffed, "I was lost in thought. I should've been paying attention."

"I can't blame you. It wasn't as if you had an exciting task." She smirked.

Now the little pieces were swept up and deposited into the trash can. Being at that low of an angle, I checked for any tiny shimmering pieces that may have escaped her broom; but it seems she got everything. I stood up and handed her the pan. She returned both to the dining room and reentered the kitchen.

"Would you like to switch?" She joked.

I shook my head, chuckling. "Nope. I think I'll manage."

She smiled wide and positioned herself at the sink again to start on the pots. She held the smile all the while she scrubbed; *that* became my new focus.

It's a sincere smile that's hard to come by. One that held such a powerful, genuine interest and appreciation. A smile that was. . . almost perfect; perhaps it *was* at one point.

A memory presented itself with vivid imagery.

"One time. . ." I started with a whisper.

Her eyes shifted to me.

"One time I dropped a glass cup onto the floor when helping my dad with the dishes. . . it broke." A weight was draped over my shoulders. The rushing water splashed against the pot in the sink as her hands idled on the edge.

"My dad was so angry that he made me clean up the glass with my bare hands. I think I was nine at the time." A pained chuckle slipped from my lips.

A moment of clarity entered my brain.

I sniffled, wiping moisture from the tip of my nose. "Sorry. I don't know why I told you that." My voice was dry.

She responded quietly, absorbing my words. "That's alright."

"Ms. Hikono?" I whimpered; eyes falling to the floor. She reached up and turned off the rushing water. Her body turned to me; a new aura emitted from her skin.

I bit my lip. "Why. . . do you guys care so much about me?"

A pause of disbelief. "Why would you ask something like that?" Her voice was tender; concerned.

"I don't know. . . It's something that's bothered me for a while; but I was afraid to ask."

She grabbed another towel from the counter and wiped her hands dry, keeping a watch on me.

I continued, "It's different now, but back then; I hardly knew Tansu at all. And yet, when my dad-" A lump formed in my throat. "-when he died, you took me in immediately. Tansu has shown me forgiveness and acceptance in ways I don't deserve. You *both* carried my burdens for too long. . ."

I started to get quiet, eyes scanning the floor, her feet, the lowest edge of the cabinet. I took a long pause as the thoughts circled around like a spinning top. Then raw emotion tuned in.

"How could you take in a stranger!?" I tearfully shouted; lashing my eyes up to hers and meeting them with powerful emotion. She was halted for a brief moment; unable to respond while she absorbed the scene.

Then her smile returned. "Well, that's easy."

She ushered me toward the dining room table. My trembling eyes followed her movements. She stood by the table, and I slowly turned to join her. To my surprise, when I sat down, she did not take the other end of the table; instead, she sat right beside me.

An awkward energy only I could interpolate surrounded us. She placed both elbows on the table and joined her hands, eyes fixated on the front lawn just outside the window.

"Tansuke is. . . the greatest thing that has ever happened to me. I love her with all my heart, no matter what. But she has had trouble in her life, as everyone does." Her fingers tightened around each other, "Growing up, she couldn't really make friends. No confidence, you see. But shyness wasn't entirely the problem. Her father's passing made everything. . ." She caught my curious gaze from the corner of her eye and looked to me.

"She didn't tell you. After all this time?"

My head shook. "No. I mean, I assumed that may have been the case, but I tried leaning more towards the *divorce* side of things." I said with raised, tight shoulders; feeling uncomfortable even suggesting that.

Her eyes fluttered and fell to the table. "I should've expected as much. She really doesn't like to talk about it; not even to me."

"How long ago?" I asked.

"It's been almost three years, now." She recollected.

My heart ached. Now I felt terrible for all the times I complained about losing my mom, considering how long ago that was compared to this.

She continued, "He was a man with a brilliant mind and an impossibly kind heart. Never putting himself before anyone else."

"What happened, if you don't mind me asking?" I asked with cautious sensitivity.

Kari ran her fingers through her hair and took her time answering; formulating a proper response.

Her voice was tired sounding. "Nakito worked as an EMT, when we lived in Rhode Island. . . He and his partner responded to a call; a teenager needed their insulin and they were the closest. Everything went well, the boy was fine, and they went on their way. Afterward, they stopped to get gas." She started to slow down at this point, "He went inside to pay and that's when a robbery took place. . . My husband w-was shot three times-" She gestured to her stomach, "-in the abdomen and. . ."

"Y-you don't have to say anymore. I'm sorry." My words left my mouth laced in despair.

She clasped her hands together again. "Soon after, Tansuke became anxious. All the time. She was afraid of doing anything, seeing anyone and going anywhere. She did everything with her dad, they were inseparable. . . In fact, I don't think she even noticed me fully until after he passed." She regrettably chuckled, voice cracking. "She always held his hand. . . even though hers were too small; she adapted and started holding his thumb."

A sorrowful frown painted both of our faces. She was palpably reliving these painful memories; enough for me to empathize with her and soak myself in her buried agony.

She continued, "I didn't have much hope left for my little girl. But, then, something amazing happened."

"What?" I asked in a hushed voice.

"You." She unclasped her hands; resting them flat on the table. "The first day she went to this new school, I expected her to come back sad, just as she always did. Quiet, lonely and angry at herself. . . she would get so *angry*. To my surprise, she greeted me with a smile on that first day and her attitude has improved immensely since then. When she met you." She gave me a big heartfelt smile.

"But. . . What did *I do* that made her different that day?" I asked in all seriousness.

"You did something no one else bothered to do. You helped her. You didn't look down on her and you did not turn her away. And since then, you have remained by her side." She said cheerfully.

"There's no way. I can't be the only one? What about her friends, or other family? I mean, even *I* had Joey growing up, and I'm the one that spoiled that." I whispered at the end.

"Back then, she was only interested in school, music and choir. We urged her to make friends, but she didn't want to; because she had him. As a result, she was shunned by her classmates; then bullied." She voiced in a depressed manner.

"So, she had no one else?"

"No one. Until you came along. *You* brought her back to life; you accomplished what I, as her mother, failed to do. And I couldn't be happier." Her voice began to shake. "When I see the two of you together, I see two confident young ladies who found their missing piece in each other. . ." A desperation emptied from her lungs. "The way she looks at you, all I see is a *purpose* in her. I'm not sure you understand just how much of an impact you have had on her, just by being here. I took you in because I trust you, just as she does."

I had my teeth in a tight clench, fighting back more tears. There was no response I could muster to accurately portray my feelings. Every word fell miles short of its intended meaning. With tense shoulders and a relaxed posture, I tried to stifle my whimpering, but it was no use. I sat in that chair, bawling like a flustered child; unable to cope with the reality presented.

Lead-filled teardrops fell to my lap, flowing like a rushing river. She paused, mouth partially gaped and eyes as wide as they have ever been. Then, she relaxed herself and closed her eyes; a motherly sigh.

She inched her chair closer to me and brought my head under her chin where she embraced me, gently caressing her fingers through my hair. *This*. . . this was the mother's touch that I have been searching my deepest memories for and never found. This is what I have been longing for.

In wake of this moment, I had an epiphany. The feelings I have for them; the pain we each carry every day, is mutual. We all grieve, just as we all strive to be loved again. In each other, we have found a new balance.

We saved one another.

Chapter 29 – Retrospective

I don't know why I feel comfort in the meek and depressing sky. Something about the way such a vast canvas of commanding layers robbed me of my awareness every time a distant rumble announced itself. It shaved away the tense wall of doubt I was building around my heart and made me understand how truly insignificant I was. A blip, a tiny speck in this verse that couldn't make an impact on anything outside of my own little world.

But that doesn't mean that what I've done, and what I *will* do doesn't matter. Inspired by the crashing rain and opaque rays shining through the wavering clouds; I can say that my life has had meaning. The storm that has raged not only in my life, but my mind as well; is finally leading to something.

From behind, a voice called my name.

"Kim, sweetie, can you please shut the door?" Kari asked almost impatiently.

Leaning against the gaping frame, I angled my head to peer at her down the short hall. The brisk air wormed its way between my legs and over my shoulders, invading the house for the past few minutes while I indulged in reverie.

I held my tongue, not wanting to disconnect from this explorative state and instead took a step into the hall. On the hangers to my right, I retrieved an old red scarf from my home and wrapped it loosely around my neck. Then, I slid on my shoes, grabbed a small umbrella and retreated to the open frame where I exited to the sprawling world and closed the door behind me.

Raising the umbrella over my head, I popped the chute and moved partly down the red brick path. A cold, steady rain continued to pour; slapping the thin black fabric with relentless determination. Such consistent tapping birthed a cathartic rhythm that revitalized a hopefulness in me. Interacting with the rain, as opposed to concealing myself within those walls was therapy to me. I spun the handle; in turn twirling the fabric sheet and disrupting the expected pattern of notes. I created a new melody, able to be altered at my will.

I smiled big.

"Alice?" I said out loud.

Her buzz rose like my beckoning voice turned a dial. But she didn't say anything back; just lingered there.

"I'm sorry. . . for getting so mad at you." I muttered with tight lungs.

The pitch of her static abruptly changed to a low burn. Then her voice broke through, "An apology. This is unexpected." She sounded tired.

"Yea, well. . . I can't blame you entirely. Some unconscious part of me allowed you in; so." My words were stiff.

"Erm, I apologize as well." She said through pinched lips, "I should have known it wasn't really you."

I smiled, "Thanks. That means, well, a lot; coming from you."

She returned to cynical, "I stand by wanting to kill her. It's our best option for survival."

I snickered, "I know. Speaking of which. . ." The rain kept my voice hidden beneath the veil of noise, "have you felt anything weird? Since the ring broke?"

She seemed hesitant, giving light sighs and unsure grimaces. "It's fuzzy. Truthfully I *have* sensed Teufel presence again but it's not like it used to be."

"Are any close enough to worry about?"

"No." She slumped; almost sad that she wouldn't have a chance to fight again soon.

Her defeated vibrancy brought forth sarcasm in me. "Aw, don't worry; we can go kill some defenseless trees later on."

She gave an unenthused snarl, then scoffed loudly; a sharp pinch in my eardrum. "So, it seems you were accepted by your new family. Touching."

My face softened with a crisp smile, "It's. . . really special. I mean, I finally don't feel like an outsider; living with one foot in and the other dangling over a cliff."

A pause. A reflective moment where I got the feeling that Alice was absorbing the rain. Something as strange as feeling her aura wander in a tight space; reaching out to feel the energies around us, is impossible to fully describe, but too noticeable. I let her roam; think.

Acceptance. . . something a Teufel probably never has and will never know. Dejected and scorned by their host, siblings and probably Sin himself. They are bastards; twisted products with obtuse purpose forged from desperation. Acceptance is nothing but a ghost of an emotion that she can only witness through me, as it entranced my soul.

"Y'know. . ." I started drearily, "I dreamt about running away, in the beginning."

My words reestablished a connection.

"So many times, did I feel that urge to just walk out the door and never look back. Let my dad either go crazy searching, or forget entirely. . . After we killed him, that thought crossed my mind again. Escape, before I got stuck."

She responded with meager investment. "If that happened, then we would have been just like all the others. Destro would have killed us, if not for your will to protect your friend."

My voice was flat, arms shaking. "Things could have gone so many different ways."

"Do you wish they had?"

Her question left me in divisive contemplation. My fingers wrapped loosely around the handle of the umbrella, gently twirling it with a sickness sloshing in my gut. The fabric of my shirt had gone cold and left me in a frail shiver. Despite this, I gave a heavy sigh through my nose and lowered the umbrella.

The rain overtook my body in an instant and penetrated every available inch of fabric, hair and skin. I tensed at the icy bite, clenching my teeth together but allowing the rest of my face to relax. I pulled back my skull, raising my face to the sky and closed my eyes. Limply dangling the protective octagon, I soaked it all in; pillaging my delicate flesh of its much-needed heat.

Submitting to the torrential tears from the sky, I experienced the opposite effect most assumingly would. Cold, shivering and overall miserable; I felt larger than myself. This mortal body has carried me through a life of unceasing hardship, degrading circumstance and abhorrent loathing; and yet, here I stand.

A heart pumping blood and a soul on fire. This rain could not harm me, could not sway me from my goals. I haven't forgotten why I rose from a puddle of my own blood. The reason I chose this path to walk; I am more than this body, this life. My time's up, and I am ready.

I opened my eyes, lowering my head to the ground and raising the umbrella over my head again. A trembling breath swelled out of my lungs and produced a wisp of mixed air.

"If you sense anything, let me know." I requested.

Alice receded to wherever it is she goes, and I was alone again. I spun myself around, weighted by my clothes and weary from such intensity inside my mind. I entered the door and shook off the umbrella outside before pulling it in and shutting the door behind me.

Kari was nowhere to be seen, but Tansu's door was now closed; whereas before I left it open just a bit. A unique detail was in the air upon reentry. A sharp culmination of static and lack of audio from the television made me feel like I walked into a different day entirely. I could almost taste the degraded quality of air; thick with dread, haunted by remorse and a somber nature. Many emotions had vacated our bodies in the past twenty-four hours, and that charge was caged in here; slowly thinning.

Right now, I needed to warm up and wash this acidic rain from my pores. With haste, I skipped across the floor and barged into the bathroom. Turning the water knob, the pipes banged and unleashed a stream. I immediately plugged the drain and stripped out of my clothes, making sure to set them in a pile. Violently jittering, I wrapped my arms around my now naked body and watched the steaming water rise in the bowl.

The loud gushing and whirring of the ventilation fan above quickly drowned out all my thoughts and left me in an in-between state. Once it filled about a quarter of the way, I stepped over the edge and dipped one foot in; hot, but welcoming. In a short time, the water rose nearly to the top and I canceled the flow.

Unwilling to tremble any longer, I endured the drastic change in temperature as my body was swallowed by the pool; undulating circular ripples with every point of contact.

Rainwater dripped from my bangs and rippled throughout; giving me a visual distraction while my body rose in temperature. A pleasureful sigh brushed past my lips as I laid my head back on the edge and eased deeper; the water reaching my armpits.

Quiet; all except for the vent above. In my mind, swirled images of Alice and her siblings shimmered between expressions of shock and anger. Vividly detailing the fights and conversations we endured and all of the confusion I faced as I adapted. It all seems like a dream, now. A ghost of a life forfeited and regained. When I think of myself at that time, in the beginning; I don't recognize me. The core elements of my existence remain, but if I found myself face to face with the *me* of a year ago, I'd want to kill her. . . Maybe, save her; it depends.

I only wonder what was in store for us without the protection of anonymity. Who will show their face; who will open their mouth? I submerged my head under the water; feeling the cold dampness lift off and be replaced by heat. A pressure on my skull tempted me to rise, but I remained. Thirty seconds. . . a minute, until I came up for air.

A soft knock shattered my dome of solitude and grabbed hold of my attention. I didn't respond, just glared at the door, wondering if the noise was real at all. Then another.

"What?" My voice echoed.

"It's me." Tansu replied softly. I relaxed my tensed-up jaw and let my breath ease out.

"You're finally up. How do you feel?" I shouted through the door.

She was quiet, not answering right away.

"Are you decent?" She asked.

"No, I'm in the tub. What do you need?"

"Nothing. I just wanted to apologize for earlier. I don't know what came over me." She said regretfully.

"I said don't worry about it. I didn't take it to heart." I reassured.

"A-are you sure?" She asked.

"Yea. But, hey, if you wanna make it up to me, maybe we can go for a walk?" I smirked, raising myself from the waterline a little.

"That sounds nice." Her voice was frail.

"Cool. Let me finish up in here."

"Take your time." She whispered.

She didn't make a sound; but I felt her presence move away from the door. I sighed, a headache forming. Looking down at my hand, I examined the dented, pruned skin. Closing my fist loosely, my arm trembled.

I wanted to get out right now, but that would be a waste of water. So I soaked it in a little longer; resting my muscles and fully submitting myself to the nothing. A daydream crept up on me. a mix of memory and fantasy where neither could truly be distinguished. Jumbled, raw; nonsensical. I discarded the images and focused on the walls, sink and my own body. Slight shame entered my brain looking down at myself. Thinking back on my shriveled husk of a soul in my mental caverns; I was reminded that this body would be in her hands by the end. I frowned.

Still sitting, I unplugged the tub and allowed the water to drain freely. Closing my eyes, I immersed myself in the soothing sensation of the water slowly gliding down my skin as it filtered into the pipes. I climbed out and dried myself quickly; starting from my head and working in descending order until I reached my feet. Keeping the towel bound to my torso, I shut off the light and exited the bathroom; lowering my head and darting into the bedroom to get dressed.

I came out wearing a fairly standard attire; jeans and a red short sleeve. My hair was somewhat flat, but it would grow lively in time. From the bedroom door, I could see Tansu standing in the hall to my left; stopped nearby her moms' room and holding something in her hand. She seemed keenly focused on this; and from here, I could almost certainly tell what it was. A picture frame.

"Hey," I whispered, moving closer to her.

"Hey." She repeated.

"What's up?" I asked.

"Nothing, just. . . Nothing." She set the frame down, on the console table and then moved some loose hair to the side.

"Your dad was handsome," I said, referring to the photo.

She didn't say anything.

"Your mom told me about him."

Her face was unchanged; but I could see the fierce contemplation going on within her skull.

"I don't know why I never told you. It's stupid." She said in a monotone.

"No, it's not."

Her eyes were glassy. "You were so open when we first met. I should have given you the same treatment."

"To be honest, I was immature and wanted attention. Plus, I can't help that I'm a little too honest, right?" I nudged her delicately.

She was still staring at the photo even after she set it down.

"Do you want to talk about it?" I asked.

She slowly turned around and faced me. Her eyes were sad, but she was not crying.

"I'm okay. I just sometimes forget to keep moving when I look at it."

My legs wobbled slightly; then I raised both arms and gave her a comforting smile. She smirked back and embraced my offer for a hug.

"Well, if you ever want to tell me anything, get it out of your system. I'd love to hear about him." We released.

She took a shaky breath. I could feel her tremble at the core.

"All right, someday." She smiled.

I tilted my head, gesturing for the living room and we both walked over; each dragging our feet. When we reached the couch, I observed the nearby window and saw that the rain was lifting still. By this point, it was just a light misting.

"So, do you wanna go for a walk?" I started.

She shrugged, not entirely invested. "We could. . ."

"We can wait a few more minutes if you want."

She nodded.

"Alright, well, pop a squat on the couch and let's watch some TV." I tried my best at sounding peppy, despite my inner turmoil.

The two of us got comfortable. I took the left arm and she took the right; curling her legs up onto the cushion and keeping tight to herself. I switched on the TV and changed it from the news, flipping through various channels until settling on an old cartoon. The volume was low, and the subtitles were on by my choice. We were stagnant, but not unwilling to solicit.

A comment, here or there was shared about the show or the day; but ultimately the room remained less than erratic. There was a moment where we sat on the couch, sitting just a few inches from each other where the channel went to commercial. The program faded to black and attempted to start the advertisement, but the black screen remained; lingering far too long. All noise was cut off, and the eerie ringing of silence vibrated in our skulls. We waited, both of us in a dreary staring contest with our darkened, blurry silhouettes in the screen.

Then the advertisement played, and I released my stare. Fifteen or so minutes flew by us; neither invested in the screen. In the time that passed, I hadn't seen or heard Kari once. That concerned me.

"Where'd your mom go?" I asked, breaking the silence.

"Um, I think she left."

"She was neck-deep in laundry, where would she go?"

Tansu shrugged, "She isn't bothered by the rain. She probably ran out of detergent or something." She seemed distant, but her voice lightened up a tad bit.

"Ah." I vocalized, then let my eyes rest on the TV but didn't take in any information. In the corner of my eye, I saw her drop her legs to the floor and lean away from the arm; sitting up straight.

"This show sucks." I said plainly.

"I haven't been paying attention." She admitted.

"That makes two of us. I'm ready for that walk whenever." I pushed my chest out, cracking my back.

"We can go now. I don't think it's going to pick up again."

I rotated to her, "But we should probably bring an umbrella just in case."

"Or. . ." She smirked slyly, "We can leave it and run if the rain starts again."

"I don't wanna get soaked for a third time, Tan." I groaned.

"Then if it starts to rain again, you'd better move fast!" She cheered, her mood swinging. Then she hopped off the couch and looped around the back; heading for the front door. I raised an elbow over the spine and crooked my head to look back at her.

"You're in a damn good mood, huh?"

"I know? I just got a burst of energy." She smiled. "Maybe you should try to smile for once, sour puss."

"Shut up. I smile." I said, turning my body and reaching for the remote.

"Oh yeah, you're always smiling. You're just a ray of sunshine all the time." She said as she slid her arms into her sweater sleeves.

"Sarcasm will get you nowhere." I stood up and switched the TV off.

"It got me this far, didn't it?" She replied.

"Only because you have me," I said confidently and met her by the front.

"That's true." She agreed.

She stepped out of the house while I searched for something to wear and keep me warm. Unfortunately, most of my warm clothes were snatched by Kari during her laundry frenzy. Which left me with only one option; Joey's leather jacket.

I stopped outside the doorframe and looked to the dark grey sky scrolling along. A foreboding weight carried in the wind. The thunder continued to roll as the sun peaked out from behind a mass of lighter-toned clouds.

"The air. . ." I started.

"Hmm, what was that?" Tansu asked

"It's, especially heavy."

She gave me a weird look, "Whatever you say, Kimmy."

My eyes lowered, and I spoke in my head. "Alice? Keep your feelers out."

Her comforting buzz reassured me of her presence. Then we started moving.

I followed Tansu; keeping one step behind her, all the while scanning each side of the road. We moved towards town with moderate haste, sustaining the immediate bracing chill. Upon reaching the first turn out of this private community, I had warmed up under the leather and Tansu seemed comfortable by her stride. I walked with both hands in the pouch pockets, while she let both of her arms sway by her side; hands balled into regular fists.

The world was desaturated and damp; but the mist was gone, and some rays of light continued shining through the clouds. We were at the point where there wouldn't be another house until we reached mine; and that is when the gurgle in my stomach began. If we reach my house, Tansu will most certainly want to go check it out. She can't go inside no matter what.

My past lives there. The corrupt energy inside those walls never left, and besides that; I'm still ashamed of my old life. I don't want her discovering how I used to live, so maybe I can divert us. From here, I could see about a quarter-mile down the road was the turn left that would lead us to my old home's strip; I had to think of something.

The sun happily pushed through the clouds and reached out to us. Its low heat patted our backs, in a way, lifting my worries. Together we walked, side by side on the edge of the desolate, broken pavement. It was peaceful, the ground still freshly wet. Stepping over puddles and pavement streams was a little game we'd play in silence.

I loved the smell of the air right now. Wet bark and leaves mixed with a cool wind that often lifted our hair. I slyly looked at Tansu. Her head was hanging low, but it didn't seem like she was going to turn around and head back. Just then, I felt something odd pinch me. Some strange feeling that tilted my head and almost pulled me out of my body. Tansu was not only staring at her feet. She held a look on her face that was even more distant than mine. Very loose, yet at the same time, extremely tensed up.

"So, it's a good thing it hasn't started raining again." I tried to reach her.

"Mm." She hummed quietly.

"All right?" I sighed.

Our footsteps were almost aligned, squishing in sequence on the wet blacktop. The air seemed sharper now; less heavy and more volatile. We finally reached the fork. To our left was my road, and straight ahead was another that ended very abruptly. An old gravel dump for construction some time ago that has long since been abandoned with a low car gate blocking the entrance. Without a word, I turned left, and she followed. My heart was picking up the pace; soon my house would come into view. We made it ten feet and another harsh wind hit us. I shivered.

"I wish I had a hat," I said, flicking up the collar of my jacket.

She didn't look at me, instead, she reached back and lifted her hood over her head.

"Jerk." I giggled, joking.

She didn't say anything. Her footsteps slowed, and she gradually fell behind. I swung around, now walking backward at her speed.

"Uh, Tansu?"

She came to an immediate halt and all at once, her energy shifted. With clenched fists and an angry, sickened expression, she scoffed at me; then began walking back the way we came. I watched her in disbelief for a moment, then cautiously followed her.

She arrived at the fork again and instead of turning right to go home, she went left. She climbed over the metal bar and then proceeded to walk down the small abandoned trail that cut through the trees. I stopped at the fence and hesitated just a moment before going under and catching up.

"Tan." I called to her.

We walked in the woods, brushing off low-hanging tree branches that grew over the thin road. I decided it best to keep a short distance from her, careful not to lose sight. It wasn't long before we came across a large clearing in the trees where all of the mounds of dirt and rock used to be stored.

She stopped at the mouth of the clearing and quickly turned to face me. Fist curled and shoulders tense.

I tried to maintain my posture, "How'd you know about this place?" I asked with a light tone.

The underside of her eyes was glaringly dark; an evil huff rose form her chest with every breath. My lungs started to rapidly shiver as anxiety grew, but I tried my best to smile.

"You know, my dad used to come here and steal dirt for our driveway. . . during winter. He never got caught." I laughed.

The back of my neck suddenly went stiff and an electrical surge coursed through my veins.

"Kim, what's going on?" Alice awoke.

I spoke inside my head, "I'm not sure. Tansu is acting very strange."

"You're right. There's some dark mist surrounding her body."

"Meaning what, exactly?"

She snickered to herself. "Twisted."

Feeling nervous, I curled my wrist and cracked it once or twice.

"Tansu, are you feeling all right?" I kept on guard, dropping the smile. The thing about her that stood out to me the most was her stance. Feet spread apart for better balance, arms raised out from the body, head lowered with eyes concentrated and straight-as-a-board shoulders. I recognize this stance in every Teufel I've seen. Even Alice stood like this right before they attacked.

"Can you even hear me? Let's head back now, all right?"

As expected, and as fast as lightning, she hunched down with teeth bared like a mad dog; she rushed toward me.

We had space between us, but she moved fast; I had to act quickly. I ripped my jacket off, widened my own feet and threw it at her face. It landed perfectly and covered her head. For just a moment, she was blinded by the leather and it gave me a chance to act. I ran forward and grappled her, bringing her to the ground and unintentionally slamming her pretty hard.

She let out a loud grunt when we hit the dirt and flailed her arms to grab ahold of me or the jacket. I held her down, trying to keep control without hurting her.

"Kimberly, take your hands off me!" She snarled.

"Kimberly?" I repeated in confusion. "Snap out of it. What you are doing?"

This was her body, but it was not her mind. A cold, radiant aura burned off her skin and tickled my own. That shadowed underline of her eyes, accompanied by her twitching and words painted a very clear picture.

Something is controlling her.

Chapter 30 – Resolve

I experienced a fleeting period where everything slowed down in my eyes. My spectral being lifted from my mortal coil and hovered above the scene as it played hundreds of times slower than actuality. From above, I could see the two of us, rolling on the ground; laughing. Overblown colors and a joyful soliloquy blissful of the danger around us. All sound was muted, and liberation embodied me.

All at once, that fantasy came crashing down as Tansu's wild struggling almost got the better of me. My muscles engaged and held her to the ground; pinned like a vicious animal. A slave; impulsive and intent on killing me. I couldn't completely focus myself; the sounds of her grunts churned my gut. Her erratic movements scattered my guard; giving her an opening. She managed to get the jacket off her face, tossing it to the side and forcing her knee up into the middle of my back. It stunned me for just a second but didn't knock me off.

Her fiery expression became mixed with tears of anguish as she cried out in a desperate plea. "Kimmy! Let me go, I have to kill you!"

Hearing her voice pierced my core, "No. . . I won't let go. I don't want to hurt you." My voice was breaking.

A sudden, heavy current of air blew through the trees, thrashing my hair in every direction. The wind licked my skin with an acidic burn and caused me to arch my back, gripping my bones. Every muscle was seized by a stabbing pain that began to vibrate intensely. My grip loosened with the pain and she didn't waste that opening. She slipped one arm free and punched me in the stomach; then kicked me off her. I hit the dirt on my side, limp but recovering as she rolled onto her stomach and stood up.

I held my gut with saliva dripping from my bottom lip.

"She's tough for a petite child." Alice cackled.

My shoe scraped across the wet dirt; trying to stand.

"It's not her at all." I exhaled, the shock receding.

I propped myself on one arm, but she ran up at a rapid pace and kicked the underside of my stomach; which expelled all the air from my lungs. I wheezed and fell back onto my face. She kicked again and again, crashing her foot into my ribs. I braced myself each and every time, but her attacks were losing power quickly.

I let her kick until I could hear the huffing and panting. Then I rolled away just before another attack; she missed and stumbled for balance while I rose to my feet and created distance between us. Alice immediately began working on the bruises while I composed myself.

I directed an upset look at her; to which she returned furious dark eyes and a trembling fist.

"Snap out of it." My lungs returned.

She grinned in response; a wide demented flare that was also reminiscent of Teufel behavior. She crept towards me, watching my movements carefully.

Getting within a foot of me, I relaxed and lowered my arms; leaving myself wide open.

With saddened eyes, I extended my voice. "Tansu, c'mon; look at me."

Rejecting my words, she refuted with a fist against my jaw. The harsh smack deafened my ears; throwing the world in a violent spin. I remained standing but shifted between my legs with a stacking headache. I took another step back, rubbing my jaw with one hand.

Alice was getting impatient. "You're wasting *my* energy letting her hit you. Subdue or kill her, I won't heal you if you continue to act foolish."

"I need to reach her." I said determinedly.

Tansu growled and tried punching me again. I used my own hands to deflect the first blow and catch the second. I held her fist tight and used it to push her away. But she just jerked forward again. I sidestepped around her continuous swinging; making circles around this one position. By now, she was completely worn out; her body sagged, and veins pushed to the surface. Whatever energy was flowing through her, was volatile.

Alice urged me, "The energy in her is unstable. If you don't do something, it's gonna kill her."

"I-I don't know what to do." I bit my lip. "Stop!" I screamed.

Her wheezing became pained; her eyes squinting as her body sunk lower. A raspy whine emitted from her lips and she fell to one knee. My chest burned, as fear entered my brain. However, a flicker of her eyes caused a release of pressure in her body. A voice boomed from all directions, causing goosebumps to coat my skin.

"That's enough, my dear."

As those words entered her brain, the veins on her skin reduced and the color washed over her face. She stood herself upright, still shaking and lowered her head.

A sudden pinch in my head. "Look out!" Alice shouted.

Out of nowhere, a hand reached from behind and grabbed my face in a tight grip. I reached up and tried to pry the skeletal fingers away. I recognized him immediately.

"Sin!?" I yelled as he held me in place.

A confident chuckle slipped between his lips, right in my ear.

"You fucker! What did you do to her?"

"This. . ." His voice assaulted my eardrums, "was an experiment. And I must say that you passed." He glared at her, then chuckled.

All of a sudden, Tansu knelt down and picked up a small stick from the ground.

"You've gotten better at controlling yourself." He snickered. "However-" Tansu held the dull end of the stick directly in front of her left eye and moved it closer until in was merely a centimeter away.

"Don't you fucking dare!" I threatened; still prying at his grip. Then, in fury, I jabbed my elbow back into his chest, but only sent a shock through my bone. It didn't affect him at all.

Alice screamed at me, "That won't work! You need my power. Give me control!"

“I-I can't focus.” My worried expression was stuck solely on her.

“You have to forget about her for now. Focus on *me.”* The conversation with Alice took place inside my ears, as always, but was not private.

Sin spoke, “You lied.” His voice was sickly sounding, “Your death was broadcast loud and clear, and yet. . . suddenly you're back.” He sounded irate, yet curious.

I threw both my hands upward into his face, scratching and grabbing at what I could. He chuckled, unphased but then decided to toss me forward between Tansu and him. I stumbled and got to my feet; furious and directing my body to him. The second I planted my feet into the dirt, I heard footsteps rushing from behind.

I turned my head just in time to have the stick slapped into the side of my face. The blow knocked me off balance; and Tansu again pounced me. This time I was the one being tackled to the ground except she was far less defensive than I was. Almost immediately she set the stick on the ground and started aggressively bashing my face.

Sin remained and pushed his voice to me; calm. “Kimberly. It's been such a *long* time. I must say, I am happy you survived. . . That being said; I need to know exactly *how* you concealed yourself. *No* Teufel hides from me.” His voice became unpleasant again.

It was hard to hear him over the sound of her fists smashing into my skull.

“She's no longer your friend; you know what to do!” Alice made her intentions clear.

In a desperate attempt to stop her attacks, I used my arms as a shield, but she went around every effort I made at blocking. My face quickly bruised and split. Then she changed it up with a punch to the forehead, so hard, it whipped my head back into the dirt below. Then, acutely burying her knuckle into my throat, blocking my windpipe.

Her flurry of fists ground to a halt and her heavy breathing picked up again. Her body couldn't keep up with whatever spell he used to control her. With her bloody knuckles still clenched, her eyes went wide and showed only emptiness. She was merely a puppet, forced to play on her emotions and intended to kill me.

My defensive arms fell to my sides; resting as well.

“I know you can hear me in there.” I weakly stated.

Her expression didn't change a bit; she sat on my stomach focused on my eyes. Suddenly, my shoulder twitched on its own. With that little movement from me, she reacted. Grabbing a fist-sized rock from the ground; she lifted it up high and slammed it into the right side of my face then slowly brought the rock back up.

The violent crash had stunned me. Everything in my eyes had bled into a solid white and a dense, ringing concussion vibrated in my skull; forcing me into a state of incoherency.

I grimaced with pain, teeth chattering, and eyes squeezed shut. I held back my agony; any sudden movements could mean another hit.

Sin's face became pensive; watching closely.

I opened my left eye a little. It was blurry, but I could see a splotch of blood on the rock. The pain on my cheek was dense, and my head shook. Though most of my face was numb, I could feel a stream of warm blood roll down under my jaw and down my neck. A high-pitched whimper of pain escaped my lips, but I will not falter.

Then, a comfortable burst of static surged through me.

"Take hold of her now!" Alice called from within.

Acting on pure instinct, my body jolted forward, swift and fierce. I took hold of her right arm and used my free hand to throw the rock to the side then immediately grab her other arm. Having a solid hold on her, I rolled her over onto her back. Now, I was on top of her with my knees planted firmly on her chest and my hands pinning hers to the ground. A long breath slipped through my lips and my body continued to shake.

She struggled and growled at me like a monster. Whatever he did to her was turning her into something she wasn't.

"Wake. Up!" I called to her. "Wake up damn you." I wept.

As I begged her to come to her senses, break free of this curse; drops of blood from my cheek and split lip dripped onto her forehead. Something happened as the blood touched her skin. She abruptly went limp and stopped fighting me altogether. Chest pounding, I carefully lifted one arm up away from her.

My whole hand was shaking intensely. Then, I placed my hand on her cheek. The moment my palm touched her, she sprung back to life and swiftly clamped her hand around my wrist and immediately began to crush it with unnatural strength. Her face was blank. Expressionless.

"Uhaaaa! Tansu, stop. Please, this is not you!" My wrist was slowly breaking.

This time, she replied with a low, rippling voice. "You. Should. . . have died-*you* did this!"

She still held my wrist tight, but I raised my other arm quickly and punched hard under her armpit. Her grip slipped, freeing me. In that moment of release, I took both my hands and put them on each side of her face, gently holding her cheeks. I got right up to her and met her eyes with mine an inch apart. Her eyes went wider than ever before as she watched my face, panting irregularly. I gazed deeply into her soul; those shady green eyes that I once admired were nowhere to be seen, just lonely darkness.

"I can't hurt you. . . Because you saved me from myself. *You* are the reason I get up every day; why I can stand to look in the mirror. You're my best friend and I will not let this darkness consume you, the way it consumed me." I felt tears under my eyes, but held it in. "Tansuke, please, let it go."

She started huffing violently, but her body didn't move. Her chest just jumped up and down and her mouth hung open as the sharp breaths lept from her lungs until she slammed her eyelids shut. Then, her breathing steadied. The world fell silent; nothing else outside from the two of us existed in a way that mattered. My head lifted slightly, turning in a semi-circle looking for Sin. He was gone without a trace. No doubt watching, waiting for me to crumble.

I waited for her delayed response; a word, a breath, anything. But she was still. My heart started to break at the thought of her not waking up. This thought took hold of me and started ripping me apart; loosening the latch I so dearly held onto. The walls of my soul were thinning, and Alice prepared herself.

Tansu was motionless; pale. All hope drained itself from my blood and my hands slipped from her face. Then, her face saddened. A cold spike stabbed my chest as her vivid green eyes fluttered open with new life.

"K-Kimmy?" She stuttered at first, then turned frantic. I could see the fear in her face. My throat got stiff with tears.

"You're. . ." I felt the blood course through my veins again.

"What. . . just happened?" She asked; not fully understanding where she was. Before I could answer, I saw her eyes widen with realization. Recalling flashes of what transpired, she struggled with the reality she found herself in.

"That thing. . ." She shook, "it made me do it; he was talking inside my head. I tried my best to stop! But. . . But-" she wailed. She appeared to be on the verge of tears, still trying to piece it all together.

I crawled off her body, practically falling over with how dizzy I felt. I had regained some strength, but my face was throbbing, and I could hardly see out of my right eye at the moment.

She sat up, and I looked to her with relief. "I understand you're scared. But right now, you need to—"

She interrupted me. "I-I did that, to your face." She pointed out.

I hovered my hand over the wound to conceal it.

"Forget it. We need to focus on getting you out of here. You're in danger."

She got close to me and moved my hand out of the way. Looking at the bloody mess under my right eye, she had a sickening stare.

"I can't believe I did this to you. I am, so sorry." She said, full of shame.

I gritted my teeth with impatience.

"Tan!" I shouted at her. "You need to listen!"

She quickly changed her posture and got serious.

"S-sure, no problem." She said obediently. "What do you need me to do?"

"I don't know where he went, and I'll bet we don't have much time before he makes a move. This guy is Sin."

"Sin? You mean—"

"Yes, the one I made the deal with. He brainwashed you, lured me out here and he's pissed. If you don't get out of here right now, he will kill you." I looked around, trying to find a means to her escape.

She paused for a moment, looking blankly at me.

"This is the demon that gave you that power?" She got angry. I knew what she was thinking.

"It's alright to get angry, and I know what's going through your head right now. But drop it; this is no place for you."

She nodded. "Okay. S-should I call the police?"

I scoffed, "No, that won't do anything. I have to face him alone." I then directed my eyes to the ground but spoke out loud.

"Hey, some healing would be great right now." I demanded.

"On it." Alice spoke quietly, almost sounding annoyed.

Tansu gave me a concerned look. When my gaze returned to hers, I blushed.

"I-uh, I was talking to Alice." I said awkwardly.

She didn't have much of a response. At that moment I felt a warm pulsating jitter flow over my face. The skin got hot, and that white transparent steam pushed out from my pores.

"What in the world." She said, amazed.

"Heh. . ." I winced with one eye closed while the steam pushed out from under my flesh, "there's a lot to all this demon-power stuff."

Seeing her childlike amazement brought me out of the seriousness for a few seconds. Alice was working in overdrive and got the wounds repaired in just under a minute.

"There. That'll have to do for now." Alice stated.

"Thanks." I smirked.

Tansu stood herself up and brushed off some dirt before extending one hand to me.

"Here, let me help you up." She offered.

I smiled and accepted. The feeling of her hand in mine, helping me to my feet, gave a tingly comfort in my chest. Her smile was enough to fire me up again; make me feel like I could stand up to him.

She gripped me tightly and began to lift. All of a sudden, I plummeted back to the dirt, landing hard on my tailbone. Shocked, my eyes shot up to her, and my world quickly turned black and white.

Sin had returned. A black tentacle made up of some sort of malevolent mass sprouted from his back and draped over his shoulder. This limb tightly coiled around her throat and one of her legs; squeezing the life out of her.

"My, such a powerful bond you two share. However, I'm not here to play games."

Another black tentacle sprouted and tangled itself around the center of her chest, ensuring she would not escape and that the damage was distributed everywhere. Her arms were bound to her rib cage and the limb that coiled around her neck held her just tight enough to restrict most of her breathing.

Sin's anger burst, "I will not be made a fool! You cannot steal my child and use my own spell to hide!"

His grip loosened for a fraction of a second, then slammed even tighter around her whole body. A loud, wet crack filled the air. Her eyes shot open, and tears flowed freely as she squealed in pain.

"Hk. . . gheh. . . K-im." Her voice screeched out, calling me, begging for my help.

She's dying. She's dying.

Something in me broke. I went deaf in both ears, and a jolt of hot electricity shot through my brain, reviving the animalistic anarchy that forced itself into a dormant state the night I killed my father. The very first, cold madness was reanimated at my very core. That well-known acidic fluid coursed through my veins as my heart rapidly crashed against my rib cage.

It took me a moment, but I hoisted myself to my feet, moving slow and patiently. Standing slouched, eyes directed at the dirt. My hair fell loosely forward with my swaying movements and both fists bound to the point of aching. She continued to gasp for air, loudly groaning in torment. This pause I indulged in only increased the tension around us.

I spoke very softly, a faint whisper with the wind.

"You will not hurt Tansu anymore, you filth." I huffed an irregular pattern. "Bastard, you put her down before—" Fists shaking, I slowly lifted my head and glared directly into his eyes. The bangs in front of my face were lifted by the abundant energy pulsating from my skin. The purple glow of absolute hatred beamed out from my Anima.

"—before I tear your arms off!" My voice exploded.

This anger forcefully wove itself through my bones. The peace that I held onto so dearly, so close, had been brutally ripped to pieces and left to rot in some shallow corner of my mind.

My shoes dug into the ground and sent shards of wet grass springing upward as I sprinted toward him. As I got in close, he lifted Tansu higher and let his hands rest by his sides.

I kicked off and sent a forceful punch at his chest. He moved to the side, then, opened one hand and playfully pushed against my shoulder. Even though it was a light touch, I was knocked to the side by some invisible force and licked by small sharp gusts of air. I recoiled back but landed on my feet and reaffirmed my stance.

His expression flattened to modest annoyance.

"Kimberly. If you plan on challenging me, I suggest you discard whatever morals hold you back. I'd hate to see you waste your one and only chance." He stated very matter-of-factly.

Standing now thirty feet apart, I ignored his jest and attempted to close the gap in the same way; blindly dashing. Five steps forward and suddenly he was in front of me. My face crashed hard into his open hand as he grasped my entire head and lifted me up like before. He punched me with his free hand then tossed me to the side. In the air, I rotated myself and hit the ground on one foot, allowing me to control my tumble and stop upright. Bent on one knee, I let out an angry breath through my nose and ran at him again.

This time as I got close, he grinned and released Tansu, disappearing instantaneously in a brief flash of white. She gasped sharply as air finally entered her lungs, and she fell from almost twice her height. I reacted quickly and caught her just before she hit the ground. Her body landed safely in my arms, and the previously built momentum caused me to skid to a halt.

"Impressive catch." Alice complimented.

I set her down gently as she coughed violently for a few seconds. She sat at an angle and held her neck and had one arm slung across her chest.

"Kimmy." She coughed, "I think he broke something. My chest hurts so much." She cried, short of breath.

She looked into my purple eyes, noting my standard appearance besides that, then scanned my face for any glimpse of my humanity.

"Just wait here and try not to move. Pretend like you aren't even here, okay?" I said sincerely.

Her eyes were still wet from the tears and worry. There was a huge red mark that lined the middle of her neck, and she rubbed it gingerly. She only nodded in response.

I stood shakily and checked my surroundings.

"Do you feel him?" I asked Alice.

"No. He isn't like Teufel; I can't ever see him until he's too close."

My brows lowered, feeling the heat rise off my body. "What do you think his plan is?"

"He hasn't killed us yet. So, maybe he's testing us? After all, we disappeared for half a year; I'm sure he's curious about our strength."

"So, he's probably not gonna kill us right away." I said, almost relieved.

"Maybe not. . . but your *friend's* life doesn't apply to the game." She reminded me. "He's using her. As long as she's here, we're vulnerable."

"But even if she gets away, he can probably just zap right to her."

I shot her a glance, but she was also looking all around us with paranoid trembling. I got myself ready for him to strike; keeping my arms raised and taut. I crept a few feet away from Tansu, trying to draw him out.

"Are you nervous?" I asked with a cocky grin.

Alice laughed sarcastically. "I'm thrilled. Ready or not, today we make a stand. Who knows, maybe I can walk away from this wearing Sin's crown on my head."

"Maybe you'll be a bloody paste." I joked.

"At least we had a good run."

I got myself about ten feet away from Tansu and glanced back. She was sitting quietly, terrified. She saw me check on her, and I smiled; trying to let her know that everything will turn out all right.

With my smile came a small, barely audible whoosh noise. Sin suddenly appeared a few feet to my left, and with his entrance, his shadow limb swung out and connected to my still torn face. He slapped the raw skin hard and I fumbled back.

"Urgh!" I grunted, my face now thumping with new pain. "Decided to show yourself, huh?"

My heart kick-started again, as I saw him standing nearby. That same old black suit, red tie and bowler hat. It's as if no time had passed at all since the last time I saw him.

Trying to catch him off guard, I jerked forward and swung my fist, but the only thing I connected with was air. Another swing, and another miss. On my feet and putting the pressure on him, I continued to swing enthusiastically, and he waded side to side. Easily avoiding my efforts. However, my first intention was not to hit him, but to push him away from her. Still, I hoped to land a good punch. I was quick, but as of now, I was only human, and he glided with incredible speed.

He spoke; arrogant, "I'm insulted. Do you honestly think that you can even touch me as a mere human?" He casually dodged.

I didn't say anything, instead focusing on my punches. But he was right; he was way too fast for me in this state. Halting my swings, I planted my feet and pulled my arms in, panting slightly. He stopped as well, now standing opposite of me; keenly watching.

I spit to the dirt and flared my teeth. "I've been waiting for this, old man. You have no idea what you're in for, now that you brought Tansu into this. I'm gonna kick your ass."

Oddly enough, his smile went away, and he got serious.

"Your anger is misguided. I am not your enemy. . . Do not forget who saved you." His words were slow, drawn out.

"You cursed me." My teeth scraped, "I was naïve and stupid. . . you prey on the broken and feed them lies of vengeance. When all you're doing is damning them to a life of misery and hatred. The only thing I can't figure out, is why?"

He gave me a yearning look and continued,

"Why? My child, your desires are not so astray from my own. I want nothing more than to be free from my chains, just as you. Such liberation requires sacrifice. . ." He paused, contemplating, "I do not wish to destroy this world."

"Bullshit. You're nothing but a monster that kills and creates more monsters. The blood on your hands. . ." I grew irate, "I can't even imagine how many souls you've destroyed."

He gave me a stern look, "I have never killed."

"Don't fucking lie to me." I spat "You killed my mother!"

His face widened with revelation. "Is that why you turned against me? A continuous lie your father has spread?"

His words stopped me, but only built upon my anger. My teeth started to grow sharp, and my skin was becoming paler. He began laughing quietly to himself.

"You have matured in many ways, but this grudge you hold will make you bleed." He said, pleased.

Barely able to contain my wrought desires, I let out a ferocious yell and ran straight at him; blinded by rage. My fists shot at him in the form of quick, straight jabs, but every single one I threw was easily avoided by a simple sidestep. To counter, he threw his limb around my wrist, only getting a slight grip and pulled me to the side; I stumbled but stayed on my feet then stalled for a moment. He stood tall and slipped both of his hands in his pockets. He wasn't even trying.

Now, a little way away from Tansu, I let loose a determined grin. Taking a moment to collect myself and released the restraints on my mind. A trickle of sweat rolled down my face and stopped at my lips; the itch made me lick it. Densely salted and chilled. My heart started pounding at the thought of feeling that energy again. The challenge ahead excited yet terrified me.

"Are you ready?" I asked out loud.

Alice reared her head back, "Are *you?*"

"Heh. I've been holding onto this for a long time. Let's show him what we're made of."

I glared at him; he was waiting patiently. He didn't seem to be rushing me at all; he just smiled creepily. I broke attention from him and instead dug at the tombs of my mind.

Submerging myself in bottled agony; I was overcome by the memories that triggered Alice over time. Every negative thought I had, piled on and screamed in my ears, but it didn't control me. In the time Alice and I had away from the threat of this battle, we learned to moderate; stoke the flame.

My head fell forward as my soul ignited within. Instantly, I found myself back in those hallways; a disturbingly lanky shadow of my former self, standing before two metal doors.

I could hear Alice calling to me from some faraway room; weak. I couldn't understand what she was saying. Snipped, torn pieces of prior conversation that lingered eternally within the timeless gaps of my brain. A distraction. The door on my left was already cracked open. I approached it and took hold of the ring handle. Dragging it open, the metallic grind bombarded my senses and splintered my translucent body. It opened, and a desperate exhale flowed into the hall. The energy that spiked around me upon its release suddenly took shape before me.

A mirror image of myself; a snapshot of the terrified girl who recently abandoned her humanity; still covered in her fathers' blood. The stitches prominently clasped her lips and she was crying; eyes black. I took her hand, gently guiding her closer until she was within my brace. Her sobbing faded away, and I took her within me; becoming closer to whole, myself.

Next, I moved to the second door. With my new stature, I was able to pry this one apart from the frame with moderate ease. The room itself was vast, but empty; devoid of any meaning or reprieve. I found myself just inside, leaning against the wall; holding a knife in her hands. I bent down to her level and saw blood on the blade. She took note of my presence and turned, revealing a vertical line down her wrist; spewing blood.

I frowned, placing my palm over the wound and wiping it away entirely. The skin closed and I whispered, *Not yet.* She leaned her head against my knee and gave a fatal sigh before turning to smoke and siphoning into my lungs. I brought myself upright and exited the room; making a mental note to return these pieces as soon as it's all over.

I turned away from the two doors and was halted by something that wasn't there before. The cage by the river. I lingered with obtuse curiosity as the memories revolved. The dusty brown mist formed, contained in the bars and took on the shape of my childhood body. She approached the bars and took hold of them, leaning in close and staring up at me with wonderous curiosity.

I crouched down and met eyes with the child; cautiously taking hold of the bar and expressing mourn in my face. The child tilted its head, then its face split in half vertically and spat a web of brown strings that attempted to reach me. I lept back and pressed myself against the stone wall. Its ravaging cords fell short.

In a crumbling, fizzy voice it beckoned; *I just want to help. Forgive?*

You manipulated Alice. I don't trust you. I responded.

The split head closed up, leaving a slit down the child's face that was bound tightly by identical strings sewn from the jaw to the hairline. She spoke again, with my tiny voice.

You could die. I could die. Let me help.

My head shook on its own, left and right. But a part of me considered what this thing was saying. However, deep down I know that my nightmares, my crisis every day and my inability to control my emotions since I was a child, all stem from this abomination. This festering culmination of Ditch energy. Despite my resolve to walk away, I mentally unlocked the latch without sharing that information with the shadow.

I got what I came for.

Back in the real world, no time had passed. My left eye twitched very suddenly. A powerful, invisible explosive wave of pure energy shot out from my body, sending a huge amount of dirt and dust into the air. This power began spiraling around me; lifting and spinning bits of dirt and grass.

"Looks like all that practice worked." Alice congratulated; unaware of my trials within.

"I guess so." My words were slightly strained. "Keeping the worst parts of me locked away until I need them. . . a good way to effectively *give* you control." I snickered.

Even though I had dived into the depths of my darkest corner, I couldn't remember my time there. I know that I did, and that was all. My skin was burning; itchy. The spiral of energy continued to engulf me. Sin removed his hands from his pockets; investment growing. The transformation began to gradually take hold. I could feel it glide over me, just as I felt the insanity attempt to grab hold. Then, all at once, the dust and blades of grass froze in the air and fell to the ground. My back was straight now as I held myself with a new sense of superiority.

My eyes were glowing purple still; brighter than before and my eyeballs had been painted black. The biggest change I experienced was the left side of my body flooded with her chalk-white skin and my hair had become darker; just a little longer.

Sin gawked at me with a dissatisfied crook on his face. "Not a full transformation? Is this a joke?"

My focused gaze scrutinized him. In this state, I could access most of her power without causing a drain effect on my body. I could already feel a difference in my worldly perception. Previously, every random noise in the background plucked in my ears, but I tuned them out. I got distracted by deeply saturated colors, small observations like the tiny hairs on Tansu's face shifting as we walked and even the sound of the air bubbles in my joints popping as I walked. All of those scattered details, bombarding me constantly, were now entirely focused on Sin.

I made a fist and brought it up to my chest. "I don't wanna overwhelm a *demon* like you with my full strength right away. Let's ease into this." I said with a cocky attitude.

"Today you face a *god* and you compare me to these lowly demons? How dare you." He furrowed his brows.

Alice spoke to me, "I think you went too far. . ."

I whispered, "Yeah, might've made him a little mad. Just hurry up."

"I'll try. Drawing all the energy from my reserves isn't easy. I have to keep my Anima balanced while at the same time, slip a little to you. It's a delicate task."

"When the time comes, jump my skin and give 'em hell." I encouraged her.

"Just don't get us killed before that." She snarled.

Without thinking, I opened my left hand and released the dense black claws from my fingertips. In the moment they tasted fresh air, I sprang forward and the background in my peripheral became a blur. My feet stomped into the dirt as I approached him at triple the speed. Closing the distance in a blink, I sprang upward and slashed at a downward, diagonal angle. He avoided it like it was nothing and chuckled.

As a follow-up to my downward swing, I continued the momentum and rolled on the ground, then quickly attempted a rising slash from below. This attack launched me two feet upward but still missing him. In the air from my swing, I sent both feet forward and kicked him in the chest; landed, then stepped forward with another slash. He pulled himself back and avoided the hit entirely.

"You *are* quick." He shimmered; disappearing for a second and reappearing five feet behind me. "I warn you, child; you are not the first Teufel to face me. You all fight the same."

I whipped around; arms bent.

"You sure like the sound of your own voice." I laughed with confidence; speaking through our melded, singular tone.

Sin suddenly moved so fast, that I didn't even see him twitch before he was right in my face. My expression widened, unable to react.

"*This. . .* is fast." He stated under his breath before a swift punch to my chest knocked the wind out of me. Instantaneously, two more punches contacted my stomach and right shoulder at nearly the same time. Then he finished off the barrage with two more insanely fast hits to my gut and face, knocking me backward and skidding on my heels.

Instinctively, my arms shot up to further defend myself until I ground to a halt. As I did, my arms lowered a slight amount and my body felt ten times heavier. With no time to recover, one of his shadow limbs had become razor-sharp and was flung upward, slicing through my shirt and a layer of flesh beneath my collarbone. One eye closed itself with the instant pain as I threw myself backward and created a twenty-foot gap between us.

I bit down hard on my lip and kept my composure. However, it was difficult to keep my head raised as all the pain from his punches washed over me like a tender flame; sinking into my flesh and creating deep black bruises.

Trying my best to ignore the pain, I ran at him and jumped up into the air; springing two feet above his incredible height and swinging my claw down at his head. He ducked slightly and reached up, pressing his flat palm into my stomach and using some wave of energy to make me hover momentarily. Then his shadow limb coiled around my ankle and whipped me back in the direction I came from. I hung in the air for a second and a half before crashing into the dirt and bouncing into a backward somersault until I came to a sliding halt.

Flat on my stomach, I gave a pained breath through my open mouth; tasting the dirt and blood on my tongue. I spit it out while attempting to pull myself on all fours.

"H-holy shit." I exclaimed; the sweltering pain radiated all over my body. "I thought your Demonic Energy was supposed to protect me from attacks."

"It *is* protecting you. He's just far more powerful than this state can handle. If it wasn't for me, you'd be dead after the first punch."

Before I could respond to Alice; I sensed him standing above me. I raised my head, only to be met by the tentacle as it started to lash my body like a whip. The limb was thin, probably about the size of my forearm, but it hit like a sledgehammer. One hit smashed into my shoulder blade, another two rebound off my ribs.

"Don't tell me all this resolve you bolstered was for this!" Sin shouted down at me.

I had enough and forced myself to sloppily roll to the side. Then, mid-roll, I stabbed my fingers into the dirt and had my claws reemerge with explosive force from directly beneath him.

Caught off guard, he pulled his head and torso back just enough for his chin to be slightly grazed and his hat to be pierced by a single nail. He puffed into a cloud of black smoke and reappeared a few feet back. I was lying on my side, one arm tucked under my body and the other hand in the dirt, with my fingers, stuck a few inches deep.

"Don't talk down to me." I demanded through strained huffs.

Retracting my claws, I partially hoisted myself up. I watched his hat flutter to the ground; he wasn't amused. His slick gray hair was now exposed, making him look much less threatening. His body remained steady and his gaze fixated on me. He reached up and with his thumb, he wiped the small cut on his chin. It had disappeared completely with his light rub.

Sin continued his offense and wavered; reappearing behind me with a downward lash from his shadows. This time, I sensed him appear and turned in time to bat the limb away with my claws; cutting it in half. Unsurprisingly, it sprouted from the nub and distracted me while he reached out and grabbed the collar of my shirt. Hoisting me up, he glared with his intrusive yellow eyes, scoffed and puffed away again.

I landed on my feet and found him to my right. Feeling dizzy trying to keep track of him, I found myself twitching at every touch from the air, or pat from my hair on my neck. Having so much space to move around in was a disadvantage for me. My main way of attacking was hacking and slashing; keeping pressure and staying close, but he's too quick. My ground phase attack can only be implanted through and up from a surface, but the only surface was the ground; limiting me severely.

Then he did something strange. He extended his right hand out, with his palm facing me and connected his fingers. Then he placed his left hand adjacent to his right, making a partial fist but pointing his index and middle finger downward. He then used his left hand with the two fingers pointed down to make a circle around his flat hand. Following the path of the circular motion, a thin streak of blue light formed. The shining trail morphed into shapes and letters; it was some type of energy glyph that circled his hand and began to emit a strangely pleasant radiance.

Then, random letters of the glyph rose away from his hand, the light becoming a tainted black. The separated letters took the shape of five large, black spheres that seemed fixated on me.

"What the hell?" Alice gawked.

Just then, one of the spheres became engulfed by a dusky flame and shot straight at me, flying through the air like a baseball. It was fast. I hopped to my left and the blurry shape went soaring past me. However, the ball had hit the ground about six feet back and suddenly I was propelled by a large burst of energy and fire. This threw me a few feet up and forward, but I was able to hit the ground, tumble and get on my feet.

A new sweat rolled down my face, "That's just great." I exclaimed.

"Should probably make sure we avoid those." Alice agreed.

I looked at where the ball had impacted the ground and saw no hole; just a black spot where the emission occurred. In my peripheral, I located Tansu nearby to make sure she was still safe. She was crouched down a small distance from the forest edge, on the complete opposite end of the entrance. From me, she sat almost a hundred and fifty feet; to Sin, it was nearly double that distance.

Then, I felt a tinge in my ear and redirected my eyes to him; he was grinning devilishly.

Alice shouted, "You moron, you just-"

She couldn't finish her sentence before Sin shot another orb in Tansu's direction. It blasted through the air with a high-pitched screeching that assaulted my eardrums as it passed in front of me. Horror encapsulated my face in the same instant my body reacted. Then, everything nearly froze through my eyes.

A huge eruption of the energy that Alice was building got released into my body; allowing me to propel myself at speeds I had never reached before. The attack cut through the air, moving so fast its image appeared almost as a large pencil. Within the last fifteen feet before impact, I shattered all understanding of my capabilities and intercepted the attack. Diving into the air and grabbing it with my bare hands; planting my feet and skidding; leaving a trail of crackling electricity in my wake and burning the ground behind me.

The sphere infected my hand with its dense flame and so I turned to Sin as quickly as I could and threw it back at him. He simply looked at it, and it turned to bitter dust.

My face was angled; determined as I recovered my stance and faced him again. Then, I switched back to my normal demeanor; unaware of exactly what I just did. To me, the events that just unfolded were resting in my recent memories like a waning dream. Looking to my right, I saw Tansu safe on the ground; wide-eyed and barely able to comprehend what was happening.

Alice exclaimed proudly, "Nice work."

"I-I don't. . . remember doing that." I questioned. Then looked at my hands; both had turned grey. The power Alice let out to assist me caused another stage of transformation. Now all of my skin was white, and my eyes were purple and black. But my hair was only half-length and dark; not the terror abyss they became when she was upfront.

"Just don't get distracted now. Keep your head in the fight." She instructed.

"Yeah. You're right." My eyes wandered to where I was standing prior. There was a long thin trail of burnt ground that emitted some visible electric charge. I shook my head.

I turned back to Sin; he was leering assertively, not shaken by my action and still held his arm straight out.

Three more to go. I thought.

Without warning, another was sent my way. I dodged it fairly easily; faster now. The attack screamed by me and flew into the tree line where it continued on for an unknown distance before colliding with a tree and exploding.

"You're doing well; just hold out a little longer." Alice praised.

"Thanks. But I don't know if I can keep dodging those."

Her voice was strained, "Gotta admit, it's a pretty cool attack."

"If only we had a ranged move like that." I scoffed.

"If only." She pondered.

"How much longer, until you're ready?" I controlled my breathing.

"At first it was going slow, but now. . . I'm going twice as fast. I feel invigorated." She grinned, getting excited.

"Sounds good. . . I think I have an idea." I said, the weariness reducing.

I hunched down and prepared myself, then started a dire sprint in his direction. Just as fast as the last one, the sphere shot straight at me. I let it get within a few feet and slowed my sprint just enough to bring my left hand in front of my face. Claws fully drawn as the sphere reached me, I swiped the backside of my nails in a downward-left motion; making contact with the spike and deflecting it to the ground. As soon as it hit the dirt, I long jumped, using the explosion to propel my body forward, flying at Sin with my claws ready.

I'm gonna get him, this time.

Chapter 31 – Guardian Devil

His eyes broadened in disbelief as my blurry image rapidly closed in. Sin promptly released the spell on his hand; causing the remaining orbs to disappear into thin air. Then, with little time to dodge, he brought his arms up in a cross-defensive position shielding his face and having his two shadow limbs layer over his arms for additional protection.

Upon reaching him, I aggressively slashed at his head; cutting through both of his shadows and creating a large gash in his left arm. My body continued past him after I made contact, but I was able to orient myself and land on both feet and stagger to a halt. My thighs immediately burned with the landing and expulsion of energy. As the dust settled, I braced myself on bent knees, recovering stamina. A raw burning radiated from my hand where I held his attack; I squinted harshly.

My eyes shot open again, but to my surprise, he was standing just in front of me. With a loud growl, he wrapped his skeletal fingers around my throat and lifted me to eye level. My feet dangled above the ground, swaying with his irate movements. He aligned his other fingers with my cheek, holding them gently over the gash the rock had left.

A demented smile, "You know what I love most about my children? The way you all turn out so sure of yourselves. You have no idea what true power is and yet you scramble with purpose."

Suddenly and excruciatingly, five needles; reminiscent of my claws but made of pure energy, shot out from his fingertips and stabbed into the open wound, stopping as they connected with my gritted teeth. My voice broke as I screamed in agony, forcing them to tear deeper into the flesh of my cheek.

"And yet every time I think there's a chance, I end up disappointed." He wriggled his fingers which tore through the delicate flesh.

Thinking fast, I reached out with my right hand and took hold of the wrist of the hostile hand. I gripped it tight, while Alice unleashed some of her energy into his skin; scathing him. With my touch, his invasive strike was retracted, freeing my cheek from the torment. Still being choked, I swung my claws at him, but he disappeared into smoke again; dropping me to the ground. I landed hard, but the discomfort in my ankles was nothing compared to my face.

"Mother—F—fucker! That hurt. . . Oh, man." I swore, my jaw trembling like crazy.

"You gotta keep your eyes on him." Alice instructed.

I saw him reappear just opposite of me, a stones-throw away. Getting fed up with his pathetic disappearing act, I openly mocked him.

"Y-you always jump back, Sin. Every time I get too close; you flee. What kind of coward are you? Even going as far as using Tansu as bait; ridiculous." I ridiculed. "What's the matter, are you afraid of a little girl like me?" I chuckled. He didn't say a word.

Formulating a strategy, I found my brain settling on just one thing over and over. Just keep up the pressure; wear him down enough to give me a better chance when Alice was ready. Maybe, I'll even get lucky and land a critical blow. Again, I stood myself up and charged him. The wind from my sprint pushed the newly flowing blood from my cheek down the side of my neck.

I dug my claws into the dirt behind me and dragged it all the way until I reached him where I fiercely slashed upward; throwing dirt all around. Unsurprisingly he dodged the attack, but I was ready. I instantly retracted my claws, used my left hand to grab him by the suit and pull myself in; driving my knee right into his ribs.

The power behind my jab was futile. Unaffected, he pulled one fist back and punched downward; crashing into the top of my head and slamming me to the ground. As my back hit the dirt, I threw my hand forward and shot my claws out again. This time my pinky nail penetrated about an inch deep into his left shoulder. A small reaction of pain irked his face and he grabbed my arm; tossing me upwards with ease.

In the air before him, he drove an incredibly fast punch into my gut. The force of his punch didn't instantly throw me back; I lingered just for a moment. A glob of spit shot out of my mouth and landed on his crude, arrogant face. A glow in his eyes triggered a cold air to wrap around us. Whispers erupted from nowhere and washed over me like a dream of a life I never knew. Pleasant, dreary.

Then, a dome of unstable power expanded from the space between us. This gurgle of unnatural vigor washed over me like a bubble of acid; curling the hairs of my body and causing my skin to tighten. Every tooth felt loose and my eardrums momentarily contracted.

After the sphere passed over me, I was harshly sent flying backward at high speed. My body rag-dolled across the ground, bouncing and skidding as though I had been hit by a semi-truck on the highway.

My brain shut down.

The world swayed around me, but not the world I had previously known. I was standing along a barren roadside. It was dark, not a cloud or star in the sky to guide me. A thick, icy fog rolled along the ground and concealed my feet.

By some will other than my own, I started to walk along the edge of the pavement. The empty strip lacked any designated lines or markers, but the borders were decorated densely with familiar trees and lanky shadows. Oblivious to anything and everything, my empty head pushed on. A nonchalant stride of mute purpose carried me in a destination undetermined, but I got the impression that I was not alone.

My eyes peered to the left, over the road and to the trees. To my surprise, I saw another traveler matching my stride. Unclear at first, it was soon revealed to be Alice. She moved in a mirrored fashion, looking back at me. We continued to move; eyes locked indefinitely without concern for the road before us. In my peripheral, I saw her rapidly approaching a figure along her path.

A ghastly figure, matching the appearance of Crism. I watched Alice face forward and suddenly Crism turned to a white mist and shrouded Alice's body. Before I could see the result of this, I realized our paths were matching. Fearful, I faced ahead to find myself in contact with a character of my own.

My mother.

I immediately forgot about Alice's existence in this place. There was no more road, no more fog or trees. Nothing but her, and I, alone.

She stood before me with a smile and an outfit exactly matching my own. I tried to speak but fell silent. Not even the ringing in my ears was present; absolutely nothing else existed. She smiled even bigger, causing her baby blue eyes to close with joy and cute dimples to form. She lifted both of her hands cupped together, holding something. I didn't want to look away from her face, but my head lowered anyway.

In her hands, was a tiny, glass unicorn.

It was dark again, but this time I could feel my body; it screamed. A cool rush of air flowed over my stillness, as my mind lingered; dazed and abstract. I lay on the ground, three inches of loose dirt piled around my impact shape. Awake; not quite remembering my dream, I tried to immerse myself again. Blinking and groaning, I shakily picked myself up to a kneeling position.

“Fuck.” Alice cursed, “I thought he knocked you out cold.” Her voice was distant; like there was a concrete wall between us.

I moaned, “Almost. . . Jes-us, what the hell did he do? M-my lungs . . . they hurt.” I stuttered and coughed. Every organ in my body felt like they had individual tears and couldn't stop pounding.

“I'm not sure, but whatever it is, it can't be good. There's something foreign in me.” She responded. It was clear by her voice that she was panicked but kept the illusion of confidence in front.

My body received backward signals. I tried to move my hand, but my neck turned. Attempting to adjust my shoulder caused a reaction in my foot. It was obvious that his bizarre wave did more than just hurt me; it scrambled my nervous system. My eyesight was darker than normal; almost as though the contrast balance of my vision was all blown out.

I barely lifted my head enough to get a glimpse of the old man. He remained unscathed and poised. I tried to stand, but a sudden sharp pain in my abdomen stopped me. I lost my balance and fell back to the ground. How my brain normally perceived my body and consciousness was thrown out of whack.

With every thump of my brain, every ounce of blood pushed through my veins; I could see in the darkness behind my eyelids, a vision of myself from a third-person view. At the same time, I opened my eyes and could see normally. These two views overlapped each other.

One moment I could see myself and another I saw the grass below me. I shook my head violently side to side. Sin stood a short distance away, watching me in agony. He didn't seem to have any interest in finishing me off right away, otherwise, he could have taken any number of opportunities.

With every passing second, I slipped deeper into the confusion of my senses. Each attempted movement was misinterpreted by my brain, causing a madness to slither from under my skin. Growing increasingly disturbed, my breathing started to become erratic. The understanding of minute details was completely skewed.

I could see the grass below me magnified ten times, I could hear the desperate sound of Tansu softly crying in the background and I could taste that glass of juice I had for breakfast this morning. These perceptions constantly switched and twisted; causing my sanity to splinter.

"Make it stop." I huffed. "Alice, make it stop, please!"

"I'm trying to find the source of this hysteria!" She beckoned, quieter than before.

I buried my eyes into each palm, bypassing the nervous confusion and pushed hard on my own skull. Slowly, my vision stabilized. The effects lessened with the added pressure on my eye sockets. I got on my hands and knees; head lowered. The land beneath me continued to swim and blur and from that motion sickness; my stomach churned. All of a sudden, I heaved violently. Vomiting a mixture which contained copious amounts of deep red blood.

"Oh god." I shivered.

"Forget about that. You're fine." Alice shouted at me, clearly lying.

I moaned loudly; the discomfort unlike anything I've ever felt.

"Can you pinpoint where the pain is coming from?" She asked.

"N-no. It feels like every inch of my body is filled with hot knives. . . and my bones. . . like, they all just split open." My arms shook immensely, trying to hold me up.

I *want* to pass out. Die; right here and now. But I can't. . . I won't; Tansu is at stake. Nevertheless, a depressing sensation came over me. Even now, after everything I have been through, I am powerless and on my knees. It's hopeless.

"So that's it!? You draw the line here, before the *real* fight begins." Alice shouted; her voice filled with detest and impatience.

"Shut up," I demanded

She started to laugh at the audacity. "You're fucking worthless."

I winced in pain. "What can I do? He's too powerful."

She paused, distracted. ". . . I think I have an idea of what he used against us." She stated.

"What?"

"My power is circling inside us. I think that attack shut down some links between my Anima and your body. I'm gonna try to force my way through." She stated, worriedly.

"How are you gonna do that?"

"Building my energy all this time has pooled it at my core. If I can reach even deeper; siphon every drop of my being and push it to you all at once; it might break through. . . But, if it doesn't. . ." She ended with a dreadful tone.

"It'll probably kill me." I finished for her. I let the risk settle in my brain and gave a heavy sigh. "I'm dead if we don't."

The buzzing in my head simmered down and she pulled back, trying to search herself. At first, I felt nothing. Left to stare into the field, hoping Sin wouldn't get impatient and just cut my head off. Then, my chest ran cold and my fingers twitched. An odd rumbling took place in my head and I could suddenly hear more voices.

Many unified calls and screams played like an old, scratchy record at the stem of my brain. I couldn't keep my eyes open while these indecipherable words pounded my skull. It felt just like it did back then when I met Lucy in the dream. Some strange connections to the woefully abandoned. It was, almost comforting.

In just a minute or two, I started to feel my skin grow warm, a soothing sensation came over me, and I briefly felt no pain. I managed to pull my torso upright, propped up like a board on both knees.

"I think, it's working." I jeered, still inhibited.

Suddenly, a tiny gust of air spiked my ears. I looked up and Sin was there again with his smug scowl. I choked on my own breath, horrified that he was this close at such a vulnerable moment. At first, he did nothing, just held a finger pointed at me. My lips trembled, anticipating he might attack at any moment. To my surprise, he talked.

"You know, Kimberly; when I look into your eyes, do you know what I see?" He sounded annoyed.

My voice trembled. "I don't care."

"Exactly that; defiance. Your father defied me, and he paid for it. You two are so very much alike."

Alice whispered, "I'm doing the best I can; keep him talking."

Not acknowledging Alice in any way, I kept my stare on him. "No, my mother paid the price for his mistakes. She was innocent!"

"And it's because of those mistakes that you ended up here. I fail to understand how the blame was shifted on me; I gave you what you wanted; you got revenge on your father. This was not meant to be a vendetta."

"You expect something different!? All those kids you cursed with your so-called gift were robbed of their lives; all because you preyed on their trauma."

He remained stoic, "And all of the other children lost their minds not long after they were reborn. . . you, however, remain intact. Why is that?"

He grit his teeth; then turned his head and looked to Tansu. Out of thin air another glyph circled around his fist as he retracted his finger. I saw this and tried to pull myself back, but it was too late. He pressed it tight against my chest and a massive surge went through me. Whatever this force was, levitated me off the ground and held me there. Arms and legs dangling, completely numb and suspended in a stasis.

As I floated there, he began walking towards Tansu; leaving me.

"W-what are you doing?" I struggled to move my mouth.

His footsteps were light in the dirt, not making an impression or dust as he casually strode in her direction.

"I can read your Teufel, Kimberly. You two have such great potential, having defeated Destro and Lyumik. You even managed to inflict damage on me. . . that alone is enough to consider-" He snickered, impressed. "if you were capable of even touching me in this form. . . I wonder?" He grinned evilly.

I tried prying my arms in every direction. The pressure behind my eyes was building.

"If I am to kill you, I must be absolutely sure that you have what I need." He spoke calmly, pondering some far-off thought.

He moved toward Tansu in a ghastly motion; she couldn't run. When he had her entangled in those dark snake-limbs, he had crushed her, breaking some of her ribs in the process. I could tell right away she was defenseless from then on. She looked at me, floating there.

"Kimmy!" She cried out as he slowly closed in on her. Arriving in a matter of seconds, he reached his long arm out to her.

"Damn it! I said get away!" My voice grew louder, echoing in the trees. The stress writhing under my skin, shook me in this invisible web.

He got a big, creepy smile on his face. "Just as your mother died for your father's mistakes, so too shall your friend die for yours!" He declared.

My arms and legs dangled still. I tried everything I could to force a movement.

"Alice! Alice, come on, he's gonna kill her!" I screamed, begging for her to force her power.

"I'm trying!"

I have to save her.

Sin lifted his arm and very swiftly—fiercely—slapped the back of his fist into the side of her head. Her face hit the dirt, but she got on her hands and knees, grabbing at her rib cage and trying to crawl away. I watched in horror, tears spilling out from under my eyelids.

I can't do it. I can't.

"Don't." She whined and dragged herself.

Sin then brought his hand straight out and held it above her. She rotated her head enough to see his fist above. He looked into her fearful eyes, then spoke to me with shaky desperation. "Free me."

Then brought his fist down with intense force directly onto her forehead. The loud smack echoed in my ears as her head bounced off the dirt. Her body eased into the ground and stopped moving entirely.

My heart, my breaths, and my rage all ceased as I watched a deep red pool of blood begin to pour under her head. In my blurry vision, I saw a light mist flow from his hand, around her body, then dissipate. Sin looked to me, his face smug and daring.

I watched with a frozen face and slacked jaw. Waiting, searching, listening for any movement; any noise. But there was nothing at all. Something deep inside snapped. The human side of my brain shut down and something else awakened. All senses narrowed, and my eyes focused on my target. I began breathing deeply, chest rising with the anger building inside. My temperature scorched, head pounding, demonically glaring at the motionless body and blood that carpeted the ground.

My brain shattered.

"Sin!" My vocal cords strained to the max, releasing this powerful call. As my voice faded and left the echo of fury bouncing off the trees, I was left wheezing, sweat dripping from my brow.

Then, a shallow voice was heard in the back of my head. It was Alice, and, strangely enough, my voice. . . a younger voice.

"Perfect."

A burning wave took hold of my bones and a sharp snap clicked at the top of my spinal cord. I started to groan as a crazy amount of pressure built inside.

The groan turned into a ferocious battle cry as the power rose higher and higher—the pain along with it. His expression changed to twisted pleasure.

My body relaxed then seized tight as the transformation slowly tried to take over. Alice's deep white skin tone struggled to push across my own flesh. It receded a bit, then quickly reversed and rapidly flooded me. My hair flailed wildly as it was given a new black coat and sharpened like a bushel of daggers. The pain of such a quick transformation was intense. Bones shifted under the tightening skin, becoming elongated and dense.

I then felt a burning sensation on my face as my lips suddenly pressed tightly together and began to sear. The skin did not get stitched, as it normally would. Instead, my lips melted together, forming one solid patch of skin. Then it began to wrinkle and scar everything beneath my nose to my cheekbones; forming an ear-to-ear mess of pinched, burnt skin.

I squealed loudly, emitting noise from where my mouth would be, but was no longer open. My muffled cries vibrated inside my head and my entire body began to quake without mercy. A new, curious sensation touched my eyes. The weirdest thing I have ever experienced was the literal spinning of my irises as the new radiant purple glow emitted from them, and they slowed to a resting position.

Along with everything else, black curved markings followed the sly, outer edges of my eyes and over my cheekbones, topped off with a few black dots being burned above my eyes but below the brows. Just like Lust, I had facial markings indicating some greater power.

This otherworldly torture crushed every fiber of my being then reformed it into something new. My body froze, then relaxed. The pain subsided, leaving me panting from my nostrils. There was a dense silence in the air. Sin was watching me hover there, very closely, waiting to see what came next. My eyes shot open and with it, a huge expulsion of energy was released, breaking this magical hold on my body.

I plummeted to the ground, falling nearly ten feet and landed upright without any loss of balance or discomfort. My head fell forward and arms relaxed. I stood like a zombie, swaying.

"I. . . don't understand. This is-" Alice, of all people, was confused.

I lifted my head up with squinted eyes, barely feeling conscious. As soon as my eyes rested on him again, I was immersed.

"Woah. I don't feel *anything*. Alice, what did you do?" I asked.

"Nothing! I followed the plan and kept building my energy. . . when he attacked your friend, all of a sudden I was-" She stopped.

"You were what!?" I questioned.

". . . *You* were *here* again." She was astonished.

I paused, and contemplated; searching for an answer that was right in front of me. The cage. "Its *my* energy. . ." I mumbled. I got a sick feeling with my understanding.

She then got an overwhelming confidence, blatantly ignoring my plight. "Do you know what this is?"

I shrugged.

"This is Ascension!" She announced with boisterous glee.

My skin made a grinding leather sound as I opened and closed my hand, stretching the ligaments. It was weird. Alice did not have full control. I still moved, but it was like we shared my brain, each making the same decision. I don't know exactly how to describe it, except that our minds worked together and worked insanely fast.

"Kim. . . Let's rip his throat out." She stated boldly.

With Alice's confidence and willingness to fight, I disregarded the turmoil in my gut and set my sights fully on Sin. "Let's."

I pulled my arm straight back with a tight-bound fist and keenly glared at him. In less than a second, I closed the near thirty-foot gap between us. Now, within striking distance, I thrust my right fist forward like a piston. He stepped to the side; his movements were much slower than before through my eyes, but he still managed to dodge.

His eyes grew wide, and a delighted smile came over him. "Y-yes." He stuttered, completely out of character. "You might be the one."

Then, he lashed out a new dark tentacle at my head; this one razor sharp. I saw it coming and ducked just in time to avoid it. As I ducked under his flailing limb, I planted my foot firmly in the dirt, then dug my elbow into his stomach. His thick skin buckled with the force. Not letting up, I continued my barrage with several insanely fast and powerful punches, every single one collided with his chest. Each and every hit rebounded off him and at the same time left a small dent in his torso.

Everything was moving in slow motion, or so it seemed through my eyes. I could see every movement he was about to make, like a shimmer of the near future, which allowed me to react faster than my own thought process.

I finished my flurry of punches with a concluding fist that sent him skidding backward a few feet. Pure instinct forced my claws to be drawn forth. The release was much smoother than before. In my regular form, the nails were like bones, jagged and rough. Now, they were sleek; almost like metal.

I slammed my fingers into the ground, and they sprouted right up from under him. One shot up and pierced through his right foot. The others missed on either side.

He glowered at his foot, the nail pushing through to the other side.

"I know you can do better than that." He said calmly, not even the slightest bit concerned with his foot.

I retracted my nails and charged at him again. This time he attacked first with his tentacle limb; he was still insanely fast. But I saw the attack coming and brought my arm up and deflected it to the side; passing by the limb and jump kicked him flat in the chest. My body rebounded off him and I landed heavily, then performed a smooth roll to the right, where I rose from the ground and punched him square in the face. He staggered back a few steps.

"Sin." Alice grumbled. "I quite enjoyed that little trick with the orbs. . ." She sneered.

His brow raised indifferently.

Still moving as one, we both focused our energy; coiling together elements of a mixture containing my own twisted soul and Alice's power. The result was a mimic from the past and present. Hundreds of strands of my own hair snapped off and rose away from my skull; collecting in three bundles above me. These strands spooled together, spinning and tightening into a dagger shape infused with our energy.

"I think I'll make it my own." She finished; a delicate hiss trailing her words.

The three magnetized floating blades wobbled in the air; twitching and yearning. Sin looked at me, a bruise on his cheek that quickly disappeared. He seemed interested in my display; but not worried. With gusto, I rose one arm and pointed it at him. In response, the closest shard above my shoulder jittered and flew in his direction at high speed.

He grimaced and used his bare hand to catch the weapon; crushing it between his fingers. As it traveled, I began moving towards him with the other two keeping up with my speed. I got close and stopped; jabbing my fingers into the dirt and making him react to the sprouting claws. Simultaneously, I sent forth the second blade at his face.

Light on his feet, Sin avoided the attack from below by leaping up and backwards. However, as he jumped up, the flying blade whizzed by and cut his ankle; leaving a trail of blood in the air. I ripped my hand free and tracked his movement closely. He landed on one foot, but before the other foot could touch down, I sent the final blade in his direction. As it shot at him, I sprinted at full speed; making a wide arch to the left and coming up on his side in the same instant his second foot settled down.

Caught off guard, I caught a glimpse of his shocked face while he turned his head to meet my demented sneer. My nails cut four ways deep into the flesh of his face; and just half a second after the impact, my airborne blade caught up and pierced through his chest.

Sin was not beaten yet. Reacting to my last attack, he angrily sent his hand downward and tried to grab me. I threw my available hand in front of his and caught him by the wrist. He used my own grip to pull me closer, then punched me in the face; but that had minimal effect.

Visibly frustrated, Sin rapidly crafted another glyph around one of his shadow limbs as it reformed over his head. The glyph shined bright like before and imbued the arm with magical properties. Growing sharp like a sword, it swung down at me; forcing me to leap back out of his range. But when I hit the ground, Sin took a long step towards me and lashed the blade at my torso.

I pulled myself to the side enough to avoid a vital hit as the tip of his limb pierced the lower half of my left rib cage; penetrating two inches deep.

"Try as you will; you will always end up here." Sin attempted to crucify me with his words. "There is nothing you can do, to stop me."

Alice crooked her neck; a confident boast. "In this six-month absence, I have been dreaming of ways to make you bleed, Sin. I'm just getting started."

I winced, but only grinned wider; a psychotic cackle trickled down my lips. The limb then forcefully ripped to the side; tearing through the rest of my flesh and leaving a deep gash in me. This was only the beginning of his assault. The singular shadow then split into three, each as sharp as the last.

One wrapped around my waist to hold me while the other two whipped me in random places; tearing sections of flesh and drilling accurate holes an inch deep. My body jerked around while the attacks continued until I had had enough.

My hair rose as another surge of power flowed out of my skin. With this unity of Teufel and my hidden power; I felt no limits. Raising both arms I caught his attacking limbs mid-strike and held them tight. He attempted to pull them free but struggled to do so easily. Using one of his arm limbs, I slashed down at the one that tied my waist; breaking me free from his hold. I quickly charged my palm with crackling power and slammed it into the dirt, creating a deafening shockwave that pushed us apart.

The shadows disappeared entirely. He recovered his stance a fair distance away, hunching forward slightly. But I quickly and accurately sent a bouquet of claws into the ground to erupt at his position. This time, they came right up from under him, piercing all the way through his torso; he was pinned. He hacked violently, as blood dripped to the ground.

Now! We both shouted within.

I ripped my claws out of the ground and replaced them with the other hands set. One retracted, the other entered the ground in its place. Right hand, left hand, right hand, left hand. . . On and on, just keeping him suspended, and pierced. Finally, to finish my assault I kept my left hand planted, hoisting his bloody torso in the air, then reared back my right arm. I focused my energy in each finger, letting the power within coat my nails with a deathly purple ink. Once the energy was charged, I released him from my stalagmite blades, allowing him to land on his feet; staggered.

Hefty white steam poured from my wounds like dry ice; healing at an unrestricted pace.

Alice spoke to me. “I need your hand with this one, Kim.”

“I’m giving you everything.” My voice was static, “But I’m slowing down.”

“Just push.”

I took a few advancing steps, generating a field of electrical potency. Each time my feet contacted the ground, a small voltage ran up my foot and exited a random part of my skin. I stopped briefly, then sprinted five or so short steps before scooping my arm at an upward angle in his direction. As I did this, the energy built in each of my nails combined into a vertical, thin strip of pure Demonic Power that manifested from my claws. This physical slice of energy hurdled towards him; ripping through the dirt and spanning a verticality of ten feet.

The corporeal slash rushed straight at him with glaring speed; ripping through the earth below. A torrent of wind was released as it crashed into Sin's torso, cutting and digging into his body before releasing the remaining energy in a massive outward surge. Crackling electricity licked and stabbed the ground, leaving many new holes and smaller dashes in the dirt.

The energy had dissipated, leaving only the rumble of its former existence to roll through the trees, and a massive plume of smoke obscuring my vision. My ears were ringing with the new silence. Panting, I hunched forward, feeling the numbness in my muscles.

“Holy shit. That was awesome.” I exclaimed between panted breaths.

"It used a lot of energy; we need to get some distance and recover." Alice replied.

Right where we stood, the two of us took stock of the situation. Examining the burnt ground and tears in the earth. I could only imagine what would have happened if this battle took place in a building or nearby town.

This reprieve lasted nearly two whole minutes. In that time, my muscles went into overdrive. I could feel the drain begin to take hold; the idea of this form going away soon was a hinderance to my focus. Then I picked up on something I couldn't quite place. A ping. . . no, a jingle?

All of a sudden, behind a blink shot one of his limbs; stretching unbelievably fast from a puff of smoke I never saw take shape. It shot out like a bullet straight at my face, snagging my attention and forcing me to quickly dodge. I somehow managed to duck in time for it to pass through a clump of my hair. The limb retracted, and he emerged from the smoke, with no injuries to be seen. A loathing grit in my teeth exhibited my worry.

However, it was worth noting that he seemed heavier than before. His shoulders were slumped and the way he held himself showed strain. I've weakened him, which means I can beat him.

Again, he launched the darkened limb from his back directly at me; this time, aimed for my chest. I easily avoided it once more, shifting my body and jumping to the left, but he faked me out and pulled the limb back with lightning speed and held out his flat hand again, this time, twisting it to the side. When he did this, my body slowed down in the air; floating again. This allowed him to materialize within a few feet of me.

Like before, he created a charged glyph and masked it over his pet shadow. This time, as it drank in the spell it started vibrating intensely; bubbling beneath the surface. With a tired sigh, Sin jabbed the tip into my right shoulder.

"Geh." A short cry came from me and a small amount of pain steadily grew.

I looked at the manifested tendril as it pierced my body. A heavy, black and brown substance began to seep out from the puncture, pouring out like chunky milk and spilling to the dirt. Without warning, an abrupt blast of similar spikes erupted from the needlepoint beneath my skin. Like a thorn-bush of pure evil.

This sting halted my voice. I couldn't even scream. Only whimper. Blood sprayed out, splashing his rotten scorn. He held me there; the black ooze painted my body as it dripped and spurted out; mixing with my own blood.

Alice instantly felt something wrong within us, "No!" Alice shouted. "Kim, get away from him!" She ordered.

"I-I can't. He's got me." I struggled to pull myself away.

"Perhaps you aren't as foolish as I thought you to be." Sin spoke quietly. "Your speed and raw power are quite impressive. . . however, this all ends here." He threatened with passive cynicism.

Then, his voice halted, and the punches came. One to the face, one to the head. Then a few to my chest and stomach. Every punch shook my body and forced the spikes to rip deeper into me. I couldn't move. Another tentacle of darkness took hold of my left arm and immediately started to pull. I felt my arm pop out of the socket and strain as the muscles began to tear.

"Ahhhhhh, dammit!" I cursed.

To his surprise, I fought through his hold on my left arm and dragged it across my body; slamming my fingers around the thick appendage. The limb cracked and split with my astonishing force as I started to pull it out of the flesh. The more I dragged it out, the more the outward spikes were drawn back into the needle, leaving vacant holes in my shoulder and surrounding area.

"This isn't the end!" My eyes still shined bright with hatred—a hatred I held on to all this time, just for him.

"I-Impossible." His lip quivered.

"Nothing is impossible if your desire outweighs your defeat. I won't stop until Tansu is safe from you; even if it costs me everything!"

I gave a final yell and ripped it from my body, taking a large portion of blood with it. I then reversed the spike on him and returned the favor, impaling him in the side with his own weapon. Sin, like the coward he is, slipped away.

I landed on the ground and rested on my hands and knees, bracing my right shoulder with the same hand. My left arm was now limp. I panted heavily as blood poured from me; my breathing increased when I moved my hand to my left arm and pushed it upward. A loud pop could be heard, and my arm was reconnected enough to regain movement.

"That was too close." Alice was sweating.

She scanned the area until he was found. He was farther away now, standing there, surrounded by a light cloud. He had healed again.

"His ability to heal is absurd. We need a new plan." She stated.

"He may be healing the outer wounds, but I know we're damaging him. His composure is lost; he's less patient. . . What do you have in mind?" I tightly gripped my shoulder, shielding the wound and trying to keep the blood in.

Alice contemplated, "We can't win like this. We need something more powerful; something that will, at the very least, cause him to finally retreat. Unfortunately, we don't have much time left before this form reverts."

"So then, what can we do?"

"Well, I was thinking we could try an *all or nothing* approach?" Alice pondered

"Haven't we been doing that?" I groaned tiredly.

"I have something more. All these attacks we've been throwing his way are the result of me being creative with my energy and having plenty of time to balance them out in my head."

"Yeah? I'm listening." I ushered her to go on.

"I've tried everything. . . but I think I have one last idea." She chuckled.

"Secret weapon?" I asked.

She scoffed, "Tch, just thought of it."

Without warning, my right arm began to heat up insanely. The scorching energy passed over my shoulder and emitted a small amount of steam, briefly healing as it brushed by, but not altering its condition too much. This current of heat left a wake of soothing ice in my arm; until it stopped in my hand, built pressure, and flowed over my skin once more. The intense heat grew; almost as if it were on fire.

A lavender purple and shimmering blue mist blended together like a little cloud. It completely swallowed my arm and hand and patiently rotated in a circle; signaling tiny purple sparks within the cloud every so often.

"Mph, it hurts." I closed an eye, the hostile energy restricting my movements.

"Kim. This is all the remaining energy of this form concentrated in one place. After this attack is spent, hit or miss, we *will* revert. You cannot miss." She growled.

"What about *my* energy?"

"It's there." She assured me.

My heart began to race as the dense body of mystical energy spun and flailed in circles. My knees bent in and my eyes locked onto Sin. His cocky stance showed disinterest, still wanting to play with me. I froze, doubt filled my mind.

My arm spazzed for a second, tightening and twitching. It's now or never. Without another thought, I sprang forward, the speed in which I ran instantly tripled. Each rapid footstep caused a small crater to form where I had stepped.

As I got in close, he predictably vanished and appeared beside me, but I was ready; I saw it happen before he knew himself. I came to a halt and skidded from the momentum, immediately turning myself and kicked at him, using Demonic Energy to power my kick. He glided to the side and avoided the blow, but I was ready for that as well.

My whole body slowed mid-kick and I reached my left hand out and latched onto his arm, at the same time, slamming my foot down to the ground, stopping in a balanced sumo-like position. I saw the confidence in his face quickly drain away.

I pulled him downward by his arm. His knuckles hit the dirt and his face was met with mine directly; eyes merely an inch apart. I released his arm and instantly shot my claws out and stabbed them into his hand and wrist, pinning him to the ground. It was quiet for a moment, until Sin spoke in frustration.

"I demand you, release me. . . I created you!" He ordered.

Alice spoke in my place with a hearty cackle "You created me but did so for one purpose; chaos! And you know what. . .?" Alice was having the time of her life. He cocked an eyebrow and gave an angry face. "Nothing will bring me greater pleasure and birth more chaos, than watching you die!"

I stared into his dark, deceiving eyes. Every memory, every emotion. Everything that made me who I was, who I am, reflected back at him. He could see the animosity in my gaze, how much I revolted his very existence and how I cursed him for my own life. All my hatred, previously spread across the people in my life, now directed only at him.

I am his nightmare; I am his greatest sin.

The lavender energy that surrounded my arm unexpectedly absorbed into my skin. The fiery element was now spinning only around my tightly bound fist; it started to shake. My bones felt brittle, but my skin felt strong. The finishing touches of this attack were readied.

Then, as if the gravity around me multiplied, my feet sank into the dirt. In a fraction of a second, my fist plowed into his chest, buried deep into his center.

It was held there, nothing happened at first, but the initial shock caused his face to crunch in and stole his lungs.

White-hot bursts shattered the air around us, creating a concussive dome to expand, then rapidly recede back into my fist.

"Yes. . ." He struggled to get his words out. "It *is* you."

"Just. . . Shut. . . Up!"

I finished the follow-through of my punch and blasted him back. With the surge of energy being released, my arm rebound and threw me backward as well. He flew about fifteen feet and hit the ground hard, bouncing and rolling until his body slowed to a stop. I flew nearly the same distance and landed almost identically, however I landed on my front and managed to get myself to a kneeling position.

My lungs wheezed, refusing to allow air into my system. My right arm was completely numb. I grabbed it with the other, holding tight. As I looked down, I saw my skin was my own again. Alice's power had faded back inside me, and I was now human once more.

"Dammit!" Alice shouted in distress.

"What is it? What's wrong?" I asked, worried for an answer.

"The attack; it backfired. Some of my energy was shot back into your arm." She explained with an angry tone. Either furious with me, or herself.

I tried moving my arm, but it would not respond. It was just dead weight; completely lifeless. There were many deep, purple bruises along my bicep, accompanied by a few gashes that formed along my forearm. Gashes that appeared to be made from energy escaping my body by tearing through the skin.

"Kim, I have some more bad news."

"Great." I panted.

She spoke with hesitance. "I'm trying to repair your body, but it isn't working. I think he did something to you with that heatwave, or maybe that ooze he pushed into you; I'm unsure."

"So, you can't heal me at all? How long will that last?"

"No, I can heal you a little bit. Around, three percent of what I'm usually capable of. . . In time, it will return."

I sat there in a contemplative state, taking in the serene breeze and enjoying the sun painted high above. The clouds had mostly moved on, leaving behind only trickles of white dust in the blue. The warm rays kissed my skin and brushed the top layer of my hair, drying the pooling sweat and blood.

I curiously looked over to where Sin had landed, wanting to know if he was still down. I wasn't surprised to find him standing. Albeit, he was bent; hunched forward and to the side a little. I could clearly see his shoulders rise and dip with his own harsh breaths. He seemed injured, unlike before his wounds had not healed yet. There was a shredded, bloody dent in his chest where I had hit him. A spiral of mangled skin and protruding bone.

"Kimberly." He called from across the field, his voice straining.

Shaking in a pool of my own fleeting blood, I lifted my back as much as I could, out of breath and sore.

"I see you are adamant in keeping your humanity. . . You have fought quite well." His body flashed white and he was gone, I heard the faint swoosh sound as I redirected my eyes to where Tansu had been lying. He stood above her and reached down, lifting her by the collar bone. My heart began racing as disgust boiled in my gut.

"Leave her alone, she doesn't deserve to be treated that way!" Tears welled inside, as I examined her body. But as he held her, I noticed something. Above her right eye and just below her hair line was a large gash, where all of the blood had come from.

Sin then used his free hand to grab her head and give it a little pinch. With that pressure, her face twitched, and her eyes innocently fluttered half-open. The moment she saw me across the field and felt his touch, her eyes shot open and began looking around desperately.

"W-where. . ." She looked to me; revulsion prominent in her stare.

She's, not dead? I questioned in my head, unable to form words.

My mind started to accelerate; thinking, planning. Trying to figure out some way to get to her. I didn't know what to do. A hollow threat followed my thoughts.

"I swear to God, if you—" I shouted.

"Do not spout the name of a figure that lies in fiction. If you swear to a god, swear only to me. I am the one who heard your cries, who granted your wish!" He screamed.

I shifted my sight, rapidly scanning for something to give me an edge, an angle, an opening—something to use and save her. It was all in vain, there was nothing, just an empty field of craters and blood.

Tansu begged, "Please. If you have to kill someone, kill me. Let her go" She cried. Sin completely ignored her. With no response, her tears began to flow heavier, until she was bawling. "I want my mom." She sobbed.

I screamed as loud as I could. "Tansuke!"

Her eyes shot to me, shaking.

"You will see your mom again. I swear on my life that you will make it through this!" My own tears fell to the earth, wetting the patches of grass beneath me.

She continued to stare at me, appearing hopeful but also cemented in cold reality. I then clenched my eyes shut in frustration. My only ace in the hole used up all my strength and left the two of us far too weak. It can't end like this.

Sin interrupted.

"I saw all I needed with this fabricated loss. This girl. . . she means nothing to me; and now, I have no more use for her."

He held her collar bone still and raised her up higher. Then, five large shadow tendrils sprouted from his back and flailed wildly. They wavered, faded in and out of perception indicating his frailty. The limbs wrapped themselves around his free arm, which he held high and at the ready, and merged together, becoming one solid weapon.

"Wait!" I shrieked at the top of my lungs.

I had nothing. Everything I've ever fought for, everything that kept me going, day after day, is about to come to an end and after all my suffering, all my efforts, I am powerless to stop it.

Chapter 32 – Inheritance

At birth we are given just two things; two precious things which we are entrusted, above all else, to safeguard. A body and a soul. I have kept my body intact, more or less over the years; ensuring the other, my soul would always have a home to reside and be warm. Until I foolishly trusted my soul in another's grasp. Since then, my body has endured many hardships. Much of its vitality lost to protect something that no longer belonged to me.

I have betrayed my body, my soul and who I am as a person. All for the sake of wreaking havoc on the lives of casually narcissistic fiends parading as people. For what, exactly? Some redemption- Payback? No matter the excuse, it seems stupid now. Because in the end, all of the choices I made that I believed to be rational and justified, have led to my body and soul shredded and spilling on to the ground. Watching my best friend face her fate while I am powerless to do anything about it. Only being kept alive by an entity which has thoroughly invaded my only tether to this world; in an attempt to claim it as its own.

All was hopeless.

"Bastard!" I shouted as I took one final effort and buried my feet, once again into the soil, somehow stumbling ardently forward. While my muscles dragged me in a daring sprint toward him, I felt violent stabbing shoot through my bones.

My legs suddenly locked up stiff, and all the momentum of my run made me tumble forward; crashing into the ground with embedding force. A trail of spitting blood led up to where I lay. I wheezed violently as the dust fluttered around me. I was within five or so feet of him, and he just looked at me with a crooked smile. Entertained by my heroic act.

I lay on my stomach and cranked my neck to see him. Fueled only by anger and the desire to save her, I started to crawl. Every movement ground my tissue down to nothing.

My mouth hung open and my raspy irregular breaths displayed my defeat. But I crawled with all my might, reaching his ankles and grabbing hold of one. His arm had released the weapon of darkness and he reached down, grabbing hold of my hair and lifting me up. I squealed in pain as I was hoisted. Bringing me up to his eye level, he then leaned in and pressed his forehead to mine.

"In my time, I never thought that the key to my freedom would be someone like you. It's. . . almost poetic." He stated, then pulled his head back.

Tansu directed her eyes to me, witnessing up close how much damage had been caused, how much I sacrificed. Angry, she addressed him.

"What did we ever do to you!?" She yelled; tears continued down her face.

Hair being ripped out by his grasp and neck strained by my bodies dead weight, I reached up with my own working arm and dug my everyday human nails into his hand and wrist, but to no avail. I had no strength to even break his skin. Sin let out a long, tired breath; taking it all in.

Then, the low static rose again.

"Shame. . . we did our best." Alice grinned in defeat, letting her high emotions slowly dissipate.

As my body slowly gave in to inevitable defeat and the cold blanket of limbo attempted to secure me, I stared into Sin's eyes. Those faded yellow, evocative eyes that buried themselves deep in my soul, continued to terrify me. No matter what I said before. In his eyes, I could see everything.

My father and his bloody demise. Joey with his confidently smiling face. Stacy and her unfair treatment. The stitches on my lips, then Alice fusing with me. Destro and Lust. Lastly, Tansu and the little time I spent with her, but most of all, what I'm putting her through because of my mistakes.

Then suddenly, I was slightly tossed upwards, his hand released my hair but quickly caught me again, this time by the neck. My eyes popped as he began crushing my throat with his shaking fist.

"Hggg . . . Gah." I gagged.

"Let your mind wither away; follow the path to an everlasting nightmare." He chanted. "Only at the brink of death will your Anima slip into my grasp."

My vision slowly faded into a misty black veil. I felt nothing, heard nothing and thought of nothing. Until a strong burst of something familiar brushed over my skin and fueled the flicker in my soul. There was a strong presence beneath me, some unknown force that plucked gently in the back of my head. His grip loosened, and I gasped loudly for air.

I could hear his faint voice.

"I was starting to wonder if I was being ignored. . . Quickly! Preparations must be made for the seal to be broken. I will need your help." His instructions were directed to someone else. I could tell by the low tone that his head was now looking downward.

There was a hum in my skull. I was trying my best to keep myself conscious, but everything I perceived as *me* was screaming. I heard his voice push through the deafened walls again.

"Are you listening!? What . . .?"

Without warning, I plummeted to the ground; landing heavily onto my back. When I hit the earth for the hundredth time, all the oxygen in my lungs shot up into the air, carrying a dense amount of blood and spit, which came falling back down onto my own face.

This effect made me question my lucidity; a final dream? I struggled to breathe, but more importantly, pried my eyes as wide as I could, enough to see Tansu lying on the ground as well. Apart from that, I could plainly see ankles and bare feet standing between Sin and me. On my back, I raised my head to try and see.

Sin spoke again, louder this time, "Now it all makes sense. All the inconsistencies, the flaws—a traitor in the midst." He spat with an acidic tongue. There was no response from whomever he was speaking. He continued, "You are no better than the rest of these filthy creatures." He growled. "After what I did for you?"

This time he got a response,

"When the last innocent fell by my hand; my eyes were opened to the truth. So long did I unjustly punish innocents at your command, for reasons I never considered. No more."

I recognized the voice.

"No! Everything I've worked for is about to come to fruition. You would stand against me!? Deny my destiny!?" He challenged.

"You will never be complete, again." This girl responded.

"Then, this is . . ." He spoke softly, sounding quite sad.

A pause in the air; complete standstill.

A vibration in the ground, then I saw a flash of yellow light. It grew brighter and brighter, nearly blinding me at first. It rapidly expanded until the shimmering edge had passed over us. I was lying inside the dimmer center of this newly formed sphere and could plainly see what was causing it. This new arrival had their back to me, though I had pieced together their identity through voice and mannerisms alone. Crism. She had her bare feet planted firmly in the ground and her fist outstretched.

Her fist was held by Sin. The two of them locked, body and eyes. A war raged between their intense stare. This fiery yellow sphere of light that swallowed us and hid the rest of the world was caused by both of their energies clashing into each other.

Like savage beasts, they unleashed their strength, sending out bursts of air that lacerated the dirt and made my hair flutter wildly. This wind tunnel of raw demonic ability was nearly overwhelming. They stood together, bound and unchanging for a solid minute, neither of them flinching, blinking, or shifting an inch. Just staring and pushing out copious amounts of destructive power.

All at once, everything changed. The light shimmered a little and then vanished completely. With it, the surge ceased, and this windy storm of aggression was eliminated. All that was left was a look of shock on Sin's face. Using more of the strength I didn't have, I dug my fingers into the dirt and pulled myself to the side, angled enough to see both of their faces. Sin's eyes were as wide as I've ever seen them, and his mouth drooped.

"That's . . . impossible." He stuttered.

I looked at Crism and what I saw completely baffled me. Her left eye. The eye that was sealed shut by scar tissue and allegedly rendered useless. . . was cracked open. Exposed enough to see a faint purple glow, which I associated with that of the Teufel.

Sin spat wildly as he screamed, "No! Y-you *cannot* do this, I am your father!"

I've never heard him this flustered. The way he shouted was desperate, like when I thought he killed Tansu. In response to his words, her jaw clenched tightly.

"*My* father is dead."

For the first time, I detected malice in her voice. In the blink of an eye, she used Sin's own grip around her fist to pull him closer, anchoring his head down to her level and loudly snapping his spine with the height difference.

They glared into each other's eyes; Sin became much calmer than he was moments ago. He chuckled to himself as sweat dripped from his brow. He spoke.

"Crism, the child's Anima is the strongest I've seen. Please, let me use it to save us; free me from The Council's laws. . ."

"If you were to regain your power, the darkness would take hold of you; birthing cataclysm."

"But!" He shouted again, then ground out his words through clenched teeth. "If I die, the gate will open; they will come." He warned.

"Then, it shall be broken." She declared.

Instantly, with her free hand, she slammed her fingers around the top of his head. From her grip, his face went totally limp. Both eyes fell in different directions and his jaw fumbled loosely. It was faint, but I could hear a fizzy breath erupt from his throat. Crism closed her good eye and left the Teufel gaze open.

A dark purple mist began to emit from her hand and surrounded Sin's skull. All it took was a tiny contraction from her hand, and his head exploded, sending chunks of skull and brain soaring in every direction; creating a fountain of blood that proudly sprayed from his neck.

Tansu squirmed away to avoid the rain of blood, while also shielding her eyes from the cruel action. The ground became littered with a chilling display of brutal homicide while the wet chunks splattered all around us. I lay there at a loss for words and watched as she released his limp hand and pushed the body back, letting it fall to the ground with a disgusting splash.

His body lie there for a moment as silence rang. Within a minute his corpse and all the scattered pieces started to make weird popping noises; the pressure in the air had dissipated.

I slowly sat up, managing to prop myself up on one arm, my right one still numb and not usable. I stared at her in disbelief and suspicion.

"Kimberly." She greeted me, her damaged eye closed and regular one open again.

"Holy shit." Alice mumbled.

My mouth was agape, eyes half closed with the pain and my whole body shaking, now for a whole new reason.

"What. . . did—" I murmured. His body held my attention. Fearfully, I stared and imagined my head exploding like that.

"What the hell?" Alice yelled in my head, piercing my ears. "What have you done?"

Crism could hear her plain as day. "My apologies. I know this was your fight. It was not my place to interfere." She again spoke in a very flat voice, just like last time.

"I don't understand. I thought you were his right-hand?" I questioned.

She looked down at his body with a loathing stare. "I was."

"Then, how . . . why did you kill him?" Alice asked worriedly, sharing my valid concern that she was going to target us.

Her big brown iris watched me with zero hostility. She ignored Alice and spoke directly to me,

"I know of your past. I know of all his human's pasts. Their pain bleeds black and wails in a language only I can interpret. . . I understand you; I am you."

She lifted her hand up and stared at the blood, which continued to drip, then began sloppily whipping it at the ground, trying to remove the gore.

"I was the first." She started, "but I am not what you think I am." She explained quickly, but took frequent pauses,

"Our encounter was some twist of fate neither of us could have predicted." She looked down at her left side, the scarred side, "If not for random chance, Sin would never have created me, he would have never created his weakness. And yet, without me, he never would have shaped the perfect anima. So, in a way it was all necessary."

Alice spoke up, "But you aren't just a Teufel, that's pretty fucking clear to me. What makes you so powerful? Powerful enough to do that to him!?"

Crism tensed her arm, the arm used to kill him and stretched her fingers, opening and closing her hand.

"It's quite complicated, to say the least. . . My body housed the first Anima, but it was not given to me as a source of power; it was a stabilizer. The power he transferred to save my life, to save his own, was *his*. . . and it was very unstable."

"You, *share* his power?" My jaw dropped.

Alice fought to find the appropriate words. Nothing she could muster would convey her feelings, so she listened.

Crism nodded. "Sin isn't what you thought. He is not some demon or fiend; he is much more than that. A higher power; a fallen power. Being such, he had a certain barrier in place; a barrier that made it impossible for any power outside of his own to destroy his body."

I took a moment to myself, shutting everything out, and just let this all sink in. In this reprieve, I averted my eyes and looked past her to see Tansu sitting upright on the ground, holding her ribcage tenderly and was watching the two of us with a pained face. She was messed up in human standards. She sat there, listening to us and didn't say a word.

Knowing all this was far beyond her understanding. She remained quiet, but she was in pain. In that momentary pause, I came to a realization.

"Wait a minute. From what you're saying, that means that this whole fight was a waste, there is no way we could have killed him?" I groaned. My face saddened.

"No. This battle had a high purpose. If I had attempted to fight him, I would have been defeated. I had to expel all of *his* power within myself, to deplete his barrier, but he would still have enough strength left over which easily dwarfs my own Anima. I needed you to harm him, distract him just long enough to make a move." She explained.

"But, why did you want to kill him? I still don't get it." I asked, my head spinning.

She was breathing kind of heavily through her nose. The whole time, never getting upset, never getting sad or angry. She just kept talking so quietly. It was hard to hear her sometimes with the ringing in my ears. While she was talking, I could see the pieces of Sin literally melt away, his body had almost vanished into a cloud of particles that seemed to flow into Crism herself. I tried to focus on her words, and this phenomenon; she didn't seem to notice.

"He has always created monsters, one way or another, with his endless cycle. So many innocent people died. . . I had to put an end to it."

Alice was just as curious as me. Growing more anxious and stirring inside, still wondering whether Crism could be trusted, wondering if she would turn on us.

She continued, "There have only been a handful of Teufel that attained power enough to challenge him. Only one had Ascended and all had failed. Others wounded him, but not to this extent. You were the first to damage him enough and give me the opening I have been striving for." She said proudly.

She never stopped confusing me with every new thing she said. Alice as well. "What sort of things?" I asked.

With an unchanged face, she said, "The ability to maintain a balance between good and evil allowed you to befriend your Teufel instead of succumbing to her. That love for your family and your Teufel as well, safeguarded your humanity and allowed you to fight with more grit and willpower than Sin could account for."

She paused.

"Perhaps, even more important than that was the deal which determined your birth. . . Sin was not aware of your dormant power; from your original link to the Ditch. He was only able to read Alice's energy, but never grasp your own."

My mouth went dry, and inversely, my nostrils became wet. It was hard to formulate any sort of response that wasn't the first question that popped into my head. My lips quivered with the buildup of emotion, "Heh. In the end, I wasn't completely worthless."

I gave no hesitation and let my head fall forward, hair was strewn around and messy. I cried. I cried for a minute or two. Just, incredibly happy that he was gone. That I was safe; that Tansu was safe.

"So, what happens now?" I asked through the tears. She stood beside me and faced the direction I was facing, like we were both looking at a sunset that wasn't there.

Hauntingly casual, she said, "The Teufel, will begin to die."

"They die?" That really shook me.

"Yes. The Teufel's life force is always dwindling due to a crack each Anima harbors."

"A crack?" Alice pondered.

She didn't seem bothered by explaining this to us. "The feature and flaw was intentionally built into their design. This crack allows energy from human souls and other Teufel to be absorbed. However, these cracks eventually splinter from the vile, writhing power inside; if left un-mended. Eventually, they will all turn to dust. Sin has a spell which simultaneously mends all active Anima; making the whole process much easier to manage."

I thought about what she said. "Can't you mend them yourself since you have some of his power?"

"Not me. . ." She paused awkwardly.

"What about you? You have some of *his* power and an Anima? What will happen to you?" I asked.

She looked down at herself, adjusting her muscles and shifting her feet in the earth. "His energy is fueled by different means; it will recover in time; keeping my human soul alive. But my Anima was just destroyed finishing him off. I will not die. . . In a way, I suppose I am his successor."

His successor? I thought.

She saw the worry form quickly in my eyes.

"I know that must trouble you, but there is no need to be concerned."

"Then, what will you do?" I asked nervously.

Her eye shifted very slightly, like she was thinking deeply. Taking her time to answer.

"The future holds many paths. All of mine led me here today, to assist in preventing a second destruction. Now, I'm afraid I have no choice but to wait and see. Other evils will likely spawn again. Sin may have been corrupted, but his presence left this world in a surprisingly better state; for the moment."

My stomach churned at the thought, but it made sense.

"You aren't saying we were better off *with* Sin around. . . are you?"

She bit her tongue, restricting her words until she could formulate a proper, satisfying answer. Staring off into the empty sky, not even blinking. A gust of wind passed us by with a gentle touch.

"The history and future of this realm are complicated; I do not have all the answers. If blessed, I may find exactly *that* in his archives; now that he is gone."

While we talked, I almost forgot Tansu was still there right in front of me, watching us; listening intently. When I looked at her, she gave me a huge, but pained smile.

"Tan, you're okay. . . right?" Relief in my voice.

"Yeah, I-I think I am." She said quietly, her words dragging. The damage inflicted on her ribs and head were not something to ignore; she needs medical attention. "I don't know what to say right now. I just want to go home and see my mom." She swallowed hard and kept the tears in.

"How do you *feel*? I mean, can you move well enough?"

"I should be able to." She said, though there was still uncertainty in her voice. Then her face became much paler, "B-but. . . Kimmy, you-"

My eyes disconnected, falling to the ground in shame. I couldn't imagine how I must look to her. But then, I was disturbed by an inkling.

The attack he used earlier had stunted most of my own healing. But the Ascendant form seemed to have fixed mostly everything up to that point. Now, most of the bleeding had stopped and the wounds appeared to close slightly; but the damage was done. Everything hurt but was somewhat manageable.

I looked at Crism.

"Is there any way you can help heal our wounds, even just a little?" I asked kindly.

"I am sorry, but I cannot."

"Oh." I replied, disappointed.

"It is not because I do not want to. I am unable to. My ability to heal was gifted to Alice when I pulled her from the Ditch."

"Y-you pulled me from The Ditch? And you-" Alice shouted; her irritancy pinched my brain.

I winced, "Alice, please. . . stop yelling."

Crism continued, "The conditions to your birth, just as all the others, was planned months in advance. However, I had my own agenda. . . Do you remember Sin's surprise when it was *you* who was born that night?"

Alice groaned. "I thought he just didn't like me."

"Sin had already prepared another Teufel for Kimberly, pre-creating a link to a section of The Ditch containing a readied Anima. However, on the night she made the deal, I had moved that link to a section holding you instead. You may recall how hard it was for you in there; always last to get a soul fragment. Never completely satisfied with what you had; starving. Accept my apology, for it was I who let you suffer."

Alice snarled. "I fought tooth and nail for any shred of a soul in there. I thought I was cursed. There were times when I believed I would wither away." She held confused fury in her breathing.

"I specifically chose fragments to feed to you. . . It was necessary; trust me. Without my interference, I fear you would have been no better than Euclipse upon birth. . . Once I placed you in Kimberly's path, I transferred my Anima's healing to you; giving you just a little extra." She confessed.

Crism took a breath and paused, waiting for us to comment. But we didn't, she continued, "That is why you did not come to this world with a name. He never gave you one because he did not know you would be the one to be removed, but *I* did."

I felt Alice tighten up. "Y-you gave me a name?" My chest ran cold as her soul shivered in anticipation. Distrust, loathing and anger all mixed in a boiling pot of emotion.

"Never properly, I quite like your adopted name more. The name I chose feels hollow now, given your life."

Alice growled, "Tell me."

"Are you sure?"

She looked at Alice through my eyes, and Alice stared right back.

"Very well. The name I chose. . . was Reius."

Alice was shaking inside; mixed around in ways she hasn't experienced. Her life, her purpose was twisted for someone else's purpose, just like mine; but she didn't know how to cope. As a Teufel, she was designed for hunger and blood; it's how her brain is wired. But in her life, that had become almost secondary.

I could feel her searching herself, questioning if her thoughts and actions were truly her own. She took a retreating step in my head and her static presence mellowed to a low hum.

"Kimberly, I know how that must feel, living a life that had been crafted since before you existed. I do not want you to think badly of yourself, and the same goes for you, *Alice*." She emphasized.

I took note of her gesture; referring to Alice by her preferred moniker. A respect.

She continued, "Although you may not realize this, thinking I did all of this for my own personal vendetta; you are precious to me. I have been watching you for over eight years now. . ." She paused, looked to the ground and then back to me, changing the pacing of her words. “From the moment you first experienced the feeling of abandonment. I want you to know that you were never alone and never forgotten.” She said very calmly, stressing her kind words but falling short of verbal emotion.

I went quiet, thinking on everything she said. She knew so much about me, about Alice. I know nothing of her. Who is she really? Then something else came to mind.

“Crism, can you tell me one more thing?” I asked sincerely.

She had turned her head and stared off into the distance, lamenting. I licked my lips in anticipation.

“As you wish.” She whispered.

“You told Alice her name, and now I'd like to know yours.” I smiled softly.

A new expression took over her face, almost stunned or trapped in a new line of thought. Her wide-eyed emotionless stare sank down. Her eye squinted slightly, and lips turned to a frown.

“My name? . . .” The way she spoke was as if her lungs released all the air in them. She sounded, in a way, confused. Her perfect plank-like stance started to sway. Her balance shifted from one foot to the other. Then she shut her eye. Her head twitched very suddenly and something I never expected from her, happened before my very eyes. A tiny, almost nonexistent smile appeared on her face. Then just as quickly vanished.

“I abandoned my name and former self a long time ago. . . It fell to ashes with the rest of my life, then blown away by my thirst for blood. And yet, when I saw the result of my coercion, I started to pick up the pieces of my soul.” She murmured.

“I would love to hear your story. I want to know how you got here, but I don’t think we have the time.” I chuckled. “Still, if I am to thank you for all you’ve done for us and mean it, I want to thank you—the real you.”

My voice started to hurt more. My consciousness was getting harder and harder to maintain with each passing minute. Crism regained her composure and looked me dead in the eyes.

“My name is, Christine Mathews.” She said in a lighter tone, just barely off her mutter.

That name—resonated with me. Some odd vibration bubbled in my chest, different to the pain. It was somehow familiar to me, though I’m sure I have never heard it before. Trying to assign a face to the name didn’t do me any good; I was drawing a blank. In the state my mind was in, I didn’t try to think about it too much. The name was a shadow that I couldn’t place.

Then I noticed something peculiar. She suddenly whipped her head to the side, looking off into the trees and stared, locked onto seemingly nothing.

“What’s wrong?” I asked.

She did not react to me. Instead, she kept staring into nothingness. Tansu also stared at her with concern; she looked at me and we both shrugged.

Then she spoke, “A voice . . . it's calling.” Her tone changed. It had an electric whir to it then quickly switched back to normal.

“Nothing. No need for you to worry.”

She looked back to me with that unchanged expression, but her stare seemed more intense, if that's even possible. She reformed her posture. The horizontally stiff shoulders rose and dropped very slightly as if taking her final breath of this earth's clean air.

"It's time." She said happily.

"Well then, thank you. . . Christine." I said with a smile.

Motioning her hand toward me, she placed it on my shoulder. Her hand was neither cold nor warm. I relished the touch; it gave me goosebumps due to the surreal nature of this situation.

Crism urged softly. "Kimberly. . ."

My eyes waned, a heaviness overpowering me.

"I'm sorry, about your mother."

Unexpectedly, a bright light erupted from seemingly nothing, engulfing everything and obscuring our vision. When the light faded, she was gone. Vanished to a destination unknown, where the world will never know of this day or of her. A lingering wind carried on for a few seconds, leaving a surrounding chill. I waited for something else to happen, some pulse or whisper; but nothing did.

Shifting my eyes to the surrounding dirt, I noticed Sin's body had completely dissipated. Leaving only blood spots, and a ravaged landscape. I didn't really understand the scale or damage of this battle; witnessing all of the craters and scorched grass. I wish I could've seen it from a birds-eye view.

Wandering in awe, I remembered her previous words. The Teufel are destined to die at any time and that means Alice will be gone soon.

"Hey, you there?" I said inside.

That familiar static charged up in my ears again. I never got used to the headache it brought.

"It's over. How do you feel?" She asked with her usual sinister tone; although lacking a smile.

"We're safe; Tansu's safe. How about you?" I chuckled.

"Pissed. This whole journey was pointless for me." She grimaced, holding on to a sharp tone of humiliation.

"Not totally. At least you helped me; by proxy you helped save a lot of people."

"I don't wanna think about that."

Out of nowhere, I started coughing violently, catching my breath in the palm of my hand. My head throbbed with each heave and when the retching stopped, I observed my palm and saw only blood. "God, I feel like shit."

"Well, I'm sorry, but you're going to feel a whole lot worse when I'm gone."

"You aren't sorry." I sighed.

There was a stillness between us. Some stubborn feeling that I couldn't figure out and neither could she.

"Ya know, I'm actually okay with this." Alice murmured.

"Yea?"

She said nothing. Keeping her mysterious feelings under lock and key; offering me only a glimpse at what she was thinking.

"By the way, thanks," I said kindly.

"Shut up. I don't want your gratitude." She hissed.

A hurt frustration painted my face. "You and your damn—" I groaned. "Look, I'm serious. Without you, there's a lot I would have never learned about my family, about the world. About myself. You had been like a mentor; a *psychotic*, bloodthirsty mentor. . . but still, thank you."

"Oh, stop; I'm blushing." She let out a sarcastic snarl.

"Tsk. Well, in any case, it's been fun. I guess." I sniffled, feeling sentimental in this time of solitude.

"It has." She said almost sincerely, with a splash of sadness.

Tansu interrupted my inner thoughts.

"Kim? Hey, I think we should go. We need to get you to the hospital."

I smiled at her. "Not just me. You look pretty rough yourself." I said with a lighthearted chuckle.

"I'm fine but- I'm not gonna lie. I don't know how you are still-*awake*."

She put it lightly with a shaky, tear-jerking voice. "Your shoulder looks like it was hit by a truck and the side of your face is just—you need help."

"Alice's healing ability hasn't returned; for now, she can only keep blood in and make sure I'm numb. . ."

"But she's going to die?" She finished.

"Pretty much, we don't know how long, but I don't think there is a lot of time." I stated regrettably.

"Then we have to move fast. If we can get you to a hospital before she's gone, then you will be okay." Her voice became hurried.

"Hold on. Before we go anywhere, can you do me a favor?"

"Of course, anything at all." She agreed.

I gestured my head away from us, directing her to the spot where we had our scuffle.

"My jacket—can you please get it for me?"

"Jacket? Yeah, yeah, sure, I'll be right back."

She stood up very slowly, but as fast as she could; still clutching her side and swinging a little. Then she moved quickly over to the leather jacket, which had been tossed aside and lying alone on the ground about forty feet away. She promptly returned with it in her hand.

"Here." She held it out.

I took a deep breath and tried to move my left arm up to take it from her. She watched me struggle to even lift my arm. A burdened sadness in her eyes just added another layer of weakness in my brain. She placed her hand on mine and smiled.

"I got it." She assured, then draped the leather over my shoulders. I felt a new comfort come over me with the weight of the coat.

"Thanks."

"Don't mention it. Now let's get out of here."

She tried her best in helping me stand as well, pulling me in to lean on her shoulder. My legs weren't injured, but everything inside was mush and my muscles were stiff. Given my dead weight plus her injuries; our movement was overall hindered dramatically.

"Tansu, are you sure you can handle this? Would it be better if you move on your own to get help?" I suggested, wincing with every step.

She got my better arm over her shoulder and brought me in as close as she could, struggling to keep us vertical.

"Don't worry. I can do it. Let's just get moving, all right?" Her breathing increased.

"You're tougher than you look." I snickered.

I couldn't help but admire her willingness to carry me. Someone like her, getting mixed up in a death battle with demons and god's; it was an incredible feat, mentally and physically. But she pressed on; stumbling and tripping every couple of feet. In our position it was shorter to try and cut through the trees and make it to the road, instead of trudging along to the proper entrance. So that's the path she chose, and she did so with vigor.

We stayed quiet, saving everything to be shared at a later time.

The walk felt like an eternity; as though I had already died and this was limbo, or purgatory. Just an endless stroll through the woods with my insides a slimy puss and my outsides falling off. Every step forward was two steps back and to the left. My eyes started to warble; every step we took made my head thump, a tremor of new pain quaking through my bones.

I felt sick, and my chest wouldn't stop vibrating. Each breath I took got more jagged and irregular. A sharp pain behind my eyes forced a yelp out of me; a horrid sensation of my eyeballs seemingly splitting in half from the inside out. My head fell forward and I groaned loudly.

"Tan, I think I need to—"

Before I could finish, my body became unbearably heavy all at once. A loud ringing abruptly pierced my eardrums and the muscles in my legs gave way. I tried to catch myself, but inevitably fell to the ground; bringing her down with me. *She*, however, managed to maintain her balance.

"Kim!"

Chapter 33 – No Garden for Wilted Flowers

Darkness.

Darkness surrounded me entirely. The air held a frosty bite along with a feeling of complete loneliness. The shadows around me began to squirm, rub against my shoulders and hair; absorbing me slowly. My mortal being fading deeper into the inky black. Until I caught the sight of a warm dome of light before me. No slow ignition, no warning. Just there.

"Make a wish, honey" A women spoke gently, echoing on and on.

"Go ahead and blow out the candles." Another voice, this one a man.

Two familiar voices prodded my brain; both instructing me, caring for me; urging me. I sat in a dark room, now aware of what exactly sat beside me in the dark. Pale masses, with faces obscured by nothing. The frail orange light softly glowed in the center of the table between us all, slightly illuminating the two sitting to my right. A third voice suddenly appeared, and with it came another mass to my left.

"Go on Kim, show them who's boss!" This one was younger, much more innocent, almost childlike.

Set on a dark wooden table before me, was an off white, frosted cake. I could barely make out the cake beneath the orange flare of candles, let alone any specific details about it. Each of these voices sounded familiar to me, some more than others. I found myself unable to question their requests.

Almost like my motions were scripted and out of my control. Following the instructions laid out before me, I took in a deep breath and blew out the candles. Six dead wax stumps emitted a frail smoke from the wick. The sulfuric smell filled my nostrils and dried on the back of my tongue; my eyes watered.

All three voices cheered for me simultaneously; two of the three began clapping. One of the frailer looking figures moved forward to set the cake to the side, but just as they were about to move it, the candles suddenly lit up again. Bright orange flames revealed the dark room again.

The cheering stopped.

"I thought I told you to get regular candles." The woman's voice sounded annoyed.

"All those damn candles look the same, Rachel. I was in a rush." He defended himself.

Rachel? I repeated.

All of a sudden, the table and the group of shadows seemed to get distant, my vision became warped like a fisheye lens and a light humming buzzed in my skull.

All the faces were shrouded still, though I could make out who they were by their voices.

My mother sighed. "No harm done, I guess."

"Um, Mr. Avery, why did the candles turn on again?" The child spoke.

She started. "Aren't they cool? They're called-" She was cut off.

"Hun, I think Joseph asked me about the candles." He chuckled. "They're called 'trick candles' they reignite when they get blown out."

"How many times do you have to blow them out?" Joey asked naively.

My mom answered. "Who knows? Maybe they will never go out. They say that trick candles are magic and if a child can't blow them out completely in three tries, then they will never grow up." She said with a happy grin.

Joey's eyes widened in excitement. "That's cool! Go on Kim, try it again."

I shuffled awkwardly in my seat. My mouth would not open to speak. The entire scene played to me, like I was watching, but still acting it out against my will.

"Give it a try sweet-heart." She said to me.

Reluctantly, I took in a deep breath. This time, it took two tries to blow them all out. Just like before, all went dark, and the feeling of isolation returned. The voices stopped when the candles were out. When the emptiness appeared, only whispers remained, whispers I could not understand. Within ten seconds the candles were alive once more.

"All right, last try." Joey's voice echoed.

My dad played along. "If they don't light up again, then you don't have to grow up."

Now, every time they spoke, I could hear disembodied, echoing words around me. Muttering random phrases every time somebody spoke.

I hesitated, looking around at their faces. I could not see them, their bodies were there, but the faces were dark.

"C'mon Kim!" Joey spoke. "What's wrong? Don't you wanna be a kid forever?"

Forever.

Forever.

Forever.

That word echoed in my head, over and over and over, shattered and lingering. Never grow up, never face adulthood. Be a kid, young and happy and innocent, until I die.

I hesitated. Unlike before, I felt my movements float like I was in water; no longer did I follow the path predetermined. I had control of my actions. I looked around in the dark, feeling eyes all over me.

My mother's voice grabbed me.

"Kiki, what's wrong?"

Everything is wrong. A voice hissed.

Her silhouette leaned in towards me, her face still hidden. I felt my cheeks start to get hot; my jaw began to tremble.

Joey exclaimed, "If you blow them out for good this time, then you can stay here. You won't have to get old." As he finished his sentence, his voice faded out and his body disappeared altogether.

My dad spoke very softly, comforting.

"If the candle comes back to life, then you will have to face it." His voice became malicious, twisted. He too began to fade at the end of his words, until he was erased.

You've come. . .

All that was left was her and I. The black hole that was her face stared at me. I stared right back, searching for something human, something I could recognize as real. My trembling face slowly descended into sorrow.

My inexplicably dry mouth trembled as I attempted to force movement. Invisible stitches held on like a ghost of who I am to become. Keeping quiet my whole life, lying, remaining abstinent to reality. Not anymore.

"M-mommy. Is that really you?" I asked, just as tears began to drip down my face.

She cocked her head, seeming surprised. "Of course, Kiki, it's me." She giggled.

. . .to join us?

"I don't want. . . to grow up, Mom." I cried, my childhood body shook, and my stomach hurt, feeling shrunken down and fragile. "I want to stay here, forever, with you, Daddy and Joey." My shoulders bounced while the tears flowed, dripping onto my legs.

"If that's so, then just give those candles a big huff." I heard a smile in her voice.

Death. . . stuck.

"But what if. . ." I started,

"Don't you worry about a thing, darling. Everything will be okay." She promised, and she too began to fade.

Everything will. . . be okay.

I watched her body get taken by the surrounding black and I felt scared.

"Mommy. . . Mommy, please don't go!" I whimpered.

Despite my plea, she was gone. The haunting whispers recited verses of hell and torment; in a language I could not interpret. Maddening cackles and demented shrieks. The darkness itself had sprung to life, reaching out for my tender flesh. Starving.

My eyes shut, and weighted tears fell; I was cold. I pulled my knees to my chest and hugged them tight, trying to keep warm, fighting the abandonment. The cake had vanished, but the candles remained. Gently flickering with an endless wick. They floated in the abyss before me, six dimly lit sticks were all that kept the darkness at bay.

I cried still.

The longer I sat in this chair, and ignored the candles, the louder the whispers grew. Every voice stabbing my ears, trying to make me understand. One thing stuck with me; one thing gave me solace. Her final words.

Everything will be okay.

It was those words that gave me the strength to do what needed to be done. It was my choice; it has always been my choice.

I lifted my head and watched the fire waver and spark.

"It's my choice." I shakily spoke. I took in a deep, deep breath and held it. Held it until my face turned blue and air began to leak from my nose.

I blew out the candles.

Darkness still, breathing stifled by a mound of dirt surrounding my face. My restriction of air did not last, as Tansu quickly came to my side and rolled me onto my back. Allowing the light from high above to blind my clouded vision.

Dust and blood coated my raw skin, and I desperately clung onto consciousness. My eyes lightly closed; she is there.

"Oh my god. Kim, talk to me!" Tansu panicked.

Her words to me came as a whisper spoken through a speaker a hundred feet away. Eyes baggy and dark. Every vein pushed to the surface of my pale skin. My fingers dug into the dry dirt while my body remained motionless, unable to move anything else. With enough effort, I managed to open my eyes to see the blurry shape that was Tansu above me. I tried to speak but fell short. My lips chapped and blue, the only words came in bursts, with a hot exhale.

"The candles. . ." I whispered.

"W-what?" She asked, frightened and alarmed.

"I'm okay." I coughed.

When I spoke, a searing pain stabbed the roots of my eyeballs. I couldn't see it, but I could feel a hot stream of blood rush out from under my lids. Falling out, then immediately redirecting the flow down the side of my cheeks and dripping onto the ground.

Tansu cupped her mouth in her hands.

"Oh my god. Y—" she whined, then shook her head side to side, denying what she could plainly see. "You're fine. Don't worry, Kim. You're fine." She choked back tears.

I blinked. My sandpaper eyes burned as my eyelids scraped against them. The vision remained, but my eyes throbbed immensely.

"I can't. . . m-move." I whispered.

My breathing slowed for a moment and I felt a gentle sleep try to take me. Darkness blanketed over my sight, but opened again quickly, trying to stay awake. Tansu sat beside me, lightly panting and rubbing her ribs beneath her armpit, then leaned in to move the hair out of my face. I couldn't feel her touch.

"Just rest here a moment." She whispered, keeping her hopes high.

The silence was my answer. For a minute, we both sat still, letting the memories of recent events settle, burrowing into a permanent place in our minds where they would remain forever. In this time of solace, it was perfectly clear to me Alice was dead. I could no longer feel her presence. The raging anger, the electric shock of her voice. The crowded presence in my soul was gone. I felt empty. Emptier than I have ever felt in my entire life.

With the emptiness came the pain. Her death brought all the wounds to surface, but on top of that, I felt sadness. Just like that, she was gone forever. And I wanted to cry for her, because she is my friend. Without her ability and me being unable to move, there was no way I'd be leaving this place. Tansu felt the untouched flesh below a gash on my cheek; a gash she inflicted on me when she was under Sin's control.

"We need to get this hole in your face cleaned up. It looks awful." She wanted to keep me listening to her voice. Keep me attentive and awake and I think she focused more on that cut in particular, seeing how she caused it. What she didn't understand was how hard it was to focus on anything except for the erupting, blistering pain that raped my body. The welcoming invitation of sleep was difficult to fight, and her voice was distant now, more than ever.

She was brushing her hand across my hair, trying to comfort me. Through the quiet wind that remained persistent around us, I felt the urge to speak. My first attempt at words fell short, only pushing out a raspy mumble. She heard this and leaned in closer. I licked my lips and tried to clear my throat, but the grinding of my muscles only made my mouth wet with blood.

I managed to cough out, “I'm sorry.”

“Sorry? Please, don't apologize.” She chuckled, still holding on to that tone of relief.

I scarcely shook my head sideways with a tremble in my lips.

“No, I have done. . . horrible things Tansu. I killed my father and Mr. Kel. I almost killed Stacy and I. . . brought my living hell into your life. For that, I'm—”

She interrupted me. “Don't apologize. It's not necessary.”

I shifted my eyes to hers and gave her a big teeth-revealing smile. A smile stained through with blood.

“My life is just one huge mistake. Even when I thought I was doing the right thing; I was always wrong.” I chuckled.

She brought her hand up and placed her palm under my jaw, lightly holding my neck. My smile went away with her touch and my teeth clenched behind my tightly closed lips. A childlike whimper grew in my throat, and I tried to fight these emotions.

“Kim, please, everyone makes mistakes. Don't torture yourself like this. You have to understand if someone could go through their life without making a single mistake or hurting someone” —she shook her head— “you just couldn't. Humans aren't made to be perfect.”

“I'm just so sorry for involving you in all this. If I was smart, I would have walked right past you in that hallway. Stayed alone forever.”

She had some sort of twitch in her eyebrow like she was fighting back the urge to slap me. Then, she sighed and pointed her finger.

“Now you listen to me.” She spoke sternly, “You may think that you ruined something in my life. That you brought a new hell with you, but I was already suffering before I met you. So, no matter what you say, in the time that I have known you.” Her voice cracked a little; and she stopped, gathered her words again and continued,

“I couldn't have asked for a better friend than you. I mean that.”

Tears rolled without me telling them to, mixing with the blood that previously came out of my eyes. I didn't know what to say. No words could suffice in expressing my genuine happiness at this moment. She looked around quickly.

“Now, you need to stop talking. We need to get you to a hospital. Then we can talk all you want, okay?”

I exhaled and got serious again. With my last bit of strength, I lifted my hand up and opened it; she took it quickly in hers. I squeezed as tight as I could. My entire arm shook viciously with the agony I was in. As my arm quaked, hers was being manipulated along with it. The gears were turning. The reality of the situation was crashing through her mind. The rational side of her brain was slowly coming to terms with this, but the blindly hopeful side was denying even the possibility of the foreseeable future. I could see the hurt in her eyes, the understanding.

Unexpectedly I felt a razor-like tear open wide inside my stomach. My body tensed up, and I felt an unimaginable pain rip through me. A fiery twinge held my muscles tightly, making even my immobilized body crunch inward and go through a small seizure. Everything started to get fuzzy and unbelievably cold.

Tansu's eyes widened, and she clasped my hand between both of hers.

Now panicking, she began to recite a prayer in a hushed tone. My small thrash halted, and my body flattened out on the ground again. There were a few seconds where I was in a dark state. I forgot where I was, who I was.

Everything went blank in my head, but I saw her face through the blur, then gazed past her head for a moment. Just to get a glimpse of the sun's rays shining through the clouds and trees behind her. The chirping of the birds, a plane that flew far overhead.

These few sounds that would be my last to hear. I took it all in as my mind slowly returned. With my mind resetting once more, a new thought was brought forward, completely out of context and had nothing to do with the situation. This thought burned in my mind. It always has, but never found its way into words until now.

"Tansu, can I ask you something?" I gasped.

"Of course." She replied quickly, willing to give me anything.

"It seems dumb-now. But why do you do that thing. . . with your hand?"

"Thing. . . with my hand?"

"Yea, that odd little fist. I've always wondered." I wheezed slightly.

She smiled a little. "You could have asked me at any time, and you choose now." She giggled with wet eyes. "It's something I do to feel closer to my dad. It was our own personal pinky-swear. His two fingers wrapped around my thumb. I do it when I feel afraid, so it's like he's still here, with me." Her words sank at the end.

In the background, thin close-together trees scraped against one another, their leaves brushing and twisting.

"That's nice." I whispered, my eyes fading in and out of darkness. I could feel my brain dimming.

She sniffled and looked at our surroundings. "Okay, that's enough sad talk. We need to get moving. I'm sure if we go a little farther in that direction, we'll reach the road. Then we'll get you help." She stated. Her determination was inspiring, but I couldn't let her on like this anymore. I knew my fate.

"It's no use." I coughed.

"What do you mean?" She said fearfully.

"I want you to go. Go to the road alone and flag down help. It will be faster if you go alone. . . Then come back." I instructed her. She shook her head in protest.

"No way. Are you kidding? I won't leave you." She refused skittishly. I paused, hearing the anxiety rise high in her voice. She doesn't get it.

"Then you can sit here and watch me die," I said with hollow eyes.

That made her go quiet and think.

"I'm—" I started. My throat started closing up. My lungs weren't working properly. It felt like my lungs were stuffed full of steel wool, making it impossible to keep a full breath. With a violent cough, blood pushed through my gums and out of my mouth.

"I'm scared. . . I don't wanna die."

She didn't say anything, just looked at me, showing a red face and wet eyes. She seemed lost in words and spirit. I could see the daylight shine through the clouds behind her, illuminating and blurring the outline of her head. The clouds shifted slowly through the sky, just going with the wind without a choice, or change. My eyelids felt heavy. I let them ease shut for a moment.

"Please," I begged. She was listening; she understood.

"Okay. . . okay, I'll go. But you hold on 'til I get back, you hear me? I will only be one minute. . . Just one minute." She choked back her cries.

"You have thirty seconds." I chuckled with a broken smile, grinding out more words.

She nodded. "Thirty seconds. You got it." She gave my hand a final squeeze then placed it by my side. At the same time, she grabbed Joey's jacket from the ground beside me and placed it over my torso, hiding the wounds and holding in fragile heat. "Keep warm, all right?" Her lips quivered.

She half stood, then paused and crouched back down. She leaned in close, locked eyes with me for what seemed like an eternity; then slowly pressed her lips to my forehead then held them there for a few seconds. Her mouth was trembling, and the air from her nose was dry. She pulled away slowly.

"I will be right back." She retrieved her stability and made an unstable dash up the pathway. I listened to her soft footsteps in the dirt. They became more and more distant until they disappeared altogether.

I was alone—now truly alone—for the first time in over a year. In a way, I missed this silence. It was, at the moment, nostalgic to me. I waited, trying to hold on, but my body was purging itself of all good feelings; leaving only the terrible pain that he gave me. I thought about Crism or Christine and everything she said to me.

This carried my lingering mind to all the Teufel I never met and how glad I am that I didn't. . . Which brought me to Alice. I never said good-bye to her, but at least I thanked her for what it was worth. I wonder what would happen to her, dying like that when she never existed in this world. What would become of her? What would become of all the Teufel when they leave here? What would happen to me?

Tansu has been gone a long time.

Ten minutes—I counted every second as best I could. Many times, I thought I heard her voice call to me. Footsteps and car brakes had been among these imaginary noises. Except none were real—or maybe they were. Maybe in the real world, I'm already dead, and this is my punishment, to lie here forever. Waiting for help. My own personal Hell; loneliness.

Another set of clouds made their way overhead. A long fat one blocked out the sun, bringing with it a cold shade. My sharp breaths began to speed up slightly, heart pounding. Random twitches flashed everywhere; pulses of electricity pinched my nerves from all angles. My eyes shot open. Then it subsided. All at once. My eyes relaxed again, closing gently.

I knew that by the time she found help. It wouldn't make a difference.

I just wanted her to leave. That way, she wouldn't see me like this, because I knew my fate. It was clear to me, she doesn't need to be here, she doesn't need to see. I know she will be mad at me. I'm even mad at myself for making her leave like that. I only hope that she understands why I had to send her away.

A rush of smooth cool wind brushed against my pale skin. Frail leaves bounced all over and around me, the dry skipping accompanied by the fresh air calmed my senses and allowed them to slow and relax. Every inch of my skin began to numb and tighten, a persistent daydream of nihility.

A very small ray of sunlight made its way through the thick cloud and trees, bringing a glow on my eyelids from the inviting light. A smile to the sky and I exhaled.

Everything is okay.

END

EPILOGUE

A door, visible only to her, appeared beside the beaten and bloodied girls. Tansu, Alice and Kim were none the wiser as Crism stepped through the glare and left the two to make their journey back to salvation. Her vision adjusted fluently as she passed through the frame of effervescent light. Without hesitation, she began walking in total isolation. Only a few short steps forward and she found herself gradually slowing.

She had forgotten the properties of this place, an odd feeling; once she had known it so well. The ground beneath her feet was comprised mostly of a white, almost sugar-like sand. She stood in place for a moment while the ground tried to absorb her. Her toes wobbled and curled in the ground; it was cold. With little extra effort, she moved forward again, each step trying to swallow her.

Her mind was taken by thoughts of recent evil and revelation. Nothing, but solid white emptiness and a dense fog occupied this place. Nothing to keep her thoughts from roaming. Adjacent to nothing, her footsteps carried no sound, no feeling. This girl was searching for a door, a snow-white tear in reality that would led her to the one that called her name in urgency. The one who should be dead.

In body and mind, she wandered in apathy. Feeling not the motion of her muscles, or the breath on her upper lip. Devoid of all feeling, she felt distracted. Still, she moved forward. Lost in this vacuum that could only be compared to that of space.

She stopped.

There was a melody, one that did not exist, but inside her head. An off-key piano played a docile tune, replicating a lost fragment from her childhood. It was then that she closed her eye. In this place, many souls and demons had passed through; brushing past each other like ghosts, unaware of any other that existed just inches away. The only way to make contact is for destinations to be linked. As of now, this place was hollow. Not a single door could be found. Nor a soul.

A few moments after she froze in place, the first sound was muttered. A tender cracking emerged from all around, no specific location could be determined by anyone other than her. She not only heard this cracking, but she could also feel it in her bones. As the sound grew louder, she opened her vacant eye and turned to her right.

She could see plainly, there was a gap that had formed in the mist; pushed aside like the parting of the Red Sea. At the end was a door, a door made of solid white light. Nearly impossible to distinguish white on white, but it was there, an outline very clearly defined in her eye.

In the frame, stood a silhouetted figure. A heavy wind pushed through the door as this mysterious being entered and the door behind them faded out of existence. The fog reset itself.

The two faced each other, a few feet apart; the silence thick enough to choke on. The first step was made by the latecomer.

“If I had to guess, I’d say you won, or should I start running?” The new voice called into the void in a sarcastic tone.

“Sin is dead,” Crism stated in a very lax manner.

“And, what about that other girl?”

“My assumptions were correct; she possessed great strength and integrity. Her abilities surpassed my expectations. . . Her Teufel was conflicted, but in the end, they were one in the same. Without them, I could not have succeeded.” She explained.

“Well, that’s great to hear. . . Did she make it?” The voice was soft, not aggressive or hurried. The tone was pleasant.

“She suffered greatly; Alice will keep her alive, but her current Anima is quickly fading. The fight with Sin proved too great for her to handle.”

“Man, that sucks to hear.” He shuffled his hand in his pocket.

“The two had just begun moving. With any luck, the other girl will make it to save herself.”

“At least someone will survive. That’s what’s important, right?” He said with a frail smile.

“Indeed. So, tell me, you-who-are so aware of the rules and limitations of Teufel; why are you here when your time is also limited? Magcrow.” Crism asked.

She spoke his name as he arrived at her front. She could see him mostly clear now. A young adult male, with gentle, but angular facial features. Soft and trustworthy, but sly eyes that bore a bright radiant purple. His pale skin almost reflected this emitting light. The bushy violet hair which nearly reached his eyes, was stoic in this place. No gust to lift the shaggy locks.

“What, don't tell me you didn't wanna see me before it ends? Don't worry I've got it figured out.” He snickered playfully.

Crism started again. “How is Kenneth? The Rift is not meant to carry human souls, I am impressed you two are able to travel this way.”

“Ken does well. With me in control, it’s far less damaging for him, but we can’t be in here too long.”

“I agree.” She stated.

There was a long pause, where the two just looked at each other, but only Magcrow was taking in her appearance. Crism, however, was struggling to maintain focus, though she did not give any indication of such a fault. She was tired, physically drained by recent events.

“Well then-” Magcrow started, but Crism picked up the conversation for him.

“There is much to discuss. Why have you called me here, putting yourself and Kenneth at risk?”

He grinned a little, “I felt the death of Sin just as I am sure all the others did. I knew from that point my time was limited. We had no choice but to seal the Anima’s crack for good.” He rested his hand on the side of his head.

Crism’s eye squinted in confusion, she avoided eye contact and stared into the void.

“You look concerned.” He poked fun at her.

Crism was indeed confused, putting her guard up. “You solved it?”

“I solved it.” His voice was cool; proud.

"Which means you are locked at your current power."

"I never was a fighter. That's why you recruited me; to replicate Sin's formulas." He replied.

Magcrow adjusted his feet and slid one hand out of his back pocket and let it rest by his side. In this place that produced no walls, no sound of its own; any noise was instantly absorbed by the fog. There was nothing to reverb off of.

"What else have you learned?"

He smirked, "The books you gave me in exchange for watching over her provided much more information than you or I thought. He kept *everything*." Magcrow went on, sounding happier and happier the more he talked about the books and scrolls.

"He took pride in his collection," Crism spoke, however, sounded disinterested.

"Well, it's a shame Sin was a bastard, because he was a damn fine scholar. The books you gave me on human souls, info on the Teufel and The Ditch are fantastic; but in all of these books there were some names mentioned, some names that I am sure would interest you." His eyes became more intense.

Crism seemed interested certainly, but ultimately had something else on her mind.

"You mended your own Anima; can you do it again?" She asked.

"What, mend another Teufel? Probably."

"But not guaranteed?" She prodded.

"I mean, now that dad's dead we can raid his archives, right?"

"I can grant you access. . . but only if you help me hunt down the remaining Teufel. Some will survive much longer than others, and we need to ensure they are put down. After that, I propose we work together to deal with this realm's fiends and demon factions. With Sin gone, they will become bolder."

"Of course, I'll help. You know I'd do anything for you. But some of that will have to wait for now." He spoke softly.

"Is there something else?"

"You didn't feel it? The shock-wave knocked Ken on his ass instantly." He explained, his smirk now gone and eyes more focused than before.

Crism became worried, almost shifting to impatience. "In order to defeat Sin, I had to exhaust nearly all of my power to tear down his defenses and finish him off. My Anima is shattered."

"Well, that's a bummer. . . So, you were too drained to notice? Gotcha."

"What power did you feel?" She now felt the urgency settle in her gut.

He took his dangling hand and ran it through his hair, then shook his head around. A few strands of loose hair were dislodged from his head, but they did not fall. Instead they were caught in the fog, they were held there and slowly drifted away. The stress in his face was rising.

"He wasn't lying when he said they would come."

"The Council. . ." She responded gently, "So soon?"

"I'd give it a week, maybe a little more before they make it down here and reclaim his power." He said in monotone.

The two pondered for a few minutes. Each feeling a sickness swell within. Crism especially. Magcrow looked to her, he seemed to still hold a small amount of worry, but there was a sincerity in his eyes. One that would only be shown between family members. A trust, an unconditional care.

"You know, it's still strange for me." He said softly.

She remained quiet.

"When I first saw you approach me that cold, bitter day; I was terrified. Do you remember? How I tried so hard to crawl away. Heh, and to see you now. Unplugged, the mask removed. You aren't the boogeyman . . . not anymore." He shook his head despondently.

Crism exhaled loudly. "What do you propose we do? This threat is not something only the two of us can face."

"We knew the risks. . . I was thinking, there may be time to save her. If we get there now, you can remove the Anima and bring it to me. I'll ensure it returns to dormancy and then we move it to its birthplace. The leaking fumes from The Ditch should provide enough for me to slow its breakage while keeping it preserved for a short time."

". . . She will have to be awoken again. All of her power will be locked away until she feeds; which means a new host must be prepared." Crism said in a low, aggravated tone.

"We'll figure it out. She's far too valuable to lose."

"Her strength is not entirely her own. Kimberly's cursed vigor will not be a factor."

"The important thing is, she can be trusted, and she's plenty strong. Unlike you or I, she can grow again once she breathes this air. For now, we just need to move her somewhere safe. After that we will have a little more time to plan." He said in a rushed manner.

He then closed his eyes, and the shimmering edges of a new door began to appear, once it was fully formed, he grabbed the handle and gave Crism another look.

"I'll meet you at the girl's place. I'll work on concentrating the fumes until you arrive with her; it'll make it easier for her Anima to slip in."

Crism appeared uncomfortable, her typically relaxed fingers seemed stiff. Magcrow noticed this.

"What's up, is there something else? We can't afford to be lagging here." He spoke softly yet stern. Crism relaxed her hand and watched him carefully.

"Sin never had all of his power. . . It was cut in half to hold the seal; then a third of what remained was forced onto me. . . It's finally whole, and yet-" She spoke almost nervously; holding back foreign emotions.

She then closed her eye and her head lowered the slightest amount. A pressure pulsed through the air, enough to give Magcrow goosebumps all over his skin. He loosened his body and suddenly the air itself began to crackle.

What was perceived to be an endless sea of white land and fog, suddenly fractured. This small dimension for travelers began to shake and split along the very fabrics of its own reality.

A harsh, wet tearing of flesh was heard and immediately suffocated in the air. From Crism's shoulder blades, unfolded a set of broken and charred feathered wings. Stretching nearly ten feet wide. A small collection of burnt and torn feathers fluttered to the ground and were quickly absorbed by the white sand. They shivered violently as Crism rose inches above the clouded ground, her body limp.

Magcrow had a bead of sweat trail down the side of his face and even retreated a step. She relaxed as her wings sustained her fifteen feet in the air. Her head rose slightly and her left eye peeled open to reveal the Teufel eyeball had become grayed, and both of her pupils were glowing a mystical, enchanted white.

Her bottom lip quivered, her face was sunken with anguish and dejection. She muttered one sentence.

"It does not accept me."

As those words fell from her lips, her body tensed up, and the wings quickly retreated into her back. Blood sprayed out and stained the white fabric of this dimension. She plummeted to the ground. Attempting to recover, she fell to one knee and rested there. Her breath would not return.

Magcrow stepped away from the door and knelt beside her. The air became still once more, as if this place and everything related to it was a dream you couldn't quite remember. His movements were stiff and reserved. Despite the discomfort in his gut, he placed his hand on her shoulder. She did not react; she did not make a sound.

He sighed. The fear plain as day in his voice.

"Well, isn't that something."

Made in the USA
Middletown, DE
09 April 2021

37311215R00224